Redbeard the Magnificent A Yankee in the Court of the Russian Tsar

by

Patrick W. Dentry

To my emerald-eyed Snow Maiden, and the brave men of the Fighting 6th Massachusetts Volunteers who brought Old Glory through the streets of Baltimore against all odds.

Visit the author on Facebook with any questions or comments @ https://www.facebook.com/MrBirdToo/

Thanks also to Chris at Walkerloo.com for his wonderful cover art.

Copyright Numbers:
ISBN-13: 978-1717477491
ISBN-10: 1717477496

Explanatory Note

When I was a boy back in the fifties and sixties, my grandfather was a country doctor out in the little village of Whitehall, Maryland. He had a small farm there with horses, and goats, and grandkids galore where he loved to teach us life's little lessons through the experiences of his patients. My favorite character he ever told us about was an old gentleman by the name of Robert Augustus Stewart. Colonel Stewart lost his whole family in the Russian Revolution and returned home with only an old Civil War pistol, a shredded double-headed Romanoff eagle button that he claimed came off the last greatcoat the Tsar of Russia ever wore, and an old moth eaten silver fox fur blanket that he cherished till his dying day. He was given a place to stay at the Confederate Soldiers' Home in Pikesville, Maryland where he lived out the last years of his life.

The only Yankee to reside at the home, Colonel Stewart was fast with a hand for an old soldier who had fallen, or one who was too weak to stand. He would sit by the side of a poor dying Rebel all night long just so the old soldier wouldn't have to die alone. Doc made rounds at the Old Soldier's Home and they would sit and talk about horses for hours, or they'd talk of the beauty of their beloved rolling hills of Maryland, or their love of France—her fine red wine and beautiful women, which both men had seen first-hand in their wars. And when Doc died and left his ten grand children without a hero, he left me a special gift, for as well as the little brass thoroughbred race horse that sat on his living room table, he left me the wonderful tales of Colonel Robert Stewart.

The Colonel had survived the first battle of the American Civil War and went on to serve the King of Prussia and three Romanoff tsars—all the while bragging that he was such a bad shot that he couldn't swear he'd ever killed a man, nor did he feel good about those that he'd hurt. I've arranged his writings into chapters using titles taken from his own words and provided references where I thought them appropriate. My check of Colonel Stewart's facts has left me stunned, for as bizarre as his story may seem, I can find nothing in the history books to discount them. His genealogy, however, proved more questionable, for I could find not a single leaf from his family tree that would claim the poor man. And now without further ado, I present Redbeard the Magnificent a Yankee in the Court of the Russian Tsar from the Memoirs of a Baltimore Stable Rat by Colonel Robert Augustus Stewart.

Patrick W. Dentry, Editor in Chief

Chapter One

A Runaway Sleigh

Steam rose from the dapple gray stallion as he stormed on through the star filled night. Higher and higher he rose up into the heavens hauling our bright red Romanoff sleigh behind him. And there tucked tight in a warm cocoon of soft silver fox, we were two lovers lost in the Vertigo.[1]

"Lovers who enter the Vertigo together will be lovers through all of time," Nadia whispered to me gently as we sailed on through the stars. Stars so close you could feel their fire. So endless and timeless, I felt like a flea on the Universe's back. There were flames coming from beneath the furs on that cold winter's eve, for the touch of Nadia's body set the whole sleigh on fire as we flew on through the firmament.

Hans had noticed we were flying too, for his great silvery head searched for Mother Earth way down below us in the snow. The colt had been scared the first time he saw Russia—just as it had scared me, but Nadia had made us both see the beauty of the Venice of the North, as St. Petersburg was known for her fine tall women, wild musicians, wide canals, and marvelous mansions painted every color of the rainbow.

St. Petersburg was a fairy tale place—full of fairy tale people who could make you laugh, make you sing, or make you cry. With just one snap of their finger they could end your life, but it was a place of love and laughter as well. All of which I experienced in that far northern city where the richest and poorest of peoples survived at the top of the world as cyclones and storms whipped in off the Baltic, which made the good days of sunshine and starlight that much better!

Babylon of the Snows some called this desolate place, for early in the eighteenth century Peter the Great had forced his bluebloods to move all the way up there from Moscow. So if the number of palaces and rich people in the great city of Peter seemed a bit out of proportion to the rest of Russia, well, the Tsar was an all-powerful man! And the Tsarevich—his son and heir apparent (or Naslednik as the Russians called him) was under the same spell.

A chance meeting with the next emperor of Russia in the summer of 1872 threw me into this cauldron of a witches' brew, and as I bubbled

1

and boiled to the top, and boiled and bubbled to the bottom, one thing was absolutely certain—deep down inside these Russians were as good a people as my people were back in Baltimore, though at times that wasn't saying much about either.[2]

The Heir Apparent was a great giant of a man standing six foot five to my five foot seven, as big and wide as any Russian bear you'll ever see. Well into his prime at the age of twenty-six (as I was at the time), the great giant loved nothing better than to twist a big silver serving spoon into a little tiny pretzel and pitch it into someone's soup. His Majesty was my mentor and my nemesis, but first let me tell you of my one and only love, Nadia Shuvalova!

Nadia was my savior, my soulmate, my laughter, and my tears! From the time our eyes first met on a warm autumn's day as she softly played her violin, I was in love with her! Professor Korsakov had come to his classroom door to shoo me away like a pesky horsefly when he noticed I was bathed in a golden light. And when he turned to see Nadia bathed in that same golden glow, he knew we were soulmates! If you say that sounds like a fairy tale to you, it did so to me as well, save for the fact that my emerald-eyed Snow Maiden made my heart sing and Professor Rimsky-Korsakov was a well-known synesthete.[3] And that golden glow that surrounded us there on that warm fall day has washed over us in life and in death, so when my love comes calling for me in a dream some night, let me fly through the sky with my fairy tale princess—lost forever in the Vertigo!

In my old man's dream we were standing inside the Royal horse barns at Gatchina some twenty miles south of St. Petersburg. This was a grand stable as big as any Moscow cathedral—lit with the golden light of a thousand gas lamps. Huge rectangular windows let in long beams of moonlight that cast shadows of naked birch trees on the ivory walls. The Farm Pavilion sat on a snow covered knoll a mile northwest of the royal palace, tucked away on a little ten thousand acre estate the Tsarevich owned. Near a block long with a huge round rotunda in the middle that you could use for a ball, though the Naslednik hated to dance, these stables held some of the finest horses in all of Europe. All tucked away in their freshly cleaned stalls stacked knee deep with a golden straw. The barns smelled of new mown hay, sweet grain, and molasses, and from the stall doors and the tack hooks, to the water pails, and the pitch forks, double-headed Romanoff eagles sparkled in the lamplight. There was not a drop of straw out of place in that stable, for someone must have used a pair of double-headed silver eagle tweezers to tidy it up. The second floor of the stables, though squatter than the first, had large square windows that looked out on the great snow covered park, and though it was but four in the afternoon on that cold December day, darkness was coming on fast.

Our sleigh came down on a mechanical lift as thoughts of Nadia and I bouncing around in that tight little space danced in our heads. With sleek curved runners of shiny steel, the racing sleigh looked like a bright red rocket ready to set off for the stars. And somewhere out there on that snow covered trail we would kiss. Our hearts beat like tympani drums!

Maybe I couldn't drive a racing sleigh like some said. We Southern boys liked our horses tucked tight between our legs where we could feel what they were thinking, but I'd lied to the Naslednik and said I was one of Baltimore's finest sleigh racers, just to get out there alone with Nadia. Not the first lie I'd ever told His Highness, but a dangerous lie nonetheless.

They led the dapple gray stallion out of his stall and his silvery withers shuttered as three burley stable hands came dancing down center aisle with long leather lead shanks trying to control the colt. These reitknechts bore scars to show they'd spent plenty of time around the working end of a horse, and each of these powerful men tried to drop their heads and give a long low bow to the next emperor of Russia, who stood six paces ahead of us like the Rock of Gibraltar. One of the many rules the Romanoffs had to keep us mere mortals in line was never ever turn your back on your betters, and try that whilst a half ton of horse flesh is hauling you through the air like a ballerina. Hans arched his silvery head backwards as he tried to bite at the boys, for he wanted to be free and he wanted to run! He threw the lads about like chaff in the wind, and then in came Haughty Herr Horse Trainer to bring order to this world of horse pounding chaos.

3

Haughty Herr Horse Trainer was dressed in a long deer skin caftan coming down to his knees, and across the middle of that loose fitting shirt was a bright red belt his wife had probably made him, for he would need all the good luck he could get! Herr Horse Trainer was the third Herr Horse trainer up, and he wore short cropped hair and a thin Van-Dyke half beard on a long stern face as he studied the colt. Haughty Herr Horse Trainer, as I'll continue to call him, since his name was as long and twisted as any I ever heard, wore his pants tucked tight into a pair of knee high cavalry boots to let us know that he'd ridden for Tsar Nicholas in the Crimean War. He carried his pride like a Preobrajenski Guardsman from the time he jumped out of bed in the morning 'til he blew taps at night.

"Get that horse under control!" he bellowed like God on high, as he searched Hans's big brown eyes in an attempt to control him with his psychic horse control powers, which weren't working so well, though Haughty Herr Horse Trainer didn't seem to notice.

Let him walk a bit, thought I, but I said not a word for the Tsarevich, who would someday become Alexander III, Emperor of All the Russias, had warned me to keep my thoughts to myself. But anyone with any horse sense at all could see that he was bringing the colt to a boil!

"You settle down now, damn you!" He hollered in his deep Russian bass. Then he hooked up a fourth lead shank to the halter and held on tight as he gave that short shank a good hard yank as he signaled the reitknechts to pitch in with their short shanks too. But they'd have needed a whole regiment of Guardsman to take control of Hans like that!

Alexander Alexandrovich stood silent and steamed as he watched the great twisting battle proceed on the stable floor. A little on the big-boned side, if you were being polite, the Grand Duke hovered over us like an oak tree in heavy winds. He had a wide barreled chest and the poorest posture God ever saw fit to give to a tsar—more like a farmer without his plow, a big farmer with a really big plow, but none the less a moujik—or peasant as the Russians said it, stooped over from a hard days' work and mad that his horse and his handlers couldn't get their acts together so they could all go home for supper! The Tsarevich carried his black fur cap stuffed in his right paw which hung down at his side like an anvil.

His hair was auburn and unkempt with long curly side-whiskers that ran down His Majesty's melancholy face to the arch of his huge jaw. His mouth was offset like a half sprung trap waiting for the next victim to step in.

I was dressed in a long red caftan that came down to just about my knobby knees, my lucky red, white, and blue belt, that Nadia had made me, around my waist, with those bulgy black pants, and soft black boots all the peasants loved to wear. In my mind's eye, I was a wild Russian sleigh racer and I knew that with Nadia's help, I could soothe that savage beast!

The Naslednik had bought the Gelderland stallion sight unseen from a German horse trader and his performance—to date had been quite abysmal. He'd broken the bones of three of his horse handlers, crushed the hand of a fourth, and his high stepping fast trot had put in some terrible times out there on the snow trail. Soon all of Russia would know of the joke they'd played on His Majesty, and if there was one thing he hated more than being stood in front of, or not bowed to properly, or being stared in the face, or talked to before you were asked to talk, it was being the brunt of a joke—he couldn't abide by that at all!

"Let's let the colt walk a bit, Your Highness?" I suggested with my eyes cast down—hoping he wouldn't notice he hadn't asked me to talk.

But that continuing to speak out of turn was one of my major sins, according to the Tsarevich, and His Majesty's eyes flared like a cobra getting ready to strike! I'd seen that look on the big man's brow before, but mostly his bark was worse than his bite.

Sasha, as I was NEVER allowed to call the Tsarevich, wore a long gray greatcoat against the cold Arctic air, though there inside the royal stables it was unbuttoned and proudly displayed the belly of a well fed moujik. Under his coat, the Tsarevich's uniform was a dark Russian green with a wide blue ribbon running diagonally across his chest. He glared down at me, the stable hands, Haughty Herr Horse Trainer, and a little lost piece of straw he spotted on the floor, and the fire of Peter the Great could be felt by all.

"That damn horse doesn't need to be walked, Colonel Stewart, he needs to be shot!" His Highness roared over that steady drumming of hooves on the wide wooden floor.

Maybe the horse couldn't talk Russian was my guess. I couldn't talk it much either when I first came, but I remained silent as ordered. Hans thrashed, and tempers flared, and the bruises began to mount, so I figured weren't rules—even Romanoff rules, meant to be broken!

"Please, Your Highness, let Nadia Shuvalova see what she can do with your horse?" I entreated with my head hanging down.

Just then, the dapple gray came ass end to me, as the Tsarevich thought long and hard about the plan we'd already made over breakfast.

Haughty Herr Horse Trainer shrieked, "That blue-eyed Yankee with his harebrained plan will get the three of them killed out there, Your Majesty! Don't let him drive that sleigh!"

"I may not be well versed in sleigh racing, Your Highness, but you have seen me fly like the wind on my English mare, and I have entered the stalls of Your Majesty's sickest horses and never once been kicked. Horses are in my blood, Sire, and they are in Nadia Shuvalova's blood as well. You can take the cost of the horse and the sleigh from my pay if anything goes wrong out there, but please let us give it a try?" And I dropped my eyes to the floor and waited for his reply.

The big giant looked down at Nadia standing silently beside me and his face slowly changed from one of sadness to one of sheer delight, as Nadia smiled sweetly up at him. She was maybe two inches taller than I was with her long red fox fur coat open to my adoring eyes. My emerald eyed Snow Maiden wore a bright red peasant blouse with just the touch of her curves showing in the golden lamplight. A handmade red, white, and blue good luck belt was around her waist, and she wore the soft black boots we all loved to wear. On her head was a matching red fox fur hat from which a tiny plume of light brown hair escaped and ran down across her face.

Nadia had calmed Hans down when he first came to St. Petersburg, for the young stallion had been scared by the hustle and bustle of the great Babylon of the Snows. Two hundred thousand horses madly raced through the city whilst the church bells rang from a hundred gold topped steeples, moujiks bellowed, and Cossacks cracked their long black whips—it was all too much for the colt. Nadia had soothed him by talking softly in his native tongue as she scratched him between his wide silvery ears, and he transferred to a rail car bound for Gatchina Palace with the grace of a seasoned race horse, so we knew Nadia's soft touch and a little more Dutch would work wonders.

Finally, with the look of a small boy with a broken toy, the Tsarevich asked, "Nadia Shuvalova, will you see what you can do with my colt?"

"Under your eyes all things are possible, Sire." Nadia said softly as she bowed her head. Then she approached the prancing stallion and spoke in her soft sweet Dutch, whilst her right hand came up and tenderly patted his silvery rump. He put that left rear hoof back down by way of a truce, and I breathed a little gentler.

"Goede jongen," she whispered, which was good boy in Dutch, and there was no kicking, no thrashing, no gnashing of teeth, just the drop of his head as he sawed around and brought his big brown eyes up to Nadia's green ones, sniffed deeply in at her tender long neck, and took in the sweet scent of spring flowers. The stallion began to nuzzle Nadia at just about chest level (to my great jealousy), whilst Haughty Herr Horse Trainer and his grooms stared on in disbelief.

The Tsarevich smiled down and congratulated himself for a job well done, as he looked over at the horse trainer like he was about to twist him into a tight little knot and pitch him into someone's soup. Of course, if our plan failed out there on the snow trail that night, it would be horse borscht he was pitched in, and I'd be paying the butcher bill!

The colt stood silently awaiting his coronation like a prince of the realm, as the horse trainer began to direct the harnessing. With the snap of his fingers, the flick of his wrist, and that haughty high grimace when something wasn't done just to his liking, off came the long shanks, and on went a bit and bridle that Hans took with ease. The dapple gray shifted a bit as the stable hands reached under his belly to adjust the straps, but he didn't skitter or raise a hoof, and when all was completed to Herr Horse Trainer's taste, Nadia stood by his side and smiled.

7

"Would you like to pat your horse, Your Highness," Nadia asked the Tsarevich as he gazed at his stallion like he'd just seen a magic trick done right for the very first time. But the Naslednik wasn't exactly what you'd call a horse person—being almost too big to ride, and he declined.

"And you, Augustus Augustovich (for my father had been an Augustus before me), would you like to stroke this fine beast before we set out?" Nadia asked with a tantalizing grin.

More than the horse I would have liked to have stroked that night, but I walked right up to the big stallion's side and gazed at how powerful he looked standing there in full harness. And suddenly sleigh racing seemed like a very dangerous sport indeed!

"Geode jongen," I said as I stroked Hans' silvery neck whilst I smiled a loving smile at the woman I loved, for like Ralph Waldo Emerson said, it was time to "hitch my wagon to the stars!"

This was a fine Romanoff racing sleigh built for speed with no doors to slow her down, just the weight of those golden double-headed eagles on each side to keep us glued to the ground. There was a small leather seat with a blanket of silver fox fur to keep us warm, and we buttoned our coats and up we climbed. First, Nadia with a helping hand from the Tsarevich, and then I popped up there—like a jockey on the 4th of July.

The stable doors came open letting in long shafts of moonlight and in blew the cold Arctic air. The barn floor had been sprinkled with saw dust, and as we skidded out into the snowy night, the scent of a great pine forest rose in the frost. The starlight twinkled down as we moved from the barn to the lane where the gas lamps hissed, and the big brass double-headed eagles lanterns glowed in a golden light, as a full moon broke through the trees and made the snow shimmer.

There was a long line of mounted Cossacks stretched out along the Farm Pavilion, probably a hundred strong. They sat their shaggy Steppe ponies with great huffs of frost coming from their ice covered mouths making little rainbows in the moonlight. Dressed in their long red cherkeskas with a sword and a dagger in black leather sheaths swinging from the right side of their waists, a rifle strapped to their backs—their long red lances in black gloved hands with the steel tips shimmering in the lamplight; as a shooting star came sailing down for good luck.

The colt was starting to feel the excitement too, for he was standing tall and proud by that long line of red Cossacks as he sniffed the air and snorted like he wanted to run. His silvery spots wreathed in the moonlight as he started his anticipatory side strut and begged to be set free!

"Dis horse is a high stepping trotter," Haughty Herr Horse Trainer broke in to my revery. "Keep control of your horse at all times, Gus!" he hollered, and nobody ever called me Gus. "And for God's sake don't let him break his gait, for if he goes to the gallop, you've ruined him!"

"Give him his head, Augustus Augustovich, and let the colt run wild and free!" His Majesty roared in counterpoint. "Now be off and good luck," he bellowed as the Cossacks hammered their lances to the side of their saddles and gave us a loud hurrah.

"Keep my Cossacks close by your side, Colonel Stewart, and don't miss the turns in the snow trail!" the Naslednik shouted as the red riders roared.

"Nadia Shuvalova, if that little Yankee attempts to insult your honor in any which way, I will feed him to the wolves!" was His Majesty's last bellow as we sailed off into the starlight.

Six Cossack lancers broke off from the long line and came into column of twos up ahead, while six more came in from behind. We were now boxed in by a tough and craggy bunch of black-bearded lancers who had been promised my head should anything go wrong, but Death didn't scare me at all that night, for up under the furs with the woman I loved, I was already in heaven!

Hans showed his high stepping fast trot as he gazed at the shaggy ponies before us. He was a big horse and the Steppe ponies could never match his stride or his speed. North into the hollow we went through snow as high as a house, as the moon cast shadows of the sleigh and her two lovers on the snow below.

9

We trotted to the bottom of a knoll and crossed a small bridge over a frozen creek, then up a low rise we went—heading for a big glass greenhouse the Romanoffs called their Aviary. Near a block long with great shafts of summer's sun streaming from its thick glass windows— the Aviary was full of exotic birds, with palm trees and tropical flowers blooming as we rode by at fifteen below zero.

Now a fast trot doesn't start out fast, it starts with a slow 1—2 1—2 rhythm, as the horse's right forefoot and the opposite left rear take off and strike down in unison. Then it's the left forefoot's turn to take off with his right rear friend and they fly through the air whilst the first two legs form a base, then boom, the left front hoof and the right rear touch down, and on and on through that dance they go. To get a horse to go from a slow to a fast trot was just a matter of rhythm, so out came my trusty Hohner harmonica and I began huffing away like the night train to Washington as the stallion kicked up great clods of snow that rained down upon us. I sucked in and blew out at an ever quickening pace and Hans took to this technique like a duck to water. We did that first half mile in nothing flat as the full moon shimmered across a plane of snow and the stars came down and swallowed us in the Vertigo!

But the Dutchman had more in him than a fast trot, so I had to keep my mind on the driving. My father had said that all creatures large and small love their freedom, and I could feel that freedom in the way the colt wanted to soar. So with a loosening of the reins just to give him his head, and a good old Southern boy's cluck, we were off like lightning on the wire! Freedom had come for us all that night and he dipped his head like a yearling in a warm spring field and started to run like the wind!

Now a gallop or a run, as we call it back in Maryland, was a three beat gait with a hind foot coming down for the first beat, followed by the opposite hind foot and it's diagonal front footed friend striking together, then the remaining front foot touches down for a third beat as the horse flies through the air like a great big Romanoff eagle. Hans galloped up to the shaggy ponies like a buzz saw and begged them to move over.

"Cossack Convoy, Right Oblique," I hollered like the officer I was.

There was nothing worse than giving an order that wasn't followed (save for running in the face of the enemy), and not one of my bearded friends would budge. We pulled up close on their heels with the snow flying in our faces and I hollered, "Cossack brothers, please move over!" But not one inch of the road would they give up.

"Didn't the Naslednik say this horse should have his head and run like the wind?" I yelled with great conviction. And suddenly it was Right Oblique, Forward March, with the red riders all moving to the right with just enough room for us to pass.

Nadia waved to the Cossacks as we flew by. They smiled their toothless grins, and nodded their fur topped heads in delight, for if there was one thing that the great horseman of the Steppes enjoyed even more than a horse race, it was the possibility of a hanging!

"We'll see you in Siberia, Redbeard the Wild Man!" their Hetman roared and they hammered their lances to the sides of their saddles and laughed.

We were on the fast train to Glory that night as we flew by the mile and a half marker with a sharp turn to the right. Tall spruce trees dropped their loads on our heads as we sailed through the sweet smelling pine forest laughing like lunatics. Hans picked up the pace with that, for Nadia's laughter set the Dutchman's blood to boiling as we came roaring through a hair pin turn at the two mile marker with the sleigh runners sizzling. We skidded sideways and came up on one runner, then slammed back down. The press of Nadia's body against mine was a magic elixir that made the back stretch but a blur. We flew past the four mile marker as great sheets of fire in red blue and green rolled up from the horizon, for the Aurora Borealis was burning bright. And there—coming out of the night like a great white tornado was a swirl of snow that rumbled and vibrated the ground! Hans sniffed the air and pressed onward at the gallop, as that mysterious cyclone came on like Death itself. Then suddenly I saw just the tad of red showing from a Cossack's long cherkeska, and I leaped to my feet and hauled back on the reins like Ben Hur before me! But the dapple gray stallion had an iron mouth and a will to match, and he would not slow down! I can't say why someone else's fear makes some people so merry, but Nadia was laughing like a banshee in heat as my knees went weak and my heart skipped a beat.

11

You could hear the roar of the red lancers as they came on in that great white tornado! At twenty yards out we closed for hard impact—saddles creaked, hooves pounded, and their long red lances flashed a sad farewell in the flickering moonlight. So to let them know we were coming out of the swirling snow, I pulled out my trusty harmonica and started wailing away like a runaway freight train!

My last thoughts were of Nadia still clutching my legs as I closed my eyes and breathed in my last breath. But there was not the clash of horse flesh to horse flesh that I'd expected, for those fast coming, fast thinking column of two Cossacks had split into two columns of one—just like the Red Sea had split for Moses! And right down center aisle we flew with the sleigh runners sizzling and the hooves pounding. Up through the hollow we went, as the Cossacks roared, "Redbeard the wild and crazy Amerikanski!" And the moon still glowed through the pine forest, and the stars still shined as I opened my eyes, and we saw His Majesty with a stopwatch in hand standing in the snow trail before us.

"You've ruined that horse, you damn Yankee!" roared Haughty Herr Horse Trainer as he stepped out in front of the Tsarevich.

But what he'd forgotten in his anger that night was the next emperor of Russia didn't like cussing, especially in front of a lady. Nor did the Naslednik care for Herr Horse Trainer having stepped out in front of him, but what the Tsarevich really did care about—and this was very important for all of us, was how well Hans had run under new management!

"Guards, get that man off the palace grounds at once," Alexander Alexandrovich bellowed as our sleigh skidded to a halt.

But before I could wrap my arms around Nadia for that well deserved kiss, the Naslednik's voice shook the ground. "You have shaved four minutes off the record time, Augustus Augustovich, and that's with the two of you aboard a sleigh built for one, Bravo my friend! Bravo!"

The Cossacks kicked in with their gravelly roar of, "Redbeard the Magnificent" as they banged their lances to the sides of their saddles in glee. **Bang! Bang!** Went that sound of their long red lances striking their pommels like a battery of artillery going off in battle. Then **Bang Bang** came another sound, more like the back of my bed board in another time and place I preferred not to visit!

"Colonel Stewart, time to wake up now, honey. Come on now, open those baby blue eyes," said someone I knew and loved. Lord how I wanted to stay with Nadia for that celebratory kiss, but it was Baltimore calling from the year 1930. As I opened my eye, there lay the body of a tired old man. Scrawny old pasty white legs stretched out before me, and the big strong arms of a horseman that had guided Hans to his victory that star filled night had been stolen by Father Time!

"Well, good morning, Augustus," the fat little nurses' aide said, as my heart pounded from the thrill of that sleigh race. "I thought you was dead there for a minute, you was having a conniption fit."

Viola was a hard working lady who had ten of us old soldiers to bed bathe, dress, and get down to breakfast. Overworked and underpaid, she was dressed in a bright white work dress all pressed and smelling of a hot iron. There she stood all four foot eight of her, ready to lift tired old soldiers from their beds with an amazing grace, and never once did she let us think we weren't helping her. Viola came to work each day with a smile on her face and a real passion to help her fellow man, so with her pail of hot soapy water at the ready, what was I to say? Dreams are a wonderful thing, they can take you away to a love one long since gone, but as a shaman once said on the road to Shambhala, "You've got to live in the moment." And a hot soapy bed bath is a hell of a moment!

"You sure has got some scars, Augustus." She said with a smile. The rules at The Old Soldier's Home were strict, the help had to address us by our military titles and last names only, but weren't rules meant to be broken? "Lordy, look at them scars!" she'd say as we played name that battleground across the wasteland of my tired old body.

First, there was the scar over my right eye from a piece of pig iron thrown off the roof of the Monumental Steam Bakery when I was a boy of fifteen—a little memento from my hometown of Baltimore. Then there was a big hole in my left shoulder from a Turkish rifle round that I got up in the Shipka Pass—all ugly and ragged. Next was a little six inch gash in my right thigh from a Boxer's sword I got way out in China, followed by a long ugly scar running across my forehead where my left eye had once enjoyed the sights. We called that one the Catherine's Quay, and the Tsar of Russia did way worse than I did that day. No, the years had not been kind, yet I still managed to enjoy a good bed bath and a bottle of Maryland rye from time to time!

"And don't forget your PS de résistance," Viola would chuckle. "That double lung shot wound[4] that you call Antietam."

That bed bath could have gone on forever, but like all things we enjoy in this transient life, it was over far too fast for me. She dried me off with a nice fluffy towel, helped me get on my underdrawers, and then sat me up on the side of the bed where we waited for the room to stop spinning. I took my glass eye out of the water glass, popped it back in place and smiled, as my old colored friend asked, "You gonna wear your blue suit today, baby?"

She knew I only had one change of clothes in this whole wide world, but I answered like an English lord, "Sure, let's wear that blue suit today, Viola," and we laugh like the old friends we were.

We'd get me dressed in my best including a vest and a short little neck tie—get my shoes and socks over my eight remaining toes (which was whole nother story), then she'd pass me my cane and help me to stand. And then with the poise of the best butler in Europe, she'd brush me off with a little brush she carried just for the occasion, and sent me off to another exciting day at The Old Soldiers' Home staring at the walls.

"You be good today, Augustus. Don't go getting into any trouble," she'd coo and off I'd go like a wayward schoolboy.

Down a long straight hallway with thick plastered walls turning yellow from age[5] I'd walk, as we made our way down to the chow hall in wheelchairs, crutches, canes, or a friendly arm to hang on to. After we ate, we'd go our separate ways. Some going back to their rooms to seek solace in sleep, some to walk outside and seek their sleep under a tree, some to sleep where the sun came in on a couple of sofas in the solarium, whilst others—like me and my rowdy friends, went down to the road to celebrate having survived one more day! The horse and buggy days were just about over, and those people out there on the Reisterstown Road in

14

their flashy new cars would fly by like a school of mindless minnows. The Modern Age was a strange age to be growing old in, for first they claimed they'd invented an unsinkable ship, and don't she go down on the first iceberg she hits! Then they brag that they've fought the War to End All Wars, and I'll be damned if there wasn't another one brewing in Europe. And when that idiot President Hoover went and said that we were in the land of milk and honey, didn't the bottom fall out of the market![6] We old soldiers knew we were truly in the Age of Bullshit! Oh, we were fed plenty of crap too—like when they said the Civil War would be over by that first Christmas. But things were moving slower in the Steam Age and we could see the manure pile growing, while now, as they plowed down the road at near forty miles an hour, they didn't even have time to wave! Well, we didn't give a damn if they waved or not, for going out to wave to the cars was just our code words for stepping out for a drink and a smoke. Down we'd go to the pike each day to talk about our glory days as we downed a little illegal alcohol and smoked our weed, and after a few hours of these wild shenanigans, we'd limp back home for our supper. Dinner was always a nice warm meal like Maryland fried chicken with passing dishes of mashed potatoes and homemade gravy—washed down with all the ice cold milk and hot coffee an old soldier could drink. Then it was time for a mid-day nap, and by three or four in the afternoon we'd have us a few hard core campaigners looking for a military escort back down to the pike. Nice work if you could find it, and though the rest of the nation was down in the dumps with the Depression, we old soldiers were living high off the hog in Pikesville! Oh, there were some obstacles to enjoying ourselves, like when they announced that the Baltimore Sun Papers was coming out to do their Memorial Day story on the last survivors of the Civil War. It was far better for the paper's circulation to catch them that were still above ground than the silent six foot under majority.

"Don't nobody go nowhere till the Sunpapers comes out," the Home's Administrator lectured to us over breakfast. He never smiled save when he crossed one of us off his list at a funeral, but he was excited that day for being in the newspapers meant everything to him.

Our Bulletin said they'd arrive at 3:00 PM, and by 4:15 their beat up old black Model T finally rolled up the driveway. There was a tall thin shaky

15

camera man at the wheel who looked like he could use a walk down to the pike to steady his nerves, and a chubby little red faced reporter in a wrinkled white suit, who thought he was the Sage of Baltimore[7] sitting right there beside him. "Sorry we're late, old soldiers!" bellowed the would-be sage over the snoring crowd, and then they proceeded to position us according to size and disposition on those hard wooden benches like we were props in a Shakespearean play.

"You there in the gray suit—keep your head up," the shaky photographer would shout, as if those Rebel boys weren't all in Confederate gray. Then just as that tired old soldier would open his eyes, the one beside him would fade away, and down would plop his chin to his chest.

Our guests were getting frustrated for they knew their Cocktail Hour was fading away fast, but they finally captured us in our mostly awake state like sachems in a National Geographic shoot down in faraway Borneo. And when they were finished, the reporter sashayed over to me and asked, "You there, you must be that damn Yankee we've heard so much about! Why do these Rebel boys let you live with them, anyway?"

Well, this was the last home I'd ever have in my life, and these were the last friends I'd ever know, but what with my ration of ice cream riding on me answering in a "civilized fashion" as we'd been warned to do, I was in a quandary. If you've got nothing nice to say, my Mother had taught me as a wild child running the streets of Baltimore, stay silent, and on to question # 2 he went. "What's your secret to a long life then, old soldier?" He said like he really didn't care.

Luck was my answer to who got a nice long ride in this world we live in, for I'd seen men zig to the right and live a hundred years, whilst those that zagged left got their heads blown off for their troubles. But that just might get me crossed off the ice cream list in perpetuity, so I gave him a little philosophy lesson.

"Life is like a runaway sleigh, there's no mortal at the reins, so hold on tight to the ones you love, sing a happy song against the darkness, and just sit back and enjoy the ride, for life is but a dream!"

Those were my words of wisdom that never got published, though they did get a nice shot of me shooting those boys The Bird.[8]

Chapter Two

Land of the Free

One warm summer's day about a month after my now notorious Bird to the Baltimore Sun, we old soldiers were down by the road drinking and waving to the multitudes when up rolled a Baltimore County Sheriff in his big black Model A cruiser. He came to a halt with his ass sticking out in traffic, wound down his window, and hollered real loud, "Are you old soldiers enjoying yourselves?"

"We sure is, Sheriff!" the Corporal, who was our leader on this blind path to sin and degradation answered. Then my old Rebel friend stepped up to the car real slow, leaned in the window, and breathed Maryland rye whiskey all over The Man.

The Corporal had been a proud member of Lee's Army of Northern Virginia and he had a sword slice across the side of his face to prove it. It was rare for an infantryman to stand and face the charge of a cavalryman, but that was our corporal. At five foot four, he was the shortest member of our Maryland Rye Whiskey Appreciation and Prohibition Can Go Kiss Our Rosy Red Asses Society (Baltimore Chapter), and he had the heart of a lion!

"You boys aren't out here drinking again, are you?" barked the Sheriff, but he knew we were, since he was being suffocated by the corporal.

The Sheriff's eyes never left that paper sack at my side as I yelled, "No sir, we're not drinking! Ain't Prohibition still in session?" Hoping they'd repelled it in the night and hadn't bothered to tell us old soldiers about it.

"Do you think I'm dumb, boy?" he yelled like I was a thirteen year old, as he put his car in gear with a loud grinding noise and drove up on the grass almost knocking the poor corporal over.

Before he could step out of that big black cruiser, I flung that half full bottle of Old Pikesville as far as my tired old arm could fling it, which wasn't half as far as I'd wished it to fly, and it let out a little shattering noise way down in the culvert. The Sheriff wasn't pleased with the sound of breaking glass, nor with what he smelled wafting in on the breeze, and the cars out on the pike were backing up fast, for those that weren't

17

directly blocked by the Sheriff's vehicle were doing what they called rubber necking in the great Age of the Automobile. We only had a skeleton crew out there drinking that day. There was me, the Corporal, Toots—who was not a bugler, and Nathan Bedford Forest, although that was not his real name, though he wouldn't go by any other. All scrawny old shriveled up shells of ourselves, each bent over till our noses nearly touched the ground, teeth missing, and damned near deaf. Toots had a right arm off above the elbow from the battle of Sharpsburg, and I had a big hole through both lungs from the battle of Antietam on the very same day—now what were the odds of that?[9] But what I'm getting at was we weren't much of a threat to society in general, or that big old Baltimore County sheriff in particular!

"Who threw that bottle?" His Honor bellowed as he pointed his Billy club at our dear departed friend in the paper sack laying there in two inches of last night's rain water.

"What bottle? Over where? What's that speak up, sonny!" We all mumbled, trying to look more tired and useless than we really were, which was a hard thing to pull off unless you had a little practice.

"Then why do I smell whiskey coming in on the wind?" The Sheriff roared like he was William Jennings Bryan.[10]

There must have been fifty cars going five miles an hour out there on the pike with their horns beeping and their fists shaking. Some had come to a complete halt—half on and half off the road, just like the sheriff, and some were getting out of their vehicles to see which one of us old soldiers had finally keeled over and would wave no more.

"Let me see that bottle down there," His Lordship bellowed.

Down in the gully sat Exhibit A—smelling like the fine rye of a Maryland hillside, and the Corporal went gimping down into the morass as if to fetch it. But just as he got to our little banged up buddy in the paper sack, don't he give what's left of our evening's libations a quick little kick and sent it way down into the darkness. Oh, he acted like it was an accident and all, though a William S. Hart[11] he wasn't.

The Sheriff was growing perturbed with us old soldiers and the crowd was starting to take sides, whilst we were longing for our supper which we could smell wafting down from our house up on the hill. Back fin crab cakes cooked in a black iron skillet, no doubt about it! They always served them up with corn on the cob, fresh cut tomatoes, corn bread and butter, a little cucumber and onion in a vinegar sauce. There'd be plenty of coffee and milk, and maybe a fresh strawberry rhubarb pie.

"You old Civil War soldiers have no respect for the law!" The Sheriff cut into my reverie, as he sawed around and yelled. "Get back in your cars, folks, there's nothing to see here—save for a band of drunken old soldiers. And who hasn't seen that before?"

The crowd all laughed, but drunken we weren't, and we took umbrage with his lies. I'd lived through three revolutions in my time,[12] and none of them ever tried to cut off a man's libations. Yet here in the land of the free and the home of the brave we were supposed to go without our alcohol and smile.

"Keep a fast horse handy and a path to the rear," my Daddy had told me when I first went off to war, and that path to the rear sounded like a plan to me. Between the law man's big black cruiser and that slithering gully of muck was a good foot of solid ground—sharply listing to the west, but just about passable, if we kept our heads about us.

"How abouts you move your car over just a little, Your Honor, so we can get by you, and we'll go back home peacefully?" I suggested like the officer and gentleman I was. That was my final offer before we did what all soldiers know to do in a pinch, which was break ranks and run!

The Sheriff was a slow thinking kind of a giant. He sort of reminded me of my old boss, the Tsarevich of Russia, but finally he said. "You boys go on now and get, but I'm not moving my car, and if I ever see you out here drinking again, I swear I'll lock every one of you up for the rest of your lives!"

"And that won't be long now!" one wise cracking bystander shouted, and the crowd laughed as we limped back home like a band of sad sacks.

So to keep from going stir crazy, I took up the pen.

When our Home's administrator learned of our little run in with John Law, he placed us under house arrest until the Second Coming or our own individual funerals—whichever came first. There'd be no more drinking down by the pike unless we wanted to join the displaced peoples of the Great Depression sleeping under a bridge somewhere. So with no outlet for our boyish minds to overcome our aging bodies, we lost our will to live! One by one my comrades began to die off. Nathan Bedford Forest went first—even forgetting who he wasn't anymore, then my old friend Toots tripped and fell, and hit his head, and it was even lonelier around the house without him. Finally one night in a horrible dream, our little Corporal took his last sword slice across the face whilst I wet his lips with a bottle of—you guessed it, smuggled in Maryland Rye Whiskey. So with nothing left to do except stare at the walls, I took up the pen like my grandfather John Stewart before me.

Robert Augustus Stewart is my name—just like my great great granddaddy who died at the Battle of Culloden. Royal Stewarts—we were, though as often as my kin lost their heads at the job, believe me, I'm not bragging. Born December 9th, 1845, my twin sister Lizzy beat me to the wire by two minutes, and never did she let me forget it. And when my Mother, Mary Ann Bloise Stewart would ask if I'd been raised up in a barn, my answer was always a proud and emphatic, hell yes! For horses and horse barns were in my blood from the day I was born till the day I die, which at eighty-five won't be long now.

My first memories of home were of a small horse barn we had out behind our house right there within earshot of the ships in the harbor. We had two fine horses there, Old Dan the unreformed gelding, who was a pure white half-Standard/half Belgium near seventeen hands tall—a little sway back but nevertheless game, and Lucky—a two year old big black thoroughbred who was as fast as the wind. Our cow's name was Mona and she lived there too, with our chickens, a mess of cats, and a stray duck named Margaret. Our barn was an old rickety affair with a red clay floor and a small hayloft up top where we'd play for hours jumping and climbing like Cheyenne braves. In the barnyard was a great mound of manure that my brother John and I would pile high, and when the stalls were all cleaned to my father's liking, we'd lay down fresh straw, put two pitch forks full of hay out for each horse and the cow, and fill a feed pail with grain that smelled of oats and molasses, and another of water. Then my brother would move us back into the depths of the barn up against a tall wooden grain bin. He'd put his hands on my shoulders and call the horses in and they'd come a stomping—huge to boys as small as

20

we were—heading straight for us like ships steaming up the Baltimore Channel. First Old Dan would come stomping in to his stall on the left, and then Lucky with his muscles rippling came back like a runaway freight train and turned into his stall without one word being said.

"I'd like to see human beings act half as civilized," said our father when we recounted the story, and you know Doc was right. To this day I'd say a horse is the more civilized of the two species, though I'd like to see them put their own shoes on.

Doc was the Veterinary Surgeon for the B & O Railroad and before you say why does a railroad need horses, let me just say, I'll get to that. But for those unfamiliar with the state of Maryland, we lie in what they call the Mid-Atlantic States right up against the Atlantic Ocean with the Chesapeake Bay splitting the state almost in half. The eastern shore is up tight to the sea—a flat and sandy land, perfect for slavery with its dusty fields that grow tobacco, or cotton, or beans, or corn in great quantities, whilst the western shore is made up of fine rolling hills where wheat, rye, and alfalfa grow on the lush green hillsides. To the west, Maryland grows steadily narrower with the Mason Dixon Line to the north and the mighty Potomac carving her southern border, so we're shaped like a pistol—the barrel of which was pointing due west into the heart of the nation. The eastern shore was the grip, the western shore the rolling cylinder, the mountain country out in the far west—the long barrel, and Baltimore? Why, Baltimore was and always will be the trigger, and not just the trigger for the state of Maryland, but the trigger for the whole damn nation!

My harbor home was a red brick town with waters so deep you could sail right up to the Light Street Wharf and come alongside Pratt Street in the middle of town. High on the hills above the Basin (which was what we called the harbor) the rich people lived in their fine brick mansions, but down in the flats where the smell of the Jones Falls took a hold of your nose and the seagulls were never silent, lived the newest members of Baltimore's society—the poor Irish, the poor Germans, the poor Italians, the poor Greeks, and the poor Blacks. And if you were on the West End and needed something on the East End toot sweet, you'd have to go down that busy corridor along the wharves at Pratt Street. The long wooden docks brought ships right up to the cobblestone streets and their masts looked like trees as they swung at their moorings. While just to the north of Pratt was a jungle of old brick buildings five or six stories tall running along the length of the Basin. And right in the center of that busy street ran the two tram lines that moved the passengers between the B&O Railroad and the lines coming in from the north.

The rails rolled in to take Baltimore by storm! From the north came the Philadelphia, Wilmington, and Baltimore Railroad with its Boston, New York, and Philadelphia traffic, by way of the President's Street Station on the East End of town. While the Northern Central came in from Harrisburg heading for the Calvert Street Station a mile and a half to the north. The B&O was responsible for all things moving south and west out of the Monumental City, for no locomotives were allowed in the heart of town, which meant each and every rail car that came down Pratt Street had to be towed by horse. Say some Boston Brahmin was shipping his fabric to Richmond, well, they'd ship the fabric from Boston by train to the President's Street Station on the East End, and then we'd haul every last rail car—one at a time down Pratt Street past the docks, and the stores until they reached the Camden Street Station on the West End. And if we had a flood, or a fire, or a blizzard and the horses couldn't get through that bottleneck that Pratt Street was, all traffic would simply cease.

"Didn't make a lick of sense," my father would say of the system. "But that's what keeps our horses fed." He'd add, for Doc was a very practical man.

Every bale of cotton heading north to the fabric mills had to go through the same drill, coming as far as the Mount Clare rail yards on the West End by locomotive, then being taken one car at a time down Pratt Street by horse teams. Every rifle made in the north that went south, or every barrel of molasses heading north from the south, every barrel of maple syrup, every keg of nails, every hundred pound sack of flour from the Baltimore Mills, every yard of fabric, every bottle of whiskey, plug of tobacco, ton of coal, bag full of coffee, and or passenger that passed through Baltimore had to be hauled part way by good old fashion horse power.

Mount Clare Shops stood at the head of the rail line coming in from Washington with a great brick round house where the locomotives could be spun around. And right there up tight to the most modern steel works in the country was the long brick horse barns we called, Mount Clare

Stables—jam packed with some of the best work horses in all of America. We had big standard breds, Clydesdales, Belgiums, half-Belgiums/half-standards, all kinds of mixed breeds, for if they could pull a rail car through town, my father would sign them up.

My brother John and I would leave our little three stalled stable up on Old Dan's back and down Pratt Street we'd ride pretending we were Grandfather John coming back from the Battle of Baltimore. That old white gelding could still draw eyes as he clip-clopped along with his head held high—the two Stewart boys sitting up there proudly on his sweet old sway back.

"In his youth, Young Dan was a fine dapple gray gelding with a sparkling harness and a silvery mane," our free African friend, Chester Harris would tell us. "He gave up a budding career as a rich lady's carriage horse—all for the love of a bay filly."

Chester was my Dad's right hand man, a tall proud Negro with graying temples who'd been sold twice down in Memphis when he was a boy. Doc said, "He was the best man with a sick horse or a stubborn mule that he'd ever seen." My father loved Chester like he was his brother!

"When Old Dan first came to the B&O," Chester would go on, "that big dapple gray had been working high up on the hillside above the harbor where the first monument ever built to George Washington stands, which is why we is known as the Monumental City. That park up there was surrounded by red brick mansions parked side by side in the Federalist fashion; so the blue bloods could get down to the harbor in a hurry." He'd say as he settled us stable boys in under a shade tree or back in the warmth of the barn on a cold blustery day for one of his famous stories. "The rich lady's husband was a ship's captain out traveling the seven seas, and that woman loved nothing more than to drive her carriage through town like a wild banshee!" He said like he was seeing her do it.

Chester would make sure we were all comfortable and although some might find exception with young boys hearing a story full of sex, and violence, and romance, well, we lads were stable boys—born and raised. We'd seen God's creatures humping since we were old enough to walk, so this tale of love and wild abandon was the stuff we all loved!

23

"Young Dan was her fastest horse in a fine stable of fast horses." The old free African would pause to make sure we caught every detail. "He was a strong young gelding with big rippling muscles, a fine silvery head, and pounding hooves!" We'd all be as silent as church mice as Chester moved on. "That rich lady would run her chase down Charles Street with Young Dan doing a fine high stepping fast trot, and when they got to the harbor, she'd wheel him left on Pratt with his hooves setting sparks to the cobblestone streets. Pratt Street was jam packed full of horses that day, with sailors laughing and drinking down by their ships, and street urchins picking their first pockets of the day, whilst the Ladies of the Evening were just coming home from a hard days' night." Chester would pause while we all thought about what a circus Pratt Street always was, and then he'd slowly move on. "Well, there was a sweet bay filly tied by the Maltby House Hotel and she looked especially inviting on that warm spring day. And although you boys all know how Young Dan came to be called a gelding, that poor horse was so much in love with that sweet little filly that it didn't matter. So, up on the bay mare's back he went, coach, rich lady, and all—bouncing like a Mexican jumping bean!"

Chester had us by then no matter how many times we'd heard his story. Thoughts of those wild gyrations going on in broad daylight on the busiest street in Baltimore, whilst the ships rocked at their moorings to the south, and the shop keepers swept their porches to the north, and the sea gulls squawked as they flew overhead, was all too much for us!

"No matter how much that rich lady hooted and hollered, he stood firm in his convictions and was drawing a crowd," Chester went on.

"Get control of that horse!" hollered a farmer with a wagon full of produce headed for the City Market.

"Have you no decency?" hollered a shop owner out sweeping his porch.

"Go for it boy!" shouted a drunken sailor as he leaned against his ship.

Chester would add more and more characters depending on how much lunch break we had, or how bad the mosquitoes were biting. But the story always built to a crescendo for the coming of Doc, my father, the hero of Pratt Street.

"The crowd was growing wild as Young Dan kept to his wild gyrations, and out of the Maltby House Hotel came the bay mare's owner. He was a tall man from a ship building company over in Fell's Point, and he didn't have time for that kind of nonsense, so he grabbed Young Dan by the bridle and tried to haul him down, but the man was no match for that love-struck gelding. The crowd was growing rowdier, as Baltimore crowds tend to do." Chester paused and then went on with the tale of my father and his great wisdom and strength. "Doc was checking a lame horse that had been injured pulling a passenger tram down the tracks," Chester said by way of explaining why Doc was so Johnny on the spot. "He was a tough six footer with broad forearms and a fine full head of curly red hair," which would make us all laugh, since the Doc we knew and loved was just about bald. "That City Passenger tram had a load of New Yorkers heading west for the Camden Street Station, and Doc turned and saw that rich lady up their gyrating away. Quick as the wind, he turned that hurt horse over to his handler and grabbed a bucket from a nearby wagon, emptied out the turnips, and ran to the watering trough."

Chester would always pause right there so we could all catch up with Doc's fast thinking, fast acting ways. "Doc heaved that bucket of freezing cold water right up across Young Dan's face, and as fast as that horse started gasping for air; he grabbed the reins and hauled him down!"

We would all clap and holler hip hip hurray, and then Chester would move on. "Well, the crowd had mixed feelings about Doc stopping their fun and some was saying some mighty ugly things."

"Could you help me down?" the rich lady yelled. "I think we could all use a drink!" And with that the crowds' mood went from fire, to the Fourth of July, as she gathered up her fans and feathered hat and marched right into the Maltby House to buy drinks all around!"

Chester would pause to let us see what a joyful place Baltimore was and then he'd move on to our Dad's fine business sense. "Doc had one round with the lady, but before he left, she said, I'll sell you that horse for fifty cents, Mr. Stewart. Doc tried to talk her out of it, but at the agreed upon price—including his harness and bridle, which she threw in as a parting gift, he bought Young Dan for the B&O Railroad."

Chester finished his tale and prepared to go back to work, but he stopped and put his calloused hands to his chin like he'd forgotten something. "Old Dan worked for the B&O for many a year and when he was sway back and pure white with age, Doc bought him back so Augustus and his brother John here could have a horse to ride. And he paid the railroad exactly what they'd paid for Young Dan—a first in the annals of B&O bookkeeping!" My God we loved Chester and we loved his stories!

But with that bottleneck down on Pratt Street, the horse stables were always a busy place with workers coming and going, shifts of horses sleeping while other's worked, harnessers, teamsters, farriers, and stable hands—the place was a zoo. So nobody even noticed ten or twelve extra boys living up in the hay loft above the horses.

Chester and Doc would see that my homeless friends got at least one meal a day from the coffers of the B&O Railroad. Doc had an account for paying extra help when the work backed up, and what with that bottleneck down on Pratt Street, the work always backed up. Chester would let us cool the horses when they came in off the rails all wild-eyed and frothy from the stress of the streets. We'd walk them 'til that feeling was washed away and then we'd wipe them down, give them some food and water, and turn them into their stalls for some well-deserved rest. Once a month we even had a fire drill.

"You never want to see a horse barn burn!" Chester would say with a tear in his eye, as he told us about a stable he'd seen burn to the ground down in Memphis when he was a boy.

He trained us to throw a blanket over the big work horses' heads so the sight of a fire wouldn't panic them. Then with just a halter and a lead shank, we'd take them out to the open air where the rail cars were lined up. Doc would be standing there with a stopwatch in hand, saying, "We've got to get faster if we want all our horses to survive!"

Up came one of the B&O's managers in a big black bowler hat and yelled, "Why in the world are these horses sitting here with blankets over their heads? Get them out on the rails this instant!"

"This is a fire drill!" Doc bellowed. "You either give us a hand, or you get the hell out of our way!" Doc wasn't scared of management.

The B&O was in stiff competition with the Pennsylvania and New York lines at the time and the bosses had sent Mr. Lewis M. Cole to tell my father how he should run things. Mr. Cole was starting to sweat bullets in his black wool suit as he stared up at Doc. "We've been concerned with your expenditures as of late, Mr. Stewart—ten dollars a month for rat control, what's that all about?"

These were the funds that fed my friends and they were earning every penny cooling the horses down, training for fires, and yes—catching rats. At a penny a rat that mounted up fast down there at the docks, but how could Doc explain that to the bean counter?

"We've doubled our work load in the last six months, Mr. Cole, and you want my men to work even harder while you're laying them off! How in the hell do you plan on doing the work without the workers to do it?" Doc was turning red and his Irish was up as he moved the discussion right off the rat catching funds. I could hear the pipers piping and see the steam coming off his bald head, and I'm sure he'd have gone on 'til he got himself fired, but suddenly there was a sliding noise from the hay loft to my right. Little Larry (who we sometimes called Worm on account of he could crawl into the tightest of places), came sailing down and landed with a big thud in a huge pile of hay.

"What was that?" Mr. Bowler Hat asked with a shocked look on his face, for although Worm weighed but fifty pounds dripping wet, he made one hell of a crash. Just his head was sticking out of that hay pile, but Doc could see him and figured Mr. Cole could too.

We boys up above were as silent as a tomb when my father finally came to his senses and said, "Why, that, sir, was a Baltimore stable rat!"

"A rat," cried Mr. Bowler Hat, "sounds awful big for a rat!"

"Well, if you ever come eye to eye with a Baltimore stable rat, Mr. Cole, you'll know what big really is," went Doc with a straight face and a winning smile, his bright blue eyes twinkling with the mischief we Stewarts loved!

Mr. Cole shook Doc's hand real fast and said he had to be off for parts unknown. After that, we were called the Baltimore Stable Rats, and the log jam down on Pratt Street just kept growing bigger. The connecting

27

lines even complained that the B&O was dragging their feet on bringing their things through town.[13]

The Steam Age was rough on its horses, but Chester had a cure for that too, for on the first Sunday of the month from April 'til hard frost, we would ride the horses through town to a waiting freight car for a trip out to the country. Our free African friend would pick out about twenty head that needed the trip the most and we'd be off. Chester would be in his happy clothes, a red flannel shirt with a loud checkered handkerchief sticking out of his back pocket, tattered blue work pants, and tired old shoes, with a smile on his face as wide as the Mississippi as he directed our loading onto a Northern Central freight car.

"Get that bay up there, Ned." He'd say real gentle like, as the bay gave Ned a little problem with the ramp. Ned, being the oldest and the biggest of the batch at a lanky six foot, had a full time job with the B&O as a horse handler, though he was on a busman's holiday.

"Come on now Larry, don't let that chestnut give you no lip," Chester coached our youngest and original member of the Baltimore Stable Rats.

"Augustus, what is you doing with that black, give him his head for God's sakes and he'll climb up there his own self!" he told me.

"Come on Tommy, bring old blaze around—don't let her chew on that tree!" Tommy was the strongest of the bunch, and Chester always gave him the orneriest horses.

Then up came the other Tom like a knight of the realm, his big black climbing the wooden ramp like he lived there. And with such a good example, in came Rob with his red hair flying aboard a huge Percheron, while nine year old Timmy came in on another tired looking bay.

"You're fine now, Dave. Bring him up, bring him up," Chester coached the taller of our two Dave's—his legs stretched so wide they looked like they'd split.

Then up came the other Dave on a sad looking swayback with his ribs sticking out. Marvin was the old horse's name. He'd once been the best work horse the B&O had, yet when his time to retire came, management wanted to send him down to the Bullock's Glue Factory to cash him out.

28

Doc wouldn't have it, so except for these train rides out to the country and short walks to the wharfs; Marvin was basically in hiding.

Finally, up came the most talented member of the Baltimore Stable Rats atop a big powerful white mare—half Belgium/half Percheron and good God almighty huge! She climbed the ramp and gained room in the box car for two, the other horses moving politely over. Her rider was Allen— a short little boy with the strength of a stevedore. He was the toughest little Stable Rat we had. His hair was cut short, as we all wore it to keep the lice at bay, and he had that relaxed seat of a natural born athlete. Allen could do somersaults up on the big mare's back and she didn't seem to mind. As the remaining horses were led up the ramp, the shriek of the steam engine signaled we were leaving, and with a swift jolt we were underway. North we went through parts of the city that we'd never seen. We saw the rich people's tall brick mansions up on the tree lined hills at Mount Vernon Place where Young Dan had lived before his libido went wild, and the brick and brand new pig iron fronted buildings four and five stories tall on the rolling hills heading out of town.

As the sun came up on that fine spring day, you could smell the sweet smell of the Chesapeake Bay, and the new grass growing, and the horses that needed a bath, as did we all. We were on our way to the Big Gunpowder Falls—watching the countryside roll by as our hearts filled with excitement. Out the wide wooden slats of the railcar we watched as we came to a place called Phoenix where the Northern Central ran right alongside the river. You could smell the cool mud and fresh water down below. Unlike the smell of the Basin back in the city; it was a sweet tasting fresh water that smelled like heaven. Silent as a church at midnight, we watched the river flow by in peaceful swirls, as the horses breathed in the cool country air and started to talk. Now, if you've never heard a horse talk before, then I know you've never spent any time around a horse barn, for a horse had about a million ways to let you know they were happy, or hungry, or ready to give you a good swift kick. But these whinnies we heard on that blue sky Sunday were the whinnies of freedom! And those whinnies of freedom spread from the horses to us boys like a wild fire. Chester even joined in with a whinny of his own, for it was good to be free and out in the country!

29

The locomotive started to slow down at a little dirt road that crossed the river via a short iron truss bridge maybe three miles north of Phoenix. I remember looking east as we crossed a dirt lane and there was a big white mansion with a slave quarters the size of the Maltby House Hotel. A mess of slaves were looking for poke sally in the weeds by the railroad tracks and I thought to myself, why don't they just run? But they just smiled and waved as the train rolled by.

About a mile north the locomotive slowed down and came to a stop on a rise by the river with a little trail dropping down maybe fifty or sixty feet to the stream. A dove cooed in the woods nearby where a great hard wood forest rose several hundred feet in the air. The crickets cricked, and the birds chirped, and the sun shined down upon us on that glorious Sunday. All we city boys had ever heard for our whole lives was the sounds of horses clacking on cobblestone streets, hammers hammering, ships' rigging ringing with the roll of the sea, hustlers selling their wares, and thousands of people yelling and screaming—all day long, every day. It was like we had entered a giant cathedral, and we led the horses down off the rail car in awe! A quail sang his bob white song on the hillside as we boys raced down to the river. The Gunpowder ran between two big wooded hills and picked up speed with a loud gurgling sound as we threw off our clothes and jumped right in. We let out loud shrieks as we hit the cold water and once the horses realized we were just playing, they moved on down to the river's edge and joined us. Chester was standing up near the tracks shaking his head and taking off those tattered shoes with a big smile on his face. He carried two heavy burlap sacks, which we all figured was supper, for Chester liked to see us boys eat.

"You Stable Rats is the craziest bunch of wild Indians I has ever seen," he hollered as he prepared to enter the waters with his pant legs rolled up. He'd been working fifteen hour days trying to keep the horses healthy, but on that first Sunday in April, we were all there to wash our troubles away! We had horses with torn ligaments and pulled muscles, horses with shin bone breaks, lacerations, abrasions, and just plain fatigue from pounding the streets. They picked their heads up and looked around at the ancient forest as they sniffed the warm spring air, felt the sun on their backs, and breathed in the first whiff of freedom they'd had in a year.

30

Chester jumped into the cold water with a mighty gasp and a, "Good God Almighty" and we all laughed as the Northern Central gave us a farewell toot. We'd be picked back up by the train coming in from Harrisburg around 6:00 PM, so we proceeded to swim, and wash the horses, and maybe eat what Chester had brought us.

Our old free African friend waded up to a low sandy island maybe a hundred yards upstream, dropped his heavy burlap bags in the sand and said he'd be off gathering firewood. Ned climbed up on a big bay's back and scouted up to the north, hollering down that he'd found a nice little waterfall, with pools, and ferns, and perfectly clear water. Me and about six of the boys scouted downriver to where a great white rock sat half in and half out of the stream. There was a hole there that was near six feet deep and were swimming for our lives when up came the work horses—first five, then ten, then twelve—all gathering around us with joy in their eyes as we jumped in and splashed them. Why, Cheyenne braves never felt as free as we boys did on that warm Sunday in April!

Allen had trained his big white mare to canter down the shallow western side of the creek whilst he stood on her back with his arms outstretched like a circus performer. We boys would all clap and cheer—a great echo coming off the wooded hillside as he did somersaults and smiled.

Timmy, our youngest member of the Stable Rats, and Worm, were up gathering firewood from snags near our little island in the stream. They were picking up their feet real high with oohs and aahs as the gravel poked at their toes. Several of the horses were gathered round them in the shallows grazing on tender shoots of wild asparagus, and there was Old Marvin—the swayback retiree trying to mount the bay mare. Spring had certainly sprung!

When Chester finally returned from his travels, he got a fire going and by 2:00 PM we were all back up on our little island with enough firewood to burn that bon-fire for a couple of days. We had our clothes back on save for our shoes and socks, and every horse was present and accounted for as we bowed our heads in prayer. "Sweet Jesus," Chester started his invocation. "We thank you for these foods we are about to receive from thy bounty!"

31

Amens and Hallelujahs were interjected with great vigor whenever and wherever The Spirit moved us, for Chester had taught us our prayers in the fine Negro fashion. We might be a band of mostly white boys, but when we prayed, we prayed pure black!

"Thank you Jesus!" we added to our rhythmic responses, and then the old free African asked the Lord to protect our horses.

"Let them rise from their injuries, dear Lord, and let them never feel the whip!" He prayed until the bacon on the fire turned us all into a band of brigands, and someone in the back row yelled, "Good God let's eat!"

Chester let out a little gasp like we were a band of incorrigible boys,[14] then he swept away a bed of hot coals and there before us was his famous black iron skillet and his Tennessee corn muffins! He lifted the top with an old rag and there was that rich golden brown crust with a big wedge of butter in a cloth sitting up on a rock nearby. He tapped at the bottom of the pan with his Bowie knife and dropped that big muffin whole to the rock near the butter, whilst he flipped the skillet back over to make us a mess of eggs. Then before we broke bread on that fine spring day, out of Chester's burlap sack came twenty bright red apples from last year's crop—one for each horse. We served them up with love and laughter for those horses were the reason we were there!

After we ate, Chester put some more wood on the fire and began tuning up his five string banza. Now you might think I spelled banjo wrong, but those that call it a banjo are the ones that are mistaken.

"You see a banza comes all the way from Africa," Chester would say proudly as he tuned her up. His calloused black fingers going almost around the fretless neck as he sat there by the fire with his legs crossed and a big smile on his weathered face. Ned and I got out our trusty harmonicas and tested the waters, while little Larry was twanging away on his Jew's harp. The rest of the lads were forming a circle around the campfire waiting for the fun to begin with a couple of gourds and a wayward wash board or two, but always before we played, Chester had to finish his banza story! "Now a banza was first made with a long stick for the neck and a big gourd for the body, kind a like a drum with strings. And them strings was made of very special things—secrets from the deepest and darkest of Africa," he'd say, and although we knew he was born a slave down in Memphis, he was a true African on that magical Sunday!

He started to strum at his banza and plucked at the strings, making adjustments as he went. "And on that Middle Passage from Africa to this white world we live in, them slavers cast all our slave things into the sea. So if we wanted a banza in America, we had to make one, and what we made from our homeland, we had to hide from the bosses, for we were in America to work—not to play the banza!"

We'd all laughed, for we were city boys who already knew this was a strange world we lived in. Chester sat there strumming away and smiled whilst the horses gathered in the stream and listened in. And when we finally cut loose with our wild mountain music, the horses swished their tails in time to our tunes. We played Look Out the Way Old Dan Tucker, Swing Low Sweet Chariot, and several others, and when it was time to leave, Chester bellowed, "Leave the fire burning, boys, someone's bound to come along and use it!"

Whatever was left in those burlap sacks was left behind too—no questions asked. We boys all imagined that Chester was provisioning a runaway army, for there was a big cave down river which was a good place for runaways to hide. In our active minds, the escaped slaves would come out of that cave, eat what was left in the burlap sacks and warm themselves by our fire, and then they'd be off for all points north, disappearing around the hills up near Monkton Mills. And since we'd laid down enough scent to block the noses of the best bloodhounds in Maryland, they would be free of the slave chasers! It was a nice story, and we rode the box car back home in silence and detrained at the Bolton Street Station with smiles on our faces.

It was dark when we hit Baltimore and most of the white folks had turned in for the night, but seeing how it was Sunday evening; the Negroes were out in force! Over twenty thousand Free Africans and a couple thousand slaves lived in the Monumental City and at least half of them went to church come a Sunday evening. So as we clip-clopped towards the center of town with the rain coming down, you could hear the whole south end singing the Lord's praises! We heard Go Down

Moses being sung by a heavenly choir from way down on Montgomery Street where the Ebenezer African Methodist Episcopal Church sang away, then an echo coming from way across the Basin from a ring shout that was moaning and groaning—and not in English, no sir, we were in the belly of Old Mother Africa, as they sang in Swahili.

The next day was a school day and if you're wondering why I haven't said much about my schooling to date, well, there wasn't much to say. My twin sister Lizzy did real good in school, but I was a boy of action and sitting on my derriere was sheer torture. My life was one of truancy, the dunce corner, and being sent home from school for various and sundry sins. Luckily, Doc was a practical man and he could see that my talents lay elsewhere, whilst my Mother, well she expected better things from a "Royal Stewart."

My thirteenth birthday was coming up fast and I'd found a part time job delivering telegrams for the B&O Telegraph Company. My first delivery was to a wealthy man up on Charles Street north of the city some three miles. This was the land of the rich with big oak trees and lots of wide green lawns. The heat was stifling that August morning as Old Dan and I trotted along. That rich man's lane was made of crushed oyster shells that sparkled pure white in the sunlight and up around a curve we went to where a huge brick mansion stood on a hill with windows taller than a horse—all trimmed in bright white marble. Dark green shutters stood on each side of those long shiny windows and out of the center of that huge white mansion was a pure white portico with gingerbread trim. The walls were painted white, the great door that my friend Allen could have ridden his horse through with his arms outstretched was white, the thirty foot tall Greek columns that ringed the portico were white, and even the marble steps that climbed up the fancy front porch were white as well.

Off Old Dan's back I jumped, tying him to a post by the front porch that had a cast iron horse head on top. I climbed the steep stairs wondering what I should say to my first customer of the day, since I'd failed to read my manual in a timely fashion. I knocked on the door twice then stepped back and stood at my best imitation of military attention and waited for what seemed like an eternity. Bang, bang, bang, on the screen door I went for a three bang combination the second try out. "This here's a telegram from the B&O Railroad and Telegraph Company," I bellowed.

There was silence. Then a katydid sang his yakety yak song from a tall oak tree behind me, then more silence. It was as quiet as a graveyard.

"Knock, knock, knock, knock," I added that fourth knock for effect and waited with little balls of sweat running down my back.

I had that strange feeling that someone was watching me as I heard a raspy whisper say, "Go around back, boy."

But that katydid must have been watching me too, because he would start and stop depending on whether I was moving or not. I stood there as still as the dead and that katydid cried, yakety yak yak.

"Are you daft boy? I said go around back!" This time the voice from the crypt within was loud enough for me to know it wasn't a ghost.

I climbed back down those twelve marble stairs and started to walk around to the west wing when all of a sudden that same ghastly voice spoke from a side window. "Take your horse around back with you, boy! Are you daft?" he gasped like the ghost of Edgar Allen Poe.

The back of the mansion looked like a mirror image of the front, and it reminded me of Poe's Premature Burial on account of that bell tower on top of the carriage house. But that silence was way too much for a high strung boy! Was I alive or dead? Only that katydid seemed to know, for even around back, when I moved he fell silent, and when I stood perfectly still—like at the back screen door, he would start in again.

"Knock, knock," I signaled my presence once more, thinking if this was the way my delivery business went, I should get paid by the hour.

Finally, an old cadaver of a man waddled up to the screen door looking like death warmed over. He would have been six foot if his head wasn't resting on his chest like it was. Hollow jawed like a dead man; he was the epitome of all things Poe. I wanted to throw him his telegram and run for the hills! "Take those shoes off, boy," he moaned.

"I've got a telegram for a Mr. ah ah..." He had me so tongue tied and twisted I couldn't even remember my name!

"I said take your shoes off, boy, and get in here." Said the old hunchback, and he disappeared as the katydid hit his cue once more.

The old mummy went rummaging around in the next room for his glasses and I was thinking he could sneak up behind me and hit me upside the head with a ball peen hammer when I least expected it! I'd wake up down in his dungeon tied to a table with a pendulum swinging over my head, and by the time they backtracked all the way up there to that mansion on the hill, all traces of me and Old Dan would be gone. So I searched that darkened room for any weapon I could find. There was a fireplace in the corner made of fancy white marble with a set of tarnished old brass ornaments—a little hunting horn on the top of each and every one. I could hear the old ghoul batting around, so with the speed only fear could bring to a small boy like me; I lifted that long brass poker from the holder and stuffed it down my pants.

Just then the old ghoul reappeared. "Now, come boy, what is it? Speak up and be quick," he croaked with breath so bad it smelled like where the Jones Falls ran into the harbor.

Strange how the slowest man I'd ever seen in my life was telling me to be quick, but what I wanted to do right then was throw him his telegram, run for the door, leap down those white marble stairs, jump up on Old Dan's back, and ride for the hills. But there was one problem with that plan, for that poker was crushing my nannies!

I stood sideways to the old cadaver as he silently stared and said, "This here's a message from the B&O Telegraph Company," as I turned and limped over to pass him his telegram—hoping he wouldn't notice that little hunting horn sticking out of my waistline.

He looked at my limp with cold disdain, like maybe he figured cripples should be drowned in burlap sacks like blind kittens were, which would have left him and that hunchback treading water too, but Good God Almighty that rod was painful! He took that telegram and started reading as I worked on how to explain that brass hunting horn, should he ask. What's that poker doing in my pants? That didn't sound right! Sorry about putting your poker down my pants—that sounded even worse! Well, you see, sir I had a mosquito bite in the strangest of places whilst you were off finding your glasses. That last one sounded like a winner to me, but before I could polish my story, he yelled, "You really are a daft one, boy! Put your boots back on and get the hell out of here!"

I took a deep breath, poked that stiff leg behind me like a bad Bolshoi ballerina, picked up my shoes and limped for the door with not a penny for my troubles. This job was a pain in the balls!

My next delivery was to the slave pens down on the southwest corner of Pratt and Eutaw Streets right in the heart of the city. I was looking for a Mr. Donovan and although the distance from the B&O Telegraph spindle where I picked up the message was but four hundred feet to the slave pens where it was going, it took me a full hour to get the job done.

It felt like a fiery furnace as Baltimore days tend to do in the dog days of August, not a breeze stirring out in the Basin as the sea gulls cried hoarsely for water. Old Dan and I walked up there to the slave pens with great trepidation, for we hated the place more than Death itself. First off, it stunk for those slavers were a filthy bunch, and secondly, even if they called their slaves stock, they didn't care for them like Doc trained us to care for our stock. My father would have horse whipped a man for treating any animal like that, only here south of the Mason-Dixon you didn't dare tell a man how to treat his own slaves! When Old Dan and I got to that wooden shanty with the high wooden fence, I saw three tall black bucks walking the fence line like caged animals, and two lady slaves sitting up in the shade by a ramshackle shanty. A white man sat beside them carving a little chunk of wood with his Bowie knife.

I was already feeling surly when I yelled, "I got a telegram here for a Mr. Joseph Donovan, is that you, sir?"

But there was no answer from that slovenly slaver who sat there whittling away as he spit a great gob of tobacco like a giant grasshopper. He wore a dirty long underwear top and a pair of the dirtiest pants I had ever seen. "Are you Mr. Donovan?" I hollered through the wooden slats.

"Ain't me, boy. Get the hell out of here!" He yelled, as he kept on whittling.

The lady slaves looked at me like I was the best entertainment they'd seen all day as I yelled, "I'm from the Baltimore and Ohio Telegraph Company with a message for a Mr. Joseph Donovan, or his agent!"

He looked at me like he was thinking about who he was and who he wasn't, but hadn't the energy to decide. I was so disgusted with my new job that I turned to walk away and hollered in a tremulous voice, "Fine, if Mr. Donovan or his agent don't care that they found one of their runaways and they're holding him up in Pennsylvania, then so be it!"

"What's that, boy? Get your scrawny little ass over here," says the splay footed slaver, for his Southern drawl was thicker than molasses.

He got up real slow from that over worked chair and headed for the gate, taking out a big rusty key from a chain tied to his rope belt. My plan was to hand him the telegram and run like hell, for he looked like a very dangerous man!

The three male slaves came nearer as they begged for water with their eyes as that toothless slaver unlocked the padlock, grabbed me up by the scruff of my neck, and hauled me in. He banged the rickety gate shut and locked it tight. I was now a prisoner just like the slaves—only I was pretty sure that at the end of the day; I'd be set free, while they weren't even sure they'd get water! I wore my best white shirt and a nice pair of brown dress pants with a pair of freshly shined riding boots, and that lowly slaver looked at me with disgust.

"You sure are a Yankee Doodle dandy, ain't you boy?" He said stretching that "boy" part out into at least three syllables. "Now what's this here b..hul..ull shit about a runaway slave?" His once white undershirt had great streaks where he hadn't spit his chew quite far enough out, and here he was lecturing me on my appearance! It was bad enough I had to act all polite like, "to the good patrons of the B&O Railroad and Telegraph Company," like the manual said (when I finally read it), but not only was I forced to sell myself cheaply—so far to the sum of zero dollars and zero cents, but I had to stand there and smile whilst being insulted by the dirtiest white man I'd ever seen!

"You damn Yankees think you're better than us boys from the Deep South, don't you, son?" He asked like he was reading my mind.

It was getting real hot out there in the haze that day. You couldn't see the harbor some two blocks away, as the heat waves rippled up off the railroad tracks casting mirages of water to the poor thirsty slaves. And in what shade was left of that falling down shack, I could just make out a pail of water with a little wooden ladle sticking out.

"Listen sir, I don't want to waste your time," I told him—since he was perfectly capable of doing that himself. "But this here is a telegram to a Mr. Donovan or his agent, and if that's you, you could make yourself some real good money by going up there to Pennsylvania and fetching him." I said as polite as a Yankee could be to a dirty filthy slaver.

"I be his agent, hell yes I is," he answered with a new found pride. "Mr. Donovan done left me in charge, but you'll need to read that message to me, boy, for I ain't got no need for reading."

Suddenly, I realized why my Momma was so disgusted with my slovenly school work! I turned over the telegram and slowly read: "To Joseph Donovan, from the Lancaster County, Pennsylvania Clerk's Office. Sir, we are holding your slave, one Ape boy, a six foot male of about twenty with exceptionally long arms and legs. You can pick him up at your convenience at the Lancaster County Jailhouse. Expenses of the Court will accrue on a daily basis."

It was all rather business like, you see, Lancaster County had gotten themselves in trouble back in 1851 for sheltering a runaway slave against the brand new Fugitive Slave Act. This fine Federal law stated that a slave owner had the right to go fetch his runaways from wherever they ran off to, and the state that the slave had escaped to had a solemn duty to return the escapee. A Maryland slaver, who lived out near our little island in the stream, had gone up to Pennsylvania to fetch his runaways and someone took a scythe to his heart. They called it the Christiana Riot and the master's son was near murdered, so since then, the state of Pennsylvania had been on their good behavior. So Mr. Donovan and the other slave chasers could just wait for the northern states to gather their runaways, and go up and fetch them back. A good male slave could bring two thousand dollars, so the slavers would just go up north, pick up their property, and everybody would be happy. Everybody except the slaves, that is!

39

"How am I gonna leave these damn darkies alone to go and fetch that Ape boy back?" The toothless wonder complained as he looked at me like I was his new found friend. Bad enough I had to read his telegram for him, but now he wanted me to do his thinking too.

"You let me give them bucks over there a drink of water and a piece of that stale bread, and I'll tell you how to pick up that runaway for pennies on the dollar."

He scratched his butt, chawed his tobacco kind of academic like (if you could call chewing your cud academic), then he scratched his rump once more like it was the seat of his thought, and told me real serious like, "Don't you try nothing smart now, boy!"

I went over and gave them each a wooden ladle full of lukewarm water. They had whip marks all over their backs and rags for clothes, and they were sweating bullets in that hot steaming sun. Their heads were down as I said, "Easy boys, I ain't gonna hurt you," like we talked to our horses, for though there was fear in their eyes, their muscles were huge and it didn't look like they had any love for us white people. They drank in the water and gnawed at the bread like that lazy cracker hadn't risen from his chair in days.

"Thank you, Massa," says the oldest of the black men; his hair graying a little around his temples like Chester's was.

"Did he just try to talk to you, boy?" barked the slaver and he started to walk over with his hand on his Bowie knife.

"No sir," I said with no respect at all, as I walked over to the ramshackle shanty and handed the lady slaves the rest of that stale bread and what was left of the water. Then I told my new friend how to go and retrieve his slave. "All you've got to do is walk east a block to Howard Street right there," and I pointed it out. "Then you head north up Howard a mile to the Bolton Street Station and get on the New York Central to Harrisburg, Pennsylvania. But be sure you get off at York!" I paused since none of this seemed to be sinking in. "At York you catch the Wrightsville, York, & Gettysburg train line east into Lancaster. It will let you off right there at the courthouse, and you can be back here by nightfall."

"Well, how abouts you watch these here slaves whilst I go north and fetch that runaway back? I'll give you fifty dollars for your troubles!" he said as he spit on his hand and prepared to shake on it.

I had a real dilemma on my hands, for could an abolitionist like me take money (and that was real good money), for watching someone else's slaves whilst the slovenly slaver went to fetch his other slave back from a run for freedom? I knew what Jesus would say on the subject, and what Old John Brown would say too, but maybe they'd seen what a fifty dollar bank note looked like—not me! Yet even if those slaves were the meanest bears that ever walked this earth, I'd have set them free, for didn't every creature deserve their freedom, just like Doc said.

So, my answer was, "Hell no, I ain't watching your slaves!"

He looked at me like our friendship was over, scratched his rump like a monkey with fleas, and said in the saddest voice I'd ever heard, "Then what shall I do with these here darkies?"

"Take them along for the ride," thinks I out loud, not really thinking he'd try it! "Why a ticket to Lancaster and back won't cost you more than two dollars apiece, and your master would pay a pretty penny for the return of that Ape boy. But you'll have to feed them up and get them some clothes, for us northerners don't like to see our slaves mistreated."[15]

And that's how a Georgia cracker and his five slaves left the Monumental City for all points north, whilst I collected absolutely nothing by way of a tip. But the fact was, he had to feed and water them, and they got to get out of town during the hottest part of the season, and that was all the reward I needed. Three days later the whole mess of them headed north in chains looking five pounds heavier and happy for a break from the heat, so you can call me a poor excuse for an abolitionist boy if you like, but ethics weren't exactly my specialty!

After that pressing dilemma was solved to everyone's satisfaction, it was on to my next assignment. The high clock tower at the Camden Street Station guided me in to the telegraph office. Inside the huge brick building was the main offices for the B&O Railroad with a large reception room for our customers and a ticket office. Out back was a long wide covered platform where the luggage from the connecting railroads could be sorted and put onboard the outgoing trains. We were the gateway to a mighty railway system that ran west into Virginia and Washington, D.C. and on out into Ohio and the Great American West. The world's most modern train station was what our sign said, and the telegraph office was right there in the southwest corner.

Someday I wanted to become a telegrapher and learn Morse code, but you had to be sixteen for that. The telegraphers sat behind their desks firing away with their messages and getting up and placing them on a little spindle by the front counter in the order they were to be picked up. The telegraph manager sat up front at a high desk like a judge overseeing the work as I came into the chattering room.

"Good morning, Mr. Sommers," I said to the top dog who was sitting there acting like he hadn't heard me. He pointed to the spindle like he couldn't be bothered with a part-time boy like me. Our employee manual stated that you were supposed to take the first message on the spindle— only word on the street was you could keep one eye on the manager, and one eye on the messages, and save yourself some trouble. Bad enough I'd worked four hours for free that day, but there was no need to kill Old Dan out there in the heat! Well, ain't there a message on the third spoke back for a Mr. Salomon down on Thames Street, which was in Fell's Point right near my home, so I did what the delivery boys called a switchero and slid the first spoke's message to the third spoke's slot and pocketed the switch. Then out I sailed down Pratt Street past the docks and the stores on my way to the third customer of the day.

Old Dan and I played Grandad John Stewart on our way to stop the British when they came for Fort McHenry back in 1814. Old Dan looked like the dapple gray stallion he always figured he was, whilst I imagined that the stick I'd picked up at the Camden Street Station was a sword held high in the air. "On to Fells Point my fine fellows, our friends are waiting!" I hollered under my breath to my imaginary 5th Regiment as we reached the mile marker heading for where Pratt Street narrowed over a little wooden bridge at the Jones Falls. All was a hustle at that narrow little bottleneck and my men were being held up by the throng. My trusty stallion and I kept pressing on for the President's Street Station just to the south a few blocks. East on Alice Anna Street we went clopping along on the hot cobblestones as the smell of the Bay blew in and the seagulls grew thicker and louder, then south on Ann Street to Thames we went, right there by the docks.

There was a block of red brick Federals staring at the still harbor and the only three story structure in the first five shops was Mr. Salomon's little jewelry store. Narrow she was with a little dormer sticking out of the top, a skinny little arched doorway on the east end which had probably been there since the Revolution. Above the jewelry shop door was a fine long cast iron holder that came to a spiraling circle about three feet out with a great shiny globe of polished copper hanging down, and back near the red brick wall was a square with a brown background and white lettering that said, "Salomon's Fine Jewelry."

A little hidden bell rang as I opened the door and announced my coming. "I have a telegram for Mr. Haym Salomon!" I cried out.

Once my eyes got use to the darkness, I could see there was but twenty feet of counter space. The rest must have been a shop in the back, as there was a little door behind a long glass topped display case that ran near the width of the narrow store. On either side of me was more glass covered displays running three quarters of the way to the door with the only light coming in by way of those two little windows. Luckily there was a gas lamp on each wall with finely polished brass reflectors that lit the room in a golden light, and there in the back standing next to his showcase stood Mr. Salomon smiling away.

"I'm Haym Salomon; may I help you, son?"

"I have a telegram for you, sir," I said and I walked across the remainder of that tiny little space in about three steps and handed it over to him.

He stood maybe five foot ten or so, a thin man in a black suit, a black bow tie tied tight to his thick neck and ruddy sun-beaten skin. His furrowed forehead rose to a thick head of black wispy hair—parted down the middle, whilst his nose was that of the tribe of Abraham—long and proud, but again ruddier than someone who worked inside.

Later he told me of the farm fields around Philadelphia that he'd worked, and how he'd saved enough money to buy this business. Mr. Salomon's grandfather had been a wealthy man who helped finance our Revolution,

43

but he'd died a pauper when Congress failed to pay him back. He took the telegram, read his name on the one side, turned it over and silently read the message. "More bills," he said with a shake of his head, and as he filed that telegram away in a desk drawer with a thousand others, he asked me in a gentle voice, "Care for some tea?"

Well, I'd never had tea with a Jewish man before (or anybody else for that matter), so I told him I'd go and loosen the cinch on Old Dan's saddle, make sure he had some water and a little shade, and then I'd be back for that tea. Outside I ran to take care of Old Dan. He was standing in the sun watching the traffic go by and I found him some shade and a watering trough, and tied my old swayback friend to a sycamore tree.

"Be back soon, Dan, me and this Jewish fellow is gonna have us some tea! Ain't that something?" I told him and he seemed impressed.

My momma had warned me that spending all my time with the Baltimore Stable Rats would be the death of me, and now with my new job at the B&O Telegraph Company, my horizons were expanding by leaps and by bounds. I straightened my shirt. It had been a real rough day, and now it was time to show some class. After all, I came from the blood of the Stewart Kings! Back into Mr. Salomon's jewelry store I bounded like I was about to have tea with the Queen. He had two little china cups sitting on the center of that long glass counter with a pitcher of what turned out to be boiling hot water. There was a plate of, good God Almighty—sugar cookies, and Lord was I hungry! He came around to the front of the counter and held out his hand, looked me straight in the eyes, and announced in a soft voice, "I'm Haym Salomon, pleased to meet you, son."

I looked up into those deep dark eyes and saw the soul of a gentle man. Casting out my right hand just as he'd done, I told him, "my name is Robert Augustus Stewart, but my friends call me Augustus. I'm pleased to meet you too, Mr. Salomon, sir."

"Where are my manners, Augustus? I'll get us some chairs from the back room," he said with a friendly grin. Beneath that finely chiseled nose was a great brown and blond two-toned mustache that twitched as he talked.

He handed me a little silver ball with holes in it and a long silver chain, what it was, was anybody's guess? But I watched and waited and saw him plunk his silver ball into the small cup and pour scalding hot water from the pot until his cup was full and I followed suite. He smiled and seemed to be following my awkwardness with great curiosity—like maybe he'd been a bungling boy once too.

"Been working for the B&O Telegraph Company for long, Mr. Stewart?" His eyes looked away just long enough for me to have some privacy, then they swung back again.

"No sir, this here is my first day on the job."

"And what a day it's been!" he said like he'd been along for the ride.

"How did you know that, Mr. Salomon?" I asked as I took a bite of those wondrous cookies.

"Today is your bar mitzvah, Augustus. The day the work world steps out to greet you. You were a boy when you set out this morning, and now you've seen that the world is a very dangerous place full of cold hearted people!" he was reading my mind. "But remember this, my friend, where there is darkness there is light! Today you have seen that there are many paths you can take in this world—you can follow the light or you can follow the darkness, but I see in your sparkling blue eyes a follower of the light. Would you like some more sugar cookies, Mr. Stewart?"

While this wonderful man had been defining my steps from a child to a man, I was busy devouring his cookies at a rapid rate. I apologized over and over, and when it was time to leave and he tried to give me a dime for my troubles, I held him off through a dozen rounds. At least once a week from that day forward, I would stop and see my good friend Haym. I'd bring the sugar cookies from a little German bakery, and we'd have a civilized conversation. Why, he even gave Old Dan an apple every time!

As my trusty steed and I headed back to the Camden Street Station for our last job of the day, I saw what Mr. Salomon meant about the light and the darkness. It was everywhere to be seen on those city streets. There were muleskinners whipping their stock and hollering like hellions, young boys and girls holding onto their momma's hands, slaves jingling by with their legs in irons—all moving in step to keep from

45

tripping. There were shop owners up on their wide wooden porches gazing out into the Basin like they were proud of their harbor home, sailors wrestling in the street—some half drunk and angry, some all smiles, ship's captains standing on their vessels with their watches in hand hollering that they had to hurry and cast off with the tide. There were ladies of the evening smiling away, whilst their good friends the pickpockets lighten someone's load. Good and bad all around us, just as Mr. Salomon had said, but on my bar mitzvah day, all I wanted to see was the good in my people. Baltimore might have it's rough edges, but you build a city by the prettiest Bay in the whole country, and you bring in the voices of people from all over the world, add rich men, and poor men, and people with callouses on their hands, and what do you get? Just the best damn city in the entire nation!

I rode back to the big brick cathedral that the B&O built and was hoping to find a close in delivery for my final job. As I shimmied past the front desk where Mr. Sommers was holding court, he had his eyes to the front like a museum statue as I stared down at the spindle. One, some three back was just a few blocks away, so I coughed and I sneezed, and with my bumbling fingers #1 goes to #3 and the great switcheroo was made. Mr. Sommers was still staring straight ahead, when all of a sudden there came a loud voice straight from the heavens. "You didn't just try and switch telegrams on me, did you, boy?" Mr. Sommers was still sitting at that high judge's bench facing forward with his mouth shut, but I swore that sound came from his lips—rumbling across those twenty foot ceilings and making me sweat.

"Mr. Stewart, I suggest you correct your error and be off with you, boy," said the voice from on high—only this time I saw his lips moving.

A little snicker went up from the telegraphers who'd returned to their clacking, and I put #3 back in its place and took the one I was supposed to take. It was a couple of miles away up on the hills above the harbor and as I walked past the front desk, Mr. Sommers barked, "Don't you ever try that on me again, Mr. Stewart!" He didn't look up, he didn't look down, and he didn't even seem to be looking around, yet the man had won my respect and set me on the path to a love for all things foreign! Foreign women, foreign places, foreign tongues—from that day forward the die was cast; Baltimore would never hold me!

Up Howard Street we rode, that big white gelding still as strong as he was in the morning, though a bit lathered—his head held high in the rippling heat. Old Dan and I climbed the hill by the harbor going up and up for close to a mile on Charles Street past some of the tallest brick buildings in the city. We hit the four legged park at Mount Vernon Place and I tipped my hat to the tall white statue of General George Washington. Then on we rode past the big brown and gray stone Mount Vernon Place Methodist Church as big as any cathedral. One square north we started to descend Monument Hill and there was a big bronze statue of General Howard in his tricorne hat up on a plucky stallion with his right hand pointing straight to where that telegram was heading.

The park was peaceful and calm as I turned right onto East Madison Street and headed for the 1st brick town house on the north side of the street. She stood some three stories tall—deeper than she was wide with a tall arched doorway surrounded in you guessed it, white marble with two eight foot windows to the side. There were three tall windows on the second and third floors with their thick wavy glass looking out on the park. Beside that brick mansion was a little private park with a high brick wall separating it from the Lovegrove alleyway, and if ever there was a better named alleyway in all of Baltimore, nobody bothered to tell me.

I tied Old Dan to the fence in the shade and up those five pure white marble steps I ran. They had an eight foot tall double wooden door with a little brass thing in the center that when you twisted it real hard, it rang loud and clear. But first I shifted my trousers, brushed the horse hair off as best I could, and tucked my shirt tail in. Then I shined my boots against the back of my pants and patted my hair, for that telegram I was delivering had come all the way from Paris, France. And the fact that that Trans-Atlantic message was destined to pass through my hands on the very day that Mr. Salomon had pronounced me a man, seemed like a sign from the Lord! I gave that brass knob a good twist and the doorbell rang and up came a six foot Negro gentleman in a black tuxedo. He opened the door with a stately manner; wearing white gloves and standing as straight as any Guardsman I ever saw. There was no gray on his black curly temples, though he wasn't what you'd call young, and he had an English accent, which I later found out was Jamaican.

"May I help you, sah?" he said in his deep bass voice.

Now, I had never been called sir before, and never heard a Negro with an English accent, but as I started to answer him three pretty ladies in next to nothing came giggling by. They went into a large parlor to the east of a huge pocket door, and I figured this was some kind of a finishing school for girls, only the girls hadn't quite finished dressing. One of the girls was a tall buxomy blonde haired beauty. She wore a sky blue piece of short little underwear with a garter belt kind of thing that no boy should ever see before he's had his bar mitzvah! The second girl or lady, I wasn't quite sure where one left off and the other one started, had brown hair tied up nice and high—big brown eyes that were warm and caring, and Lord knows what they called that thing she was wearing?

"Telegram," I said as my voice cracked high. "I have a Trans-Atlantic telegram for a Miss Yvette DuPuis!"

The butler stepped back in awe, whilst the girls gave a gasp. "Look at those baby blue eyes; have you ever seen anything so beautiful? Why, he should have been a girl," the brunette said, and my interests suddenly went from all things horses, to all things women in the blink of an eye.

"I'm Sabastian," the white gloved Jamaican cut in to my reverie, "and this here is Natalia, Jasmine, and Jennifer. Girls, why don't you go upstairs and put on some clothes, look how the poor boy blushes!"

"Don't bother on my account," I said all flustered. "You look mighty fine to me!"

It seemed women and horses had something in common; if you stayed real calm, they wouldn't crush you! And I stayed calm and ogled to my heart's content as the girls giggled and gawked. "My God, he's cute," said the buxomy blonde and I blushed even hotter.

"Do you know Chester Harris?" was my question to the butler.

"Why do you ask?" he said with the whites of his eyes rolling back in his head like he'd heard that kind of thing before.

48

"Well, he's a friend of mine, that's all. I thought maybe you'd heard of him, since the two of you are Negros?"

He laughed and his bow tie shook as he asked, "Do you know how many black people there are in Baltimore, boy? But yes," he answered with a friendly smile, "I know your friend Chester, he's a wonderful man. Would you like some ice tea, lemonade, maybe some ice cold water?"

"How about a short little rum punch?" says one of those three half-naked ladies and they all started to giggle, which made their bosoms shake like apple trees in an autumn breeze, and Lord was I happy!

"What in the hell is all this noise?" barked a voice off in the parlor to the north. The pocket door had been left half way open and there on a long backless kind of couch that I imagined a Roman lying on to eat grapes was a famous Baltimore personality, Mike Kelley, the best telegrapher the B&O Telegraph Company employed. Mike worked the Morse key so fast you could hardly see his fingers move, and they say he was even faster with his revolver. He sat up from what must have been a sound sleep and rubbed his eyes—a tall thin young man with long brown hair down over his ears, a thick brown mustache with a narrow face, and a big dimple right there in the middle of his chin.

To keep him from straying too far from his chosen path, B&O management had put him on the night shift (7 PM to 7 AM), but he must have had another job there at the mansion, I figured. Maybe he kept those finishing girls safe, was my take on the subject, though later as the ways of the world grew clearer, I realized Mike was such a good customer at The House on East Madison Street that they gave him his own parlor to rest in between jobs.

"Sorry, Mr. Kelley," Sabastian said and he pulled the sliding door shut.

We were enjoying ourselves so much that the purpose of my visit was nearly forgotten until Mr. Sebastian suggested I place that message on a silver platter. "I'll personally deliver it upstairs to Miss Yvette," he said as he handed me a tall glass of ice cold lemonade.

"I'll just wait here to see if she wants to send back an answer." I told him and for the next few minutes I doubt if I blinked.

Some twenty feet down the hall was a grand staircase which climbed eight steps up to a little four foot landing that looked like a pulpit, and then the stairs took off again climbing to the second floor. On the right side of the stairs was a bannister that dropped like a series of waterfalls, and there at the base of the steps was a magical knoll post with the most amazing gas lamp I had ever seen! Just below the flame in the center were four naked ladies leaning way back and they must have polished them regularly, for they were the shiniest brass in all of Baltimore! There was another flight of stairs that climbed up to the third floor landing, and high atop the ceiling was a huge Tiffany skylight with the afternoon sun streaming down in the long beams we called Jacob's Ladder. But those golden shafts of light were suddenly blocked by the most wondrous pair of pure white legs! Her hair was red like mine was, her bustier was a light sky blue, as were her tiny little bloomers, while her legs were strong like they'd done some walking in their time. And with each step she took down those steep wooden stairs, I watched her leg muscles contract and relax like a mongoose watches a cobra.

"Monsieur Stewart," she said in her soft sweet voice. "Parlez-vous francais?" And I didn't, but I answered oui anyway.

"Merci pour le telegramme. Je m'appelle Yvette DuPuis a votre service," she said in her siren song as she held out her hand for a kiss.

She saw me glance once more at those gas lamp ladies and asked, "Tu aimes," though tu aimes rang no bells at the time.

But what she was asking, was did I like that lamp with the four naked ladies? And I liked it all just fine—from that Tiffany skylight on the third floor landing, to her three lightly clad ladies in the alcove giggling, and her big blue eyes, and her sweet red hair, and her tiny little bustier, and those long white legs. Tu aimes, hell yes, tu aimes, tres bien!

And from that day forward, I loved everything French!

"Where are your manners, girls? Would you like to come in and talk with us?" she asked as she guided me into the south parlor where the ladies were leaning against a white marble fireplace back in an alcove.

I looked out the window to let the blush burn off. Old Dan was out there eating an apple, as the ladies clustered around me. Miss Yvette held up her telegram and started to read in her lovely French, though Baltimore and Paris were the only two words I recognized at the time. We toasted the great Comte de Paris, who'd sent the message, with a chink of our glasses and smiles all around.

Then Miss Yvette asked, "Would anyone like me to translate dees?"

Although somethings are better left unsaid, we all said hell yes and jumped up and down like little school girls! And as she breathed in and out whilst her bosoms did bounce like two hot air balloons in heavy winds, my young soul soared. At least once a week for the next two years (although the Trans-Atlantic telegraph failed in a matter of weeks), I'd ride up there to the house on East Madison Street and present Miss Yvette with her latest love letter from Paris, France.

She would read it first in the language of love, and then we'd sip our lemonade and clink our glasses as she adjusted her bodice and read with great vigor in her wonderful English:

My Love Yvette,

Your skin is so white

Like fine alabaster

If you'd be my slave

I'd be your master

With love, the Comte de Normandy

Not the best of words for an abolitionist boy to be writing in his spare time, but the ladies' bosoms would all shake, and their smiles would grow bigger, and for a minute we'd all forget about the war that was coming for us like a storm off the Chesapeake!

Chapter Three

Home of the Brave

That first year with the B&O Telegraph Company went by in a hurry, for Mr. Salomon took me under his wing and taught me politics, commerce, and the need to apply myself better at school, while Miss Yvette and her cocottes taught me to stop and smell the roses. My horizons were expanding by leaps and by bounds, but that part time job was killing me—what with the poor pay and expenses, so when they opened up a brand new job down at B&O Headquarters, it was time to move on.

"Wanted, one dependable boy who is quick on his feet and has no fear of electricity," went the advertisement. And since I hardly knew what electricity was at the time, I jumped at the chance to learn a brand new trade for the hellacious pay of three dollars a day! Once a month they shut down the telegraph to replenish the Battery, which was what they called the long line of bubbling blue jars that produced the electrical charge needed to send the signal down the wire. My job was to help the Battery Room Operator with various and sundry deeds all day Saturday and Sunday on the last weekend of each month.

The Battery Room was located down in the basement of the brand new brick goliath that was the heartbeat of the B&O Railroad; and her bell chimed seven in the morning as I arrived. A tired old man came and got me from the Telegraph Office and bid me follow him down to the dungeon below. It was cool and dark down there under the Camden Street Station. He lit an old kerosene lantern so we could see, and down the steep wooden stairs we went, breathing in the smell of fresh cut pine for the building was only a year old.

"You know what scares a telegrapher more than death itself?" the old man asked me as we went down into the darkness.

"No sir, Mr. Fred (which was what he said to call him), what are telegraphers afraid of the most?" was my hesitant answer.

I saw stacks of telegraph paper, signs and posters, an old printing press, paint cans, and over in the corner up against the southwest wall by a high half window was an old horse hair chair that Mr. Fred made a bee line straight for. Above our heads you could hear the hollow steps of people walking as my new boss rummaged around in his chair for something he must have lost. He finally fished out a pint of whiskey from under the cushion like he'd just found his long lost friend, pulled out the cork, adjusted his seat so the light coming in from the high half window lit his face, and took a long slow pull. Then he smiled, took another pull, and slowly spoke. "There's nothing more fearful to a telegrapher than lightning on the wire, boy. It'll kick your ass, scorch your hair, and kill you, if you ain't real careful!"

Apparently that was all there was to Lesson One, for Mr. Fred sat there soaking in that shaft of light and fell fast asleep. I was standing in the shadows wondering what to do if somebody came down and caught us not working, when he finally came back to life with a jolt.

"Come on boy, the day's a wasting. Let me show you the Battery Room!" He said as he hopped up out his chair like a brand new man, took out a big iron key from his pocket and unlocked what looked like a crypt. "Without the electrical charge this Battery creates, the telegraph would be but a tom tom drum, but you give her enough electricity to send a signal down the wire at near the speed of light, and suddenly the whole world knows your business."

The big iron door slowly creaked open and Mr. Fred shined his lantern around The Herd, which was what they called a long line of Gravity Cell jars all lined up like candles at a Catholics church. The stink of rotten eggs filled the air with a twang like you smell after lightning strikes a tree. It was that dangerous twang of electricity I'd soon learn to respect—a smell that said, run boy, don't walk to the nearest exit!

"One thing to remember if you don't learn anything else today," the Professor broke into my reverie, "don't you never touch nothing to nothing down here in the Battery Room, unless I tell you to, boy!"

Suddenly I realized why they were paying me so much, and why Mr. Fred needed a little time in his horse hair chair before he entered that chamber of horrors. Kind of like a zoo keeper deciding when to go in and feed the hungry lions! It smelled like hell on earth in that plastered over tomb, a room maybe twenty feet wide with not a window in sight, and I hate to mention poor Edgar Allen Poe once more, but that Battery Room brought up thoughts of that bricked over crypt in the Cask of Amontillado, set down there under the stairs in the cob webs stinking of nitre. Within two minutes, I managed to touch one of the wires to the back of my wrist and down I went—kicked harder than a mule kicks!

"That's exactly what lightning on the wire will do to you every time!" the shaky old wireman said by way of his second lecture.

It felt like my brain was erased, and my jaw ached, my arms and legs were weak, and for once in my life I was totally speechless.

"Now go on up and tell Mr. Sommers we'll be cutting their power," my mentor told me with a little twinkle in his eyes. "Tell him to stomp on the floor twice when they're ready, and we'll go right to work."

Mr. Sommers was seated at that high judge's desk where I'd left him as a delivery boy. He was overseeing eight or ten telegraphers—all hammering away at their keys. He looked surprised to see me, as he asked, "What in the world are you doing here so early on a Saturday morning, Mr. Stewart?"

"Why, I took a new job working weekends, Mr. Sommers," I told him all puffed up with pride.

"Then who will deliver those love letters to the ladies up on East Madison Street?" He asked and I realized the work place was no place to keep secrets. Mike Kelley had been helping me with those faux Trans-Atlantic telegrams and although he always seemed tight lipped to me, he must have been talking to somebody.

"I don't have time to dilly dally, Mr. Sommers. Mr. Fred said to tell you we'll be cutting your power, just stomp on the floor when you're ready and we'll get right to work."

"Well, aren't you the busy beaver. Tell Mr. Fred, message received, and Mr. Stewart," he paused and gave me a warm smile. "Good luck with your new job. Anytime you want to help us with a delivery or two, I'd be much obliged. You can even keep your old route, if you like."

Back down those steps I ran with the promise of another part time job and already counting the money! Mr. Fred was back to keeping his horse

54

hair chair warm, sipping Maryland Rye Whiskey out of a paper sack and wondering where the fire was at. "Settle down, boy, and get yourself one of them five gallon paint pails over there. They won't be done sending messages for at least a half hour."

So there we sat for forty-five minutes listening to all kinds of racket. There were trains steaming in, freight handlers hollering and dropping their loads, telegraphers clicking and clacking, passengers scuffing their feet—all echoing through the darkened basement. Mr. Fred was teaching me an important thing in life; you didn't need to talk when you had nothing to say. That was his mantra, that and beware of lightning on the wire, plus always keep an ample supply of Rye Whiskey on hand!

Finally, a loud stomping sound came from the ceiling above and Mr. Fred put on a pair of heavy black India rubber gloves, took a long curved crow bar from behind the Battery Room door, placed the pointy end down on the ground by a big brass plate, and carefully let the curved end come right up to the lip of one of those bubbling blue jars. He warned me with an outstretched hand to keep back or get electrocuted for a second time that day, and then he let the tip of the crow bar just touch the wire. Out came a streak of lightning thicker than a grown man's arm! It shot down to the ground with a sizzle and a flash, and gave off that twangy smell in spades.

"That's what you call a ground return, son!" said my boss like a little boy on Christmas morning. "They've got a big brass plate screwed underwater down at the Light Street Wharf and another one buried under the tracks down in Washington. This whole thing is one big electrical circuit, the Earth, the Bay, and those long iron wires. Just add a little galvanic current (which was what we were making), a Morse key, and a sounder, and you've got yourself the fastest communication system in the history of man!"

Mr. Fred wasn't the best instructor a boy could have—to say he was cavalier would be like saying he cared, which he didn't. He started me skimming a thick mineral oil off the top of the brew in each crowfoot jar with a steel ladle, and then had me siphon off some of the light blue broth into an old steel pail. "Just enough for the new ingredients to go in there," he told me and that was all he said.

55

The Gravity Cells had a copper crowfoot piece of twisted up metal the size of my hand sitting on the bottom that was attached to a little insulated wire that ran up and out the top, then about a third of the way down the jar was another heavy metal plate—again shaped like a crow's foot, only this one was zinc. It too had a wire that came up and out of the jar, and in the bottom of the bottle was a darker blue solution made by me dropping bluestone crystals into that bubbling blue broth.[16]

"Don't let them chunks be any bigger than acorns," Mr. Fred said by way of an explanation. "Just drop them in and remember, don't get that stuff on your hands! Let's go outside and take a smoke and we'll gather up some rainwater," he said. And up those steep steps we went, him as slow as a Chesapeake Bay terrapin and me in the rear trying to put out the fire in my pants, for that sulfuric acid sure did burn!

Outside the seagulls were calling real lazily in the summer heat and the haze seemed to be growing thicker as the day warmed up. I could see the ship's masts out in the harbor sitting as still as tombstones. We walked around to the west end of B&O Headquarters in that rippling heat, and Mr. Fred struck a match to the wall and took a long first puff of his weed. "Take off that screen from the rain barrel real carefully and don't let any leaves get in there! Now, scoop up a big pail of that fine Baltimore rain water." He had a smile on his face as he watched me work.

The old white haired man took a long deep drag and I could see his heavy wrinkles in the bright sunlight. He'd been rode hard and put up wet, but his blue eyes were sparkling as he said, "We're almost done now, son, soon the Battery will be sizzling! Go ahead and put that screen back on and we'll go back down to our dungeon below."

It was like he'd read my mind, for I hadn't told him about my Cask of Amontillado fears, and down the stairs we went like a couple of comrades. He had me drizzle clean rain water into each of those glass jars until the blue broth was up over the top of the zinc crowsfoot, and then he'd hollered stop. One hundred and fifty times I did that deed 'til the whole Herd had fresh water. Then Mr. Fred made up a stronger solution of sulphuric acid and bid me to avoid getting any on me at all.

"Now drizzle a few drops of my secret elixir into every jar," he said as he handed me the pail with that frothy sauce. That seemed to wake the brew and the smell of rotten eggs and the twang of electricity rose in the air. "It won't be long now," Mr. Fred whispered like the thing was alive. "Now slide a thin coating of this mineral oil on top of each jar to keep the electricity from crawling out and shocking you again!"

Once I did that, I stood there staring into space. "Sit down boy, you make me nervous," he said from his horse hair chair.

"You remember how that electricity kicked your ass when you first unscrewed that electrode?" he asked, and I did. "Well, it's time to screw her back on again, only this time, try and hold the insulation on the wire and don't touch nothing else. As long as that electricity is running around in that circuit from the Chesapeake Bay on down to Washington, it's like a tired old work horse pulling the railcars through town, but you let it leave that circuit for a clean shot at a target, and it'll blow your leg clean off! Go on boy, give it a try."

It seemed like the chance of me getting electrocuted had energized Mr. Fred, for he said more in that little lecture than he'd said all day. But I was real careful and the broth began to bubble, and that twang filled the air with the stink of rotten eggs and not a shock in sight.

"But where's that flash of lightning, Mr. Fred?" I asked him.

"It don't flash when it's building back up again, boy. But you give this Battery a chance and we'll be putting out over a hundred volts. Now go upstairs and tell Mr. Sommers he can have his telegraph back."

Then we went outside to get lunch and he said, "How bout a fried fish sandwich?"

"Lake trout sandwiches sound good to me, Mr. Fred, but I find myself without any funds." Half a day at my new job and a jolt of electricity later and my grammar had improved immensely.

"I'll spot you for lunch, Augustus," he said like he almost liked me.

I guess once you survived shorting out The Herd, Mr. Fred figured he'd learn your name. It was just like Mr. Salomon had said, "You've got to

57

give people a chance." And as we walked slowly down to the harbor, I began to pick up the scent of Miss Lew's fried fish sandwiches.

Miss Lew was an old free African lady who had cooked her way to freedom in some of the best homes in Baltimore. She wore a big bright colored African turban to ward off the sun, had wide chunky shoulders, and a squat little body, but the prettiest thing about Miss Lew was her warm welcoming smile!

"Augustus, how are you, boy?" Miss Lew hollered as we came up to her pushcart down by the docks at Light Street.

We hugged and I tried to lift her up off the ground which always made her laugh since my ninety-five pounds could barely budge her two hundred. Then I remembered my manners and introduced Mr. Fred to the sweetest lady in town, minus Miss Yvette and the cocottes, of course.

"Oh, I know Mr. Fred," Miss Lew told me before I got the words out of my mouth. "He's been coming down here since before you was a glimmer in your Daddy's eyes."

"How are you today, Miss Lew?" Mr. Fred asked in a warm voice, and although they didn't hug like we did, I could tell they were old friends.

"Been too hot out here for the customers today, Mr. Fred," Miss Lew complained. We all looked across Pratt Street at the few horses tied outside the shops all stooped over in the heat. "There was a crowd down at the City Market this morning," she told us nodding to the east. "But now not even the buzzards are flying."

We laughed and wiped the sweat from our brows, and then Miss Lew passed me my sandwich with extra vinegar and fried potatoes.

"I've got this," Mr. Fred said. "The boy has been working hard today."

"Working hard you say?" Miss Lew looked shocked as she put down the plate she was fixing, came right up to my face and pried my eyelids open. "You alright in there, Augustus?" the sweet little lady asked as she tapped at my head like a woodpecker. "I ain't never seen this boy work hard in his life, why, we call him the poet of East Madison Street down here at the docks," and she slapped me gently on the top of my head and said, "Watch out for this one, Mr. Fred, the boy is a rascal and a rake!"

58

"Strange that you bring that up, Miss Lew," Mr. Fred said nervously. "But I was just about to ask the boy if he would write me a poem for my wife's birthday."

"Oh, hell yes he will, Mr. Fred, or the boy ain't gettin no more of Miss Lew's fried fish sandwiches!" she said as she served up his lunch.

I swore right then and there that Mike Kelley would never be privy to another secret! And I prayed hard that my father didn't hear of my fame as a poet, or he'd probably have me gelded like poor Dan. Mr. Fred and I walked right up to the side of a big side-wheeler in from New Orleans, and I munched on my sandwich while he bent over and showed me where the brass plate was buried in the side of the dock. Fish were swimming all around its glimmering length.

"That's the ground plate I was telling you about, Augustus." He smiled and looked south towards the Chesapeake Bay and went on with his lecture. "Like I said, there's another plate just like it buried beneath the tracks down in the District of Columbia, and with that ground charge traveling through the harbor and the Bay and down the telegraph wires, those batteries we just charged, will give the whole system just enough power to send the signal flying at the speed of light. So Augustus, what kind of a poem would you write for my wife's birthday?" He shifted his questioning like a police detective.

Now, I was no poet, but between Mr. Fred pressuring me and Miss Lew signaling her new pet bear to go ahead and write the poor man his poem, I had no choice. My professional writing career began even as the last of my fried fish sandwich slid down my gullet.

"When's her birthday, Mr. Fred?" I asked.

"Next Thursday, September the First and I want to say something special to the mother of my three children, and the love of my life!"

"Well, what's her favorite flower?" I asked as Miss Lew stared on with a scowl. "We can always say something about her favorite flowers."

"She likes daffodils," he said staring out at the glassy harbor as a ship was just getting underway, smoke rising from her stack.

"Well, that's a hard one, what rhymes with daffodil, Mr. Fred?"

"Hell, you're the poet!" said the old white haired man.

"How about, let's say, Happy, Sick, or Ill…You can be my daffodil," I said whilst wondering why these adults were so much trouble?

"Yes, that sounds good, son!" And he jumped up and down like a kid in a candy store. "How about drawing some little daffodils around the sides and maybe a big heart up on top, and do you know calligraphy?"

He was going on and on like I was some kind of an artist, but if he'd opened his eyes he'd have seen it was just a mirage, like the one that was rising off the rails on that hot hazy day. We spent a whole hour down in our dungeon designing a birthday card and he didn't even go near his bottle. The card had flowers and hearts intertwined, and in a big crisp imitation calligraphy it said:

To my Dearest Ethel,

Happy, sick, or ill, you will always be my daffodil!

Love, Your Husband Fred

That might have been my worst poem ever, but the man was absolutely ecstatic! "I'll take her out to eat and buy her some flowers," he said.

"That's right, Mr. Fred, let her know you love her!" I smiled, he smiled, and then we climbed the stairs and put a double boiler full of wax on the pot-bellied stove. Mr. Fred said this would be our last job of the day, and he left me to watch the pot boil as he went from telegrapher to telegrapher showing the birthday card off. Thank goodness, Mr. Sommers had gone home for the day, for if he'd seen the serious dilly dallying we called work, he'd have fired us all!

Once that double boiler did its job, Mr. Fred showed me how to paint the wax on the battery's wooden frame with an old two and a half inch paint brush. The wooden stands were about six inches wide with hollowed out spaces for each of those crowfoot jars—all hooked together with wires to form the battery, just like a battery of artillery lined up for battle. To prevent any moisture from forming a pool of water where the charge could short out, the battery table was coated in paraffin.

I was about a third of the way done by quitting time (7:00 PM) and Mr. Fred said, "Well, you're a smart boy, so tomorrow I'm going to let you work solo. All you need to do when you start in tomorrow is melt down another pot of paraffin and finish waxing the stand. Then just give the place a good sweeping. Oh. and if you have any time, Augustus, you can get a ladder from over there," and he pointed towards the shadows where I couldn't see a thing, "and put it against the west window and repack that cast iron water pipe that's coming in through the wall where the rats ate at it. But be gentle—we don't want to lose the line to Washington?" And he laughed, though this sounded like a whole hell of a lot of instructions given in a very dark place, in a very short time, to a very inexperienced boy, if he bothered to ask me, which of course, he didn't. "The rest of tomorrow's shift is yours, my friend. You can bring your school books and study, read my paper, or rest in my chair. You'll be six dollars richer and I'll see you next month."

Mr. Fred picked up his keys, locked the Battery Room's big iron door, grabbed the lantern, and headed for the top of the stairs. "You take these and put them under the rain barrel tomorrow evening when your shift is over," he said as he pitched me the keys.

The next morning, August 28th, 1859 started out with a warm rain that blew in off the Bay. The cobblestones were glistening as I set out for work going up past the President's Street Station to that narrow bridge that crossed the Jones Falls. A little colored boy sat there fishing off the wooden trestle as we bid each other good morning. The sea gulls shrieked, and the smell of the sea filled us with joy, for Baltimore was a beautiful place in the peace and quiet of a rainy Sunday morning. On across Pratt Street I walked west for a mile to the Camden Street Station going past the ships and the stores. The B&O clock tower tolled out the half hour of 6:30 as I arrived early and banged on the Telegraph Office door.

"What in the hell do you want, boy?" the operator bellowed.

"I'm here to finish my work down in the Battery Room. Let me in?" I smiled like a cherub and waited for the telegrapher to respond. He was a lanky eighteen year old with a mop of brown hair and freckles—leaning against the door leering at me.

"Don't they just let anyone work down there in the Battery Room," he said as he let me in with a snarl.

I didn't say anything back. Just lit my lantern and descended the stairs, took out the key to the Battery Room door and there was that bubbling blue broth, and that big pail of paraffin with a paint brush sticking straight up in the center. I had to go back up and face him again to get the stove going.

"Do you know where the wood is?" I asked him real nicely. He must not have liked coffee and the stove was cold.

"What in the hell do you need a fire for, it's August, you dumb shit?"

"I've got to melt this paraffin down to paint the Herd," I explained.

"Herd? You've got yourself a herd of what down there, boy? I don't hear no moos?" He laughed and that mop of brown hair rolled down in his face.

There was no way this brute was going to help me! But then I remembered what Mr. Salomon had said about who you know being an important thing in life.

"Do you know Mike Kelley," I asked the freckle faced baboon. "He's like an older brother to me! Would you like me to have him kick your ass?"

"The wood is out in the ticket office shed, you want me to build you a fire, bring it in here," he changed his tune. Mr. Salomon was a very wise man!

The wax only stayed runny for a short time, so up and down those stairs I went heating and reheating the paraffin until almost two in the afternoon. Outside the day had turned nice, maybe eighty degrees—a big blue sky, a gentle breeze from the west, not the best of days to stick a boy like me inside a dungeon like that, but I kept to my duties as I listened to the trains roll in, and the people shuffling overhead. Finally, I ran out of paraffin and the job looked done, so I scraped up my leavings, swept the floor, and remembered Mr. Fred had said something about a lightning protector that the rats had attacked. I wasn't quite sure what a lightening protector was, but he'd made a vague sweep at that high west window and said the rats had chewed it apart. I held my lantern up high above my head and searched the floor joists for signs of a rodent.

There was a thick iron water pipe coming in near the window, and wrapped around it was several telegraph cables and the tell-tale mark of the beast—a bunch of frayed up newspaper.[17] Now, all I needed was that ladder Mr. Fred said was over in the darkness. Another train came in and as it rumbled and echoed down into that cavern, my little lantern gave me maybe twenty feet of light. There was a whole pile of ladders lying there. The first two were way too heavy for me to handle alone, so I hauled them out of the way and chose a twenty-footer to drag slowly over to the western wall. I'd seen the shop owners out on Pratt Street run extension ladders up to their porch roofs. They would set the feet up against the building, stand out at the far end and walk them up rung by rung, then they'd pick the whole thing straight up and move it with brute force and balance. But the problem with that plan was I was but a fourteen year old boy—the size of a small jockey, so that ladder outweighed me by a good hundred pounds. That water pipe was at least twenty feet in the air, so I pushed and I shoved and finally the top of that ladder smacked hard on the wall, and I was almost home. I had to rock her back towards me and haul hard on the halyard to raise the fly, as she started to sail over my head on a collision course with the floor behind me. I was cussing Mr. Fred for his lack of supervision, cussing myself for my lack of strength and size, cussing the ladder for being so damn heavy, and cussing the rats for chewing up the paper that caused me to have to climb up there in the first place! But all that cussing seemed to work just fine, for that ladder slammed up against the wall not two inches from the water pipe.

Only now I needed some new paper to rewrap the pipe with and Mr. Fred had failed to mention where I got it from. I moved a bunch of drop cloths off the five gallon paint pails out in front of the Battery Room door. There was no paper there. I looked at the stacks of paper for the train schedules by the old printing press and they were way too short to wrap around that thick iron pipe. So I set out to find a newspaper to replace the one that the rats ate. On Sundays there wasn't much going on at the Camden Street Station in the late afternoon. The last train for Washington had set out a half hour earlier and there on a deserted bench sat a nice thick copy of the Saturday Sunpaper—only as I made a leap for it, up comes a hobo, and he takes my paper to make a pillow.

"Hey mister," I asked real nicely, "could I please have that newspaper back? I saw it first!"

"Hell no," he said.

His hands were so dirty and shaky I figured what the poor man really needed was some of Mr. Fred's Maryland Rye Whiskey. And what with Mr. Fred screwing the pooch, and me being the pooch that got screwed, I came up with a plan. "I'll give you a half drunk bottle of whiskey, if you give me that newspaper, mister."

"What kind of whiskey?" he asked.

"Well, hell if I know—the kind that gives you a buzz!" I guessed. How hard could it be to talk a full as a tick deadbeat into drinking Mr. Fred's whiskey? This job was as bad as the last one was!

"You've got yourself a deal," he growled.

So down I went to the basement where I fished about in Mr. Fred's chair for his bottle of hooch and dashed back up to the hobo. We made the trade and I got back to the top of my ladder, wrapped the water pipe real tight with the newspaper, and made sure all the telegraph wires were intact. Everything looked fine to me, so I climbed back down with my lantern in hand and said to myself, I'm going to sit here in Mr. Fred's chair and take myself a little rest! I was hungry. I was tired. I didn't know what time it was, though there was a little red flare to the sky.

The next thing I knew I was on a ship at sea. I could hear the slosh of the waves and feel the sway of the boat as we rolled with the swells. There was a humming sound too—like a billion bumble bees, and the stink of rotten eggs as that ship filled up with a million clucking hens. I had chickens on my shoulders and chickens on my head, and every one of them chickens was laying rotten eggs. Then the sea began to toss that ship in the air, as the ocean came alive and tried to eat me! "**Fire, fire**," went the alarm bell and still I couldn't break free from that floating chicken farm dream! Then "**Fire! Fire!**" I heard again, only this time my eyes were wide open.

"You best get the hell out of there fast you little bastard!" the telegrapher bellowed from the top of the stairs, and the basement was full of smoke.

I could have run, but I'd sooner go down with the ship than explain why the ship done sunk—especially if it was me that had sunk her! A long craggily strike of electricity shot out of the Battery Room door and caused one of the drop cloths to explode right before my eyes! I started to stomp, which split it in two and it threatened to spread to the paint cans. Once that pile of wooden ladders started to burn, the whole place would go up in smoke, so I stomped and I kicked as I slid sideways to miss those lightning bolts streaking out of the Battery Room door! The crows' feet were melting, and the jars were breaking, and sparks were flying, and the smell of lightning filled the air, so I weaved and I ducked, and I slid, and I slipped as I begged Sweet Jesus for some assistance. Finally, I got my hands up against that big iron door and gave her a good hard heave. She slammed shut, and just then a fireman appeared.

"What in the hell is going on down here? Is that door hot?" he yelled.

I told him, hell yes it was hot! He could feel it for himself.

"This must be where the fire is at?" he pronounced like maybe he knew more about electricity than I did, which wouldn't have surprised me.

We put out the fire, ran up the stairs, and went outside, and there stood a great giant of a man staring at the Camden Street Station all covered in smoke. He was about forty years old, maybe six foot three or four with a thick-set neck, a long clean shaven face, and a fine blue suit. The big baby-faced man was staring at the train station like he owned the place, which it turned out, he did.

"We found this boy downstairs fighting the fire, Mr. Garrett. If he hadn't gotten that iron door shut, the whole place would have gone up in flames!"

All around me people were gazing up at that fiery red sky and screaming that the End of the World was coming. It was not the red of a regular sunset; it was this rolling blood red of Armageddon!

"Mr. Garrett that Battery Room is buzzing like a hive of bees," went the fireman. "Do you want us to give it a good hosing down?"

65

"Do you think it's on fire in there?" Mr. Garrett asked and the fireman said no, he doubted it was still burning what with me sealing the door, but it sure as hell was humming like a hive of bees!

"For some reason that electricity is going haywire in there," I said to my baby-faced boss. "But if that electricity and the water from the fire hose mix, we might have ourselves an even bigger problem."

"What's your name, boy?" the Boss man asked.

"Robert Augustus Stewart, sir."

"Any relation to Doc Stewart, from down at Mount Clare Stables?"

"Yes, sir, he's my father," I bragged with my chest sticking out.

"Well, I'm Mr. John Work Garrett, and I'm pleased to meet you," he said holding that big barrel chest high in the air. "You did a fine days' work, now go home and get some rest. We'll talk about this in the morning."

His curly side-whiskers danced in the blue green light of an Aurora Borealis that boiled out of the sky like the blue broth in those bottles below. As I walked home, I saw the cooper ground plate Mr. Fred had shown me bubbling away and the whole harbor was an eerie blood red as the Northern Lights rolled across the sky. I could hear the Negros singing Go Down Moses and I thought of The Lord turning the Pharaoh's river to blood. "Let my people go," Moses had said, and the drums of Africa were pounding!

"The natives were restless last night," Chester said to me the next morning. Most people that heard those drums would have taken it as a threat, but we were abolitionists—tried and true, and we knew it was the call of freedom echoing off the blood red Basin!

I went to school that Monday morning still frightened that somehow I'd caused the whole thing to happen, and as I sat there counting my sins, up walked my father. Doc was dressed in his work clothes, a pair of tall riding boots covered in horse manure, a dirty white smock with some horse blood on it, an old tie tucked into his shirt's fourth button down, and a frown on his face directed at yours truly. He asked my teacher if he could borrow me, which wasn't a good sign at all. I got up behind him on

Old Lucky's back as we rode past Fells Point with me praying Mr. Salomon wouldn't see me under guard like that.

"What do you think you did this time?" Doc asked like he might be growing tired of my wayward ways.

"I think I did good, Doc." I told him, though I wasn't quite sure.

We rode past the President's Street Station where the trains came in on the East End, then past that bottleneck bridge at the little creek, and on down Pratt Street we rode heading west. When we entered B&O Headquarters you could still smell the smoke and the sulphur of last night's fire. The telegraph was still down, and the Battery Room still buzzed, and no one seemed to know what had caused it. We climbed the central stairway that took us to the Board Room on the 2nd floor, being ten minutes early for our meeting. Doc and I looked out the tall windows at the streets of our city and you could see all the way up to the Washington Monument high on the hill above.

They came for us a few minutes later. There in that room were ten business men in their dark black suits talking and smoking cheroots around a big mahogany table. Mr. John Work Garrett was right there in front. He was slightly taller than Doc and about twice as wide, his double chin coming down over his fine white collar. He flicked that cigar and chuckled with his friends, then all of the sudden we caught his eye and he called the room to order with, "Gentlemen, our guests have arrived."

As he spoke, every last one of those finely dressed gentlemen nodded their heads at everything he said. Doc and I moved up and shook his hand—taking him and his friends by surprise. The great giant stood briskly, and pressed our flesh.

"Gentlemen, this is Doc Stewart," and they all nodded like damn if he wasn't. "And this is our latest member of the B&O family, his son, Robert Stewart." They all nodded again—like damn if he didn't know every one of his employees by name. "The reason they are here today gentlemen is to allow us to show our gratitude for the boy's bravery in the unfortunate fire." He went from eye to eye down his row of hirelings and every one of them stopped their shifting and coffee searching ways and smiled for the boy that had saved the Camden Street Station.

67

"Doc, if I may call you that? Your son showed little concern for his own safety when the fire broke out," went the man in charge.

Actually I was sleeping at the time, but why go into the particulars when he was doing so well?

"The fireman said that if he hadn't acted so wisely and closed that Battery Room door, the entire Station would have gone up in smoke," said the boss. Mr. Garrett took a long puff of his cigar and searched his friends for any inattentiveness.

Doc and I stood there in front of him like we were being sold on the block. "So on behalf of the B&O Railroad," great here comes the good part, I thought to myself. "I would like to present (here comes my shiny new fifty dollar gold piece) our youngest B&O employee with a..." He was fishing in his front pocket and I was all excited! I thought of a new suit of clothes for me, and a fine English saddle for Old Dan and a new dress for my twin sister Lizzy. And maybe Doc and I would get invited to stay for coffee and cake—my, wouldn't that be a wonderful thing?

Well, I won't say what he had to push out of the way to finally locate my prize, but there it was—a brand new shiny silver dollar! His little puppets all started to clap, as they signaled for the major domo to come and drag us away. Sadly, there was no cake and no coffee for me and my father. We were sent on our way with that silver dollar and a pat on the head.

"Your first brush with management," Doc said as we left, like maybe he thought my life was worth more than a silver dollar too.

They were hollering for me to come back to work down in the Battery Room after that, but I never went back down in that dungeon again! First off, the place was a fire trap, and secondly there was no natural sunlight, and a boy like me needed lots of sunlight to survive! And thirdly, the place came real close to blowing up again a few days later when on September 1st (Mrs. Fred's birthday) we had another solar storm—bigger than the first one was. A scientist over in London by the name of Carrington[18] was pointing his telescope at the surface of the sun when he saw two giant flares coming straight for us. Within hours the solar storm hit and the parts that were dark turned light, roosters crowed though it was two in the morning, birds flew and hunters shot them, and the

68

Northern Lights rippled across the sky all the way down to the Caribbean. A telegrapher in Washington was nearly electrocuted when electricity flew from his Morse key and set him on fire, while the telegraphers up in Boston could send signals to Portland without even using a battery. I'd seen enough of amps and volts to last me a lifetime, and I took a new job as a teamster hauling the rail cars through town once I graduated from eighth grade.

Although I was the smallest lad on the B&O Horse Handler payroll, my team could do the most work! My horse team and I hauled freight cars from the Philadelphia Street Station on the East End of town to Mount Clare Yards on the West End—one at a time. Two miles back and forth—trip after trip—day after day, but the time passed quickly and my young boy muscles turned into the muscles of a man. I grew to a full five foot seven with my Dad's wide forearms, and weighing in at a hundred and twelve pounds. My dream was to become a jockey someday and every chance Mike Kelley and I got, we would ride the streets of Baltimore like Cheyenne braves!

My Mom and Dad gave me a horse as a graduation present, for Old Dan had passed away. We called my new horse Gunpowder after that wonderful stream out in the country. He was a three year old chestnut thoroughbred race horse who broke his leg plowing through an inside rail. Doc had bought him for a dollar when the owner wanted him put down, and we hung him in a sling in the B&O stables. I brought him food and water—played my harmonica and talked to him as he hung there mending. Once he could place weight on that busted up leg, we took him out to a little park south of the Mount Clare Rail Yards for an easy walk. No bridal, no saddle, just me and my horse watching fall come on in all its glory.

"He won't hurt himself," my Dad told me. "Horses have more sense than a man about these things. Just don't spook him or make him run!"

Mike Kelley and his bay mare, Louisville, would come over to our private horse park, and sometimes the way they played, it didn't look too slow to me. But as February came on and it was time to test Gunpowder with a rider aboard, there was no limp, no loss of stride, no signs of pain, and above all, no fear of flying, for within a month he was taking jumps.

Mike Kelley still worked the night shift, so he had plenty of time during the day to help me improve our steeplechase course. I'd bring up logs with my B&O horse team and we'd build a few timber jumps as Louisville and Gunpowder stood by our side. When I got done my railroad work, or sometimes if my lunch break was about to begin, or there was no boss around to bother me, we'd do a little riding on Company time. We quickly realized it was really about being one with your horse, and one with the ground you were riding on that made a good steeplechase racer. Oh, you had to know how to balance over your mount as you sailed through the air, but if you and your horse were in two different places when you took off, that's probably where you'd both land!

The B&O horse farm was just south of the Machine Shops with long lines of stables, rooms for the hands, Chester's little shack, and a couple of one acre fields for the horses to graze in. On the east end of the compound ran a four foot fence where Mike and I made our starting line tight to the corner of an old red barn. Chester or one of the stable hands would come out with a little stop watch in hand and start us. A couple hundred yards out there was an irrigation ditch where the horses would gallop through foot deep water then climb the muddy bank to head south at the gallop, taking a couple of jumps over post and rail before we came to a water jump. We'd sail across that creek, and then uphill we'd head jumping a wide chicken coop,[19] then a brush jump, then a tall timber jump in close succession. As the hill leveled off, we had a big five rail jump, then a hundred yards more and another tough jump—this one made of seven foot Green Mount Cemetery privet, which the horses could clear by swishing right through it. Then downhill we'd race to a fence by the railroad coming in from Washington—taking another big timber jump as we came hard to the left. And this was where the course got tricky, for we didn't always know where the clay pits were, so we had to slow down and neither that bay mare, nor my chestnut gelding cared for slowing down! We'd fly hell bent for leather down the east side of the Brick Yard past their ovens where we had a nasty double timber jump, then up and around the old mansion on the hill like we were demons possessed. Back around the brick yards and over the stream we'd fly as we hollered to the horses, for we never used whips! And although

Mike and his powerful mare always took first place, Gunpowder and I always came in a close second.

When I went to see my Jewish friend down on Thames Street one Sunday, he told me of a rich man's horse race that was scheduled for the third Saturday in April. "Just how good do you and your friend think you are?" he asked like he was planning to bet on us.

"I think we've got two of the fastest horses in Baltimore," I swore. We can cover three and a half miles in a little over nine minutes.

"Is that good?" Mr. Salomon asked as he ate a sugar cookie with his tea.

"Damn right it is, oh sorry!" I apologized, for my new job at the B&O Horse Works had taught me to cuss real good.

"Mr. Ridgely and I aren't exactly on a first name basis," he said somewhat hesitantly. "But I know a person who can print you up some cards, and the two of you can ask for an audience with the great man. He's a very," he paused to pick his words real carefully, "he's a very noble man, and if you can impress him enough to get invited to his horse race, you and your friend just might win this cup!"

Mr. Salomon pulled a white silk cloth off the tall cup and I gasped for it was as big as a house and shining bright silver in the lamplight!

"Oh, and Augustus, there's a thousand dollar purse to the winner, five hundred for second place, and third place will win you or your friend a hundred dollars!"

It was the first time I'd ever seen Mr. Salomon excited. There he was jumping up and down believing in me and my friend and a couple of horses he'd never seen run—Lord how I loved that man! And just as he promised, we had cards printed up in two days' time that said:

Mike Kelley of Lawrenceburg, Kentucky, and Robert Augustus Stewart of Mount Clare Stables. We wrote in our best cursive on the back of each one: "Dear Mr. Ridgely, we would very much appreciate an audience with you so we might discuss the possibility of entering your steeplechase race."

We sent them by special currier to his plantation up at Hampton House. Then we waited and waited and finally on the 15th of March (The Ides don't you know), we received our answer:

Sirs, I would welcome a conversation regarding our little horse race. Please arrive at noon on March the 30th for a little light lunch and tea.

Yours truly,

Mr. Charles Ridgely

"You ever heard of the Ridgelys of Hampton House?" I asked my free African friend as he went over my jumping one evening.

"I'll tell you if you promise to stay centered when you jump that poor horse. You spend more time throwing him off balance than any jockey I know!" Chester preached.

He wrapped his frock coat tighter as a cold breeze blew in off the Bay and said, "Now I ain't saying the Ridgelys is bad people, Augustus, but you see that bunch of old buildings right down there," and he pointed to the northwestern shore of the Ridgely Cove just at the base of the hill we were up on. "Them peoples down there had slaves working an iron forge like dogs," he went on with that little stutter he'd get when he didn't know how to say something to a white man. "They was... they was real cruel down there![20] So you be careful what you say to them rich folks up in Towsontown. They ain't the same peoples as you and me."

Saturday March 30th promised to be warm and the smell of springtime filled the air. By noon we knew it would be 70 degrees and sunny in this land of pleasant living we were pleasantly living in. Mike wore a nice English tweed hunting coat and matching vest, a pair of fine tan britches tucked tight into a brand new pair of tall English riding boots. His Colt revolver was tucked in a leather holster pointing backwards on his left hip for that quick cross draw he loved so much. His long brown hair was combed back out of his eyes and that thick handlebar mustache made him look dapper. Six foot tall, thin and handsome, Mike looked like the kind of man you shouldn't trifle with, and who the hell would?

Meanwhile, my dark blue suit was a bit too tight in the butt and the chest, too short in the arms and legs, and my Sunday best shoes were a tad too worn, for we Stewarts weren't the richest folks in the Monumental City. My red hair was cropped short like the railroad boys wore it, and at the last minute I swapped out those shoes for my riding boots so at least Gunpowder would recognize me. Then out to the country we rode. I hadn't been north of the city since the fall before and you could see how the whole place was growing real fast.

Towsontown proper was a sleepy little village with a tall stone court house and a little jail surrounded by wide green lawns and big new houses with flowers popping up and birds singing away. Not those squawking seagulls either, these were country birds—red winged black birds, cardinals, and robins—all with their wondrous songs of spring. We climbed the hill north onto Old York Road with less than a mile to go.

"Don't you start in with your abolitionist ways," says Mike in his strong Kentucky drawl as he adjusted his holster and straightened his tie. "You let me do the talking and just nod your head, you got that, Augustus!"

"What if he asks me something?" I asked my buddy just to get his goat.

"If he asks you something, answer him with something brief, not one of those rambling stories you like to tell."

We made the right turn off the macadamized road and went down a dirt lane heading for the Ridgely mansion high on a hill to the east. We were surrounded by a large apple orchard, the bees buzzing, and the sweet smell of flower blossoms in the air. The horses liked the new surface we were on and started to canter towards the huge mansion they called the Hampton House. The private lane meandered through the estate of ten thousand acres with greenhouses growing oranges and lemons, fields of winter wheat, corn fields being cultivated by slaves with long hoes, stone horse barns, stone mule barns, dairy cattle grazing away on lush green hillsides, and everywhere you looked there were slaves sweating away. They were raking by the forsythia bushes—all abloom in their yellow haloes, slaves down on their hands and knees picking weeds from the daffodil beds that Mrs. Fred would have liked to have seen. All was order and beauty at the Hampton House, and slowly the tower atop the huge mansion started to peek out of the tall green trees.

I was busy practicing my silence, but from that first telegraph delivery where the old man with the ball peen hammer was planning on murdering me; I remembered that rich folks liked to have the rest of us peasants go around to the back door. "Back door, Mike," was my whisper, and he nodded at me. And as we brought the horses around nice and slow, people were looking out from five or six windows on all three floors of that fine Georgian mansion. There were white faces, and black faces, and a couple of faces that looked like ghosts.[21]

We dismounted at the bottom of a set of white marble stairs they'd probably dug from their own quarry (well the slaves had dug). Eight of those shiny stairs flickered in the sunlight—surrounded by a white marble railing and a nine foot door with tall windows to either side, all wrapped in sparkling white marble. Mike gave the knocker a good hard bang and up comes a butler in formal attire. He was maybe thirty with white gloves, a tuxedo and tails, just like Sebastian wore; only Tom wasn't as tall and stately as Sebastian and he had a rather shy way about him.

"May I help you gentlemen?" He kind of sighed.

"Why, yes, you may," says Mike all distinguished like and I swear his southern drawl grew stronger. "We have an appointment with the master of the house, if you could please tell him we're here."

"Does you want to see Mr. John Carnan Ridgely, or his son, Mr. Charles Ridgely?" the timid butler asked.

"Well, Tom," says Mike scratching his head, "we got ourselves a dilemma on account of we got an appointment to see one of them two Ridgelys at twelve o'clock, only we don't know which one. Maybe you can help us?"

"Yes, sir," the better dressed than me butler answered and went silent.

"Why, I guess we need the farm manager Ridgely," I broke in cuzz the clock was ticking, "which one was he again, Tom?"

"That would be Mr. Charles Ridgely," the shy slave said as he folded his white gloved hands and smiled at our having solved the problem so fast.

"Mr. Charles Ridgley, that's the one!" Mike agreed—looking at me like I needed to remember my oath of silence. We had five minutes left, but that Tom fellow was so pleased with his answer that he just stood there and grinned.

"Well, can we see this here Mr. Charles Ridgely?" I finally blurted out, and Mike looked all flummoxed at my lack of discipline.

"Mr. Charles is down at the Lower House," Tom told us with his eyes flashing. "You've got to get back on dem horses and ride down to the bottom of the hill," he said, as he pointed to a long white farmhouse in the meadow below. "See dat white building right dere; he's down there working on his farm business. I hope you ain't late, Mr. Charles don't like people what's late!"

Not only did these Ridgelys have a back door finer than most people's front one was, but they had a whole nother house to conduct their business in. We leapt on our horses and galloped down to the Lower House which looked to be near a hundred feet long with a fresh coat of white paint, green shutters around the six tall windows, a big front porch, and a farm door—painted green like the shutters were. It was a pleasant enough building that sat far too close to the slave quarters for my taste, but like Mike said, I needed to keep my abolitionist thoughts to myself.

Suddenly, around the corner of the house came a young slave boy howling like a banshee. Behind him were two little curly-headed white girls chasing him with death in their bulging brown eyes! They were the ugliest little girls I had ever seen, and in their hands they held long wooden swords that they whacked across the poor slave's back. And not only were they the ugliest little creatures on God's green Earth, but they were the meanest ones too!

"Welcome Massas," the slave boy said as he came to a halt and bowed low while the white girls beat him.

"Girls, don't be hitting that boy!" I yelled automatically—since bullies were my main weakness in life.

"We aren't girls and don't be telling us what to do with our slave!" Yells the tallest one, maybe ten years old—dressed in a wide lace collared white shirt and a shiny blue vest with a matching cape, puffy blue pants tucked into long white socks, and dainty little black patent leather shoes. He was a kind of Three Musketeer complete with a curly black wig and a painted on mustache, and how the hell was I to know I'd gone and offended our host's sons?

"That's right, don't be calling us girls!" whines the smaller one who must have been about two years younger than the first one was, and dressed just as strangely.

"Are we gonna stand here and talk with these cretins till the cows come home, or do we need to see a man about a horse?" Mike cut in.

"Cretins, we know what cretins is!" says the taller one.

"I'm going to tell my father what you called us," cried the short one with his big brown eyes as deep and dark as any dungeon. He came right up to Mike, and shook that little wooden sword in his face.

"Who might your father be?" Mike asked with a friendly smile, but I had already guessed.

"Our father is Captain Charles Ridgely of the Baltimore County Horse Guard Cavalry," says the older of the two musketeers with a rich boy's sneer. "Father was on the Harvard boxing team and he'll kick your ass for what you've just called us!" warned the little one with wide jaws like a boxer dog.

We'd have stayed there forever being grilled by those two little hoodlums in their curly black wigs, only their father came out, looked at his pocket watch, and frowned down at us. He was around thirty years old, a proud and stately six footer with a regal face, a long noble forehead, a narrow patrician nose, and a fine dark brown mustache with a crop of chin hair we called a Van Dyke.

"Are you the lads about the horse race?" The country squire hollered.

"Papa, these men called us girls and cretins too!" popped off the first musketeer as he demanded satisfaction.

Their father was already put out at our being late and he took his wrath out on the slave boy. "Henry, how many times have I told you to keep those boys away from the Lower House when I'm working?"

The last we saw of that little black slave he was hauling up the hill towards the mansion begging for mercy as the two little musketeers beat him about the head and shoulders with those nasty swords.

"Come in lads, I'm Captain Ridgley," said the cretins' father, though he was in a long gray frock coat with white pants, as civilian as we were.

He led us into his work place, his spurred riding boots jangling across the wide wooden porch. We did our handshakes and niceties—starting with: "My, aren't those smart little boys, Captain Ridgely, sir. And won't Harvard be happy when they matriculate?"

I looked around to see where that "little light lunch and tea" was at, and all I saw was one big roll top desk and one wooden chair on wheels. There were a few paintings of old dead Ridgelys on the wall and that was it. But right over that huge mahogany desk was a big framed Harvard University Diploma, Class of 1850—just in case we hadn't come to grips with the fact.

"So, you boys want to enter our steeplechase race?" queried our host and before we could do more than nod, he went at me with a long list of questions. "Mr. Stewart you say," and he paused and stroked his long chin hair as he stared into my eyes like he had me hypnotized. "Are you any relation to General George Hume Steaurt?"

Doc called that line of the Stewart family the Stewarts that couldn't spell straight, on account of that extra e they threw in. He said my grandfather John called them the Stewarts that straddled the fence on account of their actions in the Revolution, but we were there to get invited to a horse race not to talk politics.

"Distant relatives, sir, but I admire what General Steaurt has done with the Maryland Militia," was my bold faced lie, for he was turning our state Militia into a band of Secessionists.

"So you're a State's Rights Man, Mr. Stewart?" He asked as he stared down at me with his snake eyes trying to work their way into my brain.

"Oh, yes sir, I most certainly am," I told him as I looked right back.

"Mr. Kelley," the Captain changed his tack on my southern friend, "You say you're a Kentucky man born and raised, did you ride to the hounds?"

"Oh, yes, sir," answered Mike. "The Lawrenceburg Hounds were the most famous fox hunting club in all of Kentucky. My father and I rode with the hounds for many a year, Captain Ridgely, sir."

Later Mike was to tell me that they only had two dogs on his father's little tobacco farm—one was lame and the other was blind, and the only running they did was to supper, but our Captain was very impressed. He glanced down at Mike's Navy Colt, smiled at his fine English riding boots, and gazed at his big horseman's thighs.

"What do you do for the B&O Railroad, Mr. Kelley?" His Lordship asked.

"Oh, I'm a master telegrapher," Mike boasted.

"And are you any good with that gun?"

"Some would say so," Mike told him. "And some can't say nothing no more!" Mike's Southern twang grew stronger as he talked to the fourth master of Hampton House (once he out lived his Mom and Dad that is).

"Ha..Ha..Ha," Captain Ridgely laughed in a strange staccato. "Ha.. Ha.. Ha..," just like that. And I'm not saying it that way because I can't describe a laugh. Ha...Ha...Ha was all he had. "This calls for a brandy, gentlemen, I have found my new 1st Lieutenant!"

He reached into his roll top desk and pulled out an old clay jug and some glasses, and gave us a toast with what he said was last year's Apple Jack Brandy, and all on an empty stomach. That brandy burned and felt good at the same time! He topped us off, and we stood there smiling away as the room took on a glow of its own.

"You see," said our now flushed captain, "my current 1st lieutenant has absolutely no experience at war. He's lazy, he lacks any sense of strategy and tactics, and the poor lad can't even think for himself."[22]

Then he reached for a map nearly four foot long which he laid out on the floor before us and began to unravel his harebrained plan. The room was spinning and his face was taking on otherworldly dimensions, and maybe I was forgetting my manners, but my stomach needed something in it that wasn't on fire! "Captain, sir," I begged with my stomach howling, "How about that little light lunch that was promised?"

Mike seconded my emotion and the good captain called for his slave who was sitting behind the kitchen door. "Bring those sandwiches in here at once, and bring us another bottle of that Apple Jack brandy."

I was figuring Mike and I might have to spend the night, since I probably couldn't hang on to a horse. We started to giggle as our deranged leader went on with his cockamamie plans—all three of us sitting on the floor like school boys playing at marbles. "Once we burn the bridges to the north of Baltimore and block the Union troops from entering town right here and here," he told us as he pointed to a couple of places he'd marked off on his map. "We can move southwest for Washington right through here," and he pointed to a little spot near Bladensburg, where my grandma Bloise had her farm.

"We'll cross the Anacostia River into the District of Columbia like Caesar crossed the Rubicon," and he pointed to a little spot on his map he had marked off for that. "Then we'll ride down New York Avenue to the President's House and capture that long legged ape and make a slave out of him!"

Great, goes my drunken mind, we're going on an ape hunt in the District of Columbia—won't that be nice? And then I realized this fine man from a noble family actually had plans to take Abe Lincoln prisoner, and we were to be his henchmen! I was munching on those little watercress sandwiches and I thought to myself, Sweet Jesus are we in trouble! Mike rolled his eyes back in his head, and suddenly I realized our leader was surrounded by a band of abolitionists!

"Oh, and I forgot the best part of my plan," went the lunatic in charge.

"Once we cut Fort McHenry off from Federal support, we'll ride down there with the whole Maryland Militia and take the star fort by storm!"

We started to giggle hysterically, and Mike's head was nodding like a woodpecker on a piece of beech. He rose to his feet—wobbled a bit, looked down at me with a big shit eating grin and said, "Sir, I got to go see a man about a horse."

"It's just down the hill to the right there by the slave quarters," says our wild-eyed leader, and I leapt up and mumbled, "Me too!" Don't leave me alone with this lunatic!

79

When we returned, Captain Ridgely stood at the Lower House door pulling at his beard like he thought he might have made a mistake choosing us for accomplices, but as soon as he saw Mike and gazed at his mighty horseman physique, the captain settled down. He walked over to his roll topped desk, leaned over and picked up his quill and wrote out a short note that said: "Please provide Lieutenant Kelley with a Baltimore County Horse Guard uniform and all the accoutrements. You may charge it to my account. Captain Charles Ridgely, Commanding"

"Take this to my tailor, Mr. Guis down at the corner of Howard and Fayette Street, and do keep me posted on Union troop movements through Baltimore. And Lieutenant Kelley, the next time I see you, I expect you to be in uniform."

"Well, what about me, sir?" I asked His Holiness in my drunken stupor.

He looked down at me like he looked at little Henry—a bug to be squashed unless you could teach it to work silently. "Lieutenant Kelley, please tell your man to follow the chain of command. If he has something to say, he should say it to you, and you can tell me—only if it's absolutely necessary."

"Yes sir," said my new lieutenant. "But what about the lad's uniform?"

"The enlisted are expected to purchase their own uniforms," His Lordship answered with a haughty shrug of his shoulders. "But you both should be in uniform when you return here next."

Only Captain Ridgely would think of dressing his brand new spies in full Rebel regalia right in the heart of Union held territory.

Chapter Four

A Storm off the Chesapeake

We were so shocked by Captain Ridgley's treasonous plans that we forgot to get permission to enter his steeplechase race, figuring we'd just go on with life like it never happened. But then we thought what if Fort McHenry really was attacked by the Rebel horde, or they really did go and kidnap President Lincoln right out of the White House? Still there was not a soul in Baltimore that we could tell! We couldn't tell Marshal Kane for he hated Lincoln with all his heart. Nor could we ask the Governor of Maryland, Thomas Holiday Hicks for any help. He was a proud member of the American Party or Know-Nothings, and although the Know Nothings knew for certain that they didn't like foreigners, Catholics, and Jews, they hadn't quite made up their minds on Secessionists yet. The Baltimore City Mayor was out too, for Mayor Brown was what we called a Copperhead who believed the South had a perfect right to secede anytime they liked. If we marched over to City Hall and said we wanted to report the commander of the Baltimore County Horse Guard Cavalry for conspiracy to commit treason, Mayor Brown would have probably said, I'm sorry, boys, but that's out of my jurisdiction.[23] We also had a Rebel arms dealer by the name of Ross Winans in town who would feed you to the fish if he heard you were a loyal American. Whoever we told of Captain Ridgely's plan, they needed to have the power to stop him in his tracks, or we'd be dead for sure! Then I heard a bugle call from across the harbor as the flag was raised at Fort McHenry and it came to me, we could ride down there to the ramparts red glare and tell the Yankee commander.

The next day was perfect for the clandestine work we set out on, with a fog so thick you could cut it with a knife. We rode south for a mile down Light Street barely able to see each other, and then the route turned east as it headed down an old dirt lane where we were enveloped in the gathering gloom. For two more miles we rode in the sea smoke, being worried we'd ride right past Fort McHenry and into the Patapsco.

"Who goes there? Halt or I'll shoot!" went a faceless voice in the fog.

Louisville and Gunpowder jerked their heads up high and snorted as they skidded to a halt. Mike and I froze in the saddle.

"Are you a sentry?" I blurted out when my heart started beating.

"I asked you who you was first, now who the hell are you?" hollered the invisible voice. I heard a musket cock and the hair on the back of my neck stood up.

"Ain't no reason to point that thing at a friend," Mike said in a calm southern drawl. "We're here to see your commander. This is Fort McHenry, ain't it?"

"Well it might be stranger, but where'd you get that drawl?"

Mike was to hear that a million times, you see a Baltimore boy sounds like a Johnny Reb to someone up North, and like a Billy Yank when he's way down South, but a Kentucky boy always sounds like a Rebel to everyone. And Fort McHenry couldn't afford to let Rebels inside!

"Listen here soldier," Mike tried his hand again. "If you and your friend there," for he could feel another one in the gloom, "would let us down off our horses, you can search us all you want."

"Good idea," says the second deeper voice that sounded like a tug boat coming from right behind me.

"Step down off them horses real slow and we'll take ourselves a peek. Nate you watch that Southern one, I'll keep my eye on the city boy."

"I'm a loyal Union man, so point that Springfield elsewhere!" I barked.

"Springfield, how the hell did you know this here is a Springfield rifle?"

"We Union boys know all about you soldiers down here at the Whetstone Point. We know there are only about fifty of you guarding this huge star fort with your brand new Springfield rifled muskets. And we even know some of you boys are regulars with twenty years' service fighting the Seminoles, Cheyenne, and Sioux."[24] I said, for they were our heroes.

"Walk over there real slow," he said, and he poked me in the back with his long steel rifle.

"You too, friend," says the squeaky voiced one to Mike.

We came up to what looked like an old hen house, with just a flicker of light coming out of an old rickety door. "Well, go ahead and open it," said the fog horned one as he rammed his rifle into my ribs.

There was a little ramshackle table inside with a kerosene lantern sitting in the middle of the roughhewn floor, and judging by all the chicken feathers and the wall of chicken wire that made a little jail out of one side, it had probably been a hen house at one time or the other. I wasn't real sure these fellows were soldiers until we stepped into the light, but they were. A six foot pimply faced squeaky voiced private, and a five foot five little dwarf of a corporal, who was as big around as he was tall.

"I guess you boys want this?" Mike said, as he drew his Navy Colt and gave it to them butt first.

"Why in the hell didn't you disarm the man?" goes the fat one to his pimply faced friend.

These two were a real dangerous pair, and I wondered if we'd ever see Fort McHenry with them leading the way through the heavy fog?

"We need to see your commander right away!" Mike told the corporal.

"Well, why didn't you say so in the first place?" he answered. "Nate you got them blindfolds?"

"Well, I got one of them," says Nate in his high pitched voice. "But corporal, you blew your nose on the other one. I think it's in your pocket."

They led us the last three hundred yards with me sure I was gonna catch a cold. A little breeze was starting to blow in from the Bay and sea gulls were singing somewhere up there in the unseen heavens. I'd have kicked up my heels and sung a few bars of The Star Spangled Banner as we went through the sally port, but that Springfield rifle was still stuck in my ribs.

"Sergeant major, bring the tall one with the pistol in first!" ordered a gravelly voice in the inner Watch Room.

They left me sitting there blindfolded as Mike went in. The room smelled like a hundred year old tomb, though fifty years down by the sea will do

83

that to a place. Maybe ten minutes later, they brought Mike back out and by the way they slammed him down, I'd say he was still blindfolded.

"Your turn, Firebird, don't piss your pants!" went some real helpful member of The Watch, as they shoved me into the back room.

It was a plain brick lined chamber with a lantern burning on a big wooden desk, a picture of President Buchanan on the stucco wall. There at the desk sat a tall dark haired Army officer with a high forehead and the eyes of a hawk. He had two lines of those bright brass American eagle buttons running down the front of his dark blue tunic, and his epaulettes said he was a full blown captain. But the most amazing part of him was his big black beard—as thick as a brick and down to his chest.

"Where is your friend from, boy, and why is he here in Baltimore?" His questions were fast, disjointed, and in search of the smallest discrepancy.

"Mike is from Lawrenceburg, Kentucky, sir. He ran away from his father's tobacco farm when he was but a boy of thirteen, went to Washington to learn the telegraph, and then came on to Baltimore."

"How old are you, son?"

"Sixteen, sir," he stared at me hard, so I changed it to, "fifteen and a half."

"And what do you do for a living?" Every time I gave him an answer he would check it off his list, but I could see he was bouncing around looking for holes in my story.

"I'm a horse handler for the B&O Railroad."

"Who's Captain Ridgely?" Now, we were getting somewhere!

"He's a low down good for nothing snake in the grass that plans on taking Fort McHenry by storm!"

"Like the man, do ya, boy?" My inquisitor asked with a little chuckle. He was some kind of a New Englander—upstate New York, maybe Vermont, I couldn't tell for sure, but he had a smile on that black-bearded face and that was a very good sign.

"That crazy Harvard man has his own private band of Rebel cavalry up in Towsontown, sir, and they're planning high treason, I swear they are!

Why, I sat there and watched his sons beat a poor slave half to death and he didn't even lift a finger to stop them!"

"Are you an abolitionist...," he paused looked down at his notes and went on, "Mr. Stewart?"

"Yes, sir," I told him with pride. "But I'm also a patriot and that Captain Ridgely bragged he'd go down into Washington and capture President Lincoln and make a slave out of him, sir! He needs to be hung! Ain't that the price for treason these days?"

"Sergeant major, untie the boy, he's convinced me of his loyalties," went my new Yankee captain. "Bring in his partner; I might have a job for these two."

So in came Mike all unfettered with a pleasant smile on his face, as his green eyes twinkled. They sat us down in old wooden chairs right before Captain Robinson's desk and he said, "Fort McHenry needs all the friends she can find in these troubled times, gentlemen. If you boys can help us with a little subterfuge, I'd be greatly beholding."

"Pardon me for interrupting, sir!" I said. "But what is that subterfuge thing?"

"Chicanery, trickery, bluffing, call it what you will, Mr. Stewart," says the second captain to command us in less than a week. "We want you to stay close to the Maryland Militia—report any strange activities."

I had my eye on Mike to see what he thought. At our last strategy session I knew exactly where he stood with Captain Ridgely in a matter of seconds, but Mike's face was a blank slate. "We was hoping to never go back up to Towsontown again, Captain Robinson, sir," my old Kentucky friend finally said. "They're all crazy up there, and it's a dangerous place to be taking a fifteen year old, if you ask me, sir."

Begging off on account of his partner being too young for the job, now that was too low a blow for someone who called himself my friend! I wanted to defend Fort McHenry just like my Grandfather John had done back when the British came for us in 1814. Still, I stayed silent and let Mike do the talking, but the more he tried to get us out of the captain's plan, the more the captain wanted us in it!

85

"You two would be perfect for this job," said the black bearded Yankee. "Captain Ridgely will never suspect you are Federal spies, since he recruited you himself."

"But he says next time he sees us, we have to be in uniform, sir." goes Mike. "And they say it will take two weeks to get my uniforms made."

"Two weeks, no way!" our new captain told Mike. "Do you know how many good German tailors there are up in Baltimore, Mr. Kelley? Where did Ridgely tell you to go for your uniforms?"

"Guis Tailor Shop at the corner of Howard and Fayette under the bank, sir." Mike looked surprised that he was discussing tailors with the Fort McHenry commander.

"Good taste," says Captain Robinson. "Harvard grad you said?"

"Yes sir, Class of 1850," I pitched in with great pride for my first captain's college credentials.

"Oh, Mr. Stewart, welcome back to the conversation," goes our new boss. "So how do you feel about our plan?"

"Oh, I'm game, Captain Robinson. And I'd like to try and steal that poor slave boy, if I could, sir. He don't need to be beat like a donkey!"

Mike frowned at me and the captain smiled, and the sergeant major, who had been standing behind us quiet as a church mouse, laughed out loud. "He's a game one, sir—a regular fighting banti rooster, well worth the pay if you ask me!"

Pay, thinks I, who said anything about pay? And suddenly I was off to the races, if these people were thinking of paying me for getting Captain Ridgley hung, I'd die a happy man—no matter what transpired!

"But the next time we come up to Hampton House, Captain Ridgely said he wanted information about Union troop movements through town," Mike stuttered. "We can't hardly be giving him that kind of information, can we, sir?"

"That's the beauty of this plan, Mr. Kelley, we can do anything we like!" goes our commander as he jumps up from his desk and stands a good six foot two with his black beard flying. "We'll have your Horse Guard uniforms ready for you in two days, Mr. Kelley. Just go directly to Franz at the shop you just mentioned and whisper to him that I sent you. The Germans are the best Republicans[25] in all of Baltimore. And when you ride to Towsontown, I want you take this message to Captain Ridgely."

Captain Robinson was talking so fast he almost lost me. "Tell him you got this right off the wire." And he wrote out a note that went as follows: Cabbages arrived, all heads present and accounted for—one gross grade A." and he signed it with his name and handed it to Mike. "Tell him you saw two companies of fresh troops marching straight for Fort McHenry and let his imagination do the rest. Then if you boys have had enough of spy work, we'll cut you loose. Now come on fellows it's payday!"

Out of his desk drawer came a bag full of coins, and they weren't just any coins either, no sir, they were 1849 Double Eagles—twenty dollar gold pieces minted in San Francisco, California. Lady Liberty was on one side with a nice little crown and some stars around her head, and a big overfed American eagle was on the other side holding up the National shield. Captain Robinson counted out six of those beauties for each of us boys, and I looked over at Mike and we were officially spies!

"These lads won't need their blindfolds anymore," the captain told his sergeant major. "Good luck and God bless America!"

We all joined in with that blessing to our birthplace, even the old bald headed sergeant major. I looked at the stripes on his shoulder and said to myself; someday I'll wear that insignia too. And as they marched us out of Fort McHenry, the sun burned through the fog and Old Glory was flying high. Mike and I came to attention right there beneath her big white flagstaff and gave our country's flag the best salute we ever made, for this was the land of the free, and the home of the brave, and we were about to help save her from the Rebel horde!

As we jingled up the Old Fort Road we were amazed at how many landmarks we'd passed in the sea smoke. First, there was the Dixon's Brick Yard on the south side of the lane—so close we should have bumped into her fences, then the grove of trees in front of the Patapsco Chemical Works—where I must have felt that gathering gloom. Then down to the little church of St. Lawrence and the Chase Brick Yards

87

where we should have been wallowing in the clay pits, but for God's help. We rode on into the city to start our new career having been blessed by the Lord—of that we were certain.

Mr. Guis's clothing store was down in the basement of the bank with high half windows looking out on the bottom of horses and half people going up and down the busy street. Suits and hats hung on racks, but there was not one military uniform in sight.

"May I help you, sir?" says a man with the strangest mustache I'd ever seen. It started out all thick and well combed at the lip, then climbed up like a honey suckle vine on each side of his narrow face.

Mike whipped out his letter from Captain Ridgely as the man stared down at his Navy Colt. Mike was a stately young man—hard not to admire, but it seemed to me the mustachioed man lingered a bit longer than was natural for a man who liked ladies.

"Captain Ridgely said you carried Maryland Horse Guard Uniforms, but I don't see any here. Guess we're in the wrong place." Mike said as he prepared to make an escape.

"Oh, no sir, we have a whole room full in the back! Come with me," mister curly que mustache said with great glee. "We have the finest selection of military uniforms on the whole Eastern Seaboard, and to tell you the truth—save for those Maryland Guard Zouave uniforms, I haven't seen anything as becoming in years! Second Lieutenant, sir?" he asked with a pregnant pause.

Mike stared at the grand row of uniforms in a dumbfounded state. There was The First Rifle, First Artillery, First Cavalry, Fifth Infantry, Fifty-third Infantry, and the Battalion of Baltimore City Guards uniforms all hanging at eye level with their loud swirling colors—all from the famous First Light Division. Then there was the Law Greys, the Towson Guard, the Garrison Forest Rangers, the Howard County Dragoons, the Patapsco Dragoons, the City Guard, and the Maryland Guard—the latter being the outfit that modeled their uniforms on the famous fighting Frenchman—complete with a red kepi, a bright red Garibaldi shirt, a blue tunic with bright red trim, and puffy dark blue pants with a red stripe down the side.

Not to mention all that shiny brass from the shoulder epaulettes that sparkled in the noonday sun.

"He's a 1st Lieutenant," I stepped in like a good orderly should.

"Very fine," said the salesman with wonder in his eyes as he gazed at Mike's powerful rank and tender young age and began to salivate. He took the Horse Guard sample uniform down off the rack and there was a little written list of accessories attached to the hangar. Each uniform had its own belts, sashes, shoulder straps, special buttons, and even their own particular undershirts, underpants, and socks. The Baltimore County Horse Guard uniform was dark blue with a single row of brass eagle buttons running straight down the chest. There was a gray sash coming across the right shoulder and down to the side of a wide black belt for the pistol and sword, but the finest part of the whole uniform was the big brass epaulettes draped down over the shoulders!

"Do we get our swords here?" I asked not being able to control myself.

"Well," says the salesman, "you really need to be fitted for that. Some men are tall," and he gazed fondly up at my 1st lieutenant, "and some are not!" And he pursed up his lips like he'd just sucked on a lemon as he looked down at me.

"Look, Mike, I know we haven't eaten lunch yet," I said, "so let's get this uniform fitted and we'll go up to Barnum's Hotel.[26] I'm buying!"

Strange how I could order him about even though he was the officer and I was the private. But first, our friendly salesman took a couple of measurements around Mike's neck, chest, arms, and inseam (good God).

"You will not believe this," says Mr. Tweedlelydee as he leapt to his feet, "but that uniform on the rack just might fit you!"

"And if so, can we have it as is?" I asked, thinking how wonderful it would be if one of us was to show up in full dress uniform as ordered.

"I thought we were just going to get measurements today?" barked the officer in charge.

"Which would be faster?" I asked Mr. Nancy.

"Well," he said with great excitement, "this is extraordinary, and I'd have to check with my manager, but we'd merely try it on, do the final fitting, and your 1st lieutenant could walk out of here in uniform today."

"And how many fittings does it usually take?" I asked.

"Three or four for most of the Maryland Militia officers," says our new little buddy. "But it took Lieutenant Merryman seven fittings, and he still refused to accept this uniform because he said it didn't show off his hindquarters like it should."

"Do you hear that, Mike? We can be out of here before the sun goes down, then its steak and potatoes and ice cold beer on me! What do you say, Lieutenant Kelley, sir?"

"Fine, but I want to wear my pistol when I go out of here," he barked.

"So where do officers get their swords, holsters, and weapons from?" I asked the helpful salesman.

"That's entirely up to the individual," said he. Then with the back of his hand to his mouth he added, "Canfield, Brother & Company at 229 East Baltimore Street," like it was a military secret.

"Fine," I said. "You get that fitting done toot sweet and I'll go pick up the lieutenant's sword and holster. Let's strike while the irons hot!"

"Well," says the gay blade of a naysayer, "your lieutenant will need to be personally fitted for that sword," which I ignored completely.

"How about I take Louisville and your pistol along with me, Lieutenant Kelley?" I begged. "Your horse needs a walk and how can I get you the right holster without a proper fitting?"

Mike was standing up on a little wooden platform with a full length mirror before him and one to each side, as our new friend brushed his proud blue uniform and pulled at it in a dozen places.

"Go ahead take my revolver," said Lieutenant Mike utterly hypnotized by the man in the mirror.

"Do you have that little note from Captain Ridgely we gave you?" I asked the clerk as he worked away.

"I'll need that back for my manager on your return," he said as he handed it over like I had leprosy.

I left Mike with his admiration society of two (him and his little friend with the honeysuckle mustache), with a reminder for them to call the tailor in and get going on the refinements. Then I climbed the store's steps to Howard Street, untied the horses, mounted Gunpowder, and led Louisville seven city blocks to Canfield, Brother & Company—a three story brick building on the north side of the road.

Now Baltimore Street was a raucous place, with drunken sailors from all over the world—gangs roamed the streets, and I kept one eye on the store clerk and one eye out the window on my horses. He too had a working arrangement with Captain Ridgely, and on his walls were all kinds of guns, knives, canteens, cartridge boxes, hats, belts, knapsacks, epaulettes, saddles, and swords. And although I was only there to buy my lieutenant a sword and a holster, that shiny new saddle with a long hole down the middle caught my eye. Captain Ridgely had said I'd have to pay for my uniforms, but he didn't say a thing about my accoutrements!

"You say Captain Ridgely's promissory note will cover all of this?" I asked with my fingers crossed.

"And you are Lieutenant Kelley?" asked the skinny salesman, as he read the note a second time.

"Yep that's me. It helps to have a father that rides to the hounds with Captain Ridgely and his swells up in Towsontown." I smiled like a smirking young rich boy would and waited to see if he agreed.

"Then buy away, lieutenant. What can I help you with first?"

"Well, I need two of your best saddle blankets in grey and one of those saddles over there," I told him pointing at the brand new McClellan[27] that would cost me a years' pay.

"You sure know your saddles, there lad," and then he corrected himself, "I mean Lieutenant Kelley. That saddle is the latest and greatest the US Cavalry has to offer."

"Can you jump with that saddle?"

"You're the first one to ask, I guess you can," goes the man as he scratched his head.

"Well, then I best take two of them. Can't have Captain Ridgely trying to steal mine, can we?" And we both had a good laugh on the Baltimore County Horse Guard commander.

"How bouts you help me carry those saddles out to the horses and we'll see how they fit? Bring those two saddle blankets along with you, and we'll be ready to parade down Baltimore Street." As long as I barked out orders and put on airs we were getting along fine, and we traded out the saddles and blankets in a breeze. I told him to save our old things and I'd send someone around to fetch them, then back to the store we went.

First, I needed to make sure I got Mike's sword, and since I wasn't in a mind to get one myself, I picked out a Bowie knife and a nice leather sheath for me. "If you don't mind me saying so, Lieutenant Kelley, sir," goes my favorite purveyor of all things military. "That one sword looks a bit too long for you, and the other a tad too short."

"True, my good man," I said with a smile, "but up on a horse I might need a real long one, while down here on the ground, won't it be fun to use this little pig sticker?" He laughed and said he knew why I'd made 1st lieutenant at such a tender young age.

Mike needed a fine black leather holster for that Horse Guard uniform and Bart (that was the salesman's name) set me right, testing them all out until we found one that fit his Navy Colt perfectly. Then we moved on to two canteens, two haversacks, two fine sets of leather saddlebags, eight cans of the best Chicago bully beef he had, two large tins of gunpowder, pistol primers, and a hundred .36 caliber balls, a large box of matches, 2 pairs of long underwear in small, three pairs of socks—size eight, English riding boots—again in size eight, ten pounds of cornmeal, a large black iron skillet with a cast iron top, and last but not least another Bowie knife, in case the real Lieutenant Mike wanted to skip the sword.

"If I can have my note back, kind sir, I have uniforms to fetch, and if you can give me a receipt, I'll see that Captain Ridgely gets it."

I signed my Lt. Kelley to the receipt in big flourishing letters, took the bill in an envelope for Captain Ridgely to gawk at, thanked Bart, and promised to come back real soon for my old gear. Then I secured all my new contraband to the horses, mounted Gunpowder and felt the smoothest, firmest, sweetest saddle ever known to man. And maybe, if I'd been a better boy with a bigger conscience, my horses wouldn't have looked like we were setting out for the Lewis and Clark expedition, but that was Captain Ridgley's price for his treason!

When I got back to the clothing store, I was afraid to leave the horses alone—what with all that gear aboard, so I bent over to see down into that shop window and there was my 1st lieutenant regaling the help with stories no doubt of his military prowess. Out came that little devil with the wrap around mustache who said, "I'm here to keep an eye on your things; Lieutenant Kelley says to come right in and bring him his pistol!"

Mike was enamored by his own magnificence! He slid his new black belt around his sash and set his sword aright, then took out a newly purchased tin of wax and lightly brushed his thick brown moustache, as that dimple in his chin grew deeper.

The manager (he was the tall one in the hound's tooth suit) took a look at Captain Ridgely's order and nodded. "Yes, it's our honor to serve the Baltimore County Horse Guard Cavalry and God Bless the Ridgelys of Hampton House."

When we mounted up, Lt. Mike noticed his new saddle right off. "Is this a McClellan saddle?" he asked all excited like. "Where in the world did you find it, boy?"

"Boy? You see a boy you spit on him," I said in anger. "You got to snap out of it, Mike!" He was losing himself in all that glory.

He stood there like that statue of General Howard up on Charles Street as a horse drawn tram went by. "Augustus, I think I'll skip that trip to Barnum's Hotel," his honor in the black feathered hat said sharply. "I need to go up to The House on East Madison Street and show Miss Yvette this beautiful uniform. Who could imagine me, Mike Kelley, being a 1st lieutenant?"

Those were my exact thoughts as well, but as we split for the day with plans to meet the very next morning and ride up to Towsontown, I told him, "Don't forget to send that message about the cabbages!"

The next morning about 8:00 AM, I came down the Lovegrove alleyway past the brick courtyard to the east of Miss Yvette's where an ancient brick wall stood guard all covered in ivy. I came through the gate into the courtyard past the huge oak tree and silently climbed the steps to the side door. Sitting at the dining room table was 1st Lieutenant Mike Kelley in his Horse Guard regalia having his first cup of coffee and talking with the new maid, Margaux.

I tapped on the window real quiet like and they let me in. Margaux was a good two inches taller than I was, probably sixteen—a gorgeous slim girl with curly shoulder length brown hair, green eyes, and the smile of an angel. She was right off the packet from New Orleans with that sweet cinnamon skin of a Creole, and I was in love the first second we met!

"Je suis heureux de vous recontrer," I whispered as I kissed her hand.

"Je suis heureux de vous recontrer aussi," she told me back, so we were both pleased to meet each other.

Margaux had a tiny little waist, and as she touched me while I was pouring my coffee there was a spark that set me on fire!

"Du Sucre?" she asked.

"Non, merci," no sugar for me, I answered her slowly.

"Crème?" Her eyes were on fire as our hands touched again.

"I need you to keep sight of what we're doing today, Augustus," Mike cut in. "Get your mind off Margaux, if Captain Ridgely catches a whiff of this plan, we'll both wind up in shallow graves. You spend far too much time thinking of women for a boy your age!"

All this coming from a man who slept in a whore house, ate in a whore house, and probably wished he'd die in a whore house too! My friend was possessed by the spirit of a Southern gentleman, and as I looked over at Mike with those huge brass epaulettes coming down off his shoulders, I thought this could be somebody's blue blooded son of the South.

"I want you to keep your mouth shut today," he lectured with great authority, as he touched his napkin to his mouth.

94

Usually Mike acted like an older brother who didn't much care what I did, but after that Horse Guard uniform went on his back, he was like the emperor with his brand new clothes. His buttons sparkled and his fine black Hardee hat sat there on the dining room table with its long black feather glistening in the lamplight.

I gazed at Margaux in her tight little maid's uniform as she dusted in the south parlor, and my heart did a pitter-patter.

"Remember today we're gonna get ourselves fired!" Mike said sternly. "This ain't no kind of sport for boys like us. We're the chase the girls and make them cry kind of boys. We ain't cut out to be spies!"

Mike was right, neither one of us was what you'd call Harvard material, but then I thought back to Captain Ridgely up there strutting about Hampton House. We weren't the dumbest boys in town!

"We just got to play it by ear, that's all." I told my commanding officer.

"Don't be starting with that playing it by ear again, Augustus!" goes Mike in a tirade. "Do you have any idea how much trouble you're playing it by ear has gotten us into?"

"Well, I ain't the Master of the Lawrenceburg Hounds, so don't be putting it all on me! All I'm saying, Mike, is Captain Robinson and the boys down at Fort McHenry need our help, and the Lord has put us right here for a reason, so let's just play it by ear today."

"You, sir, are way too big for your britches," he told me, which might have been true since my pants were a tad too tight. But my mind was made up—no matter what Mike said, we were going to play it by ear, if I had anything to say about it!

Up to the Lower House we rode with Mike's sword jangling against his saddle. "Who needs a sword in this modern age of warfare?" he asked, but I wasn't allowed to answer.

All the way in from the macadam road we'd seen slaves working away. They were moving the milking herd out to pasture, planting the corn, training the horses, and tilling the ground. There must have been a hundred slaves out there sweating away, and I was thinking that my first move as an abolitionist would be to come up there to Hampton House

95

some night with a stolen freight train and load up every slave who wanted to make a run for freedom. We'd head north as far as the New York Central could carry us, then off we'd run for Canada. Why, Miss Harriet Tubman couldn't have come up with a better plan.

The Lower House looked abandoned when we got there. There was one little colored boy whittling away on a homemade whistle as his legs dangled off the long white porch. The only time those slaves got any freedom was when they were young, which seemed like a tease to me, but from birth 'til maybe three or four years old they were left on their own to grow. This little four year old cherub was smiling a happy smile and blowing on that whistle trying to make it work—taking a notch out here and blowing some more, then whittling away. He was dressed in rags, but the buttons on his tired old shirt had that Ridgely stag imprinted on them—just like the stag that stood watch over their front door.

"Is Massa Charles in?" Mike asked the boy as he whittled.

"No sir, he's up at the Ice House torturing Little Henry!"

"Torturing Little Henry?" I asked. "What did Little Henry do to deserve getting tortured?"

"Oh, Little Henry don't have to do nothing to get tortured around here. My Momma says Little Henry is the official Hampton House whipping boy, though she's been known to whip me a time or two too!"

He just kept on whittling like we weren't there, a big smile on his tiny dark face like he didn't know what was coming for him. Every time I saw that place with its promise of beauty and grace, its gentility and class, I wanted to take a torch to it, for who takes a child like that and makes a slave out of him?

"Where's that Ice house at, son?" asked Mike as he tossed the sweet boy a penny.

"Oh, it's up there by the side of the mansion, Massa. Up on that grassy knoll," and he pointed it out.

As we trotted up the hill over open turf there came a deep hollow voice that seemed to vibrate the ground. It was kind of muffled like Captain Ridgely was far away in a cave somewhere. The hair rose on the back of my neck. Louisville and Gunpowder raised their heads and snorted. Trembling echoes filled the air. It was definitely Captain Ridgely somewhere out there hollering, "You get down there Henry and find those damn wigs! You hear me, boy?" That echoing voice of our Rebel commander rumbled across the plantation like far away thunder. "Why in the world did you let those boys go down there in the first place, Henry?" went that angry voice.

"I was hollering for them to stop, Massa, but dem boys don't listen to a thing I say!" another voice screeched with that strange vibrato.

We dismounted and searched near a big oak tree where the sound seemed to be the loudest, and there was a series of steep slate steps that descended down into an underground cavern.[28] There was an arched doorway at the bottom of the stairs—maybe eighteen steps down, with a heavy wooden door that was about half open, and that's where the sounds seemed to be coming from.

"Get down there damn you, Henry!" goes our great leader in a fit of rage. "Those wigs cost me ten dollars apiece!"

"Captain Ridgely, sir," Mike called down the steps. "This here is Lieutenant Kelley of your Horse Guard Cavalry, sir." There was silence, like maybe the captain was thinking he was hearing things too, and then Mike hollered, "Captain Ridgley, we come bearing news of troop movements through Baltimore!"

Our leader came to the half open door and looked up. He was dressed in an old farmer's change of clothes with wide wooden shoes like the Dutchmen wear, a pair of old torn and tattered pants his father had probably thrown out, and an old flannel shirt—most probably his father's too. He had a big wide brimmed straw hat on his head, and let's just say he was not the fine looking figure of a Baltimore County Horse Guard officer that we'd expected to see!

"Well, Lieutenant Kelley," he said with a little blush on his wide-jawed face. "Pardon me for being in the midst of my farm work." He seemed embarrassed—not for the strange outfit he was in, nor for that big straw hat on his head, and not in the least for those wide wooden clogs—no sir, he was embarrassed for being caught nearly working!

97

"Let me set this boy to searching down here, and I'll be right with you," he yelled. There was a little more ranting and raving, and then up the steps came our beloved commander, who took off that ugly hat at the top of the stairs like he suddenly realized how strange he might seem.

We tried not to stare, but his tired old farm pants were folded up at the cuffs, and those boney white ankles stuck out and took your breath away. We were seeing a whole different side of Captain Ridgely that day!

"Captain Ridgely, sir, we have word of reinforcements for Fort McHenry," Mike reported, sitting tall in the saddle as he smiled.

"Quiet, lieutenant," said our leader in crime as he searched for spies nearby. "Come with me and I shall find us a place where we can speak privately." He was clogging along in those big wooden shoes through the heavy dew as we went down the hill to a little family graveyard.

"Your uniform looks absolutely superb, Lieutenant Kelly!" our good captain said as he made sure we were alone. "And where did you find those McClellan saddles?"

I waited for Mike to answer. He looked so fine in his dark blue uniform, but it was the same old Mike Kelly I knew from the day before— searching for an answer that just wouldn't come to him.

"Canfield and Brother down on Baltimore Street," I piped in and the captain sighed like who could afford to shop there?

The little graveyard had a high brick wall wrapped around it with a slate top that finished it off nicely, and a creaky cast iron gate. There was the First Master of Hampton House, Charles Ridgley Jr., buried in 1790 with his wife Rebecca. Then came the Second Master, Mr. Charles Ridgely Carnen—who changed his name to Charles Carnen Ridgely just so he could inherit the place. A three time Governor of Maryland, he was lying there at rest with his wife Pricilla. The Third Master, Mr. John Carnen Ridgely and his wife Eliza were up at the mansion—still very much alive. Captain Ridgely's dearly departed were all lying there quietly in the drizzle as the want to be Fourth Master of Hampton House gazed around behind every tombstone checking for spies. "Here lieutenant, we can talk over here," he said, signaling Mike to the back corner of the graveyard. "You watch the horses, private!" His Majesty said, so I was damn near out of earshot.

"Well," Mike told him real secret like, "while I was working at the telegraph office last night, a Yankee lieutenant came in from Fort McHenry with a message for the War Department."

Mike pulled out the copy of Captain Robinson's message and handed it to the man in the wooden shoes. At first he seemed not to want to touch it, like maybe he liked playing soldier, but the real down and dirty side of committing treason was something else entirely. Finally, he took it—unrolled the message and read it in a slow and lawyerly fashion.

And just as he finished reading, I came in with the final blow, yelling from afar, "That's not all, Captain Ridgely, sir. I was out training my gelding south of Mount Clare Shops last night and I saw three rail cars full of Yankees detrain and head for Fort McHenry."

"What time did you see them, boy?" He hollered back as he gave me a look like he wished he hadn't let me into his Horse Guard Cavalry.

"It was about 7:00 PM, sir, and they were armed with brand new Springfield rifled muskets!" I laid it on thick.

"So let's see," goes our Harvard graduate turning that massive brain of his into a calculating machine. "Cabbages arrived, all heads present—one gross grade A. You said three rail cars full of troops, private? Did they look like Regulars to you?" He was leaving no stones unturned.

"Yes sir, right back from the Indian Wars," I lied having noticed that it was getting easier and easier.

Mike was making eyes like, cut that shit out, but our captain was like a blue fish on the line making a run for the Bay. It was a beautiful thing to watch a man who thought he was so damn smart be so damn dumb!

"Excellent work, gentlemen! This information must go to General Steaurt at once! Can you carry it for me, Lieutenant Kelley?" he asked as he strutted about the graveyard like Hans Christian Anderson.

"Help me, I'm dying. Help me please!" goes a faraway voice in that strange hollow echoing wail.

"Captain, sir, I think I hear someone calling!" I yelled.

I ran for Gunpowder, leapt up on his back, kicked him in the side and up that hill we galloped with Louisville right behind us, on account of somebody's orderly hadn't tied her off well. And as we galloped along in the tall wet grass towards that huge mansion on the hill, I was thinking how strange these days at the Hampton House were. Why the place was an absolute lunatic asylum!

"Help me, I'm dying," yelled Little Henry. "Help me please, somebody help me!" And then there was silence.

I came off Gunpowder's back like a Cheyenne brave, hit the steep stone steps and slid down into the chasm—busting my shin. It was dark in that cold pit of despair and I sailed through a long corridor of slippery rock for maybe ten or twelve feet, then suddenly the floor came out from under me, and down I slipped into the frozen void. I caught myself on an old wooden ladder and in the half-light coming in through the door I saw a rope. The rope was taut like somewhere down there poor little Henry was hanging! I pulled on the rope with all my strength as I clung to my purchase and begged Sweet Jesus for His help.

"Hang on Little Henry; I'm coming for you, boy!" I hollered, but there was no sound as he hung there limp as a frozen sturgeon.

I pulled and pulled on that rope and still I couldn't get Little Henry to budge, so I started down the ladder. The icy slabs pointed straight up at me like the teeth of a dragon. If I slipped in that ice house, I'd have gone in and never come out, but I wasn't giving up 'til I saved Little Henry!

"Catch hold of my leg, Henry," I bellowed, but Henry was quiet.

I could feel the frozen fuzz of his hair just touching my toe and I dropped down to the last rung, kicked poor Little Henry upside his head, and cried, "Wake up little brother, come into the light!"

He did too—first just coughing a couple times, then clutching onto my leg as I pulled us rung by rung up the icy ladder. My arms were ready to fall off by the time we hit the top, but Little Henry hung on. He was frozen, half-hung, damn near dead, and kicked in the head, but once we reached the top, we kept right on going—half sliding, half crawling for

100

the door. Up the eighteen stone steps we crawled to the warmth of old Mother Earth. The day had warmed to maybe sixty degrees and compared to those sheets of ice down below, the cold drizzle felt like a warm bath to us! We just lay there not saying a thing as we stared up at the gray sky, and then Little Henry started thanking the Lord for our deliverance.

When he got done with his prayers I told him, "Little Henry, you got to find yourself a new job—one that ain't so damn dangerous!"

We both laughed 'til we peed our pants and Little Henry whispered, "I never did find them curly little wigs!"

I gave him my socks, my brand new pair of long underwear, fifty cents—I had in my pocket, and twenty matches care of Captain Ridgely's accoutrement account. Little Henry was afraid his Massa would come up there and make him go back down in that ice house again.

"I won't do it," he whimpered. "Wouldn't you say I almost died down there, what's your name, anyway?"

"Augustus," I said. "And I think you did die down there and maybe that born again Henry ain't nobody's slave! So if you want to go hide up at the end of your Massa's lane until we're done here today, I'll ride you back to Baltimore and get you on the Underground Railroad."

"You'd do that for me, Massa Augustus?" he said with tears in his tender brown eyes—the frost still clinging to his curly hair.

"When you woke from the dead down there in that frosty pit of despair, I called you my brother, Henry, and my brother you are 'til our dying day. So if you want to make a break for it, just say the word."

"Freedom," cried Little Henry. "Freedom and Kingdom Come!"

So off went Henry for the bushes, while the horses and I went back down to the graveyard where the powers that be hadn't even noticed we were gone. As far as the captain was concerned, Little Henry was still down there searching for his wigs. It was like the Lord had placed a curtain between Little Henry and his tormentors! I stood there by the cemetery gate watching Captain Ridgely play soldier in his Dutch farmer clothes—it was grand entertainment for a boy like me.

"I shall go up to Hampton House and don my riding attire, Lieutenant Kelley," says that scarecrow with his long brown Van-Dyke soaked to the bone. "And then we shall talk about taking this information to General Steaurt toute de suite."[29] The old boy's wooden shoes had really made a mess of the Ridgely graveyard. In the Stewart family, we didn't step on our loved ones' graves, and I'm certain somewhere up in Heaven the captain's relatives were cussing him out!

"Here, Captain Ridgely," goes my lieutenant as they came through the cemetery gait. "You can take the private's horse to Hampton House, sir. He'll be happy to give you a leg up."

I could see right through Mike's little plan. He had failed miserably to get us dismissed from the Baltimore County Horse Guard Cavalry and figured let's get the red head's temper up and he'll get us fired for sure. But we now had a chance to take this act of treason all the way to the top of the Maryland Militia, so I gave the good captain a leg up, taking that muddy left wooden shoe in a cradle and giving him a good healthy boost up. Then I came to attention and saluted him smartly.

"Lieutenant Kelley," goes our lunatic in charge, "you may wait for me at the Lower House with your man. I'll only be a few minutes."

There was no thank you for the leg up, or for the use of my horse. But I just smiled and said, "My, ain't Captain Ridgely looking lovely today!"

Gunpowder galloped up the hill towards the mansion as we walked back to the Lower House. A copperhead slithered across my path and made Louisville rear. Lieutenant Mike told us both to calm down; though it wasn't his feet the serpent was near.

"Give me your Navy Colt and I'll blow him to hell," I volunteered, but the snake was away before Mike said a word.

"Remember we're getting ourselves fired today, Augustus. Don't you go screwing things up!"

What we really needed was for Captain Ridgley to think so highly of us that he didn't put his slave boy missing with our having left the plantation. The day was starting to warm up—the gray sky just a little lighter, and up on the long white porch we went, tying Louisville to a little statue of a colored jockey. The door to Captain Ridgely's office was unlocked and there on his desk was a jug of that Apple Jack Brandy—only this time, neither one of us wanted to partake.

"Here's some nice cold coffee, Lieutenant Mike," I said to my boss.

"Don't be getting into the man's stuff," Mike replied sternly.

"I thought we were getting ourselves fired today? Won't digging around in the man's private affairs, drinking the last of his coffee, and eating his stale muffins do the trick?"

He just stared at me and shook his head. "You ain't never planning on growing up, are you, Augustus?"

"You got that right. Wow, look at the jaws on that lady," I interjected, for the ambrotype of Captain Ridgley's wife showed all the bad traits of our cavalry commander, with big brown eyes much sterner than his, and a strong jaw the size of a good healthy boxer dog. She wore her hair exactly like her two musketeer sons, and it was uncanny to see a husband and wife that looked so similar.[30]

"You keep an eye out that window for our great white leader and I'll go through his desk with a fine toothed comb," I said having fun, for this spy work was a pleasure to me.

Mike settled down with some cold coffee and a stale muffin and he started returning to his old self as we dug deep into Captain Ridgely's desk. He watched out the window with his legs propped up on the sill, and I narrated my findings.

"We got two 1859 bills for racing carriages the father bought—at two thousand dollars apiece, then a second notice on the one, no both of them are outstanding." I stuck our bills from the tailor and the military shop right there with the unpaid carriage bills, figuring we'd be off to war before the captain got wind of it, but if anybody ever asked, we could swear on a stack of Bibles that we'd turned them in.

"We got bills from the spring of 1860 and 1861 for corn seed, wheat seed, seed potatoes, grain for the horses, a couple of slaves, and if our Captain Ridgely is the farm manager of this here plantation, they might need to hire themselves a new one." I told Mike as I went through the papers of a failing farm.

Fifteen minutes had gone by and still Captain Ridgely was nowhere in sight, so deeper into the roll top desk we went—well into his private correspondence with his old Harvard friends. The lads were busy settling the issue of States Rights in a civilized fashion:

"Dear Charles,

Our country is big enough to split in two with nary a problem, and if the South is allowed to continue her slave trade, we in the New York banking community would wholeheartedly support you."

There was another letter from a Harvard friend way down in South Carolina that said they would be happy to send Palmetto Republic Militia to the aid of their sister state. "Just let us know, and they'll be there."

A half hour had gone by with this drivel and I put everything back in perfect order, took a break and drank the last of the captain's coffee— split the last of the stale muffins with Mike, and we both cursed our Confederate commander for running so late. Rich people didn't much care about wasting the little man's time, so into the side drawers we went, and there we found the mother lode of military intelligence! There was an entire file on the Maryland Militia, and another on the Baltimore County Horse Guard Cavalry, but the one letter that really stuck out from the crowd was the one from General Steaurt with that extra e thrown in.

Gentlemen,

In order to respond rapidly to any invasion by the Northern states, we should begin training to fight out of uniform and ready for action at a moment's notice. Acting as private citizens, we will not need the Governor's consent to be called out.[31]

Sincerely,

Major General George H. Steaurt

Now that was a big thing, for by law the State Militia could only be called out by Governor Hicks—the Know Nothing wild card that nobody could get to commit. He wasn't saying he was Union, and he wasn't saying he was Secesh, but what all the slavers hated about him was he didn't own slaves, and by their reasoning, that meant he couldn't be counted on to deliver Maryland up to the Rebels. We had to get that information to Fort McHenry fast, for if the Militia went over to the Rebels in force, they could drag Maryland kicking and screaming right into the Confederacy.

Just then the boss came galloping down the hill from Hampton House as Mike hollered, "Put them papers away! Here comes the cavalry!"

Captain Ridgely was dressed in his dark blue uniform, his Hardee hat's long black feather flying in the breeze. It was hard to believe it was the same man we'd seen standing there with his boney white ankles sticking out of those worn out pants, but there he was, a fine Horse Guard captain—sitting his stallion oh, so perfectly, his long saber slapping to his side, and a big grin on that bull dog face. Behind him up near the mansion, a slave ran with Gunpowder heading straight down the hill. Better to have him run the horse than let him realize he could ride it. I stuffed that treasonous letter right down my pants and prepared for action!

"Bravo, Captain Ridgely," hollered Lieutenant Mike. "That's a mighty fine looking stallion you're up on this morning!"

That thoroughbred the captain rode was a big-boned hunter that I swore had some Belgium in him. He was snorting and prancing as they came to a halt, and I ran out and took his reins.

"That chestnut of yours is superb as well, private," he told me with a look of envy. "I'll give you a thousand dollars for him."

"No thank you, sir!" I told him with as much respect as I could muster.

"Fifteen hundred dollars then, soldier! A horse of that caliber deserves the finest trainer money can buy," he told me—like the wealth of the master determined the quality of the horse.

Well, I'd seen how the Ridgelys treated their things, and I'd be damned if I'd leave Gunpowder with him for one more second! The more Captain Ridgely pushed for my horse, the more I wanted to kick him in the shins and ride for home, but Lieutenant Kelley was hoping that would happen, so I tried to stay calm. "Gunpowder already has the best trainer in Baltimore. Chester Harris of Mount Clare Stables," I told him with pride. "And I'll wager you a twenty dollar gold piece that my gelding can take that stallion of yours right here and right now!"

"Ha..Ha..Ha..," goes the captain in that strange staccato laugh. "The lad has spunk. Ha..Ha...Ha, but does he have a twenty dollar gold piece?"

I reached into my pocket and pulled out a Fort McHenry Double Eagle and shook it in his face. "Consider yourself challenged, captain, or call yourself a coward!" I yelled, invoking the Code Duello.[32]

Mike smiled, as he figured we were fired for certain! By the Fool's Code Captain Ridgely had to run the race as challenged, or fight a duel for me having called him a coward.

Ridgely's servant jogged down and I caught Gunpowder by the reins and leaped up in the saddle as I stared at my former commander with a cold defiance. The captain went as white as a ghost as he searched for words, then he sawed his stallion around like I wasn't there and hollered, "Lieutenant Kelley, this boy is dishonorably discharged from my Horse Guard Cavalry—get him off my property!"

"What of the boy's challenge, sir?" Mike asked His Lordship, for they taught the Code Duello in Kentucky too. "You either accept a man's challenge, or you fight a duel for your honor, sir, and you are no coward, are you, Captain Ridgely?" Mike yelled as he lost his religion.

"I'll not contest my honor with a Baltimore street urchin like him," he bellowed as he pointed at me. "Nor with an ill bred Kentucky dirt farmer like you, Mr. Kelley, so get the hell off my farm—the two of you!"

So with no hope of a duel and no chance for a steeplechase race, we threw him a backwards bird as we flew over the first jump we came across. I'd never been fired before, but damn if it didn't feel good!

"We need to slow down a bit as we get to the woods," I told my ex-lieutenant, and out stepped Little Henry from the thicket with a sheepish grin. He was bedecked in my complimentary long underwear and nice warm wool socks, his hair finally back to its natural curly black.

Mike was in a happy mood as we slowed down to greet our little runaway friend. "Who is this?" he asked, tipping his Hardee hat with that tall black feather flying proudly.

"This is Little Henry," I told Mike. "He's the one that was trapped in the Ice House trying to fetch those curly black wigs. He almost died down there, and I promised him we'd help him escape."

Mike just smiled and that dimple in his chin grew deeper as he said, "Nice to meet you, Henry. Climb up behind my little red-headed friend and we'll be on our way to freedom."

I figured we could ride out to the Quaker Meetinghouse near Sparks and get poor Henry on the Underground Railroad, but wondering around in Horse Guard territory with a runaway slave didn't sound too smart. Little Henry said he could hear the train whistles blowing out near Bellona Mills on a rainy night, so my next idea was to ride out there and hide under a train trestle 'til the North Central came steaming down. We'd hop the train while Mike took the horses back home the long way, but our ex-lieutenant thought we should go straight down Charles Street through the heart of the city.

"Who's gonna suspect a Maryland Militia lieutenant of stealing his captain's slave in broad daylight?" He asked, and the rest of his plan was brilliant. "We'll come in behind Miss Yvette's house in the dark, put our horses away and hide Little Henry up in the hayloft," Mike said as we trotted south with the little runaway bouncing along behind me.

We came in the back alley to The House on East Madison Street after sunset just as Mike had planned—hid Little Henry up in the hayloft, cooled down the horses, watered and fed them, and went in to get some supper. The girls were all up when we came in and the big crystal chandelier over the dining room table flickered across some of the prettiest women in all of Baltimore. Margaux was standing by a side table polishing silverware, and we smiled like young lovers as the ladies gawked at Mike's magnificent uniform.

"You best go out and feed Little Henry," Mike said—his Hardee hat with that big black feather being passed around with gasps.

Margaux dished out a bowl of beef bourguignon with great chunks of beef and potatoes and carrots all floating in a fine brown broth, and I knew I was in love when she asked if I'd like some.

"Non merci," I answered and out the side door we flew—me with two cups of coffee, and Margaux with Henry's dinner. It was getting a little chilly out there, and as we brushed against each other—the sparks flew.

"Do you speak any English, Margaux?" I asked, as I stared into her eyes.

"Of course, Augustus," she said, with her warm sweet breath blowing on my neck. "We speak three languages in New Orleans—English, French, and Creole. And of course, there's always the language of love!"

Margaux leaned towards me and we kissed, then on we went to the horse barn calling for Little Henry. He'd fallen asleep up in the hayloft, so Margaux and I climbed up the ladder and sat down beside him. She took a twig of timothy hay and tickled his nose, and when he finally woke up, he uttered the smartest words I'd ever heard.

"Sweet Jesus," he said with his eyes the size of twenty dollar gold pieces, "I've done seen me an angel!"

We lay there in the hayloft and talked of our families and homes till three in the morning. Henry said he missed his Momma, for she always told him a Bible story before he went to bed each night, and could I please pat his head and tell him a tale from the Good Book.

"Well, I'm not much on religion, Little Henry, so I don't have any Bible stories to tell you." I whispered real gently so as not to wake Margaux. "But I'll pat your head if you promise not to tell anybody."

It was the least I could do for tearing him away from his Momma!

Chapter Five

Wolves in Sheep's Clothing

The next morning Mike got up early and rode down to the tailor shop to return his Horse Guard uniform, which they were happy to do as he tipped them a Fort McHenry gold piece to cover cleaning, wear and tear, and the loss of that Hardee hat, that Miss Yvette and the cocottes just couldn't part with. But as far as the rest of our accoutrements went, Mike said we'd let that sleeping dog lie.

Little Henry was on his way north for Canada in less than two days, for when I stopped down to the harbor to buy him his first fried fish sandwich, Miss Lew knew just what to do.[33]

Our next mission was to go down and warn Fort McHenry of the Rebel's treasonous plan! Security had improved on the approach to the star fort, and they now had four guards and a light artillery piece pointing straight up the dirt lane towards the Chapel of Saint Lawrence Mission.

"What are you boys up to on such a fine Baltimore morning?" a big Irish corporal asked as we came to a halt by the Guard House door.

"We're Captain Robinson's scouts come to talk with our commander," Mike told him with pride.

"Ah, yes," goes the corporal in his fine Irish brogue. "We have orders to watch for a good looking Kentucky boy, and a little freckle-faced redhead on fine thoroughbred race horses. And those sure are some fine looking horses you're up on, boys. You lads may pass."

White caps were brewing out on the Basin as two guards at the sally port let us in. The sergeant major smiled and opened the inner door to Captain Robinson's office, and our black-bearded leader walked over to greet us. He was in a jolly mood as he bellowed, "Well, boys, I'm surprised to see you're still alive, what with all the trouble brewing in Baltimore."

"The Baltimore County Horse Guard Cavalry took the bait, sir." Mike reported. "Not only did Captain Ridgely believe you were reinforced, but we were about to hand carry his warning to General Steaurt of the Maryland Militia when..." Mike paused, as he looked at me critically, "unforeseen circumstances arose."

"What unforeseen circumstances, Mr. Kelley?" asked our captain as the hoods of his eyes came down like a cobra getting ready to strike.

"Well, the lad here kind of lost his temper, sir, and he called Captain Ridgely a coward for refusing to race him, which by the Code Duello could have caused a duel. But Captain Ridgely really was a coward, sir, and he dismissed us from his Horse Guard Cavalry."

"Pardon my interruption, sir!" I told our Yankee commander as I turned beet red and began to relive the circumstances of our untimely discharge. "But that slimy bastard was trying to steal my horse!"

"Captain Ridgely—a fine Harvard graduate, trying to steal your horse, Mr. Stewart?" Captain Robinson said like he was shocked.

But I couldn't tell from his war torn face whether he was mad at me for getting us fired, or having fun at my expense, but all that anger, all that embarrassment, all that hatred I held for people like Captain Ridgely riding herd over me, my father, Chester, and all the sane people of Baltimore, came oozing out!

"There was more to it, Captain Robinson, sir!" I said pushing on with my story. "First the man almost killed one of his slaves down in this giant ice house, and then he stomped all over his poor dead kin, and then, Captain Robinson, sir, he kept us waiting for over an hour when he said he'd be back in a couple of minutes. So when he ordered me to sell him my horse to him, I kind of lost my religion, sir!" I stopped to catch my breath and see if our leader would be so inclined as to send me down into the Fort McHenry dungeons, but he was smiling like the cat that ate the canary, and so was the sergeant major and Mike Kelley too!

"And did you even have a weapon to duel with, Mr. Stewart?" Captain Robinson asked with a feigned look of surprise.

"No sir, none but this Bowie knife!" I answered. "But I'm sure Mike would have lent me his Navy Colt, if I'd asked him real nice."

Captain Robinson busted out laughing and the sergeant major pitched in, while Mike Kelley started to weep till he cried, though what was so funny about a boy trying to defend himself from a common horse thief, I couldn't see it! So out of the backside of where my long underwear had once been, I pulled out what was left of General Steaurt's letter. It was a bit damp—a little bent in some strange places, but still legible, and I passed it over to Captain Robinson.

The captain put his spectacles on and read it once, then twice, and the hoods of his eyes grew dark and ominous. "How did you come by this correspondence, Mr. Stewart?"

"Well, I was reconnoitering Captain Ridgely's desk during that long wait he gave us, sir, and here's this note from the leader of the Maryland Militia saying they were planning on striking while out of uniform. That word subterfuge you taught me the last time we met came to mind, sir, so I stuffed it down my pants. There was a letter in there from South Carolina offering help as well, but I didn't snatch that one up."

"Wolves in sheep's clothing," Captain Robinson said as he shook his head in disbelief. "These Maryland Secessionists are a vicious lot, we should hang every last one of them! Do you lads like fried scallops? Our cook is excellent with them," were his next words, I swear it.

So off to the chow hall we went. Our captain was right too, those fried scallops had a light crispy batter and tasted like they'd just swum up the Bay. Served with fried potatoes, pickles, butter and rolls—and all the coffee we could drink, we were as happy as clams! There were maybe twenty soldiers eating at a long table—Captain Robinson up at the head like a proud father watching his boys eat. After our meal, the sergeant major gave us a tour and up on the ramparts we went. We watched the ships steaming up the North Branch of the Patapsco River for the Pratt Street docks. Baltimore was the largest port south of the Mason-Dixon and her deep water harbor outflanked Washington, so if the Rebels wanted to take the Monumental City by sea, they had to take Fort McHenry first! We patted the huge cannons that were trained on the narrows and wondered how far they'd shoot?

"Far enough for the Secesh to think twice about attacking us by ship," said the sergeant major with a devilish grin. "Let them Rebels come, we'll show them what Fort McHenry is made of. Why, look at that paddle wheeler flying her palmetto flag[34] as she steams north for the Basin without even a nod to Old Glory."

Even though they'd already seceded, the ships from South Carolina were still steaming in—picking up slaves, shipping Mr. Winans' armaments south, and bringing tobacco and cotton in for the northern markets. And when our tour of Fort McHenry was over, the sergeant major escorted us back down to the Duty Room where the captain sat with two stacks of twenty dollar gold pieces, ten in each stack. They sparkled in the lamplight as he smiled like a proud father.

"You lads have done a fine job, but the rebels will be getting word out on you any minute now. It won't be safe here in Baltimore anymore. So you best take this money and run, boys!"

"Begging the captain's pardon," I cut in, "but Baltimore is my home, and I won't rest till she's free! You can keep your gold, sir; this here is a blood feud now!" I stood at attention before his desk, a small lad in civilian clothes—head held high, the blood of a fighting Highlander coursing through my veins.

"And you, Mr. Kelley?" asked our black-bearded captain.

"I'm not from Baltimore, sir, but I call her home now. We'll do your bidding right here in the Monumental City, if you don't mind?"

"Wonderful!" says Captain Robinson, "I was hoping you'd say that, this money will help you with your," he paused as he thought of just the right word, "endeavors. I want you to scout out Mr. Winans' weapons factory. They say he has a Steam Cannon in there that can throw four hundred lead balls a minute over five hundred yards. A weapon that powerful could go through a regiment like a scythe through wheat, but be careful lads; we've lost three agents nosing around his depot! One more question if you don't mind, Mr. Stewart," the captain added. "Did you make true on your vow to steal that slave? I think you said his name was Henry."

"How can you steal something that never should have been owned in the first place, Captain Robinson, sir?" was my answer. Something Chester had taught me a long time ago. The Captain smiled and dismissed us— his ignorance being his bliss, for according to the Fugitive Slave Law that our Congress had passed, he would have had to help get Henry back to his owner, if he knew he was stolen.

The next thing I did on that fine spring day was go down to my parent's house. My Momma wasn't talking to me, for I'd disappeared like a tomcat weeks before.

"Where have you been, Robert Stewart?" My father asked in a state of shock, his gray hair looking thinner than I remembered it.

"Doc, you know I ain't been to work in a while," was my opening line that didn't go over too well. "I've been helping Captain Robinson and his boys down at Fort McHenry out."

"Helping, Robert Stewart? What the hell does helping mean?" my Dad asked in the gruffest tone I'd ever heard, as my Momma sobbed loudly in the corner.

"What I mean, Doc, is I'm," and I couldn't say spying—my Mother would have shot me! "I'm an un-uniformed Union soldier." If it was good enough for the Maryland Militia, it was good enough for me. "I'm a paid agent of the United States Government working out of uniform and undercover from the hallowed grounds of Fort McHenry."

"At fifteen years of age?" My momma cried as she cussed the day she gave birth to twins.

"Fifteen and a half," I countered, "soon to be sixteen!"

"Soon to be sixteen is right!" my father said with fire in his eyes. "We are going down there right now and I'll tell that Fort McHenry commander that you're but a boy of fifteen. I know for a fact it's illegal to take a lad under eighteen into the service."

"Just a boy is right, Doc," I said softly. "But there's a War coming for us all real soon, and we've got to break free from the Rebel horde, or there won't be a Baltimore to come home to when the war is over!"

There was silence and the sobbing ceased, and for the first time in my life, my parents actually listened to me. "You two can give me a hug and a kiss goodbye, or you can tell me to get the hell out of your house," I told them proudly. "But my mind is made up, until Maryland is free of these bloody slavers, I'll fight them even if I was but a boy of four!"

So with a hug and a kiss from my mother and father, and a scratch between the ears for Old Lucky, Gunpowder and I were off. My sleeping quarters from then on out was the hayloft at Miss Yvette's barn.

We started looking for Mr. Winans' Steam Gun the following day. It was supposed to be stowed in his private depot which sat on the Ferry Bar out in the harbor—a huge complex with warehouses, docks, and railroad tracks weaving in and out. Somewhere in there that Steam Cannon sat and we planned to be the ones that found her! We borrowed Captain Robinson's telescope and dragged an old wooden rowboat down to the Basin, then took turns rowing until we got down to the Maryland White Lead Company, where we got out our crab lines and pretended we were in search of the State's favorite crustacean. Mike hooked an old rotten chicken neck to a large fish hook and pitched it in the churning waters, while I lay down in the flat of the boat and trained the telescope on Mr. Winans' Depot. It was busy in there even though it was a Sunday. Stacks and stacks of barrels and boxes, mounds of cannonballs, and crates of gunpowder, and right in the center was a dock that stuck out into the Harbor—all full of boats going this way and that. There were schooners, paddle wheelers, and tug boats steaming alongside her wharf with their steam horns blowing and people running about. We saw three ships from the Palmetto Republic loading up boxes of what could have been rifles, gunpowder, and shot—all supplied to a Rebel state that had already seceded and was planning to attack Fort Sumter in the very near future. We rowed along in the white caps trying to look like crabbers, when suddenly a steam tug came scooting out of the harbor heading straight for us! The black smoke poured from her stack and she kicked up a wake as she bounced across the waves.

"Oh, shit!" cried Mike, who was at the spy glass lying in the flotsam. "Here comes the Rebel Navy!"

"Then drop the telescope over the side," I yelled.

The skipper of the tugboat was up in his pilothouse training his spy glass on us as they came on like thunder! Three or four of his crew came up to the gunwales with shotguns in hand and glared down as they prepared to run us over. "Heave to!" one of the henchmen hollered from the port side, and since they were traveling at six or seven knots and we were but drifting with a rising tide, heave to sounded just fine.

I wondered, should I leap right or left when they tore us in half, but they cut their steam at the last minute and the bow of that tugboat sunk back down as we collided with a bang. We were knocked off our feet and the bullies laughed as we bounced around in the bottom of the boat.

They threw us a rope to tie off with and covered us with their scatter guns, as one yelled, "Put your hands up, boys! What in the hell are you doing in these private waters?"

"We're just crabbing," I told him, "and not having any success at all. Would you mind if we came in there by your docks to try our luck?"

"Jesus Christ," goes the red-nosed idiot pointing his twelve gauge shotgun at my head. "We've got a couple of city boys trying to catch blue claws in ten fathoms of water!"

"What's wrong with that?" yelled Mike, "Them deep water crabs are the sweetest kind, aren't they?"

"Do you boys know how to swim?" hollered the red-nosed gentleman looking all disgusted at our lack of crabbing skills.

"Why, yes sir, we do!" I said in a fit of not looking forward.

"Well, then you're in luck," he added as he cocked his weapon. "Strip down to your birthday suits, boys. Let's see what you're really up to?"

The rest of the bullies had evil looks on their faces like they were about to end our lives. But as long as we were above ground and able to hear the seagulls sing, there was no reason to panic, for weren't we Fort McHenry spies!

"Throw them pants up here you little shrivel dicked sons of bitches and let's see what you've got in your pockets?" barked the red-nosed idiot.

His partners all chuckled at our turning blue and shrinking down under, as we heaved our pants up for inspection. Never give up the ship 'til she's sunk, was my thought on the subject, as we stood there stark raving naked and freezing our balls off.

115

"Twelve cents and a postcard of Jefferson Davis—a real nice likeness in the tall one's pants," the man with the twelve gauge shotgun hollered up to the skipper. "Some lint and some hay in the little red head's pockets. You been sleeping in a barn, boy?" I nodded sheepishly at the scatter gun and Mr. Red Nose smiled right back. "Today is your lucky day, boys, you've got exactly ten seconds to jump, and don't you never come back to Mr. Winans' waters!"

We jumped into that stinging cold water, and if we were shriveled dicked before we jumped in there, we were a couple of girls when we hit the water! We gasped for air as we came up, and there was the sound of four shotgun blasts unloading on our poor little rowboat. The incoming tide was with us, so between strokes we closed on the limestone cliffs of the Whetstone Point. We were in the water for close to an hour, and could hear the lads in the tug boat laughing as they commented on how she went down stern first.

The climb from the water was another harrowing experience, for the waves tried to crush us into the tall stone cliffs. Straight up over those sharp jagged rocks we climbed, naked as jaybirds. There was a little farm between us and the Fort Road and we ran from spot to spot Indian style—hiding behind a hay mound here, and an outhouse there. Our bare foot prints were all we left in a freshly plowed field, and then the Chapel of St. Lawrence Mission's tall wooden cross guided us in to a little house next door that had laundry drying on a line. We were high and dry in fifteen minutes' time, to return the next day with the borrowed clothes— freshly washed and pressed, for we weren't thieves.

Our next plan was to stay as far away from Winans' Depot as we could whilst searching for that troublesome Steam Gun. The first thing we did was burgle the B&O law office up on the second floor of the Camden Street Station for anything pertaining to Mr. Winans. We climbed the creaky wooden stairs in the dark and went by that Board Room where they'd paid me a whole silver dollar for risking my life. Mike used his lock-pick to open the door to the Legal Department, and we had engineer's lamps that lit in red and green to read by. We read those red and green papers until our eyes popped out, but we never found one word about a Steam Cannon.

This sleuth work seemed a lot safer than going near the Depot; and we finally found the name of one of Mr. Winans' lawyers—a Mr. Hill, so we were off to search his office. It was the evening of the 10th of April, at about 2:00 AM with the city sleeping and the stars popping out as we walked the half mile from Miss Yvette's to the lawyer's place at St. Paul and Fayette. The Hill Building was a big three storied stucco affair— eight huge windows across on the St. Paul's side by five big windows facing Fayette. It had a big open porch that sat low to the road with six tall archways, and the windows were shining in the street light as we stepped onto the porch. We'd checked the City Directory and some thirty offices were listed there—eighteen or nineteen being lawyers, a shoe maker, a Real Estate Broker, a Justice of the Peace, a Surveyor, a tailor, a florist, a barber, and a hair dresser. Why, we even had the name of the janitor in case somebody asked! And save for a dog barking a square to the east, we had the place to ourselves.

Mike jimmied the lock and we walked right in and got ourselves comfortable, then we lit our trusty engineer's lamps and read Mr. Winans' private history of legal fights with the B&O, the Philadelphia & Reading, and even the Tsarist Railroad in Russia. It seemed there wasn't a railroad the man worked for that he hadn't tried to sue, but the one thing we couldn't find anything about, was that Steam Gun. And as the sun slowly rose over my harbor home, we started to hear wagons rumbling across the cobblestones. First, there were just farm wagons heading for the Centre Market, then horses clip-clopping along with men heading to work in the early hours of a fine red dawn.

We doused the lantern—locked Mr. Hill's private office, and were about to step out on the porch when we heard the sound of a man with jangling spurs coming our way in a hurry. Should we duck and wait for the dandy to pass, or should we run? My thought was to dig a hole straight to China and let him pass, but Mike must have figured let's take the bull by the horns, and right out the front door he went, almost knocking the man over!

"Who the hell are you?" The tall man squeaked, for though he was at least six foot tall, that voice of his was a high falsetto.

"We're the painters Bill Jones (the janitor) sent in to finish the attic," goes Mike like a master liar.

"And where's your paint brushes and drop cloths, boys?" Goes Mr. Squeaky with his fine questioning mind.

"Why, we're painting the whole place," Mike tells him—coming right up to his face. "We'll be up there for three or four days, so there's no reason to break down the job site."

The whole time I was standing behind Mike nodding my head like a trained monkey. Painters we were, a three or four day job, no doubt about it. "Then Mr. Hill is going to rent out the place," I expounded.

"That's strange," the man squeaked in that high key of C, as he pulled a Dragoon pistol out of his waist belt.

We called that kind of a pistol a horse pistol, since it was as big as a horse, but, if you ever shot one you'd see why duels were held at close range. Although it kicked like a cannon, where the ball went was anybody's guess.

"My office is on the Third Floor of this building and I haven't heard a word about any renovations. You stand fast now, boys, the police will be coming along on their rounds real soon!" And he covered us with that dueling pistol.

I was thinking that since Mike was blocking the man's shot, maybe I should jump off the porch and run like hell. We had an unwritten rule— as all good comrades must, that when the time to cut and run came, it was every man for himself! Then Old Squeaky started delivering a Civics lesson with that big old horse pistol waving in our faces.

"The Law is sacrosanct and any crime against the legal system (which must have included breaking and entry), was a crime against Humanity!" he roared like a high soprano.

Now, I never said Mike was a model of civility, but having that huge pistol waved in his face was a bit too much! He grabbed that long barrel with his left hand and caught the barrister with a jaw raising undercut with his right. The gun went off—the bullet breaking a window across the street, while we boys took off for the hills.

118

"Why did you have to go and make up that story about renting out the place?" cried Mike as we sprinted north for Miss Yvette's.

"You're the one that said we were painting the attic," I screamed in my own defense.

We took the rest of the day off just to rest and recuperate—being fresh out of plans. Mr. Winans may have looked like an old white headed grandfather to some, but he was a cold hearted killer, and the whole town knew it! We figured most of his workers were Irishmen and when an Irishmen wasn't working, he'd probably be off drinking somewhere, so we went down to the Celtic drinking hole and listened in.

Just about a mile north of the Winans Depot, there was a little Irish pub across the street from the Cross Street Market. It was our plan to go in there with forty silver dollars in hand and see what kind of information we could get. The bar was not twenty feet wide and but twice as long, and we parked ourselves up at the north end on the narrows to be away from the mayhem. It was jam-packed with Celts washing the taste of the night shift away. One old drunk sat near us at the back corner of the bar, and from time to time he would pick up his head, look around in a lonely way and bellow, "I want to say something!" Nobody seemed to care if he did or not, and he seemed to sense this lack of interest, for down would plop his head to his chest, and he'd stare into his shot glass in silence. Then up he'd come for Round Number Two and yell, "I want to say something!" This babble went on for over an hour and the drunk seemed to scare the lads away, so we went down and sat dead center of the bar. Try as we may and try as we might, not a word could we discern save for beer, prick, piss, bloody Brits, and crock of something, though we didn't know what the crock was full of. They were an animated bunch, but there wasn't a single word about that Steam Gun.

By 2:00 PM our Irish had improved to bull shit (cac tarbh), horse shit (cac capaill), and we now knew what went in the crock (cac, which was shit as well), but this intelligence gathering mission was going nowhere fast, and we were getting really snockered. We'd have stood up and wedged our way to the front door, but just then a mob of five or six Maryland Guard Zouaves came rushing in hollering in good God

119

Almighty English, so we decided to order another pint and stay for the festivities being spoken in our Mother tongue.

Tall and proud they were—all dressed in dark blue tunics with bright red trim, baggy blue pants with a red stripe down the side tucked tightly into light gray spats. They wore a red Garibaldi shirt under their tunic that showed in the front with a bright red kepi on their heads, and these boys from Company G of the Maryland Guard Zouaves were recruiting for the upcoming Second American Revolution as they loved to call it.

"The war has started fellas!" bellowed the corporal of the Zouaves. "At 4:30 this morning South Carolina opened fire on Fort Sumter!" He waved his red kepi in the air and called for a cheer. "This round is on the Maryland Militia, first Fort Sumter, then on to Fort McHenry!"

We were heading for the back door when a Zouave officer came in the front, and as God is my witness, it was Mr. Sacrosanct himself, only now he wore the wide brass epaulettes of a second lieutenant. His shoulders were way back and proud as he stood there looking around the rowdy crowd with some trepidation, for he was a blue-blooded man, a civilized man, a man Mayor Brown would later describe in his fine book of fiction[35] as being, "a quiet man," though if I had his squeaky little voice, I'd have been quiet too!

"Mike," I hollered to my daydreaming friend, "It's that lawyer that shot at us up on St. Paul's Street. We've got to run for it!"

Mike was so busy gazing at the colorful uniforms, especially the one with the brass epaulettes that he didn't hear me. "Kelley," I yelled on my second try. "Get your head out of your ass, there's that man with the big horse pistol!" But my friend was still frozen to the spot.

Just then the Zouave lieutenant let out a high pitched shriek and it was directed at me. "There's that little red-headed street urchin that broke into my Law Offices, and my God, there's his friend! Get them, boys!" And the race was on!

It was standing room only in that narrow bar, as we ran for the back door. There was an outhouse out back with a line of irritated Irishmen waiting to go in there, so making any headway against that sea of drunken Celts was a difficult task.

120

"Catch those damn Yankees!" went the barrister's shrill cry.

The Zouaves were pushing and shoving at the drunken Irishmen as they came on like warriors. "Watch out for that tall one with the dimple in his chin, he just about broke my jaw!" their commander squealed.

Well, I was pretty dangerous too—when cornered, but one thing I had on my old friend, Mike Kelley, was an ability to size up the situation and run like the wind. We were making almost no progress against that long line of bathroom goers, so out of desperation I turned and hollered, "I heard that Zouave officer yell God Save the Queen down at The Horse You Came in On!"

We ducked and we ran leaving the Irishmen to do our dirty work. They might have liked Jeff Davis better than they liked Old Abe, but they'd be damned if they'd stand for a toaster to the Queen in their favorite bar! The last of the Zouaves were gathered up and pitched out the front door just as Mike and I made our way out the back. And right there by the side of the outhouse we got our first lead on that Steam Cannon!

The man was the kind of fella that after he finally relieves himself, sticks around by the line to have a smoke and a chat. There he was bitching in his perfect Baltimorize about how a Mr. Davidson wouldn't give poor Mr. Winans his Steam Gun plans. "With that weapon we could take Baltimore by storm!" He swore as he took a long pull from his weed.

So, with the name Davidson and the knowledge that the Zouaves just might figure out how to get around back that hundred feet it would take them to catch us, we made a hasty escape. The next day we'd set out to find the man behind the Steam Gun, but on this day in April when Fort Sumter fell, it was hard enough just wading through a sea of Rebels. The church bells rang and the people cheered. They waved their palmetto flags and fired their guns in the air, and when we got back to the house on East Madison Street, there was a long line that stretched up the Lovegrove alleyway all the way to Eager Street.

We slept in the barn that night and the next morning we didn't even go in for coffee. Neither of us wanted to see the bedlam that the mere talk of war had unleashed on our happy home. We rode south towards the Harbor making plans to eat breakfast somewhere nice, for those twenty dollar gold pieces were burning holes in our pockets. And while we waited at Barnum's Hotel for the steak and eggs, and corn beef hash, and fried potatoes, and some lovely German rye toast with butter all melted on top, we sat at a corner table and drank Rio as the businessmen rushed off. We had the big ball room to ourselves, and there was white linen and silverware in great abundance.

"Let's split up and go to every hotel in Baltimore with a telegram for this Mr. Davidson fella," goes Mike as he cut a big chunk of blood red steak, stabbed a piece of eggs over easy, and obliterated the two of them.

I was too busy drinking the best coffee I'd ever tasted to answer. He chewed, swallowed, and spoke again. "We can flush him out I know we can, Augustus. But how about I treat you to a haircut and a shave before we start out?" He said, like maybe I was looking a little bit ragged.

Barnum's City Hotel was one of the biggest grandest hotels in all of Baltimore; and downstairs in the Beauty Parlor, Captain Ferrandini—one of the most famous men in Baltimore, held court. Besides being a Captain in The Knights of the Golden Circle[36] which was very strange since they didn't seem to like swarthy foreigners. Cipriano Ferrandini was the impresario of the Barnum's Hair Dressing and Barber Salon and there were four fine chairs there for the men—all covered in leather with bright shiny steel levers and pulleys to put their extremely refined customers into a multitude of positions whilst their European trained barbers did their best to shape you into the proud man only they could make you. The ladies went east and the men went west with just enough room between the two sexes to keep the ladies from hearing the sometimes blue talk. Captain Ferrandini was standing there pontificating on the evils of Lincoln as we entered.

He was shaving a fat man with three chins as he waved his straight razor in the air and hollered, "An act of war, sir! South Carolina says the election of that black ape Lincoln was an act of war that required their secession, and I think we can all agree with that!"

He paused as we entered, like who let the riff raff in? Then he went silent as he stared at us suspiciously. His three colleagues leapt up from their chairs surprised to see anyone show up at ten on a Saturday morning— especially two city boys of questionable means. They were nevertheless eager for our business and offered their chairs.

"Thank you gentlemen, but I'd rather wait for Captain Ferrandini to cut me," I told the three of them politely as they studied me hard.

Not that I cared much for the way he tossed that razor around, but the captain was a very famous man! And to say you had a shave and a haircut from such an illustrious person, sounded like something you could tell your grandchildren.

"I'll wait too!" Mike said sheepishly.

We sat there in those fine leather chairs and read the New York Times, The Baltimore Sun, and even the Charleston paper from April the 10th that said war would soon come—and didn't they get that one right! Captain Ferrandini stood about five foot six or seven, and he carried himself like a proud little lion. Maybe forty, with a thick head of dark curly hair and a wide black mustache that was tweaked at the ends, his wild brown eyes scared me to death, to say nothing of how the poor triple-chinned gentleman must have felt when he saw that razor fly by his jugular vein! He left half shaved and screaming, as Ferrandini bid him good riddance, then the dark-eyed maniac yelled, "Next!"

Mike pushed me forward like a human sacrifice and with a nod of his head he said, "Take the lad first."

The wild-eyed barber slipped a white linen cloth around my neck and pinned it tight, then he started working at his straight razor with a strop—staring at me silently as he slung his arm forward and backward. One of his flunkies flung a scalding hot towel over my face, as I twisted and fought for air, but finally that towel came off. I was catching my breath, when down plopped a big pile of hot shaving cream. Then the barber of Seville took his right index finger and carved a little hole for my mouth, as he began to chat with Mike.

"I could not help but hear your southern drawl, sir." He said as he hacked away at my head—red hair falling like chaff. "If you don't mind me asking, which southern state do you hail from, sir?"

"Kentucky, Captain Ferrandini," goes Mike like he knew the man well, "where the women are fast and the horses are beautiful."

My fast cutting barber friend smiled, and I wanted to remind him whose head he was rampaging across, but quite frankly the less attention he gave me, the better I felt.

"What are you doing in Baltimore, Mr...?" the barber inquired.

"Ladew," Mike told him like he'd said it a million times, "Mr. Percy Ladew of Shelbyville, Kentucky, at your service, sir."

The Barnum's barber put down his scissors and shook Mr. Ladew's hand without even so much as a by your leave to the head he was cutting on.

"I've been sent here by a mutual friend, Captain Ferrandini," goes Mr. Ladew oozing southern hospitality like sap from a maple tree. "You might know him as JD?" Then Mike winked at the little Italian.[37]

He halted my haircut without any warning and gazed at the ceiling searching his brain for a Mr. J.D.

"You know, a Mr. JFD," Mike said by way of a second chance, "the F being for Finis."

Suddenly a lamp went off in my hair dresser's head as he figured what I had yet to grasp. "Should I send my staff away so we can speak privately?" went the wild-eyed barber.

"Why that would be absolutely magnificent!" says Mike in a drawl so thick you could smear it on toast.

The captain dismissed his men and told them to close the door as they went. Then he unhooked my drop cloth and set me free without even asking if I was satisfied. He signaled to Mike to come over and sit down in his chair, but Mr. Ladew wasn't having it. He gave the Barnum's barber a silver dollar to cover my hair cut and said, "You come sit beside me, Captain Ferrandini. Boy, you go stand by the door!"

I made a mental note to protest when we were alone, but I had never seen Mike so theatrical before. And although he was a really bad actor, Cipriano Ferrandini was even worse!

"Jefferson Finis Davis, do you mean, sir?" asked the mustachioed hair dresser in a hissing undertone.

"Exactly!" went Percy Ladew with a knowing smile. "I bid you hello from your friend in Richmond. He has heard much about your good work down in Mexico.[38] We are in search of Mr. Davidson's Steam Gun."

Now, I finally saw what Mike was up to. He was enlisting the craziest man in all of Baltimore to help us find Mr. Winans' Steam Cannon.

"Would there be a reward for putting President Davis and this weapon together?" asked the only Italian hair dresser that I knew of in the Knights of the Golden Circle.

"Why of course," Mike said with great excitement, "One thousand dollars in cold hard cash, and ten thousand more when the gun is delivered to Richmond." Mr. Ladew had taken over my old Kentucky friend, and my respect for him was growing by leaps and bounds!

"I'll see what I can do," went the wild-eyed barber. "Meet me at the Basilica tomorrow morning for the eight o'clock Mass, and make sure you bring the money." He whispered.

Then the door to the Barber Shop came open and a female helper in a starched white dress came in and hollered that Mrs. Bonaparte was ready to have her curlers removed, could the captain please come quickly. Spy work was strange work indeed, and these were very strange times!

We waited for the darkness to come then rode down to Fort McHenry, taking care not to be followed. Two sentries guarded the large brick sally port—one with a lantern and the other with a loaded musket in hand. Captain Robinson had the fort locked down and was taking no chances. The Corporal of the Guard checked our saddlebags, patted us down, and confiscated Mike's Navy Colt before we were allowed to go in. They took us to the Watch Room where our old friend sat reading Hamlet. We came to attention before his desk—saluted, and he put down his book and returned the salute with a big furry smile.

"Something is rotten and it's not in Denmark, gentlemen!" he said philosophically. "What news do you bring me from Baltimore?"

"Well, sir," goes Mike standing as straight as any officer in the Horse Guard Cavalry ever could, "we got us a lead on that Steam Gun, only the man needs a thousand dollars for the information up front."

"A thousand dollars?" said the captain with a look of shock. "Do you think he's playing you, Mr. Kelley?"

"Well, it could be, captain, but if anybody in all of Baltimore is up to no good, this man is the one!"

"Do you know his name?" asked our Yankee commander.

125

"Cipriano Ferrandini, that crazy barber up at Barnum's Hotel."

"You boys have lit into a hornet's nest this time!" Captain Robinson gasped. "Ferrandini is tied in with some of the most influential men in Baltimore, Mr. Kelley. He's a high captain in the Knights of the Golden Circle,[39] but knowing that motley crew, I'd say they'd never give up that Steam Cannon to anyone. Still, Washington is sending us help to destroy the damn thing, so you need to find it fast, and get back here with its location!"

He hauled out his big leather sack and laid out five stacks of ten coins each of those shiny double eagles to make a thousand dollars for Captain Ferrandini, and another ten double eagles for each of us boys. Oh, we tried to pass on his money, but the captain wouldn't have it. He said that whole sack was his espionage funds; and we were the only two spies left alive on his payroll.

"You boys take the money and run," goes our black-bearded captain. "For if those Rebels get that Steam Cannon set up in the streets of Baltimore, we'll all be running!"

We came to attention and saluted the finest officer we'd ever met, and back out to the streets we went with Ferrandini's money in a royal blue sack. The next day we awoke before six on pins and needles. Mike cleaned his Colt at the dining room table while I got up a pot of coffee. It was a Sunday so the girls were all sleeping.

"Do you think I should have a pistol?" I asked my friend, for Mike was teaching me how to fire his revolver.

"Do you want to shoot your foot off, Augustus?" he said and that was that.

At exactly 8:00 AM on that Sunday morning, I walked right into the Baltimore Cathedral with a four pound sack full of golden double eagles. I sat down next to that wild-eyed barber and slid him over his thousand dollars in gold, then got up and left.

Mike waited out on Charles Street watching the side exits, while I went a block to the south on Cathedral Street and waited there by some marble stairs. We had a shrill little whistle we made with our index and little

126

finger—a single note followed by two high pitched doubles when it was time to meet up. And out came Ferrandini from the Church's front door nervously twisting at his long black mustache. He was bundled up in a black wool overcoat and under his arm was that royal blue sack, and as he came slowly down those stairs, I swear I could hear it jingling. Ferrandini walked slowly down to Mulberry Street where he proceeded to walk west, but before I could let out my call, two strangers in dark suits with black bowler hats rode by. I stayed silent in the shadows and let them pass, and just as they moved down Mulberry about a half a square, two riders I recognized came up from behind them in a grand parade of the blind leading the blind. It was the two biggest bullies in all of Baltimore—Marshal Kane's sons. They were following the men in the bowler hats that were following Cipriano Ferrandini. Once the Kane brothers got down Mulberry Street to the corner of Park Avenue; I let out my high pitched whistle and Mike came trotting up on Louisville.

"We got us a little complication here, Lieutenant Mike," I told him as I mounted Gunpowder. "That crazy Barnum's barber is being followed by two well-armed men in bowler hats, but that's not all, they're being tailed by the Kane brothers!

"What do we do now?" Mike asked like he was out of ideas.

"We just play it by ear," I said to him proudly. "And thank God, I brought along Captain Robinson's telescope!"

Ferrandini was a block and a half ahead on the wet brick walkway as he approached Howard Street. The bowler hats were a half block behind him as our telescope steamed up, then a half block further back and way too close for comfort were the Kane brothers—all traveling at a funeral pace. I could see that royal blue sack in the barber's hand as he sauntered along. At Howard Street the little Italian hair dresser stood facing us for ten minutes whilst the rest of the parade came to a halt. Then the tram car came south down Howard and stopped to pick up the captain and five or six others and headed south for Pratt Street with the smell of the Bay in the air as the drizzle came down.

Several times we saw Guildenstern and Rosecrans (we called them that in honor of the play Captain Robinson was reading), looking eye to eye with the Barnum's barber, or the Kane brothers, and we were starting to wonder if they weren't all in league. Captain Ferrandini signaled to one of those pairs and climbed up into the City Passenger coach going out Frederick Road to the west. We sat back about a quarter of a mile with the telescope trained on the strange procession. Up would come that coach being pulled by four horses with Ferrandini inside, then Rosecrans and Guildenstern on their big black stallions, followed by the Kane brothers waving their arms as they talked endlessly. We were blessed to be learning our trade with men who never looked back. Finally after six miles of endless drudgery, we came to our destination and the Barber of Seville dismounted from the horsecar in front of a series of long white buildings tucked away in a forest near Catonsville.

Guildenstern and Rosecrans were biding their time about two hundred yards back, and we cut down a dirt road to the south where they were building an Insane Asylum (how appropriate). About a third of a mile down the dirt lane we tied our horses to some low hanging branches by a little stream and made our way back north on foot. Mike checked the primers on his Colt and said, "If I start shooting you run like hell, Augustus! We'll meet back up at the house on East Madison Street."

It was good to have a fall back plan, however basic, and we moved through the hilly woods like a couple of Cheyenne braves 'til we were across from the complex maybe a hundred yards out. We lay down in a wet patch of red undergrowth and took turns with the telescope. There was a two story white house with a notched roof that looked like the Alamo—two windows up top, two below, and a little square door with a small roof over the entryway. Standing there in the rain was a Corporal's Guard of four boys in their steel gray uniforms—collars buttoned tight, old Mexican War style dragoon hats on their heads. Their muskets were at the present arms as Ferrandini came forward and saluted.

We couldn't find Rosecrans and Guildenstern, nor the Kane brothers, which troubled us some, but the view wasn't great from the weeds we were in. Out of a big building with a tall white cupola that had a palmetto flag flying came the Headmaster, for the sign said this was the St. Timothy's Hall School for Boys and Keep Out!

Firing came from the forest maybe two hundred yards off. Firing like a platoon in full volley—first muskets, then revolvers fired off fast. Gun smoke rose in the woods to our west, and Captain Ferrandini mounted up and sped off for the forest where the shooting came from. We heard two loud rounds of artillery going off with a **boom boom**! These school boys could load, fire, and reload everything from their pistols, to their rifles, and a couple of cannons.

Carefully we crawled forward through the underbrush to get a closer look, and there came an ominous throb of a steam engine. Thick black smoke rose in the air and you could hear the pounding of her piston. Then out came that shrill whistle that told us she was ready to roll, followed by a loud **hiss …hiss …hiss …hiss …hiss …hiss …hiss …hiss …hiss …hiss …hiss …hiss** in rapid succession as we heard trees being shredded like kindling wood. Tops of big oak trees two feet across quivered and came crashing down, for we'd just seen the famous Winans' Steam Gun in action! Cheers rose from the woods and we heard officers calling their men to attention. Sure the boy officers had voices that cracked, but anybody that commanded a weapon that powerful, commanded our respect. We crawled back deeper into the forest to dig that hole to China and began to hear the creak of harnesses and horses digging into the muddy hillside as they hauled the big gun back to its hiding place. We saw the Artillery section wheel the huge steam weapon into an old rickety barn. The boys brought her in like professionals, unhitched the team, and left the still smoking gun without a sentry, as they headed off for their dinner.

Mike and I snuck in there and climbed up in the hayloft and gazed at the mighty machine. It had a big metal plow poking out front with four huge freight wagon wheels, a tall black smoke stack, a wide boiler just like a locomotive had, and a metal drum that was bigger than a whiskey barrel where the rounds went in.[40] We'd just seen her mow down an oak forest like it was timothy hay—yet standing there smoking away, she looked like a steam driven fire engine.

In less than five minutes up snuck Guildenstern and Rosecrans. They entered the barn with great stealth and stared at the huge weapon like they couldn't believe it. Then up came the Kane brothers, who whipped out their Army Colts and hollered, "Put your hands up!"

The bowler hats did as they were told. "Put on these handcuffs," says the younger of the Kane brothers, "and we'll go and fetch the captain."

"That sounds like just the job for you," says the older brother as he brushed his black hair back out of his face. "You go and find that little Italian stallion, whilst I keep my gun on these here spies!"

"No, you go and find Ferrandini, I'll stay and watch these boys," went the baby brother in a fit of independence.

"It was your idea, damn you! You go and find that little brown eyed bastard!" went the first born of Marshal Kane's loins.

We'd have tried to help the bowler hats out but the Marshal's sons were armed to the teeth, so we stayed silent up in the hayloft as that first itch of poison ivy came creeping in, and Lord did it make me itch! Doctors say it takes eight hours for the itching to start, but you take a fair skinned boy like me and you rub poison ivy all over his privates (a man has got to go to the bathroom, don't you know), and you can cut that time in half.

The Barnum's barber finally arrived all bug-eyed as he tried to adjust to the dim light of the barn. Under his arm was a long black leather bag that he held like his mother's ashes, and he settled his gaze on the two characters in the bowler hats and let out a bloodcurdling scream.

"Where are the two boys I told you fools to watch?" His mustache started to twitch and he turned a nice shade of purple.

"This here is all we got!" hollered the eldest Kane brother. "These two fellas were following you since you left the Cathedral, so we took them prisoner and figured you'd be happy."

"You idiots!" bellowed the only dark hued member of the Knights of the Golden Circle. "Did I not say to watch for a tall Kentucky boy on a bay mare and his little red-headed friend on a chestnut?"

"Well, yes sir, you did, but that ain't no reason to call us idiots!" goes the baby brother Kane, who apparently took exception to being called an idiot more than his big brother did.

130

"We have to find those two boys right now!" Ferrandini howled. "You," he said pointing to the younger brother, "bring those two along. We've got to get up a search party! As for you," the wild-eyed barber of Seville yelled to the older brother, "you stay here and guard that Steam Gun and this money with your life! Go lock that back door and when we leave, lock this one. Nobody but me gets in here, do you hear me?" The captain was throwing out orders like an old campaigner, and if the two men in the bowler hats were the Federal agents that Washington had sent to destroy that cannon,[41] we needed a new plan and toot sweet about it!

We were trapped up in that hayloft with an armed man down below, but Mike settled that in a heartbeat. He climbed down the ladder as quiet as a church mouse, picked up a handspike and hit the older Kane brother upside the head. Down he went with a loud thud as I came down scratching like a hound dog in heat. I bent down and opened that alligator skin bag praying it was full of calamine lotion, and I almost forgot my own prickly affair; for there were our gold coins in that royal blue sack, on top of a hefty pile of crisp new bank notes. There were hundred dollar certificates from the Bank of Georgia, the Bank of South Carolina, Canal Bank of Louisiana, the New England Commercial Bank, and four or five others—all to the tune of ten thousand dollars! And Sweet Jesus be praised, there were the plans to the Steam Cannon too! We began to celebrate, even though technically we were still locked up in a barn.

"Let's get out of here!" whispered Mike all excited like, as the elder Kane brother began to groan. Mike clubbed him again for good measure and I said, "I've got to throw a couple of these iron balls in the bag for Captain Robinson and the sergeant major to see. Why, they're as big as a walnut." And that too made me itch!

Then I saw an iron tiller that was attached to a hinged lever on the side of the Steam Gun, and right there on the work bench beside it, like the Lord had left it there for me, were the wrenches we'd need to take her apart. But the real miracle that day was the hinged lever, the spring, and a little steel gear I lifted all fit right there in Captain Ferrandini's bag with all those bank notes, the plans, and our golden double eagles! We made our silent escape from the barn as the search party hunted. You could hear the Italian stallion screaming out orders like a fishwife as the torches

131

moved through the woods. We snuck back across Frederick Road and when we got to the horses, I threw that tiller, the springs, and that little gear thing right in the creek. Then we rode off for Fort McHenry.

"You're the luckiest boys I've ever met," Captain Robinson said when we arrived at the fort. "That money was probably from the Knights of the Golden Circle and they would have never parted with that Steam Gun."

The sergeant major locked the bank notes and plans away in the safe and smiled like a proud uncle. I gave them their complimentary two ounce balls, which we estimated could fly a few hundred yards—not the five hundred that was rumored.[42]

My next two days were spent flat on my back in the Fort McHenry Sick Bay staring up at the ceiling with my little friend and his two buddies begging for attention! Every soldier in the place stopped by to wish me well, and with an, oh, my God here, and a Jesus Christ there, my affliction was the talk of the town!

On the second day of my recovery, Mike Kelley stopped in to see if I wanted to take a ride up to the house on East Madison Street before we went off to war. Mr. Lincoln had called for seventy-five thousand volunteers to come and save Washington, and we were off to join the army as soon as I could sit a horse. But, if those sweet ladies had seen the condition my condition was in, they'd have put me in quarantine for a month, so Mike went alone to the House on the hill. I figured he'd be at least a day or two saying his goodbyes, but somewhere just around midnight, he showed back up ranting and raving about a treasonous West Pointer he'd like to kill, and how I needed to get myself dressed, for we were off for Washington.

"Slow down, Mike," I told him, "and don't wake little Marvin over there with the mumps!" My sick bay roommate had just fallen asleep.

"You were right about those Steaurts with an extra e in their name!" Mike hollered in a loud half whisper. "They are lowly snakes in the grass!"

"What's going on?" I asked as I covered my little buddy (and I don't mean Marvin).

"It was standing room only at Miss Yvette's tonight," Mike said with a sad look on his face, "and I was sitting there in the dining room with the off duty girls drinking coffee when through that pocket door to the south I heard this braggart saying he'd just resigned from the Union Army and was about to take Baltimore by storm."

"We'll kill every damn Yankee that tries to cross Pratt Street!" he swore, and that really got me since he was still in uniform!" Mike went on as he frothed at the mouth. "I wanted to fight him right then and there, but I went upstairs and got my things and headed out to the barn. But when I brought Louisville around front and looked in the window, there he was leaning against that white marble fireplace in the alcove like the King of Siam still talking his high treason!"

"What happened next?" squeaked poor little Marvin who looked like he'd just swallowed two mice.

Mike looked at Marvin and then he looked at me, and he hollered, "Well, enough was enough, and I walked right back in the front door, heaved that pocket door open, and walked up to that mouthy West Pointer. I slapped him across the face with my riding gloves and said, sir, if you're half as brave as you say you are, step outside and meet your Maker!"

"Are you calling me out, you young hooligan?" he yelled.

"I am indeed sir, I told him, by the Code Duello I challenge you!"

"Well, I'm a gentleman," said the haughty young Army captain with that extra e in his name. And gentlemen don't fight with piss ants like you!"

"If you were a gentleman you wouldn't be standing there in your Union blues talking treason against the country you swore an oath to defend![43] Come outside and fight me, or I swear I'll drag you out!"

Little Marvin was sitting up in his bed trying to swallow hard as he hollered bravo. I was thinking it sounded a whole hell of a lot like how Captain Ridgely treated me—one set of rules for the rich man and another set for the rest of us humans.

"The next thing I knew, Miss Yvette was standing between the two us pointing to the door and telling me to get the hell out, as she called Sebastian to come quick and bring his scattergun," Mike cried.

"She had to get you out of there, Mike!" I told him. "Or you would have killed the man."

"Come morning I'm riding to Washington," says Mike with a scowl on his face. "You can ride with me, or you can stay behind, but the next time I tell you my troubles, I don't expect you to take the other man's side!"

Mike stormed off like the love sick lover he was—not realizing this would be the last time he ever saw Miss Yvette. War was coming for us all that night, and just like the End of the Worlders had said when the solar storm hit Baltimore back in '59, time was speeding up, and death and destruction were on the rise!

Our weather took a strange turn that night and we awoke to high winds, cumulus clouds skittering across a deep blue sky, five foot white caps out on the Basin, sea gulls screaming to gain headway in the windy gusts, and a chill in the air at forty-two degrees—strange for a mid-April day. Fort McHenry had never looked so clean, and I was finally able to pull on my pants! Gunpowder and Louisville were out on the Parade Grounds grazing on the fresh green grass as Mike and I walked out to catch them.

"You know I'd go with you to Washington, if I thought I could sit a horse that long," I told my friend who was still in mourning from the night before.

"I'm sorry about last night, Augustus. I guess Yvette couldn't have me bothering her customers like that. What was I thinking?"

Mike was dressed in his best riding clothes—a pair of fine English riding boots, a white shirt and a light brown herringbone jacket and vest, with tight tan britches. He'd liberated the bigger caliber Army Colt from the eldest Kane brother, and it sat on his left hip facing backwards.

I was walking like a bowlegged cowboy—carrying my saddle and gear out to the mounts. It would take me a few more days before I could travel, but at least I could say my goodbyes. Gunpowder gazed around his private pasture with the Stars and Stripes dancing in the stiff breeze, and he didn't want to leave Fort McHenry either. I put my blanket on his back—smoothed it out and threw that McClellan up and cinched it tight. Then I slung the saddle bags up behind him with all my gear and a twenty pound bag of feed on each side, care of Captain Robinson and his boys, and went up to let Gunpowder nuzzle me.

"Thanks for taking Gunpowder to my Grandma's farm, Mike. I'll catch up with you in Washington."

"No problem." Mike answered. "You take care of yourself, Augustus. You want to say goodbye to your horse in private?"

I did and I told that big strong gelding, "I'll be seeing you in a couple of days, old Hoss. You be good and keep Louisville and Mike safe, and when we next meet we'll all go and join the cavalry."

A strong wind was blowing Louisville's mane and her pink nose was flaring as she watched Old Glory flap. The soldiers gave Mike and the horses three cheers as they rode off, for they knew how we'd disabled that Steam Gun and got over on the Knights of the Golden Circle. The rest of the day I just moped around—a man without his horse is a lonely man, and a man without his best friend is twice as lonely!

The following day I was ready to venture out to the Cross Street Market in a creaky buckboard with the Army cook and his team of horses. He was out of uniform and armed with an Army Colt and a double barreled shotgun, and was charged with buying the fresh fruit and vegetables the fort would need. We rode slowly up the dirt road to the market near the Irish pub where the Zouaves had chased us, and the cook dropped me off at West Hill and Sharp Streets. I hopped the passenger tram as it climbed north for Pratt and arrived at Mount Clare Stables as the last notes of colors drifted across the Basin.

Mount Clare Shops was bustling that day liked I'd never seen her bustle before. There was hammering and shouting as the night faded into day and the red sky rose in its glory. The horse handlers were busy moving the stock, as the harness boys mended their leathers. I caught a glimpse of Doc back in the bowels of the barn with a hurt horse and I hollered, "Doc, what's going on in here?"

He looked up and smiled—his blue eyes merry to see one of his sons, as he gently let the Belgium's leg back down on the ground and sent her off to the farrier. Doc signaled his assistant to hold up on the next horse and said, "I thought you'd be gone for a soldier, Rob?"

"Any day now, Doc," I told him with a little sadness. "But what's going on in the barns this morning?"

"B&O management has decided that we'll be pulling all the passenger cars through town.[44] We told them we haven't enough horses for that, but you know Mr. Garrett? He won't take no for an answer. Chester is over on the East End trying to come up with a plan, for there are troop trains due in any minute. I've got to get back to work now, son."

"Doc, wait a minute," I hollered over the hustle. "I'm supposed to catch the next train to Washington, but I can help 'til one comes."

"I thought you'd never ask," he said with a broad Stewart smile. "Grab a harness and a horse and make yourself useful."

I put the horse collars on a team and set the harnesses, ran the traces in line, and took them outside where we tied them by sections all prepared to ride when the Yankees arrived. Mike's friend Kowalski had riders ready to race the third of a mile from the telegraph office at the Camden Street Station to Mount Clare Stables with the latest news, for we didn't want to tip our hand as the Rebels were gathering for a fight.

Next door to the stables, the boys at Mount Clare Machine Shop were busy welding freight cars together. They didn't trust B&O Management either, so they welded seats into sturdy old cattle cars and put together a steam engine and a tender to make the trip to Washington, should the scheduled train fail to show up.

My father rang the fire bell and we horse handlers mounted the right lead horse in our teams and prepared to ride out. "Remember boys, we represent the B&O Railroad and all that is good in America today!" Doc cried out. "Keep your teams together, keep your eyes on your task, and God be with us all, now let's ride my boys!"

When we turned north on Howard Street, we sounded like a battalion of cavalry as the hoof beats echoed off the cobblestone streets and across the tall brick buildings. The secessionist mob ran before us and behind us, shaking their fists and calling for blood. As we drew near the Bolton Street Station, the mob grew to over two thousand, screaming and yelling, cussing and spitting—shaking clubs in our faces, and snarling like wolves! I spied the police hovering in the shadows down on John

Street, maybe a hundred of them against a mob twenty times their size as we brought the horse teams into the open space between Foster and John Street where we waited for the train from Harrisburg to come in. Across the street you could see Mayor Brown—a neat little man in a dark black suit with a pencil thin moustache standing next to his big burly friend, Marshal Kane. Up on the train platform where the Yankee boys would detrain, the gangs of Baltimore were gathering. The strange thing was the Secesh were standing right beside their sworn pro-Union enemies—something I'd never seen in my life. Then I saw the Knights of the Golden Circle up there passing out gold[45] and I realized why they were all on the same side.

"Get out of here you B&O bastards," the hooligans yelled as they shook their clubs and showed their teeth. "Leave these damn Yankees to us, we'll see them through to their destination, see them through to Hell!" A toothless Plug Ugly hollered and the crowd went wild. Soon the train would come screeching in and the Pennsylvania Volunteers would be attacked by over two thousand men.

Doc and Lucky trotted over to the policemen and my father addressed them like the proud Highlander he was. "Men, these poor boys coming through town today don't want to be here anymore than we do!" Lucky was stomping back and forth before the law men, his ears back, nostrils flared like a young stallion. My father sat up there like General Howard's statue up on Charles Street—calm and stately. "We can let these rascals tear Baltimore down, or we can take her back from this motley mob, for I'll be damned if the Blood Tubs, and the Red Necks, and the Plug Uglies, and the Black Snakes, and the Rip Raps will rule my world! Come with me, lads, and show the world that Baltimore is the land of the free and the home of the brave!" He hollered in a voice unlike the polished politicians that were sitting there doing nothing.

"Stand down, Mr. Stewart!" barked the black-bearded Marshal, and I could see the Mayor slinking off in a hurry.[46]

"Am I to believe a citizen of these United States has no right to speak?" Doc roared. "Come with me, lads, and show the world what Baltimore is made of!"

And to a man the Baltimore police moved forward like a wave moving in from the sea. The mob moved out into the railyards north of Cathedral Street and waited for their prey. Even Marshal Kane joined in the chase, and then in came the train from Harrisburg. It hissed to a stop and first to come off was a band of United States Regulars in their Union blue uniforms—some fifty strong from Company H of the 4th Artillery under an old Mexican and Seminole War veteran. He was a forty-six year old Pennsylvania man—proud and tall, with a big puffy Van-Dyke, wavy dark hair, and a high thoughtful forehead. He came off the train, took in the mob to the north, our horses to the south, and right away commanded his men to detrain and form ranks.

Doc rode up to the major and said, "We're here from the B&O Railroad, sent to tow you through town, but you'd be better off going by foot, if you ask me!"

"Who came up with this plan for my men to be split up and hauled through your city like so many cabbages?" The Union commander bellowed over the roar of the mob.

"That would be my boss, Mr. John Work Garrett, President of the B&O Railroad, a man not well known for his common sense," my father answered with a smile. "I can lend you my horse for the ride down to the Camden Station where the train for Washington will be waiting."

"No thank you. I'll stay right here on the ground with my men, for on the ground we will fight. I am Major John Pemberton, what's your name, friend?" he asked as he looked around at the howling crowd.

"I'm Charles Stewart, and these are my men from the B&O Railroad."

"We're not going to the Camden Street Station, Mr. Stewart," the major hollered. "My men and I are headed for Fort McHenry."

My ears pricked up at the thought of reinforcements for my friends down at the Whetstone Point. I jumped off my horse and ran over and hollered in his ear, "It's a little over four miles to Fort McHenry, sir, but I can get you there faster than anyone can!"

Just then, a yell came up from the mob. "God bless Jeff Davis and to hell with you slave stealing Yankee bastards!" And the rocks flew!

138

There were five hundred Pennsylvania Volunteers headed for Washington that day, and not one of them had a live round! Major Pemberton took the new recruits under his wing and ordered them to form ranks and follow his fifty Regulars who were armed with Springfield rifled muskets. They took the position of honor to the front with bayonets fixed, which kept the mob back just a bit, but not out of brick range. There were rocks and bricks, and brick bats, and clubs, cussing in your face, and stomping on your feet, fists shaking, middle fingers flying, rotten fruit splatting, people pissing in your path. And all along the way a sick laughter rose in the air. From time to time a soldier would go down—felled by a brick or a paving stone, but the Marshal and his men did a fine job keeping the rioters back. Until we reached the Camden Street Station that is, for just as the men from the Machine Shops had figured, the train to Washington was not there!

The mob multiplied like Jesus's fishes, all pitching stones and waving their weapons as they shrieked like banshees. Should we wait at the Camden Station as the mob grew bigger, or should Major Pemberton break off and leave the Volunteers to their fate? No one seemed to know. No one, except my father!

"Keep pushing west on Camden Street, boys!" he yelled to the Volunteers. "Break south for Fort McHenry, Major Pemberton! Augustus you go with the major and good luck to you, son!"

It was the first time he ever called me Augustus, though I didn't have time to savor it. We moved south for Fort McHenry being chased by four or five hundred toothless beggars, cussing and heaving rocks. By the time we hit the dirt road down to the fort, there was not one rioter left on our tail. And when we finally made it to Fort McHenry, Captain Robinson and his boys stood up on the ramparts and cheered.

The lads from the 4th Artillery came to attention on the Parade Ground with their Springfields unfired and saluted Old Glory who blew in a cold stiff breeze. Had that mob not held back for fear of their bayonets, we'd have all been torn to shreds. One poor old black soldier who'd been marked by the mob for total extinction went down a hundred times, yet he always got back up again![47]

"Mr. Stewart," yelled my old friend Captain Robinson, who was talking with the Yankee major. "We just can't get rid of you, can we, son?"

"I'm on the next train out of town, captain, I swear it!" was my answer.

The boys from the 4th Artillery surveyed the massive star fort that they'd just entered. There was well over two thousand feet of high brick walls to cover with a hundred men, but our strength had just doubled and Captain Robinson was pleased.

"Major Pemberton tells me you handled yourself well out there on the streets today, Mr. Stewart. He also tells me the B&O Railroad's plan for ferrying troops through town was absolutely abysmal. Before you get on the next train leaving town, we need you to guide Corporal O'Malley up to Camden Street Station so he can send an important message to our troops in the field. Then you are to get yourself gone by God!"

His stiff new major went red in the face at our familiarity, and I wondered if he'd keep Fort McHenry half as safe as my captain had?[48]

"Here's a chit to ride the train to Washington, Mr. Stewart. Now get!" were my black bearded captain's last words.

Just outside the sally port, Corporal O'Malley and his two buck privates had saddled three ponies for the ride to the city. O'Malley was well armed with a Henry repeating rifle, two Army Colts, and a sawed off shotgun. The latter hung from a thick leather strap around his neck, which he promptly handed over to me once I mounted.

"Can you use this, boy?" the corporal asked as I climbed aboard.

"Is it loaded?" I asked.

"Both barrels," he told me as we jostled along.

"Then just cock it back and fire the damn thing, right?"

"Cock it back, hold on tight, and then fire it, little one," he said with a smile. "That shotgun kicks like a Tennessee mule!"

I went on guard behind him as we slowly rode up to B&O Headquarters in the darkness of a rioting city. They were burning pro-Union offices and breaking into stores, and word on the streets was the town fathers were having a big meeting to decide what to do next.[49]

"Do you trust any of these men, Mr. Stewart?" the corporal asked in a whisper as we arrived at the telegraph office.

"That big burly one over there, that's Kowalski. He's good people! You can trust him with your life." I told the big Irish corporal.

"Mr. Kowalski, would you please come over here?" Corporal O'Malley said softly, signaling him to a quiet corner.

"Kowalski," he whispered as he bent into the man's ear. "My captain wants to send a message, and we ain't writing nothing down?"

Kowalski looked at me with a grin and said, "Sure corporal, what do you want me to send?"

"To all commands: Detrain and come through Baltimore by foot prepared to defend yourselves, or don't come here at all! And sign it, Captain John Cleveland Robinson, Commanding Fort McHenry."

When Kowalski was finished, the corporal paid him with a fifty cent piece for the Telegraph Company and a twenty dollar double eagle for himself. "When's the next train out of town?" the corporal asked.

"Not till tomorrow morning, everything is in flux," Kowalski told him.

"I'm not supposed to leave here until I put this boy on the next train out of town, but the captain said to come right back, what should I to do?" went my big Irish friend.

"Give me an escort up to the Mount Clare Stables and my Dad will put me on the very next train, I swear it." I promised.

We rode up to the horse barns and when I first saw Doc he was standing back by the Tack Room door picking glass from the withers of a big nervous mare. Her eyes were wide open with fright, and Doc never once looked up. "What is it this time?" he asked as he continued to free the glass from the mare's side with a pair of forceps.

"This is Corporal O'Malley from Fort McHenry, Doc. He wants to have a word with you, please."

"Is my son in trouble again, corporal?"

"No, sir, Captain Robinson doesn't want this boy getting killed, and he has charged me with seeing that he's on the next train out! Could you personally see to that, sir?"

"Corporal," Doc said as he stitched that jagged wound shut. "I swear by the flag that flies over Fort McHenry, he'll be on the very next train." The big mare whinnied and Doc added with a hearty laugh, "And you can tell your captain you heard it right from the horse's mouth."

The corporal reached into his pocket, pulled out a jingling bag of gold coins and tossed them to me. "Captain Robinson said to make sure you took this with you, lad." I'd made six hundred dollars in a little under a month—not counting the contraband Captain Ridgely had contributed. Spy work was fun and it paid well too!

"How did the Pennsylvania Volunteers make out today, Doc?" I asked my father with my fingers crossed.

"Those cattle cars the B&O Machine Shop boys cobbled together saved them, Augustus! The mob stood on the roofs pounding away, but those sturdy old freight cars just wouldn't collapse. They left for Washington pulled by a locomotive the Machine Shop boys had just put together. Sweet Jesus was with us, Augustus; we need to thank him in prayer!"

I climbed up in the hayloft above the horses where my friends and I use to play and slept peacefully for the first time in a week. There were no dreams of the evil Steuarts with that extra e in their name, nor thoughts of the Knights of the Golden Circle plotting to destroy our great nation, nor the smell of the Rebel hordes with their rotten teeth and nasty breath calling for blood. No screams of fear from the poor scared horses, no gunfire, no Blood Tubs, and no Plug Uglies. The horse barns were a place of peace and quiet that night, and I slept the sleep of a baby!

Chapter Six

Homo Homini Lupus

I awoke the next morning to Chester whispering, "Get up boy, we've got horses to feed down on the East End."

All the German breweries[50] had lent us their horses to tow the troop cars through town, and they were hidden in a lumber yard down on Canton Street. It was still dark with a little light drizzle—maybe sixty degrees with that incessant sound of the sea gulls crying as they felt the sun rising somewhere off to the east. This day had dawned without a sunrise and would be a day of great trials and tribulations, a day when I saw the worst and best of man—just as Mr. Salomon had said.

We filled the freight wagon with hundred pound sacks of feed. By using my knees to kick a little purchase in the bag, wrapping my arms around them real tight, and leaning way back; I shifted the grain up onto the wagon trying to make it look easy, as Chester watched me and grinned.

"Are you boys about loaded?" Doc yelled as he prepared to mount Lucky and come part way with us. He'd already been over to the East End that morning and was worried, for the Rebels were already gathering out on Pratt Street. "We'll stop at B&O Headquarters and see what news they have of the trains coming in, then you and Augustus can head over to the Philadelphia Station." Doc said to my old free African friend. "Then you're on the first train out of town, Augustus! And Chester, you be careful out there, these slavers blame your people for all their ills!"

The rain had stopped and the fog was blowing off and as we rode up to the Camden Street Station her bell boomed out eight o'clock. "Let's go inside and get some coffee," Doc said. He dismounted and tied Lucky just off the arched doorway. We brought the freight wagon to a halt just to the east and caught up with Doc in the main hallway as he headed for the Telegraph Office. Mr. Sammons was there in his high backed chair bidding my Father good morning as we entered.

"Can I get you gentlemen some coffee?" he asked, and we all said yes.

"What do you know of the troop trains coming in this morning, Mr. Sammons?" Doc asked as he blew on his scalding hot Rio.

"From what we've heard, the train left Philadelphia at one o'clock this morning, but she hasn't made the ferry at Havre de Grace."

"That's a pretty slow run isn't it, Mr. Sammons?" Doc asked with a worried look on his face.

"Slow indeed, but she's hauling thirty passenger cars full of soldiers from Massachusetts and Pennsylvania."

"Well, we best get a move on!" Doc said as he took his last sip. "We haven't the horses to haul half that many—not even in shifts."

Chester and I ran for the door to catch up with my father and just as we reached the stairs going down to Camden Street, up came Marshal Kane.[51] Usually the Marshal stood two or three inches taller than Doc, but my dad looked down on him that morning.

"You're just the man I wanted to see," Marshal Kane barked with an evil glare. "If you ever come between me and my men again, Stewart, I swear I'll lock you up for the rest of your life!"

"Can we talk about that later, Marshal Kane?" My father asked politely. "We've got railcars coming in to the President's Street Station packed with Volunteers this morning. You need to get your men over there right away to protect them!"

"Why, Mr. Stewart," says the Marshal with a sickly grin. "I thought you were the B&O's horse doctor, not their road agent. Your Director of Transportation has told me that the cars will be coming straight in to the West End today, so here at the Camden Street Station we'll wait."

"You've lived in Baltimore all your life, haven't you, Colonel Kane?" Doc asked the black bearded bully. "So you know damn well our cars have to be pulled one at a time down Pratt Street past the docks and the stores. We need to send some protection over to the East End right away, or they'll be hell to pay when the boys come in!"

"That's it," Marshal Kane bellowed like a wounded bull. "Sergeant McComas, arrest that man and throw him in the Middle District Jailhouse!"[52]

"What are the charges, sir?" the good sergeant asked.

"Just lock him up like I told you to, and while you're at it, lock up that damn nig..." he started to bellow. But before he could get the rest of that terrible slur out of his mouth, Chester jumped up on Old Lucky's back and was off for the territories.

"Shoot that black son of a bitch," the Marshal screamed, as I went back into the train station real slowly. One advantage of being short was people tended to look right over you, so slowly I stepped out of the last Depot door—silently climbed aboard my buckboard, and signaled the team to head east. Snakes aren't as likely to strike if you move real slow, and Colonel Kane was the biggest snake I'd ever met! Doc was right, how could the Yankees get past the docks, and the stores, and the gathering hordes without a police escort? Why, it would be a massacre, and the Marshal knew it![53]

At Light and Pratt Street, a huge South Carolina side wheeler was tied up with her palmetto flag flying, and down her starboard side were swivel guns being readied for battle, while to the north the un-uniformed Maryland Militia sat up on the porches and out on the roofs—drinking coffee and sneering as I rode by. You could see the red Garibaldi shirts of the Maryland Guard Zouaves, and the silk stripes down the sides of their pants. They were digging up cobblestones and building stone walls, and didn't that "road crew" as the Mayor later described them, even have a band tuning up down at the Centre Market playing Dixie and La Marseillaise in an off key way. Why, I even saw an artillery piece being hauled down Concord Street towards the bottleneck bridge over the Jones Falls. Once that cannon was set up at the crossing, they would have the Yankees boxed in on the East End—far away from the politicos sitting at B&O Headquarters pretending all was well with the world.

I got the feed down to the horses hidden in the Mathews and Son Lumberyard and warned the horse handlers to batten down the hatches, for war was coming like a whirlwind! Around 10:00 AM the pilot train (a single locomotive and a tender) steamed in. Its whistle echoed through the whole East End as it sailed down Canton Street to the President's Street Station. They told us the troop train was about an hour behind them and a rider took the news to Camden Street Station just in case the powers that be decided to send help.

145

A great wave of sound rolled down Canton Street when the pilot train came in, and that roar of the masses spread up President's Street to Pratt like the rumble of a great tidal wave! An ungodly roar of thousands and thousands in a communal growl of stone cold hatred, and the evil echoes of that wall of sound traveled on down between the tall brick buildings, and out onto the docks, and bounced off the ships in the harbor, and crashed into the waves of sound coming back. Those swirling sounds spooked the seagulls into their first silence of the day, for there was awe in the air as that power of the people was unleashed. And when I heard that primal scream of anger, I thought of what Mr. Salomon had said about man's inhumanity to man, "Homo homini lupus," he said. "Man is a wolf to man!" And the wolf pack was awakening!

At exactly 11:00 AM the troop train came in with its whistle blowing. It pumped out thick black smoke as the thirty railcars lined up for a quarter of a mile to the east of Presidents Station. A tall bearded major in his crisp blue uniform came down onto the train platform and looked around as the mob howled for his blood. He was a proud man with a long patrician nose—his dark hair just over his ears, his shoulders held high. I walked right up, came to attention, and gave him a crisp Fort McHenry salute, then passed him my note from Captain Robinson.

"And you are?" he asked before opening the chit, his cheery red cheeks showing he was younger than I first thought.

"I'm a Fort McHenry scout," I told him with pride. "Come to bid you welcome to my hometown of Baltimore, Maryland, sir."

"Well, I'm Major Watson of the 6th Massachusetts Volunteers, pleased to meet you, son."

"Will you be marching to the Camden Street Station on foot today, sir?" I asked, hoping they'd follow my captain's directions.

"We will, lad," went the young major—his brass eagle buttons glistening as the sun tried to peek out. "I see you're in need of a ride this morning. Well, move on back and show this note to my men in the rear. They'll bring you over when they make the march."

Then out stepped the regimental colonel. He was a young man of maybe thirty. Tall, as almost all men seemed to a small boy like me, and he had a look of sheer shock on his face as he heard the roar of that wolf pack and saw their teeth flashing! Colonel Jones came out of his stupor and gave the major an evil glare—probably for wasting time talking to a small boy, and I turned and walked fast for the rear cars.

Twelve cars back there were two old freight cars that looked like the cattle cars the boys at Montclair Shops had cobbled together the day before. The rest of the conveyances were the standard fifty seaters with a bathroom inside, while the boys in those cattle cars were out on the tracks looking for an alternate solution to a very pressing problem. Down Caroline Street they went by the droves to a lumber yard with a high wooden fence. The lads had pried open a few boards for access to their own private latrine, and as they returned to their railcars, I decided to ask them if I could make the march over to the West End with them.

"You don't want to ride in here, boy!" they all said to a man. "We ain't got no bathroom!"

"Well, we'll be marching by foot to the Camden Street Station to pick up a brand new B&O passenger car for Washington real soon, so that won't be a problem." I told them like the railroad man I thought I was.

"I think you've got that wrong, Old Hoss," goes a big Irish Sergeant as he gave his leg a mighty shake and buttoned his trousers. "Those horses up front are hauling our colonel away even as we speak."

He was right too; at exactly 11:30 the first two rail cars headed north from the President's Street Station under the tow of our B&O horses. It didn't matter if we'd risked our lives to send a message to detrain and march across town ready to fight; the senior officers were being hauled away like so many cabbages just as Major Pemberton described it!

The Irishman ran for his railcar with a final shout, "I'd run for the next car back, if I was you, boy. It smells like an outhouse in here!"

I ran back to the next rail car in line—one with a water closet and a fresher stance, climbed aboard, and asked for the man in charge. This was a fine car indeed with twelve rows of double seats on either side of a narrow isle and a small water closet in the rear. Near fifty feet long and filled to the brim with blue clad soldiers, she'd be a hard pull for four horses, and I prayed the mob didn't pick us apart.

147

It looked like a gypsy camp in there—what with the soldiers' heavy packs all strewn about, their tall Hungarian shakos hanging off seat backs and rifle barrels. Their beautiful gray caped coats were folded up as pillows and back rests—one even down on the floor with a couple of dice on it. The only thing that looked orderly in the whole place was two rows of seats up front where the officers sat quietly. Ten hours of steady bouncing had left them all pretty lethargic, but as I made my way to the front of the car, a fresh face stirred their curiosity.

"My name is Augustus Stewart, sir," I said to the first sergeant I came across.

He was a tall thin man with blondish hair and his men called him 1st Sergeant Lamson. He looked down at me like what's this boy doing on my train and started to point to the door, as I handed him my note. The sergeant unfolded it slowly as the boys gathered round, then slowly he read with his lips moving so that some of the men knew the gist of the thing before he even got finished. "You must be a Senator's son?" he said by way of a first question, and I shook my head no, though the men had already taken that up as a well-known fact. "You are a Fort McHenry scout?" he asked like he couldn't believe it.

"Yes, sir," was my answer—not realizing how small or how young I must seem to these well fed Yankees.

"Sir, do I look like a sir to you?" 1st Sergeant Lamson laid into me.

His men were all giggling. They'd seen the 1st sergeant testing a man before, but I wasn't there to piss my pants, I had some campaigns under my belt too, and I let him know it!

"Look sergeant, I know I'm just a boy, but what's about to happen out there in the streets of Baltimore is what we all should be talking about. There are thousands of Militiamen[54] preparing to attack us in a well-planned trap! So you best make plans to defend yourself, and you best say your prayers, and if somebody has an extra rifle they can lend me, I'll be happy to learn how to use it!"

There was complete silence like nobody ever talked to the 1st sergeant like that, but when he broke into laughter, his henchman joined right in. After that, the boys of Company D and me were best friends. We sat there on that railcar for over an hour waiting our turn to be hauled through the city one railcar at a time as the mob screamed for blood! The lads just sat there watching the mob grow bigger, as the 1st sergeant taught me how to load and aim a Springfield rifled musket.

A new recruit had joined the 6th Massachusetts in Boston just two days before. His name was Private Charles A. Taylor, and he hadn't had much training with the rifle either, so the 1st sergeant put us together as a team. The private was a blue-eyed pale faced man of twenty-five who had been issued the gray cape coat and black leather cartridge belt of the 6th, but nothing more—save for that shiny new Springfield rifle. 1st Sergeant Lamson got me half proficient with the task of loading it, and then he let Private Taylor do the rest by way of a review for the two of us.

"So you're a painter?" I asked as we loaded another rifle from a long line being passed. "Do you climb high on the roofs of Boston?"

"I'm not that kind of a painter," he said with a twinkle in his sharp blue eyes. "I'm a portrait painter. Say you had a scene in Baltimore you'd like committed to the canvas, I'd be the one to paint her. And if you were to hire me right now, what would you have me paint, Augustus?"

"Oh, that's easy, Private Taylor," I said passing a loaded musket back to the next customer. "I have friends here in Baltimore that are what you call ladies of the evening," and the whole car fell silent! "They live in a fine brick mansion high on a hill above the harbor, and all day long they traipse around in these skimpy little pastel pieces of underwear." You could hear a pin drop in that crowded railcar as I told them of the lovely ladies of East Madison Street. Even the officers up front swung round to listen—whilst outside the mob howled!

"The madam of the House is a beautiful blonde haired lady from Paris, France named Miss Yvette DuPuis, and as God is my witness, she has the sweetest smile and the whitest thighs that I ever saw!" You could hear the mob chanting outside, but inside that railcar, Company D of the 6th Massachusetts Volunteers couldn't be waylaid from my story!

"Go on now, tell us more, boy!" said 1st Sergeant Lamson with a smile on his face, and some said he had a new Company favorite.

149

"Well, if I was going to ask you to paint me a portrait of anything in this whole wide world, Private Taylor," I said proudly to my new found friend, "it would be of those lovely ladies in their fancy pastel bustiers, standing high atop their third floor landing under a Tiffany skylight as the evening sun shines down in those great shafts of light we call Jacob's Ladder." I closed my eyes and smiled as we were washed in that golden light, and somehow that simple story of Miss Yvette and her cocottes distracted us from our fate. That hour traveled by as fast as any in my life, while the next one would travel so slowly I thought we were in Purgatory!

There came a rumble of thunder from the west and we all fell silent. Five minutes later we heard more booming from up on Pratt Street,[55] and I could hear horses screaming like I'd never heard them scream, for war had come to Baltimore! Then the mob tore up the bottleneck bridge over the Jones Falls and chased the last railcar back to the President's Station where we were trapped like fish in a barrel. Four companies of the 6th Massachusetts and over a thousand Pennsylvania Volunteers were stranded a mile and two tenths from the Camden Street Station, and nobody was coming to help us. We had to move fast or die!

"Company D get your covers and coats on and prepare to detrain," ordered their young Captain Hart up front of our railcar.

Captain Hart had the rosy red cheeks of a farm boy and a smile on his face as he threw on his big gray coat, adjusted his sword, and placed his tall Hungarian shako on his head. His hat had a big bugle and an eagle in brass on the front with a fluffy white ball sticking out of the top, and as the captain went to don it, the roof of the railcar knocked it off. New Englanders are a practical lot, and as the good captain was nowhere near the tallest man in the Lowell City Guards, the rest of Company D waited to detrain before placing those old-fashioned hats on their heads. With their arms full of packs, and rifles, and accoutrements, they fought to stand and exit the train, and once they landed on solid ground they put those shakos on and helped each other prepare for the march.

"You'll never make it across Pratt Street you slave stealing bastards!" the mob cried as they shook their brick bats and yelled, "Best start digging your graves, you Yankee bastards!"

150

Two hundred and twenty-eight brave souls (two hundred and twenty-nine counting me) detrained to make the march that day. The rest of the Regiment was already over at the Camden Street Station with the Baltimore town fathers and we prayed they'd come back and help us! But as I looked at those brave Yankee soldiers who were about to make the march through a mob of ten thousand, I never once doubted we'd make it! For even though the wolf pack was howling like Death itself, we had the cause of freedom, our Springfield rifled muskets, and Old Glory to guide us! Our officers lined the four companies up in column of fours—Company C the Mechanics Phalanx up front with Captain Follansbee commanding. Then came Company I—the Lawrence Light Infantry, then Company L—the Stoneham Infantry with that big Irish sergeant that I'd seen buttoning his trousers carrying the furled colors, followed by my adopted friends of Company D, the Lowell City Guard, and me bringing up the rear.

"Men of the 6th Massachusetts, column of sections, forward march!" roared Captain Follansbee with his sword held high as we wheeled right up President's Street heading north for Pratt. And as we took that first left step, the mob unloaded. There were brickbats, and rocks, and sharp pieces of lumber, oyster shells, chunks of marble, bottles and pieces of pig iron flying by! We hadn't gone ten steps before two thousand people blocked our path, and when I say blocked, I mean they stopped us in our tracks!

"Company halt—one two," goes Captain Hart up at the head of our squashed little Company of fifty men in response to the Regimental command, for we couldn't move an inch against that mob!

The crowd loved it when we stopped, for they could dance up, show their derrieres and act real brave. And the strangest thing of all that day was I didn't see one unhappy face! They were smiling and laughing and showing their teeth like the wolves they'd become.

"6th Massachusetts," Captain Follansbee roared, "fix bayonets!" We did with a mighty hurrah, which caused the mob to fall back. But when they saw there was no room in that pushing and shoving mass of humanity to use a bayonet, they got brave and moved back in. We would have been crushed right there but for a hundred Rebel boys who came sashaying

151

down President's Street in a high stepping strut bearing a blue and white palmetto flag. Their buck-toothed leader swung that flag right in our captain's face and dared him by penalty of death to even try and touch her glory. And when they couldn't get the captain to bite, they moved down the column and stopped before a big bearded corporal.

"Go ahead I dare you to touch her you son of a bitch!" Their leader screamed at the top of his lungs, and he spit in the corporal's face.

The corporal just stood there as still as a Guardsman—eyes forward and shoulders back. He wasn't scared of those filthy beggars, but he wasn't going to start the Civil War with his anger!

"6th Massachusetts," called our captain three companies up. "Attention, Column of Fours, Forward March, Left, Right, Left!" And we were off; being led by that strutting man with his palmetto flag.

"1st Sergeant Crowley," bellowed the curly-headed Captain Dyke of Company L just ahead of us, "Unfurl the colors, for are we not in the land of the free and the home of the brave?" And we all bucked up!

Old Glory caught the breeze off the Bay and unfurled in a flight of freedom as the former citizens of Baltimore almost forgot their treason and started to salute. Then came the first mortal wound of the day—it was that tall bearded corporal from Company I who'd been spit on. He was there by the side of Fawn Street with his head caved in, as the mob tore his rifle from his hands and dragged him off.[56]

Out from the mob ran a loyal Union man who caught the buck-toothed Rebel by surprise and captured his palmetto flag—throwing it to the ground. They caught him and he was dragged back in alley nearby and murdered, but that South Carolina flag met her fate too, for first Company C went marching over her, and then Company I. One big burly Secesh grabbed her back up and was tying her to a makeshift flagpole, when the lieutenant from Company L broke formation and smashed the Rebel's face in with the hilt of his sword. He stripped that palmetto flag right out of the Rebel's hands, and tucked it inside his tunic.[57]

Sniper fire opened up on us from the roofs to the north. The rebels were on the tall brick buildings sighting in as puffs of black smoke rose in the air. The whiz of bullets rained down upon us and ricocheted off the pavement like angry bees, whilst the City Fire bells wailed, and the wolf pack roared! And suddenly there came a sharp whack to my head—followed by complete and utter darkness.

One minute I was there watching the mob prepare to devour us whole, and in the next breath I was simply gone! There came a little bounce here, and a jiggle there, and beneath me the Jones Falls was peacefully flowing. Private Taylor had tucked me under his arm like an easel as he climbed over the stringers of that torn down bridge. The colors went up and over the barricade and I saw a 6th Massachusetts boy lying there dying, as the mob tore his rifle from his hands.[58]

"Put me down, I'm fine," I yelled, as The Spirit moved me!

There were broken down farm wagons, ship's anchors, cotton bales, flour sacks, lumber scantlings, and even an artillery piece sitting there by what was left of that old wooden bridge. A dead Rebel lay in what was left of the barricade,[59] and if it hadn't been for Private Taylor's brave deeds that day—I'd have been murdered for sure! We fought our way west for the Camden Street Station, and got to see what being caught in a crossfire can do. The walls to the north were sparking with rounds fired from the ships in the harbor, as rounds ricocheted off the cobblestones flying south, and those rounds from the Rebels going this way and that were doing more damage than our muskets!

My right eye was gushing blood, but my left eye was working fine as Private Taylor fired and reloaded his rifle, while I kept the mob back with my Bowie knife. Our big Irish sergeant held the National flag high as we pushed on through the shrieking mob. He was taking hard hits as bricks struck his caped coat and lodged on his sleeping roll. Bullets ripped through his coat and snapped off his buttons, but our color sergeant would not go down.

We drew closer to our flag and fought on like lions!

At Gay Street we busted through another stone barricade the Mayor's "road crews" had put up, and fought hand to hand across those tall stone walls as we moved on for the Camden Street Station at a crawl. And to the surprise of many a Rebel who reached down to squash this little Yankee bug; I stung deep and often!

153

Private Taylor was growing more proficient with his musket at every shot, and when he wasn't busy reloading and taking careful aim, he was parrying and thrusting like he'd been a soldier for a thousand years. The game had changed up at the head of the Basin where the crowds were even more massive than down on President's Street. At Pratt and Commerce they almost stopped us in our tracks as they charged in gangs—screaming as they came!

At Gay Street, I saw Sergeant McComas and a couple of Baltimore City Policemen (the first I'd seen all day) trying to drag some obstacles away from our path. The crowd was pelting him with sticks and stones and still they tried to help us. At Light Street near the western end of the harbor, the smoke swirled from the rifle fire coming from atop the Maltby House Hotel. Private Taylor was loading his rifle as I swung my blade, and just as he prepared to take aim on a sharpshooter up on the green tin roof, a huge paving stone came flying down. One minute he was there with that blue twinkle in his eyes, and then he was gone![60]

I grabbed up his rifle as the wolf pack closed in, and there was that lunatic lawyer from the Maryland Guard Zouaves leading a charge on our colors. "Take that damn flag, boys!" He squealed in that high key of C, as they came on like a tidal wave.

And to say both our blood was up that day would be a bold faced lie, for both of us had turned into wolves! But this little wolf had a Springfield rifle at the ready, and that barrister only had his horse pistol on him.

"Lord, don't let me miss!" I prayed, for that shot was for Private Taylor.

I fired from the hip and that Zouave lieutenant went down—though I did too, for that musket had a hell of a kick. Sergeant Lamson scooped me up and set me on my feet, while Sergeant Timothy Crowley, our color bearer from Company H of the Watson Light Guard, yelled," Nice shot there, lad!" as he smiled like a proud big brother.

Old Glory waved in the breeze as we huddled in the shelter of her stars and her stripes! And then I saw the strangest thing of all, for though it had not rained since early morning, there was Mayor Brown nervously waving an umbrella in the air and yelling at the top of his lungs.

"For God sakes, don't shoot, hold your fire, men!" And although he later said in his fine book of fiction that he yelled that command at the 6th Massachusetts, I swear it was a plea to his voters up there on the roof of the Maltby House Hotel. The politicians were finally coming out of the Camden Street Station like rats off a sinking ship. Just one square out from B&O Headquarters, Marshal Kane appeared with that buck-toothed man who'd waved the palmetto flag.[61] And although some would say Marshal Kane was a hero that day, I'd say he was a two-faced coward who should have been hung for his treason![62]

The Marshal and thirty or forty Baltimore City Police took up a position to our rear and the mob backed off from that direction. Colonel Kane stood there with his weapon held high and claimed to have saved the day, but the only problem with that tall tail (and there were many tall tales told that day) was we still had thousands of fighting mad Marylanders between us and our train to Washington! We passed a busted up rail car with a team of four dead horses still harnessed to the burned out shell,[63] their eyes staring up at the heavens asking me why? Volleys were being fired into our ranks from all sides and brave Captain Dyke with his curly black hair went down, as did the 3rd lieutenant from Company L. Then 1st Sergeant Lamson was struck in the head with a paving stone and we helped him along the best we could. Lieutenant Lynde was next to go down in that supposed safe zone Marshal Kane had made us. He was stabbed with a Winans pike—knocked down to the ground and kicked a hundred times as the Rebels made their last attempt to crush us. And when we finally mounted the train we found out that the first men over had locked the doors and couldn't hear us pounding.

"Open the damn door!" bellowed Lieutenant Lynde, as he hammered away with the hilt of his sword.

Finally, the train door opened and we helped 1st Sergeant Lamson get in. He was confused and hollered we needed to go back and fetch 1st Sergeant Ames,[64] but Sergeant Lamson was hurt real bad and we held him back. We entered the last car on the line with a rush, as the mob hammered away at our railcar. The boys of the Fighting 6th calmly reloaded their muskets—at least those that still had a round left, and there we sat and waited for the train to pull out as the wolf pack roared.

My right eye ached and there was no water to wash it out to see if it still worked, but all around me men were hurt far worse than me. They were gut shot, bones peeking out of crushed arms and legs, caved in heads from bricks, and bats, and cobblestones, cuts and bruises from being dragged across the city streets, kick marks, black eyes, pike stabs, swelled up lips—we were all beat to hell. But we were happy, for we'd made the crossing against all the odds!

"Keep the shades drawn tight, boys," barked an orderly who was sent back from our colonel to quiet us down. "Colonel Jones doesn't want the people of Baltimore worked up, so furl those colors!" he bellowed.

I learned that day that there were two kinds of officers, one led from the front like Captain Dyke, Captain Hart, our 3rd Lieutenant Rowe, and Lieutenant Lynde, for they'd fought tooth and nail right beside us! Then there were those like Colonel Jones who led from the rear spending their time issuing orders for us to draw the blinds and furl the colors, while wounded Lieutenant Lynde did a head count.[65]

"I see the boy made it across," Lieutenant Lynde said to my new best friend, Tim Crowley, who sat next to me with Old Glory still unfurled. "Fine job out there today, 1st Sergeant Crowley! Fine job indeed, to all you men!" he added with a grimace from his kicked in ribs.

I sat in the lee of 1st Sergeant Crowley—safe in the loving hands of the Fighting 6th. The mob was still howling outside, throwing bricks and cobblestones as we sat there waiting to pull out. Rumor had it, Colonel Jones wanted to go back and teach the mob a lesson, but it sounded like braggadocio to me, for if he really wanted to come out and fight, he could have met us half way. It was time to shake the mob and head south for Washington. Mr. Lincoln needed us badly!

We left the city by fits and starts and finally pulled ahead of the mob as they fired their last shots.[66] Nine miles out of the city where the main trunk line headed south for the capital we were run off on a siding to wait for a northbound train to pass. We waited for close to two hours not knowing if the Secesh would catch up, and Colonel Jones never even bothered to throw out a picket. There in the rear car we sat with Lieutenant Lynde lying across two seats in agony.

156

1st Sergeant Lamson—two seats ahead of me, was calling out for the lads from Company D to close ranks and fight on, while 1st Sergeant Crowley was smiling away at that sweet music of Sergeant Lamson's nightmare. Tim looked like he'd stuck his head in a beehive. Every one of his brass buttons was shot off and his lips were bleeding, but that smile was as wide as the Mississippi!

My ears were ringing from the roar of the mob, and the shrieks of the horses, and the cries of the wounded, and the fire bells ringing, and the ships in the harbor blowing their steam horns, and in my fitful dreams, the city fire bell rang as Mount Clare Stables burned. The Stable Rats covered the work horses' heads with their coats and led them out to safety as the horses screamed. The next thing I heard was a soldier from the 6th Massachusetts mumbling something way back in my brain— something that didn't quite sound right!

"What's that darky doing walking up here like he owns the damn place?" He mumbled, and I heard the cock of a Springfield rifle.

My good eye popped open and there we were dead in the water at Relay with a soldier of the 6th leaning his rifle way out the window getting ready to shoot. An old Negro man was coming slowly along the railroad tracks from the east with a wide splay footed gait and a limp that favored his left leg—a quick little hop step that I'd seen a million times before, for it was my old friend, Chester Harris.

"Don't shoot! Hold your fire!" I yelled like Mayor Brown before me.

"That ain't no darky, that's my free African friend! He's a good Union man, Lieutenant Lynde, I swear he is! Can we let him in?"

"Alright, son," he said with pain in his voice, "but be quick about it. We'll be leaving for Washington any minute now."

Chester was limping worse than ever as he came slowly up to me with his eyes wide open in shock. And I realized just how bad I must look, for he went white as a ghost, and Chester was a very dark Negro!

"It's me alright, Chess. Don't worry it looks worse than it is," I told him to calm him down. "What happened to you? That limp is hellacious."

157

"Those policemen that was chasing me, Augustus, they done shot poor Lucky right out from under me," he said with great sadness. "I've been walking west since they gave up the search. It looks like you boys need a good doctor in here? Well, I reckon I could help you, if you'd like?" Chester said by way of volunteering. "Just let me go and fetch some hot water and clean rags from the station."

"Private Green and Gerry go with this gentleman and give him a hand," said our wounded lieutenant with a groan as he tried to sit up.

The two privates were only beat up a little bit and they were happy to go stretch their legs. When they returned with the scalding hot water and rags from the train station, as well as some slightly used horse bandages, the first person Chester picked to work on was me.

"Pardon me, sir, but this boy has been in my family since he was a little baby," Chester told Lieutenant Lynde. "If he's still got an eye left under that mess of blood, I've got to relieve the pressure so he don't go blind!"

Lieutenant Lynde nodded and Chester gently washed the dried blood out of my eye—just a little at a time. Finally, there was my eye poking out, a little bit bloody and swollen but at least it worked. The boys of the 6th all gathered round me and let out little gasps as the eyeball was exposed— the blood oozing from a deep gash above my eyebrow. They all agreed that I was one tough little son of a bitch, as a private from the fine state of Maine came up with some thread and a needle, and Chester stitched me up without a howl.

"What in the world hit you like that, Augustus?" he asked to distract me.

"A chunk of pig iron thrown from the roof of the Monumental Steam Bakery, can you believe it, Chester? I'm telling you; those people out there were wolves!"

"Worse than wolves," goes 1st Sergeant Crowley. "Wolves kill to survive, that mob was killing for the fun of it!"

Chester kept on sewing as I talked. "They killed my new friend Charles Taylor, Chester. Smashed his head in with a paving stone! And the horses, my Lord, I could hear them screaming. They clubbed them to death, Chester, and burned their bodies![67] Who does that to a horse?"

"It's gonna be all right, Augustus," my old friend said, but we knew it would never be all right as long as those Rebels ruled Baltimore!

"Chester, I don't ever want to go back home again," were my words as he jabbed hard to get another stitch in.

"This too will pass," he said as he worked. "I felt the same way about Memphis when I left as a boy, but you can't let them slavers ruin your memories of home, or they've beaten you, Augustus! You've got your Momma and your Poppa, and all your sisters, and your brother John, Miss Lew, Mr. Salomon, me, and all the lads down at Mount Clare Stables who love you! That's the Baltimore you've got to keep in your heart, now hold still before I accidentally sew your mouth shut."

While Chester worked he wasn't just healing my wounds, he was healing my soul, just like he did with those work horses out on our little island in the stream! Next, he went up to poor Lieutenant Lynde—his cheek bones drawn up in pain, though he stayed silent as a Guardsman.

"What's this?" Chester asked as he took the Rebel's palmetto flag out from under the lieutenant's torn and tattered tunic. The men of the Fighting 6th all started to cheer, for that low down good for nothing South Carolina flag had kept the Winans' pikes from killing our lieutenant!

The captor of the Palmetto Republic's white and blue flag had fought like a lion, and he smiled bravely as Chester wrapped his rib cage real tight with a long wide horse bandage, then put that palmetto flag right back around his chest nice and tight like. On Chester went through the wounded—cleaning the blood out of 1st Sergeant Lamson's ears and wrapping his poor crushed head, setting broken arms and legs here, washing out deep cuts from being dragged through the streets—the lads all whistling at their bruises. There was no crying and no whimpering for we were the boys of the Fighting 6th Massachusetts Volunteers—baptized in fire on the eighty-sixth anniversary of the battles of Lexington and Concord. Born in freedom and ready to die to set other men free, we sat there proudly as my old friend worked his magic.

Finally, the train pulled out of Relay and we arrived outside the capital around five that afternoon. We were greeted by the sounds of a cheering crowd. The wounded were unloaded as we formed up on Major Watson's

159

command. Chester and I went round to the rear of the column for we were but unofficial members of the regiment, but 2nd Lieutenant Stevens came and asked if we'd do him and the boys of Company L the honor of marching with them to the Capitol dome where they were putting us up for the night. Lieutenant Lynde and 1st Sergeant Lamson were just being loaded into an ambulance and we gave them a big cheer, and prayed that Captain Dyke survived![68]

Major Watson almost cried as he saw the remnants of his beloved 6th so beat up by the mob, while Colonel Jones had that haughty look of a hero as he detrained with his nose in the air. That wispy moustache of his was freshly waxed and his uniform was as crisp and clean as the day he left Boston. He stood tall like he'd fought right there beside us, as he drew his sword and sang out the regimental commands to bring us into column of twos for the march. For three squares we went over the muddy streets of Washington as the crowds cheered.

We'd survived the attacks of over ten thousand Rebels, and we swore that the Lord was with us, so with our heads hanging down in prayer at the Capitol Rotunda, Chaplain Charles Babbidge gave thanks.

They fed us outside at a long low table full of fried chicken, fried potatoes, bread and butter, boiled cabbage, and kale. Milk must have been in short supply, but we had all the coffee we could drink.

Major Watson came up to me there under the trees and said he was glad I'd made it to Washington. "What Company did you come over with, lad?" he asked like he cared.

I told him Company D and Company L with 1st Sergeant Timothy Crowley and the colors leading the way.

"Good men to fight your first battle with, son. Thanks for your help and take care of that eye!" said the regal major with a fine salute.

A military band began to play and some nice ladies in their crinoline dresses went round darning the tears in our clothes. Miss Clara Barton was there as the sun went down—helping to stitch up those that hadn't gone to the hospital. And while we were all watching the stars pop out, I thought of the poor lads still surrounded down at Fort McHenry. If Old Glory could survive her trek across Pratt Street against a mob of ten thousand, then Captain Robinson and his hundred men could hold out 'til we came back to help them, and that's what I prayed. "Sweet Jesus; help me set my harbor home free!"

When our prayers were over they turned the Press loose on us. Mostly they wanted to hear from our officers, so we lads in the ranks were safe, save for our color bearer, who was swamped worse by the newspaper reporters than he was by the Maryland Militia.

"Did you think you would ever get the National flag across Baltimore?" they asked my big Irish friend like it was a chess game.

"We gave as good as we got, and with the help of the Lord we survived," our 1st sergeant told them modestly, and he was right.

Tim Crowley was maybe a year or two older than Colonel Jones, and the 1st sergeant was a tall good looking giant, so as he spoke to the Press on the Senate Floor, the colonel's face grew redder and redder. And to keep the Press interested in the man at the top (as they should be), our good colonel told them that he hadn't detrained his men in Baltimore as planned because the horse handlers had whisked him away so fast he didn't have time to give the order. Why, he just panicked when he saw the wolf pack getting ready to attack—some men are not made for war!

Then one of the fine members of the Third Estate—I think he was from the Baltimore Wecker, came over and asked me in his strong German accent, "Are you the little red-headed boy what saved the colors out on Pratt Street?"

"I didn't save the colors; Sergeant Crowley did!" I told him and started to move away, when he said what I really dreaded. "Well, did you shoot dead a well-known lawyer as he charged Old Glory?"

In the Age of the Telegraph word traveled fast,[69] maybe not as fast as those horses that pulled the colonel's rail car through town, but it was my opinion that Mr. Squeaky was caught in the crossfire—not shot by me! He'd been coming straight at me when I fired that rifle, and I saw him swept sideways when he went down, so unless I could shoot a bank shot, which I certainly could not (not even in pool), it was my belief that the barrister had been struck by a rebel round.[70] So my answer to the man was, "I didn't shoot anybody!"

After all, Doc was locked away in the worst jailhouse in Baltimore and somehow, I'd be setting him and Fort McHenry free! So having my name in the newspapers would only complicate things.

President Lincoln had just joined us on the Senate floor, though I was too short to see him. He planned to shake every hand in the place, though the first hand I shook was a tall stately man from Mike Kelley's home state of Kentucky. This fine Southern gentleman stood well over six feet and had two big horse pistols stuck in his belt, a huge Bowie knife in a brown leather scabbard hung at his side, and he had the sharpest piercing brown eyes that I'd ever seen. The big man was dressed in a dark blue uniform with well shined black boots and brass spurs poking out from under long dress pants. He wore a pair of huge brass epaulettes on his wide shoulders with the rank of colonel showing, and the man had that stately grandeur that I was only to see a few times in my life!

"Have you ever used that Arkansas Toothpick in anger, friend?" He asked with a big broad grin. He saw the reluctance to talk in my eyes—plus I didn't know what an Arkansas Toothpick was, and he settled me down by introducing himself in a calm and noble fashion. "I am Cassius Marcellus Clay of Madison County, Kentucky, at your service, sir!" Then we shook hands like a couple of senators.

I'd heard of Cassius Clay for he was a brave emancipationist living in the heart of a slaveholding state. Near murdered by his fellow Kentuckians on several occasions,[71] he liked nothing better than a good hard fight! And now that war had come, Colonel Clay had great plans to free all the slaves as soon as possible, and he wasn't bashful to talk about it.

"So as I was saying, Mr. Stewart," he said after I'd told him my name. "Have you ever had occasion to use that Bowie knife in anger?"

"You bet he has," 1st Sergeant Crowley stepped in like a proud big brother. "There's many a Maryland Militiamen walking the streets of Baltimore wondering how they got them deep nicks in their shins."

We all laughed like the warriors we'd become, as the 1st sergeant went on to tell our new friend how I'd fought like a banti rooster out there on the streets of my hometown—slashing and whacking away with my Bowie knife, as my friend, Private Taylor fired his Springfield rifled

162

musket, reloaded, and fired once more. "And when his friend went down," the good sergeant went right on bragging, "the lad took up his comrade's rifle and killed a man who was charging our colors!"[72]

"And this is Chester Harris, Colonel Clay." I burst in to change the subject. "He saved my eye and our lieutenant too!"

"Nice to meet you Doctor Harris," the Kentucky colonel said and he shook Chester's hand. And then he asked us the strangest thing. "Do either of you know the way to Annapolis, Maryland?"

"I believe I do, sir," I spoke up first, though I'd never been there before.

"Well, you two would be perfect for a little expedition I'm planning," he exclaimed with a mischievous grin. "Take my card and come see me at Willards' Hotel on Monday morning. You don't want to spend your life in the infantry, do you, son?"

The great man left as fast as he came in. Like he was picked up by a whirlwind and raised to the heights, then gently put down somewhere else on the Senate floor—the toughest, roughest, most genteel man I had ever met, gone with the wind. When we later greeted the President, it was like seeing the moon when you'd just come from the surface of the sun, for nothing could touch Cassius Marcellus Clay for the fire in his soul, and the freedom in his heart!

We fell asleep on the hard stone floor only to be awakened in the early hours by Colonel Jones sitting up in the Senate Pro Temps' chair pontificating to a member of the Press about how Mayor Brown had fired at the Secesh mob.[73] I couldn't take another second of his lies, so Chester and I said farewell to my friends of the 6th Massachusetts Volunteers and headed for the peace and quiet of my Grandmother's farm.

There my Grandma Bloise raised chickens to sell eggs, the only cash she had since my grandfather died. She also had one old cow for her personal needs, and a middle aged mule named Milton. Milton use to help my Grandpa plow the forty acres they had, but now all he did was eat and bray. My Grandma could still hoe her garden, or find her bird's hidden eggs, or shoot a fox out of the hen house, though she was well over eighty, and as we approached her farm that bright sunny day, I could see Gunpowder grazing down by the Anacostia River.

163

I swear he spotted Chester's little splay footed gait from a half mile away, for he raised his big chestnut head and whinnied loud enough to wake the dead. He galloped towards us like the charge of the Light Brigade and we had a grand homecoming. Even Milton the mule remembered me and Chester, for each spring—except for this one, we'd come down to help open the garden. Out from the little farmhouse came Grandma Bloise to see what the fuss was, for with Gunpowder whinnying and Milton braying it sounded like a carnival had come to town. But when she saw how beat up her grandson was, her knobby knees went weak, and Chester had to catch her before she went down.

"Robert Augustus Stewart," she said as she regained her composure, "have you been fighting again, boy?"

How do you lie to a Grandmother that you love like life itself? The answer is you lie just fine, if you don't want to scare her to death. "Grandma," I lied, "my horse fell on a jump, and this here is all that's left of me!"

"Don't you be lying to your old Grandma!" she said as the color came back to her cheeks. "First off, your horse has been here for nigh on three days, and secondly, I heard you scream when you got hurt in Baltimore yesterday afternoon!"

"What do you mean you heard me scream, Grandma? I never screamed!"

"Oh, you screamed alright, and I heard you!" she swore.

Chester stood there with his wide white eyes. A hundred years earlier they'd have called my Grandma a witch and burned her at the stake, but she weren't no witch, she was my Grandmother!

"My God, let me look at you son," she said as she brushed at the dried blood in my hair and stared at my eye and asked, "Who did that stitching there above your eyebrow, Robby?"

"Chester," I said. "The Lord sent him along to save me, Grandma."

"That ain't exactly true, Mrs. Bloise," Chester told her with his head hung down. "Augustus, I mean your Little Robby here was with a whole train full of men from the 6th Massachusetts and they saved my life, Ma'am, the lad's just being humble."

164

"Well, whichever way it went," says my sweet little Grandmother, "once again, Mr. Harris, I'm beholding to you—those are some mighty fine stitches you laid in there. Did he bellow when you put them in?"

"Not once, Mrs. Bloise," went Chester with fear in his eyes for he'd never seen my Grandmother's otherworldly powers before. "I didn't hear him yelp once, Ma'am, and the boys of the Fighting 6th said he was one tough little son of a...," he paused and his eyes grew wider, "gun!"

"Let me get you two some towels and a bar of soap and you can go down to the river to wash up. Your uncles use to love bathing in the creek after a hard days' work. I'll go gather some eggs and fix you a nice country breakfast."

We splashed in the creek and tried to laugh, but I was too bruised and banged up to enjoy it. Those flying rocks had given me bruises that were more black than blue and I ached all over. Still, that soap and the stinging cold water revived me. We dressed in some old clothes of my uncles and walked up to a very late breakfast. We had biscuits and homemade wild blackberry jam, sausage and scrambled eggs, fresh butter that was turning orangey-yellow with the season, and cups and cups of hot Rio.

"That horse of yours pined for you terribly, Robby," my Grandma told me as she passed me the biscuits. "He pined away like a little lost puppy. Why, we had to lock him up in the barn when your friend Mike Kelley rode off, for that gelding jumped the fence twice!" I smiled at my Grandma and ate my breakfast, and forgot all about the war.

Grandma's little farm was a haven of peace. A quail sang his Bob White song out in the meadow, and we took my uncle's old bedroom and slept through the afternoon—the tree frogs singing away. In my dreams my painter friend, Charles Taylor, came to me. He was painting a portrait of the girls from East Madison Street in that golden light streaming down from the third floor landing. And as I awoke to the fading light of another day near gone, I hoped somewhere—in a higher place, Private Taylor would continue to paint! It was about six-thirty on that warm spring evening. I smelled crab cakes cooking in a black iron skillet! Grandma Bloise always believed in drowning your sorrows with your favorite foods, which I agreed with wholeheartedly.

165

I went down stairs and there she was, a small woman with delicate fingers who use to play the piano before she moved to the farm and raised a mess of kids. She was maybe five foot tall when you stretched her out a bit, and she'd adjusted to the unexpected death of my Grandfather by taking on all the farm work. And still she had time for her grandkids, and her Church, and for making the best back fin crab cakes in the entire Universe!

Grandma had a smile on her wrinkled old face as I came into the kitchen and hugged her. "Oh, I'm glad you're up, Robby," she said as our blue eyes (some said the same blue eyes on the two of us) met. "If you sleep the whole day, you won't be able to sleep through the night."

The crab cakes were sizzling away on the wood stove and I saw that she'd cooked two loaves of rye bread that were cooling on the window sill. Toasted rye bread, some fresh picked baby lettuce, a healthy plop of Grandma's homemade mayonnaise, and a nice thick crab cake was exactly what her Little Robby needed!

"Grandma," I said with peace in my soul and love in my heart, "I feel so much better now that I'm here. It's like I'm a little boy again!"

My Grandma started crying! She held me tight in her arms like I was but a four year old and stroked my head real gently. I knew that very instant as she soothed me, just how poor Little Henry must have felt when his Momma rubbed his head—he gave up a lot for his freedom!

"They killed the horses, Grandma," I cried like a sniffling baby. "They were just doing their job and the mob tore them apart! Why are men so cruel?"

"There, there, Rob!" My Grandmother soothed as she bucked up and swallowed hard. "All this will pass; you've got to let it go, son."

Chester had told me the very same thing, and I wasn't sure if this was something adults said to mean things got better over time, or that you'd grow to forget what was troubling you, but I'd never forget how those horses had died—not in this world, and not in the next one!

"Now go and wash up for supper," Grandma said as she wiped the tears from her eyes. "I'll go and call Mr. Harris in from the garden."

"I thought Chester was sleeping right there beside me?"

"Oh," she said with a tender smile, "he told me you were snoring like a freight train climbing the grade to Harper's Ferry and got up about two o'clock and went out to work the garden. No wonder your father loves him—he's a saint. By the way, Robby how is your father?"

Grandma Bloise always had a way of sending your thoughts one way then hitting you up with a question from the other direction. And how do you lie to a clairvoyant grandmother? Do you tell her, her son in law is doing just fine, or do you blurt out he's locked up in the worst jailhouse in Baltimore? Or do you just change the subject as fast as you can and say, "Grandma, look how Milton watches every move Chester makes like they're the closest of friends."

As the old gray headed free African moved down the row of peas with his hoe, the mule moved right along with him. So, partially to keep from returning to the subject of my father's unfortunate fate, and partially because I thought it sounded like a good plan to me, I asked, "Did Mike Kelley leave me a cigar box full of money, Grandma?"

"He did," she said, "and I was going to ask you about it."

"Well, Grandma, you don't farm with that old mule anymore," I said in an attempt to move right on through my father's whereabouts. "So why don't you let me buy Milton off you? After all, Chester needs a mount to help me win back Baltimore!"

"What do you mean; win back Baltimore, Robert Stewart? You are without a doubt the strangest grandchild I've ever known!" she said with a look of surprise. "How can a boy and his old colored friend take Baltimore back from a horde of Rebels? Don't be ridiculous!"

"That hurts, Grandma," I told her in my best salesman's pitch. "It won't be just Chester and me coming for those Secesh. They'll learn the hard way that there are plenty of loyal Union men and women in the Monumental City."[74]

"You are far too much like your Grandfather John Stewart," she cried, but I took it as a compliment. "The first time I ever saw that red-headed firebrand he was facing a Jeffersonian Democrat on the Dueling Grounds

167

right within earshot of this farm,[75] for those Federalists were not afraid of a fight!" She went on like she was looking through time and seeing my grandfather John instead of me standing there. "But you hot headed Highlanders have to learn how to control your tempers, and you Robert Stewart, have to learn how to choose your battles!"

"This is real personal to me, Grandma, so with or without that mule, I'll be going back to Baltimore. I don't rightly know how, or with whose help it will be, but I know we'll return and set my harbor home free! Now, how bouts I give you three hundred dollars in gold coins for Old Milton? The War is coming on fast and the price of everything will be rising sky high, so you can use the money to live off."

"Let's leave this foolish talk till tomorrow after church," Grandma said to me sternly. "No more talk of death and destruction, Robby. Do you want me burning your crab cakes? Now go and wash up. You talk way too much for a boy your age."

"Chester," she hollered out the kitchen window, "Supper's almost ready, wash up and come on in!"

We ate that second peaceful meal of the day under Grandma's new rules: No talk of War—no talk of Death—and no talk of retaking Baltimore!

Grandma ate but one little crab cake sandwich, while Chester had two, and I ate three—though in my defense, that rye toast was kind of small on the ends. After helping her clean up the mess, me and Chester went right back to bed.

In my Grandmother's house, everyone went to church on a Sunday morning and the Sabbath was always a full day of prayer. She wouldn't let us hoe the garden, or tie up the peas, or hill the rest of the potatoes— we just went to church, and read the Good Book, as the crickets and the tree frogs sang. Then Grandma lit the kerosene lamp, put it on the kitchen table and said, "Rob, let's talk."

Chester was out with the livestock gazing at the stars, so we could plan his special gift without him knowing it. He'd need a mount for our campaign, and that Fort McHenry money had no better purpose than to feed my Grandmother through a long cruel war.

"Rob," Grandma started her story as she sat down at the table and held my hand. "When Milton was a young jack and you were but a four year old freckle faced boy, Grandfather Bloise and I looked out in the garden one day and there the two of you were by where the pea patch now stands. You were holding Milton's tail in your hands and leaning way back trying to get him to go in reverse, while that stubborn young mule had his head turned sideways looking at you like you were crazy!"

I could almost see me out there the way she said it. Stubborn beyond belief—that mule had nothing on a little Stewart boy.

"Now, as you know a mule can kick harder than a horse can kick and a young jack can crack a skull wide open, so you were on Death's doorstep and didn't even know it, but Milton sure did! Your Granddad and I weren't sure how to save you, for if we panicked, the mule would kick you, and if you kept hauling away at his tail like that, he'd have kicked you too! Finally, your Granddaddy just walked up there real slow and laid his hand on Milton's neck and stroked him as he prayed.

"Good Lord," said your Granddaddy and he said a special little prayer, whilst I caught you up and whisked you away for a well-deserved spanking. And do you know what his prayer was, Rob?"

"No, Ma'am," I said not knowing where she was going with her story, though I could never remember her spanking me. "Your Granddaddy prayed in a sweet and gentle way, Dear Lord let this mule always stand over this boy and defend him through thick and through thin! So if you are planning to head back to Baltimore to set your harbor home free— which is crazy," my Grandmother said with tears in her eyes, "you can take Old Milton with you, but don't insult me or your Grandfather's memory with talk of any money!"

"Augustus, Mrs. Bloise, come quickly!" Chester hollered from outside.

There in the night sky was a great rising moon that had just busted through the trees and it was shining like a silvery platter. And the strangest thing of all on that mystical night was the moon was surrounded by a halo of three different colors. Great circles of red, white, and blue surrounded that rising moon,[76] and if that wasn't a sign from the Lord—nothing was!

169

"My God," said my sainted Grandmother. "It's true Rob, your mission is blessed!" And she hugged me.

Grandma made me take my Granddad's old English saddle and his saddlebags too. She said they would just sit back there in the barn and collect dust, and with a good cleaning I brought them back to life. I gave Chester that fully accoutered mule as a gift—telling him it was my way of saying thanks for all he'd done for me and the boys of the Fighting 6th. By midnight on that magical moon lit night, Chester and I went off to bed with plans to ride out for Washington the very next morning.

Monday, the 22nd of April was another fine spring day as we awoke from the peace of my Grandma's farm. It was a cool clear morning that promised to become a warm spring day as the sun started to cook things up. A red-winged black bird sang its shrill song down by the river while Grandma waved goodbye. Crickets cricked at a slow Southern pace, as we came upon a team of ten oxen dragging a cast iron arch for the new Capitol dome. Whips were cracking, slaves were singing, and the winds died down as Chester told me the bible tale of Balaam's ass one more time. "Why do you beat me, have I not been a good servant?" the little donkey had asked his master. And once we got past those oxen, we picked up steam for the last mile down Pennsylvania Avenue.

Willard's Hotel was a conglomeration of five or six buildings all no more than four stories tall parked just a few squares from the President's House. Baltimore's Barnum's Hotel would have made this hovel blush for there were no high-class ladies in their fine hooped skirts walking about their lobby, just frumpy couches full of frumpy old men sitting there smoking their cigars in a dark musty mist. Dark and dingy we'd have called that lobby in the Monumental City, and we waltzed right in and rang the front desk bell. We waited a long while till a surly little desk clerk in an itchy black wool suit showed up and looked at us like he smelled a skunk.

"We're here to see Colonel Cassius Clay," I announced proudly.

"Get that darky out of here right now!" he hollered by way of a reply and pointed to the F Street door.

Chester was already heading there before the moron finished his tirade. We'd been in the capital for less than an hour and already I hated the place, for if you weren't a Senator's son, or a wealthy planter, or the President Pro Temp of the Senate (or sitting in his chair), you might as well lay down in the gutter and let the whole world walk over you. And suddenly, out came my Bowie knife before I even had a chance to think, and I put it right between the clerk's palm down thumb and his right index finger with a loud twanging sound. Grandma was right, I needed to learn to control my temper, but it had been a very bad week!

The clerk went white as a ghost with his mouth wide open and seemed ready to play nicely when I said, "Now, if you would please apologize to my friend here and direct us to Colonel Clay, we'll leave you to your own devices."

"So..So..Sorry, sir," he said to Chester as the chatter broke out again in the smoke filled lobby. The clerk pointed to the dining room door and said, "Col..Col..Colonel Clay is in there, k...k...kind sirs."

Now it was my turn to be worried, for Colonel Clay was an emancipationist—no doubt about it, but he definitely had Southern sensibilities, and to march right in there with Chester in tow while the man was eating his breakfast might have got us both tossed out the F Street door. Luckily, Chester was worldlier than I was and he walked right up to my ear and whispered, "Just go in there and talk to the colonel." Then he said loudly so all could hear, "I's got to go and see a man about a horse, Massa Robert," and he swung around for the door.

Chester always said the best way to disarm a touchy situation was to, "get them laughing." But surveying the tables full of rich men, and hearing them jabbering, I was more afraid than when we faced that mob!

"Over here, Mr. Stewart," a voice rang out and there was Colonel Clay standing by his breakfast table waving a white handkerchief.

A strong tall man in a deep blue uniform—his two horse pistols sitting peacefully on the table, that big long Bowie knife at his side, he was the grandest man I'd ever seen! The colonel was surrounded by junior officers—junior to him anyway, a major, a captain, and a 1st lieutenant, all in the uniforms of the Washington Guard with the same big brass epaulettes that the colonel wore. By the way they all stood up when the colonel stood; they seemed to be blue-blooded Sons of the South. When President Lincoln had found himself all alone in Washington with the Virginians moving in for the kill, Cassius Marcellus Clay and his friends from Kentucky had formed their own private army to guard Old Abe 'til the volunteers arrived. Colonel Clay introduced each one of his brave officers and after the niceties were over, I sat down at the table all littered with the remnants of a wondrous breakfast. The half-eaten ham and a biscuit on the major's plate looked especially inviting! I can't remember their names anymore, but the major, who was very well fed, said he had a boy my age back in Frankfurt, and he begged me to finish his breakfast.

"How'd you get that big cut on your head, son, and that bloody eyeball?" went the 1ˢᵗ lieutenant—a fine looking blonde headed boy with a long Van-Dyke and a slow Kentucky drawl.

"Gentlemen," goes Colonel Clay as he wiped his mouth with his napkin, "This lad was with the 6ᵗʰ Massachusetts when they crossed Baltimore on the Nineteenth of April. I have it on good authority that he can handle both a Bowie knife and a Springfield rifled musket, so beware gentlemen, for his bite is worse than his bark! Now if you'll excuse us please, I need to talk with Mr. Stewart alone."

They all nodded at me like I was a little rattlesnake coiled up and hissing and since Colonel Clay seemed to like that image (though my Grandmother would have boxed my ears), I barked to the next waiter that came by to hurry up and bring me my Rio. And once I had sipped the finest coffee this side of Barnum's Hotel, Colonel Clay started right in— his piercing brown eyes gazing at my red one like he wondered if it still worked. My Fort McHenry spy training kicked in and I perused the room for anybody eavesdropping, which they weren't. Just a room full of rich men feeding their faces as the colonel's strange plan unfolded.

"My Radical Republican cohorts and I have come up with a plan to bring a very important person to Washington to meet with the President," he whispered as he leaned low and talked in my ear.

"She'll—I mean this very important person—will be traveling incognito and it will be your duty to rendezvous with them, and sneak them through Maryland. Am I clear so far?" he asked as he sipped at his brew.

The only thing that was clear was that the colonel had slipped up the first time he'd said "she" and he'd be damned if he was going to divulge her sex again. Which meant his fine plan was already starting to fray at the ends, but I smiled and hoped it got better.

"You'll meet this very important person on the Annapolis docks," Colonel Clay went on—smiling away like he loved spy work just as much as I did. "They will be looking for a little red-headed boy with the biggest revolver on the North American continent and his old gray haired slave. And when they walk up to you and ask what kind of pistol this is?" And he brought this huge revolver in a brown leather holster up onto the table with a bump and a thump as the other patrons stopped eating and stared. Not that they hadn't seen plenty of pistols in Washington before, but this thing was a monster with a .42 caliber nine shot barrel up top and a little added attraction by way of second barrel down below that held a .62 caliber buckshot round. It was called a LeMat revolving pistol, and it was without a doubt the biggest pistol I had ever seen! The dining room went silent as they watched and wondered what Cassius Marcellus Clay was up to, and I wouldn't have minded knowing that myself, for so far his plan had a whole lot of mystery and not much substance.

"Now once you rendezvous with this secret person who shall remain nameless, you'll bring them straight back to Washington to meet with President Lincoln!"

My new leader looked like he'd said all he had to say. So that's when I asked him about taking on a third partner.

"Who would that be, son?" he asked—like maybe a boy my age didn't realize the importance of secrecy.

"I believe you have a man named Mike Kelley working for you, sir. He's a tall eighteen year old Kentucky boy with a thick brown mustache and a dimple in his chin, and he rides one of the finest thoroughbred mares this side of the Mississippi." I said as he interrupted me.

173

"Is she a white faced bay mare by the name of Louisville? I tried to buy her off the lad just the other day. But no matter what I offered, he would not sell her!"

"Well, don't hold that against him, general," I told the big man with the Bowie knife—giving him a field promotion that made him smile. "That bay mare can jump like a jack rabbit and Mike Kelley can ride like the wind! You give him to me for this secret mission, sir, and we'll get that very important woman through to Washington!"

"How did you know it's a woman?" this Yale graduate asked, and I just shook my head and told him I read minds.

"Fine, I'll get you your Lawrenceburg boy," he said as he signed for his and his staff's breakfast and my three cups of coffee.

"We'll meet again tonight in Georgetown at 8:00 PM," and he handed me a calling card with his friend's name and address on the back.

When we arrived at the Senator's place some ten minutes early for our meeting, we were struck by the home's simple beauty. It was a long two story brick affair with two front doors facing east. There were little half windows from the basement below peeking up, and two little brick and white marble stair bridges that brought you up to the doors. At the southern edge of the mansion—butting directly up to another narrow little two story townhouse, were two tall brick archways with wide wooden gates that led back into a cobblestone courtyard. There was a stable back there that could hold six horses and a grand carriage, though Senator Wilson[77] only had one horse and a dusty old buggy. Right through that big arched gateway we rode like we owned the place, and there he was watching us come—a man who would change our lives, though he didn't look like much at the time. He was big alright—but soft like a businessman with long strawberry blond hair and wide shaggy sideburns, a huge forehead and a beardless face, a double chin, and the perfect smile of an a politician.

"Are you the boys Colonel Clay has sent me?" he hollered with his narrow blue eyes staring at us. He was in a dark vested suit with a black necktie and baggy black pants—his hair combed way back to show that hellacious forehead.

174

"Yes sir," I said having paused awhile hoping Chester would take over, but Chester didn't like talking to strange white people.

"Come in gentlemen," Senator Wilson bellowed. He was a cheery fellow, maybe fifty years old. "Colonel Clay tells me you're a survivor of the 6th Massachusetts's march across Baltimore. What was that like for a boy your age?"

"It was like being caught in a bear trap with the best men you could get caught in a bear trap with," I told him proudly. "The Fighting 6th fought their way out of a real tight place that day, Senator Wilson, sir!"

"Colonel Jones told me your Mayor Brown and Marshal Kane were both very helpful when the mobs went berserk," the big man said. "He told me that the Mayor even fired on the mob."

"As far as I'm concerned Senator Wilson, both Mayor Brown and Marshal Kane should be tried and hung for treason!" I barked, for how long could that lie go on? "And if your Colonel Jones had come out of his rail car long enough to see what was going on out there on the streets of Baltimore, he'd have known that himself!"[78]

"My, my," Senator Wilson sighed. "Colonel Clay was right, you are a little banti rooster! You could prove extremely helpful, Master Stewart!"

A horse galloped up at ten minutes after the hour. It was Mike Kelley up on Louisville all hot and lathered from their ride across Washington. Chester and I greeted him at the door with great big bear hugs.

"I'm Mike Kelley from the Clay Battalion." Mike said to the Senator, and then he shook the great man's hand and said, "Colonel Clay begs your forgiveness, Senator Wilson, sir, but he has been called away, and says to go on without him."

"Well, gentlemen," goes the new man in charge. "Let's get started. This plan is simplicity itself. You lads will be heading to the City Docks in Annapolis to rendezvous with a very important person who shall remain nameless."

The Senator took a long pull at his tea and I swore there was just a wisp of Maryland Rye Whiskey. "They will be looking for a small red-headed boy with the biggest pistol this side of Kansas City, and that's you," he said nodding at me and that cannon Cassius Clay had given me. "And his old slave friend with a rope around his neck," he added pointing to Chester.

I thought to myself, Colonel Clay had said nothing about Chester having to wear a rope. Why, every red-necked Secessionist in Annapolis would want to take a pull at him!

"Our very important person will come up to the small red-headed boy," and our leader dipped his head once more at me—going as slow as he could so as not to lose us. "And they'll ask what kind of pistol is that?" Then he took another pull of his tea and smiled like he'd come up with the plan himself. "And you'll say, this here is a Grapeshot pistol."

Mike had a big absent look on his face like oh shit, here comes the hangman, while Chester's eyes had gone to those wide white saucers of surprise! And I, well, I was wondering, when would I meet an adult in this world that wasn't trying to kill me?

Chapter Seven

Go Down Moses

If Robert Burns was right and the best laid plans of mice and men do often go astray, this plan the Senator was making was destined to fail. And if it failed out there on the Annapolis docks, we'd all go down with the ship! To make matters worse, according to the renowned senator from Massachusetts, there was no time for any questions.

"You lads can sleep over the stables tonight, so if you would be so kind as to harness my horse and carriage up, I'll be on my way to the Round Robin to meet some old friends for drinks."

As he disappeared down Beal Street, we figured we were just a little sideshow to him and his politico friends, so we had a moot court to practice the points we needed to discuss before we signed on. Like: How much were they paying us, and who would buy our supplies, and most importantly, who would notify our next of kin—in case things took a turn for the shitter? Then we filled the Senator's two kerosene lamps and waited in the darkness for his return. It wasn't till four in the morning that he finally came waltzing back in, and as he stumbled down off his carriage, we lit the lamps and court was in session.

"Oh, I forgot that I had house guests!" he said as we startled him out of a stupor.

"We'll unharness your horse and cool him down in a second, Senator Wilson, sir." Chester told him politely.

"But first we have some questions," Mike added, holding the lantern up to His Honor's face.

He must have been quite busy that evening for his coat was off and twisted up on the floor of the carriage with his bow tie hanging out of the pocket. His long white shirt tail was out, and his big baby face was smiling away like the Cheshire cat that ate the Cheshire canary. He stood there leaning first to the north, and then to the south, then way back to the northeast in a slow unsteady roll.

"Don't take this the wrong way, Senator Wilson, sir," I said, having forgotten my next line.

"What the boy is trying to say," Chester leapt in to my rescue, "is this is the most marvelous plan we've ever heard!"

"But, we never got told what we were to be paid, and we'll need money for supplies, now won't we?" Mike hit his line right on cue.

"I thought Colonel Clay was handling all that!" Senator Wilson said with the sweet smell of Maryland rye whiskey filling the barn.

"Colonel Clay is heading off to Russia[79] any day now," Mike told him with a worried look, for the Senator was now our only leader.

"We'd work for free if we could, Senator Wilson, sir," Chester added almost truthfully. "But peoples has got to eat!"

"Of course you do fellas," says our new commander. "Let's go into the kitchen and cook up a great big breakfast, and we'll settle this once and for all. I've got ham and eggs. Does anyone know how to make biscuits?"

"Oh, I make the best biscuits you ever ate," Chester answered, and we all marched into that big dark mansion like long lost friends.

By dawn all was settled and sealed with a toast. "If we are to win this war, gentlemen, we must emancipate the slaves as soon as possible, and that's exactly what our secret guest will address with President Lincoln!" Said the Senator, then he peacefully passed out.

We left for the Georgetown Market with nice full bellies, gold coins in our pockets, a warm burning sensation in our gullets and a sense of justice in our hearts! Some called Senator Wilson the worst kind of names for his Radical Republican ways, but he always dealt fairly and squarely with us, and we loved him like a wayward uncle.

Down High Street we went to the shops by the Potomac—stopping first at a livery stable where we asked if they had any old farm carts to sell. Right there in the corner was a pile of hay atop an ancient old gray two wheeled market cart like the Lord had left it there just for us.

"How much do you want for that two-wheeled wagon?" I asked.

"Fifty dollars," says the brown bearded blacksmith.

"Fifty dollars!" echoed Mike. "Do we look rich to you?"

178

"There's a war coming, boys, and everything will rise in price," he said by way of an economics lecture. "The Secesh are leaving Washington by the droves after Colonel Clay made them sign letters of loyalty and every conveyance is going at a high price."

"Fifty dollars is way too much for that old ancient market cart," Chester added and we were about to walk out.

"Look, I like you boys, and beings you're my early birds today, I'll knock the price down ten dollars! What do you say?"

"Make it fifteen and lend us a broom and some soap and water to get that pigeon crap off and you've got yourself a deal!" Mike bartered back.

So for thirty-five dollars we bought an old English farm cart with a walnut seat and a double shaft of what looked like mahogany to us. We lay my Granddad's old saddle and saddlebags down in the four by five foot bed, hitched Milton to our new acquisition, and commenced to shop. We bought four fine woolen blankets with nice colorful stripes from the state of Maine (the nights were still cold there on the Potomac), twenty pounds of coffee, twenty pounds of flour, ten pounds of sugar, four small smoked Virginia hams, beef jerky, beans, bacon, salt, pepper, a bushel of last year's Western Maryland apples, a hundred pound sack of horse feed, gunpowder, shot & ball, percussion caps, and the new rim fire rounds for Mike's Henry repeating rifle, then we returned to the Senator's house and slept over the stables.

That Wednesday we were invited to a farewell dinner with Colonel Clay back at Willards Hotel. He wanted to see us one last time before he set out for Russia, though Chester bowed out as he had a bad taste of the place. Mike and I met Colonel Clay in the lobby at six o'clock sharp. The Dining Room was like a ghost town after the Secesh had pulled out, and even that surly little desk clerk had gone south. We had a table for six—just the three of us, with fine linen tablecloths and matching napkins of light blue and real silverware sparkling in the lamplight. We ate Chincoteague oysters, followed by diamondback terrapin stew, then a nice roasted canvasback duck right off the Chesapeake, and all the butter and rolls a boy could eat! I put a few of the latter in my pocket for Chester as they were the nice riced potato kind he loved, and though three or four of the waiters saw me do it, they were so busy fussing over Colonel Clay, that I could have walked off with the table, the silverware, and that big tureen with the turtle soup in it. It was a glorious meal!

The colonel was looking marvelous as usual, his dark blue tunic was sparkling with two rows of American eagle buttons running down the front, his long dark hair combed free and easy, a clean shaven face, and brown piercing eyes that said, "Damn if I'm not having fun!" And everybody around him was having fun as well!

"My son, Green, is just a tad older than you are, Mr. Kelley," says the colonel as he sucked down an ice cold oyster.

We waited for him to swallow as I quaffed my milk. Then he went on with his story like we were nobility. "He's gone down into Kentucky with old Bull Nelson, which was why I wanted to buy your mare."

Mike was silent, thinking the man was making a second bid (just like Captain Ridgely did), but Cassius Marcellus Clay was not that kind of a rich man. He saw the first time out how much Mike loved Louisville and he was in no way trying to buy her.

"You know why I hired you, Mr. Kelley?" Colonel Clay asked as we cut into that tender young duckling.

"Cause I hail from the same state as you do, sir?" Mike told him like he knew all the answers.

"That and the fact that you're from Lawrenceburg, for you see, when once I was on a speaking tour there, the crowd turned ugly, and there I was face to face with death by a hundred blades. Of course, I had my horse pistols and my trusty Bowie knife with me, but there was a good hundred people ready to strike. Then this huge man stood up from the crowd and said he'd had the pleasure to serve with me in Mexico and anybody that wanted to harm Cassius Marcellus Clay, would have to walk over him and all his cousins too![80]

He paused for a second with a big old southern smile, and said, "And you know how many cousins a Kentucky boy has, don't you, Mr. Kelley?"

The two of them had a big belly laugh over that, so I reckoned cousins were thicker than fleas down there in the blue grass. Next the colonel gave us advice on how we should never come and go by the same path, never let a stranger ride up beside us and chat, never ever tell a stranger your business, and never camp out in the open where cavalry can ride you down—the latter having made him a prisoner in the Mexican War. We talked of horses, the beauty of Mexican ladies, how it was the colonel's great pleasure to meet a couple of fine fellas like us, and how he wished he wasn't going off to Russia, for he would have loved to be in on our great adventure! And when we finally finished our strawberry rhubarb pie, we all shook hands and went our separate ways without one word being spoken about that secret plan.

The next day we washed the Senator's carriage, mucked out his stalls, and cleaned up his stables. His former stable boy should have been shot for the way he'd left the place with the manure up to the horses' hocks. We worked the rest of the week washing and currying the horses and Milton, fixing the two squeaky wheels on the market cart, and generally making ourselves useful.

On that Friday, Mike and Senator Wilson set out for Annapolis to go over the rendezvous point with a fine toothed comb. The Senator always wanted to be a spy, so armed with a quick drawing well-armed body guard like Mike Kelley; he headed for Maryland's capital to make sure it was safe for his very important person.

We had the run of his mansion while they were away; and that Saturday we took fresh fruit down to the wounded lads of the Fighting 6th. They were staying at the Washington Infirmary on North East Street and 4th, a big white building with a portico sticking out of the front that held a huge American flag that was flying proudly as we rode up. There were maybe thirty boys in there—many with head injuries from bricks and cobblestones, but gunshots and pike stabs were common as well. The wounded were lined up in a ward of pure white—long lines of beds in a barracks like fashion with clean white sheets and white woolen blankets.

Why, it was so white and fresh in there that 1st Sergeant Lamson thought he was in Heaven! The poor man had been beaned in the head pretty good and things still weren't quite right with him. He'd lost a good ten pounds since we made the march down Pratt Street, and his pasty white legs stuck out of that hospital gown and I wanted to cry. His head was

181

shaved and he had a big caved in place near his temple where the paving stone had hit him. The 1st sergeant sat there in a big rattan wheelchair staring out the window. He shook from time to time, though he didn't seem cold, but what hurt the most was he didn't seem to know me!

"1st Sergeant Lamson," I said in a soft gentle voice, "I'm the Baltimore boy you taught to load a Springfield rifle. I've come to bring you some fruit," which was two oranges and a pint of fresh picked strawberries.

"Sorry you died and went to Heaven, son!" he said sadly. "But ain't it a beautiful place up here in the clouds? Who's your colored friend?"

"Oh, this here is Chester Harris," I said with a tear in my good eye. The hurt one still didn't blink and I'd taken to wearing a patch to keep the dust out. "He came in with us on the train. Don't you remember, sir?"

"Sir, did you just call me sir?" goes the 1st sergeant and I knew he was in there.

"Yes, sir," I said and he got the joke. "Can you walk, 1st sergeant?" I asked with my fingers crossed.

"Not much," he said, and the boys all around him shook their heads no. "We don't need to walk here in Heaven, son. We roll around in our fine golden chariots," and he patted the tall India rubber tires and smiled.

My talk was wearing the 1st sergeant out, but I swore to come back and see him soon. Seeing what havoc one hour of war had created made me realize what a serious thing it was.

Mike and Senator Wilson came back that Sunday from their scouting mission, and that following Tuesday our boss got a telegram from Governor Andrews up in Massachusetts. That Very Important Person was on her way, so we set out with strict orders to be at our rendezvous point in three days' time. Chester drove the market cart as Milton trotted along slowly behind us. We stopped by a field on the Bladensburg Turnpike just outside the District of Columbia to pick up all the first cut hay we could stuff over our treasures, figuring if we were stopped by Rebel patrols in Maryland, we'd say we were farm boys taking a load of hay to Annapolis. As far as how we'd get back across enemy territory, we all prayed that Very Important Person was wearing a good disguise!

All went well until we crossed the Anacostia River into Bladensburg and Old Milton decided to have a revolt of his own! His ears were way back, his teeth were showing, and he was bound and determined to take the River Road to Grandma's, instead of heading east as directed. Chester clicked and clucked—slapped the reins across his back, and even cussed him a little, but that old mule just wouldn't listen.

"Well, now I can see why Balaam beat his ass, you take this stubborn beast, Augustus!" yelled my old free African in total frustration.

My plan was to let the horses go ahead and when Milton saw they were leaving him he'd get going of his own accord, but that plan had one weak spot in it, for it assumed Milton was a stupid beast of burden—not the master tactician he really was. He kept nudging towards the River Road as Mike, Louisville, Chester, and Gunpowder got smaller and smaller on the horizon. So in a fit of not looking forward, I took out my LeMat, pointed him towards our destination, and let her rip.

Now Milton was raised on a peaceful farm and he'd never so much as gone on a midnight coon hunt, so that cannon blast from my Grape Shot Pistol startled him into a stampede straight for his home! We sailed down Grandma's dirt lane with Milton braying hello to Grandma, the cow, the garden, his stables, and the chickens. Behind us came my cohorts flying along in the dust—laughing like hyenas.

Grandma Bloise had a happy look on her face and hollered, "Rob, you're back so soon! Did you miss your dear old Grandmother?"

"Not as much as Milton did," I told her truthfully.

The next morning—the first day of May, before we set out for the second time, Grandma gave Milton a good talking to, telling him how he and me were hitched at the hip, and how that prayer my Granddaddy made when I should have been kicked in the head, was a firm deal with the Lord that even Milton couldn't break! "You do what little Rob tells you to do, Milton," she told him face to face, and I'll be damned if he wasn't the sweetest mule that ever there was the whole rest of the Civil War.

After that, my coconspirators voted me the official mule skinner, so Chester was up on Gunpowder, and I was bouncing around in that creaky old farm cart. The sad thing was my big chestnut gelding seemed as happy to give Chester a ride as he'd been to serve me.

Prince George's County was drying up fast that spring and we made twenty miles down dusty roads to the little town of Queen Anne on the western side of the Patuxent that second day out. We crossed the river on a narrow little trussed bridge in the dark and camped in the woods on the eastern side. That evening there was quite a lot of traffic coming west out of Anne Arundel County (which we were now in), and we doused the fire and moved deeper into the woods so as not to be seen. We rose the next morning before sunrise and pushed on for the Maryland capital. When we came to Taylorsville, we planned to take the noon ferry over the South River, but Milton wasn't having any of it. I think he figured if the Lord wanted a mule to ride in a boat, He'd picked the wrong mule! Luckily, there was a bridge to the north where we crossed at Milton's leisure and by eight o'clock that evening we were making camp on a grassy knoll just above Annapolis—within earshot of the St. Anne's church bells, the smell of the Bay washing up the hill.

The following morning we walked down Church Street leaving that stubborn mule and the horses hobbled in the woods. Annapolis was a hodge-podge of brick and timber buildings—its dirt lanes making it look like a lazy southern town in a little backwater, nothing like the grandeur of my harbor home. The Yankees had landed at the Naval Academy a few days before and everyone seemed certain they would come and punish them for their Secessionist ways, so they were all hiding.

We took up our position at the head of the docks—Chester with his rope around his neck as ordered, and me, the little red-headed banti rooster with the biggest pistol in North America sitting there in a cold wind waiting for our mystery guest. Mike took his place in the room he and the Senator had rented in a three story brick building not a hundred yards to our west. He and his rifle kept watch over us as we hunkered down on the docks whilst an oysterman came in with his single masted sailboat. About ten in the morning, two market carts pulled by swaybacked horses clopped up and two old farm ladies—both selling fresh strawberries that looked absolutely scrumptious, started to set up shop in the sun near

184

Chester and me. We were just about to sashay over to get us some berries when the old ladies began to argue.

"Move that wagon, Martha Gibbons!" goes the first little lady in a calico dress. "I seen this spot first."

"You push on now, Melba," said the short one in home spun brown. "Sell them bitter berries over at the City Market like the law says."

"And what makes you so wonderful you don't have to follow the rules?" goes the calico one with venom in her voice.

"My rheumatism is acting up today, and I need a place in the sun," goes the homespun one.

"My rheumatism is twice as bad as yours ever was, and this here is my place in the sun, so you get away, you old hag!"

On and on they went until they scared the oysterman off, while Chester and I were trapped trying to blend in with the docks. Finally, a policeman came up and told the two "ladies" to cast off, and neither one of them wanted to move the twenty yards to the City Market, so our fresh berries disappeared to the east towards the Naval Academy. Then up comes the officer of the peace. I saw Mike pop his head back in the window real fast, while Chester closed his eyes and played dead, leaving me to face the law man all alone.

He wore an old weathered black suit with a little blue ship's pilot hat, a whistle and a club, and he was staring at my huge revolver with his eyes wide open. "What are you boys doing out here lying on the docks on such a cold and blustery day?" he asked.

"I'm waiting for my uncle to come in from Savannah," I said looking up at him with my pirate's patch on and trying to look harmless.

"What happened to that eye, boy?" went the observant law man.

"Well, my Papa just up and died, sir, and we was taking him to the undertaker, when the mule that was hauling the cart hauled off and kicked me," was my lie du jour.

"And did you get your father buried alright?" he asked as he stared down at that rope around Chester's neck like he'd just seen a rattlesnake.

185

"Yes sir, and thanks for asking," I answered. "But my Momma sent me here to meet my Uncle Ted. We're going on to Baltimore to try and sell this here slave to help pay for my daddy's funeral."

"What's your name, son?"

"Stewart Roberts, sir." I lied like a rug.

"And where are you from Stewart Roberts?" He asked as he thought he saw a movement up in the third floor window to our west.

"I'm from the little town of Queen Anne down in Prince George's County, sir. We've got us a little tobacco farm down there."

"And when's your uncle coming in from Charleston?" He asked trying to catch me in a lie.

"He's coming in from Savannah, sir," I corrected him. "He should be here any day now, Your Honor."

"Well, I'll let you wait here as long as the town stays deserted like this, but once people start coming out and taking to the streets again," he laid the law down. "I want you and your slave off the City docks!"

"Yes sir," I told him and wondered whether he meant three or four fine citizens of Annapolis, or maybe a couple dozen, for who knew when that Very Important Person would arrive? He started to walk away—staring up at that opened window at Green and Market Streets, when he stopped and turned around real fast.

"You know, son," he said like he couldn't believe it, "maybe in Prince George's County you can treat your slaves that way," and he pointed at that hangmen's noose around Chester's neck (which wasn't my idea at all). "But here in Anne Arundel County we treat our slaves real good, so you slip that rope off the poor man's neck, right now!"

"This here rope keeps the snakes off, sir—it ain't the boy's idea, it's mine!" went Chester, who opened his eyes like Lazarus.

"I don't give a damn whose idea it is!" goes the law man—mad that Chester had spoken without being asked. "Take that damn rope off your neck right now, boy!"

186

So there we were with half our props missing, though I figured anybody that couldn't see we were their rendezvous people by the size of my pistol, and the fact that we were the only two souls out there on the docks, couldn't be too very important to anyone! The next fly in our ointment came when I had to take a bathroom break, for it turned out the public rest room was nearly a half mile away. Chester said he wasn't going to get himself hung trying to use a white man's bathroom and the argument was on.

"Well, where do you Negros go when you've got to relieve yourselves?" I asked with my bladder begging!

"Some back alley far away from a white man's stares," he said with a grin, and it was almost the same grin that Milton had on him when we arrived back at my Grandmother's place. Whether it was my size, my age, my happy go lucky attitude, I noticed that when I was supposed to be in charge, things quite often took a turn for the shitter! We argued some more and finally I signaled Mike that we were off to the bathroom. Down Green Street to Duke of Gloucester we went, then west on Market all the way to where the road dead ended at a little bay. There we came to a rickety old double outhouse setting out over the water.[81]

"I ain't going in there!" says Chester with a touch of fear.

"Well then, just stand here and wait," I said at the end of my rope!

"That ain't a good idea neither, Augustus. Some slaver might come along and steal me!"

Chester had a point; Annapolis was a very Southern town. In Baltimore our slaves could go this way and that without a soul watching them, but the further south you went the more nervous everybody got about a slave walking around free.

"Look Chester, I'll go in the Ladies' side, there ain't a lady in sight," I said in my best command voice. "And you hop in the Men's side and do your business toot sweet."

"And get a good beating for using the white man's bathroom? No way," Chester argued.

"Have you seen one single person trying to use this bathroom?" I asked.

187

"No, but they might!" my free African friend retorted.

"And I might wet my pants if we keep on arguing," I said in a hell of a plight! "Please Chester come on in—you get a stall, I get a stall, I'm begging you! Don't make me use this pistol on you."

Chester laughed and he went right in.

The wind was still blowing out of the North bringing cold air down from Canada as we walked back to our rendezvous. White caps danced across the harbor, but the afternoon sun was getting stronger so we slept in the lee of a life boat turned upside down on the dock, as Mike kept his over watch in silence. The only excitement we had all afternoon was when a one clawed crab came down unannounced with a seagull right behind him. The one armed blue claw put his back to the life boat and snapped at the bird as it tried to eat him. Who would live, and who would die? That was the question, but the bird finally flew off with his prize in his beak and things settled down. The smell of the sea, and the incessant cries of the seagulls, and the warmth of the sun finally lulled us to sleep.

Chester had nuzzled up against my shoulder to keep warm and he snored, as I heard the bump slide of an old crippled black woman coming our way slowly. Bump slide, bump slide she came on holding her left leg out stiffly. She was a short little lady with a red checked bandanna on her head—wild bug eyes, short cropped hair, and an angry stare—a little drool running down the side of her chin, and with that bump slide gait she came on at a snail's pace. The old black woman was in a brown homespun dress with a frail little shawl around her bent over shoulders, and hanging around her neck upside down, and still very much alive, were two hens tied by their scraggly legs. They were talking chicken talk as she bump slid along, all five foot of her coming straight for us. I was about to shoo her off, when she took a feather from out of one of her hens with her right hand, while she signaled me to stay silent with her left. Then she bent down and tickled Chester's nose.

Mike didn't know whether to raise his rifle in our defense, or just try not to laugh, but there he was half hanging out the window with that rifle in his hands, as that short little black lady played a trick on Chester. Several times he almost woke up as the old cripple tickled him. He'd scratch at his nose and move about a bit and almost sneeze, and she'd stop, and then off to tickling him some more she'd go. His eyes finally came open, and he let out a shriek.

"Sweet Moses," he hollered and the old woman shushed him.

"You have a nice nap there, Panther?" she said like she knew him well, and the two of them smiled like long lost friends.

Chester rose and towered over the old black woman as he asked, "Where's your ship, Miss Moses?" like not only did he know her, but— and this part made no sense at all, she was our Very Important Person!

"My ship came in at the Naval Academy this morning and it took me the better part of a day to figure out I was waiting at the wrong dock."

Who was this short little lady with the wild rolling eyes, and why would President Lincoln need to talk with her so urgently? And, why, oh why, did she call my old free African friend, Panther? These and many more questions spun in my head as we followed her (at a distance by her direction) up the hill past the St. Anne's Church, then on out to our hidden campground. She seemed harmless and docile on the stroll up the hill, but once we reached camp, she was a whole nother person.

"You two ride ahead with the horses, the boy and me will take the mule cart and follow behind." She said like she was use to giving the orders. "We see you circling your horses to the right and we'll come on, but if you circle to the left, we'll hide."

And then we moved out. Me busy trying to figure out who she was, and her busy trying to tie her chickens off in the hay.

"This here is Milton, my Grandmother's mule, and my name's Augustus Stewart," I said—hoping to draw her out.

"Where are we headed, boy?" she asked with a sideways list of her wooly head—a big dent in her skull just visible under that red bandana.[82]

"Wherever those two riders lead us, Ma'am," was my answer.

"You can call me Miss Harriet when we're alone," she said, "but don't call me nothing otherwise."

189

That's when it came to me, this little woman, who limped like an old lady one minute and stood straight and strong like a general the next, could be none other than Miss Harriet Tubman—the famous abolitionist from Dorchester County, Maryland! She was sitting right there next to me, gazing out at the sandy countryside as we headed for Washington. Miss Harriet had the second sight like my grandmother had and I swear she was reading my mind as we went. It was maybe three o'clock in the afternoon with a stiff breeze blowing in from the north; and I was sitting to the left of her on that old farm cart, when out of the blue she asked me, "Are you an abolitionist, boy?"

"Yes Ma'am, I am, though I've only helped one slave escape in my life, and I didn't guide him all the way to Canada like some people did." We smiled at each other like we were in on a secret.

Miss Harriet was the kindest, most thoughtful woman I'd ever met (save for Miss Yvette and her cocottes), and me and Milton became her trusty companions. I was star struck and babbling like a drunken barrister as we headed for Annapolis Junction twelve miles to the north. Up ahead, the two horses trotted along making circles to the right at the top of each rise and all was going just fine. The Elkton Railroad connected with the Washington Branch of the B&O at the Junction and ran into the District of Columbia, so just as Cassius Marcellus Clay had instructed us, we were heading back to Washington by a different route.

"Why did you call Chester, Panther, Miss Harriet?" I finally asked, for that question above all others puzzled me most.

"That's his story to tell, if and when he wants to, Augustus!" she said. "Just let that sleeping dog lie."

Miss Harriet didn't like to talk much, but she sure was a good listener! I went on and on about how I hurt my eye, and how the Secesh murdered the 6th Massachusetts Volunteers in cold blood, and how they slaughtered the B&O horses—who were only doing their job, and how Marshal Kane had locked my father away in the worst smelling jail in all of Baltimore. Then I told her how the Rebels had burned all the bridges and cut the telegraph wires, and any day now they planned to take Maryland head long into the Confederacy.

The hours ticked by as we followed the horses and I told her, "If I'm talking too much, just tell me," but the poor lady couldn't get a word in edgewise.

"What do you know about John Brown?" she asked out of the blue.

"I know he was a brave man who died a brave death," I told her with confidence, for I'd seen him go!

"You've met John Brown?" She asked with excitement in her voice, as Milton pricked up his ears to hear the story.

"Well, I ain't exactly been introduced to the man," I apologized. "But I gave him his last benediction and got a nod of his head in thanks."

"You saw John Brown hang?" she asked like she was calling me a liar.

"Oh, yes ma'am, I most certainly did! That Winter's day was as warm as the spring with bees buzzing and forsythia bushes in bloom when they brought John Brown down on a buckboard with his coffin beside him."

"Go on, child," she said, "but don't you lie to Miss Harriet."

"That gallows was surrounded by a thousand soldiers," I proceeded as the cold wind blew down and froze us to our seats. "Out ahead marched a column of soldiers. No civilians were allowed anywhere near him, but I was a small lad of thirteen, so I moved closer to the gibbet."

I was silent for a second thinking back to that warm December day. His hanging had stuck in my head undisturbed for two years!

"Go on now, child," says Miss Harriet and Milton picked up his pace, thinking Miss Harriet had been talking to him.

"He climbed down from the wagon and walked bravely up the gallows stairs without any fear. And the old gray bearded man looked out over the Blue Ridge Mountains like he was in Heaven," and I started to sob.

"Sweet Jesus," she said! "You're a good lad, go on!" I smiled up at her bravely and went on thinking of his hanging like it was yesterday.

"And just as he was about to have that canvas bag drawn over his head, I yelled God Bless you Mr. Brown! He smiled down and gave me a nod."

Miss Harriet patted my head and told me what a good boy I was. We were losing the light and almost to Annapolis Junction with Chester and Mike about a quarter mile ahead. "Go on, Augustus," she said softly. "Did he have a quick death?"

I fell silent trying to put it in words, for the poor woman seemed to know him well, but what I, and everyone else on the ground that day, had seen was a slow and painful strangulation. Oh, they dropped him from the scaffold alright, but the rope wasn't long enough to break his neck. The poor man hung there and choked to death, and even after he quit kicking, John Brown's heart refused to die.

"Go on boy, tell me more," she said with tears in her eyes. "Don't hold nothing back from Miss Harriet!"

"Well, they just hung him and that was that!" I told her and I threw off that pirate's patch and both my eyes were crying!

We rode on into a reddening sky in silence save for the clip clop of Milton's hooves. That night we made camp at a narrow branch of the Little Patuxent about a mile from Annapolis Junction. Chester and Mike both wondered why we of the mule cart clan were so quiet, but Miss Harriet and I were thinking of poor John Brown. We huddled together on that cold and windy night and awoke on the 4th of May to a big chill in the air.

Miss Harriet went off to pray while the sleet rattled down as we boys made a fire. Our firewood was wet and Miss Harriet hollered from the woods, "Make that fire bigger, boys, for I've just heard from the Lord!"

So we built a huge bonfire and Chester made his famous Tennessee corn bread in his black iron skillet and sliced up some Virginia ham, while Miss Harriet's chickens contributed a couple of eggs. The coffee pot boiled and hissed as the sleet came down covering everything in a thick sheet of ice as we gathered around the campfire to hear what Miss Moses had heard from the Lord. She still had that woolen trader's blanket wrapped around her tiny little shoulders—two wide stripes of green and red at the ends and a big smile on her face. First, we said grace—the most beautiful grace that I'd ever heard, for Miss Harriet and the Lord were on a first name basis. She thanked Him for our bounty like she was thanking an old friend, then we ate and warmed ourselves by the roaring fire. And when we were all done eating, she cast off the traders' blanket and stood there like a general making ready to address her troops.

"I had a dream last night that the Union Army took Baltimore back from the Rebels without one soul being hurt from either side!" She started in and we all wondered where this was going? "And our little band of four was leading the way to freedom for many a friend in the Monumental City—it was a happy day!" Miss Harriet stood there by the crackling fire with her hands held high and cried, "Can I get a witness?"

I pitched right in with an Amen, Sweet Jesus, as Mike looked at me like I'd been hit in the head, which of course, I had!

"What about your mission to see President Lincoln?" asked Chester with those wide white eyes of surprise? "Senator Wilson said we were to bring you right back to Washington."

"Oh, the President ain't ready to emancipate anybody yet," she said with total conviction. "And when the Lord changes your plans, you don't stop to ask him why! Come on now, Panther, it'll be fun raising a little Cain with Miss Moses, now won't it? Think of it, not one wounded soldier on either side to take this poor boy's city back, and maybe we can even get his father out of that jail and free Fort McHenry in the bargain!"

Not that I'm saying Miss Harriet didn't get her visions from the Lord, but our conversation the day before had sure lit a fire under her. "Let's break camp and head for Baltimore, we have a city to save!" she roared.

Chester knew better than to argue with her. Every time she got a message from the Lord, she was as lively as they come—almost like watching those Gravity Cell jars boiling blue from the Solar Storm.

"Come on now, saddle them horses, boys! Let's get this show on the road!" she hollered as the sleet turned into snow.

Miss Harriet was in a talkative mood that morning as Chester and Mike rode out. She started by telling me why Chester was called Panther. It seemed there was a place maybe twenty miles north of Baltimore on the road to York where the slave catchers kept a special eye out for runaway slaves. Nobody but nobody could sneak passed that slot that they called the Sign of the Panther.[83] "Nobody until Panther came along, that is!" Miss Harriet told me as she brushed the snow out of her eyes and reminded Milton he had a job to do besides listening. "A little less listening and a little more trotting, Mr. Milton," she told him gently.

"You see Panther was a conductor on the Underground Railroad down in Tennessee in his youth, and although he'd sworn off it when he came north, the challenge was way too much for him." She went on.

I stayed silent; for Miss Harriet was so charged up by then that no prompting was needed. "Panther found his self a perfect way to get by the slavers," she told me with a big smile, as she kept Milton moving with a slap of the reins. "He would have his slaves escape on a Saturday night and wait in a cave just south of a little island he'd found in a stream. Come Sunday morning he'd bring a band of orphaned boys up from Baltimore by train with a herd of old work horses to swim in the river and muddy the waters. They'd make a big bonfire and once he was sure the coast was clear, he'd move them runaways up the river to the steep hills near his private island. They'd hide by a little creek that came out of the hillside with waterfalls and pools of cool water, and there they'd wait for the boys to leave them a roaring fire and a sack of food."

Miss Harriet sat there on that ancient market cart with snow coming down and smiled like she wished she could have come up with such a plan. And as our little mule cart lumbered down the icy road to Relay, I realized I'd been an abolitionist for longer than I thought.

The snow began to swirl and Miss Harriet hauled back on the reins and said, "Is them boys up there riding circles to the left or circles to the right? I can't hardly see them!" She whispered as she set Milton to trotting back for an old tobacco barn maybe a hundred yards off.

Barn gray with wide wooden slats, the drying shed was empty at that time of year. I dismounted and quickly slid the long board out of its slot on the door and raised the little wooden latch to swing her open, but there at eye level was a barn beam running cross ways at the door that looked like it was a tad too low for the high wooden wheels of the market cart to clear. Miss Harriet jumped down and brought Milton in real fast and there wasn't a sixteenth of an inch between those metal rims and that beam, as if the Lord had found us that exact market cart just for its height. We ran the wagon all the way in and there we sat in silence.

Through the wooden slats you could see the storm raging outside and there sat our wagon wheel tracks leading straight to the drying shed like a big arrow, as I started praying like a priest on Sunday! Miss Harriet came out of a trance just then and said, "You don't have to worry about dying today, Augustus. You're gonna live to be a very old man. I saw you lying in the snow beside a big carriage with your face half blown off and that didn't even kill you. There were two women there who loved you, son, and one will set you free, while the other will drive you off to freedom," she whispered, as she pulled out her Navy Colt and cocked it.

The mounted Militia came on at a canter. There was maybe five or six of them and I was sure our tracks would give us away! But in the time it took them to ride to that barn; the Lord had dumped enough snow on the ground to cover our tracks.[84] Snow so deep and white that none of the Rebels even suspected we were in there!

"Randall, get off that mare and go in there and see what's in that drying shed," said the one Secesh we could just barely make out in the blowing snow. He was up on a skittish roan.

"I can see the whole damn place just fine from here," goes Randall, "and there's not a damned thing in there save for a tobacco rat or two."

My LeMat was out and I planned to put that single shotgun blast right through poor Randall's skull should he get more industrious. That would leave nine shots to take the other four or five riders out, while Miss Harriet and Old Milton made a run for it. Miss Harriet had a forty thousand dollar reward on her head—dead or alive,[85] and I swore they wouldn't get paid on my watch!

"Boyd, how bouts you dismount and open that drying barn door real slow so we can tell the commander we done checked every nook and cranny," went the one that wanted to be boss the most.

"Who done died and made you the boss?" goes Boyd, and it was then that I learned one of the true weaknesses of the Rebel Army.

195

You see when a man decides he wants to be a Rebel; he tends to throw authority right out the window with the bath water and the baby. And when you throw authority out the window and everyman thinks for himself, and thinks as slowly as these boys thought, why, you're bound to get a few flies in your ointment!

"Let's just burn the son of a bitch down," goes the next man with a fine idea, and Miss Harriet and I started to worry!

"You want to tell Mr. Gibbons we done burned down his drying shed?" goes the brains of the outfit. "Let's go find us a warm fire and forget about the whole damn thing." And off they rode—finally in agreement.

Mike and Chester met back up with us a little later and said they told the Secesh they were scouts for Captain Ridgely's Horse Guard Cavalry coming back from Washington with plans to ride down and steal Abe Lincoln real soon. We rode on through the blizzard and reached Relay at nightfall with the storm still howling. Nine miles out of Baltimore and closing fast, Miss Harriet said we should keep on pushing for the Monumental City, but the horses were tired and we all needed a rest, so we pulled into a little stable and borrowed a stall. Two big thoroughbred race horses, a mule, a market cart, and four frozen people, all huddled together—true friends in a storm!

The next morning we crossed the Patapsco River at Smith's Bridge and came into town by way of the Washington Road right next to our old steeplechase course. The storm was still blowing and you could barely make out the old Carroll mansion up on the hill, while the B&O horse farm looked lonely and deserted. We hid in the woods near the mansion and watched for any movement.

Across the tracks to the north, the Mount Clare Machine Shop was going great guns—you could hear the big steam engines growling, and the steel saws grinding, and the welding torches burning off, so we came on down and took possession of our old stomping grounds. There were railroad sidings between us and the Machine Shop—filled to the hilt with freight waiting to head south, but there in our private stables, we were tucked away peacefully. We dried Louisville, Gunpowder, and Milton—helped ourselves to the B&O horse feed, and picked our own private stalls to sleep in. When I awoke on the morning of the 6th of May, it had stopped storming and the sun was out. The birds were singing, and the sky was blue, for spring had returned to my harbor home. Miss Harriet and Chester had gone off on foot and Mike was keeping watch by the door.

"Where do you think all the B&O horses went to?" I asked Mike.

"The Secesh cut the rail lines out of the city, so there's no need for horses anymore," he told me.

"Still, I doubt they'd take all their stock down to Bullock's Glue Factory," I said to him nervously. "Hell, those horses are worth something—even if they're not hauling freight."

"Them they didn't killed in the riots," Mike reminded me sadly. But there must have been fifty head down at The Farms, while up at Mount Clare Stables, there was another couple hundred, and they were all gone.

When Chester and Miss Harriet returned from their scouting mission, they looked very worried. Miss Harriet was back in her crippled old lady costume with those two live chickens round her neck, and Chester wore a big floppy hat and a pair of scraggily wool pants with about half of an old white shirt, and his big splayed feet padding along in the mud.

"Dem Secesh is riding rough shod over Baltimore, boys!" goes Chester with a sad look on his face. "They're riding around in the tens and twenties at the gallop, trying to keep the natives down. One minute they're in Black Town claiming there's a slave uprising, and the next minute it's the Germans on the West End that need to be taught a good lesson. And every horse I saw belonged to the B&O Railroad!"

"You think Mr. John Works Garrett is a Rebel?" I asked.

"I doubt that Mr. Garrett is a Secesh, but somebody sure is being free with his horses."[86] Chester answered with the shake of his head.

"Miss Lew said the slavers are passing out whippings at the drop of a hat, and tossing many a free African into the slave pens for God only knows what!" Miss Harriet added with a look of disgust.

"And that's not all," Chester went on, "there must be ten or twelve ships in from South Carolina, Georgia, and New Orleans."

197

"I got to go see this for myself," I said, knowing there was no way we'd let the Rebels take Baltimore without a good hard fight!

"Not with that black eye and them stitches hanging over your eye," goes Chester. "You're a famous man now, Augustus!"

Luckily, we had a bottle of medicinal Maryland Rye whiskey on hand to get me ready for the stitches being struck. Chester snipped a knot at the end of a long row at my eye brow and pulled real slowly. Out came a little drop of blood and he was done.

Miss Harriet took a sniff and said, "Good work there, Panther, it's as clean as a whistle," as she poured a little whiskey on the scar.

Then Mike held me and Chester cut off my fiery red locks and shaved me right down to my pale freckled skin. Next they carried me out to a huge tin watering trough—full to the hilt with melt water from yesterday's snow. Out of the mule cart came my last change of clothes and a Fort McHenry gold piece—it was time to go see what was left of my city.

"You ain't taking that pistol along with you!" Chester told me like he was in charge. "The Secesh see that big old revolver on a boy your size and they'll sweep you away to the Middle District Jailhouse with your daddy."

"How about my Arkansas toothpick strapped to my leg under these ugly plaid pants, can I at least take my knife?"

"Let him take that Bowie knife, Panther!" Miss Harriet barked, and we all knew who the big dog was.

"What about Mike, don't he have to wear a disguise?" I asked.

"Mike's disguise is that fine Southern drawl and his Army Colt revolver setting right there on his left hip pointing backwards!" says Chester with a grin. "Besides he didn't get described in the Baltimore newspapers as having saved the colors by shooting a well-known lawyer!"

"Remember boys, the Rebels control Baltimore," lectured Miss Harriet. "Stay low, go slow, and keep your eyes open!"

I could see why John Brown called Miss Harriet the General, she wasn't about to strike 'til she made a plan, and sending out spies in advance was part of every good plan. We were off for the first place a good scout needed to go, which was Miss Yvette's House of Love!

When we turned the corner off Charles Street and saw what was left of our once happy home we almost cried. Every window in the place had been busted out—the front door was ripped off its hinges, and as we got closer we saw thousands and thousands of baseball size stones lying all about. We crunched in over busted up glass, the furniture all broken to bits, the curtains torn to shreds, the good china shattered, and even the fine Persian rugs were destroyed. Upstairs the windows on the second floor were busted out too, the feather beds torn apart—duck feathers flying everywhere. But on that third floor landing it was as if the Secesh hadn't the energy to go any higher, even the Tiffany skylight was intact. And as the morning sunlight came streaming down, I thought of Private Taylor up there painting away. I was glad that the haters had torn the House on East Madison Street down—for it was now a place where the spirits could play! We left with sad smiles on our faces thinking of all the joy that place had brought.

A neighbor told us Miss Yvette and her cocottes had survived and gone off to Paris. Mike—in a somewhat melancholy mood, said he'd go down to the bars along Baltimore Street and see if any of the ladies had stayed, while my plan was to go and see my old friend Mr. Salomon. But first, I had to go home and see my Momma.

The old homestead looked lonely—the barn deserted, what with Old Lucky's death. "Momma," I hollered from the front porch, "I'm home— it's Rob, your prodigal son."

The little woman with her graying hair (most of which I'd given her) came running out. I picked her up and swung her round trying to keep that mangled side of my face to myself.

"You need to sit down, son; I've got some bad news! Your father and Lucky never made it home after the riots and I fear they may be dead!"

"You can put those thoughts behind you, Momma," I told her softly. "I saw Doc handcuffed and taken to the Middle Station Jailhouse before the riots even began. He ain't dead, Mama, he's just incarcerated!"

She was so happy she cried and clutched at me with her chunky fingers. "Should I get him a lawyer and post his bail?" were her words.

"No Ma'am, you can't go near him or that stinking jail!" I scolded. "We need Marshal Kane to forget all about Doc while I come up with a plan to set him free!" Then to change the subject and try and get the old girl to smile, I said, "And by the way, here's a kiss from your Mother," and I kissed her on the forehead.

"You saw Grandma Bloise?" she asked with a thin smile.

"Yes ma'am," I told her. "Got to eat her strawberry rhubarb pie and hoe a few rows of her peas. And she gave me her mule, Momma!"

"You mean that big jack of your Grandfather's that almost killed you?"

"Yes Ma'am, that's the one—only now he's older and wiser, just as I am, momma. Now give me a kiss and a hug, I've got to run."

It was on to Mr. Salomon's jewelry store. I'd have brought along some sugar cookies from our favorite bakery, but the Rebels had trashed the place. Their windows were busted out and a handmade sign was posted on their door that read, "Go back to Germany you slave stealing bastards!" Apparently there was nothing worse than a slave stealer, for they yelled it at us as we marched across Pratt Street, and they wrote it all over Miss Yvette's walls, and now they were writing it on the busted up door of a little German bakery that made the best sugar cookies in the whole damn town!

When I came to Mr. Salomon's jewelry shop, I was shocked by all the ships tied up across the street from him, and even more shocked for where they came from. There were ships in from South Carolina, Louisiana, Georgia, and Virginia.[87] All busy stealing what they could before the war started in earnest. Inside his store was the biggest change of all, for the neat little wood and glass counters had given way to a hock shop affair of all things silver and gold. There were two guards at the door, both armed with double-barreled shotguns, and a third man inside with an Army colt. Mr. Salomon came out of his back room to greet me, and he didn't even look up. There was no time left to sit and drink tea with a friend, just a, "I can't talk today, Augustus," was all he said.

Baltimore had changed for the worse since the riots. The people all moped around with big blank stares on their faces. Yet standing out there by the docks in front of Mr. Salomon's shop, I could see Old Glory flying high down at Fort McHenry. I knew someday the Stars and Stripes would return to set us all free!

When I got back to our hiding place down at the B&O Horse Farms, I heard either Milton or Miss Harriet (or maybe the two of them) snoring. General Tubman liked to do her scouting at night and being a general she slept during the day, while Milton didn't much care when he slept. My old friend Chester was sitting on a five gallon pail by the barn door looking out at Mount Clair Shops as he whittled away on a small piece of beech. He watched the smoke stack over at the Machine Shop belching out a thick black smoke like we horse handlers use to watch our cook blow smoke rings from her old clay pipe. She'd sit up there on the porch peeling potatoes for thirty or forty men and light up—give it two or three good puffs and try to blow a smoke ring through another one. We'd all clap and cheer when she did, but now Chester and I were all that was left of the horse crew—hiding in the stables like a couple of criminals.

"Remember how Inez blew them smoke rings, Chester?"

"I do and I was thinking the same thing," he said with a faraway look, for we both longed for the simpler days before the war came and changed us. "So how is home today, Augustus?" Chester asked with a sad look.

"Busy," I said. "Busy, doing nothing! Why, I saw not one face with a smile. They all walked around with their heads hanging down—afraid that they'd say the wrong thing and get a good beating. Why, even Mr. Salomon didn't have any life left in him, Chester. I tell you the place is a ghost town, full of hollow twisted up souls just waiting to be set free!"

"And what would you do to help them out, Augustus?" he asked, putting down his whittling and putting his arm around me.

"I'd give those Secessionists what they fear the most," I swore!

201

"Which is what?" Chester asked with a look like I'd finally gone mad.

"Well, if slave stealing bothers them so damn much, we need to give them a slave stealing extravaganza!"

"You is crazy!" Chester cried, but his eyes lit up like the Fourth of July!

"Crazy as a fox, Chester, what we need to do is steal so many slaves—so quickly and so completely, that the slavers can't hold their heads up!"

"Amen to that, brother!" goes a woman's scratchy voice from behind us. It was Miss Harriet who had awakened and was smiling away with her bandanna off showing that hole in her head where the iron had hit her. She was to say many times, that we were kindred spirits on account of us both having been hit in the head by a chunk of pig iron, and I was on fire that day! We'd steal a slave ship right out of the harbor—head north for the head of the Bay, and bring her in where we could make a run for Delaware and all points north.

"And with the War on," went General Tubman with a big wide grin, we just might not have to go all the way to Canada!"

"So where do we get a crew and a ship to sail these runaways off to freedom?" Chester asked like he enjoyed the story, but it would never work.

"Miss Harriet always says the Lord provides," I told him, "and docked at Fells Point this very moment is a ship fitting out for the Deep South. She will be full of slaves by the end of the week. We'll just borrow her and her crew and sail off for Freedom and Kingdom Come, as Little Henry describes it."

There was total silence save for the incessant sea gulls crying outside as Miss Moses and Panther looked at each other and weighed the odds. True, we'd all be hung if the plan failed. Well, actually the Rebels had sworn to burn Miss Moses at the stake, but wasn't it all worth it?

"You want us to commit piracy on the high seas?" came Mike Kelley's voice from back behind Miss Harriet, "and kidnapping to boot! Are you crazy, Augustus?"

Miss Harriet wasn't the type to get snuck up on, but she was so engrossed in my plans that she'd let Mike come right up to her. She leapt in the air with her Navy Colt drawn and almost shot him. The General simmered down when she saw it was one of her bodyguards, but according to Mike this whole thing was insane.

"Thank you for drawing me on to the best part of my plan," I told him. "We won't be committing piracy, nor kidnapping if my plan goes right, for we'll return the ship and the crew when we're finished with them!"

I was so proud of that part—even if it had just come to me, but Mike—being the ex-Horse Guard officer went right on picking holes in my plan. "What if we kill a sailor or the Federal Blockaders attack us out on the Bay for the slave ship we'll be?"

A retort boiled up in my brain where the pig iron had touched me, and I said, "You tell me, Mike Kelley, who are those Rebels gonna bitch to anyway? It ain't like their part of the Union anymore!"[88]

Even Mike had to shake his head and grin. The seagulls continued to sing outside, but there was silence in the horse barns, for save for Old Milton's continued snores, the plan was accepted unanimously.

We proceeded to hone the operation. Chester and Mike started gathering supplies. Miss Harriet went around town seeking out them that would join us on our ship to freedom. She sent word to her friends up in Delaware via coded telegraph messages to prepare a place for our coming. Mike would take her cyphered messages out to Germantown on the deserted Philadelphia–Wilmington line and wait up to a half a day for a message to come back. Miss Harriet would send: Church picnic planned for one hundred souls. Has you got enough chickens to feed us? Which meant we planned to bring one hundred runaways, could they take care of that many peoples?

They'd telegraph back: We can provide all the chicken you need, you just provide the congregants. And that meant, bring them on—as many as we could steal!

My job was to keep track of the ship we would be borrowing—possibly by getting aboard. The Chesapeake was her name—a 4th Rate three-masted, schooner-rigged, screw-propelled steamship out of Savannah,

Georgia. She weighed slightly less than six hundred tons and was tied to the dock right across from Mr. Salomon's jewelry store. None of the slaves were aboard her yet, but the slave hotel was nearby to keep the stock fresh for the long voyage south. The ship's crew worked on her rigging and patched her sails, and I saw her take on fresh water in huge kegs, and sacks of corn meal, which would probably be made into a kind of a mush once they went to sea, for you had to keep the stock well fed if you wanted a good price in Savannah.

"Excuse me, sir!" I said to her captain as he limped off the ship the next morning. "Got any need for a cabin boy who is good with numbers?"

"Where you from, son?" he asked me suspiciously. He was a squat little white bearded gentleman that reminded me of Ross Winans, only with better kempt hair and a bit more manners.

"Right here in Baltimore, sir. But my Daddy done died and I want to go south where his kin live, for my heart is set on joining a Georgia Regiment."

"What outfit, son?" he asked with the start of a smile.

"Why, the 1st Georgia Infantry, of course! I promised my daddy I'd serve her well!" I lied.

"A dollar a week would be the best I could offer," he said looking me over like I was a slave on the block.

"God Bless you sir, a dollar a week is just fine by me!" I told him.

"Then get up there and put that corn meal away!" He yelled like I was already late for work. Shorty will you show you where to stow them."

The only man I saw as that first hundred pound sack sailed down the ladder and crashed to the deck below was a big brooding giant in a pair of bell bottomed pants—barefoot and bare-chested to boot. He gazed up through the hatch as the first sack came down and sprayed dust all over his freshly swabbed deck. "Who the hell are you? And what the hell are you doing on my boat?" He roared.

Not the best of introductions, I'll admit, but Shorty was a man of few words, most of which weren't repeatable! He must have stood six foot six—though below decks he was stooped a bit. The big man had himself a bucket of water and a swab in his hands, which I was shortly to learn how to use.

"I'm the new cabin boy," I told him. "And you must be Shorty?"

"Get down here, boy!" he hollered and I shimmied down the ladder to below decks where he towered over me like David's Goliath.

Shorty took that swab and gave it a great wide sweep across the back of my knees and put me down to the deck. I was thinking maybe his nickname was reserved for those with a higher rank than me, but then he started laughing and yelled, "Bet I made you piss your pants, you little shit?" And I realized Shorty was what you call a bonafide bully!

I could have gone along with him and said yes I've wet my pants, but the truth was that pig iron that hit me upside the head hurt way worse than that slam to the deck ever did. So being the fool that I was, I called his bluff and said, "I'll bet you a week's pay, that my pants are as dry as the Gobi Desert."

He looked at me with an evil glare and said in a strong southern drawl, "My name is Bosun's Mate Third Class Nelsen Pettigrew, and don't you never ever call me Shorty! Now get them sacks below deck."

The first and second mates were both on shore leave, but the third mate—who was really just the bosun's mate I wasn't to call Shorty, took a real disliking to me. He had me move the corn meal down to a little room on the third deck with a padlocked door, then set me to swabbing like a lowly galley slave.

"Shorty (as everyone else was allowed to call him)!" hollered the Skipper. "Where the hell is that new cabin boy at?"

"Below decks, probably sleeping," Shorty hollered back.

"Get him topside to the forecastle right away!" I could hear the Skipper bellow, but what in the hell was a forecastle?

I put down the swab and started climbing the ladder, for any fool could figure out what topside meant, and doesn't Bosun's Mate Pettigrew grab me up like a one clawed crab and hold me dangling right there over the hatchway. "Did I tell you to stop swabbing?" he growled.

"No sir, Bosun's Mate Pettigrew!" squeaked me as I hung there praying. I heard the captain call again and I tried to break free.

"You ever heard of the chain of command?" Shorty started to lecture—dropping me to the deck with a painful thump.

Apparently, the Skipper would tell my bosun's mate what to do with me, then he would get word to me when he saw fit. Once the first and second mates returned from their shore leave, it seemed like it would be a pretty tedious way to communicate, but then Shorty was the one with my fate in his hands, so I nodded and headed back to my swab.

"Where the hell are you going?" bellowed the big burly bully. "Get your scrawny little ass topside and see the Skipper where he stands!"

I wasn't sure if Shorty forgot where the captain stood, didn't want to tell me how to get to the forecastle, or just wasn't quite sure what a forecastle was (like me), but when I hit the light of day there was the captain frowning away up on a little rise in the main deck. He wore an old sea cap and had wrinkles on his face like the roll of the sea.

"You said you can figure, right, lad?" the Skipper asked.

"Yes sir, I have an eighth grade education," I exaggerated a little having flunked math twice.

"Go to my cabin aft and fetch me a paper and pencil, and make sure it's sharpened. You do have a knife, don't you?" Well, General Tubman had sent me out sans arms that day. So once more I had to catch hell with a lecture that went, "You damn Yankees don't know shit about the sea!"

I went back and retrieved the paper and pencil—sharpening the latter with my teeth, and then we were off for a place I would have liked to have skipped. There was an old three storied brick warehouse a few squares down and when we opened the door it smelled like an outhouse. Chained up on all sides were various and sundry slaves—their one ankle cuffed and hooked to long iron rods in the floor. There were baby slaves, and big slaves, girl and boy slaves, and old aunties with bandanas like the one Miss Harriet wore—all sobbing away, for they knew they would never see home again! As I coughed and hacked at those terrible smells, my captain just stood there with a handkerchief over his nose.

"Ah, Captain Crowell," goes the skinny little slaver. "We've got a nice crop for your next run down to Savannah."

"I hope you hose them down real good, Mr. Shepard! Those darkies smell mighty foul. Boy..." and he slapped me across the head just to break the spell. "Make me three columns marked small, medium, and large, and as we go down the line you mark a slash in the one that I say they are—understand me?"

My math skills weren't the greatest, but my spy skills were tops, and I figured since we were probably gonna be using his calculations to come up with the ship's weight, I best exaggerate to cover the extra customers we were planning on bringing aboard. So when he said medium, I put down a large. A small was a medium, unless he looked at me sideways. A large was any buck you didn't want to be discussing slavery with in the dark, or anybody he spoke of while his head was turned. We were going down the line with me watching the Skipper's eyes before I placed the slash in the inappropriate space, when there before me and causing me great concern, were the sweet green eyes of Miss Lew!

Now maybe I failed to say Miss Lew was a green-eyed Negress, but she sure as hell was, and when our eyes first met, my mind just froze—even though I knew she should be marked down as an extra-large. Captain Crowell would have a head count from the slaver, and if I was off by even so much as one slave, he'd have fed me to the sharks!

"Wait a minute, sir." I pleaded, hoping he'd take pity on me. "I think I've got something in my eye, could we start over?"

It must have sounded true, for when he looked at that swollen red eye of mine he halted and said, "Well, just wipe the damned thing out and let's get back to work! Where did we leave off?"

"Right here at this old green-eyed lady, I think you said she was a large?" I gave Miss Lew a little wink when we passed just to let her know something was brewing.

When we returned to our ship, the Skipper made me come and compute out the weight of his "cargo" as he called them. It was thirty pounds for a small, a hundred for a medium, and a hundred and sixty per large, and praise Jesus my math skills were up to snuff, as I added ten pounds to everyone. With ten small ones, ninety-six mediums, and twenty-one large, we had a total of eleven thousand one hundred and thirty pounds—minus what I exaggerated, of course.

"Plus ten pounds of irons each," added the Skipper real pleased with my math, and I tagged that on too.

That brought us to a grand total of twelve thousand four hundred pounds, and with those ten bags of corn meal (at 1000 lbs.), and the kegs of water—what with a pint a pound the world around, the ship would be heavy in the water when she cast off. Out past the Baltimore Basin, when we hit the Chesapeake Bay, there were Federal Blockaders waiting to take up the chase, and although the Chesapeake was a sleek steam propelled ship, the captain kept his eye on her weight.

The first and second Mates returned to the ship—none too happy with the Skipper for taking on crew without their approval. The next morning they'd bring the slaves aboard—all hobbled in irons, but on what was left of this last day in port, I was turned back over to the loving care of my favorite bosun's mate.

"You know when I called you a bilge rat," Shorty cried with an evil glare, "I didn't know how true that was, but you are about to go down in the bilge and find out!" The big giant pointed to a little hole in the lower deck. "Climb in there and start bringing the stones out."

It was dark in there and smelled just slightly better than the slave hotel with a great mound of old slimy rocks weighing twenty to thirty pounds each—all bathed in a broth of rotten sea water and rat shit. And the rats down there in the bilge were the size of Doberman pinchers! I wrestled one of those great gooey stones between my legs and tried to hold it there as I climbed the ship's ladder with only my arms like Shorty had told me.

"Jesus Christ, Shorty, what are you making that boy do? Rig that damned sling right now!" went the second mate in my defense.

My favorite bosun's mate just stood there with his head hanging down and took the criticism without breaking a sweat. Apparently, they had a canvas sling and a long rope to raise the stones from the bowels of the ship and it was a two man job. No one climbed the ladders with those rocks between their legs—no one except me!

Shorty was up on the main deck hoisting my rocks the last leg of their trip back into the Basin, and I told him I needed a break as I heard a stranger come aboard. I scooched back to the stern just under the captain's cabin and listened in to the Skipper's conversation with a man whose voice sounded very familiar.

"Maybe you know Jerome Patterson Bonaparte, Captain Crowell, or Mr. Thomas Winans?" he went throwing out names like you throw out rotten tomatoes, and sure enough that was the voice of my Barnum's barber. "These great men—on behalf of the Knights of the Golden Circle have sent me here to arrange for a shipment to the eastern shore."

Captain Ferrandini had somehow risen to the top of an All American outfit, and his henchmen, the Kane brothers were probably somewhere nearby. "We have a fifty mile sojourn to the Eastern Shore that will pay you handsomely, Captain Crowell. Just drop our cargo at Port Herman and we'll pay you a thousand dollars," said the darkest hued member of the Knights of the Golden Circle I ever saw. "But you must leave tonight if you want the job!"

"And what will we be carrying for such a hefty price, Captain Ferrandini?" my Skipper asked like the horse trader he was.

"You'll be carrying cases of Harpers Ferry Rifles right off the rack[89] and all their ammunition, plus two thousand pounds of gold and silver. You need only sail fifty nautical miles to collect a thousand dollars in gold, Captain Crowell! How can you lose with a plan like that?"

"Well, first off, I'll lose my passengers if I sail ahead of schedule," the Skipper told him.

"The Knights of the Golden Circle will take all your first class cabins, and to sweeten the pot, we'll take all the berths in steerage too."

"That won't be possible, sir," the Skipper said like he was almost sorry. "We have a consignment of slaves filling the hold this cruise and they won't load till tomorrow morning."

"Why not make our little run north to Cecil County tonight, then return to Baltimore for your slaves in the morning?" Ferrandini begged.

"Would if I could, sir, would if I could," the Skipper exclaimed. "But once we reach the Craighill Channel the Federals will be all over us. Lincoln may have silenced the guns of Fort McHenry, but it's a whole different story out there on the Bay. And once General Butler attacks Baltimore from the west, we may not be back for a very long time!"

"Fine," said the captain as he twisted at his mustache, "We'll take all the first class cabins, and pay you an additional one thousand dollars in gold, but we need to have you load our cargo and be off at first light!"

That was another one of those flies in my ointment, for what with the extra guards and treasure aboard the Chesapeake it might be hard to take over the ship. Still, if we could steal the KGC's gold and the slaves as well, wouldn't that be a wonderful thing to tell your grandchildren about!

"The Chesapeake is a screw driven steamship, not a hauling service, sir." goes the Skipper all huffy and out of sorts. "You need to bring me the goods, if you want them shipped, Captain Ferrandini."

"All I have with me are four well-armed men and over twenty crates of gold, silver, and weapons—way too heavy for them to handle. What if I give you one of those crates of precious metals to cover the expense of moving it aboard, on top of the two thousand dollars already discussed?"

I was busy below deck adding up the new weight of the cargo in my head (although all that talk of money distracted me some), and unless Port Herman was as deep as the Boston Harbor, we'd run aground well before we ever docked.

"What's in Port Herman that's so important?" asked Captain Crowell.

"Nothing that you need to know about!" went the wild-eyed barber of Seville. "But you need to load this ship and set sail by first light tomorrow morning, if you want our money, and that's final!"

If the Chesapeake was getting underway in the morning, how was I to get word to my friends? I tore off a piece of the paper I'd added the slaves up on and wrote a brief note to my comrades that went as follows: Ship sails at first light tomorrow! I'm stuck here aboard the Chesapeake at Thames Street—best play it by ear if you ever want to see me again! Help me, please, help me!

The next part of my plan was a bit trickier, for it involved trusting an old friend who may have fallen in with the Rebels. The last time I'd seen Mr. Salomon he was knee deep in the Knights of the Golden Circle's gold, but I needed him now or our plan was sunk!

"Boy, get your scrawny little ass up here," bellowed the first mate, who definitely didn't like the captain taking on new hands. "Take this note over to the man in charge of that Jewelry store and get his answer."

As I dashed across the street, I prayed to Sweet Jesus that Captain Ferrandini didn't stop in to see his gold for he would definitely recognize the boy who had cheated him out of eleven thousand dollars and a working Steam Gun! "Sweet Jesus, this is Robert Augustus Stewart," I prayed. "Could you please come down here and help me?"

Then into Mr. Salomon's store I ran. The guards were busy packing up large wooden crates full of silver candelabras and serving trays. I dashed over to Haym standing by his weighing scale and pretended to look for just the right broach, whilst he pretended he didn't know me.

"Can I help you, son?" he finally asked and I passed him my note.

"Can you see this note gets to the B&O Horse Farms as quick as you can, please, Mr. Salomon? Just hum a few bars of Go Down Moses and somebody will come along." I whispered but one of the guards looked up just then, and it was the oldest Kane brother.

He had two brand new Army colts on his hips and two large bumps on the back of his head. I was praying my short hair and bruised up eye was enough to keep him from recognizing me as he hollered, "Who in the hell let you in here, boy? Go on and get the hell out!"

"Oh, you must be in charge, sir, is that right?" I asked him brazenly as I stared at the ground like Mr. Salomon had taught me to do with royalty.

211

"What of it?" goes he like he wanted to fight.

"Well, I've got a message from the captain of the Chesapeake across the street right there," and I pointed to our ship bobbing in the Basin.

"Give it here and get the hell out!" growled the Marshal's first born son.

"My Skipper said to wait until you gave me an answer," I told him, standing my ground.

He opened the note and read with his lips moving—telling me every word, which was, "We will need you to have all the crates packed and loaded aboard the Chesapeake by first light tomorrow morning."

"Ain't no way!" he growled. "We've only got half our shipment here and the rest is with my father over at Police Headquarters in Baltimore. We can't possibly have them crated up and shipped over to the East End before ten tomorrow morning."

"Well, maybe you'll have to get a second ship for the rest of your things." I suggested, but the big bully didn't like me talking back.

"Not if the KGC says otherwise!" he barked. "You tell your captain once we get to Snow Hill and the Eastern Shore secedes from the state of Maryland, he'll be making plenty of money off the Confederacy, so he best waits to cast off 'til after ten, if he knows what's good for him!"

Those flies in my ointment were coming on fast, though at least now I knew what the Rebels were up to. But could my old friend, Hayam, get word to my comrades before we set sail? That was the question!

But seeing how I might end up on the Chesapeake for the whole ride down to the Deep South, I came up with a plan to get in the Skipper's good graces. "I've got a way to get them crates loaded aboard the Chesapeake, Captain Crowell, sir." I told him. "We could get a good strong crew of slaves from that slave hotel and have them do the heavy lifting for us."

"You're a smart boy," he said and he patted my head. Then he wrote out the following orders: Give me ten strong bucks in leg irons and have them ready by 8:30 tonight. The remainder of the stock is to be brought aboard in full irons by 7:00 AM tomorrow morning.

I walked over to the slave hotel and after delivering the captain's message; I was leaving when right there before me sat Miss Lew all trussed up in chains and crying like a baby. I dropped my pencil and bent down real slow as I whispered, "Miss Moses is coming for us all! We're going to the Promised Land, I promise you!"

When I got back to the Chesapeake, she was like a ship on fire with men running everywhere. Coal was being shoveled below decks where her great boiler would gobble it up and turn the steam into horsepower to turn the shafts that drove the propeller at a rapid rate. The big bronze screw would spin, we'd fly up the Bay, and before those damn slavers knew what hit them, we'd have their gold, and their slaves, and they'd be the laughing stock of Baltimore—just as I planned!

At 7:30 PM I reminded Captain Crowell that we needed to go and fetch the slaves. The Skipper was busy with his navigational charts, but he thanked me, and said, "Take Bosun's Mate Pettigrew and two scatter guns with you, and bring them down here right away."

"But sir," I said, "that bosun's mate has been picking on me something fierce, and he surely won't do a thing I say!"

The captain put down his ruler and looked at me as he said, "I'll give you two dollars a week and a nice promotion to an officer's rating, and the bosun's mate won't be able to touch you, Ensign Roberts."

What could I say to that, except thank you and play it by ear, but my real thought was: I'd hand Shorty an unloaded scattergun, while mind was double shotted just to level the playing field. But those slaves in our work detail must have heard the word about Miss Moses coming, for they were as docile as lambs. I had them all lined up by the side of our ship and ready to work ten minutes ahead of schedule.

They took a couple of fence posts and strapped them to the top of the crates making four little handles and hauled each crate like they were in the deepest and darkest of Africa. We stowed the crates all along the gunwales on the main deck—tying them tightly, save for the crate delivered to the Skipper's cabin as Captain Ferrandini had promised.

"Take the slaves below decks, Mr. Roberts," our captain said with a big pleased smile. "And see that they get a taste of beer for their troubles."

213

I sent Shorty to fetch us two one gallon pails from The Horse You Came In On three squares down—one for the slaves, and one for the crew by way of a peace offering from their brand new ensign.

The first and second mates glared down at me in a fit of hatred. If ever they got a hold of me, I'd be swimming in the Bay. But then, if the Lord decided to come aboard the Chesapeake, those Rebels might be the ones that were swimming!

Sleep that night was sporadic—what with the constant bumping of the ship against the dock and me being a landlubber who didn't much care for all that rocking going on. I slept on the deck just outside the Skipper's cabin just in case the crew tried to kill me. Each hour the ship's bell would ring—like three bells in the mid watch was one thirty in the morning, and then the Town Bell would ring on the mainland at two, whilst it was four bells on the ship. I had terrible dreams that I was locked away in a clock tower—not knowing my job, and finally, at two bells in the Morning Watch—which was five AM, I heard the Skipper moving about in his cabin. I pulled myself together and was standing there waiting with a nice hot cup of Rio when he finally came out.

"If we can get these slaves loaded fast this morning, Ensign Roberts, we can be off with the tide."

That might have been good for the Secesh and their KGC gold, but it sure as hell wasn't any good for me! I was shaking in my boots—not knowing what to do, and not wanting to see Georgia too soon!

"Mr. Roberts," says the Skipper as he sipped his brew, "go to the slave hotel and tell them there's a dollar tip for bringing the slaves right now!"

"Aye aye, sir" I said, and up Thames Street I ran—too dumbfounded to even ask Sweet Jesus for His help.

I brought the slaves back down dragging their chains—the little baby slaves crying, a great line of humanity clinking along as the good citizens of Baltimore stepped out of our way. There was a gentle hum coming from the throng, and if you listened real closely, it was Go Down Moses being sung as the light came up in their eyes! We were on the fast train to freedom that morning, only where the hell was the conductor?

I hadn't said a thing to the Skipper about the second KGC shipment, and as we were locking the slaves away, I heard a commotion out on the docks. "Stand fast!" the first mate bellowed to someone coming up the gangplank in a hurry.

"I am Mr. Percy Ladew!" Mike's voice reverberated through the entire ship. "Here with orders from Richmond to come aboard!"

"And that's supposed to mean something to me?" went the first mate.

"Where's your Skipper, boy?" Mike ceremoniously cried.

"Can I help you, sir!" went the voice of Captain Crowell who seemed duly impressed, for Mike had arrived in a palatial carriage drawn by six pure white German beer horses.

Go light with your story there Mike, I prayed, for just down the road the Kane brothers would be coming! There was nothing to do—save pray, which I did with a, "Sweet Jesus if you're coming along on this cruise up the Chesapeake today, please don't let Mike blow his story!" And lo and behold, the Lord must have been listening, for I heard Mike say, "Captain Crowell, I represent the Confederate States of America—sent here to see that the Knights of the Golden Circles' treasure arrives safely on the Eastern Shore. I presume you have my stateroom ready? I will be bringing my own personal slaves aboard momentarily."

"We have no staterooms available?" goes the Skipper real nervously. "What did you say your name was?"

"Mr. Percy Ladew," Mike said with his strong Southern drawl dripping molasses. "President Davis will be saddened to hear you can't find accommodations for me and my slaves, but good day to you, sir. Bentley," he hollered down to Chester on Thames Street dressed in a tuxedo and top hat that looked suspiciously like Mr. Sebastian's. "Hold that carriage; we'll be seeking another vessel to Snow Hill."

"Not so fast, sir!" goes the Skipper with alarm in his voice. "How many personal slaves did you say you have, Mr. Ladew?"

"Twenty-seven, not counting the pickaninnies, with probably a dozen of the latter," Mike told him and I thought to myself, I've got to get above deck and see this for myself!

"And what's in that sea chest of yours, sir?" Our Skipper was a cautious soul even when he respected a man's social rank, and there at the base of the gangplank was a huge sea chest the size of a good healthy coffin. Six tall slaves supposedly belonging to Mr. Ladew were standing there waiting to carry it aboard.

"Oh, that's my personal belongings. I've got the official seal of the sovereign Confederate State of Eastern Maryland, orders from President Davis for our official secession,[90] and my private collection of weapons," Mike, I mean Mr. Ladew, told him.

"Unfortunately, Captain Ferrandini bought up all the State Rooms, but I guess I could let you have one since they're all empty," said the Skipper with the tip of his hat.

"Cipriano Ferrandini, a little Italian fellow with a surly smile?" Mr. Ladew asked the Skipper like he knew him.

"One in the same, sir," goes the Skipper, wiping the sweat from his brow as he watched the day start to fizzle away.

"Well, that Barnum's barber is but a high captain in the Knights of the Golden Circle, sir, whilst I am a full blown high colonel."

I was praying that Colonel Ladew's little barber friend didn't show up just then, for the clock was ticking! But, like I said, Sweet Jesus had come amongst us on the Chesapeake that day, and even as the slaves carried Mike's huge sea chest up to his State Room, the worm was starting to turn in our favor.

"Can I assume we will set sail as soon as my belongings are loaded?" went this fine southern gentleman as he looked at his stopwatch that said Haym Salomon on it, and he gave me a little sideways wink.

Up the gangway the big box came with those African fellas making it look easy. The first mate, who still wanted to murder me, didn't even blink as he stowed it in Mr. Percy Ladew's State Room. I was thinking of poor Miss Harriet in there gasping for air and wondered what I should do?

"Where's that damned cabin boy at? Get up there in the crow's nest," the second mate bellowed! I must have climbed maybe three or four stories up that scrawny mast as the seagulls dove at my head shrieking like banshees. There was a little foothold up there—more like a hummingbird's nest than a crow's nest, and my knees were knocking as the eastern sky went red. Thunderstorms flashed to the east maybe twenty miles out on the Bay, but I heard no thunder.

"That's where you'll stay for most of the cruise you little son of a bitch!" the first mate yelled by way of instructions. And just as I got use to the place, I had to come back down as he bellowed, "What in the hell are you doing up there? Get down here and give me a slave count!"

Down in the hold I went—lickety-split, and there was one hundred and twenty seven souls chained up in those cramped quarters; all begging for water. So until the next time the petty officers decided to choke my chain, I passed out fresh water and comforted them. Some of the slaves were but five or six years old, and I swear if my weapons weren't locked away in that sea chest with Miss Harriet (at least that's where I figured she was), I'd have come out blasting.

"Cabin boy!" shrieked the first mate. "Get your ass up here and report on the double!" My days as an ensign were over!

"We've got one hundred and twenty-seven slaves down in the hold, First Mate Hinmann, sir!"

One of them was the best Lake trout sandwich maker in all of Baltimore, though I kept that to myself. How poor Miss Lew had been served up to the slave catchers was anybody's guess, but she was being brave and bucking up well—humming Go Down Moses with the rest of the choir. That song gave them hope and tied them to our plan, for we were heading for the Promised Land, though only God knew how!

Captain Crowell was below deck in his cabin checking the depths to Port Herman, which was up the Elk River on a peninsula called Bohemia, while the first and second mates worked me to death. We had a skeleton crew aboard the Chesapeake that morning, for they wouldn't be rigging the sails 'til they hit the Atlantic.

"Once we get to Norfolk, we'll pick up a crew for the run down to Savannah," says the first mate to the second—the two of them sweating away as they saw to a dozen things. "What in the hell are you doing spying on your superiors?" yelled the first mate as he caught sight of me slinking in the shadows. "Get back up in that crow's nest, damn you!"

So up the rat lines I climbed, gazing down at the busy ship as I went. The Chesapeake's funnel was spitting out thick black smoke as she got up steam. Great black puffs rose up over Fells Point as they climbed towards my narrow perch. Out on Thames Street I could see people just starting to hit the streets, and I swear maybe two squares down Alice Anna Street, I saw that little Italian stallion with the Kane brothers heading our way with a couple of fully loaded wagons.

Colonel Ladew came out of his First Class cabin just then. He'd taken off his dress coat and was standing there with his arms crossed and ready to draw. The Skipper came out of his cabin and walked towards the bow of the ship. He stopped beside Mike and asked him something, but I couldn't hear what it was, for the sea gulls, and the thumping of the steam engine, and the sounds on the docks were rising.

Colonel Ladew shook his head no and shouted, "We're not waiting for Captain Ferrandini to arrive—let him take the next ship over!"[91]

If that crazy Barnum's barber got there before we cast off, our whole plan would be ruined, and just then the first mate yelled, "Captain Crowell, this ship don't sail till the cargo is stowed!"

Even though these fellows had technically seceded from the Union and didn't have to stand by any Federal Maritime regulations, slaves were never listed on a ship's manifest as people—they were listed as cargo. And just like fire was feared on board a ship at sea, loose cargo was even more of a danger to the crew of the Chesapeake. I was staring down Thames Street, praying that Captain Ferrandini and his caravan got caught in traffic, when Colonel Ladew hollered, "Prepare to cast off, you can put my slaves anywhere you like, now let's get underway!"

Down to the hold went the whole flock of Ladew slaves, so we now had one hundred and sixty-six pieces of living cargo. And as we steamed past Fort McHenry with her guns run out, I saw Captain Robinson up on the ramparts with his spy glass in hand. The Secesh threw him The Bird (and a bare backside or two) as their palmetto flag flew, whilst I gave him a proud salute. Freedom was rising in the air that morning!

"You keep a close watch for shoals out on the Bay you little one-eyed bastard," bellowed the first mate with his hands cupped. We steamed by the North Point Light with the seas beginning to build.

The ship picked up steam and turned to the starboard as we went into the Craighill Channel with me up on that little swaying crow's nest. And there beneath us came a great brown Leviathan—growing bigger and bigger as I wondered what the hell I was seeing? The thing seemed to be curling up out of the bay like the tail of a whale, as I let out a shriek! "Hard to the Starboard," I bellowed!

"Hard to Starboard," echoed the worried first mate, for he knew I wasn't the seafaring sort.

"Hard to starboard," added the second mate real worried as well.

The Chesapeake heeled hard to the side almost pitching me into the sea as that mountain of brown came up to the surface then disappeared. And no sooner had we cleared that little undersea island (they were actually called the Six and Seven foot knolls), then another huge brown whale came up to sink us! There was just the faintest sound of a metallic ping as the screw of the Chesapeake hit something hard.

"Full stop!" yelled the Skipper at the top of his lungs. "Full stop, and put somebody up in the crow's nest that knows what they're doing!"

We'd hit that second knoll with just a glancing blow, but as I was about to learn the hard way, a glancing blow was sometimes enough to ruin a propeller. Since we hadn't the crew to rig our sails that would mean a slow trip back to the Baltimore Harbor, if we could find a tugboat?

There were four men on the main deck staring into the murky waters as I came down the mast in disgrace. The Skipper—frothing like a rabid dog, the first mate—glaring at me like I'd scuttled her on purpose, the second mate pulling at his beard with murder in his eyes, and the engineer who was hanging over the ship's stern trying to see if the screw was still on.

"No telling how bad that propeller is banged up, sir!" goes the latter with a big wrench in his hand. "We'll have to send down a diver."

"Let's toss this little son of a bitch in and see what he comes up with," yelled the second mate as he grabbed me up by the scruff of my neck.

"What do I know about propellers, boys?" I cried as I searched the crowd for a friend. "Skipper, tell them I'm just a baby. We need someone with more experience than me!"

"Not really," says the first mate with blood in his eyes. "We just need someone who sinks!"

"Listen here, boy!" cried the Skipper like he'd never made me an ensign. "Just dive down there and see if the screw is held tight. It has four bolts where it attaches to the shaft and we need to know if they're still on."

"Into the sea," screamed the second mate as he pitched me in. I bobbed up and down with that heaving ship threatening to crush me. The water had warmed since April, but it was not what you'd call comfortable, and I looked up and saw one of the sailors climbing the mast, whilst Colonel Ladew was coming up on the main deck.

"All passengers back to their cabins," hollered Captain Crowell. "We've got this handled, sir! Go back to your cabin, right now! Get the scatter guns out, Mr. Hinmann," the Skipper yelled to his First Mate. "Shoot anyone that steps foot on the main deck!"

"Get down there, son," barks the Engineer as I treaded water and gulped for air. "You should feel that propeller just by the rudder—feel for the bolts holding her on, and give me a count."

"Now dive boy, dive!" yells the second mate, pointing his scatter gun at me.

I dove straight down till I smacked into that big bronze propeller and clung on for dear life. It felt pretty tight, though a hundred and ten pounds ain't much to test how a screw is held on. Then up to the surface I went gasping for air.

"Get your scrawny little ass back down there and see what's what!" screamed the black-bearded second mate and they all began to laugh.

My belief in adults was waning fast, for first they put me up there in that tiny crow's nest without a second of training, and then they made me a diver to do God only knows what? But down I went and around the back side of that big sharp blade I swam, feeling where the back of the propeller joined the shaft. The engine was still huffing and puffing, and if

220

they put that thing in gear, I would have been ground into sausage! There was one bolt that I knew for sure was still on, then two bolts before I came up for air. And with another point from that scatter gun, I sent my feet flying high in the air and swam back down into the murky waters where I sat under the curve of the Chesapeake and listened in.

"Damn, the lad's done gone and drowned this time," goes the Skipper with little concern.

"Good riddance," yelled the first mate.

"Amen!" went the second.

"Who's next?" asked the engineer, and they all fell silent.

Back down I went, and when I finally came up again, they were very impressed. I'd counted three bolts and that was it. Three bolts held that propeller to the shaft. I'd have told them four, if it would have helped my case, but three bolts was all there was!

"Damn!" says the engineer. "Let's test her out and see what's what. Three bolts just might hold at half speed."

"Sail ho!" hollered the new boy up in the crow's nest. "It looks like a Federal Blockader coming on fast! She's out there along Love Point (the northern tip of Kent Island) maybe twelve miles to the starboard."

"All ahead half speed," hollers the Skipper before they hauled me in, and as that propeller started to twirl and the waters began to suck me under, my whole life passed before me! "We'll head for Poole Island and cast our live cargo into the sea so we can make better speed up the Bay," hollered the Skipper, as they battened down the hatches for the big storm that was coming.

The crew all put on their rubber slickers, as the second mate bellowed that all civilians were to stay in their cabins or be shot on sight. That huge thunderstorm came tearing across the Bay like a big black banshee growling and throwing lightning bolts our way! Once we were in the eye of that storm, the Yankee Blockader wouldn't be able to see us anymore, but before we disappeared into that dark swirling tempest, our crafty captain heeled to the starboard. He knew what that word subterfuge

221

meant and he held his course till we disappeared into the flashing clouds, and then he went on a new tack to come in behind Poole Island.

"Cabin boy (which was me after my untimely demotion) get down there in the hold and start unlocking the slaves!" Captain Crowell yelled as he pitched me the keys.

"Mr. Hinmann," he yelled to his first mate, "I want every last piece of living cargo including Colonel Ladew's slaves over the side as soon as we come in the lee of Poole Island. We'll pick them up on the run down the Bay—them that survives, that is!" And they all laughed.

I ran to Colonel Ladew's cabin and banged on the door as the storm began to roar and the ship began to quake. The door opened a quarter of the way and a big black hand drew me in. There was Chester with a scatter gun, Miss Harriet in a bright red bandana with her Navy colt in hand, and Mike passing me my LeMat with that big Henry Repeating Rifle at his side.

"Go now," he whispered. "We heard it all! Get down in that hold and start setting the slaves free just as the Skipper told you!" And he pitched me his Henry, as I tucked the LeMat in my belt.

"I'll go with him!" Miss Harriet said, as the thunder roared and the lightning struck, and the seas threatened to swallow us whole!

We were cast about like pins in a bowling alley, but Miss Harriet and I made it to the hold where we started unlocking the seasick cargo. And when they saw Miss Harriet amongst them a, "Praise Jesus!" rose in the air! Up the Chesapeake Bay we flew—the thunder and lightning firing off like a great sea battle all around us, as Miss Harriet talked to her children in a calm and gentle voice.

"When the Lord was out on the waves of Galilee," she yelled over the crashing storm. "He said oh ye of little faith, why are you so afraid?"

That calmed everybody down—even the little baby slaves who had been frightened by the strike of the lightning and that stinging taste it left in our mouths. One hundred and sixty-six souls, one hundred and sixty-eight counting me and Miss Harriet—all singing Go Down Moses as we prayed to Sweet Jesus for our deliverance!

"Get those damned slaves up here on deck!" shrieked the second mate from the hatch above as the ship shuddered in the boiling seas.

"I'll go up and start taking prisoners, Miss Harriet!" I yelled over the roar of the storm.

"Fine, but leave that LeMat right here in the hold for one of my men," she ordered like the general she was.

"Leave the LeMat? Why do you want me to leave my LeMat?"

"We all know what kind of a shot you are, Augustus, and you just might hit something you aim at with that Henry rifle!" She roared with a great big smile, for General Tubman always loved a good battle!

The second mate was looking down through the hatch screaming at me, "Hurry up with those damn slaves! We're coming up on Poole Island."

I pointed the rifle right at his belly and yelled over the close crack of a lightning strike, "Why don't you come on down and join the congregation?"

He was hog tied and gagged in two seconds' time—one down and a dozen slavers to go. Chester headed for the Engine Room and I joined him there. The first engineer volunteered to switch sides with his stokers if they could get off the ship when we did, and we passed the rest of the Secesh up to the main deck as we came up to the island with the storm churning the waters into a swirling vortex. It was maybe a hundred yard swim to shore in rough seas, and Mike hollered from the bridge to come and get his prisoners. There stood both the Skipper and the first mate, and two or three other crew members with sad frowns on their faces.

"You mean you ain't Colonel Ladew?" Bosun's Mate Shorty asked Mike, as we escorted him and his seafaring friends to the starboard side.

"All ashore that's going ashore!" I bellowed as we prepared to throw them in.

"We'll drown in those seas!" the first mate whined! "We got rights you know," he yelled like a Boston lawyer, but he was the first to go in!

"This is piracy on the high seas and that's punishable by death," goes the second mate.

"You won't make it to Hampton Roads before the Rebel Navy scoops you up," he hollered as he went in next.

But we weren't planning on making a run for the mouth of the Bay. We were heading for a place not five miles north of where the slavers were heading. The Lord worked in mysterious ways!

"Once that Yankee blockader breaks free of the squall, she'll put her carronades into you from a mile off and you'll all be crab food," goes the Skipper before he entered the waters with a blood-curdling scream.

Mike hollered for us to get the crates of gold, and silver, and guns, and ammunition over the side as fast as we could. The Skipper was right; those Yankee carronades would cut us in half well before we could explain who we were. But the same crew that had loaded the KGC's gold on the Fells Point dock were now the ones who were unloading her fast. Down went their treasure, and the cases of Harpers Ferry rifles, whilst the crew of the Chesapeake floundered ashore.

"Here boys, you can have your palmetto flag back," I yelled as I flung her into the swirling waters. "And don't you ever come back to Baltimore no more!"

We sailed on for the head of the Bay—a King's ransom in gold, silver, and armaments lighter, as a rainbow formed over the Eastern Shore. The congregation came up on deck and breathed in the sweet air of freedom. There were big ones, and small ones, little babies clutching at their momma's breasts, all happy to be heading for the Promise Land and Kingdom Come just as Little Henry had described it.

Up into the shallows of the Elk River we ran to the dock at Frenchtown with our propeller still hanging on. There like the good shepherd she was, Miss Harriet led her flock down the gangplank and up an old abandoned railroad to Delaware.

And on the wings of that very same tempest that took us to freedom that day, General Butler and his Yankee Army entered Baltimore, freeing my father and Fort McHenry as well. All without one soul being injured on either side,[92] just as Miss Harriet had prophesized!

Chapter Eight

Up a Tree in Bohemia

For four long years my friends and I fought for freedom and when the war was over, I decided to leave my homeland for the peace and quiet of Europe. My ship over was Cunard's iron hulled RMS Persia whose record time from New York to Liverpool was nine days, ten hours, and twenty-two minutes, though with this Jonah aboard, she took twice as long. When we finally reached Liverpool, I kissed the ground I walked on and headed for Paris, hoping to find Miss Yvette and her cocottes.

Campaigning with the cavalry had left me tanned with a big red beard, forearms the size of anvils, and weighing in at one hundred and thirty-one pounds. I was a nineteen year old Yankee warrior, not the scrawny little fifteen year old boy the girls had known, and I wanted to show myself off. But I never found them, though I tried real hard. And as the summer heat started bearing down, and the river Seine sent off her muddy mist, I missed the smell of the sea, and the song of the seabirds, and decided to do what all rich men do at that time of year, which was head down to the sea!

The Rothschilds weren't the only ones who made their money with the telegraph.[93] My friends and I did quite well trading with the enemy in imported Brazilian coffee and British gin in exchange for fine southern tobacco and southern whiskey, the proceeds of which we reinvested wisely. Say the Rebels captured a ship with thirty thousand bags of coffee aboard,[94] well, we'd buy all the coffee we could afford on the New York Exchange and wouldn't the price soar! Or, say we saw 10,000 bales of cotton going up in smoke on an Atlanta train platform; well, we'd use the talking wire to buy Egyptian cotton before the news broke all over the world, and wouldn't the price of cotton go up like the rockets' red glare! Being up front with the Army where things happened fast meant our little nest egg grew until at War's end, some would say, I was a very wealthy man. And what better way for a wealthy man to spend his time than sitting on the beach by the azure blue sea, drinking wine, and watching beautiful women! I'd have stayed there in the French Riviera forever but for the actions of two horny lovers I knew.

Nice was nestled on the shores of the Mediterranean Sea with palm trees, beautiful blue waters, lovely women, and a nice warm breeze. My plan was to train my new thoroughbred, Yvette, to become a fine steeplechase racer, for I missed my cavalry days. A Baltimore boy can handle the boredom of a quiet life by the sea if he has something he likes to do with his time, and riding my mare by day, and drinking absinthe by night, suited me fine!

Nice was nice, but Port Abri du Cros de Cagnes was even nicer, and I rented a room in the little fishing village there at the harbor where I could watch the boats go in and out of her crystal blue waters. During the day I'd sit under a palm tree on the beach and read Robinson Crusoe or the Adventures of Alice in Wonderland as I sipped red wine. Then at sun down I'd go eat some of the best fish on the Continent—cooked in the Sardinian, or the Italian, or the finest French fashion. After a long lovely dinner, I'd spend an hour or two sipping absinthe under the stars with my fishermen friends, who loved to bitch about the Frenchmen who'd recently rolled in. The Sardinians—like Nice's own, Giuseppe Garibaldi, had pitched in with the other Italian States to throw off the Austrian yoke, and the Italians, in order to thank their French allies, had given them Savoy and Nice as a gift. So with the Frenchmen flooding in like the ten plagues on the Pharaoh, it was another of those migrations that sets off friction all over this world—and where there's friction there's long nights of drinking and cussing, which sharpened my Italian and Sardinian immensely!

But all that easy living weighed heavily on my soul and some mornings I found myself sipping white wine with my breakfast and cognac with lunch. Then one evening in late June after a little too much absinthe and The Adventures of Alice in Wonderland rolling around in my head, I saw three of my Sardinian drinking buddies being sucked down a hole in the sand. I was surrounded by a silence so sharp you could cut it with a knife, and as the waves crashed around me in the morning light, I lay shipwrecked like Robinson Crusoe. It was time for old Redbeard to give up the Green Fairy![95]

My sweet little landlady, Signora Fungini (who was as tall as she was wide with short hairy arms and legs), gathered up my half empty bottles of absinthe, brandy, wine, cognac, scotch, and whiskey, and took them away to the city dump. Spring water from the best fountain in Port Abri du Cros was all that would pass my lips from that day forward, and for exercise, besides my steeplechase racing, I added rowing to the list; buying a little red row boat—complete with a net, an ancient limestone anchor, and a pair of long wooden oars from a fisherman's widow. Each morning, I'd go out to the sea and row my boat maybe a mile or so as the sun came up over Nice—all alone in the silence as the clouds skidded by.

The peace I'd been seeking when I first came to Europe came to me there—it was the true peace of being one with the Universe, and one with my oars, and one with the deep blue sea! Happy in the emptiness my Zen Master would say on the road to Shambhala later in life. I'd strip naked and jump into the water and swim like I'd never swum before—the Mediterranean surrounding me in a silent cocoon. And as my mind healed from the memories of a cruel war, my body became that of a little brown galley slave.

Signora Fungini started to worry for my sanity to the point of suggesting I take up drinking again. "A young man needs a young woman to be happy in life," she said in her flowery Sardinian at dinner one night. "It's not right that you spend all your time out on the sea alone, Signor Augustus. You have another life locked away in that sea chest of yours. You have to let it out, if you want to be free!"

Every day after that, I'd saddle Yvette and we'd ride east for Nice where we'd look at the sailing yachts out in the harbor, and listen to the sea gulls singing their screechy songs. The July sunsets of Nice la Belle were a time for celebration, and all that were fashionable presented themselves along the cobblestoned streets by the shimmering sea—on horseback, or in sumptuous carriages, dressed to the nines with happy smiles on each and every face, for in the Provence Cote d'Azur, which was the official name of the new region of France, happy faces were an absolute must.

The prettiest women in all of Europe were there along the Promenade des Anglais in their bright crinoline dresses with freshly curled hair—their perky breasts pointing straight to the heavens! And as the sun went down in a fiery flare and the Champaign glasses clinked, and everyone laughed, and the brass bands played a merry song—it was a good time to be alive, and good to be young, and love was in the air! Everywhere!

Of course the best looking women on the Promenade were taken by the pantaloons rouges or red-panted French officers. The poor sergeants, corporals, privates, and civilians like me hadn't a chance in the great Second French Empire.[96] The cavalry officers were especially sought after by the women of Nice—the richer the better, and as the soldiers tweaked their fine trimmed goatees and sat their gorgeous steeds, the ladies in their horse drawn carriages swooned and threw them flowers.

At first I dressed like a Sardinian with baggy blue pants and a bright red Garibaldi shirt, but that outfit couldn't cut the mustard with the women of Nice. Oh, I had the maids and the seconds throwing flowers at me, but not one of those high-class ladies ever looked my way. I decided to open my sea chest and bring out the heavy artillery, for locked away since our Victory Parade,[97] was my old cavalry uniform, bought and paid for with my trading with the enemy money, and only worn that once. You see, we didn't wear uniforms in the 3rd Indiana, for we worked behind enemy lines—climbing telegraph poles to listen in on the Rebels.[98] But once we won the war and the Grand Army of the Republic prepared to march in a celebration parade, we all dressed in our Sunday best. True I was but an enlisted man, but the stripes on a sergeant major's arm aren't exactly unattractive. That tight high-collared deep blue cavalry tunic came out of my sea chest and though all the yellow braid said I was a trumpeter; I doubted the women of Nice would notice.

Lieutenant Klein had said he needed a trumpeter to ride with our colors, and since he'd spent so many nights around our campfires listening to me wailing away on my trusty Hohner, he told me, "if ever there was a man in the 3rd Indiana that deserved to make bugler, it's my sergeant major." Oh, I knew it was a joke and all, but just knowing my friends would get a kick out of it was all I needed. After all, we'd laughed when the Rebels chased us, and we laughed when we beat them at their game, and we laughed when crying was just too hard to do, so when the war was all over it was a real good time to laugh some more!

That tight little shell jacket had one row of flashy brass eagle buttons down the center on a thin line of yellow braid with a great yellow trapezoid across the width of my chest—six lines of braid running cross ways. I wore a black leather belt with the crossed cavalry swords on my buckle, a big Bowie knife on my right hip instead of a sword, and a black leather pistol holster on my left hip with my trusty LeMat facing backwards. On my arm in bright yellow were my three sergeant major's stripes forming a V with three half circles of yellow lace climbing above. That high blue collar had three lines of yellow braid and when a soldier stood up tall and proud, it added two inches to his height. On my head was a fine French kepi of dark blue, while my britches were sky blue with a narrow yellow stripe down the side—tucked tight into a pair of well shined English cavalry boots. Signora Fungini had cleaned and pressed my uniform—polished the brass and the boots, and sent me off to see the mayor to get permission to carry my weapons.

"Of course, signor, said the chubby little Italian with a smile on his face. "I have two brothers who fought in your army. Just don't go shooting any citizens of Cagnes-sur-Mer, unless they are French, of course!"

When I returned to Port du Cros my sweet little landlady had not only prepared my dress uniform and all my accoutrements, but she'd also braided Yvette's mane with some red, white, and blue ribbons. My mare had a white blaze across her face running from between her soft brown eyes to her nostrils, and my landlady and her three little children had washed her so well that the pure white of her face and her fetlocks were as clean as a Sunday dress shirt. Her head was held high like she knew those ribbons looked good and she snorted and wanted to be off.

"Hurry, you must go signor," Signora Fungini begged, as her children stood back and smiled like cherubs. "The sun will be setting soon!"

Barefoot and as poor as church mice, the Funginis were the apples of my eye, and as I mounted and saluted my Port du Cros family, they all gasped at their American hero and his beautiful mare! Down the Promenade de Anglais we rode as the setting sun turned everything to a golden glow. We rode east to the Opera House where the gas lights were lit and the palm trees swayed, and there were gasps from the crowd when they saw Yvette. Roses and sprigs of pink Bougainvillea were passed our way from slow moving carriages with gorgeous ladies smiling up at us. My heart did a pitter-patter as we trotted along. There were horse teams of twos and fours—all well matched pairs, with sparkling harnesses and high stepping gaits—some even with feathers flying from their heads, for sunset in the city of Nice was a circus extraordinaire!

A bright red Romanoff carriage came down the Promenade with a driver that looked like he was one of George Washington's servants—only in green with red trim, a powdered wig and long white socks to the knees. The glittering carriage displayed the golden double-headed Russian eagle on each door with two beautiful women inside—both in exceedingly low-cut dresses, clucking like hens for Yvette to come over. They each passed me a rose the color of their dress (one yellow, one red), and according to custom, if I felt the same way about them, I'd pass it back for a kiss. My heart was thumping like the roar of the sea and as I stared down into the unfathomable depths of those four lovely breasts—that feeling of oneness with the Universe returned to me!

I was so entranced that I didn't hear the steel-chested cuirassier yelling, "Keep moving Yankee, you're blocking the Promenade!" He must have hollered it at me fifteen times before the spell of the Oneness of the Breasts was broken. That captain of cuirassiers in his shiny chest armor rode up close to Yvette and struck me across the chest with his riding crop. "I said move on, Yankee!" he roared in his finest French as his shiny chest plate sparkled in the setting sun.

His helmet too was glistening gold—great red fluffs of his captain's epaulets sprouted from his armor at each of his overly proud shoulders, and of course he wore those red pants that all the pantaloons rouge loved so well. He wore a pointy little black goatee and glared at me with the beady little squint eyes of a senator's son.

"Move on, you damn Yankee!" he yelled, and then he paused like he had a better idea, and called for two cuirassier cavalrymen to come over. "Do you have a permit to carry that pistol, sergeant major?" he roared with a haughty disgust for all things American.

I counted to ten like Lieutenant Klein had taught me, but the cuirassier captain wouldn't ease up. His horse was digging into Yvette's side trying to push her away from the two Russian girls, while the two troopers on their stomping black steeds were trying to catch my reins and haul me away. I sawed my mare around sideways and hollered, "I have permission from the Mayor of Cagnes-sur-Mer to carry my weapons!"

"Well, you are not in Cagnes-sur-Mer, monsieur!" goes the French officer with an evil smile. "You're in Nice, and I must confiscate dees weapons!"

In the 3rd Indiana we were trained to ride away from trouble as fast as we could, and we were never to hand over our weapons to anyone! For four long years that rule had worked, so I swung my mare around and we flew off for Port du Cros at the gallop, as I threw him the good old Digitus Impudicus. The race was on, but once we reached the Var River Bridge, my weapons were legal, although from that day forward, I was a persona non grata in the city of Nice.

I had to be content with my memories of those two Russian beauties, as I lost myself in my steeplechasing. Yvette was a natural born jumper and as she learned to approach a jump just right, we began to sail over everything we went for. Her stables were about a quarter of a mile west of the place I rented, and every morning we'd go up in the olive groves above the deep blue sea and build a timber jump or two. "Just don't hurt the trees," said the Sardinian farmer who charged me next to nothing for the privilege. Somedays Yvette looked like an Army mule going out to work in those peaceful groves. It kept my mind off the drinking and the women, until I almost forgot those ladies.

But one day when Yvette and I were out testing the track, up came the two Romanoff sisters (distant cousins of the Tsar they said). They were mounted on fine Arabian stallions with a Cossack lancer as an escort in his long red cherkeska—a rifle in a black leather scabbard on his back, and a long red lance in his hand. The bearded warrior was on a scruffy little Steppe pony that I called Little Suli, since his rider and all the Muslim boys I'd ever met were named Suli before him.

"We finally found you!" the older one yelled like she'd found King Solomon's gold.

She was a big-busted, broad-shouldered, curly-headed, tomboy of a girl with black baggy pants that could hardly hide the curves of her very athletic body. Wearing a white peasant blouse with flowers embroidered

231

across the plunging neckline, her green eyes drew me in like a moth to the flame. But as I looked at her little sister, perhaps a year younger and a bit smaller than she was—her deep dark eyes started to draw me in too. While the older sister's Arabian was a jet black stallion, the younger girl's horse was a beautiful dapple gray, and he sniffed at Yvette like he wanted to devour her—just like I wanted to do to his rider!

I was wearing an old, white long underwear top—a bit dirty from the track making routine, a pair of tight tan English riding breeches, my tall brown riding boots—muddy from a day of hard labor, and a big smile on my face as Yvette sawed around and kicked at the younger girl's horse. The last time they'd seen me, I was in full cavalry regalia and I was wondering how they spotted me dressed like a moujik.

"Good to see you ladies!" was my opening line in the language of love—having talked only Sardinian for the last few weeks.

"We are the Romanoff sisters," says the older one as she presented her hand for a kiss. "My name is Natasha." I sniffed her beauty in a long slow inhale as I kissed her hand and bowed low in the saddle.

"Augustus Stewart, at your service, mademoiselle, and who is this little sister?" I said with my heart pounding like a tympani drum.

"Her name is Anna," said the more talkative one who was nineteen like I was—her eyes flashing a fiery flirt. "She's a little shy, for she has never met an American before."

I reached out and kissed the young beauty's hand and there appeared a lump in my throat which I figured was my heart, for it was beating at the fast trot. White clouds skidded overhead and the palm trees swayed, and I fell in love for only the sixth or seventh time in my life!

"Look the American is blushing," Natasha said to her little sister who was blushing right back.

"I think he likes you, Anna. Well, would you like me even better, Amerikanskiy, if I beat you at a horse race?"

She kicked her stallion in the side and set out down my steeplechase track like lightning on the wire! Anna and their Cossack guard (who I called Suli the First since I'd never met one up close before) set off a few lengths behind her. I clucked to Yvette and we were off—up through the olive groves we galloped, with our hearts pounding! First, I overtook the Cossack (actually he was a Circassian), and his little black pony. Circassians were Muslim hirelings of the Russians who came from way out in the Steppes—true horse country since the beginning of time. The Cossacks copied the ways of the Circassians right down to their long red cherkeska, and my Lord could that Muslim boy ride! Even with that long red lance in his hand, Suli the First could leap the tallest of jumps on that tough little Steppe pony. He was hard to pass on the sandy ground, but pass him we did. Then it was on for Anna and her dapple gray Arabian. I passed her in a heartbeat and moved on after her older sister. Finally the long legs of my mare and the hard training prevailed and Yvette took the lead from Natasha's stallion. We headed back down the hill to the sea at a blistering pace, then out into the Mediterranean we galloped.

"That was the best ride I've ever had," said Natasha totally out of breath—her rib cage going up and down as I praised the gods above!

But I realized right then and there that if that red-coated Circassian was coming along with the girls every time they came, my best bet was to stay with the older one, for how could you out-ride that dusky lancer unless you picked the faster sister! Every day, rain or shine, the ladies and that swarthy Suleiman the First would arrive at our track and help me build jumps and race the day away. Those Russian girls could work as hard as any man could, and eventually their bodyguard trusted me enough to quit bringing his lance along. The Romanoff sisters would bring a little picnic lunch in a wicker basket. We'd have caviar, Champaign; a fine beet salad—it was all so grand, but before we would spread the picnic blanket and eat, we would always have a little steeplechase race. Natasha and I would always take first and second place, leaving Suli and Anna far behind.

Then, just after a lovely day in the olive groves, the girls simply stopped coming. Yvette and I would wait at the starting gate for hours on end and no one would show up. After a week of sheer loneliness, I left my weapons in Cagnes-sur-Mer and set off in search of my lover, for I needed Natasha like I needed to breathe! It was like I was back in the 3rd Indiana again—binoculars in hand riding the hills above the city of Nice searching for the woman I loved. I saw peacocks on manicured lawns where palm trees and flowering bushes abounded, a Russian maid making the double-backed beast with an Italian gardener in a bed of red begonias, fine bright red carriages with golden Romanoff eagles on each door, but never did I ever see Natasha or her sister!

Finally, I gave my English mare a rest and took to rowing out on the sea to search—going all the way down along the Promenade like only a lonely lover would do. Summer was in full progress and it was warm at the work, so I stripped down to a pair of cutoff old riding pants sans shirt and turned as black as an Ottoman Turk.

"You must wear a hat when you are out on the sea, Augustus!" my sweet little landlady warned me, but I didn't care if I lived or died without Natasha at my side. She was all I thought about—day and night.

Then one blue skied Sunday as I prepared to set out on my love-struck journey—putting two goat skins of water and a tin of sardines in the bow of my boat, up rode two Circassian riders with their long red lances in hand. My heart soared, for one of them was my old friend Suli the First. He had a stern look on his black-bearded face that made me think there was some kind of trouble, while his friend was a big mean looking badmash with a sword cut across his cheek that said all you'd needed to know about him.

"Suleiman—my friend, where have you been?" I bellowed in my newly learned Russian. He just looked at me sadly and nodded to his left where his friend with the jagged scar sat looking like he wanted to kill me.

"Princess Bonaparte commands your presence, you Amerikanskiy dog!" The scar-faced Suli said in his halting French.

"You can come peacefully, or on the tip of my lance, it makes no difference to me!"

Wasn't he a jolly one! But my trusty LeMat was back at Signora Fungini's and all I had on me was my Bowie knife. I was barefoot, bare-headed, bare-chested, and bare-butted save for my tight little cutoff pants, hardly an appropriate uniform to go meet a Bonaparte Princess in.

"Can I dress first?" I asked the evil looking Circassian, but he wasn't taking any questions.

"You climb up behind Suleiman just as you are, Amerikanskiy!"

They were going to parade me down the streets of Nice on the back of Suli the First (a clear cut sign that someone wasn't happy), and when the scar-faced fellow bellowed for me to pass him up my Bowie knife butt first, I knew I was in trouble! But what would the ruling family of France possibly want with a man like me? That big scar-faced Musulman kept his dark eyes glued on me as I leaped up behind my ex-friend Suli. The Bonaparte's mansion was high up on the rocky cliffs of du Mont Boron Hill on the far eastern side of Nice—a place I'd ridden by several times in my search for Natasha, but the red-panted French guards at the gate had scared me off. The steel-chested cuirassiers were still there at the gate, and I swear the Captain of the Guard was that Froggy I'd shot The Bird to before we started our race. I recognized the haughty way he sat his horse and the way he pulled at his goatee like he was checking to make sure it was still on.

"Open zee gates!" he ordered in his gruff French, and he huffed and he puffed, and turned his head sideways so as not to look at me.

Up to the great limestone palace we rode, the Cossacks' long red lances held at the ready. There were palm trees and flowering shrubs all across the huge lawn and the gardeners wore the dark green livery of the Bonaparte family with little symbols of well-fed bees on their breasts. Those fat little Bonaparte bumble bees were everywhere from the wrought iron gate and the privet hedges, to the wooden railings around the high-ceilinged porch. They were even on the doors to the three story mansion as we waited to be let in the back door. I'd seen the same fat little bumble bees on the front door in Baltimore when I delivered a telegram to Napoleon the First's nephew. "Here's a quarter for your time, boy," he said; only he owed the B&O a whole dollar.

They took me into the palace with its shiny marble floors and giant potted palms and up waddles a fortyish big-boned lady with a large moon face that looked exactly like my Baltimore Bonaparte.[99] She was dressed in a gray crinoline dress with wide whalebone supports that didn't do a thing for her full-bodied figure. The Princess looked down her pig nose at me and said, "Look what you've gone and done, you dirty American!"

Surrounded by a good twenty of her dandies, I was thinking maybe that absinthe was coming back on me! First, there was that uncanny similarity to the Baltimore Bonaparte, then my half-naked state in a mansion full of strangers who were painting a huge mural of some kind of satyrs and nymphs frolicking around in a great green forest. She brushed the strawberry blond hairs on my chest and touched the exit wound from that double lung shot as she licked her lips like I was the soup de jour, and then she spoke just like the Red Queen spoke to poor Alice.

"We've checked your bank account, Mr. Stewart and you can surely afford this little deal of ours, so listen real carefully—your life depends on your answering yes!" She barked with her bulging eyes gazing at my galley slave body. "For a hundred thousand francs you can marry the girl you have made pregnant and be off for an estate in Russia to live out your days in comfort," she said in Miss Yvette's language of love.

Sweet Jesus, this is Robert Augustus Stewart, I prayed like a priest with a pregnant girlfriend. Could you please come down and help me talk to this crazy French lady! Natasha and I had done some pretty risqué things in our time, but none of them could lead to pregnancy—that I knew of. But at least I knew what the charges against me were, and marriage to Natasha would have been like heaven—whether I'd made her pregnant or not! I was ready to sign on the dotted line, when that pigheaded Princess oinked out the name Anna as my wife to be, and suddenly I knew I was innocent of all charges!

No wonder Anna and Suli the First had gotten slower and slower in those steeplechase races. They'd been off playing hide the kielbasa while we were searching for a place to heavy pet! But once that swarthy little curly-headed Circassian came popping out up in Moscow and my pale skin got accustomed to the lack of sunlight, the girls' father would put two and two together, and both me and Suli the Sire would get our throats slit! I wasn't having any of it, but to soothe the Queen of Hearts (and make a fast escape), I joined in on her sick little plan.

"I do love Anna, Your Majesty!" I said, if only in my dreams. "And yes I'd be happy to pay you a hundred thousand francs for the honor of marrying her. Let me go home and get my best dress uniform and I'll pick up the money when the bank opens tomorrow."

"Oh, no you don't, you'll have to spend the night!" she commanded. "Maybe you could pose for one of my naked satyrs while you're waiting?" She added in a nicer tone.

The satyrs were cavorting on a canvas maybe thirty feet long by twenty feet tall—taking up most of the high-ceilinged drawing room with palm trees and a little tropical meadow full of flowers and all kinds of unsaintly satyr things going on.[100] The artists that were painting this perverted pastoral scene were a real strange bunch! Some of the women were topless, as an artist or two tried to figure out just how to paint those wood nymphs being ravished by a centaur or a satyr—or sometimes one of each (though Lord knows how to tell them apart). I was hoping their priest would show up after Mass that morning to see why these good Catholics were skipping church. But that lusty old Princess definitely wanted poor little Redbeard to join in her sick twisted games! It had little or nothing to do with her cousin's honor—that was perfectly clear. What she wanted was me, and then, in the morning—when she'd used me up, I was to pay her a hundred thousand francs. Talk about getting screwed!

"Thank you kindly, Your Ladyship," I said with the best of manners. "But I've got a very important date, so how about I return in the morning with the money, and you can have your little soiree without me?"

She was taken aback by that, but her big tall butler stepped in. He was a sad-faced fellow and he hollered, "Keep him here, Your Majesty! These Yankees are a shifty lot!"

Here they were fleecing me out of 100,000 francs and farming me out for a night's wild abandon, whilst they called me and my countrymen shifty. These Froggies were even worse than the Sardinians said they were!

"Shifty you say?" I said as I frothed at the mouth. "Why, either you let me go home this very instant, or the whole thing is off! You can have your Cossacks skewer me right here if you like, but I ain't paying you one red dime unless I get to go home and get dressed!"

"Play acting, Your Highness," goes the butler with attitude.

But once Princess Mathilde realized I wasn't up to being the evening's entertainment, she kind of lost interest in me.

"Send two of our Cossack guards back with this little brown man," barked the Red Queen, "and tell them to slit his throat if he tries to escape! We will see you back here by noon tomorrow with the money, monsieur, or I swear I'll have your head for this!"

That bossy butler led me out the back door where he told the two Sulis to escort me home. "When the banks open tomorrow morning, take him there, and then bring him back to the palace tout de suite. And Princess Bonaparte says to slit his throat should he try to escape!"

Circassians were Muslims to the core, so they didn't drink, and they didn't smoke hashish, and ordinarily they didn't even go in for out of wedlock sex. So how was I to distract them long enough to make my exit? Things had definitely taken a turn for the shitter!

"How could you do this to me, Suli? I thought we were friends!" I whispered up there on that pony, being careful that scar faced Suli didn't catch wind of our conversation.

Suli the Sire dropped back a few paces, and then he whispered, "At least the baby will have a horseman father."

"Two horsemen fathers," I whispered in a raspy want to shout voice. "And what will you do when I take Anna to my bed?"

He almost fell off his Steppe pony when he heard that, for he wasn't the fastest of thinkers. "You wouldn't do that to your old friend Suli, would you, Augustus?" he said like we were hitched at the hip.

That crazy Circassian actually thought he could stay around and roger my wife while we raised his love child, and all the while that Romanoff grandfather wouldn't notice how swarthy his grandson was getting. It was bad enough he was going to be my firstborn's biological father, but wanting me to give up the best part of a good marriage, he was flat out crazy! Oh, I knew the whole thing was academic, but I needed to escape these two Sulis if I wanted to live!

Suli the Second was starting to smell a rat—what with all that shushing and whispering going on, and he turned around in the saddle and glared like maybe his Russian was better than Suli the First figured. The Sulis were of the Adyghe tribe from way down in the Caucuses, and they were so far from home that anything their great white masters told them to do was just fine by them. If that pig nosed Princess said slay your red-bearded captive, these Muslim boys would definitely do it!

We rode back through Nice with everyone looking at my half-naked backside bouncing along behind a red clad Cossack. Once we reached the fishing village, the two Circassians took me into Signora's Fungini's house. The dear sweet lady was sitting there at her table chopping an onion for the evening meal.

"Who are your friends, Signor Augustus?" she asked with a smile on her face—nodding to Suli the First like maybe she'd seen him before, or maybe she hadn't. Sardinians were a crafty lot.

"These gentlemen are here to see that I take all my money out of the bank tomorrow and turn it over to this French Princess by the name of Bonaparte," I said.

"Princess Mathilde-Laetitia Wilhelmina Bonaparte?" my little hairy landlady asked.

"That's the one!" I told her, wondering how she knew.

Signora Fungini took a quick cut with her butcher knife that took a chunk out of her table and said in her warmest Sardinian, "Do you want me to cut their throats, Augustus?"

"Not quite yet, my lady," I answered back in her native tongue, praising Sweet Jesus for making me so quick with languages, for the two Sulis had no idea what we said.

Suli the First was leaning against the door with his hand on his pistol—nice and relaxed like, while Suli the badmash had his big curved Cossack sword in his hand and was smiling a sick twisted smile like he'd love to slice me in half.

"Fine, we don't kill them now?" my landlady said with a nod of her head. "But can we put them to sleep, signor?" She was the fastest thinking short squat little hairy Sardinian lady that I'd ever met, and this was just the stuff that my playing it by ear was made of!

"Putting them to sleep would be great, signora," I said like we were talking about the weather. "Yvette and I must be out of here on the morning train or that fat little French lady will have my head!"

"We're having mushroom soup for supper, Signor Stewart," she goes in Italian and Suli the Second raised his head like he'd heard that word before. "You boys head off for the hills above town and pick the plumpest mushrooms you can find," the signora told us, and as it turned out my badmash friend was a mushroom connoisseur.

We came back with a big batch of wild mushrooms and Signora Fungini went through them real carefully—boxing Suli the First's ears for a few bad picks. Then we sat out under the palm trees to relax as the sun went down while she prepared supper. The two Sulis kept their weapons at the ready and neither one of them would take a drink, just as I suspected. At dusk our hostess called us in and after we washed, she ladled out the thick creamy soup and sprinkled some dried mushrooms on top, then gave the first bowl to scar-faced Suleiman—who promptly passed it over to me with a glare. Behind his back, my squat little landlady signaled that it was fine to eat, so I dug right in.

I noticed the next sprinkle of dried mushrooms that came from her hand weren't those white to tan ones—they were a rusty brown, and she did a sly hand swap as she dropped them in Bowl Number Two. Both those boys got the rusty brown mushrooms and dug in like they hadn't eaten in a week. Mine was good, but theirs was better! Maybe fifteen minutes later my two Circassian mess mates started to get real hot and asked politely if they could slip off their cherkeskas. Suli the Second sopped up the last few drops with his homemade Italian bread, while Suli the Sire was grinning like the proud father he'd soon become. They were giggly and looking at their hands like they never had such hands before, and when Suli the First said he couldn't possibly finish his second bowl of soup, I slurped it down before I remembered we had a plan in progress!

In fifteen minutes, my hands were looking real funny too! If you waved them real fast you could see six or seven sets of little tanned fingers

240

sliding by your view. Signora Fungini took one look at me sitting there at her supper table sweating like a whore in church and she boxed my ears and said I was the craziest Yankee she ever met! But those special mushrooms she'd put in our soup had the two Sulis speaking in tongues. Suli the Sire sounded like a mountain stream, while Scar-faced Suli sounded more like a baby wolf. Signora Fungini was looking kind of strange too, as she asked me why I'd eaten Suli the First's soup.

"What was in that soup?" asked badmash Suli like he wanted the recipe.

"Liberty caps,"[101] said the signora in a slow deep vibrato, for we were all about to go down the rabbit hole!

"Come on boys, let's go and see the stars pop out," I said, and when we waddled outside the stars were as big as marbles and brighter than I'd ever seen them before! First one, then twenty, then a sea of fifty thousand popped out, and they weren't silent stars either—they twanged and they bonged as they skidded across the sky. The two Sulis were lying on the sand looking up at the heavens as my escape plan finally came to me! "Signora Fungini, could you please go and ask my fishermen friends to meet me and my buddies down at the docks? We are going for a little row on the deep blue sea!"

Her face looked like it was going to peel off—big smiling lips, hair springing from her nose and chin—a voice that reverberated in a deep solemn bass. "What in the hell are you up to, Augustus?" and if I'd known my name at the time, I might have answered.

Down to the docks we flew and my Sardinian fisherman pals helped us get situated in my little red rowboat. Suli the Sire tried to paddle with his long red lance, while Suli the Second was laying as still as the dead on the rowboat floor staring up at the heavens and praising Allah above. The two cousins didn't even notice the boat that was towing us slowly out to sea as they lay there and gaped. And they didn't notice me going quietly over the side as I swam back in from a quarter mile out. My friends rowed the two Sulis some two miles out to sea where they sat peacefully star gazing until they came to their senses the following evening.

I was about half sober myself when I made it back to shore and Signora Fungini had my things just about packed. Her son had gone and retrieved

Yvette, and she was ready to go. Those mushrooms were so strong that according to my landlady it was a miracle I could stand—much less walk, but she helped me dress in my Union best, watched me clean my LeMat and my Henry Rifle—twice, load up my climbing spikes, and fill my saddle bags with dried sardines and olives, and extra underwear. Then she packed my India rubber coat for the rain, put my important papers away in a waterproof pouch, and even gave me a map of Europe for the long journey I was about to make.

"Where are you going, Signor Augustus?" asked my favorite chef with a sad look on her face.

"Sooner or later, to Hell, Signora Fungini, we all know that," was the words that first came to me. "But for now, I'm heading off to Russia to see an old friend who can help me with this Bonaparte Princess thing."

Ambassador Clay was still in St. Petersburg and I wasn't going to let the Queen of Hearts ruin my reputation in Europe. I'd tell my mentor what she was trying to pull and he'd know exactly what to do. So I cashed out my bank account and by ten on that hot Monday morning—June the 18th, 1866, Yvette and I set out by train for Genoa, Italy. Then it was on to Milan, and finally Vienna—making the entire journey in less than twenty-four hours.

But there in Vienna came the first fly in my ointment, for you see on the very same day that the lusty Princess had called me in to her palace to make me a satyr in that pornographic mural of hers, the Prussians had invaded Bohemia. All the trains to Prague (and then on to Berlin) were stopped by the upcoming hostilities, and no Americans were allowed north of the Austrian capital. I traipsed over to the telegraph office and sent a telegram to the US Ambassador to Russia that went as follows:

Dear Ambassador Clay,

Thought I'd stop by to show you the improvements I've made to your LeMat pistol. Will need a pass to cross the Austrian and Prussian lines! You need anything from down here in Vienna? Yours Truly,

Augustus Stewart

I'd added a bored-through cylinder to the revolver he'd given me and she now took metal cartridges. For three days I waited for an answer, killing time visiting the Royal palaces and government buildings of the Hapsburg princes who'd led the Holy Roman Empire for hundreds of years. They had horse stables there with huge hand carved marble watering troughs with not a straw out of place. The next attraction Vienna held for a boy like me was their schnecken, which were these little walnut encrusted cinnamon buns we called snails back in Baltimore. They were so good I made room in my saddlebags to take several dozen. I also bought extra bullets for the LeMat and the Henry, feed for Yvette, matches to get a fire going, canned Chicago bully beef and vegetables—for war was a bad place to go hungry in!

Vienna's streets were all cobbled and civilized with tall mansions at every turn, but as civilized as the place seemed, the citizens weren't very friendly at all. True my bugler's uniform was a little worse for the wear from riding in that cattle car some seven hundred miles, but when I went up to the Viennese to ask them a question, they'd poke their noses in the air and act like I'd just stepped in horse shit. I'd become pretty good at talking German from my time up in Western Maryland recovering from that double lung shot wound, but when I asked for those delicious snails in the tongue that the three sisters had taught me, the Viennese acted like I was speaking Swahili.

When I was shot and left to die after the battle of Antietam, up came those three lovely sisters![102] Their pig farmer father reluctantly loaded me up in his buckboard and took me home to Hogmaw Hill, where I learned to talk German. At first it was just single words like bosoms, bed bath, and bustier—the latter being the same in French. Then we got into matters a bit more tricky like: "I think three bed baths a day just might kill me!" But the point of my little sojourn down memory lane was that my German was impeccable, and the Austrians knew it. Even the Austrians cocottes were surly, so I took to visiting the Stock Exchange where the only smell they knew was the smell of money. There I bought Prussian stock at pennies on the dollar, for even the Berlin markets thought the Prussians would lose their war with the Austrians. But I figured the Prussian mouse was about to eat the Austrian master and I bet the house on it!

243

Then finally, I received word from St. Petersburg that went as follows:

Augustus,

See the American Ambassador in Vienna for your pass through the lines. If you could please bring me a jar of Limburger cheese, I'd be much obliged. Can't wait to see that old LeMat pistol, and you of course!

Your old friend Cassius Marcellus Clay

The US Embassy in Vienna was another fly in my ointment, as they kept me waiting two days to see the Military Attaché. He turned out to be an old friend of mine from my Civil War days—a man who had once been left with the last horse in General McClellan's remuda. Man Killer was her name, a big mean roan with the bite of a lioness, and although the colonel had distinctly told me to leave him any horse but her, I had left him the mare by sheer accident, I swear it.[103] Well, the colonel hadn't much of an eye for horses and he was mounted and off for the territories before he even got wind of who he was up on. They found him somewhere down along the Long Bridge to Virginia setting on his keister and calling for blood, and not only hadn't he forgotten about the way the mare had tried to kill him, but he also remembered the little red-headed private who went over to the cavalry just before he could have me shot. There I stood, a strong young sergeant major, while he was still the same colonel he'd been at the start of the war, and I think that troubled him more than setting me loose on Bohemia!

"Are you still on active duty, Sergeant Stewart," he barked like he didn't know what a sergeant major's stripes looked like.

Balding with a little pouched belly and the tender white hands of a pronounced paper pusher, the colonel was wearing his blue tunic with two rows of buttons. His Hardee hat was setting on the desk—a big black feather jutting out just like Captain Ridgely wore it. I was standing there with my cavalry kepi in hand, and answered. "No sir, I was honorably discharged right after the Grand Review."

"Then why in the hell are you traipsing around Europe in your Union blues?" he hollered so loud his Marine guard jumped.

244

"General Clay himself told me to come quick and in uniform, sir!" I lied. And I handed the colonel that return telegraph from St. Petersburg that said to bring him his Limburger cheese.

"He wants Limburger cheese?" went His High and Mightiness puffing up his chest like he was a warrior.

"No sir, that's code," I said as I started to have fun with this daft West Pointer who couldn't make general in four long years of war.

"And what is it code for, soldier?" he goes like he sure as hell hated being left out of the loop.

"I'd like to tell you, colonel, I really would. But it's on a need to know basis. Now you can keep me here while the clock is ticking on this Limburger thing, or you can give me my papers and set me free, but that's all I can tell you, sir."

The poor man looked like he wanted to cry, but then he recovered and told me to sit down like we were in the Principal's office. He started reading me the riot act about how once in the Theatre of War I was to conduct myself. "There will be no assisting either side in any military endeavors, sergeant." He said like he'd now forgotten that I was a civilian. "You'll be traveling as what we term a Military Observer and these papers will allow you access to either side, but you travel at your own risk. The United States Government can bear no responsibility for your capture, imprisonment, or loss of life, liberty, or limb, is that perfectly clear?" He pretty much covered all the bases, and if I was going to set out by sunset with General Clay's Limburger cheese in tow, he needed to put a lid on it.

"Thank you, sir, you've been most helpful." I told him. "I'll make sure to give Ambassador Clay your respects." Then I jumped up like he'd told me to (which he hadn't), and made for the door like there was a fire (which there wasn't), mumbling, "Godspeed, Marine, and good luck with that colonel!"

Yvette and I were off for Prague—my plan being to head north through Bohemia faster than the oncoming Prussian Army came south. We'd sneak around their flank and head for Berlin through the Riesengebirge Pass, then on to Russia where General Clay would help me defeat the

245

Red Queen. I didn't want Anna getting into any trouble (Suli the First had already taken care of that), but if I ever married, it would be for love—not because somebody forced me to!

Prague was a disorganized mess when we got there. Troops were being loaded up on railcars like cattle as their officers strutted about like barnyard ganders. There were Austrian Dragoons in long white tunics and sky blue pants wearing tall steel helmets that had no place in modern war, and cuirassiers in their black metal chest plates with shiny steel helmets that would set a sniper's heart to singing. There were Feld-Jagers, which were sharpshooters, in long white tunics and dark blue pants with tall topped kepis—a big brass double headed Hapsburg eagle on the front of each and every one. While other Feld-Jagers were in solid gray uniforms with tall black hats all covered in a great mass of green feathers. There were cavalry uhlans with funny flat-topped leather hats that they called a czapka—long lances in their hands like the Cossacks carried. But mostly what I saw was flocks and flocks of great coated infantry. And under that dark gray coat was an old gray tunic and dark blue pants with worn out boots—no good at all for marching in the mountains. On their heads they wore a tall black shako like the 6th Massachusetts wore at the Battle of Baltimore—only with a green leaf on top that signified they were Austrians—not that their snipers could see that in a woods full of green leaves. The Hapsburg horses might drink out of hand carved watering troughs, but their infantry looked like a band of beggars. Oh, they were proud alright, just like we were proud before the battle of Bull Run, but my last thought before we set out, was that I hoped they brought plenty of shovels with them, because the grave diggers would be having a Field Day out there!

We rode northeast out of Prague up into the mountains with a full moon to guide us through pine forests as thick as I'd ever seen. Steadily we climbed for the pass above Munchengratz, and from time to time there would be Austrian sentries posted on the steep dirt roads. They'd hold their lantern up to my bugler's uniform—whistle at my sergeant major stripes, and ask what a young American like me was doing out in the mountains of Bohemia?

"I'm a military attaché," I'd say and they'd nod and give Yvette a pat on the rump.

But you can't make any time marching on a road full of soldiers. There's artillery that can't cross bridges or climb a muddy hill too fast, infantry that stop to dangle their feet in a fast moving stream, proud officers that refused to step their men off the road, and generally the whole thing is complete and total chaos. We would sometimes take little backroads to bypass a tight bridge or a steep defile, and at the regulation cavalry pace of four miles an hour it was a long trip from Prague to Munchengratz. We finally entered the little medieval town surrounded by tall craggy mountains, and the place looked impregnable. The Austrians had an army of a hundred thousand men waiting to intercept the Prussians right there as they came down from the mountains, so I figured I better keep on moving at the fast trot, if I was to remain a noncombatant.

Up through the strange twisted outcroppings I rode to a little town three miles east of Munchengratz, and just as I thought I was free of the Austrians, there came a strange slapping sound like a battalion of hookers being spanked with wet towels. And that slapping sound was heading straight for me down a dark twisted road, so we galloped down into a little village hell-bent for leather to find a hiding place. The houses of Bosen formed a tall stone wall on both sides of the narrow lane with no place to run and no place to hide, and if that wasn't a company of Austrian uhlans coming our way fast, I was a senator's son!

"This is me, Augustus Stewart!" I prayed to the Great Creator. "Any help you could give me would be greatly appreciated!" And don't ever underestimate the power of prayer!

I didn't have to ride but 50 feet further to find a little cobblestoned lane going up beside an ancient church that sprouted from the hillside. We hunkered down in an old stone-walled graveyard as the uhlans flew by, their wet lance pennants slapping away bringing back fond memories of happier days. So much for breaking free of the Austrian Army, for a storm was coming and the streams were rising, and the Armies of the Hapsburg Emperor were on the move.

247

There were times in war when being attached to an outfit meant you were fed and provided with daily rations (beer, bread, and sausage in the Austrians' case), so we up and joined the Austrian artillery, despite that lecture the colonel had given me. A mounted battery of brown-coated soldiers with dark blue pants, all wrapped in those oversized greatcoats came out of Munchengratz hauling their cannons down the muddy lane. We tagged along as they headed for the high ground at a place called Breda Hill with the steam rising from our horses and the rain pouring down. The lads unlimbered their cannons and started to clear the ground of logs and boulders, as I reported in to their major.

"An American observer and by God a hauptfeldwebel!" says the big blonde curly-bearded man sitting atop a gorgeous white stallion.

What a hauptfeldwebel was, and what a hauptfeldwebel wasn't, I couldn't say at the time, but I stood there in my rain soaked Union blues as he stared at my arm, and soon enough I figured that a hauptfeldwebel must be a sergeant major. He read my pass two or three times, noting my rank and shook his head in amazement.

"You can take your horse down to the south side of the hill and tie her up in the graveyard at the little church of St. Bartholomew, sergeant major," he said politely in English—his blue eyes sparkling. "And you can stay there, or you can come back and join us. My men would like nothing better than to teach a Yankee cavalryman how to shoot their cannon."

When I returned, he looked surprised as he studied the Prussian lines with a long brass telescope. You could see an army of little ants coming down out of the mountains by the thousands. The ants that were moving fastest were undoubtedly mounted, though they were just little black dots across the wide valley. At about three in the afternoon a few batteries of Prussian artillery opened up on us with a whiz and a bang. That curly-headed major looked over at me to see if I'd jump, but I'd been under fire before, and I wasn't about to let the Austrians see me shake. We had twelve guns lined up in our battery just below the crest of Breda Hill. They were mostly rifled eight pounders, and the major ordered his men to open fire on the Prussian infantry when we could see the black on white flag of Prussia with her Eagle flying—his talons unfurled.

248

"How's your eye, sergeant major?" quipped the artillery commander, as he watched the Prussian rounds fly by our heads and impact the hill above us.

"Good enough to see you need to elevate a few degrees if you want to hit anything from here," I said, and he had me calling in rounds.

"Good eye, der Speer,"[104] bellowed the major as he took out a curvy white Meerschaum pipe with a long black stem. He flipped back the pewter top and packed it carefully from his tobacco pouch, then struck a match and blew a perfectly shaped smoke ring within a smoke ring just like our old cook use to do.

There was no danger if your major refused to quake, and when the firing started in earnest and the rounds rained down, the Prussian Krupps began to find their range. One caisson about twenty yards to the starboard went up in a great fiery blast while our blonde haired major puffed away at his pipe. From time to time he would look my way to see if his little Yankee friend would flinch, but flinching wasn't in my nature, for we Stewarts were fighting fools! You could just make out the arms and legs of the Prussian ants as they came on, which meant they were about eight hundred yards off. Luckily our Jagers with their green feathery hats were down in the pine forest below and soon enough their withering fire began to add to our cannon rounds.

A Prussian round came sailing down and buried itself in the mud at my feet with a sizzle! I threw myself behind a little stump and waited for the end to come with no time to trouble Sweet Jesus about it.

"And lucky too!" yelled the major as his big white horse sawed sideways, for that round from a factory I probably owned controlling stock in, failed to go off!

After that very personal attack, I joined in with the Austrian artillery— first by hauling rounds from the caisson to the gun some six yards off, then by taking up a rammer from a fallen comrade and learning a brand new trade. Once the shell went in that big round hole in the front, you rammed her home and stepped back as the gun captain let her rip. Then, as the crew hauled her back into firing position, you used the other end of the rammer—the sponge to soak the tube down so the next round

249

wouldn't go off in the barrel. It was very exciting work, but to save time—when the going got rough (and we were about to be overrun), you skipped the sponging and loaded the next shell as you prayed she didn't go off in your face! We fired round after round like that 'til we were deaf, some with blood dripping from their ears.

The Prussians were beginning to use their needle gun rifles and they poured it on. Men went down all around me with little thunks and loud screams. Then a Prussian artillery round came roaring in and took the two front legs right off the major's white stallion. It set our noble commander down to the muddy ground still smiling, as he picked up his pipe from the mud—wiped it off, and took a long puff. You could hear that sharp crack of the Jaeger's rifles in the pine forest below, and the answering return of those dammed needle-nosed rifles and just as it seemed we would be overrun; the order came to limber up and be off.

The horse handlers came galloping up from the backside of the hill— each team heading for what was left of their caisson, and just like clockwork we limbered up and were gone. Yvette was waiting for me there in that little walled graveyard, her head up—her nostrils flared. She acted as if she didn't recognize the black powder-stained, mud-soaked silhouette of her master as she circled wildly amongst the tombstones while I tried to mount. Three miles back we limped into the little town of Gitschin where we watered the horses and rested on a city street as darkness came on like Death itself. The Prussians were on our tail and a night fight broke out with the fires of Hell surrounding us there. But when we heard that our leader, Clam Gallas had run off and left us without ammunition, we ran too, heading straight for the fortress of Koniggratz down to the south. Some twenty miles we ran through the long cold night as the rain chilled us to the bone, my bugler's uniform hardly discernible from the Austrian artillerymen's brown. But as we slowly slogged up to the city gates, there was that Yankee colonel I'd left in Vienna. He was standing in the torchlight with his Austrian general friends, and didn't he recognize me like a mother recognizes her child!

"Sergeant Stewart, front and center!" he bellowed.

Yvette and I fought our way to his side through the slithering mob. I saluted the perfectly dressed colonel as I stared at the Austrian dandies and wondered which one of those bastards was Clam Gallas?

"Why are you covered in mud, sergeant?" says my old Civil War friend as his Austrian buddies looked on with disgust. "Is that gunpowder that covers your face? Please tell me you haven't been fighting!"

That was the depth of my colonel's worries. And just as I started to cuss him out, up came my artillery major on a borrowed horse. He saluted his grandees in their pure white uniforms, as they sneered down at his mud covered body. Then he said to my colonel, "Dis man vast the best damn cannoneer apprentice that I ever did see!"

The colonel was livid! "I want you cleaned up and at my headquarters in the field at first light on Tuesday morning, Sergeant Stewart," he barked over the sound of the whole Austrian Army slopping their way back into the fortress city. Then he turned to his general friends and said, "The riffraff we let into our American Army!" And they all laughed, though soon all of Europe would be laughing at them.

Our rations that night were cold sausage and a little cold sauerkraut— there was no beer or fresh bread to be had. In my nightmares, Napoleon the First was attacking with his Imperial Guard in long black columns. They went down like bowling pins as we fired our rounds, but more Froggies arrived to replace them. Then with a head the size of a dirigible flying high in the sky, Princess Mathilde showed up calling to her red-panted cuirassiers. "Cut off his balls, boys, cut off his balls!"

When I awoke, I realized those magic mushrooms Signora Fungini had fed us must have messed up my head, for that dream was one of the strangest I ever had. But there was more important things to worry about, for I had to make my escape before the colonel had me passing out watercress sandwiches at his Fourth of July Party. Several bridges cut over the Elbe River inside the walls of Koniggratz and the Austrians had posted guards to pick up any shirkers. At midnight the next day, as the city's clocks chimed and the moon poked out through the thick clouds, Yvette and I set out. I showed the guards my pass from General Clay and they let us by.

We headed north up the river road with a thunder storm guiding us on and travelled more than five miles before Yvette refused to go any further. I dismounted and checked ahead and there were three strands of heavy wire stretched across the road, so I got my wire cutters out and tried to cut them, but they were thicker than telegraph wire and they wouldn't budge. We back tracked to a small bridge over the Elbe— crossed to the western shore and before us was a little railroad station at the end of a long tree lined lane. I could hear the Austrian soldiers talking up there, so I swung wide walking south down the river valley searching for an alternate route. And just as I found a path heading north by northwest through the forest, several shots rang out, and a horse galloped by without his rider.

"Help me! Help me, please!" came a voice in High German maybe a hundred yards to the north.

Doc had trained me to help when I could, so I walked up there real careful like in the darkness. I could hear another man up closer to the little railroad station crying that he was trapped under his horse, followed by some Austrians screaming that they'd caught a Prussian.

"Help me!" goes the closer one, and I was worried he'd bring the Austrians down on us. "Der Hintern! Der Hintern! I'm shot in der Hintern!" he roared loud enough to wake the dead.

I ran up to him, knelt down and touched his backside trying to see where he was hit. He was lying in the wet grass on his stomach all spread out, and in a flash of faraway lightning I could see he was a Prussian officer.

"You keep groaning like that and I'm running off," I warned him in my best Mecklenburg familiar, and lo and behold he spoke the language.

"Don't hurt me," he pleaded and that brought back fond memories!

"I ain't gonna hurt you, captain," I whispered. "But let's stop crawling, so I can see what's what. And captain, we need to be quiet!"

The lad had a butt wound that went in the right cheek and out again, then in the left cheek and out once more, and it was bleeding real bad. My double lung shot wound would get me drinks at any bar in America, but this poor Prussian with his quadruple butt shot wound would be able to drink for free on all seven continents, provided he lived!

"There, there, captain," I said quietly—trying to calm him down, as a cold wind washed across his bare buttocks. He was younger than me and frail by the weight of him as I draped him over my knee.

I asked him his name just to get his thoughts off the pain and he groaned, "Captain Vogel von Falckenstein, nephew of General Ernst Vogel von Falckenstein, don't you know?" Which I didn't, and how the hell would I? But what I did know was this poor boy would probably live if I could stop the bleeding, and he'd most certainly die if I didn't! So I ran back to my saddle bags and started grabbing things I might need.

"You must go back and find my picklehaube," he barked, and I didn't know what a picklehaube was.

"We'll get you another one of them picklehaubes when we get you to safety, Captain Vogel von whatever, now keep quiet or the Austrians will come down here and capture us too!"

"Vat do you mean, capture us too?" he yelled as he flinched when I jammed a clean sock in the first hole I came across.

"That other man up by the train station was singing a song about being from the Prussian 2nd Army as they dug him out from under his horse." I told the young captain as the second sock found its mark with another loud howl that echoed through the darkness.

"You have got to go back up there and kill those Austrians!" he hollered like I was a new recruit.

"Maybe you can't see too well in the dark, or while you're lying on your belly, sir," I broke the news to him gently, as the third sock went in. "But I'm just a bugler and a sworn non-combatant. There will be no murdering of Austrians from me!"

He was silent for a bit, figuring his next move as I rammed sock #4 into position with another unasked for scream. I packed his seat with my folded up last pair of clean underwear, and pulled up his drawers real tight around my handiwork.

253

"Now try and be still while I fetch my horse," I said, and just then the telegraph wire above our heads started to sing!

"Vat's dat?" he bellowed.

"That's the telegraph wire, sir," I whispered. "Now please no more shouting! We're in enemy territory!"

"Cut zee damn ting!" he screamed at the top of his lungs!

I fumbled in my back pocket for those telegraph pliers, shimmied up the rain slick pole, and with a snip and a twang I cut the wire. And didn't that message to Austrian Headquarters go kaput.

"Vell den, don't just stand dere! Pick me up und put me in das saddle," he ordered like the Prussian prince he was.

The lad was definitely use to getting his way, and I realized that if the Austrians hadn't sent riders down to see what all the commotion was about by then, we were probably safe. And since the fates had given me a general's nephew who just might see me through the Prussian lines, I might as well take advantage of the situation. Wasn't that what playing it by ear was all about?

"Now captain, I ain't in your Army!" goes me as I started to bargain.

"I know," says the bright little captain, "you're a lost American!"

Well, I wasn't exactly lost—I had a map, though it was far too dark to see it, and since the Austrians were spread out like fleas on a blanket—that map wasn't much good, but how in the hell had that little Junker[105] made me for a Yankee? I threw him up in the saddle—where he squawked so loud I thought the Austrians would surely open fire.

"Take the end of that wire and twist it around the pole at horse head level," he barked, "then tighten the other end around one of those trees in case the Austrians follow us."

I'd seen that trick done before. You see a horse will drop his head when he's running, and if you set the wire just over where his head should be, you could catch the rider off guard, and well, he wouldn't be riding anymore!

"Quickly now, quickly!" he yelled in his Mecklenburg familiar, and Lord how that brought back fond memories of the three sisters! His voice reverberated across the wet fields and along the river valley.

I could see the light from an open door up there at the train station and heard the sound of riders heading our way fast. We headed off down the lane with the captain crying that his ass hurt, and me crying he was a pain in my ass!

There came a loud twang, then the distinct crash of one of them, followed by the second hitting the ground with a loud thud. Their horses galloped off down the main trail to Koniggratz, so I was still without a mount.

"Go back there and see if they're carrying any messages," says my new leader in crime.

Life was strange, if I'd let that Prussian prince lie there and bleed to death, the two Austrian boys would have still been alive, but there they were staring up at the heavens. I slid the long leather tubes from around their floppy necks and said a little prayer.

"Sweet Jesus, this is Augustus Stewart. I'm sorry for the part I played in these two messengers deaths, may you accept them into Heaven, dear Lord," and I closed their eyes.

Then I led the wounded captain out of there in silence. He must have felt guilty too, for it was the first time he was quiet all night. The moon went back behind the clouds and all went dark as the winds of war began to howl. We headed north across the wet farm fields trying to get past the Austrian Army. You could see their campfires through the mist, as their sentries called out, and the corn fields rattled in the cold wind. I was shivering so loud you could hear my teeth chatter, and my butt shot captain woke with a start and yelled he was freezing. He already had half my clothes and now he had my rain slicker as well. Still the boy whined, so off came my cavalry tunic and up under his derriere that went too. To the south—maybe a quarter mile across that muddy field was the little village of Nedelist with a thousand campfires setting off Will-O-Wisps glowing in the mist. You could see the tall spire of their church and hear the town clock chime out as we went slowly by with that endless digging

255

sound all around us. Another half mile and we heard even more digging at the little town of Chlum.

"Do you hear that?" goes my blue blooded captain as the sound of strange talking filled the air. "That's Hungarian!" he whispered. "They'll get a surprise when the Prussian 2nd Army comes sweeping down out of the mountains. We have to get word to the Crown Prince at once!"

Maybe my patient wasn't such a bad scout after all were my thoughts as we bypassed the little town of Maslowed, for we were coming up on the Austrian flank. It was silent over there—save for a town bell ringing out five in the morning, and we had a quarter mile to go to the top of the hill where a line of huge trees waved in the wind like a medieval fortress.

"Captain Vogel von Falckenstein," I whispered nice and gentle like. "It's time to wake up, sir."

The captain was hugging Yvette's neck for warmth and probably taking the weight off his wound as well, and he whispered, "The general will kill me for being shot in der Hintern!"

"Were you doing your duty when the Austrians shot you?" I asked.

"Yes, we were scouting the Elbe River crossings north of Koniggratz," he told me as we rested by two giant linden trees.

"Then you have no reason to be ashamed," I told him—trying to buck the poor boy up. "Don't you Junkers take pride in all your marshal scars?"

He laughed under his breath as we stood in the lee of those two huge trees, and then he said, "Am I going to die, der Speer?"

We were all going to die sooner or later, but unless I'd missed something, the captain would be around for many a year. And since there was not a person in sight but the two of us, and my young officer needed to raise his morale, I told him a story from my checkered past.

"When the three sisters rescued me from the dying pile after the battle of Antietam, captain, they asked their Papa—the pig farmer, if they could take me home to Hogmaw Hill like I was a little lost sheep. Their father pronounced me mausetot (dead as a mutton chop) from the seat of his buckboard some fifty feet off, yet the girls took me home anyway and

256

worked hard to save me. And as I recovered from my wounds and we started my rehabilitation, he warned his daughters that I was dead to shame—gar kein Schamgefuhl haben, I think were his exact words. And when I failed to heed his warnings to stay away from his daughters, he said I was, "gehirnamputiert sein" which was dead from the neck up, and once again he threatened to make me mausetot. But the moral of the story was it just wasn't my time to die. And it ain't your time to die either, sir. So you've got to buck up! Ain't we in search of the Prussian 2nd Army?"

It was a bad idea to buck up the captain like that, for he bellowed, "Get up that linden tree, sergeant major and see what's what. If we can find the Crown Prince's Army we can attack the Austrians right here!"

I always loved flank attacks. If done right you could roll up an enemy's line like you were opening a can of hermetically sealed oysters. Why, if General Lee had tried to out flank us at Gettysburg like Old Pete[106] had wanted him to, it might have been a real bleak 4th of July back in '63. And if the Prussians had a whole nother army coming down out of the mountains, this would be one hell of a flanking attack. But I was real tired—having slogged six or seven miles in the mud and the rain with just that long underwear top and my cavalry pants to keep me warm. I had some food in my saddle bag, but the captain was sitting on it. Why not dismount—give Yvette a little rest while it was still dark, eat a little breakfast, and catch our wind, if for nothing more than my morale. But my morale wasn't something Captain Vogel von Falkenstein thought about!

"Get up zat tree dis instant, der Speer!" he yelled like I was his lackey.

He was sitting up there on his high horse, well, actually it was my high horse, with my tunic, my newest pair of long underwear, and my freshly cleaned socks all tucked under his butt as he ordered me about. I'd have argued with him, but any delay on my part would have set His Majesty to hollering even louder, and did I mention we were in enemy territory! So I skidded and cursed and got my foot stuck in a little hollow in that big old tree, and there I was five feet in the air. I couldn't see any campfires to the north where the Prussians were coming from, but the captain wasn't satisfied and ordered me to climb even higher. Up I went to maybe ten

257

feet—taking one step forward and two steps back as those muddy boots slid along the wet bark of that giant tree.

I was watching the Austrian campfires down to our south, when my trusty commander yelled, "Zee Norden, you nincompoop! Zee Norden!"

Well, he wasn't calling me a nincompoop when I was patching him up, but there he was sitting on my horse yelling disparaging words at the top of his lungs! I shimmied around to see north and there was not one campfire in sight. Dawn would have just about broken on a regular day, but on this 3rd of July 1866 the darkness refused to leave. I heard a tawny owl hoot in the pine forest nearby as if to say, "There's a crazy American up a tree over there!" Then a hoot came back from the very top of the tree I was climbing in confirming the fact for all the other hoot owls to hear. But try as I may and try as I might, I saw not one Prussian campfire to the north of us!

"Can I come back down now, captain?" I begged with my legs crossed, for I had to take a leak something fierce!

"No, go higher," he yelled in his officer's voice—not caring who the hell heard him or what state my bladder was in!

"They must be up there somewhere—check for campfires," he hollered like I didn't know what a campfire was.

About a foot over my head was a thick limb whose presence I could feel more than see, and by leaping into the air and catching its sides, I could dig my fingernails into the bark just long enough to slide back down. With a little hop and a prayer I'd land from whence I came, making climbing sounds that the captain figured was progress. There was no way I could go any further without breaking my neck, and I'd seen enough of that to last me a lifetime!

"I have to come down and go to the bathroom, Herr Captain!" I begged, but my little friend just wouldn't listen!

"You vill stay up zer till you see zee Prussian campfires!" he barked. "Go higher, der Speer! Go higher!"

I decided to call a mutiny right then and there! I'd drop down on the little bastard's head—bust his neck and drag his body off to the Austrians.

They'd be so busy preparing for the Prussian attack, that I could probably make a run for it. True my stock would be worth next to nothing if the Prussians lost this war, but sometimes you've just got to choose between being alive and being rich. But just before I made the plunge, there came the loud flapping sound of wet pennants slapping against long lances—only I wasn't thinking of cocottes anymore, for there I was ten feet in the air as somebody's cavalry came on at the charge!

"Vat's dat?" hollers my captain real loudly, just to make sure they knew where we were.

I was contemplating whether the fall would kill me, or if it even mattered anymore, since out of uniform and with a Prussian captain by my side, I'd surely be shot as a spy! The rush of a hundred lancers shook the ground so hard that the rain on the wide green leaves sprang off and soaked me. And in my panic, I hollered, "Nun ist es aus! (It's all over now)," which was what Helga had hollered when her father rushed the barn. But didn't my little butt shot buddy think I'd yelled, Raus, which meant get out and get out now! Which he sure as hell did—with my horse, my weapons, and the last of my schnecken!

"We'll be back for you, der Speer—stay put and you'll do fine," he yelled as he rode north like a bat out of hell.

The Austrian lancers came on in a rush and skidded to a halt right under my tree. Their lance tips were dancing around right there by my privates as one of them hollered, "I heard someone gallop off to the north, should we chase them, major?"

"No, let them go!" their leader said, as he wiped his monocle with a nice clean handkerchief and stared up at me in the half-light of morning.

I stopped breathing and became one with the tree, and he put his head back down and pointed to the west and yelled, "We'll scout out towards the Swiepwald," which was a forested hill about a mile to the west.

As they rode off, I prepared to climb down and take a long awaited leak, but to paraphrase that Scottish poet, the best laid plans of mice and men do often go astray—and I mean often when I'm involved!

Before I could take one step closer to old Mother Earth there came the jingle of a thousand canteens rattling against soggy men, and bayonet scabbards banging, and feet slogging through the mud right across the wind chopped corn field as thousands and thousands of Austrian soldiers came marching by. For over an hour two Austrian Corps came on and the only thing that kept me smiling was the white tunics and sky blue pants some of them wore, for wasn't I dressed in the very same fashion—just in case they looked up at me! True the stripe down the side of my sky blue cavalry pants was yellow and theirs was red, but who the hell would notice in the middle of battle? And just as I got up the nerve to stand and take a well-deserved leak, don't a battery of Austrian artillery come right up under my perch and start to unlimber. They were all business as they prepared to open fire in support of their advancing infantry, and I figured it was now or never for me to stand and relieve myself, for who would hear me peeing with all that artillery going off?

"Sweet Jesus, this is Augustus Stewart, kind sir!" I prayed as I slowly stood on creaky knees and prepared to open fire. My plan was to just let out a little trickle. It would run down the tree to Lord knows where and no one would be the wiser. But once more those words from Mr. Burns came back to haunt me, for my bladder opened fire like Mount Vesuvius! It ricocheted off the tree and hit a brown clad artilleryman right between the eyes as he sighted his cannon.

"Vas is das?" he said as he looked up at me and my little friend trying to look innocent.

"Guten Morgen," goes me with a sheepish grin and a flow that just wouldn't quit, for there I was stuck up a tree in Bohemia peeing like a horse!

"Keep your piss to yourself, scout," he hollered up at me. "We are trying to work down here!"

The blast of their cannons lifted me right out of my perch, and from about eight in the morning till half past eleven, I hung there like a butterfly in high winds. I had rounds coming in from the east and rounds from the west, southern rounds flying north that looked like telegraph poles, and rounds coming south straight for my head. I prayed to Sweet

Jesus like I never prayed before and finally the Austrian infantry began to pull back. But as the Prussian Army began to stream down from the mountains, the firing grew stronger and the rounds came so near my perch that they raised the hair on my neck as they shrieked by.

I began to pray even more prodigiously! Two hundred cannons firing at once sets off such a din that even though I was screaming to Sweet Jesus for His Divine Intervention, I couldn't hear myself scream. That crescendo of cannon fire from the Prussian 2nd Army was the hardest to take as they sighted in on my little linden tree.[107] The rounds roared by and the ground shook, while down below the brown clad artillerymen manned their cannons.

The Austrians must have realized that they were being outflanked[108] for their army finally came streaming back from that hill above me with what was left of the two Corps running for home. They headed down into the little town of Chlum and the last ones to limber up and ride off were my artillery buddies. And as God is my witness, not one man or horse from that Battery had been killed or wounded in the fight, and I like to think it was my prayers that saved us! Even the leaves of those two giant trees were untouched, and as I finally climbed down, a little gray Bohemian wax wing with his tufted head and stripes of red, white, and yellow was busy eating the little brown berries as he chirped away.

Up came a squadron of blue clad Prussian lancers and I slid down and landed on shaky knees whilst a bunch of their infantry started to rough me up. A staff officer came up on a big gray mare and bellowed to his men to leave me alone. "Are you the little American who brought us in on the flank of the Austrian Army?" he yelled in English.

I was in a state of shock, my long underwear top soaked to the bone, my pants and boots scraped brown like the bark of that tree, but I nodded my head at anything he said—as long as he wasn't shooting at me!

"Captain Vogel von Falckenstein is in the field hospital and he asked me to see to your safety, der Speer," said the monocled major. "The Crown Prince would love to meet you, once you are ready to ride."

"I was born ready to ride!" I answered with a sheepish grin.

He signaled one of his men to give me his horse and off we flew to meet Crown Prince Friedrich Wilhelm. He was up at the outskirts of Horenowe studying the Austrian lines, and around him was a gaggle of Prussian uhlans looking at me like I was the strangest little sergeant major they'd ever seen. The major and I just galloped right up past the prince's cavalry escort and sawed to a stop in front of the next King of Prussia.[109] The Crown Prince was a tall fine looking young man with reddish brown hair, and two great mutton-chop sideburns coming down his regal face. He wore the blue field tunic of a cavalry officer, with wide red cuffs, and a high white and blue striped collar, a proud chest full of medals. To say he was the most magnificent warrior I'd ever seen would have been to cut him short, and there he sat atop a fine black stallion that his Mother-In-Law, Queen Victoria had given him.

"Captain Vogel von Falckenstein told us of his harrowing escape from the enemy, and how you sacrificed your own safety to send him off for our Army, der Speer." His Majesty said as I bowed low in the saddle.

His entourage looked on in amazement as the Crown Prince conversed with a rain soaked little beggar in a dirty filthy long underwear top—all covered in giant linden leaves. I was still in shock, but it seemed, somehow, I'd become a hero to these Prussians!

"Captain Vogel von Falckenstein told me how you cut the telegraph wire to Koniggratz, killed the messengers,[110] and sent him off on your mount to find us, der Speer. We owe you our deepest gratitude. Now what would you do, if you commanded my Army?" His Majesty asked with a twinkle in his royal blue eyes.

"Well, how many men do you command, Sire?" was my first question to His Royal Highness.

And when he said one hundred thousand, I whistled and gave him a big Stewart grin. "If I had a hundred thousand men right here and right now, Sire, I'd go down there and kick some Austrian ass!"

And we did too![111]

All because Suli the First couldn't control his libido!

Chapter Nine

The Welcoming Committee

The Seven Weeks War was what the world called this campaign, and my friend, Fritz was everybody's hero! And when the war was over, the Prussians invited me to stay on, but first, I went to Russia to see my old friend Cassius Clay about that Bonaparte problem. He was busy chasing ballerinas, fighting duels with his Bowie knife, and befriending the great Tsar-Liberator, Alexander II—Emperor of Russia, Finland, and Poland. General Clay promised to help me defeat the Red Queen, and I returned to Prussia to start my new job.

General Moltke believed in doing your homework before you made war, so he sent me to France disguised as a rich American where I traded in horse flesh and steeplechased my way across their beautiful country. If my Prussian handler needed me to check the fortifications around the fortress of Sedan, I'd head there and sketch them out, and if they needed someone to find out about the brand new Mitrailleuse machine gun that was so secret the French forgot to train their men in its use, I'd play cards with the Armaments Commissioner and wouldn't he let me fire it. I even found time to go back to Port du Cros to pick up my sea chest and see Signora Fungini and my Sardinian friends. Yvette and I climbed back up du Mont Boron hill and went to see Princess Mathilde too, and not only was she very civil to me, but she sold me a fine horse at a fair price, and never once did she ask me to pose for her pornographic murals.

Four years of peace was good for my soul, but when Napoleon III declared war on my Prussian masters, I went back to the Army for the nine months it took us to pound them into dust. But when the peace was signed and the new nation of Germany was born right there at Versailles Palace, my job was over.

The Germans were working up a treaty with the Russians called the Treaty of the Three Emperors (Austria being the third man in), and they promised me a full blown major's rank in the Russian Army, if I'd go up there and help the Ruskis get their Telegraph Service in order. The train left the Berlin station with smoke belching from her stack as we chugged east into Poland. My Momma had said I was born for trouble, and I was in Dutch with the Russians before we even hit their border.

I was studying their strange language as a warm summer breeze blew in through the window, and the sway of that train and the swirls of those letters lulled me to sleep. There was Natasha and Anna in their white peasant blouses all sprinkled in the ice cold waters of the Mediterranean. Then the train would hit a bump and there would be that book of Russian staring at me like an open grave. I learned Polish pretty easily while working the night shift as a trainee with the U.S. Telegraph Service back in our Civil War. It was a boring job for a boy like me, but Mike's friend, Kowalski taught me his mother tongue as we waited for the messages to come in. We'd sit there and talk about Poland for hours, how her maidens were the fairest, her horses the swiftest, and her wodka (as Kowalski pronounced it) the smoothest in all of Europe. Because of that, my Polish was passable, but this Russian was killing me fast! Oh I could speak and understand it a little thanks to the Romanoff sisters, but that strange alphabet made for some major problems.

Sitting across from me on those high leather seats was a fat little Polish priest. He would watch my lips move to the tune of the Russian, and every time I looked up he'd shift his questioning eyes away. Down would go my face into that boring book and as I brought my eyeballs back up again, he'd be staring at me—like he didn't see me catching him, then he'd look out the window and pretend he was praying.

Kowalski hadn't taught me the kind of Polish I could talk with a priest, but finally the jolly little Father let out a laugh and said in his finest broken English, "Dat dam Ruski is a rough dam language to learn, tak!"

"Tak," goes me, which was yes in Polish. "Prawdziwe cholernie ciezko," which was: real damn hard, and he laughed.

"You spik Polish real goot," he said with a spark to his eyes, "amerykański?"

"Tak, jestem Amerykaninem," I told him proudly, showing off my cavalry uniform with those bright yellow sergeant major stripes, for the rule in Russia was if you were in the military, you wore your uniform at all times. And since I hadn't bought my Russian uniforms yet, my good old Yankee uniform would have to do. Once the Father knew I spoke his language he babbled on so fast that all I heard was something about a wagon and some food.

Just like me, that fat little priest loved to eat, so we headed to the Dining Car. Except for the two Russian officers sitting there smoking their cigarettes with long ivory holders, we were the only ones in there for it was a tad too late for breakfast, and a tad too early for lunch. The tables had clean white linen and shiny silverware—crystal water glasses that bobbed up and down, and fancy folded up napkins standing as tall as the Pope's hat—all jiggling away with the sway of that train.

"Vee vould like a table for two, preferably by a vindow," the priest joked, for they were all by windows in that long plush car.

The two Russian officers, I believe they were captains by the pogoni on their shoulders, were staring at my sergeant's major stripes on a bugler's uniform like what the hell is that? The taller of the two spat out, "Amerikanskiy" and something about not having a cattle car, and I realized that being a Russian major would be a very strange feat.

"Don't try and spik Polish right now, amerykański," the priest whispered. "No Polish is allowed by order of the Tsar!"[112]

That seemed like a pretty harsh rule (considering we were in Poland and all), but since technically I was an employee of the Emperor of Russia, I dropped the subject and spoke only English and Mecklenburg familiar.

We ate Zupa grzybowa, which was a wonderful mushroom soup that was almost as good as Signora Fungini's only we didn't get to hallucinate, then we ate Baranina—a grilled mutton the Poles really loved, then Klopsiki, which were meatballs in a tasty tomato sauce, with a side order of Kapusta kiszona—just like the German sauerkraut we ate up on Hogmaw Hill. Followed by gallons and gallons of fine Polish beer, so I slept most of the way in.

As we came into the Warsaw Station—full of fancy carved wood and stain glass, my priest friend woke me up and reminded me not to speak Polish. We hugged and said goodbye as he headed off for his Parish while I looked around for someone to move my sea chest. All around me was a great sea of people going this way and that as they caught trains on several lines. There were dozens of Russian soldiers in their baggy forest green uniforms with big frowns on their faces and short little black whips in their hands. The porter followed me down the train platform with a little open wheel barrow—my sea chest aboard, while I carried my new Winchester Repeating Rifle in a brown leather scabbard that Mike Kelley had sent me. We were just passing a third class car where an old widow in threadbare black got her chicken cage stuck in the train door as she came out. The more she pulled at it, the tighter it was trapped, and the old woman was starting to use every cuss word Kowalski had taught me, as two Russian soldiers circled her like buzzards. If that had been my Grandmother standing there with her chickens stuck, I'd have wanted someone to help her, which I did, of course. I freed the wooden crate full of chickens and placed them down on the platform real gently, and then I gave her my hand and said softly, "Pomoge Ci babcie." Which was let me help you grandma in Polish.

Those kind words in her mother tongue had just left my lips when a big giant of a Russian corporal took a whack at my cheek with his thick black whip and commenced to yelling, "Brak polskiego w Polsce," which was No Polish in Poland! And I'll be damned if he wasn't yelling it at me in good God Almighty, Polish! There must have been a chunk of lead inside that whip for it sliced me clean down to the bone. He hauled back to let me have it again, and I put my LeMat up his nose!

"What in the hell are you doing?" I yelled in the German the three sisters had taught me.

The big brute apparently didn't speak any Mecklenburg familiar, but the universal language of having a pistol rammed up his nose brought him to a halt. His three green clad friends converged on me with their whips held high, while they watched their corporal for orders.

"Keep them hands to yourself," I warned them in what little Russian Natasha had taught me. "I'm Major Stewart of the Emperor's Own Imperial Guard!"

I figured if Napoleon Bonaparte had himself an Imperial Guard, then the Tsar of Russia must have had one too. Their officer came running up with his ancient single shot pistol waving in my face. He was a skinny thing—the skinniest Russian I'd ever seen. My guess was he'd failed miserably at some desk job up in St. Petersburg and they sent him out in the field to get rid of him. He trembled and said, "Did you say you were from the Tsar's Imperial Guard?"

"Da," I said. "I'm Major Augustus Stewart, coming in from Berlin on special orders from the Crown Prince of Germany."

All the while the big giant with my LeMat stuck up his nose was being as still as possible—his eyes crossed, and taking shallow breaths. His three privates stared intently at him like what should we do? I thought of trading him off for that scrawny lieutenant, but I could tell I'd have gotten the worst of the deal, for not one of those lads looked to their officer for anything.

"Reach in my back pocket and take out my orders," I told the scrawny lieutenant. "You'll see my story is true," which mostly it was—save for that part about the Imperial Guard.

He lowered his pistol and carefully lifted my orders, unfolded them like he was the consummate paper pusher I thought he was, and read slowly that sure enough I was an officer in the Emperor's Own Army—and wasn't it signed by the Russian Minister of War himself. He looked real close at the cut on my face—and face cuts bleed real freely, and he said in the poorest excuse for German I have ever heard (and believe me that pig farmer up on Hogmaw Hill was no scholar), "I'm terribly sorry about this misunderstanding, maior!" The next thing he did surprised me even more, for he took that weighted whip from the train station floor and don't he strike my prisoner right up side his head (just about exactly where the big man had struck me).

"Do you know what you've gone and done?" he bellowed to the giant with the now quite bloody nose that my LeMat was still just barely up.

My prisoner stood there all confused as the blood flowed—great globs dropping to the train station floor. That pistol had been just about torn from his nose and he bled like a stuck pig, but he remained silent.

"You've gone and struck an officer of the Tsar's Imperial Guard, you imbecile!" bellows his lieutenant as he winds back for a second crack. "You know what the punishment for striking an officer is, don't you?"

Having served in the armies of the world, I figured he meant death—probably by a slow hanging! But in Goliath's defense, how the hell was he to know I was an officer when I was dressed like a Yankee bugler? Blood streamed down the poor moujik's face, as the lieutenant switched from the bad German he was yelling for my sake to the Russian that sounded ten times worse. He would lecture the big bleeding giant as he swung that whip like a drunken coachman, then look to me for approval (which he wasn't getting) and go right back to thrashing the man. Oh I'd seen beatings like that on the streets of Baltimore when an unruly slave stepped out of line and looked a white man in the eye, but never had I ever seen an officer lay a hand on an enlisted man like that—that was what God made sergeants for!

"This man will never strike another officer," goes the emaciated lieutenant, and if he'd kept that up, I'm sure he'd have killed the man.

But enough was enough, so I grabbed the whip out of the unfit to lead officer's hand and stuck my pistol in his face to see how he liked it. "Stand down this instant or I'll let her rip!" I barked as I cocked her back. My first command ever given in the Russian Army, and it was given in; you guessed it, my best Kowalski Polish!

He stared at me with fear in his eyes and thunk went that whip to the floor. Strange how silent and deserted the place was, the four enlisted men quietly wondering where this would lead, their lieutenant gone crossed eyed staring at the barrel of my pistol, and me wishing I could go home and face the Knights of the Golden Circle and their little baby, the Ku Klux Klan, for they'd be easier to deal with than these crazy Russians!

"You aren't a German, are you, Herr Maior?" the frightened lieutenant asked—his eyes bulging as he stared down the barrel of my Grapeshot pistol.

"No, I'm a Yankee, born and raised," I said with a sinister smile, as I lowered my weapon. "I've got to catch the next train into St. Petersburg. Where would that be loading?"

"The train for the capital doesn't leave for two hours, Herr Maior," says the bug-eyed lieutenant with a quivering voice.

268

"Would you care to join me at the Russian Tea Room for some refreshments while you wait, Herr Maior."

So off we went while that pistol whipped corporal was told to stand guard over my things. First, we stopped at the Doctor's office and I went straight to the head of the line, and when the Doc was all done sewing me up, my scrawny little lieutenant friend told him to send the bill to Military Headquarters and chuckled like it would be a cold day in hell before he ever got paid. Then off we went for tea, only The Russian Tea Room didn't have much tea to sell. Mostly they just had rows and rows of big bottles of vodka. They had birch bud vodka, blackberry vodka, peach and pear vodkas, cherry vodka, blueberry vodka, and even a fairly nice tasting black bread beer. The place was full of boisterous Russian officers who seemed very impressed when the lieutenant told them I was on my way to St. Petersburg to join the Tsar's Imperial Guard. They'd never heard of a foreigner being admitted to the Guard before and I was a little worried, but when they found out Cassius Marcellus Clay was my mentor, they all shook their heads in wonder. They even asked me if I got that Bowie knife from the mighty Marcellus, for he was known to be handy with the Arkansas pig sticker.[113]

"No, this particular Bowie knife," I told them as I passed it around, was a gift from Captain Ridgely of Towsontown, Maryland. My first military commander when I was but a boy of fifteen.

"Fifteen!" they all whistled! "You were fighting at fifteen?"

"Yes, sir, and I took my first wound within weeks," I proudly said, showing them that pig iron scar above my eye. And once they saw my double lung shot wounds, it was free drinks for Old Redbeard for the rest of the night! I drank like a dog of war and was accepted by my Russian comrades—save for a sullen colonel who sat in the corner. He seemed to take quite an exception to my trumpeter's uniform, my sergeant major's stripes, my dusty cavalry boots, my country of origin, my long unkempt red hair and beard, and even my Bowie knife seemed to upset him.

"Vat ist your specialty, maior," he asked with downcast eyes while the rest of us were enjoying a nice game of Mumblety-peg.

"Military intelligence, Herr Colonel," I said. "Specializing in the use of the telegraph and a fast horse to keep the army advised of their enemies' strengths and positions."

The rest of my drinking buddies seemed interested so I expounded. "You know that saying homo homini lupus, don't you colonel?" It was obvious he didn't, though some of them did. "Well we're the eyes and the ears of the wolf. We'll intercept your enemy's messages and ride for Headquarters like a fiend from Hell, then it's up to you fighting boys— the teeth of the wolf, to do what you do best!"

"So you're a scout?" he cried with a look of disgust on his puffy red face. "I've never heard of using foreign scouts before!"

Well, he probably never heard of ciphering his telegraph messages either, and that was the whole reason they sent me to Russia.[114]

It started to pour outside and I thought of my things sitting out there getting soaked, and the poor corporal with his face split open, so I said to the pasty lieutenant, "Well it's time for me to leave, old salt, I'm pretty sure I can find my way back to the train station alone."

"Oh, you don't want to go out there on the streets of Warsaw alone," he said. "The Poles will catch you and string you up like a ham!" I wanted to say I felt safer with the Poles than with that bloody colonel in the corner, but in some circles that might seem rude.

"I'll see myself out, fellas," I told them unapologetically. "Me, my pistol, and this Bowie knife make a threesome no Pole will ever harm!" They all laughed and I left with a good buzz on.

Warsaw was a cold and rainy place; you could almost feel their loss of liberty—their sadness, their grief! The Russians had them on a 10:00 PM curfew and there wasn't a soul on the streets as I weaved my way back to the train station. My pockets were full of food I'd filched for my bloodied corporal, who while I was ensconced in those drinking games, was bequeathed to me by his worthless lieutenant.

"Go ahead and take the big son of a bitch!" he said in his drunken stupor, "It will save me the paper work of having him hanged."

"Give me that in writing!" I barked—almost scaring myself with the force of my voice, for that black bread beer was mighty powerful.

"What in writing, Herr Maior?" he asked incredulously.

"Write out the corporal's orders saying he's to be assigned to me and sign them," I ordered. "I'll not have the poor lad shot for desertion on top of all the rest of his problems."

He left the spot for his trooper's name blank because he had no idea what the poor man's name was, and I put the deed to the unknown corporal in my back pocket. As far as I could figure, the big brute belonged to me until death do us part.

He was lying there sleeping in the lee of my sea chest clutching my Winchester as the rains came down. I could see the dried blood on his face starting to rinse off as he snored. Now, how do you wake a soldier who's twice your size, and might have a hair trigger to boot? You don't kick him, that would surely get your leg broke off! You don't shake him—who knew what that would do? And you sure as hell don't blow reveille on a trumpet—even if I had a trumpet to blow! The only thing I figured would keep him from killing me was my trusty harmonica at ten paces off, so I played Swing Low Sweat Chariot as I got ready to run.

One eye popped open and he looked at me like I was a bad dream. "Corporal," I said in Kowalski's mother tongue. "Time to wake up, son. Would you like to go and see the doctor?" But the man declined.

I guess you could say I was a bit nervous, him being my first enlisted man I ever addressed as an officer, but how was I to break the news that his trusty lieutenant had gifted him to me? "Let's get you and my things in out of the rain, corporal—what did you say your name was?" Was my sly way of getting his name.

"Yakovich," he said. "Yakoff Yakovich," and he dropped those soft brown eyes down low like he wasn't supposed to look me in the eye.

"Well, I'm mighty sorry I stuck my pistol up your nose!" I said with great regret as I gave him a hand to rise. "Your lieutenant, I forgot his name (just as he'd forgotten Yakoff's), wanted to hang you for hitting an officer, but I told him hell no!" Then I broke the news of his change in

271

command as gently as I could in the Polish we both spoke. He nodded his head like that was fine by him.

"You get that end of my sea chest, Corporal Yakovich, and I'll get this end. Now let's get in the station and get something to eat." I said, hoping he'd see I wanted to be the kind of officer that worked with his men—not the kind that beat them.

Oh, I'd seen plenty of popinjays in my time—they'd stand back and let the enlisted men die by the droves, and when the shooting was over, they'd step out of the ranks in a nice clean uniform and let the world see what a hero they were. But that wasn't the kind of officer I planned to be—no I was trained by Doc and Chester to do a fair days' work for a fair days' pay—just like the enlisted men. We carried the sea chest inside, laid her down on the floor of that great cavern and started wiping the rain off, as the citizens of Poland looked on in fear. But Corporal Yakoff Yakovich didn't have his little black whip anymore, and he took off his soggy green fatigue cap and hung his head low. We sat there in silence eating the food I'd lifted—my Polish nearly exhausted and neither one of us wanting to talk Russian. And when we finally boarded the train, we stayed silent for six hundred and fifty miles.

My first site of St. Petersburg on that mid-May day was of a great city full of horses—more horses than even Baltimore had, horses with bells ringing and pictures of Saints hanging from their backs, horses taller and stronger than I'd ever seen before, with fine leather saddles, shiny silver buckles, and polished black bridles, horses at the walk, at the trot, at the canter, and even at the gallop—all going this way and that on the wide city streets. There were great mansions and palaces of every color of the rainbow with onion shaped gold spired churches that took your breath away. Some said the Emperor had contributed the gold for the church domes from the sale of Alaska in penance for keeping two wives,[115] but I learned fast that what you heard on the streets of Piter was better left unsaid!

Corporal Yakovich and I checked into the Taleon Hotel on the busy Nevsky Prospect, cleaned up a bit, ate lunch, and walked all about that bustling city full of sparkling canals and gorgeous women—no wonder they called her the Venice of the North. The Russian people must have been mighty religious for they had twice as many churches as we did back home, and whereas in Baltimore our tallest building was the B&O's Camden Street Station, St. Petersburg's tallest structure was the Peter and Paul Cathedral. Yakoff and I rested under the trees there by the Neva River as the sea gulls sang and the six foot six man of steel started to talk.

"Are you a religious man, Herr Maior?" he asked as we stretched out on the grass and enjoyed the spring sun.

"Only under fire," I said, glad that finally I had someone to talk with. "What about you Yakoff Yakovich—are you religious?"

"Not since I was a child of six, sir," he said with a tiny little tear in his eye. We lay there in that warm sun and watched the puffy white clouds go by as he told me something he'd probably told no one in all his life.

"When I was six, they put me on a train bound for Russia with all the other Polish orphans. I prayed to the Lord that a nice gentle family would adopt me," he said with a lonely sigh. "Being big for my age, I got as far as Minsk when a farmer hauled me down off the train and said I was to be his serf for the rest of my life! Seven days a week he worked me in the fields like an ox, and when he got drunk, which was often, he whipped me—till at the age of fourteen, I'd had enough."

"Good for you!" goes me thinking of little Henry and his escape from the Ridgely plantation. "What did you do then?" I asked my comrade.

"Someone stuck a scythe through the man's heart and we all ran!" he told me, and we lay there in a long silence and breathed in the fresh air of freedom as we soaked up the sun.

"They told me at the Orphanage that my father had been an officer of the Emperor, so I figured I would go and join the Russian Army," Yakoff added. "But not once since then have I prayed to the Lord."

"Have you ever been under fire, Corporal Yakovich?" I asked, for that always caused me to talk with the Lord quite profusely!

"Only a few shots here and there with the Polish guerrillas, but they were as bad a shots as we were," he told me and we laughed.

273

We got up and headed on to see the burial place of the Tsar's. They had Peter the Great buried in there, Elizabeth, his daughter, Tsar Peter III, whose wife Catherine the Great had him murdered by her lovers, and Paul, their son, who wound up being dragged out from under his bed and strangled in his night clothes. Oh, they had some nice tombs[116] but notice we ain't talking about too many of them having died of old age! Politics were real rough in Russia and that fact wasn't lost on me.

We returned to our hotel in a quite subdued mood. There's something about seeing two hundred years of leadership all lying there dead in one big room that humbles a man. Yakoff and I didn't have three words to say that evening, save for his warning that come morning, we were reporting in to Military Headquarters. That night I slept in fits and starts. I'd start to sleep and have a fit thinking someone was trying to drag me out from under my bed to strangle me like that poor Tsar Paul. I awoke in a sweat and there was Yakoff over by the door sleeping on the floor like a Great Dane puppy. He must have been having dreams of his mortality too, for he was twitching and flopping his feet like he was in a foot race with the Devil. A word to the wise, don't ever visit dead people's graves right before you sleep! And just as the morning birds started to sing, and the sky lightened in the east, and I figured all the ghosts of St. Petersburg were gone, I fell soundly to sleep. There I was on the French Riviera under a palm tree in the sun with Natasha undressed and about to mount me, as the sea gulls screamed, and the blue sky sparkled, when all of a sudden Yakoff was shaking me awake!

"Time to report in, Herr Maior!" he hollered. "Regulations say you must check in within twenty-four hours of arriving at your Duty Station."

Yakoff passed me my long underwear, my suspenders, threw my cavalry pants on me like I was an invalid, and jammed those riding boots on my feet so hard he nearly broke my toes! Then he threw my trumpeter's tunic on me, and I was surprised. The big giant had spent the last half hour making it presentable—all that yellow braid shining in the morning sun. He'd even sewn major's pogoni on my shell jacket's shoulders. Where he got them from? I don't know, but I was now a major sergeant major—and a cavalry trumpeter to boot!

"Thank you, Sergeant Yakovich," I said to my trusty batman with a field promotion that made him smile.

"Oh, you know I'm just a corporal," he goes and I noticed his uniform was squared away, his hair was combed, he was shaved, and he looked damn presentable—despite his fresh facial wound.

If he ever showed back up on the Army pay roll, I'd be surprised! When I was recovering from my double lung shot wound, the Army of the Potomac listed me as Killed In Action. And when I returned three months later to try and convince them that I was still very much alive, they said, well, if I hadn't died at the Battle of Antietam like their paperwork said I had, I must have deserted, and they refused to fix it. I had to sign back up under an assumed name—that's how easy it was to fix red tape in America, and from what I'd seen, these Russians were at least as inept as we were. So I'd be making Yakoff's pay from there on out, or I wasn't a major sergeant major!

"Enough talk, maior," goes my big buddy who dragged me down the stairs to a waiting carriage. "Military Headquarters!" he bellowed to the driver. "And make it fast!"

Now a St. Petersburg izvozchiki, which was what they called their carriage drivers, were a real wild crowd. The fatter they were, the more they charged, and that izvozchiki must have been the most expensive coachmen in the whole city. He wore a bright red shirt, wide blue and white striped pants, with a sparkling silver belt around his ample middle, a long white beard like Santa Clause wore, and rosy little cheeks to match. On his feet were those black felt boots that all the moujiks loved to wear, and with the crack of his long black whip we were off!

I'd never ridden in a troika before—three great dapple grays, the center one with that tall wooden frame they called a duga over his head, the two outside horses running wild and free. Oh, they were harnessed alright, but it was a loose affair which allowed them to run like the wind. It seemed pretty flimsy to me, but the coachman controlled his charging steeds with ease—weaving in and out of traffic like a man possessed.

I settled back and enjoyed the ride while Yakoff chewed his nails.

"You are Amerikanskiy, da?" the izvozchiki roared over the rush of his horses, and I smiled and said my first Russian words ever said in Russia proper which was, "Da!" meaning yes.

I was as proud of that da as I'd been when I first penned a French poem to Miss Yvette! I had a good ear for language, and soon I'd be spouting Russian like I spouted the language of love. But Corporal Yakovich broke into my little chat and hollered something to the jolly coachman that caused him to crack his whip even harder as he bellowed to the troika to pour it on! We were weaving in and out of traffic like we were on fire, hooves clacking—nearly side-swiping a turnip cart, and arrived in front of the Russian General Staff Building just as the bugle blew.

I was panting almost as hard as the corporal was when we entered that long shiny hall. The place was packed to the gills with all kinds of Russian officers in wild Napoleonic uniforms. There were hussars with tunics that were louder than mine and uhlan cavalrymen in dark green and red trimmed with miles and miles of gold braid, fancy bear skin hats, and brass helmets with double-headed eagles aboard, swords as big as a tree. I figured I'd just show them my papers and that would be that, but no—those Russians didn't work that way. They formed us up in great long lines, then about as fast as a glacier melts they'd call one man at a time to a tall little table where a surly bureaucrat in a vested black suit sat at a high stool stamping out orders as slow as a snail. Just about everyone got sent back to a different line once we got to the high table, because we (like a dunce), had failed to have all our ducks in a row. I was there all morning and didn't see one soldier go through the series of closed doors behind the paper pushers—one door for each red ribboned line we stood in. My big burly batman came back from trying to sign in (to no avail) about an hour later and brought me two hard boiled eggs (pealed) and a big long chunk of black bread, which I devoured before my disgusted officer friends. I'd seen General Grant eat his meal that way, a dusty old man on a dusty old horse gnawing at a stale piece of bread, but these Russians weren't buying it.

By noon, I'd waited my way to the high table with the man in the black suit, but when he looked at my papers his little rubber stamp was nowhere in sight. "You are a foreign national and foreign nationals have

276

to be cleared by the Foreign Office before they can be in this line!" he bellowed. "You must go now, and don't come back 'til you've been to the Foreign Office."

After lunch with some cognac to stiffen our resolve, we found the Foreign Office down by the Winter Palace, and after two hours in that line, I passed the door that was marked Ninth Undersecretary of the Foreign Office. They told me to have a seat 'til Old Number Nine came back from his lunch, and since there was no one around to tell me otherwise, I did what any Baltimore boy would do on such a fine spring day, and I pried his window open for a breath of fresh air. He must have been a chain smoker for the windows were yellow and stuck, but outside you could smell the ground warming up, and I could see some lovely ladies walking my way from the university, so I began to wave to them like the Queen on coronation day. Just then, in came Old Number Nine! He was a wiry fella, maybe six feet tall, and he wore that same black vested suit that they all wore with the same pair of wire rim spectacles, and the same sad empty look on his face. But when he saw me breathing in the fresh air of spring through that open window—a window that hadn't been cracked in all his years as Ninth Undersecretary, he was livid! "Close that window at once!" he squealed in Russian.

And sadly (for me), didn't he have a four inch wide light brown birthmark on his forehead that was shaped exactly like the State of Iowa! I mean complete with that little south east dip at the Mississippi River! Oh, I should have been looking all sad and remorseful, but spring had sprung and what with that map of Iowa on his forehead, what was a boy to do? It wasn't one of those barrel laughs—just a little giggle—nothing to go ape shit over, though that was exactly what old Number Nine did! First, he made me close the window, then after he sat there for a few minutes and stewed, he went into a tirade in Russian, which was kind of funny too, since I didn't have much of an idea what he was saying. But from the similarities to Polish, there was something about how he hated "mercenaries" and "especially smart ass American ones." I was glad he got all that off his chest, but then he pushed his horn rim glasses way up on his head near that map of Iowa, and didn't I start grinning like a Cheshire cat. Well, in case you're ever cornered by an Undersecretary of Anything (Number Nine or otherwise) remember this, or suffer the

277

consequences, don't smile, don't look smug, don't open his window, and sure as hell don't you never—and I mean never ever, start giving his birthmarks names of United States! He stuck his index finger in my face and shook it like a rattle snake as he lectured. This wasn't the welcoming committee I'd expected to get!

Now I could take the dressing down, an ex-enlisted man can take a lecture from his superiors like no other creature on God's green earth, but what I couldn't abide by, was that pasty little finger being waved in my face! He lectured on about how mercenaries were going to be the downfall of Russia, and then I swear he said old Abe Lincoln had brought the ruination of America by freeing our slaves.

"Don't wave that thing in my face, or I'll bite it off!" I warned him in what I remembered from one of Natasha's lectures.

And the next time that index finger came flying by; I latched on to it like a blue clawed crab! He let out a high pitched screech that froze me in place, and before I even had time to spit him out, a couple of guards were dragging me off.

But at least I was making my way up the Chain of Command, for they pitched me right into a chair in the Eighth Undersecretary of the Foreign Office's office. He was staring at me through these big thick glasses that made his eyes look ten times bigger than they really were, but I bucked up and found no humor in it!

"Major, if you really are a major?" he started (in Praise Jesus, pretty bad English), his suit coat unbuttoned like maybe he wore a shoulder holster in there. "Why did you bite the Ninth Undersecretary? You cannot go around biting people in Russia. This is a civilized nation full of civilized people."

Well, the big-eyed man had a point, but if he'd been getting the lecture I'd been getting, he'd have probably bit more than Number Nine's finger off. Still he didn't look like the type to trifle with, so I dropped my head in feigned remorse and let him lecture on.

"We believe in discipline and order here in Russia, and your biting the Ninth Undersecretary was most definitely out of order, maior."

I told Old Number Eight that it seemed to me his finger bit buddy was spending a whole hell of a lot of time on some really extraneous subjects, and maybe he should be the one getting the lecture. Then I said, if that's the way they treated their hired help in Russia, he could just release me and I'd go home to America without any hard feelings. And that's when he broke the bad news!

"You could be put to death if you tried to leave Russia right now, Major Stewart—for you are the property of the Tsar! We hang deserters here in the Motherland, maior! Hang them slow and sure! And unless you want to meet Frolov the red-shirted hangman,[117] I suggest you calm down."

Being hung for biting a loud mouth bureaucrat—now that was a tale to tell your grandchildren about, only I'd be dead. I calmed right down by counting to ten, then twenty, then thirty, and finally when I hit forty—backwards, I was ready to be a bought dog of a mercenary. But when the Eighth Undersecretary got to the letter of introduction from the German Crown Prince, he changed his tune.

"I see by my records, Major Stewart," the big man went on in a gentler fashion, "that you are an accomplished warrior (now that was debatable, but hearing any compliment at all just then was like throwing a drowning man a rope). I'm sorry for the delays," he said with a nervous smile, "but we must check everything, oh, so carefully in these troubled times."

Then he waved the guards out of the room and reached into his top desk drawer and pulled out a bottle of ten year old cognac and two nice little crystal glasses. We drank a toast to brotherhood, and a toast to the Tsar, and I'd have added a toast that the Ninth Undersecretary's finger healed fast, but I didn't want to push it.

"We'll clear you for work with the military, maior," went my new found friend, "but the Ninth Undersecretary's notation still stands as far as you being a security risk to the Telegraphic Service. If the Army wishes to ignore our recommendations, then it will be on their heads if you fail them." Spoken like a true bureaucrat, but who cares if the Russians got their telegraph system in order? Give me a place in the cavalry and I would die a happy man!

I returned to the Imperial Staff Building the following morning and stood in one of those red ribbon lines until well past lunch before I came to that high desk where I'd left off the day before. This time the little mealy mouthed paper pusher passed me through to a second room of scribes sitting at their high stools scribbling like Santa Clause's helpers. Mostly they asked you the same questions they'd asked on the other side—trying to trip you up on who your grandmother was. And even as they asked me those trifling questions, Russia's Armies were marching east to take Uzbekistan,[118] and you'd think they would have need of a good telegrapher to tie all that together.

Sworn in with a room full of brand new officers—most in their shiny new uniforms of greens and gold, my poor little bugler's suit still had to do until someone came along and chose me for their branch of the service. Each morning at 8:00 AM we would show up in the Officer's Pen and wait like the cocottes in Miss Yvette's front parlor for someone to come along and put us to work. What really hurt was seeing that nobody that passed by even took a look at poor little Redbeard!

The weather went from nice and spring like to almost summer with the White Nights calling me outside. The only exercise I got was at night after they let us go home. I'd bought a couple of horses and we would ride south into the flat marshy countryside and practice our shooting and riding 'til well past midnight.

Boris was my new horse's name, Boris Bonaparte. He was a four year old large headed Orlov with a high arched neck—broad through the chest and very intelligent. Yakoff and Little Suli the Second, which I named his Steppe pony because I had the honor of paying for him, would watch Boris and I jump all kinds of obstacles. We would ride out into those pearly white nights—drink wodka, and shoot my Winchester rifle at anything that moved. Little Suli the Second stood about fourteen hands—big for a Steppe pony, but small by Boris's standards. Yet whenever there was a big decision to make, like should we cross that churning stream full of ice cold snow melt, he would be the first one in. Light tan like a deer, Little Suli the Second was convinced he was the far superior horse—despite his diminutive size. And if it hadn't been for those evenings in the field, I'd have surely gone crazy!

Finally on the Friday afternoon of my second week in the Officer's Pen, my big chance came. From time to time someone would enter and look through the stock, ask us a few questions, and be off again. We lost maybe five or six officers that way and still the weather grew nicer and the boredom grew worse. But on that lucky day in May, in comes this slight little general with two great walrus like tusks of black beard splitting at his chin. His shoulder boards were sparkling in gold, with a nice straight chest and the short little bow legs of a cavalryman. General Iosif Vladimirovich Gurko was his name—a man I would grow to know and love, but on this day he was a man on a mission, for he was in search of officers to fill out his forces for the summer war games. Talk in the Officer Pen was whoever went up against the Imperial forces down at Krasnoe Selo could expect to lose badly, and lose a few men—for that tradition of a hard fought mock battle went back to the days of Peter the Great.[119] General Gurko checked the cut of our jib, our rank, the length of our hair, and even our smiles. The first officer he selected was a one-eyed captain named Rot with a big black patch over his eye from a Circassian's sword.[120] General Gurko had gone right for him as he went around the room looking at cuirassier officers with their shiny steel chest plates, and infantry officers in solid green with red trim—some with sky blue pants—some with white, all as disinterested as Miss Yvette's cocottes on a Sunday night.

"What rank are you, soldier?" General Gurko asked me.

I explained the confusion at Headquarters and how I planned to buy my Russian uniforms as soon as I got picked for a branch of service, but I was sure enough a Russian major. All of which bored him.

"Do you have any field experience?" he asked with an eye on my scars.

"Oh, yes sir!" I answered him proudly. "I've got four years with the Union Army in our Civil War and..."

"An American, why didn't I see it?" he cut in with one eye high and the other down low—his eyebrows looking like two squiggly caterpillars that were wrestling for an advantage.

"I rode with the Prussians against the Austrians and French," was my next try at escaping the Officer's Pen. "Even rode with General Sherman on his march to the sea!"

He looked me over a bit more and must have figured anyone who would go around in that kind of an outfit wasn't all there, and moved on at the quick step.

"I took a sniper's round right through the chest at the Battle of Antietam, General Gurko, sir!" I told him as I pulled up my tunic to expose that double lung shot one more time. He stopped for a moment and there was that hole were the Minie ball had gone in, and the bigger meaner looking exit wound—healed all jagged and ugly where it came out again.

"Do you spik Russian?" He asked with those penetrating eyes searching my soul and I answered da, since he didn't ask me how much.

"But can you run a battalion, major sergeant major?" he queried with a big grin on his fury face.

I figured I could command one better than Colonel Jones[121] ever did, so I answered, "Oh, yes sir, I most certainly can!" And the rest was history in the making.

Chapter Ten

A Barn Full of Uhlans

We were to report to General Gurko's headquarters south of St. Petersburg at six o'clock Monday morning, and if I'd known Mondays were considered unlucky in Russia, I'd have asked for a days' delay. The tailors said it would take at least two weeks for my uniforms to be made, so there I was the first American major sergeant major to ever run a Russian battalion!

We arrived at the general's mansion on the road to Tsarskoe Selo on time and his aide invited me into the ballroom where the general had his office set up. There were paintings on the walls all covered with sheets and in the center of that big empty room was a huge table piled high with his papers. At ten AM the general finally came in, his boots spit polished to a nice high sheen, his golden pogoni shining in the sunlight, and a cup of steaming hot tea in his hands.

I stood in the far corner under the supervision of his aide de camp, as we waited for a signal to step forward. But first the little bow-legged man met with a couple of senior officers and leisurely discussed some fine points on his maps—chatted about their families, and then sat back and read the newspaper. Once or twice, I thought I saw his fury brown eye brows twitch my way, but just like that priest on the train into Warsaw, I couldn't quite catch him at his game.

"Lieutenant," he finally barked, "go and fetch de major some coffee."

"Major Stewart," he said and it echoed across the high-ceilinged room like a big bass drum. "Come join me!"

I walked right up, saluted with a click of my heels like the Prussians had taught me, and he said I could give that right up and never do it again! Then he said, "Coffee black?" like he knew how I liked it.

"I see de Crown Prince of Germany spiks highly of you, Major Stewart!" His Excellency said with a tad of respect. "You were at Koniggratz?" he asked with his eyebrows crawling.

Right there swinging in a linden tree, but I just said yes sir, as he read on through my records.

283

He was the same size as me—both little jockeys, yet somehow General Gurko looked ten times bigger than I was.

"Do you know what dese War Games are about, maior?" he asked with those thick brown eye brows crawling.

"Yes sir, General Gurko," I answered. "Since the times of Peter the Great, you Russians have held War Games to prepare for real battle."

"Dat's right, maior, go on!" he said like I was doing just fine.

"Well, sir," I hesitated—thinking should I say what was really on my mind, and then of course it came out. "Some say we're here to be crushed by the Imperial Guard—just cannon fodder for them to ride over."

I swallowed hard and wondered why my brain had so much trouble telling my mouth to stay shut. He looked at me with his face turning red and said, "You are right, maior, we were here to lose to de Imperial Guard, but dat was before de Emperor put me in charge!"

"Amen to that, General Gurko, sir!" I blurted out as a smile lit my face. "I've been on the winning side in three wars now, sir, and I rather like the feeling!"

He stood up and slapped me across the back, and then we went to the maps strewn across his desk and he told me, "We will hold dis line from here at Lake Duderhoff to just north of Krasnoe Selo. Dis bridge right here," and he pounded on a point where the lake grew narrow, "we must keep dem from crossing dis bridge. You head dere tomorrow morning with your battalion and fortify it, major sergeant major."

"Can we tear it down, sir?" I asked, figuring if the bridge wasn't there it would make crossing it that much harder.

"Don't ask such a question of your old General Gurko," he said, but his eyes were saying oh, hell yes! He was a smart man, for if I hauled down the bridge and it was considered a foul by the War Game judges, or the town fathers demanded their bridge be built right back again, well, it was all on his new major's head—not his. He paused a second to phrase his next question, then asked real slowly, "I see from your records dat you spik Polish real well, maior."

284

Well, I could cuss Polish fluently, otherwise I'd say my Polish was about passable, but who was I to correct my general? So I nodded my head and said tak, and he went on with a big grin spreading across his furry face.

"Even doh we only keep our draftees two years, dey are sometimes more trouble dan dey are worth, Maior Stewart." He was picking his words carefully like maybe what he was about to say shouldn't be said. "I want you to talk to your officers and NCOs and tell dem dey are to give dere orders in both Russian and Polish from dis day forward. Oh, and maior, vee never had dis conversation, do you hear me?"

Once again, if the plan blew up in my face, I'd be the one catching hell. But orders were orders and even though I got a good beating in Poland for speaking Polish, I was now to speak it in Russia, by order of General Gurko. "I like you boy, you will make your old general proud," he said, then we went to the maps and started our planning.

Soon it was dinner time and we had that Zupa grzybowa I loved, and a nice plate of Baranina, and lots of spring water, for my general never mixed business with pleasure. "You like dat damn Polish food, don't you, major sergeant major?" he asked with a grin.

"My Mom said I had a hollow leg, sir!" I bragged as I finished up his mutton chops.

"Two hollow legs, I'd say," my little bow-legged general said merrily, and we passed the rest of the afternoon studying strategy and tactics.

"Wodka!" he yells to his lieutenant when the work was all over, and I knew General Gurko was a Pole![122]

We toasted the Tsar, the Crown Prince of Prussia, Abraham Lincoln, my home state of Maryland, and Mother Russia as well, and by the time Yakoff and I set off for Krasnoe Selo, I was three sheets to the wind— possibly four! Arriving a few hours later in the moonlight we found our battalion campsite with rows and rows of white canvas tents.

Corporal Yakovich helped me get my boots off and I fell asleep in the commander's lumpy old cot. There'd be plenty of time to meet the men in the morning so I drifted off to sleep. I heard my soldiers singing songs by their fires and dreamed of a great battle on a floating bridge. The next thing I knew Yakoff was waking me. It was three in the morning by my father's watch and I got up out of that bed and stepped outside to see my two sentries turning white as a ghost.

"What's a matter, boys, haven't you seen a major sergeant major before?" I asked in Polish, but there was no answer from the sentries. "Corporal Yakovich, could you go and find the Officer of the Day, and see why these two men have gone mute? And bring me some hot coffee, please, that General Gurko sure can drink!"

We had a march before us of some three miles down to the Mozhayskaya Bridge, and it would soon be time to wake the men and get them moving. I watched the embers of last night's fires and felt ready for anything.

"Major Stewart," my loyal corporal said as he handed me my first steaming cup of hot Rio.

"The Watch Officer will be here momentarily, sir." He said with a grin and then he added, "The guards were speechless when they first saw you, because you just stepped out of their dead colonel's bed! They are wondering if you slept well in there, sir?"

"Yes, I slept well, you heard me snore." I told my smirking corporal.

"Well, apparently sir, the good colonel died in his sleep a few nights back and no one has dared to step in there—save to remove the body. Word around battalion is you're one hard little son of a bitch!"

Not only was I wondering what the poor man died of, and whether it was contagious, but how could I burn his tent down without the rest of the men seeing that I was as scared as they were? It proved a morning of many questions, for up came a young officer in his fresh pressed greens. He was a blue-eyed blonde haired lieutenant—maybe six foot tall with a happy go lucky grin, and didn't he speak the King's English better than I did.

"I'm Lieutenant Shingleoff," he said in his friendly way. "I love everything about you Americans!" And we shook hands like we were back in Kansas. "I just read a book about your Major Forsyth and his fifty scouts fighting off an attack of over six hundred mounted Cheyenne and Sioux warriors,[123] said the blue-eyed boy. "Ever heard of him, sir?"

286

"Sandy Forsyth?" I asked, for I'd served with a General Sandy Forsyth down in Virginia. He was Little Phil Sheridan's right hand man and it sounded like something Sandy would do.

"Yes sir," the lad cried all excited like, "Major Sandy Forsyth—one in the same, maior. You know him?"

"I sure do, son, Sandy Forsyth is a fighting fool!"

The lieutenant couldn't have been more than sixteen. He was probably from a well to do but not politically well-positioned family, since he'd wound up in my bastard battalion. Nevertheless, he was a friendly chap, and since he was such a fine linguist, I decided to take him into my staff.

Then up comes the Watch Officer—a tall surly captain all full of himself. Maybe six foot two with great wide shoulders, he looked down his nose at the little major sergeant major before him. His fine green uniform had crisp red piping and was freshly pressed, while his boots were as clean as a whistle, which meant he must not have done much walking while on watch that night. He saluted me in a haphazard fashion and said with a touch of disrespect, "I am Captain Leonid Leontieff."

"Captain," I said in a pleasant enough voice, "please have the bugler blow reveille."

"I figured you'd want to blow that yourself, maior." He said. "After all, isn't that a bugler's uniform you're wearing?"

"And what do these pogoni on my shoulders say?" was my quick retort.

"Oh, they are definitely a major's pogoni, sir!" he said rudely. "But the question is—what are those sergeant major stripes on your arm?"

My blood was boiling and I was seeing red, but shooting the first captain I came across could hardly improve my standing with a brand new battalion. "Reveille, captain, then box up the late colonel's things and see that their sent to his family with honors," I told him as he stared at me with a hatred you could feel like a hot poker.

"That is hardly the kind of thing a captain should do, maior," he said with his Muscovite brogue, as he looked over at my blue-eyed lieutenant and prepared to send the order downhill.

"Before you say another word, Captain Leontieff," I said sternly as a warning to my senior captain. "You can show these shoulder straps a little respect or I'll send you packing—now blow reveille, damn you!"

Reveille was blown—the men woke up, and the campfires were stoked sending off columns of smoke in the cool spring air, as the soldiers climbed out of their tents and groused about the early hour. I gave Captain Leontieff plenty of time to get his household chores in order, and then sent him out to gather up the officers and NCOs, praying that the rest of the Russians weren't as surly as he was. The first one to show up under the trees that morning was my old one-eyed friend from the Officers' Pen, Captain Boris Rot. We shook hands and smiled like old comrades.

"This is some outfit they gave us, maior," my friend said with a twisted grin, that black patch over his eye making him look like a pirate. "Polish and Belarus boys with six weeks of training, and they still barely speak a word of Russian. And have you met our senior captain yet, sir?" asked my one-eyed warrior. "He's a rich Moscow boy, and nobody can do it like they do it in Moscow. Why, the man claims that his family had Catherine the Great over for supper on a regular basis. He's a real martinet and on top of that, he's never been under fire!"

"Most martinets haven't been under fire, Captain Rot," I told him and we laughed, knowing full well how a man acts when he first sees the elephant[124] is the real test of his military talents.

I liked Boris from the first time we met, which was why I named my horse after him, but just knowing Captain Leontieff rubbed someone else the wrong way made me stand a little straighter and smile a little wider. Weren't we there for a War Game, and weren't you supposed to have fun when you gamed? After all, nobody was going to get killed!

I was running General Gurko's plan through my head and thinking it just might work, though I wished Boris could have been brought in on the secret. There were four companies to a Russian battalion with about two hundred men in each company, which was led by a captain, two or three junior officers—like my blue-eyed lieutenant, plus a 1st sergeant, a quartermaster sergeant, four senior and maybe a dozen junior sergeants,

288

and sixteen corporals to run the platoons, plus perhaps another dozen clerks, cooks, bakers, and orderlies, and one hundred and fifty some odd privates. That was over eight hundred men under my command, and me a virgin major. You tell me that ain't a fly in somebody's ointment!

So I decided to join forces with Captain Rot right then and there. I would be the titular head of the battalion—from time to time putting my two cents worth in, while Boris ran the battalion on a day to day basis. Yakoff would keep the undercurrent of mutiny down to a bare minimum by his sheer size and loyalty, and we'd all get by in the sweet by and by.

The officers and NCOs gathered round my table—some grinning at the little red-bearded Yankee in a bugler's uniform. "Gentlemen," I started in, "my name is Major Stewart of the Emperor's Own Infantry and I bid you good morning!" They weren't the quietest or most polite bunch I'd ever addressed, but they settled down just fine. "I've been at this business since I was a boy of fifteen, so don't expect to get over on me! Do your job, fight to win, and treat your men like human beings, and we'll all get along fine." So far the crowd was still sitting, which was a very good sign.

"And gentlemen, since most of our troops speak Polish as their Mother tongue; I will expect commands to be given in both Russian and Polish."

That was a sticky wicket I'd just presented to them and the NCOs and half the officers leapt to their feet and wanted to scalp me!

"Here's the best deal I can offer," I said and I could see Captain Rot shaking his head, like No Deals—No Deals, as his good eye started to twitch. "If you can march the battalion to the Mozhayskaya Bridge in two hours' time, form them up and fire three rounds at my chosen target, you can belay that last order. But otherwise gentlemen, the next man to question my commands will be sent to General Gurko in chains!"

Captain Leontieff wanted to argue some more, saying his family didn't win the honor of having Catherine the Great over for dinner because they spoke Polish. But I put the whole group to laughing by saying, "That's right, captain, they probably spoke German, since we all know Catherine the Great was a proud Prussian Princess."[125]

"You dare make fun of the Leontieff family?" he said with a glare.

289

"Clock is ticking, gentlemen!" I bellowed. "We'll be marching in light order—rifles, haversacks, canteens and blankets. Three rounds by Company fire at the Mozhayskaya Bridge is your task! I will be waiting for you there. Corporal Yakovich, get my horse, if you please!"

While the surly captain prepared the battalion to march, my little command group of Yakoff, Captain Rot, and my blue-eyed lieutenant headed south by horseback. We made it to the bridge in less than an hour and then the four of us went off for a cup of tea at the Railway Station, as the sun shone over the marshlands—a golden mist rising from the land of lakes. I bought a dozen handmade brooms at a small country store and my blue-eyed lieutenant asked, "What are those for?" while I passed him up three to carry.

"When Captain Leontieff and his men finally show up, they'll need targets to shoot at, now won't they?" I told him.

The bridge was about seventy feet from shore to shore. An ice cold stream maybe six feet deep spread into two wide lakes to the north and south. So if the Imperial forces wanted to cross from the western shore, this would be their only route for several miles. A marsh ran down to the stream with willows and weeds so thick they couldn't simply wade across. I snuck over to the enemy side on Boris's back and stuck the brooms in the muck with their heads sticking up. Standing maybe four foot tall, the twelve brooms stood waiting for the battalion to arrive. And there we waited for two hours, then two and a half, and finally by the three hour mark they were trying to move from column of fours to a two deep firing line with orders being bellowed in nothing but Russian. I heard more cussing than company commands, yet the officers and NCOs kept on trying, which spoke highly of their perseverance.

I took my place to the right of the firing line and once they were ready, I hollered in my best Russian, "Battalion take down those brooms, ready, aim, fire!"

When the smoke cleared, all the brooms were still standing. "Battalion, Attention," I bellowed from up on Boris. "For six weeks of training that's pretty shitty shooting, gentlemen, and you didn't break any records getting down here!" I hollered in good God Almighty, Polish.

Maybe these draftees just weren't cut out for Army life, or maybe they just needed a little inspiration. "Today," I went on in my best Kowalski Polish, "we are going to try a little experiment!" I could see their ears prick up like a horse when you bang his feed pail. "We will give all our commands in Polish from now on, gentlemen, and if you promise to do the best job you can, I promise that we'll treat you like human beings!" There was a stirring in the formation—primarily from the sergeants and junior officers who thought this smacked of Socialism, but the Poles and the Belarus boys all started to smile. "I was born a poor stable boy in Baltimore, Maryland," I told them all nice and humble like, "and my father use to say if you treat a man like he's stupid, he'll act stupid every time." There was a mumble of agreement coming from the ranks, so I pressed on into uncharted waters. "But if you treat a man like he has a head on his shoulders, he'll come through for you when you need him! In my hometown, we had a Polish hero in our Revolution named Casimir Pulaski.[126] He was a great friend of Liberty and Justice for All."

I didn't know it at the time, but he'd been outlawed by Russia for fighting for Polish freedom before he ever crossed the pond, but my Poles seemed to know it. And that red faced Muscovite captain must have known it too, for he was glaring at me like I'd rogered his wife!

"And since our battalion has no name, gentlemen, I'd like to call us The Pulaski Battalion after my hero Casimir Pulaski, and our colors," Sweet Jesus, why did I go on so? We didn't have any colors, and there was not a flag in sight.

I looked around staring at the blue sky and praying some colors would materialize, and there before me—right across that beer colored stream were our twelve virgin brooms sitting up there proudly. So Boris and I swam across, though we could have taken the bridge, and with a sucking sound I pulled the first broom out of the muck and hollered, "Company A come on over and take your colors!"

After Company A swam across and got their brooms, I called, "Company B come into the waters and take your colors too, my boys!" They got their three brooms, and so on and so forth through Company C and Company D we went—like Napoleon passing out his eagles.

Now Shakespeare might have said that was much to do about nothing, and I'd have almost agreed, but what those brooms represented, was our battalion was born a new with thoughts of freedom and justice for all of us! And although you couldn't speak Polish in Poland, in Russia—under the eyes of our little Polish general, you sure as hell could! And just as the last broom was being passed out and the swimming began in earnest, three wagons full of provisions and a platoon of Engineers arrived with a note from General Gurko.

"Major Stewart, after thinking about your desire to "improve" the river crossing, I send you these Engineers."

My plan was to sink a tall spruce tree in the center pilings with a block and tackle on top and start lifting the bridge boards from the western shore. We'd move east taking every piece of lumber with us, and build a fort to keep the Guard from crossing at the narrows. My doodles weren't the greatest, but the Engineer captain took them to heart and with the help of eight hundred men we had that bridge torn down and converted to a Daniel Boone style fort with deep dug pilings and a thick oak board wall that even the Imperial Guard couldn't breach without a good hard fight. That night the Pulaskis were diving off the mizzen mast as the wood smoke from a thousand Imperial campfires wafted down from their camp just across the river. My men began to sing, and the balalaikas rang, and their new major played them a solo on his trusty harmonica.

We blew Reveille at eight the next morning and while our gruel was cooking in big iron pots, Corporal Yakovich and I rode east to the railroad tracks to send off a message to General Gurko. He'd moved his Headquarters down to the Krasnoe Selo Railroad Station a few miles to our north, and we were to send him a report each morning.

I brought Boris up alongside the tall wooden pole, took off my boots, and passed them over to my big moujik friend for safe keeping. I didn't want to scratch that complimentary McClellan saddle that Captain Ridgely had given me for it was holding up real well. I'd seen Captain Ridgely waiting for a train in Paris back in 1870 and had almost gone over and thanked him for that fine saddle, but he was with that mirror image of a wife (and first cousin) and she was lecturing him about his propensity to over-tip. So I turned tail and ran like us cowardly men do when we see a powerful woman, and we never did get to say another word in this world, or hopefully in the next one either![127]

Anyway, Yakoff held my boots as I carefully climbed the telegraph pole, grabbed the cross bar and swung up top like the Pole Monkey I still was. I got out my pocket key—spliced into the wire, and tapped out:

General Gurko,

Improvements to the crossing completed. Imperial Guard came by last night and cussed up a storm regarding their missing bridge, but we never touched their western shore. Our Polish is growing by leaps and bounds. Got any orders? MSM Stewart, which was short for major sergeant major—which he loved to say, and then we waited for an answer.

First, there came a message from the Mozhayskaya telegraph station that asked who the hell we were? Then about fifteen minutes later there came a second message from Headquarters saying we were to continue our training, no special orders, but we were to: "Remain vigilant, and remember the War Games will begin at 0600 tomorrow morning."

Yakoff and I returned to camp to eat breakfast and then we set off on a little scout. Captain Rot was in charge of eight platoons (two from each company), who were planning on widening our battlements. He wanted to take down the mizzen mast as it would interfere with any imaginary grape shot we fired from our three cannons General Gurko had sent us. We sent four platoons of foragers to find firewood and anything edible, as well as all the wooden staves they could cut. I'd seen Mr. Winans' pikes used to good effect in the Pratt Street Riots, so my plan was to use them in our little mock battle with the Imperial elite. They could hardly kill anybody, so they were perfect for a fight with the blue bloods! Captain Leontieff and the rest of the officers and NCO's that needed help learning Polish were turned over to our draftee school teachers, while myself with Lieutenant Shingleoff and Corporal Yakovich at my side, took two platoons (their brooms held high) from each company to reconnoiter. We headed for the southern tip of Lake Duderhoff through farmland, swamps, and marsh armed with our Baranov rifles and hand-cut staves, and kicked up deer and fox as we went. And just when I

293

decided to turn our little scouting expedition into a provisioning trip—for I'd heard elk tasted real good, we got a little surprise!

Coming north up the road we were heading south down, we heard that slapping sound of lancer pennants, and since we were occupying the left flank of General Gurko's army—they had to be Imperial lancers, coming our way in a hurry. We went to ground in a ditch full of muddy water with Little Suli the Second and Boris lying flat amongst the men as the Guardsman came slapping by. It was a full platoon of Imperial uhlans in their summer white blouses and sky blue pants, their flat-topped leather helmets glistened in the sun and you could hear that jingle of their tack as the horses came on at a run. My plan was to wait until they passed and then set up a nice little ambush for their untimely return. We found a blind curve in the road by a swamp full of small willows and quietly set up a couple of five foot timber jumps. I gave orders for the men to fire their rounds straight up in the air and come out screaming when we returned, then Boris and I were off for the rear of that lancer column.

I left my men under the watchful eye of Lieutenant Shingleoff, as Boris and I trailed behind the lancers. And when we came alongside their Tail End Charlie, I hauled his lance from his hand and fired off a round from my LeMat which sent him charging northward—taking his whole platoon with him. We swung round and galloped south with their captured pennant flapping in the wind as I called, "Come and get me, boys!" at the top of my lungs.

By the time that column of uhlans sawed around and joined in the chase, we were a furlong ahead. I could see those sharp lance tips sparkling in the sunlight as I blasted away with my Grapeshot pistol to let the Pulaskis know we were coming like lightning on the wire. Around that blind curve we went, Boris holding his line like a champion, and he took that torturous double jump of birch brush like a steeplechaser as I hollered, "Rise, Pulaski's! Rise up and strike!"

And just as the first lancers went over the brush jump, the Pulaskis unloaded—live rounds sailing skyward like fireworks on the Fourth of July! Down went their captain with horses and men going down all around him—a great mass of flying feet and screaming horse flesh. Now, I hadn't figured on killing any horses, but they were down all around me, and then to my dread, didn't that uhlan captain rise up and draw his sword for a fight! The Pulaskis were game what with all that talk of freedom and justice I'd been feeding them, so I did the only thing I could think of and rode right up to the cavalry captain and placed my revolver upside his head and cocked it back.

"Put down your weapons!" I barked. "You and your men are my prisoners. Pulaskis fix bayonets and skewer the next lancer to move," I ordered and peace was restored.

We had managed to capture thirty Imperial uhlans and their mounts a good sixteen hours before the War Games even began, and praise Jesus not one of their horses had to be shot! But how could we break the good news to our general?

In my illustrious military career it had been my experience that nothing ever came of rushing a thing like that, so we found an old barn to park our prisoners in, tied them up, watered and fed them—so we couldn't be accused of mistreating them. Then with one platoon of Pulaskis left behind under the supervision of my trusty Corporal Yakovich, we prepared to set out for Fort Daniel Boone like nothing had happened.

In my defense, I clearly stated to my men that the Imperial lancers were not to be hurt! "Brak kulki," I said before they reloaded their rifles, which was "no balls" just like Kowalski had said about General McDowell.

The rest of my crew returned to camp in silence—each man swearing to keep his mouth shut 'til their little major sergeant major figured out how to explain that barn full of uhlans! It was a nervous night for us all— never knowing if some Pole or Belarus boy would start bragging. We ate, we smiled, and we stayed silent—not wanting to risk a slip of the tongue.

"Where's the rest of my Company?" Captain Leontief demanded when we got back to camp. I told him I posted them to guard our left flank, which was true enough, though he reminded me that Lake Duderhoff would keep us safe in that direction.

I figured once the War Games began and the Imperial Guard ran over us, (as they always did), maybe just maybe capturing and imprisoning the Tsar's elite cavalry wouldn't be an issue. That was all I could cling to as

I tried to sleep, and in my dreams the Red Queen was back again—calling for my balls to be cut off! Her Baltimore half-brother stretched me out on a long wooden rack, and as I was pulled tighter and tighter there came a great fire across the horizon. Thunder rolled through the wastelands of my mind, as the sweat rolled down my body. I awoke in a cold sweat full of fear and trepidation and there was that sound of thunder coming from off to the north with a shrieking sound like a herd of elephants was stampeding!

I sat up, relieved that my dream was over, and listened carefully before I yelled, "Come men it's time for battle! No bugles, no fire, and no fanfare, for I'll be damned if the Imperial Guard aren't moving on us!"

Fort Daniel Boone must have scared them off and they were coming across the wide expanse of Dolgoye Lake with a pontoon bridge, was what I figured—for I'd heard that screeching sound many times. Our sister battalions (there were four to a Russian regiment) were lined up along the lake to our north where the sounds seemed to come from, and I sent the blue-eyed lieutenant up there to see what was what, while the rest of us dressed and prepared for action. When Shingleoff returned on his frothing stallion he said that the regimental colonel was pulling back with General Gurko's blessings, and unless we felt we could hold the line against the whole Imperial Army, we should fall back too.

But retreating while the Imperials were crossing a pontoon bridge without any harassment rubbed me the wrong way, and it did Captain Rot as well! "How about we sneak up there and screw up their plans, maior?" my one-eyed warrior suggested.

And since chaos was my middle name at the time, I said, "Oh, hell yes!"

I galloped up to that telegraph pole, put my muddy boots on my fine McClellan saddle, and hauled myself up to the top by the light of a blood red moon. I could hear drums beating and bugles blowing up to the north, though it was but three in the morning.

"MSM to General G," I tapped out. "I think we can delay the Imperial advance by hitting their bridgehead. Would you like us to try it?"

Less than a minute later the answer came back: "If you can delay them for just one hour, we might be able to trap some of them on our side of the lake. General G." Lord how I liked my little Polish commander, for playing it by ear was his favorite game!

When I got back to camp, Captain Rot was already working on the particulars. "We'll leave two thirds of the battalion (or four hundred and eighty men) to guard the crossing," he said, "for we haven't done all this work so the Imperials could trick us into moving from a position of strength."

Some majors might have been jealous of a man who took over so naturally, but I was relieved, since my last plan had opened a can of worms. Captain Leontieff, on the other hand, was taking this change in command very poorly. He didn't go to officer school down in Moscow just to play second fiddle to a self-made warrior! Leontieff was complaining to all that would listen, and I told him to stand down and shut his trap.

"But maior, I out rank Captain Rot," he argued.

Hell, I outranked Captain Rot too, but he didn't see me having any trouble with it. Once that fire was put out, Captain Rot explained how he had a special Forlorn Hope for someone just crazy enough to do the job. "But it will probably mean the end of a brilliant military career," he said with a grin as he looked at me and laughed.

"I'd love to be your Forlorn Hope, Captain Rot," I volunteered, even before he went into the particulars. After this mock battle, the Russians would probably send me packing—if I was lucky, or they'd shoot me if I was not, so why not go out with a big bang!

My one-eyed captain told me that he and his men would sneak up as close as they could to the Imperial bridgehead on the eastern shore. They'd fire off a few rounds of blanks and start screaming as they brought up Boris and the supply horses to drag the pontoon bridge off her moorings. We'd trap those that had already crossed on our side of the lake and fight on until they squashed us. The horses were already being harnessed as we talked.

"You and your men will crawl forward on the western shore and see if you can cause chaos and mayhem on that side of the bridge," he said like it wasn't much of a plan, but what else could we do?

297

Knowing we'd be swimming most of the time, I left all my weapons behind save for my Bowie knife, and dove into the ice cold waters to swim across with one of those Pulaski brooms. The ten men I took along with me were armed with Baranov rifles, which we threw in a little punt with our boots and uniforms. Everyone dressed quickly on the opposite shore as the sun began to rise in a blood red blush with that full moon freakishly leading us into battle. I ordered my boys to load their pieces sans balls—Brak kulki, I distinctly hollered, and we just walked slowly up to the pontoon bridge with our rifles in hand looking like a poorly dressed Imperial work crew.

The whole meadow was jam packed with long columns of elite infantry and cavalry waiting to cross. There was even a battery of horse artillery lined up as we walked along gazing at the long rocking bridge stretching maybe two hundred feet across the lake—waves being spread by the strutting horses and marching men. And although, the plan was to wait until Captain Rot opened fire from the opposite shore, there was the most perfect chance to wreak havoc right then and there, for up on the bridge all alone and looking absolutely magnificent in his pure white uniform was a tall proud general on a huge white horse!

The man had pure white hair, and a pure white mustache, and his pure white stallion held his head up high as he did a little side stepping strut that caused the bridge to chatter. The White General waited until he had a good twenty feet of bridge clear in front of him—waving to his men like he'd already won the battle, and I couldn't take the excitement any more! So I raised my colors high in the air and ran up behind him and gave his big prancing stallion a good hard swat across his rump that sent him running for the sun, as I hollered, "Pulaskis rise up and fire!"

They did too! And it created such a panic, what with the White General bearing down on his men and knocking them off that swaying bridge, that we had the element of surprise on our side! And in war—even mock war, surprise was a huge advantage!

"Pulaskis to me!" I bellowed.

There before us waiting to go over next was a big heavy set colonel with a bright blue sash across his chunky chest that made my men gasp, though it didn't mean a thing to me. You could tell by his gorgeous black horse and the cut of his jib that he was a Royal of some sort, and there at the head of a tough looking outfit they came on with bayonets fixed.

"Pulaskis reload," I ordered thinking there wouldn't be enough of us left to sweep up with a broom—the only weapon I had, save for my Bowie knife. Oh, I'd heard there were deaths in these War Games, but to tell you the truth, I'd never been so scared in my life!

"Fire at will," I yelled figuring that would be the last anybody ever heard of Redbeard the Wild & Crazy American, as my Pulaskis had taken to calling me after we tore down that bridge.

But then Sweet Jesus and a little miscommunication stepped in, for in my haste I'd accidentally left out that part about "no balls!" Every round that came out of those Baranov rifles was a live round and went skittering across the sky with a big ugly hiss and a sizzle! And although the Pulaskis couldn't hit the broadside of a barn door, those hissing sounds sent the colonel running for the rear! And his untimely retreat took his whole front line with him, and his frontline took the second line too!

I'd seen a stampede or two in my time and believe me once the line commences to caving in on its self, it's all over but the running. That gave us a little time to start whacking and hacking away at the bridge's moorings; for once we were afloat it would be harder for them to come back and kill us. But then my luck changed from good to bad, as one of my men tapped me on the shoulder and said, "maior, look," and pointed east towards that red rising sun.

There coming back across the bridge at the gallop with his sword held high was the White General on his wild-eyed stallion, and Lord was he angry with me! I'd seen Chester catch a runaway horse out on Howard Street one day by grabbing him by the bridle, but Chester weighed damn near twice what I weighed, and that horse he caught didn't have a general aboard with a big sword held high in the air! Still I owed it to my men to try and stop him, or at least go down with the ship, so I moved out front on that swaying bridge and set my feet nice and wide. I was bouncing from foot to foot as I prayed: "Sweet Jesus, I'm sorry to be such a troublesome soul, but could you come down here and help me toot sweet? And if that don't work into your schedule, dear Lord, could you just keep me from running?" I prayed and church was over!

"Keep your eye on the ball! Keep your eye on the ball!" I remembered my father telling me when we played baseball out in the Camden Yards, and my ball was the big white horse's head bouncing and frothing as it came on like a hurricane. That broom would be of no use to me, so I flung it at the oncoming general and leapt for the stallion's head, wrapping my arms up in the reins as we sailed off the bridge.

There I was all tied up and twisted, the flying horse slobbering all over me—his big brown eyes full of terror as we sailed through the air! Suddenly something hard hit my head and the lights went out. Oh, I knew when we hit the water, but as the cold depths sucked me under that big kicking war horse, the land of the living slowly disappeared.

Now, I'd been knocked out a time or two, so I knew what that burning smell of the Battery Room meant, and the hollow echoing sound of the world you weren't in and the one you weren't out of, and that burning in your crotch as you peed yourself pleasantly, but never ever was I unconscious underwater before! It was like I was in Heaven as the harps began to play, but on the wings of a prayer I don't even remember making, there came a loud splash, and I was picked up by a great giant who carried me ashore and squashed the water right out of me.

"Breathe, Major! Breathe!" said my big moujik friend. It was Yakoff Yakovich come to save me! I gasped for air and stared up at the big full moon that was glowing down even as the sun burned hot red in the sky.

Then I saw the Off White General all tied up and gagged right there beside me on that bouncing bridge. And there was his off-white horse—no worse for the wear, hauling away at the moorings with the rest of my four legged friends, which included all the lancers' horses Corporal Yakoff had brought along. We were a good ten feet off shore as I coughed and gagged and thanked Sweet Jesus for a job well done, and I could see Captain Rot fighting his way to our side—pitching any and all that wouldn't surrender right into Lake Dolgoye. We'd taken that pontoon bridge just as my scar-faced captain had planned, and General

300

Gurko got the hour he needed to set the trap on the Imperial Army. It was a victorious day as our cannons opened fire.

We all started to cheer, "Hip, hip, hurray for General Gurko!" and even "God bless Redbeard the Wild and Crazy American!"

"We heard the gunfire, Herr Maior," said Yakoff who was dripping wet too, "so we galloped to the sound of the guns!"

He let that sink in slowly, as it was clear that his major was a bit touched in the head. Then he went on about his mutiny at Fort Daniel Boone.

"Where's the maior? I asked Captain Leontieff," Yakoff told me sadly, "and his men pointed west across the water to where we are now, Herr Maior. Stand down, corporal, Captain Leontieff hollered. Tell me exactly where those horses came from and don't you lie! So I told him, the maior had given me orders to ride to the sound of the guns—which you had in a dream and off we rode."

"Don't worry about Captain Leontieff," I told my trusty corporal, "for when this is all over, they'll probably hang every one of us."

"You're bleeding pretty bad, Major Stewart," went my blue-eyed lieutenant. "Whoever hit you almost took off your ear!"

"That Guard general over there struck you, sir!" said a listening soldier as he pointed to our trussed up captive sitting there squirming away. "He hit the maior with the flat of his sword just before they went into the water."

"We best bandage that ear, sir," said my blue-eyed lieutenant who had a black eye of his own.

"Never mind me," I told him. "I want the USS Pulaski underway before the Imperials come back and murder us!"

General Gurko was still booming away with his artillery up to the east, though I could distinctly hear a good dozen whistles trying to blow him to a halt. The Imperials were not going to accept their defeat by a band of brigands—even if they had cheated by starting way ahead of schedule. The next sound I heard was the shrill whistle of the War Game judges shrieking for us to come back to shore. We were to untie the White

General or suffer the consequences! It took over an hour trying to paddle that pontoon bridge back to the western shore, and the whole time the Imperial Guardsmen were screaming for our blood.

"They cheated and snuck up on us," they roared. "They hit our general's horse with a broom!" One irate major with a big feathered hat yelled, "Hang them all and send them off to Siberia!" Though why they had to hang us before they shipped us off to Siberia was anybody's guess.

We untied the White General as ordered—even removed the gag, and although he was out numbered ten to one, he barked out orders for us to start rowing. So we paddled with staves, the stocks of our rifles, and even our brooms, for at that point I believe they would have shot every man jack of us had we disobeyed him! And when we finally reached the western shore, they carted me off in a cabbage cart.

We bounced up the hill to an old wooden theater where they marched me up on a stage. There were cuirassiers in their steel breasted chest plates, hussars with their wild colored jackets, and even the commander of the Imperial uhlans was there when he should have been out looking for his men. They were up on their feet shaking their fists and calling for my blood—save for this giant who sat with his back to me in the orchestra pit at a large oak table. He was bent over his papers like a moujik at the plow, but I could see the same sky blue sash across his chest that the gun-shy colonel wore. And up steps that chubby colonel with his dark black hair combed way back out of his snarly face, his piercing gray eyes glued on me as he screamed, "That little bastard dared to fire live rounds at a royal Romanoff!" And the room went wild!

"Silence!" yelled the big giant in the orchestra pit as he rose to his full six foot five. He must have been the first in line to the Russian throne, for the room fell silent in the blink of an eye.

"Live rounds came straight for my head, Your Majesty!" the big man sobbed like even recounting the story was too much.[128]

The great giant before me wore the green fatigues of a common soldier, though his shoulder boards said he was a full blown colonel just like the man that was screaming. He wore that sky blue sash and had the same steel gray eyes as the gun-shy colonel; only this man was definitely in charge. So I dropped my eyes to the lime light as Mr. Salomon had taught me to do with royalty and prayed to Sweet Jesus.

"What's your rank, soldier?" The heir apparent, or Naslednik, as the Russians called him, asked in English, having recognized that I was mostly in the uniform of a Yankee cavalryman.

"I am Major Robert Augustus Stewart, Sire," I said humbly. "I was sent here by the Germans to help you with your Telegraphic Service." I went on, hoping he'd see how far I'd been dragged from my chosen path.

"Humph," he said like he couldn't believe they were hiring short little mercenaries like me for his father's army. Then he hit me with the first direct question of the day. "Did you or did you not order live fire on my poor dear brother?"

My mother had told me sometimes a little white lie is better than telling the truth, and if I was to say to the next emperor of Russia, "Oh, yes Your Highness, I forgot to tell my men no balls when they reloaded— ain't that a little bit funny?" we'd have all been hung! So I answered with my first perjury of the day. "No, Sire, I most certainly did not! If the colonel thought he felt live rounds flying by, it was probably mud in the barrels, for we'd just waded across Lake Dolgoye."

That had come to me as an inspiration when I looked down into the crowd and saw the off white general standing there in a puddle full of muddy water. But the room went wild with that lie!

"Take him out back and shoot him! That man is a liar!" they yelled, 'til the Naslednik raised his hand over his head again, and they all fell silent.

"What do you think of our Baranov rifles, maior?" His Majesty asked.

Was I to answer him truthfully that they were less than stellar? Or did the big man want me to lie? If I could just look him in the eyes I might have been able to tell which way to go with my story, but judging by his size fourteen shoes (which was all I could see with my head hanging down) it could have gone either way. Still, if they were going to hang me, what did it matter? So I told him the truth.

"Well, Sire, they jam real easy, they misfire fast, and generally speaking they're a real piece of shit!" I told him without pulling any punches.

There was a wave of shock spreading across the room from a mere mortal like me cussing in the presence of the next emperor of Russia and defiling a fine Russian rifle in the bargain.[129] But the Big Man was so pleased with my answer that he laughed out loud and invited me to hop down and stand right there beside him—me coming up to about his nipples. He put a huge hand on my shoulder and smiled down.

"And how many rifles did you have out there at the pontoon bridge, Major Stewart?" he asked with that big paw still on my shoulder.

"Ten, Sire. Ten unloaded Baranov rifles was all we had," which they were, once we fired them.

"Ten rifles, that's all you had?"

"Yes, Your Majesty!" I answered with my eyes staring down.

"You mean your regiment turned and ran at the shots of ten rifles, colonel?" the big man bellowed at his baby brother. "And how many of your men were killed or wounded, Grand Duke Vladimir?"

"None, Sire," went my nemesis with death in his eyes. "But the Amerikanskiy he lies! They were definitely firing live rounds, I heard them hiss by my head!"

"You are certain those were not live rounds, maior?" the Tsarevich barked and I jumped and almost wet my pants again!

"I swear on my mother's grave, Your Highness," but my mother was still very much alive.

Those steel gray eyes of His Highness's were digging into my soul and the big giant pushed back his thick brown mustache and showed me his teeth that needed a good cleaning. "We have people interrogating your men even as we speak, you will die a slow death if you lie to the Naslednik!"

Well, I figured we would all die a slow death if we told him the truth, so at least we had a moment of suspense before the dying began. I prayed that the Pulaski Battalion held up under questioning, as I lied like a rug to the next emperor of Russia, Finland, and Poland.

304

"Colonel I want you to take your regiment on a forced march south and don't come back until I telegraph you!" said the Heir Apparent to his baby brother.

"But Sire, what about that little Amerikanskiy!" he screamed.

"Did I ask you to speak, colonel?" went the steel eyed giant and I realized His Majesty's rules were many and wide, but speaking when you weren't spoken to was a capital offence. "Now go!" he said, and from that day forward Grand Duke Vladimir hated me.

So charge #1 was dismissed—unless the Pulaskis broke under questioning, and on to charge #2 we flew, as the Off White General took the stand. He was still dripping wet and I swear I saw a little baby trout jump out of his pocket, that long white mustache hanging down sadly beyond the corners of his mouth.

"General, what is your case against Major Stewart?" asked the Tsarevich like he was starting to grow tired of these trumped up charges.

"Your Highness," he bellowed turning a deep shade of purple, "this Amerikanskiy struck my horse a powerful blow across his rump and sent us careening down the pontoon bridge nearly drowning several dozen of my men. Only with great effort did I turn my stallion around, Your Majesty, and I charged back to recapture the bridge, and then...," he coughed up a little lake water for effect and proceeded like a half drowned man. "He lunged for my horse and pulled us both into the ice cold waters of Lake Dolgoye."

"Were you not in a War Game with the major at the time?" asked the big giant with a smile spreading across his face as he looked down at the little mercenary before him and thought of my mounting crimes. "And were you able to pay the maior back for his insolence, general?"

"I struck him across the side of his head with the flat of my sword, Your Highness, but the little devil wouldn't let go of the reins!" he answered.

"Judging by the look of the poor major's ear, I'd say the two of you are about even, wouldn't you agree?" went the Tsarevich, and the whole room waited for the White General's answer.

305

"But then, Your Majesty," Old Muddy Waters went on with his whining. "His men captured me and tied me up like a…" he paused and coughed up some more lake water, "like a netted sturgeon" he added, and the whole room burst into laughter.

Now the Naslednik was having fun! Here was this little jockey in a Union bugler's uniform, boots squeaking, scars all across my face, fiery red hair and a red beard like Ivan the Terrible, freckle faced, and blue-eyed with the manners of a French courtier, being attacked by the White General for just doing my job. Tell me war—even faux war, ain't a little bit funny!

"General," barked my new lawyer in charge with his eyes burning through the Off White General's soul. "I think you and Major Stewart should call it a draw and shake hands. You behaved nobly out there, and you paid our new officer back for his insolent ways. Now go and get those wet clothes off before you catch pneumonia. Are there anymore charges against the major?" His Majesty bellowed!

I prayed to Sweet Jesus that those kidnapped uhlans didn't show up on cue, but the room stayed silent.

"Are there any more crimes against the Imperial forces you have committed today, Major Stewart?" my new benefactor asked like he wouldn't be surprised.

"No sire, not today," I said like a Boston lawyer. "The rest of the morning was kind of boring."

His Lordship roared and his flunkies all joined in. "Gentlemen, this inquiry is over," he roared with a slap on my back that would have sent the White General's horse flying. "Get back to your troops and redouble their training, and we'll put this loss behind us."

The next thing he did was very strange indeed, for he grabbed my jaw in a vice like grip and took a long hard whiff. You see, Russians don't accept the bravery of a drunken man—any drunk can do brave deeds. You've got to be sober for them to be impressed and he let go of my jaw, smiled down at me, patted my head like a little puppy, and said, "You truly are an amazing fellow! I am the Grand Duke Alexander Alexandrovich Romanoff and I'm pleased to meet you."

We were all alone after his men plowed out—save for a tall thin white goateed general who turned out to be the Tsarevich's Uncle Niki. They were overseeing the War Games, and as they stared down at their maps and wondered what had gone wrong, I said, "The vicissitudes of war, Sires," like I was a sage.

"You know General Clay?" asked the ramrod straight Uncle Niki as he pulled at his goatee, for it was one of Cassius Clay's favorite sayings.

"Yes, sir," I told him with my chest sticking out.

"A friend of that wild Kentuckian, no wonder the boy is blessed," went the next tsar of Russia, who then asked me another strange question. "I see by your uniform that you are a musician, Major Stewart. Tell me who was playing that fine piece down by the crossing the other night on a mouth organ?"

"Oh, that must have been me, Your Highness," I said with just a little pride. "That's my harmonica sitting right there on Your Majesty's desk next to my Bowie knife."

"Well, let's drink to the first victory of the Opposition Forces since the times of Peter the Great, and the little Amerikanskiy that God has sent down to play in my band!" His Majesty said with some mystery to it.

We held our glasses high and toasted the Tsarevich's father, Emperor Alexander II, Tsar of All the Russias, and with our glasses refilled we toasted the Opposition Army and General Gurko for being so fast on his feet, followed by a toast to the Crown Prince of Germany for sending me to Russia in the first place. The room was spinning by then and I'm pretty certain I blacked out, but the moral of the story is never drink with two men who are twice your size! Not if you want to keep your job.

Chapter Eleven

Gatchina Blues

I awoke all curled up on a polar bear rug in strange quarters with a splitting headache and a cotton mouth, not even sure what country I was in—much less whose tent it was. But it was a huge affair decorated in a Spartan style with a big wooden desk, two hand-carved chairs, a single iron cot, and room enough for an orchestra to stretch out inside. And judging by the way the grass was all matted down; I must have slept through the entire performance. I looked out the tent flap with blood shot eyes and there were guards posted at every corner. Then three colonels showed up and said I was to be relieved of my command and sent to a place called Gatchina. They'd even gone to the trouble of fetching my batman, our horses, and all our gear—minus our weapons, which wasn't a good sign!

There was a freight car waiting for us at the Krasnoe Selo Station and when we climbed aboard, not one of those colonels even bothered to wave goodbye. Yakoff looked a bit perturbed as the padlock clicked, and once we grew accustomed to the darkness in that rocking railroad car, he let me have it with both barrels.

"How do you get in so much trouble so fast, Herr Maior?" he asked, as if I could remember a damn thing!

We were locked in there for what seemed like an eternity—what with my head pounding, my terrible thirst, and the horses stomping about. One minute I'd been the proud victor of the summer War Games, a military genius loved by all (save for the gun-shy Grand Duke and the Off White General), and the next minute we were Gatchina bound for crimes unknown. I climbed up to gaze out a small hole in the rail car where a knot of wood had fallen out and there were birch and maple trees flying by as miles and miles of flat marshy swampland told me we were heading back north through the Neva Delta. Once we arrived at the freight yards south of St. Petersburg, our rail car was separated from the rest of the flock and we were left to sit on the siding in the sweltering heat. We figured it was better to be warm in the city of Piter than freezing in Omsk[130] and we sat there silently and stared at the walls.

With a bang and a boom we finally hooked up to another locomotive and an hour later the steam engine let out a long shrill whistle and began to slow down at a little station out in the country. The ramp came down and outside under a deep blue sky was a Cossack lieutenant and six blue clad lancers all lined up to greet us. The black bearded officer wore a long blue cherkeska down to his ankles with the crisscross lines of bullets across his chest. His well-polished boots glistened in the sunlight as he bid us to come out. I'd seen far too many of those long wooden lances to be impressed, but the way they held their weapons was totally different from the Imperial uhlans we'd tucked away in that barn. These lads held their lances like they were extensions of their hands—relaxed not jerky, all ready to pluck out an eye, or pick a nose—for every Cossack was a free man and did what he damn well pleased with his lance! They were like the Dog Soldiers of the Cheyenne Nation—wild warriors born on a horse—with tall fur caps, baggy blue pants with a bright red stripe down the side tucked into tall black riding boots, jewel encrusted curved cavalry swords, and a rifle strapped to each and every strong back. And although I was a very small man on a very large horse, and Yakoff was a very large man on a very small Steppe pony, the Cossacks didn't seem to notice at all.

"We are to escort you to Gatchina Palace, Major Stewart." The lieutenant said, as he sat his glorious Don stallion—a golden glow to the pony's withers as he and Boris looked eye to eye.

The Cossacks rode with their legs hanging down real loose—not as far down as Yakoff's long legs were hanging, but then none of them were as big as he was, nor were their ponies quite as short. The only person I knew in all of Russia that was my corporal's size was Alexander Alexandrovich, whose Royal palace we were apparently approaching. It was a big brown castle all stretched out on a hill with four tall towers. Boris's ears were way back as he tried to warn me the place was evil.

"What is your name, sir?" I asked the sotnik—which was Cossack for lieutenant, putting out my hand to shake his.

His only answer was, "They say your trombone instructor is waiting for you, maior, and we must hurry!" And then he just snickered.

309

"My what?" I asked, almost falling off my horse!

"Your trombone instructor, Herr Maior, he's waiting for you at the palace!"

"But I don't play the trombone!" I told him as I turned beet red.

"Well, the Tsarevich must think you do!" went the now laughing Cossack officer. "And what the Tsarevich thinks, he usually gets, so I'd start learning, if I were you! But Major Stewart," he added very respectfully, "could you answer one question for me?"

I figured word had gotten out about that barn full of uhlans, or my heroic handling of a charging horse with a general aboard, and I said, "Sure my Cossack comrade, ask away."

"Did you really sleep in a dead man's bed?" asked the blue clad Cossack.

If I'd known the colonel had died in his cot before I crawled in there, I'd have rather slept in a cave full of rattlesnakes, yet, as far as that sotnik needed to know, I was brave to the bone. "Why fear the dead when there's so many live ones out there that want to kill you!" I told him with a Stewart twinkle to my big blue eyes.

The lieutenant nodded to his men like I was the brave soul they'd heard about, and we rode on towards Gatchina Palace in silence. It wasn't much of a hill that the palace was up on, for in the Neva Delta where the great muddy river spreads out through the swamps and lowlands; there wasn't much high ground to be found. The Cossacks sat their mounts a little straighter as we approached—their black-bearded faces taking on cold absent stares as we came up to the green clad guardsmen at a little white and black striped shack. There was an arched stone bridge that led to a wide gravel square, and the place was huge.

"Tsar Paul tore up the gardens his mother and her lover had planted and made this whole area into a private Parade Ground," said the Cossack lieutenant. There before us staring north like we weren't even there was a tall bronze statue of the snub nosed Tsar Paul in his tricorn hat, right hand resting on his long staff as he stared critically at his army—still out there marching. In Russia the ghosts of yesteryear share space with the living, and I could feel the phantoms out there on the Parade Ground.

310

"The Kingdom of Shadows" the Russians called this alternate world where the dead go on with their lives in the same places that we mortals share. We were just a splash of light on their eternal canvas!

The Parade Grounds were over a thousand feet wide and five hundred feet deep to Gatchina's front door, with two long wings of the haunted palace wrapping around that central courtyard like the sides of a great stone coffin.[131] Boris could feel the ghosts of Gatchina too, and he snorted as if to say, "Let's get away from here while we still can!" But I ignored him and we rode on. And there, by the Palace Wing off to the left, was a long black funeral carriage with four black horses in shiny black tack, parked by the main door to what they called the Kitchen Wing. A tall cadaver of a man in black stood there by his hearse. Yakoff didn't want to go one step further, nor did Little Suli, nor Boris, nor any of the Cossacks, nor their fine Don ponies. Nor me either!

"This is where we leave you, Major Stewart." said the sotnik with relief in his voice. "We will take the horses over to the Farm Pavilion."

I dismounted and passed Boris's reins over to my trusty corporal. Then just like John Brown before me; I went alone and on foot to see what was what with that slack-jawed gentleman in the funeral attire.

"You are the Tsarevich's new trombonist, da?" asked this ghostly man with the stench of death coming from his rotten teeth.

Scary he was with long white fingers that showed every bone as he opened the back door of that ghostly carriage. He took out a leather tool case with wrenches and screw drivers and opened it up by the coffin rollers with care, then out slid the first long brass horn in a big black case. He passed it to me and shouted, "Sixth Position!" like it meant something to me. "Sixth position, please," he tried again, then seeing I had no idea what the Sixth Position was, he shifted me around like a manikin 'til he figured I was just about there. Holding my left hand and the horn up close to my body while my right arm was straight out, don't he yell, "Seventh Position," like any fool should be able to find the Seventh Position once you've been to the Sixth! He jerked at my arm and started measuring and adjusting, and finally, he gave up and put that trombone away and looked at me like I was some kind of criminal. Then

311

out of the hearse came trombone number two—a little bit shorter than the first one was (but just as cumbersome), and when he cried out Seventh Position this time, I stuck my right arm way out. And didn't he start fighting with my left hand, as apparently my fingers weren't curled just right. Finally, he decided the third trombone fit me just fine and after making several adjustments he was almost done. He must have had a funeral to be off to and told me the Tsarevich said I'd settle with him.

All I had on me was a five ruble gold piece, the rest of my funds being tucked away in a Berlin bank, and why in the hell would I be buying a trombone when I didn't even play one? But the answer to that question was plain and simple, for just as the sotnik had said, "What the Tsarevich wants, the Tsarevich gets!" And the cheap son of a bitch wanted me to pay for that trombone!

"How much is it?" I asked nice and politely, buying time before I broke the bad news to the undertaker.

"Four hundred rubles," he said, which was probably why he brought the hearse along, in case I keeled over from the shock of it.

"You got to be shitting me!" I said in English, but I'm pretty sure the malcontent understood me just fine.

"Three hundred rubles, and that's my last offer," he said.

"Well, I don't have it on me," I told him apologetically, but he was not pleased with my answer.

He started cussing worse than the Off White General, and I'm sure we'd have gotten into a fight right there by the palace doors had not the Tsarevich's majordomo come running out. He was a big round man— maybe five feet tall by five feet wide, dressed in colonial garb with a red and green livery, high white knee socks, and old fashion buckled shoes just like my old friend Ben Franklin wore. At his round middle was a great circle of ancient keys that jingled as he walked—a white wig on his head that bounced with every step, and a look of concern on his face as me and that trombone salesman were about to square off.

"Do we need the Palace guards?" went my Ben Franklin look-alike with his belly bouncing.

"This damn Amerikanskiy is refusing to pay what he owes me!" said the salesman, and he put his hand on me like he was gonna to drag me into that funeral carriage.

I could smell the last lilies to go in and was just about to haul off and hit him when the jolly little majordomo came to my rescue. "Just hand me the bill, I'll see that it's paid," he told the man sternly.

"I don't have a written bill made up yet," goes the trombone salesman, like he probably didn't want the Tsarevich to get wind of his milking the American. "But I'll send it right down when I do!"

"Very well," says my fat little friend—signaling a nearby sentry to stand down. "Follow me, Major Stewart. We are making a room ready for you and your trombone even as we speak."

We entered the belly of the beast through a door by a dome topped turret and swirled forever upwards through wide stone hallways and mammoth rooms that wanted to swallow me. The Grand Palace must have been vacant because all the statues had long white sheets over them and our footsteps echoed through the empty halls. We headed north for the peak of the Grand Palace curve where we wound our way up two sets of twisting stone stairs to the top floor, then walked east down a long corridor all the way to the other end of the palace with me dragging that trombone along. Then we entered a steep stone staircase that rose up through what they called the Clock Tower—which was a tall stone turret on the northeast corner of the palace. The majordomo was out of breath by then, taking a break to search through his ring of rusty keys for the door to the tower's fourth floor cell.

"They're here somewhere," he said, sticking an iron key halfway into the ancient keyhole with no effect, and then trying another one that didn't work either. Finally, a key went in with a hollow grating sound and the door creaked open to reveal what looked like a giant yellow spider web. There were cobwebs on the ceiling, cobwebs on the floor, cobwebs in the corners, cobwebs covering a painting that was covered by an old yellow cloth. I began to itch before I even went in. Nine hundred rooms in that Royal Romanoff palace and don't they want the little foreigner to practice his trombone in the one with all the spiders in it! But being the fine officer and gentleman I was fast becoming, and a bit afraid of my new Boss, I stayed silent and watched the festivities unfold.

"Don't worry, maior, the maid is on her way," the chubby little man told me as he stared at the mess, his cheeks blowing like he was playing my horn. He started swatting at the thick yellowy spider webs and coughed, for even he knew it was no place for a human being to be!

Over in the corner was a small iron cot covered in cob webs. There was a small bed stand with a wash bowl—some more cobwebs there. A little yellow wide-eyed Jesus icon was sitting there staring at me—all covered in cobwebs too! On the wall under that old yellow cloth was a painting of Tsar Paul in all his glory—that little snub nose sticking up in the air like what's that musty smell I smell? That huge stone turret cell had five sides to it—maybe twenty-five feet wide with fifteen foot ceilings and a loud grating sound coming from above us where an ancient clock rattled along. Four tall yellowy windows looked out towards a park full of lakes and forests shimmering in the midday sun, and in came the maid in her crisp white uniform huffing and puffing from the climb up those stairs.

She had a broom, a mop, a bucket of hot vinegar water, clean sheets, and a horse blanket in her hands. Small, muscular, all her curves in the right places—the only fault I could see was that tuft of wiry black hair coming off her chin, and a head the size of a full grown Orlov. But it had been several weeks since I'd seen a woman, so that horse head and those chin hairs seemed to grow on me. She worked away swatting at the cob webs—setting the bed stand free of that yellowy mass, and even washed that little three by five yellow Jesus icon who was smiling away. He was a little hot yellow Jesus with dark brooding eyes and a pair of the brightest red lips I had ever seen.

I took that broom and started swiping at the cob webs high on the ceiling to about the ten foot level with a hop, skip, and a jump, but the two Russians swung round and looked at me like I'd rogered the Emperor's wife! Doc always said the more hands the better, but apparently in this high classed society I was now in, things were done differently.

"She'll take care of that," the majordomo said with a look of disgust.

314

"Put down my broom!" said the horse-headed lady with her chin hair standing on end like a dog getting ready to fight.

Then the majordomo excused himself saying he'd go and get a man with a ladder to hit the cobwebs a bit higher (since it obviously bothered me), and the maid finally gave me a chore. She seemed quite scared of that old rusty bed and she dropped the horse blanket to the cot like it had leprosy. "That's the bed poor Tsar Paul was murdered under!" she whispered and crossed herself nervously. "And that's the last painting of Tsar Paul before he was dragged out from under there and strangled to death. Do you want the painting left covered so you can sleep at night?"

Sleep? Who said anything about sleep? Why, I figured this was to be my trombone playing room—far away from everybody's ears, not the place where I'd hang my hat at night! That clock up in the stone tower was clacking away the rusty seconds like Poe's tell-tale heart. No way was I sleeping in a dead man's bed—that ship had done sailed, and not even the next emperor of Russia could make me do it! And just as I was about to have a tirade, who steps in, but the Grand Duke Alexander Alexandrovich Romanoff himself.

The maid dropped to the cob web encrusted floor with her head bowed low—me bowing low and saluting the big man. Many times in my life the Tsarevich would show up just as I was saying or doing something that could offend him, and he was offended by many things in this life, but I smiled and prepared to lie like a rug.

"So Major Stewart," he said in a deep gravelly voice as he stared down his nose at me. "How do you like your new quarters?"

Those steel gray eyes were drilling into my soul as I stuttered, "Fi...Fi..Fine Your Ma...Ma...Majesty. That's a wonderful view of the lakes to the north—couldn't ask for a better place to call home!"

As I lied, I was looking into the deep dark eyes of that little yellow Jesus icon sitting there by the side of dead Tsar Paul's bed, and he seemed to be worried for my eternal soul as his eyes rolled back in his head. And there on that west wall was that painting of Tsar Paul with that stubby little nose saying, "Just wait 'til I get you in here all alone in the dark!"

315

"We'll have to keep you locked up at night for a while, Major Stewart," goes the Tsarevich all apologetic like. "Until I can thoroughly trust you, that is, for we have our women to protect, don't you know?"

And as the clock over our heads struck six and vibrated me across the wide stone floor, he and the maid left out the door. I could hear the key turn in the rusty lock and there I was hungry, homesick, thirsty, and forlorn. There was a thunderstorm coming in off the Gulf of Finland, darkening the White Nights as it spread its sounds of doom—great flashes of lightning and crashes of thunder, as I asked my little Sweet Jesus to please tell Tsar Paul to keep his eyes to himself!

About an hour later the storm broke hard on Gatchina Palace—hail rattling down so loud I missed the seven o'clock bell. But then there came a loud knock at my door and the guard handed me a canteen full of water and a plate of cold sausage and sauerkraut—compliments of the Tsarevich, as well as a chamber pot, a small kerosene lantern, and a couple of matches—God be praised! Let there be light was the word of the day, and suddenly those extra two pairs of eyes didn't seem half as scary! Still, I had to decide if I was going to sleep on the floor with the spiders, or dead Tsar Paul and I were going to come to an agreement, and if that lamp hadn't enough kerosene in it to work all night, I'd have probably gone with Tsar Paul's take on the subject and slept on the floor. But having had a few rough days, and what with that storm still battering us hard, the vote was a tie—and in my book, a tie goes to the living!

The next morning the majordomo showed up with some black rye bread and the best butter I'd ever eaten (they had a dairy right there on the premises), a pint of ice cold milk, and written orders from the Tsarevich for me to hop on the train to St. Petersburg and pick up my uniforms. My chubby little majordomo friend said the Naslednik didn't want to see that bugler's outfit ever again.

"What time does the train leave for St. Petersburg?" I asked the big burly gentleman in the Ben Franklin outfit.

"He looked at me like he was surprised and said, "Why, the train leaves Gatchina anytime you like, Herr Maior! Just give them this slip of paper and you'll be on your way."

The Romanoffs kept a brand new locomotive with several well-appointed cars on the siding all ready to go at a moment's notice, and up in St. Petersburg there was a Royal carriage waiting to pick me up. We scooted through morning traffic to the tailor's shop and they had the whole set of seven dress uniforms waiting for me. I'd only ordered two, but the next tsar of Russia had raised the ante, and of course I got the bill! Before heading back to the Royal Palace, I strolled about the Venice of the North on a little shopping spree. I bought dried cherries and apricots to see me through those long hard nights, backup candles, a lantern, a gallon of kerosene in a big tin can, two large boxes of matches, extra wicks, three books, two large white silk scarfs to cover those staring eyes, and some lip balm in case I really had to blow that horn.

When I returned to Gatchina in my brand new forest green major's uniform with my English riding boots shined to the bright brown color of Dead Tsar Paul's eyes, my chamber pot was empty, my bed was freshly made, and there was a written invitation sitting right there by my little Sweet Jesus icon that said I was to meet the Tsarevich for lunch. "Bring your trombone along with you, Major Stewart!" went the note with a golden double-headed eagle embossed on the top.

But first things first, I put those fresh white scarfs over Sweet Jesus and Tsar Paul's prying eyes, being too superstitious to move them. Then I moved my chair around so I could read with the sun behind me—gazed up under the bed and didn't see any signs of a struggle, hid my kerosene in the white marble fireplace up back of the flue with some backup candles and a box of matches, for night was when The Spirit World came calling on Redbeard the Scared!

That sword I was wearing was a thorn in my side as I descended those long spirally stairs from my Clock Tower cell. We never wore a sword in the 3rd Indiana, for if those ten shots from my revolver weren't enough, or the fifteen shots from my Henry rifle couldn't cut the mustard—a fast horse would do the trick every time. But there I was stuck up a clacking Clock Tower burdened with a long shiny sword and an even longer trombone in a big black leather case—and me with what some would call shorter than most appendages.

The gist of our little private lunch that day was that the honeymoon was over! His Lordship was expecting me to play that brass horn like the maestro he imagined me to be, or pay the piper for my lies. We ate cabbage soup and a few slices of black bread like a pair of moujiks, and then the Tsarevich got out his trombone.

"Follow me!" he bellowed like a moose in heat and the funny thing was I couldn't get my horn to give out one note, much less produce any music. I did manage to spit on His Majesty several times and that turned out to be Rule Number One—never spit on the next emperor of Russia!

"You have lied to me, Amerikanskiy!" goes the big giant with death in his eyes, and they locked me back up in my turret cell as he huffed and he puffed and he threatened to end my life!

Every day for a week we met for the same bland lunch out by the naked statue of Venus in the Private Gardens (just below my window) as the sun shone down upon His Majesty and me. He'd yell and scream about my failings as a human being in general and a musician in particular, and how my telling him lies would be the death of me, but I knew damn well that I'd never told him I could play the trombone—that was just wishful thinking on his part!

The Tsarevich had a conductor's baton made of ivory—long and nasty it was, with a great wide walnut handle, and he'd whack away at me every time my notes were less than perfect, which was always—and the welts were rising. Why, if I'd had my trusty LeMat at my side, I swear I'd have shot the big giant and let his gun-shy brother take over.

The next day was a Sunday and after a days' rest to think on my sins, His High and Mightiness decided to try a new tack. "Remember when you were inebriated when we first met, Major Stewart?" the big man asked, but I didn't. "Well, you started crying and said that when you caught that double lung shot wound, it affected your breathing." Although I had no recollection of that ever happening, I liked where he was going with it. "You even showed my Uncle Niki and I those terrible scars."

"I'm sorry I made a fool of myself, Your Majesty," I told him, putting the trombone down on the garden grass and gazing up at that Venus statue with her marble breasts pointing straight to the heavens.

318

"No, that's not the point at all, Augustus." We were on a first name basis by then—me being Augustus, and him being His Majesty. "The point is, maybe there is something medically wrong with you? I feel like such a brute!"

He was right about that brute part! I had bruises from his bloody baton all over my arms and back, plus a blister on my butt from sitting so much, cracked lips from that steel mouthpiece, and partial deafness—all because he wanted a trombone player for his private band.[132] I was relieved that the Tsarevich had finally figured out my deficiencies and praised him for his insight—only that backfired too!

"You will be going to the Military Hospital up in St. Petersburg tomorrow morning to be examined by the best doctor we have. Only then will we know the extent of your injuries," he said with a sad face. "Take the rest of the day off, maior."

I was off like greased lightning to see my horse at the Farm Pavilion, having gone without horses for far too long! Yakoff had made a place for himself there at the Royal stables riding out with the Blue Cossacks each day. When he saw me in my new major's uniform—my red beard trimmed neatly, my riding boots polished, and even that slapping sword at my side, he hardly recognized me. Boris on the other hand began to whinny before I even stepped out of the Royal carriage. We rode for hours on the wooded trails.

"How are they treating you, Herr Maior?" my moujik friend asked, his loose fitting infantry fatigues making him look like the peasant he was.

"Wonderful, Corporal Yakovich," I lied. "I've got my own private suite and a fine view of the lakes to the north, and the Tsarevich and I meet every day for dinner and a little trombone playing practice." I paused to contemplate just how to put those music lessons in perspective, and proceeded. "We discuss philosophy and music to our hearts content and nary a harsh word is spoken." I didn't tell my corporal that they locked me up at night like a common criminal, hit me and beat me for my off key ways, and made me sleep in a dead man's bed! My Momma said there was no reason to bore the rest of the world with your own private problems, so we just rode, and we laughed, and we drank a little.

319

"Did they give you your weapons back, Herr Maior?" Corporal Yakovich asked. The big giant was sleeping in the Farm Pavilion hayloft up above the horses, and save for the Cossacks—who spoke little Polish, he was not speaking to anyone.

"No, but I've got this nice long sword," I bragged though every time we took a jump, or broke into a gallop, that thing beat me worse than the Tsarevich did.

"Tomorrow I've got to go to the Military Hospital in St. Petersburg," I said all worried like. "That lung shot I may have showed you (and I had—several times) is acting up and the Naslednik says I've got to go get it looked at."

"Will you be all right, maior?" went my only true friend in all of Russia. I could see by the way his eyebrows scowled that he was very concerned.

"I'll survive, Corporal Yakovich. But would you like to come along and keep me company?"

"I would, what time would you like me to bring the horses around, sir?"

"Oh, we won't be taking the horses, corporal, the Grand Duke Alexander Alexandrovich is loaning us his train!" I told him all puffed up with pride. "The train leaves at 9:00 AM. Now, I'll race you and that scraggily little Steppe pony back to the barn!" And off we galloped.

Yakoff was amazed that we were the only ones riding the train the next morning. It wasn't a common train either, what with its posh leather seats, crystal gas lamps, mahogany trim, and even a bathroom for your private needs. A fine Romanoff horse drawn carriage was waiting for us at the St. Petersburg Station and whisked us away to the Imperial Medical Academy right in the heart of the city.

"Good luck, maior," Yakoff said sadly as he waited on a bench.

My doctor was a graduate of the prestigious Surgical Academy, a Dr. Alexander Borodin, who was also a chemistry professor who wrote and played music in his spare time. Not really practicing medicine anymore, he was seeing me as a personal favor to his benefactor, the Chief of Surgery. The preposterous nature of the Tsarevich's request to find me fit for trombone playing duty was a conundrum better passed down the line as far as it could travel, and it had landed right there on Professor Borodin's desk—all covered in papers. The good doctor was maybe ten or twelve years older than I was (me being twenty-six at the time), and he had a big black handlebar mustache and a dark serious look on his long noble face. Maybe six foot tall, he shook my hand and asked me to please sit down. "So what seems to be your problem, Major Stewart?"

What I really wanted from him was a note saying I should never—ever play that damn horn again, and how do you bring up something that strange to a man of science? So, naturally I fell back on my pièce de résistance and removed my tunic to show him my double lung shot scars. Then I explained how I'd come to Russia to set their Telegraph Service in order—skipped over the part about biting Old Number Nine, and went right on to having accidentally bumped into the Tsarevich, and how he somehow got it in his big thick Neanderthal head that I could play the trombone! Now, the Professor was a smart man, but I could tell I was leaving him in the dust.

"You can't call the next emperor of Russia a Neanderthal, major," he said, "though I have friends who might agree. The Chief of Surgery's note says: See if this man can play the trombone? What am I to make of that, Herr Maior?"

"Well," I said with a little twisted up grin, "since I never could play the damn thing, couldn't you just write no, and sign it with your name?"

But no! He had to poke and prod and gasp at my double lung shot wound, saying, "I have never seen anyone survive such a thing!"

"So will you write me that note or not, Doc?" I begged, for I had a bad case of the Gatchina Blues!

"That I cannot do, Major Stewart," he told me as he twisted at his long black mustache. Then with sparkling eyes he seemed to sense a solution. "My friend teaches Instrumentation at the St. Petersburg Conservatory, you can put on your clothes, major!" he abruptly added. "Perhaps I could write a note to the Tsarevich suggesting you see him for…," and he paused for just the right word, "remedial work."

Remedial work sounded like me to a T. "Fine, Doc, anything to get me away from that big bully," I said and he looked at me like I was crazy.

321

Yakoff and I had a nice lunch in the city and bought some more supplies, and then we boarded the Royal train and headed back home with my note from the doctor. His Majesty was busy, but when he was finished we met for a few minutes in his study. It was up on the Mezzanine Floor of the Arsenal Wing—to the east of the Central Palace, and he had windows there that looked out on the Private Gardens and my little Clock Tower cell, which must have been why he asked me if I'd been up half the night practicing. I was running through kerosene like Sherman ran through Georgia!

Anyway, His Highness opened the note from Dr. Borodin and sadly read: "To the Grand Duke Alexander Alexandrovich Romanoff. Your Majesty, I had the privilege of examining your friend Major Augustus Stewart, and his Civil War wounds would have killed a lesser man. These severe chest wounds may very well explain why he has so much trouble playing a horn, so, with Your Highness's approval; I would like to refer him to a friend at the St. Petersburg Conservatory, if Your Highness agrees?"

The Boss looked at me sadly like, "hang on son, we'll save you," and three days later he was heading up to St. Petersburg to set up my lessons. Luckily for me, the director told the Tsarevich that the whole idea was utterly preposterous! Not one of his music professors could take time from their busy schedules to provide "remedial studies" to an amateur like me. That was the best news I'd heard in years 'til I realized saying no to a Romanoff prince was like waving a red flag at a bull!

"We'll see about that, Augustus Augustovich," which was what the Tsarevich took to calling me when he found out my father was an Augustus before me. "My Aunt Elena Pavlovna is a great patron of the Arts. You will go to her palace and plead your case."

Now, notice he didn't say, "Oh, I'll handle that for you, Augustus Augustovich." No that would have been too easy! The Romanoffs were good at creating problems, but solving them was always somebody else's job. So two days later I traveled back to the Babylon of the Snows to see the Grand Duchess Elena Pavlovna.

I thought Gatchina Palace was huge, but the Mikhailovsky Palace[133] seemed twice as big, although once the Grand Duchess brought me into her den with rugs on the walls all cozy and quiet, I felt right at home. She had a big brass samovar going and she talked to me like a human being. The poor old lady was very sickly—all hunched over in pain, her hands withered and twisted. She was wrapped in a long silk dress of black; her auburn hair (probably dyed) was parted in the middle. Yet as sick as she was, she still had a fine smile on her face, and was as warm as my Grandmother Bloise.

"Amerikanskiy, da?" she asked with an open mouth like she didn't get to see many Americans around there. She poured my tea into a fine porcelain cup, then asked, "You didn't know Abraham Lincoln by any chance, did you?" for she was a big fan of the Great Emancipator.

"No ma'am," I said as I took a sip. "I shook his hand once and he was a real tall fella."

"And what about Ambassador Clay?" she said with a hearty smile.

"General Cassius Marcellus Clay was my mentor, Madame," I said in my best Miss Yvette French. "I worked for him at the beginning of our Civil War, and I love him like a father!"

"A Parisian accent, how wonderful!" she said. Her tired old face becoming that of a girl again as we talked of our love for Paris and all things French—save for their politicians.

She was a lover of the arts, music, and dance, and a hell of a lady. And although it was obvious that her time here on earth was just about over, the old woman's love for life was still burning bright inside her.

"So you never actually played the trombone before, monsieur?" she asked with a big Cheshire grin.

"No, Your Highness, like I've told everyone that asks me, I don't even like being in the same room as one of those long unruly horns!'

"Then why, Major Stewart, do you want to take trombone lessons at the St. Petersburg Conservatory?" she asked as she poured a drop of cognac into my tea just to calm my nerves.

"Well, that's the thing, Your Majesty," I said—glad to finally get to the point with someone sane. "It's the Grand Duke that wants me to play it!"

Her smile grew bigger as she became a young girl again, then Elena Pavlovna took a double shot of cognac and threw it back and laughed like a banshee! "Augustus Augustovich, they say the Tsarevich calls you, may I call you that too?"

She could call me anything she liked as long as she kept that twenty year old cognac coming! We talked about Miss Harriet Tubman and how we snuck the slaves out of Baltimore and poured the Knights of the Golden Circles' gold in the Chesapeake Bay. We talked of horses and France— our love for good schnecken, and then I stayed for supper. And when I went to leave her palace that night, she promised to get me into the Conservatory, for if there was one thing the Romanoffs loved more than money or power, it was being on the inside of a private joke on one of their own. One so deep I never did get it.

Three days after my visit with the Grand Duchess, I arrived at the Conservatory at the corner of Demidov Lane and the Moyka River Embankment as the bells of Saint Isaac's Cathedral announced the hour of eight in the morning. I waited at the door with my trombone in hand and up came a tall man in part of a Navy uniform. He was wearing bedroom slippers; a pair of spectacles pushed up on the top of his wild brown hair, and had a long Van Dyke beard of the same brown color.

"You must be the Amerikanskiy Grand Duchess Elena Pavlovna has talked so much about," he said. "I'm Nikolai Andreyevich Rimsky-Korsakov." He put out his hand to shake mine, and went on, "I visited your homeland during your Civil War. I saw New York, Washington, and Baltimore, lovely places all of them."

I was dumfounded that anyone in all of Russia could have been to my harbor home, but I thanked him and we got ready to play—him on the piano and I on my horn. After letting out what sounded like a wounded goose being strangled by an arthritic man, he took off his spectacles, cleaned them real good—closed his eyes for a quick little prayer, then said, "Try that again with a little more feeling."

I blurted out a few more notes and the poor man looked totally shocked. "Do you play any other instruments, major?" he asked in a hopeful way.

"Oh, yes indeed, I've been playing my harmonica since I was a boy!" and I whipped out my trusty Hohner and played him a nice little riff.

"Praise Jesus!" he said sounding relieved. "You are a musician!"

"What do you mean, Professor Korsakov?" I asked, for I'd never considered myself a musician before.

"You see Augustus Augustovich—may I call you that," he asked. "I see colors when people are happy and when they are sad. Colors that help me see into someone's soul, and you sir were enshrouded in a field of black as you tried to blow that trombone, while when you played your mouth organ, your aura changed to a solid gold."

I figured the Professor must have been eating some of Signora Fungini's mushrooms since never before or never thereafter did I ever meet a man with such talents.[134] But the fact of the matter was Rimsky-Korsakov could actually see what the trombone did to me! And when I realized that I finally had someone to listen to my problems, I unleashed my tales of woe, telling him of that raspy old clock clanging over my head, and that Jesus icon staring at me critically, while that Dead Tsar Paul painting scared me half to death! Oh, and did I fail to mention, that giant of a Tsarevich whacking away with his ivory baton! All that darkness came rushing out, and then Nikolai said something wonderful.

"Look, maior, you and I both know you will never play the trombone the way the Tsarevich expects you to play, so from this day forward why don't we spend ten minutes on the basics in case His Majesty asks, and the other fifty minutes we'll spend playing your harmonica. Does that sound fair?"

Fair, hell, I could have kissed the man! And out of gratitude, I asked Nikolai to lunch. And when I returned to the Conservatory to fetch him, there was the most wondrous violin music swirling through the air—like the music of a snake charmer in faraway Arabia.[135] The music drew me up to his classroom door and through the window I saw a thin tall beauty with her back towards me drawing her bow across her violin as those lovely notes swirled through the air. That music drew me away to a time without place and a place without time, and even before our eyes first met, I knew I had found my soulmate! But when she turned and our eyes locked in love, my heart pounded like a tympani drum, for there before me was my emerald-eyed Snow Maiden!

And even though Professor Korsakov had seen the golden glow on the two of us as our love first flared, he refused to tell me her name. "I am not a matchmaker, Augustus Augustovich," he scolded as he sat at his piano day after day. "She is a noblewoman from a family of great wealth and power, and you are but a foreign mercenary, and a commoner to boot. Now keep your mind on your music, if you please, Major Stewart!"

"Look Nikolai Andreyevich," I told my music professor. "What if someone had kept you away from Nadezhda?"

Nikolai had just gotten married and he was giving off his own golden light, yet try as I may and try as I might, he would not divulge the name of that beautiful woman. Each morning we would have tea and we'd talk about the weather, and music, and what we thought love was all about, but no matter how I prodded and pried, he would not say a thing about that gorgeous violinist. But like a good horse trainer he had me blowing that long brass horn for forty-five minutes before I even knew it.

"Your real problem Augustus Augustovich," goes the Professor one day, "is that you can't read music."

That was news to me. I always watched to see whether the notes went up or down and played accordingly. But he tried a little experiment and gave me a new song—one I'd never heard, and I'll be damned if he wasn't right.

"Here's our dilemma," my professor said as he scratched his head and pulled nervously at that brown Van Dyke. "You are progressing well with your trombone playing, and I'm thinking why lose the time teaching you how to read music, when your mind already knows which note to play? You get me the list of songs the Tsarevich plans to perform at his Christmas Recital, and we'll make sure you've heard every note a thousand times. That's probably our best chance at success."

So I got the list of Christmas songs—His Majesty being ecstatic to see me showing interest, and we began to work hard, the Professor on his piano and me on my horn. I memorized every up and down note, every rest, and every crescendo—I even took to practicing when I got home

326

from my lessons. The Grand Duke was so proud of the sounds he heard coming out of my horn that he and his wife would take their tea in the Private Gardens down below my Clock Tower just to listen in.

His Majesty's wife, Maria Feodorovna, was a real beauty—petite just the way I liked my woman with curly black hair parted down the middle— her ears so soft and tender, a long noble neck, and a narrow waist, and the body of an absolute goddess. Her eyes were a velvety brown and when the Tsarevna (which was her title) smiled, my heart would skip a beat. They would sit sipping their tea by that white marble statue of Venus in her birthday suit as Redbeard the Court Trombonist played from his tower above. Fall in all its golden glory came on as I serenaded the pair, and I began to have impure thoughts about my boss's wife!

And then came our first practice session with the boy's in the band. His Majesty must have figured he needed to refine my social skills before I conversed with his blue blooded friends for there in my freshly painted (and cobweb free) room, with my Sweet Jesus icon buffed to a high yellow sheen, and the frame of poor dead Tsar Paul's painting actually dusted and clean, a fine new goose down mattress, and a brand new pillow for my head, with a new wool blanket on that freshly made bed, was a little white envelope with a note from the Grand Duke that read: "Would you please join my wife and I for dinner in the Mezzanine at nine o'clock. Bring your best French," as he'd heard from his aunt what a fine Frenchman I'd make.

Their private dining room had a low arched ceiling with two small square windows that let in a modicum of light. There was not enough room in there for twenty people, which was the way the Tsarevich liked it. There before me was the next empress of Russia already seated and sipping her water out of a crystal glass as His Majesty stood with his hand outstretched—like maybe we should shake hands, or maybe I should kiss his ring, or maybe this whole thing was a big mistake. The Tsarevich grabbed me in a mighty bear hug and gave me those customary kisses and hugs that the Russians loved and then came the real awkward part, for although I'd seen his lovely wife from my tower many times before; we hadn't actually met. There she sat with her hand out stretched for me to kiss, and those soft brown eyes were drilling into my soul.

I could see her narrow waist as she breathed in and out, so I dropped my eyes like Mr. Salomon had taught me, and gave her a little peck on the wrist. There was just the three of us for dinner that night, which was a good thing, since they didn't have much to eat.[136] The maids in their nice white dresses brought in a small tray of already sliced roast beef, some raw radishes that the Tsarevna said were absolutely exquisite, and one small loaf of dark rye bread for the three of us, plus a big bowl of cold beet soup. I was figuring on roasted duck and pheasant under glass, and glasses and glasses of fine French wine, but we only drank water and the food was very plain. Maria Feodorovna was a lovely lady, and as she ate tiny little bites with her perfect little mouth and commented in her perfect French about each and every morsel, her husband frowned, and I fell in love just one more time!

"My husband says you are a great warrior, majeur. Is that true?" she asked with her sweet lips looking, oh, so tempting.

"Not really Your Highness, oh, I've seen the elephant a time or two, but I'm a scout and a telegrapher by trade."

"You're too modest, Augustus Augustovich. This lad once took down a charging horse with a general aboard, something I'll wager few men in this world can do," the Tsarevich bragged.

"And how did you come to be a trombonist, majeur?" Maria Feodorovna asked with an inquisitive grin, her little pixie ears looking oh so sweet.

"The vicissitudes of war," I said in my Baltimorese, for she made me feel right at home. She smiled and said she'd heard the same words spoken by the American ambassador, General Cassius Marcellus Clay.

"Well, Ambassador Clay was the one that taught me that word, Madame! He was my mentor when I was a boy. The finest American I have ever known, save for Miss Harriet Tubman."

"Harriet Tubman?" she said, surprised by my list of important friends. "Wasn't she a slave stealer and an emancipator extraordinaire?"[137]

"As my old free African friend, Chester Harris use to say, Your Highness, you can hardly steal what no man should own!" And we laughed as the Naslednik scratched his head in wonder.

I hadn't relaxed with anyone enough to speak my home style English in years, but Maria Feodorovna had drawn the city boy right out of me. I sat there making small talk with the next empress of Russia in the language of my harbor home as her big brown eyes caressed my blue ones. That's when the first of many thick serving spoons spun my way all twisted up in a tight little knot and splashed into my cold beet soup, as the Tsarevich glared down at me!

"It's not polite to stare, Augustus Augustovich! Keep your eyes to yourself!" he roared.

"Forgive me, Your Majesties!" I begged with my head hanging low.

His High and Mightiness paid me back in spades that night with our music lesson beginning early and ending late. First, he had me running scales for nearly an hour 'til my lips turned blue, and then we went over each of the songs we were to play for his Christmas Recital—then more scales just for the hell of it. All the while he was whacking away with that conductor's baton like Balaam spanked his ass![138]

The next evening his friends showed up for our first group practice and they dined with the Romanoffs until well after midnight. Two cuirassiers in their steel breast plates with big long swords escorted me down to the ground floor in my dress uniform when dinner was over. There was a huge room there—maybe a hundred feet long by a hundred feet wide that they called the Arsenal Hall with a grand view of the Private Gardens out ten tall windows. The guards parked me there to wait for the rest of the band, and there I sat like a race horse at the Starting Gate as they enjoyed their brandy and cigars out on the veranda. Then finally they arrived and I stood up with my trombone in hand and waited to greet them.

"This is the little Amerikanskiy I came across recently, gentlemen," the Tsarevich said like I was some rare butterfly he just caught down in the deepest and darkest of Borneo. "He doesn't play the trombone half as well as he told me he could." Which was a bold faced lie, but who was I to question the next emperor of Russia?

That was my formal introduction to the boys in the band, with not even a handshake. The rest of the quintet consisted of the following: A big tall cavalry colonel with a white goatee and a huge black mustache with enough medals on his chest to sink a battleship. He was on the cornet and trumpet. Then there was a major of cuirassiers, his steel breast plate shining in the gas lamps—a short little man, though when Yakoff saw him he said he was taller than I was. Next was a gay blade by the name of Prince Vladimir Mesherskii on French horn and clarinet, and didn't that big Nancy have his eyes on me! As straight laced as my Boss always was, he ignored everything that the Prince threw at me. Then finally on the oboe, trombone, tuba, and French horn—depending on the song we played, was His Majesty the Grand Duke Alexander Alexandrovich.

We were tearing through the Christmas songs with me to the rear taking hardly a whack, when don't His Highness throw us a curve ball! "I have a new song to add to our repertoire." He announced with great fanfare.

I dropped my eyes in prayer and said, "Sweet Jesus this is Augustus Augustovich, kind Sir, please give me a song I know!"

And I'll be damned if The Lord wasn't listening, for the new song was Oh Tannenbaum, that fine German tune that the Secesh had murdered with their Maryland My Maryland. We Yankee Marylanders use to make fun of their tune by singing, "Which despots heels are on thy shore," meaning the despots were quite possibly the slavers who were trying to steal our state away, not old Abe Lincoln like the Rebels meant it. And thus I knew the gist of the rise and the fall of the notes almost like I was reading the music. We played a total of ten songs that night, though the Tsarevich said we sounded like a bunch of drunken moujiks. We played Good King Wenceslas, Silent Night, Hark the Herald Angels Sing, God Rest Ye Merry Gentlemen, Joy to the World, While Shepherds Watched, The Twelve Days of Christmas, We Wish You a Merry Christmas, God Rest Ye Merry Gentleman, and of course my new favorite, Maryland My Maryland by way of Oh Tannenbaum.

"Would you like to stay and enjoy a cigar and some cognac out in the garden?" asked the Tsarevich after we finished.

I declined, for I had my trombone lessons in the morning and they were tiring me out. I went to bed at 3:30 only to rise again at 6:00 AM to head for St. Petersburg, and then it was back down to Gatchina Palace to practice some more, then a little horseback riding with Yakoff and the

Blue Cossacks. We'd ride the trails out to the northwest of the Farm Pavilion—throwing up a jump or two and betting heavily on the outcome. Then at precisely 11:00 PM each evening the blue bloods would show up in the Arsenal Hall and we'd play 'til maybe three or four in the morning. Then it was off to bed in my Clock Tower cell for a couple of hours as that rusty old clock clacked away like Poe's pendulum, followed by reveille and another busy day.

My nerves were so frayed that when the church bells rang at St. Isaacs one day, I jumped up and almost peed myself. And all that time, I was sleeping in a dead man's bed with a little yellow Jesus staring at me critically! You try that and see how sane you stay? Poor Old Redbeard was withering away—and nobody seemed to notice!

The Naslednik finally noticed I was looking poorly, and he probably figured I wouldn't live 'til his Christmas Recital, so he doubled the rations at lunch. He and his wife would be smiling away, as I tried to stay awake, and the strange thing was, just like those boys in the band, they almost forgot I was there.

"I wish you would spend less time with Prince Mesherskii!"[139] My favorite brunette would say to my bully Boss right in front of me, like I was a fly on the wall.

I wished to spend less time with that prissy Prince too. Why, if he goosed me one more time, I swore I'd cold cock him, though that may be a poor choice of words!

"You stay out of my business, Minnie!" goes the Tsarevich with a big red face and I tried to blend in with the silverware.

Then at 11:00 PM sharp it was post time and the Grand Duke put his band through our paces. He was particularly rough on me that night—not only striking me with his baton for coming in too soon, and too late, and too flat, and too sharp, but for, "the inflection of that last note you just blew," whatever an inflection was? At three thirty in the morning I was falling asleep at my horn when he finally dismissed me.

The boys in the band looked outside at the snow coming down and they decided to spend the night. "Would you like to join us for a little cognac, a cigar, and a trip to the Banya?" goes Prince Mesherskii with a boyish

331

grin. That meant they were going to take a long naked steam bath and roll buck naked in the snow after beating each other with these little birch branches. Why, I'd have sooner had my teeth pulled with a rusty pair of pliers than get naked near that Prince!

"Thank you kindly," I said with all the respect I could muster. "But six in the morning comes awfully early, and I have my music lessons up in St. Petersburg early tomorrow morning."

"A hard working Amerikanskiy!" goes my gay blade friend, patting me on the rump like I was his stallion.

I left as the boys in the band prepared to take the hottest steam bath known to man. Up to my cell I climbed. The cuirassier guards locked me away while the Northern Lights played on the sparkling snow—great sheets of greens and golds swirling through the heavens. The Aurora Borealis had visited us after the battle of Fredericksburg back in 1862— twelve and a half thousand crawling blue casualties lay on a snow covered hill as the Northern Lights played across their dance of death. Behind a low stone wall up on the hill above us, the Rebels were praying, for they'd never seen the Aurora Borealis before, and they were sure the End of the World was coming for us all. And that night in Russia, all that death and destruction came back to haunt me!

My trusty little Sweet Jesus flickered bright yellow in the eerie light as his deep black eyes stared into the darkness of my soul. I saw the blood of Fredericksburg on the snow outside, and smelled the foul smells of death all around me. And just as that raspy old clock hammered out four in the morning, there came the strange creaking sound like the lid of a coffin being opened somewhere nearby. The smell of a musty tomb filled my room, as my knees knocked and my heart pounded, and then a pair of tiny warm feet was pressed up against my ice cold ones, followed by a pair of nice warm breasts to my chest, and suddenly my fear of the afterlife was over!

We kissed and we rolled about like two strangers in the night, ready to set the world on fire as the Northern Lights danced through the sky. I could hear the Lord's a leaping out in the garden and figured it was riders up for Old Redbeard too! We took high jumps, and low jumps, doubles, and triples, even a chicken coop or two, and then we lay back and cuddled a bit before the second race began. On and on we went through that magical night and in the morning when I awoke, I swear my little Sweet Jesus icon had a grin on his face, and that Tsar Paul painting finally looked at me with respect.

When Tsar Paul ran Gatchina Palace they say he had thousands of rules. His soldiers had to wear tight little Prussian uniforms with powdered wigs, and the birds weren't allowed to chirp before seven in the morning. Well, my mystery maiden laid down plenty of rules for me too—there was no light allowed in my room once the bugle blew, no loud sounds of ecstasy, no passionate love bites, no talking, no going south of the border, why even my icon had to be covered with his little silk handkerchief before the games could begin. Gatchina rules were many and various, but believe me, I wasn't complaining—not one little bit!

Day after day this routine went on. Up at six to catch the train to Piter, back at noon to practice my horn, lunch with Sasha and Minnie, then some riding for outdoor exercise, followed by a little light dinner. Band practice with the lords a leaping came next, then back to my cell by four in the morning for some good hard steeplechase racing.

They were burning my candle at both ends and I was quickly running out of wick! My lips turned blue, my skin went gray, and I was down to a hundred and five pounds—so weak I could hardly stand—much less blow that bloody horn. Professor Korsakov took one look at me before class one morning and asked if I'd like to go to the hospital.

"Look at you," he said, "you're a bag of bones. What you need, Augustus is to see that young violinist. She'll put some life back in you!"

"Which woman would that be, Herr Professor?" I asked with a weak mind and a worn out body.

"You know, the girl who made your heart sing as she played her violin, you remember her, don't you, Augustus?" he asked. But I was not well.

I passed out coming down the railcar stairs that day, hit my head, and Yakoff had to carry me into the palace. And when Maria Feodorovna saw the condition I was in, she hollered, "Someone call the Doctor!"

"My God," said the doctor as he took up his stethoscope and listened to my lungs, "this poor man has walking pneumonia!"

Walking pneumonia, hell! I had the too much trombone playing, over worked, over sexed, under fed, raspy clock ticking over my head kind of pneumonia, and that was the worst kind you could get! Doc Hirsch told the Tsarevich he couldn't put me back in my stone tower turret without killing me, so the Romanoffs packed their things and moved back to St. Petersburg. The Anichkov Palace was right in the heart of the city, where a fever almost took me. And when I finally awoke from days and days of bad dreams, there was the Naslednik praying at my bedside.

"I'm sorry Dear Lord that I worked this poor boy down to the bone, but if you let him live, I promise to be a better master from this day forward." He said with tears in his eyes.

I kept my eyes shut tight and listened to the big man pray as I realized that if I'd done him wrong in any way, it had to stop! There'd be no more fornicating, and no more lies, and as I slowly opened my eyes, there on my bedside table was my sweet little Yellow Jesus icon smiling away.

"Where did you get that glorious icon?" Alexander Alexandrovich asked as I came to my senses.

"He was with me up in my Clock Tower cell, Your Highness and he must have followed me here," I answered as truthfully as I could be.

My new life of truth and honor had begun, and I was figuring on how to tell Maria Feodorovna the fun was over, when in came my trusty corporal with some interesting news. "I just had a talk with that upstairs maid from Gatchina—the one with a head the size of a healthy Orlov and those bristly chin hairs. She sure is a beauty from the neck down," he snickered. "She was asking about your health, Herr Maior, and she called you her little pillow." He said, which just might explain the rash I had!

As I convalesced in my suite on the third floor of the Anichkov Palace, I read the illustrated version of Jules Verne's Twenty Thousand Leagues Under the Sea that the Tsarevich and his wife had given me. My room had high ceilings and gold gilded mirrors, and the windows looked down on the Fontanka Canal. Over my head was a huge gas candelabrum that lit Mr. Verne's wonderful words, while room service brought me caviar,

334

oranges, and champagne at my slightest whim. That mattress in there was the finest of goose down, and I had sheets of silk with warm wool blankets. My old friend Yakoff slept on a cot by my door to let whoever that night visitor was, know Old Redbeard was closed for business!

A week after I went down, Dr. Hirsch pronounced me fit as a fiddle, but I was so frail my first day back at trombone practice that Yakoff came along to carry my horn. When we arrived at the Conservatory, the Professor had the samovar going and a little surprise, for there chatting away with Nikolai was that emerald-eyed Snow Maiden that had taken my breath away the first time we met. She was absolutely beautiful—her long regal neck like Nefertiti, her thin little waist and warm sweet smile drawing me in like we'd been lovers forever!

"Countess Nadia Shuvalova, may I introduce, Major Augustus Stewart of the Emperor's Own Infantry." Professor Korsakov solemnly said.

"I'm pleased to meet you," I said in the language of love as I kissed her hand and smiled. And as our eyes met, the tympani drums beat and I knew I had found my soulmate once more! She asked me where I'd learned to speak French so well, but I could not say a word.

"The Major is fluent in several languages, Countess Shuvalova," the professor pitched in. "But he is still quite weak from a recent illness, so please forgive his lapse of consciousness."

Oh, I was conscious alright, but my heart was in my throat. There before me was the true love of my life, and as we talked and we laughed—drank tea and ate schnecken, the sparks flew, as did the time.

"I'm sorry Major Stewart but our hour is up," the Professor said somewhere back in my mind.

And when I asked Nadia Shuvalova if I could walk her home, or take her to tea, or anything else she would like me to do, she politely said, "No thank you, Major Stewart," in her perfect English, then smiled a perfect smile, and flashed me those perfect eyes! "Come to my Uncle's home this evening, maior," she said in her mother tongue, "and you can ask him yourself. If he says yes, you can escort me anywhere you like."

I ran home to the palace to ask Alexander Alexandrovich if he would write me a letter of introduction to Nadia's Uncle Peter, not realizing the

Naslednik would take exception to me finding love on company time. He was sitting in his library reading my copy of Jules Verne, so I stood at attention and waited for the big man to finally look up. About a half hour later, he placed a gold book marker between two pages, closed the book real slowly and said, "What is it this time, Augustus Augustovich?"

"Well, Sire," I said with my eyes cast down. "I think I've found the woman of my dreams, and I was wondering if you could write her uncle a letter of introduction, Your Majesty."

"Who is this unlucky girl?" he asked, and when I told him it was Nadia Shuvalova, he roared, as he stood and did a little jig like a circus bear.

"Nadia Shuvalova is only the most sought after young lady in the Land of the Firebird, and her Uncle Peter is the most dangerous man in Russia! How is it you came to meet her?" he asked as he stopped dancing and stared down at me.

When I told him we'd met at the Conservatory, and that she'd won my heart with a violin piece reserved for the angels, he first warned me not to blaspheme the angels, then asked me what I was doing chasing women when I was supposed to be perfecting my trombone playing skills? "Absolutely not!" said His Majesty, like it was final. "And don't say another word, or I'll have you flogged!"

"Flogged, what's this all about?" came a voice we all knew and loved, as Maria Feodorovna came into the room. In public, the big giant wouldn't take any questioning from anyone, but in private, Minnie ruled the roost. She sucked the whole story out of him in seconds, then smiled and put a gentle hand on my shoulder, and gave me a pat on the head. "Why, Sasha, you know the major has given us his all, time after time," she said with a knowing smile. "Who are we to deny his love for this Shuvalova woman? Now you write Count General Shuvalov a nice little letter of introduction. It won't kill you to help a friend out." And armed with that short little letter, I set out for the Shuvalov Palace.

It was but a few minutes' walk up the Fontanka Embankment, the canal now frozen and sparkling in the golden lamplight. And as I came up to the two little arched wooden doors in the middle of the palace block, I had no idea what to do next. Do you knock and wait for an answer, or do you enter, and then brazenly announce yourself? The Romanoffs always had guards at their doors, but here at the Shuvalov Palace there was just a big tall door on a busy street. Then a sweet voice cried down from a second floor window, "Are you planning on standing there all day Augustus Augustovich, or do you want to knock and come in?"

Just inside the unassuming doors the majordomo waited—all decked out in the colonial garb that the Russians loved to dress their help in. He said General Count Shuvalov was waiting for me at the top of the stairs in the Grand Ballroom. So I went through a long narrow hallway covered in white marble with small Greek columns of more white marble, and as I climbed up that grand white marble staircase, the room opened up before me like a white marble heaven. And there at the first landing with maybe eight steps to go before the staircase split in two and sailed upwards from both sides of the room, stood the Count General, and he wasn't smiling!

He wore the forest green uniform of a Russian cavalryman—right up to the well-polished knee high riding boots with spurs, a long sword, and a pistol in a fine leather holster. On his chest were rows and rows of medals. His short dark hair had a high widow's peak, and he had a big gray mustache below his haughty nose. "I only agreed to see you, maior, to explain why you and my niece can never see each other," he said with a frown.

We stood on those marble stairs in silence with his foot about to give me the boot, as I handed him up my papers and rendered him a fine salute. That big room took me by surprise, rising from the simple door and narrow hallway into something bigger than a cathedral. I looked all about—thinking I caught the sight of Nadia up there on the second floor landing as His Eminence read the Naslednik's note.

"And who was this man you took down on a galloping horse, Major Stewart?" asked the ramrod straight general as he hovered above me.

"It was the White General in charge of the Guard Units at the summer War Games, Count General Shuvalov," I answered respectfully.

The big man laughed like a sea lion, then invited me up to his library. We entered a gold gilded room full of gold gilded books, with a long mahogany table all covered with liquor in gold gilded decanters. I reminded myself of what happened the last time I drank with the nobles and was on my guard.

We drank to the Tsar, and we drank to the Tsarevich, and we drank to the Empress of All the Russias. Then we drank to Nadia's poor dead mother, who'd died when Nadia was just a little girl of five. I could see that he loved Nadia more than life itself, but then so did I, so I stayed hopeful.

"And her father, Count General, who was he?" I asked, as I tried not to slur my words.

"He was an officer in Tsar Nicholas's Army," said the Count with a little tear in his eye. "Killed in the Crimea, he never got a chance to see his baby daughter." And we drank a toast to him as well. "Nadia is like a daughter to me, maior, and although you are not of her station in life, I like you, so you can escort her to the Conservatory, or the Tea Room, or even out shopping—if she wishes." He paused as he thought up the ground rules. "But if you touch one hair on her head, or even try for a kiss, I swear I will have my Cossacks cut you in half!"

That went well for a first meeting, and unlike my last toasting session with the Romanoff princes, I was still standing when the toasts were over. But the Tsarevich, being damn near a teetotaler (despite what the Bolsheviks said), wasn't pleased with my liquored up ways when I returned to the Anichkov Palace.

Maria Feodorovna—on the other hand, gave me a big Russian hug and the customary kisses, which made her husband come over and try to break me in half with his hugs and kisses too. We were a hugging and a kissing trio that night, for love was in the air!

Chapter Twelve

Nixa's Bride

My plan was to talk Professor Korsakov into giving a little soiree so Nadia and I could get together on a more social basis. Oh, I rode with her to the Conservatory six days a week like a good bodyguard should, but I wanted more than her friendship—I wanted her love!

"You don't want to tempt Peter the Fourth," the Professor said when I broached the subject. "As head of the Secret Police, Nadia's uncle is a very dangerous man, Augustus, and he wouldn't hesitate to crush you!"

"I want no part of the man, Nikolai Andreyevich," I said to comfort my musical friend. "It's his niece I long to love!"

"You have rich people in Baltimore, do you not, Major Stewart?" the Professor asked, as he shook his head like I was totally daft.

"We do Nikolai, that we do," I told him with a big wide grin. "But we keep them behind a great stone wall so the rest of us mortals won't pollute the air they breathe."

"Well, in Russia, Herr Maior," he bantered right back, "we not only have walls to keep the moujiks out, but we have Cossacks to cut them in half."

"If I was to pay all the expenses of a little soiree to be held at your apartment, Nikolai, would you agree to invite Nadia Shuvalova for me?"

Silence reigned in the classroom that day. The Professor wasn't expecting me to become an accomplished trombone player, and soon the cat would be out of the bag with my Boss. I only had a few more weeks to win Nadia before the whole house of cards came tumbling down.

"Well, Professor, what about it?" I asked loud enough to wake the dead.

"It depends on whether you can help me with a little problem of my own?" he said with a devious grin.

"You name it, Professor Korsakov, and I'm in!" I answered without even stopping to think.

"My old friend, Modest Mussorgsky, won't move out of our apartment, and quite frankly the place is feeling a bit cramped now that I'm married.

So, if you could find a way to get the Imp to move out of our apartment, I'd definitely host your little soiree."

"No problem, Professor," I said all excited like. "My corporal and I can toss him out on his ear this very morning!"

"It's not like that, Augustus Augustovich," he said sharply like he wished he'd never brought it up. "Modest was my Best Man and we both love him like a wayward brother. I don't want him tossed out of the house on his ear; I want him to go by his own volition."

I wasn't exactly the subtle type, but I figured what Professor Korsakov meant was, if anybody could get the Maestro to go astray, it would be a wastrel like me. So I agreed to try and entice The Imp, as his friends all called him, away from the fold without him even noticing he was gone.

"And Augustus," says the Professor with a worried look on his be-speckled face, "we never had this conversation! Do you hear me?"

Oh, I heard him alright. Should the plan blow up in my face, well, who knew what a foreigner like me would say to a sensitive man like Modest Mussorgsky? But as long as we got that soiree going, I'd have stopped at nothing to remove that Imp from the premises!

"What conversation?" I said, happy to have a challenge in life. "Why don't you let me pay you for today's lesson, and we'll skip the rest of the session so I can go and work up a plan."

I'd been whittling my trombone lessons down with a longer and longer tea break and Nikolai hadn't even noticed, so buying a few more man-minutes[140] was well worth the money. The next day, Herr Professor looked a bit guilty—possibly for conspiring against a friend. His pogoni usually sat high on his shoulders, but on this day his shoulders were stooped and his epaulettes sagged, and he looked tired and troubled.

"I was thinking about you last night," he said as he took a sip of tea. Usually he barked out orders like the naval lieutenant he was, but on this morning he was solemn and subdued. "You are truly in a ridiculous position, are you not, Herr Maior? How strange this must all seem to a man who has come half way around the world to play a trombone that he never could play!"

340

He was right too, being a Yankee in the Court of the Russian Tsar was a rough business to be in, but I'd have fought bulls with my bare hands to be with Nadia! The mere mention of her name made my heart soar and I longed for her love more than anything in this world!

Nikolai told me his new bride would love to have me come over after class to talk about hosting our soiree, and I figured that was code for discussing the disappearance of one Modest Mussorgsky. But once more my Professor corrected me. "Now Augustus, remember Nadezhda doesn't know you're there to lead The Imp astray!"

"Nikolai Andreyevich, do you want the Maestro to move out of your house or not?" I asked, for these Russians were killing me with their strange innuendos and shadowy ways.

"You get rid of him, or there will be no soiree!" he answered.

Now we were getting somewhere, that piano playing man needed to get himself gone! Dumping his body in the Neva was definitely out, so basically the ground rules were: the Professor's wife couldn't know we were leading the great composer astray, nor could The Maestro suspect he was going anywhere fast. Then I remembered something my old free African friend, Chester Harris, had taught me when I was rushing the jumps up on Gunpowder's back. "You got to let the horse chose his path to the jump, Augustus! Don't rush him. He's the one making that jump. You just sit back there and make yourself scarce, that he'll do the rest for himself." And that was exactly what I needed to do with this wild Russian musician, he was crazy enough to find his own way out of the house—all I had to do was give him a nudge.

"How about we skip the rest of today's session so I can go pick up a few house warming gifts for Nadezhda?" I said and the Professor bought it lock stock and barrel.

I couldn't meet the Professor's new bride without some kind of presents, so off to the market my moujik friend and I went through a Russian snow storm of epic proportions. Yakoff was waiting up against the frozen Moyka Canal as the snows came down—maybe ten inches on the ground since I went in, the wind whistling out of the north. Little Suli the Second's shaggy coat was full of curly lines of tiny snowballs, while

Boris's snow covered back had gone from jet black to pure white and fluffy. Corporal Yakovich was in his long gray greatcoat with a wide fur hat wrapped around his black-bearded face, smiling away like a cheerful snow man, for those Russians loved their blizzards.

"Where are we off to on such a fine morning, Herr Maior?" he hollered over the raging storm.

"We're off to the markets at Gostinny Dvor to buy some house warming gifts for Professor Korsakov's bride." I said. "And to see a man about a horse, if he's home," I added with great anticipation.

"Oh, you don't want to buy a horse in the dead of winter, Herr Maior! Buy a horse in the spring and you won't have to feed him through a long hard winter, that's the way you buy a horse in Russia."

Well, hopefully, the horse I was after wouldn't need to be fed through the whole winter. But if I had to pay the Maestro to take a trip around the world, it would have been money well spent, as long as we got that soiree going!

The whole time we shopped, I kept thinking of plans to expedite the great composer's exit. We bought a dozen fresh oranges and some tea from China, and I thought of hiring some cocottes to entice him away, then a crystal vase, and a big bunch of hot house chrysanthemums, and I thought of getting him drunk and kidnapping him. Then thoughts that Modest Mussorgsky might help me celebrate my twenty-seventh birthday came to me, for I'll be damned if it wasn't the 9th of December! We bought a small ham, a dozen eggs, a pound of butter, a pound of cheese, and enough flour for me to make the Professor's bride (and hopefully the Imp) the best Maryland biscuits they ever ate.

Yakoff and I kept our heads down as we headed south past the Anichkov Palace, so the Tsarevich wouldn't spot us not working. We crossed the bridge of the four horsemen all covered in snow, then turned right on Liberty Street and headed into the wind as it buffeted us about. For six long squares we fought that hard north wind till we came to Furshtatskaya Street, and there we turned right and rode on to Building #25 where Rimsky-Korsakov, his bride, Nadezhda, and good old Modest Mussorgsky lived.

I hollered to Yakoff, "Do you want to come in and meet a famous Russian composer?"

"No," the big man answered with a tip of his snow covered hat. "We Russians," and he looked at Little Suli and Boris—who looked like Yetis all covered in snow, "will wait outside in our element, Herr Maior."

Up a flight of steep stairs I climbed to Apartment #9 with the sounds of a sad (and big by my reckoning) baby pounding on a piano. The stairs shook from the dark colored notes, and not one of those notes was in harmony either—just a clang, bang, boom, like the piano had been turned into a big bass drum. Could that be the sad dark tune of the Maestro? I knocked on the door kind of fearful like for those weren't the notes of a sane man at all, and finally after much pounding, someone heard me and the delicate face of a beautiful lady with long brown hair poked out.

"You must be Augustus Augustovich?" she yelled. There was a sheepish smile on her face like she didn't know how to explain those tortured notes, so she pretended they weren't there. "Come in please, my husband has told me so much about you, Major Stewart."

Whereas, I was at a distinct disadvantage regarding the lady of the house, for Nikolai Andreyevich never talked of his private life—save to ask me this one little favor. He had not said his bride was petite and beautiful with lovely brown eyes, he had not told me her smile could melt a winter's snow storm, nor had he said she could yell like a longshoreman as she offered me tea over the roar of that poor tortured piano. All I could see in their parlor was some maps of Japan on the wall, yet definitely that baby grand was in there somewhere!

There came a silence so sharp you could cut it with a knife, as I gave the house warming presents to my lovely hostess. It was as if the being in the next room was listening in and waiting to begin his banging once he got the gist of our conversation. I tried to figure out if we had enough rope in our saddlebags to tie the man up and get him to an asylum, but Professor Korsakov would have probably frowned on that.

"Who is this little Amerikanskiy that comes to disturb my peace?" Came a squeaky little voice from the other room. Nobody had said how big the Imp was, but I subtracted about four feet of rope when I heard him.

343

"Why, Modest, this is the American major that Nikolai talked about," said the Professor's wife. "The one whose Cossack friends call him Redbeard the wild and crazy American, don't you remember?" But there was no answer. "He's come to visit us," she added, as she cut the bottoms off the chrysanthemums and placed them in the vase I bought her. "Would you like to come out and meet him, my darling?"

"No thank you, Nadezhda!" the Maestro said like a mouse in the corner. "Tell him to go away—Modest Mussorgsky needs no guests today!" And then he fell silent again.

I was thinking if I didn't at least meet the man, how could I play it by ear regarding his soon to be disappearance. It was obvious the Professor's wife loved him like a brother, and what with the Professor's decree that there would be no soiree unless he left by his own accord; something had to be done—and toot sweet about it! So I walked right in to the parlor to see the little man sitting there at his piano with his wild black hair, little brown house slippers on his tiny bare feet, a pair of long baggy black pajama bottoms with knobby little knees, and a tired old bathrobe to keep him half warm as the winds of December howled outside. His round little belly poked out and touched the piano keys, but of all the strange feelings he set off in me, I somehow knew that we would be friends!

"Have you ever heard of the Old Believers?" he asked in his beautiful Russian to see how much of a foreigner I was.

"Nyet," said I, as I dropped my eyes as if he was royalty, for as crazy as the little man seemed to be, there was a magic in his heart and a power in his soul that made mere mortals bow before his glory.

"Well, the Old Believers wanted Russia to never change," he said with his green eyes twinkling. "They burned themselves by the thousands to protest the ways of the new Tsar." He went on like a history professor with his wild eyes beaming. And in his high pitched voice that made his words sound like a symphony he added, "Why, they even nailed themselves into their own coffins!"

"And what did that prove?" I asked in my simple Russian (which was improving on a daily basis). "Once that lid to the coffin was closed, nailing it shut from the inside still gave them an out, didn't it?"

344

He stopped his rantings and smiled a glorious smile as he considered my perplexing question. And then like the sun had broken through a dark cloud in the sky, there before me sat the Imp with a big beaming smile!

"You are a warrior?" he asked like he couldn't believe it.

"Well, I've been in the wrong place at the wrong time once or twice in my life, but I'm an Army scout and a telegrapher by trade. Right now, believe it or not, I play the trombone for Alexander Alexandrovich Romanoff." And I smiled like ain't life a little bit funny.

He laughed a big belly laugh, stood up, and gave me the kisses and hugs of a proud Russian, then said I must excuse him, he had an opera to write and no more time to socialize with anyone, even if he did like them.

"Have you had your breakfast yet?" I asked him gently, for the smell of cognac was on his breath, and I knew many a drunk who was off his feed in the mornings.

"Not hungry!" he said as he went on beating that piano.

"Let me help with the meal, Augustus Augustovich," Nadezhda roared over the banging and the clanging of that baby grand, and we set out to make breakfast together.

Double paned windows looked out on the snowy street below and the winds set them to singing a high pitched siren song as the Maestro pounded away. There was an old overstuffed horsehair couch, a mahogany table, and a painting of flowers on the wall. A tall stove was in the corner, and it covered the whole western wall all the way up to the ceiling in an off-white tile. And that constant beating of that baby grand just went on and on, as I tried not to notice.

"Can I get some wood and stoke your fire?" I hollered to Nadezhda as she pulled the food stuffs out of my big canvas bag.

"The wood is down on the landing," she bellowed. "Nikolai bought some nice dried birch—it burns slow and leaves the smell of baked bread in the air."

"And speaking of baked bread," I bellowed back, I'll make you the best biscuits in all of Maryland, if you make us an omelet?"

345

That endless (and tuneless) banging went on as The Imp beat away at an opera he was trying to write,[141] while Nadezhda and I yelled to each other about my harbor home. How it wasn't cold enough to do much ice skating, which was another of her favorite sports. But before long we had those biscuits rising in the oven, and that omelet turning a golden brown on the stove, as I remembered Yakoff standing out there in the blizzard.

"Can my poor corporal come in from the cold and have a bite to eat, Nadezhda?" I asked, feeling guilty for forgetting him out there.

"Of course he can!" she answered with a merry smile. "We have a stable around back you can put your horses in."

I could just barely make out my three friends in the blowing snow. Little Suli was standing in the lee of my big snow covered Boris, while right there between the two of them was Yakoff, as snug as a bug in a rug.

"Let's get the horses in the barn and go up and have breakfast," I yelled over the fury of the storm.

"Come in out of this beautiful weather? What for, Herr Maior?" The big man stood there like a snow covered statue of Peter the Great and laughed, as he watched the shock in my eyes from seeing well over a foot of new snow since I'd last been out there.

"Well, would you come in for a little late breakfast and some American style biscuits before we set out on our next adventure, or would you rather wait on the street and get frostbit?" I asked and suddenly the big giant was ready to seek shelter. We put the horses away, watered them and borrowed a little hay from stall #10, and then up those steep stairs we climbed, with me warning Yakoff that there was a mad man inside.

"This is Corporal Yakoff Yakovich," I said as we entered the apartment.

The pounding ceased as the great artist listened in. "Yakoff, this is the Professor's wife, Nadezhda Rimskaya-Korsakova. Corporal Yakovich once saved my life. He's the salt of the Earth, Madame." I said in my best Miss Yvette French.

My shy corporal just stood there with his head hanging down trying not to drip snow on the Korsakov's rug. He was indeed a humble soul— humble, huge, and hungry!

346

"Come eat, Yakoff Yakovich?" our hostess said and suddenly we were a room full of friends.

Even Modest Mussorgsky laid down his "music" and came into the kitchen. He looked up at Yakoff in his corporal's tunic and I in my major's uniform and said, "Is this great mountain of a man before me what the British call your batman, Herr Maior?"

"My batman, best friend, keeper of the horses, comrade in arms," I said with great pride. "I've seen this man capture a platoon of Imperial lancers and ride their horses to my side when I needed him most!"

Yakoff wouldn't look up from the plate he was making; being forever a peasant he didn't feel comfortable in the presence of intelligentsia. Oh, he could look me in the eye, or tell me to go to hell, but we were boys from the city streets, and soldiers as well. Modest kept staring at Yakoff's giant parts—his big sausage size fingers wrapped around the fork, his shoulders near the width of the table, and his arms the size of well-proportioned oak branches. And as the poor half-starved drunkard watched my friend devour his food (four of my Maryland biscuits with butter slid down his gullet in a flash), the Maestro was suddenly hungry.

After that fine breakfast, we all entered into song, Nadezhda playing the four handed piano with the Imp, while I played my trusty Hohner, and Yakoff sang a beautiful baritone. We wailed away through that blinding blizzard with the screeching windows providing a high soprano, and when we left, we had a dinner date with the Maestro himself. It would be a birthday to remember!

We thanked our hostess for her welcoming ways, and told Modest we'd be back for him at eight o'clock sharp. But we needed a place to hang our hats—somewhere the Imp wouldn't want to leave once we got him there. Money was no object, for my end of the year dividends had come in from the Krupp Cannon Company and they were doing just fine. We stopped at a quaint little three storied hotel a few blocks south of the Anichkov Palace—right there on the Nevsky Prospect to find a room for the night. It was a charming place on the south side of the street with high marble ceilings and a fine restaurant down in the basement.

347

"I want your best suite," I told the manager as he stood behind the lobby desk and stared. "And it must have a piano—preferably a grand, can you provide such a place for us?"

"That would be our Emperor's suite," he said with great pride. "But unfortunately, maior, that suite is taken. I do, however, have the Empress suite on the same floor, but there is no piano!"

But if I was to keep the Maestro's attention long enough to get our little soiree going, we would definitely need a piano! So I slid the man a ten ruble gold piece and said, "How bouts you move that other party out of the Emperor's suite and move us in there toot sweet?"

He shook his head as if to say, "Move on Amerikanskiy, the Nevsky Hotel is no place for a moujik like you!"

"Well, could you move that piano into the Empress Suite if the people in the Emperor Suite agreed to it?" I continued to bargain. "I'd be happy to pay for any inconveniences."

"Actually, sir," he said with little pursed up lips, as he pulled at his mustache and frowned, "that couple doesn't wish to be disturbed!"

Being it was a Saturday that close to Christmas, plus the fact that they had a nice suite to rent us and it was my birthday and all, I signed on, telling the surly clerk that I wanted him to talk with the occupants of the Emperor Suite as soon as they stuck their heads out for air.

"How long will the maior be staying," he whined like he'd really like to have that suite back as soon as possible.

"Well," I told him in all honesty, "I'm hoping right on through the spring. But don't you worry, I'm a big tipper!" We now had a place to park Modest Mussorgsky for at least the time being.

"Where to now," Yakoff asked as we rode off into the swirling snows.

"We've got reservations to make for dinner, and tickets to buy for the ballet," I yelled over the roar of the blizzard. "If watching a bunch of ballerinas bounce up and down doesn't do the trick, nothing will!"

Dinner reservations were at 9:30 sharp, the Bolshoi at 11:00 PM, with an après ballet meal and drinks planned till dawn at a fashionable St.

Petersburg restaurant. Then in a drunken stupor, I would park the Maestro in the Empress Suite and work on getting him that piano.

That evening, after we took long hot baths in our private suite and dressed in our military best, we hailed the fattest (and most expensive) izvozchiki in the city of Piter. His team was a troika of three huge bays, and under the silver fox fur blankets we crawled, as the snows came down and the winds howled. He cracked his long whip and we were off to steal Modest Mussorgsky!

And had I known how easy it would be, I wouldn't have been so nervous, but the dinner was grand, and the ballerinas were better, and as we left the Bolshoi Theater the snow was piled up to well over three feet. Our izvozchiki was out by the fires the drivers burned to keep warm as they waited for their fares and we discussed our plans for the rest of the evening. Modest had sent his card back stage to the dancers with three dozen hot house roses I'd brought along for the occasion, and we exited the theater four ballerinas richer than when we went in. Two of the tall dancers were at the Maestro's side in their red fur coats, and two with my moujik friend, who looked dashing in his full dress uniform.

"I can't get all seven of you home in one run," yelled the izvozchiki as he shook the snow off his furs to prepare for the ride. "And I'd like to be off the streets early tonight, maior; this storm is coming in hard!"

"Fine," I told him—knowing how cold the horses must get with that bitter north wind stabbing at them. "We'll eat at our hotel."

"The Nevsky Hotel, maior?" yelled the friendly coachman.

"Yes," I answered. Can you take this gentleman," and I nodded at The Imp standing there beside me with two ballerinas in hand, "and our guests back first, and then return for me and my corporal?"

"Da, Amerikanskiy!" he hollered with joy, for not only had I already paid him well, but I promised a big tip when the evening was over.

So off went the coachman with his long whip cracking as the corporal and I hunkered down around the blazing fire. Never go out in Russia unless you are dressed for the occasion—Yakoff had taught me, and we had our heavy greatcoats, and thick warm boots, and great wide mittens to survive half the night if we had to. The coachman came back an hour later saying things were getting real hairy on the streets of St. Petersburg.

"If you want we could put you and your horses up at the Anichkov Stables tonight, it's but a few blocks from our hotel, and we'll walk back over to our room once we've bedded you down." I told our fat friend.

"You'd do that for a moujik like me?" he yelled over the screaming blizzard.

"We are all moujiks out here in this storm tonight," I said with great pride, for wasn't I a Baltimore Stable Rat! "Take us to the Anichkov Palace and we'll bed you and your horses down, and buy you a big farm breakfast in the morning." And off we flew like lightning on the wire.

It was 3 AM before Yakoff and I returned to the Nevsky with the night manager complaining that when Modest and the four ballerinas had arrived; the Maestro was seen lifting paintings off the wall as they ascended the stairs in a drunken stupor. "Every step he took up those wide wooden stairs he'd lift a painting from the wall, Herr Maior. He'd pass them back to the drunken ballerinas, who were laughing so loud they woke the whole hotel. We had the gendarmes here for over an hour, but the Maestro wouldn't open the door. You'll pay for the damages, won't you, maior?"

As long as we had Modest Mussorgsky out of the Professor's apartment, I'd have paid for anything! But when I asked the night manager about whether they'd gotten round to checking on that piano, he wasn't as helpful. "The day manager told me to be sure and walk the Duchess's dachshunds at 6:00 AM, but he said nothing about any piano," the little man whimpered.

"Well, as soon as you see any signs of life up there in that Emperor's suite, you go tell them I'll give them a thousand rubles for the use of that piano!" I told him, for Modest Mussorgsky needed a piano like a rat needed cheese!

"Yes sir," he answered, "but that door to your suite is locked tight—four policemen couldn't budge it."

"Just get me and my friend here a couple of blankets and a pillow each and we'll sleep on the floor outside our door. No need for anymore commotion." After all, we had Modest Mussorgsky surrounded!

The blizzard was still busting along by noon the next day and nobody was moving in the darkened halls as Yakoff and I slept. Finally, at two in the afternoon we heard the furniture being slid back and there stood the four ballerinas looking somewhat disheveled but nevertheless pleased.

"We have to be back at the Bolshoi for a 4 o'clock show," they told us, as they declined a little light meal.

So after piling the girls inside a sleigh and sending them home with their complimentary paintings in hand, Yakoff and I went down to breakfast. We drank our coffee and ate our eggs as we made conjectures about what shape the Maestro would be in. As we climbed back up those hotel stairs, we heard the wonderful music of a grand piano with two people playing a four handed piece. And when we looked inside the Emperor's Suite, there was Modest Mussorgsky in his pajama bottoms (and nothing more) sitting beside a buxomy blond haired lady as they tickled the ivories together!

"These are my friends I haven't told you about, Miss Lear," goes The Imp with a little nod towards the two of us standing at the door looking shocked and amazed. Their arms were entwined as they played like lovers, though he couldn't have been in there more than an hour.

"Lads, may I present Miss Fanny Lear,[142] my new employer!" the Maestro said with a well-satisfied grin. "Miss Lear has asked me to move in with her, boys." And that's how we got rid of Modest Mussorgsky without him even knowing he was going!

"And how long do you think you can keep this charade up?" I asked him when I brought him a fresh change of clothes the following day.

"You mean the piano playing or that other thing?" he said with a little jiggle of his hips, for the Imp had decided he was God's gift to women.

Miss Lear was in a relationship with a Romanoff Grand Duke, and he who must have been quite daft, for when the Imp wasn't playing the piano for Miss Fanny Lear, Miss Fanny was playing house with the Imp!

"Has Modest found himself a woman?" Nadezhda asked when he failed to come home.

"Yes Ma'am," I told her with a few facts missing.

"Well, then, Augustus Augustovich," she said with great joy in her voice. "It's time to get a list of your soiree quests together."

"There are you and the Professor," I told her, "and Yakoff and a date."

"Wait a minute," Nadezhda interrupted with a grimace. "Your friend Yakoff is a moujik—a servant—a batman, a common soldier, you can't have him at a soiree with your countess friend."

That meant all my Cossack friends were out too, and the only High and Mighties I knew were Minnie and Sasha. Two names I was never to use!

"You couldn't possibly expect the next emperor of Russia to come to your soiree?" the Professor's bride said. But who else did I know?

"Maria Feodorovna would love to spend time with a band of merry musicians like The Mighty Handful,[143] and as long as Sasha wasn't expected to dance, we could count him in." So now we had seven, though Modest Mussorgsky would always be considered questionable.

"You need to have at least a dozen people for a soiree not to be considered an intimate affair," the Professor's wife preached. "Nadia's Uncle Peter will never let her go to an intimate soiree with a man like you!"

We finally came up with eleven people; if Modest Mussorgsky showed up alone, twelve if he brought Miss Fanny Lear along with him. Our other guests were mostly members of the Mighty Handful, for Professor Rimsky-Korsakov was so happy with the disappearance of the Maestro that he'd put his heart and soul into helping me find my guests. Nadezhda said her husband had a friend named Tchaikovsky who just might fill the bill, "though he's a bit on the effeminate side; and doesn't Alexander Alexandrovich detest such men?"

"Well, actually, not to tell tales out of school," I told her as I thought back to that Prince Mesherskii fellow and his roving hands, "some of the Tsarevich's favorite friends are likers of men."

"What?" she asked with her eyebrows rising like she'd never heard it described that way.

"You know, men that like men. His Majesty gets along fine with his gay blade friends, and I doubt this Tchaikovsky fellow will even raise an eyebrow."

So we were over the top with more than twelve people. It was now officially a non-intimate affair. Yakoff and I hand carried the invitations to all comers with Nadia Shuvalova first on our list.

"Of course I'd love to come and hear the Mighty Handful play! Can I bring my violin?" she asked all excited to meet the great men.

"Of course you can, Nadia." I told her with my heart in my throat. "You can bring anything you like, for this soiree is for you!"

Saturday the 16th of December was a beautiful day—the blue of the sky and the white of the snow washing all my cares away. We carried in boxes and boxes of food and drink up those steep wooden stairs. The guests arrived at ten that evening, and we chatted endlessly about the upcoming Christmas season. I met Tchaikovsky and his cousin Alexei, César Cui and his wife Malvina, and Alexander Borodin with his lovely wife, Ekaterina. Doctor Borodin remembered my double lung shot wound and Maria Feodorovna overheard us talking and wanted to see it, but the Tsarevich glared down at me and I declined.

I'd never seen the two of them in a social situation, but His Majesty stood and smiled with the other men talking about symphonies and elk hunting like he was just your run of the mill Preobrajenski colonel.[144] Most everybody but Tchaikovsky and his cousin, and Modest Mussorgsky—when he finally arrived, were dressed in their military uniforms, but when the Maestro arrived with his buxomy blonde haired American at his side, the party really got going!

"Your Highnesses, may I present Miss Fanny Lear of Philadelphia fame!" said Modest like a prince of the realm.

Miss Fanny and her grand duke lover were later to get into trouble, but at this time in her life she was Big Medicine! "Pleased to meet you, Your

Majesties," Fanny said with a low curtsy and the room fell silent, since they bowed to their Royals in Russia.

I'd forgotten how brazen we Americans were, for the lady was definitely a fraud. Oh, she was from Philadelphia alright—I could hear it in her o's, but that high-class way she carried herself was definitely a piece of fakery. Half English—half Boston Brahmin, why, that accent was so bad I almost laughed in her face, but as long as that soiree progressed without a hitch, Miss Fanny Lear could have spoken Swahili. But what really worried me, was Nadia had not arrived by midnight!

Finally we heard a six horse team pull up outside with a carriage fit for a king. It was Nadia and a man old enough to be her father. We all tried not to look out the frosted windows as the coachman helped them down. They rumbled up the wooden stairs and Prince Yusupov entered the room first like the King of Siam, almost failing to bow before the next emperor of Russia.

He was in civilian clothes—a dark suit, a long silver fox fur coat and matching cap which he kept on before the Tsarevich for far too long. His eyes were dark, his oily black hair combed way back out of his sinister face, with his side whiskers springing up in a curly little mustache that sat high above his haughty lips. He seemed to look right through us as he offered Nadia his hand, and in she came looking lovely in a long green dress that matched her eyes. She paid her loyalties to the Romanoffs in the proper fashion—something the richest man in Russia was loath to do, and then that awkward moment of silence when all had been introduced, save me.

"I am Major Augustus Stewart," I said when the rest of the room fell silent.

"Tell them more, my friend!" goes the Naslednik in a strong proud voice. "You are Redbeard the Wild and Crazy American—the man who once took down a general on his charging horse, don't ever forget it!"

Minnie was standing proud by His Majesty's side, knowing that the Tsarevich was usually so shy he would never speak in such a boastful manner about anyone. But like a big brother who sees his little brother being embarrassed, Alexander Alexandrovich stepped right in.

354

The Prince wouldn't talk to anyone save for the Tsarevich, the Tsarevna, and Nadia, as the Table of Ranks decreed. But Maria Feodorovna was busy chatting with Dr. Borodin and his wife over in the corner, while Nadia was turning the pages for Modest Mussorgsky as he played a lovely piece on that baby grand. Prince Yusupov kept looking at his watch like he had somewhere better to go. He'd nod at whatever the Tsarevich said—half listening, and then stare up at the ceiling as if to say, Lord please let this soiree be over!

Professor Korsakov was telling me he never realized I had such a death defying chest wound, but I could tell he was really trying to distract me. My plan had been to look Nadia in the eyes and confess my love, but now my plan was ruined! I walked slowly over to the Naslednik so he would have someone to listen to his story and came up under the lee of Prince Yusupov. His shifty eyes were frozen on Nadia, and his hand was on that golden time piece like a horse trainer watching his filly run a slow race.

"Who is that fine looking young man in the corner with that nice trimmed beard, Augustus Augustovich?" asked His Majesty.

I told him that was Peter Ilyich Tchaikovsky and the teenager was his cousin come to turn the pages. There was a roar coming from Miss Fanny Lear's corner. Her audience was being enlightened to the latest in London scandals. Nadia looked across the room at me with her emerald green eyes sparkling and I swear she smiled a glorious smile! Now horses I knew, if they liked you, they wouldn't bite you or kick you, but a woman that was a whole different story. I was lost in love and didn't know what to do, so I just smiled back and prayed to Sweet Jesus.

"Nadia Shuvalova, come, girl!" yelled the long whiskered prince as he interrupted the Tsarevich's story. Right through my ear he sent that message like I was but a speck of dust. "We have a party to attend at Grand Duke Vladimir's new palace, come girl, come!" He barked.

Nadia didn't respond. She was enjoying herself over by the piano talking with Maria Feodorovna and the Imp. The crowd had been growing merry what with the music and drink, and the wild stories Miss Fanny Lear was telling, but that made the prince even madder. He let loose with a few expletives loud enough for the Tsarevich to hear, and as I may have mentioned, Alexander Alexandrovich didn't care much for cussing. Especially when there were women present—one of which was his wife, and he gave that surly prince one of his deadly stares.

"Oh, tell me Nixa's bride hasn't heard cussing before, and I'll go and apologize," Prince Yusupov hissed.

Now the Naslednik wasn't always raised to be the next emperor of Russia—his older brother Nicholas (or Nixa as only his family was allowed to call him) was first in line to the throne. But, after Nicholas was betrothed to Maria Feodorovna, the poor man up and died, so not only had Alexander Alexandrovich inherited his brother's job as the Heir Apparent, but he'd also inherited his brother's wife to be. And in some people's eyes her marriage to poor dead Nixa was official, so they said (behind the Tsarevich's back, of course), she was Nixa's bride, which was a terrible thing to say to my Boss! And not wanting to see the Tsarevich twist that filthy prince into a pretzel and ruin my soiree, I took Yusupov's elbow real gently and started to guide him away.

"Unhand me you little red-headed dwarf!" he yelled, and didn't he pull my right pogoni right off my shoulder. Now in Russia you didn't go relieving an officer of his shoulder boards unless you planned to fight a duel to the death! The room fell silent as the Tsarevich gasped; for he knew what a torn epaulette meant.[145]

There I was staring up at the man who had torn it off me, as I turned a nice shade of red and yelled, "Winchesters at a hundred and fifty yards. I'm calling you out, Prince Yusupov!"

Now according to the Code Duello, it was the Prince's choice of weapons and range, since I'd done the challenging. But dueling was about defending your honor, and no one had to die for a torn pogoni. Winchesters were only good to about a hundred yards out, so Lady Luck would decide our fate.

"Fine," he barked, "how many rounds?"

"Five!" I told him—knowing full well it would take all of that and a miracle for me to hit anything at a hundred and fifty yards.

"My Second will contact yours," yelled the Prince. "Nadia Shuvalova, come with me now!" he bellowed, but Nadia was not having it. "Very well, then," the Prince cried out. "Let's see how your Uncle Peter likes your insolence, girl!" And he was gone.

We spent the rest of the evening singing and dancing, for there was something about a man's impending doom that brought joy to a room full of friends. And as we swirled about without a care in the world, my love for Nadia grew and grew. We danced a mazurka to Tchaikovsky's piano, and did a high kicking Cossack dance as the Maestro tore into the ivories. Our little soiree laughed and made merry till the winter sun rose in a steel gray sky, and then Minnie, Sasha, Nadia, and I all piled into the Royal Romanoff sleigh—covered in furs and rode home. Nadia and I stood before the doors of the Shuvalov Palace in a hip high snow drift and kissed goodbye like the lovers we were, and then off into the frigid morning light our sleigh raced for the Anichkov Palace.

"We'll sleep a few hours, Augustus Augustovich," the Naslednik said with more joie de vivre than I'd ever seen. "Then it's off to Gatchina to get your rifle."

"Gatchina, Sire?" I asked with some worry, since I figured it would be spring before they found two Winchester Rifles in all of Russia.

"Of course," he answered like a boy on Christmas morning. "I kept your weapons locked away for just such an occasion."

Four hours later we were steaming south on his private train with our horses, our gear, and a strong but not unreasonable fear of impending Death! We were greeted by a frozen expanse of Imperial wealth as cold as any ice box, but the staff stoked the fires and slowly the Arsenal Wing was brought up to a balmy forty degrees, as the winds howled and the windows screamed. His Majesty, Yakoff, and I climbed the marble staircase to the Mezzanine and went into his study, and there by a big mahogany desk was a huge gun locker. The Tsarevich reached under the main drawer and came up with a key and unlocked his treasure trove. Inside were several shotguns and shells for same, a Baranov rifle, and several pistols including my trusty LeMat. In the back corner sat my

Model 1866 Yellowboy Winchester Repeating Rifle, her brass receiver glistening in the lamplight.

"I even have your Bowie knife, Augustus Augustovich!" says the Tsarevich like he'd already invented a tale of my latest adventure. "Now let's go out and see how that Winchester shoots!"

I knew if the shots were off by much, it wouldn't be the weather or the Winchester's fault. I was the worst shot in the 3rd Indiana.

"Have the horses saddled, Corporal Yakovich," the Naslednik ordered. "And summon my huntsmen! We'll ride out to Beloye Lake and fire a few rounds before dinner. Major Stewart bring your weapons along," he roared like a lion.

We bundled up in our fur coats and fur hats and extra thick boots, with gloves that had a little slits to let your fingers stick out, and mounted our shaggy horses for the short ride north to the lake where the huntsmen met us. He was mounted on a big brown Orlov that Boris seemed to remember from the Farm Pavilion, and they were chattering away like long lost brothers.

The huntsmen was an old moujik with cloth wrapped feet—standing there in an elk hide coat with a tall hood—a gray beard peeking out of what was showing of an old weathered face. He bowed low to the Naslednik, and His Majesty's eyes had a twinkle that seemed to say, "Now let's see how this Yankee can shoot!"

I knew the first round would kick a bit, but it almost tore me off Boris's back and stung like a yellow jacket. The target, an old kerosene can maybe fifty yards out, just sat there looking lonely.

"How far apart did Your Highness say that duel would be fought?" asked the gray bearded huntsman with some irony to it.

"One hundred and fifty yards," says the Tsarevich as my stock took a tumble. "But, I imagine we could shave that right down to a hundred."

Alexander Alexandrovich was not the kind of man a piss ant like me wanted to argue with, but being struck by a .44 caliber round didn't sound like fun. So I bucked up and lied like a Polar bear rug!

358

"I'm just a little bit snow blind today, Sire. Give me a few shots and I'll be dropping rounds in at a hundred and fifty yards, you'll see."

Two boxes of bullets later (at fifty rounds a box), I was finally able to hit that kerosene can. My coaches were cussing and hollering, "Hold your breath, don't hold your breath, relax, keep both eyes open, close that left eye, squeeze the trigger between heart beats, Augustus! Jesus Christ, are you blind, boy?" They bellowed like elk bulls in mating season!

Between me and my heart was about forty pounds of winter clothing, and my fingers were frozen to the bone, so how was I to feel my heart beat? Besides, the only thing out there was a kerosene can, you want my heart to beat hard; put something out there that can shoot back!

"We'll try again tomorrow morning," goes the Tsarevich with his mustache frozen and a mighty frown on his big giant face. He and his huntsman just hung their heads in shame as we rode back to the palace.

It was as silent as a Nun's wake at dinner that night, the Naslednik, my big corporal, and I eating at the little dining room table up in the Mezzanine. I wished Minnie had come along. She could make the Tsarevich smile when all else failed, and after he saw me shoot, he wasn't even talking to me.

"So, tell me Yakoff Yakovich, when did you join the Emperor's Army?" His Majesty asked as we ate our cabbage soup in near silence.

Yakoff, with a big chunk of black bread in his paws, answered in a most polite fashion, "I was but a boy of fifteen, Your Highness. A half Russian—half Polish Jew that nobody wanted, save for my size!"

"Being big has its disadvantages, does it not Corporal Yakovich?" the Tsarevich asked like sometimes he felt the very same way.

"And being small means I'm a harder target for Prince Yusupov to hit," I said trying to lighten things up.

"You need to learn how to keep your mouth shut, Augustus Augustovich, and how to shoot that damn rifle! Tomorrow you will work with my huntsman till your arm falls off. It's not every day someone has the next emperor of Russia as their Second!" I swear he said all of that.

359

The next day the Tsarevich's Blue Cossacks gathered round like crows before battle, and it didn't take them long to note how that crazy eye of mine pulled to the right. They rode out on their snow covered ponies to either side of the range with their long red lances waving in the air wherever my wayward rounds went in. The lads had set up a betting board with columns for each shot, while the five lines down were marked: Over to the Left, Over to the Right, Hit the Target, Under to the Left, and Under to the Right. They were prepared to rob the rich gamblers on each and every shot, which was why they took to calling me Redbeard the Magnificent.

"That's it!" hollered the Naslednik like he'd thought of the trick. "Now keep sending men all the way out to the hundred and fifty yard marker— only you best spread out a bit. Redbeard's a little wild today!"

By lunch, I was deaf in both ears, my shoulder was falling off, and His Highness had to send his private train back to St. Petersburg for more ammunition. Which he was probably putting on my tab, just like the trombone, the music lessons, the uniforms, and my room and board, for he hadn't paid me a single kopek since I came to Russia!

His huntsman just looked at me—shook his head real sad like and said, "And you call yourself a warrior?"

"Well, actually, I'm the Tsarevich's 1st Trombone!" I retorted.

The Tsarevich broke in with what he thought was bad news. "Well, to tell you the truth, Major Stewart, I wired the Conservatory this morning and ordered up a brand new trombone player for my Christmas Recital. One with—how do you say, more longevity to him."

He must have figured I'd be sad, so I frowned, as I did a little jig in my head. Why, I'd have let half of St. Petersburg shoot at me to get out of that band!

The Emperor and a squadron of his Red Cossacks showed up from his nearby palace of Tsarskoe Selo the following day. A hundred riders in their long red cherkeskas with bright red lances and rifles slung across their wide strong backs, toothless smiling bearded brutes—come down to check on my shooting. They stayed all day comparing notes with their Blue Cossack brothers whilst the Tsar and the Tsarevich looked on.

360

The Central Palace was fired up, for the Emperor and his concubine[146] would be staying a few days for the festivities. All of Alexander II's sporting friends would be down by the next morning, so the servants pulled the sheets off the statues and paintings and fired up the furnaces in the Central Palace to a tropical sixty degrees. Prince Yusupov showed up with his friends on his own private train, having put on an extra team of horses. The train doors came open and out stomped four matched pairs of pure black Orlovs with big black feathers sticking out of their huge proud heads, and shiny black leather harnesses, and footmen in black, and a driver—in deep jet black, and you guessed it, a big black Royal sized carriage with wheels that stood higher than I did. He must have figured that funeral theme would scare me to death, and quite frankly, it was working!

The Tsarevich was worried about my immortal soul and he told me he'd talked to his priest and if I was to be, God forbid, killed out there on the dueling grounds (and he crossed himself a dozen times), "We won't be able to bury you in hallowed ground, so we want to bury you out by Tsar Paul's tomb."[147] Why, I'd have sooner been buried in the Romanoff pet cemetery, for at least it had a fine view of my Clock Tower cell where I'd experienced the good, the bad, and quite possibly the ugly! So I declined his offer, though out of gratitude for risking my life for his honor, His Majesty promoted me to a full blown colonel.

That night before the duel, Sergeant Yakovich, whose rank had risen with my first wish as a newly made colonel, came to my room and said, "Nadia Shuvalova has arrived, Herr Palkovnik. She awaits you in the Palace Chapel."

I headed there in my favorite moujik outfit—a pair of long wool underwear against the cold Arctic air, big baggy black pants, and tall black boots, a red Garibaldi shirt like old AP Hill wore on his day of battle, and a bear skin Cossack cap in my hand, the walk being inside the palace. But when I got to the Central Palace hallway, the red clad Convoy Cossack guards said no one could pass as the Emperor was holding Court in there. I had to go outside in the snow and cross Dead Tsar Paul's Parade Ground in the darkness of a star filled night, so I put my fur cap on tight against the winds of winter and marched through the drifting snow to the door of the Kitchen Wing as my footsteps squeaked like little baby seals.

A shooting star glided across the sky and I made a wish that Nadia Shuvalova and I would be standing there looking up into the Vertigo the very next night. And there she sat in the back pew—the eyes of a dozen bejeweled icons staring down at us as we kissed. It wasn't the kiss of passion a man gives to his sweetheart, for this was a church of God.

"Augustus," she whispered tenderly and I wanted to tell her my Christian name was Robert, but she went on too quickly. "Come away with me to Finland where we can raise horses and little baby Stewarts to our hearts' content!" She said, but it was a good hundred miles to the Finnish border and the middle of winter, and not only had Prince Yusupov insulted me and my regiment, but he'd also insulted the Tsarevich and Tsarevna too, so I told her no, I couldn't do that. I might not have been the bravest man in Russia, but on that star filled night, I became a fighting Highlander (just like my Grandfather John before me[148]), and nothing Nadia could say or do could change my mind.

"Someday I'll be happy to run away with you, Nadia," I whispered as the candles flickered before the Holy icons. "But tomorrow morning I must go to the dueling grounds and fight. And if I die out there, I'll meet you in another life, for you are my soulmate through all of time!"

"If you love me so much, Augustus Augustovich," she said, and I cut in.

"My name is Robert Augustus Stewart, and my father's Augustus is his middle name too, for he is Charles Augustus Stewart!"

"And as stubborn a pair of mules as there ever was," she growled like a lioness as she got up to leave. "How can you sit there and talk of your love for me when you are preparing to go out and die?"

As she ran out of the Chapel crying, I whispered loud enough for all the icons in the whole world to hear, "I swear by all that is Holy, I will not die out there in the snow today!"

But Nadia didn't hear me, for she was gone in the night! There I sat in the silence contemplating my mortality until Sergeant Yakovich came for me in the first light. "It's time to eat, palkovnik. Are you hungry?"

I was always hungry, so we went to eat with my horsemen friends. The Chow Hall was full of the wild riders of the Steppes, and as my sergeant and I came in to the low ceilinged room full of Cossacks they bellowed, "Huzzah," as they pounded their fists on the tables and chanted, "Redbeard the Magnificent" at the top of their lungs.

"And here's to all you unfaithful Cossacks who have bet against your Yankee friend," I said as I pitched them the good old digitus impudicus.

The room went wild with laughter, so I whipped out my trusty Hohner and one last time before the bullets flew, I played some wild mountain music. Their officers came in and yelled at us, for the Emperor and his lady hadn't descended to breakfast, and we were to, "let them rest." That too got a good laugh from the bawdy horseman of the Steppes; for once you've seen a stallion mount a mare, you know there's no rest to it! We ate like thrashers and laughed like wild beasts, for we were the Tsar's wild horsemen with no regrets, and then it was Post Time!

The Royal Palace sat on a low rise above the dueling grounds and there under the jack booted feet of that Tsar Paul statue, a thousand people of high station spread out for a good view of the duel to the death. Once our fight was over, they'd all go back to the palace for cards and tea, but in the early hours of that cold winter day our duel took center stage.

Prince Yusupov rode up in his gaudy eight horse hearse. His black clad footman ran forward and dropped the folding stairs, and out came the man with a big black stovepipe hat on his head. The judges bowed low to the bushy side whiskered prince, and the Naslednik tipped his hat too. All was convivial till Prince Yusupov saw my dueling outfit, for that bright red shirt was a bit too much for his royal blood and he snickered and stuck his nose in the air.

Up to the Judges' Bench at the midway mark we went with a buzz of guffaws from the rise above. Those Russians couldn't just let us go out there and blast away—like the boys at the O.K. Corral, no they had to ask us if we couldn't come to an agreement in a civilized fashion and put this dueling behind us. But did the pompous prince bring a needle and thread along to sew my pogoni back on, or did he wish to apologize to the Tsarevich for bringing up Nixa's bride? No, he was ready to fight, so the show must go on—after all we had a crowd to please!

Before me on the table were the two Winchester rifles waiting to be loaded by our Seconds. Prince Yusupov chose my custom made Yellowboy, which I'd been practicing with for three days—not the best of omens.

"Yakoff," I called under my breath, "go quickly and place a thousand rubles on Hit the Target for that last shot, and a thousand rubles for you anywhere you like!"

Seventy-five yards across hip high snow we trudged. The Naslednik and I on foot, whilst the bewhiskered Prince climbed back in his eight horse carriage and had them deliver him to his mark.

"Remember, Augustus Augustovich," His Majesty said like maybe this time it would sink in, "keep both eyes open, and feel for the beat of your heart before you squeeze the trigger."

And this time, I could feel my heart pulsing fine. His first round came sailing in and missed me by a foot. Then it was my turn to shoot and I put one within twenty yards of that pompous ass. The Cossacks waved a pennant where the round went in and I made a mental note to give it some Kentucky windage. His second shot was way too long, while my second shot was a tad closer and straighter as I walked them in like the Austrians had taught me up on Breda Hill. His third round came whistling by my ear and I felt like I was back up that tree in Bohemia! I fired round three, which missed by a mile, the Cossack pennants waving wildly. Then in comes round four from Yusupov's cannon and it skipped across the snowy ground and damned near hit me. My fourth round flew in a shallow arch, and judging by the wave of the Cossack lances, it was maybe five yards short. I swallowed hard and waited for that last round to come in, but having cheated Death four times, Number Five came in real slowly! It finally arrived with a crack and a thud and dug into the frozen ground at my feet, and then like a mole all hopped up on mushrooms it came straight at my left foot and took off my little toe and his nearest buddy. I jumped up and down screaming with a great smoking hole in my boot and blood pouring out all over the snow!

Many a bet had been placed on the Prince "Hitting the Target" and the gamblers were celebrating up on the hill. Now a better man might have called it quits right then, what with the Prince having fired his last shot and first blood having been drawn, but you see how much brotherly love you can muster for a man who has just shot off your two favorite toes?

"I believe it's my turn to shoot!" I hollered to the Judges, and the crowd fell silent. Oh, he was a hell of a ways off and sheer luck would be the only way I'd hit him, but do you think his rifling mole of a fifth round didn't have some luck to it? I told the Lord that I didn't want to kill the man—just scare him, and crossed myself like I'd seen the Tsarevich do. Adjusting for the distance, and adjusting for the wind, I waited for the rest between heart beats, and then I squeezed the trigger. And didn't that big old .44 caliber round fly straight and true—taking off the Prince's stovepipe hat without so much as putting a crease in his long greasy hair.

The Cossacks all screamed that my shot was an over, but the Judges said, "No, that hat was part of the target, so it was hit the target for Old Redbeard the Sharpshooter! Nadia came running down from the blue blood section with her silver fox fur coat open and hugged me right there before God and Uncle Peter himself. Then I was taken off to the palace to have Dr. Hirsch stop the bleeding.

"You're lucky it didn't take off your foot, Augustus," said the good doctor who was getting use to his American patient. "But you must be still or you could bleed to death."

The Tsarevich said it was customary for the victor to look in on the loser, but what with Prince Yusupov's hatred for all things foreign, he'd never come round to see a moujik like me.

"Well, maybe we should go give him our condolences for that hole in his hat?" I quipped with a weak smile.

"What you need to do right now, my brave little friend," said the next emperor of Russia, Finland, and Poland, "is go up there to the Palace Chapel and thank The Lord above for saving your sorry soul." Which I'd already done a thousand times to my little Yellow Jesus hanging there under my shirt smiling away!

Chapter Thirteen

A Season of Love

We were formally asked to join the "harlot" as the Tsarevich called his father's 2nd wife before God, and the Emperor himself, for a little light lunch after the trials and tribulations of a very busy morning. The Central Palace was clogged with the Tsar's hangers-on who gazed at my limp as I came in balanced on an ebony cane. We were to stand and eat in the military fashion with a buffet stuffed with all kinds of scrumptious things, but first there were those awkward moments where you had to grovel and kowtow to your betters.

The Tsar-Liberator was standing there in Tsar Paul's suite—near as tall as my Boss with a straight wide chest, his blue eyes watching his private luncheon progress. His dark brown hair was combed back in a wave, with a rakish mustache that dashed into a curly pair of long brown side-whiskers that flowed down the sides of his tanned and good looking face. He was in a dark green uniform with his hands crossed over his chest, and his golden epaulettes sparkled in the sunlight coming in through the windows.

"Is this the little Yankee that gave Prince Yusupov a new lease on life?" His Highness asked, though he already knew the answer.

The Royals were under the impression that my last shot had been intentionally high, but luck was the name of the game that day. And the sheer luck of striking his hat off at a hundred and fifty yards was enough good luck for me to be a very rich man, while Prince Yusupov was a lucky man for not being any taller! But as the Tsar talked about what a remarkable shot I'd made, I realized how much romance these Russians had in them.

"Was that Cheyenne or Sioux that you yelled when the bullet hit your bone?" he asked like a boy at a carnival sideshow.

I lied to His Majesty and said, "Definitely Sioux, Sire! My Cheyenne is a bit rusty right now."

Nadia was off chatting with the Emperor's 2nd wife before God. She was a gorgeous woman with long blonde hair and a buxomy body—just about the Tsarevich's and my age, which was thirty-one at the time. Princess Dolgurokova had gone to the same finishing school as Nadia and they chatted like old friends about their crazy professors.

"They tell me you know General Clay, Colonel Stewart." Alexander II said in his perfect French, as he stood there and ate a little smoked salmon on a piece of black bread.

"Yes, Sire," I said with high respect, "and he gave me this revolver when I was but a boy of fifteen."

"Did you know he refused to take his hat off unless I took mine off first?" His Majesty asked. "He was the only man to ever be photographed with his hat on when it should have been off before the Emperor of All the Russias."

"Well, that would be Cassius Marcellus Clay to a T, Your Highness," I said with my eyes cast down. "He has a very high opinion of himself."

Alexander II chuckled as he looked at his princess laughing away. His eyes twinkled as he said, "Do you see how Princess Dolgurokova smiles when she talks with your Nadia, Colonel Stewart?"

"I wish Nadia could smile like that at me, Your Majesty," I said sadly. "But her Uncle Peter won't let her come near me, Your Highness. What am I to do, for I love her more than life itself?"

"What if Princess Dolgurokova was to make Nadia Shuvalova one of her Ladies in Waiting?" he asked as he twirled at his long brown mustache.

The old boy (he was fifty-four at the time) was on to something, for Ladies in Waiting had to be noblewomen (which Nadia was), and they had to get along with the woman they served, which she most assuredly did. So I told the Tsar that was a wonderful idea, figuring if he saw fit to put her on the payroll; it wasn't my place to question the Emperor.

"Send Count General Shuvalov in," said His Higness to his hetman, and in less than five minutes, Nadia had her job as a Freilini or Lady in Waiting, while her uncle and I shook hands and swore to be friends.

There before us in that thirty by forty foot room at the base of the Clock Tower I'd spent so much time in, were all the things Tsar Paul was said to have had with him when he was dragged out from under that very same bed—this being the 2nd very same bed I'd seen in the palace. His old uniform—Prussian in style, that big walking staff with a clock on the top, his tight little marching boots, even his tricorn hat—they were all there like we were in a Tsar Paul museum.

"Why don't you give your little friend Tsar Paul's walking staff, Sasha!" giggled the Tsarevich's gun-shy brother, Vladimir. He stood there in his colonel's uniform near as big as his brother having skipped the duel, though he showed up for the lunch.

"At least my little friend didn't turn and run when he was shot at," the Tsarevich said in my defense.

I started to feel faint, and my toes (or rather the lack thereof) ached as I listened to the two brothers banter, but what could I do? I couldn't sit down and prop my leg up before the Tsar of Russia. But the blood was oozing out all over Tsar Paul's parquet floor and the room began to spin!

"Excuse me, Sire, but I've lost a lot of blood today, and although I'd love to stay and talk with Your Highness, I…" and suddenly the room went dark! Oh, I could hear them talking as my crotch burned (which was a bad sign, though it felt real good at the time), and down I went to the floor.

"Should we put him up on Tsar Paul's bed?" asked the Tsarevich who sounded real worried.

"Someone call the doctor!" ordered the Emperor as he tried to take charge.

"Augustus, are you alright?" begged Nadia with her hand on my shoulder as they lifted me up and placed me on dead Tsar Paul's bed.

"Those Americans are such pansies," went the biggest pansy in the room, the gun-shy Grand Duke Vladimir.

I was thinking of playing possum to avoid all the embarrassment when I woke up, for I had definitely peed myself right there in Tsar Paul's bed! My stock went from blue ribbon to down in the dumps in a heart beat, and they carted me off to my room with snickers and snorts sweeping through the Central Palace.

After that little faux paus, Yakoff and I were sent to the horse barns in exile. But we took over the Gelderland stallion and taught him to run, and once the colt found his perfect pace of the gallop, my stock began to rise again.

We had two weeks to get Hans ready for the New Year's Ice Race which sounded like plenty of time 'til I tried to drive a racing sleigh. Luckily Nadia pitched in to teach me the proper techniques. Princess Dolgurokova didn't wake up till eleven or twelve in the morning, and once she did, her Ladies in Waiting were kept busy picking out the best dress to read a book in, or trailing about the royal townhouse after the Tsar's illegitimate children, or picking out the shoes she would wear before the Tsar deflowered her, so Nadia could sneak off to help us train.

The location of the New Year's Ice Race wouldn't be known until the very day of the race, so wishing to train Hans on all the various widths, and curves, and long straight a ways that we might encounter down in the canals of St. Petersburg, we set out each morning to test a five verst section. There was a saying in Russia that a seven verst detour to avoid a mean dog wasn't much,[149] but asking a horse to run five versts, which was 3.3 miles on sheer ice surrounded by high granite walls that could eat you alive, was a whole nother story!

Every morning, Nadia Shuvalova and Scheherazade, her Arabian mare I'd bought her, Yakoff on his shaggy Little Steppe pony, Suli the Second, me up on Boris, and Hans the Gelderland stallion with his racing sleigh in tow would choose a route through the city canals to run on. The Neva River flowed northward into the Gulf of Finland and to tame the Delta from constant flooding, a series of canals were dug by Peter the Great's Swedish prisoners. Venice of the North they called the city for her fine canals—all lined with huge blocks of granite that Catherine the Great had her convicts put there when they ran out of ditches to dig. The widest of the canals was the Neva at the northern head of the city, which brought the main waters of the river through town in a wide sweeping hook to the west like a great giant scythe. Then like strings of pearls dropping down from the northern neck of the capital came the Moyka Canal, the Catherine Canal, and the Fontanka Canal—all running across the heart of the city. Our job each morning was to mark out a five verst route that may or may not be the race course we'd run on New Year's Day. We knew the crowds (over fifty thousand—they figured) would need lots of room at the start and the finish line, but with near twenty miles of canals to choose from, the course could be anywhere.

So we marked out our race course each day and Nadia would give me a little nuzzle and say, "Go with God, Augustus Augustovich!" She would head to the finish line with a stop watch in hand and wait for Yakoff to fire a shot from my Grapeshot Pistol. I studied the curves to the right and the curves to the left, and where we'd dive down into the depths of a narrow canyon with a bridge so low it would take your head off if you didn't duck real fast, and Hans would fly! I learned more and more about driving a sleigh as we went. The first thing to remember was those rock lined walls could shred you like kindling wood if you weren't real careful. The second thing was we were running on ice, which meant even with cleats, we were always sliding. If we made a ninety degree turn off the eighty foot wide Moyka Canal onto the sixty foot wide Catherine's Canal, you best have that slide figured out in your head, or that granite wall would step out and grab you!

I'd never been what you'd call a brave man before, but once my love for Nadia began to grow inside me there was no way I wanted to die! So I would try to keep Hans from going crazy by singing Christmas carols as he ran—the same ones I'd played on my trombone, only at the slowest pace I could muster. I even took to tying my lucky little Yellow Jesus icon to the nose of the sleigh so I could see his red lips smiling up at me as we skidded sideways ten inches from a granite wall. And every time Hans tried to murder me, I'd pray like a pregnant nun!

Yakoff called this my Religious Period since every time he saw me fly by I was begging Sweet Jesus to slow the damn Dutchman down! But quite frankly, it worked, for just like Miss Harriet would ask the Lord to send her a snowstorm in the middle of May, my percolating prayers kept Hans just about under control. Nadia taught me to shift my weight with a little sideways shimmy that would cause the sleigh to change directions just a few degrees as we sailed for a tight turn. She'd get down there on the ice and take over the sleigh—shift her gorgeous hips this way and that, and that racing sleigh would negotiate a tight turn like we were on a magic carpet.

Having had so much luck with my Garibaldi outfit in the past, I decided to don the same uniform on the day of the race. So with my bright red shirt, two pairs of long underwear, my baggy black moujik pants, and soft black boots, plus a big furry Cossack hat—given to me by an adoring fan, I was ready to risk my life for the honor of the next emperor of Russia. My big red beard sparkled in the frosty air of the Anichkov Stables as we prepared to set out with my lucky icon tied to the front of my sleigh smiling away like a Cheshire cat.

"You have all done a fine job of bringing the colt along," the Naslednik said—his breath freezing as he spoke, his greatcoat open, and his medals clattering.

Beside him stood the next empress of Russia, Maria Feodorovna in a long red fox fur coat. She was holding his hand as their love grew stronger. Nadia was teaching me about love too, the give and the take, the warmth of a hug—the sweet taste of a kiss! My emerald-eyed Snow Maiden's long silver coat was opened to the elements and I could just make out the curves of her soft warm breasts. But there was a race to be run and like Doc always said, "Keep your mind on your business and you won't get hurt!"

So off to the Starting Line we went with over a hundred thousand people filling the snowy streets of Piter as a bright blue sky lightened the way and music filled the air. They had jugglers, and food carts with steaming treats, minstrels, and magicians, I even saw three separate dancing bears that had skipped hibernation just for the occasion. Ours was the first of two ice races that day, and we were to begin at noon as the church bells rang in the New Year. The race was to start on the Moyka Canal near New Holland Island with the big yellow Yusupov Palace just to the south. We would start five horses across with nearly a mile of relatively straight running before the first wide curve to the right. By then, the field would be spread out for the sharp turn onto the Catherine's Canal, then a half mile straight away, followed by multiple curves and low bridges with a blind curve and another low bridge at the finish line. At three o'clock the troika race would be run, but on that morning as we trotted

371

down the Nevsky with the crowds shouting joyously, all eyes were on us!

"Redbeard the Magnificent," they cried and I waved as Nadia and Yakoff threw candy to the little children.

Boris held his head up high and seemed to think it was he they were there to see, while behind us the Tsarevich came on like an expectant father. His Majesty had a long lead shank hooked to Hans' bridle—the Romanoff red racing sleigh in tow, while Hans was wrapped in a fine red blanket as he showed off his high stepping trot to the jubilant crowd. I saw sword swallowers, fire-eaters, pick pockets, police, and ladies of the evening (out for the earliest work of the season), rich men, and poor men, with poor ladies begging, and rich women sighing. And all along the way, the Army was out keeping the streets open for our grand procession. When the soldiers spotted Alexander Alexandrovich, they snapped to attention and gave him a passing salute and a mighty Hurrah. His Majesty kept his gloved hand tipped to his fur cap and grinned. Usually he was shy around the citizens of St. Petersburg, but with the excitement of the race and the jam packed throng, and the candy our team was throwing out, he looked like a proud prince of the realm! Minnie rode beside him on a fine English mare and waved to the crowd as we proceeded to the starting line with our hearts pounding.

"Don't let Vlad's horse beat you, no matter what, Augustus!" cried the Tsarevich over the sounds of the mob. "I can tolerate losing to anyone but him! You hear me, palkovnik?"

Grand Duke Vladimir had dashed out to buy himself an ice racing horse just a week before the race. Said to be the fastest horse in all of Europe (and the most expensive too), Vlad's Swedish Warmblood was a big buckskin with his head held high, and he was the favorite of the day.

I watched Scheherazade's gorgeous bay coat shining in the morning light, as the woman I loved waved and threw sweets to the children. I loved her and she loved me, and someday her Uncle Peter would realize that our love could not be extinguished, and he'd let us marry!

It was close to a mile and three quarters from the Anichkov Palace to the starting line and we pushed on slowly through the cheering crowd. When we got to the Moyka Canal all covered in snow, the sidewalks on both sides were jam packed with revelers. The Cossacks rode out ahead and cleared a path, and then down on the ice we went—just the sleighs, and the drivers, and a column of charging Cossacks.

"We'll see you at the Finish Line, my love—Go with God!" Nadia hollered as we rode down into that stone lined canyon.

"Don't let Hans get the better of you, Herr Colonel!" Yakoff bellowed with his beard having turned into a big ball of frost. My big black Orlov looked back like he wished me good luck, and then Boris was gone with my friends and my lover.

"Remember, palkovnik," yelled my master as he hauled the Romanoff red blanket off Hans. "Don't let that brother of mine beat you!"

Maria Feodorovna just smiled a simple smile and waved goodbye.

The Cossacks ran the pedestrians off the ice in joyful preparation for the race. Their shaggy ponies would charge after someone and the crowd would cheer and howl as the pedestrians ran for the wall. A wrought iron railing topped the canal—a swirling sea of movement and laughter as the crowd waited for the race to begin. On either side of the embankment were two and three story mansions of every color of the rainbow— sparkling in the noonday sun.

Vlad's buckskin with his big Finish driver in an elk skin coat was up against the north wall, Prince Yusupov's big black Orlov—the biggest of the batch with a black-bearded driver all dressed in black was next, a tall chestnut Holsteiner, whose driver was dressed in loud yellow down to his toes, was in the middle, then me and my dapple gray stallion, with a big strong gray Kladruber with short ears and a big roman nose to my right—his driver being a little guy my size in a sky blue coat. On the sides of each sleigh were the coat of arms of the owner—the golden double-headed Romanoff eagle on my red sleigh and Vlad's sky blue one as we moved up to the Starting Line. Prince Yusupov's sleigh had double lions that looked like squirrels holding up a huge stage full of Yusupov props, while Count Stroganov's Kladruber presented with two gray foxes holding up a double eagle with a bear aboard. The big chestnut Holsteiner had a pair of golden lions that held a big pointy crown that would break your leg if you ever bumped onto it. But one thing that all the sleighs had in common that day was a pair of shiny sharp runners that could cut you in half!

"Gentlemen, the course is five versts long," bellowed the fattest of the five fur clad judges, "from here to Catherine's Canal, then west to the Lion's Bridge. No physical contact between sleighs, gentlemen, and no whipping another man's horse!" And then with a quick, "Get set," and the shot of a small cannon, we were off!

We rumbled past the Yusupov Palace all stretched out five across, but by the first bridge we started to spread out. Vlad's buckskin was pulling to the lead out in the center with the Finn cracking his long black whip. None of us wanted to be too close to those granite walls as that whip hunted, and the pack spread out even more. About a length and a half behind the Warmblood, Hans and I were doing just fine as I realized the one thing we hadn't practiced was sliding sideways with another sleigh sliding sideways beside us.

"Sweet Jesus," I prayed to that dark eyed icon who smiled up at me. "Get me through this day, Dear Lord, and I swear I'll make Nadia Shuvalova my wife!" Some might say that was blaspheming, but I'd heard people ask the Lord to get rid of their warts, and if I hit that granite wall going thirty miles an hour,[150] I'd sure as hell have more than warts to worry about!

On the left of Vlad's Warmblood came Prince Yusupov's Orlov with his big black-bearded driver cussing and screaming as he cracked his whip, which reverberated across the ice like the shot of a cannon. The chestnut Holsteiner came up on Vlad's right, his driver in loud yellow swinging his whip like a wild man. Back maybe three lengths off the pace, I watched as the two horses tried to overcome Vladimir's buckskin. But like everything Vlad ever touched, that big Finn had been chosen for his dirty tricks, and he cut the sleigh right then left to let them know they couldn't pass without being driven into the stone walls. Still on they charged from either side. Hooves thundered, sleigh runners sizzled, and the crowd roared as we went whizzing through a tight turn. The Palace Square came up on our left and the flying snow cut my visibility in half.

"Easy, Hans," I hollered, and the colt responded by backing off, while behind me I could hear the gray Kladruber coming up fast on my right. He was breathing hard as his driver hollered "easy" in that Mecklenburg familiar I knew so well. We were coming up on a great black chasm where the canal split. Up ahead, Prince Yusupov's big black made a run at Vladimir's Warmblood. A length behind and on the inside came the chestnut Holsteiner moving up fast for a tight little threesome that could never make that turn onto Catherine's Canal. Maybe twenty feet narrower than the Moyka Canal and at a right angle, those stone walls came up like a meteorite!

I hauled back on the reins as I called for the Dutchman to slow down, while the boys up ahead poured it on! If Prince Yusupov's big black fell back far enough to make the turn safely, Vlad's driver fell back just enough to block him. And if the Orlov, who reminded me of Boris, went faster, Vlad's driver would crack the whip and speed up. He was letting that whip swing wide to spook the big black and caught him in the nose with blood spurting out all over the snow. There was no way they could both enter the Catherine's Canal, and the Prince's driver flew straight down the Moyka and out of the race. And then there were four.

We made that hard right with the Holsteiner on the inside a half a length ahead of Vlad's buckskin. There were thousands of legs flying by our heads as the crowd roared, and the speed mesmerized, and the narrow stone walls became a tunnel of death!

I could see the gold-topped steeple of the Kazan Cathedral coming up fast on my right and gave Hans the go ahead to start moving up. Inch by inch we gained ground on the two frontrunners who were busy battling it out. The buckskin and the chestnut hammered away at each other banging sleighs as Vlad's crooked driver took to his dirty work. And just as we hit that little footbridge where the canal cut right, the Finn hit the chestnut right across the face with his whip. Blood ran down the sides of his cheek as he shrieked, and the blood of my forefathers boiled up inside me! Hadn't the Judges said, no whipping another man's horse? That poor horse was running blind as we went under a low narrow bridge with golden griffon wings[151] as the sleigh ricocheted off the granite wall in an explosion of sleigh parts. And as that sleigh disintegrated into a thousand

375

pieces, the driver was still hanging on to the reins as he slid out in front of us in a dance of death. Hans cut hard to the right to avoid running over him and then there was but three of us!

We were running to the inside of the Grand Duke's buckskin and I clucked to Hans and let him fly! There was a mile to go to the Lion's Bridge with six hundred yards of straight away before the course became a fish hook flying left and right.

"Comrade," I hollered in Mecklenburg familiar to the gray's German driver. "Come on up, and we'll give this Finn a good fight!"

The big roman nosed Kladruber still had plenty of fight left in him and his driver cracked the whip, and on they came. So with that big gray moving hard on the left of Vlad's buckskin, and I on his right, we began to move up at a blistering pace. If Vlad's driver cut for me, I'd swing wide while the gray stretched his legs and ran for the lead, and if the Finn started in on him, Hans and I would make a run for the front. As we approached the last curve to the Lion's Bridge, we were running three across with not an inch to spare as those granite walls closed in like a buzz saw! We made our last curve to the left with a hundred yards to go as Vlad's horse went banging into the side of the gray.

"Pick on someone your own size!" I bellowed and the Finn swung wide and let that whip fly across Hans' silvery back, which set my stallion to flying even faster.

The Finn's next strike of the whip hit my left wrist. It stung and it burned, but as it wrapped around my forearm like a boa constrictor, I gave it a tug and pulled him off balance. He didn't fall, for the Finn was a big bastard, but being distracted for just a second, the gray had a chance to break for the lead. And as we slid under the Lion's Bridge in a flash of three sleighs, I didn't even have time to see the lions go by!

Prince Stroganov's long nosed gray came in first as the crowd went wild, while the Judges said Vlad's Swedish Warmblood and the Gelderland stallion came in a close second at exactly the same time. Grand Duke Vladimir came thundering down on the ice and said he'd seen it all from his vantage point and, "That little Amerikanskiy grabbed my driver's whip and wouldn't let him pass!"

376

He went into a tirade about my cheating ways and the judges were about to award him second place, when riders came in from the far side of the course and reported how the Finn had forced Prince Yusupov's horse out of the race, and nearly killed the Holsteiner's driver! And thus by the closest of margins, Hans and I were awarded second place.

The Tsarevich would have preferred a first place finish, but once all the fouls were known to him, he cut me some slack. And when the Tsar's own Red Cossacks came up hollering Redbeard the Magnificent on account of all the money they'd won, the Naslednik almost seemed impressed.

"You are making quite a name for yourself, Redbeard." went my Boss as he smiled and waved to the adoring crowd. "Now what would you like to do with yourself?"

"Well, Sire," I said with a big proud grin as the crowd roared on. "Why don't Sergeant Yakovich and I take over your racing stables?"

His Majesty didn't look too excited, but when the Royal couple went off for England that summer, he sent me and Yakoff ahead to scout out the talent. "Don't pay an arm and a leg for the cream of the crop, Augustus," he told me like the skinflint he was. "But get a good strong second tier and we'll make a race horse out of them, or I'm not the next emperor of Russia," and he laughed a big belly laugh, for the man was finally starting to enjoy himself.

We landed in England and Scotland Yard was certain we were a couple of spies. "How can an American serve a Russian Tsar?" asked the little Scottish gentleman in a bowler hat.

"The same way a Highlander can serve the bloody Brits," I responded, but he failed to see the similarities.

Those English horse traders tried to take every ruble we had as their thoroughbreds had been doing quite well on the Continent. "You want second tier horses, go to France and see what they're eating for dinner," said one wise cracking horse trader, not knowing I'd lived in France for four wonderful years and never once did I eat horse flesh. By the time Sasha and Minnie arrived, we had two mares, a stallion, and several geldings picked out.

Maria Feodorovna's little sister was married to Queen Victoria's son, Bertie, and the Tsarevna and her sister, Alexandra, had planned all winter for the official Romanoff visit. The girls had bought matching outfits to wear to every event. Petite little ladies with curly brown hair and the long chins of their Nordic ancestors, they looked like identical twins. And didn't the visiting Shah of Persia take a liking to the girls—much to my Boss's ire.[152]

Alexander Alexandrovich had been playing second fiddle to the Shah since he got to England and he wasn't pleased. But His Majesty thoroughly enjoyed riding the countryside in pursuit of his brand new horses with Yakoff and Redbeard the Horse Trader.

"Can that stallion jump?" asked the Naslednik as he gasped at the price the Englishman was asking for a strong bay stallion.

"He can with the right man aboard," said the blue blooded man in the herringbone jacket, and I volunteered to put his horse to the test.

Those jumps were as close to a Maryland hillside as I'd seen in a while, and I sailed over many a tall post and rail fence to his surprise. "Who taught you to ride?" he asked like only the English could ride like that.

"Well, I'd say the likes of Jeb Stuart and the Gray Ghost himself, your Lordship!" I told him with pride. "For those Rebel boys could really ride, and they shot pretty straight too. You get them riding after you with blood in their eyes and you best learn to ride fast, if you wanted to survive!"

"You were in the American Civil War?" he asked like he was calling me a liar, as the Naslednik smiled on. "You don't look old enough!"

"Well, I was fifteen and half when first blood was drawn and stayed long enough to see every day." Minus the days spent convalescing with the three sisters up on Hogmaw Hill, which I didn't count because it was like heaven to me!

"What's your flat out bottom price for this big bay?" I asked the Laird with his nose in the air.

The horse was a powerful three year old with strong legs and an intelligent head—perfect breeding stock for Maria Feodorovna's bay mare back in St. Petersburg. What I liked the most about the colt was how he took a crap right there before His Lordship and the next emperor of Russia without any remorse.

"As disrespectful as you are, Augustus Augustovich!" said the Tsarevich in his native tongue.

"And as full of shit, Sire," I quipped back to His Majesty in Russian.

"An American who speaks Russian," says the Englishman in surprise. "My, what a find!" Like we Americans didn't take kindly to speaking in foreign tongues.

"We need to buy this stallion, Sire!" I said in our lingo, as I made a look of distaste for the Englishman to read on my face. "Let's just ride away and see what His Lordship does?"

Yakoff shook his head like he agreed, the horse was a dog. The two big Russians in their vested suits looked like a couple of moujik brothers stuck at a funeral for their great uncle in borrowed suits.

"Maybe another time, Your Lordship," went Alexander Alexandrovich as we trotted away.

We didn't get more than ten feet before the man cut his price in half. Horse trading was in our blood, and though the Naslednik's official trip to England was a big disappointment, he enjoyed the time spent scouring the countryside for horses with his two moujik friends. Minnie and Sasha went on to Denmark (her father was the Danish King), whilst Yakoff and I took the horses back to Holland to find a Gelderland mare for Hans.

"You are the little American what pissed in your pants in Tsar Paul's bed, Ja?" went the first Dutch horse trader we came across, for the world was growing smaller by the day.

I wanted to shave off my beard and assume a new name, when Yakoff came to my aid, by saying, "And I'm the big Russian what pissed on your boots, Ja?" as he took a nice long leak on the Dutchman's brand new English riding boots.

But we did find a beautiful mare for Hans that day—another gorgeous dapple gray Gelderland with a long flowing mane and a lovely disposition. We loaded her on a box car and headed home for Russia with all the other horses in tow—getting back home to the Babylon of the Snows in less than a week.

Nadia was very happy to see me! Her work as a Freilini was a farce, for besides helping the Tsar's 2nd wife before God pick out the right color rouge to wear while His Horniness ravaged her, there was little for her to do. At least twice a day[153] the Emperor would send a rider from the Winter Palace bearing messages for Princess Dolgurokova to read at their townhouse on the English Quay. The girls would all gather round her and go over each and every word (like Miss Yvette and her cocottes), and when the excitement of what the Emperor had written reached a crescendo, wouldn't Alexander II show up in the flesh. He'd give his poor little illegitimate children a pat on the head, and his 2nd wife before God a good hard rogering, then dash back to the Winter Palace where his empress lay sick in her bed.

"They're not in love; they're in heat, Augustus Augustovich," Nadia would say. And all of Russia knew it!

Why, the Naslednik and his poor brothers and sisters could hardly show their faces without someone laughing behind their backs. The work of the government slowed to a crawl as the ship of state sailed on in a sea of lust! Then one day, as Yakoff and I worked away at the Royal Stables, two gendarmes in their strange metal fire helmets came marching in and said I was wanted at the Municipal Police Station.

"Can I go and get my uniform on?" I asked, for I had on my horse trainer clothes. But no, I was to climb into their carriage with no questions asked. North up the Nevsky we flew to the Moyka Embankment where the Police Station stood. Up a flight of winding stairs to a second floor office we went, and they plunked me down on a hard wooden chair. There I sat for pretty close to an hour, until the door to the meeting room opened and out stepped Modest Mussorgsky.

"Please don't talk gentlemen!" ordered the tall American. He wore a wide lapelled black suit with a black cravat around his neck, black pants, and shiny black almost dancing shoes with a rather shaggy black beard and wavy pitch black hair. He had his sights on me as he held the door open for the Maestro to leave.

"Thank you for your help!" he said in his perfect Russian.

Maybe this was about those pictures the Imp had taken from the Nevsky Hotel? But I'd already paid for them. Or maybe the ballerinas were charging my friend with some sexual improprieties, though they looked pretty happy when they left that day!

"Come in, Mr. Stewart." The man in black said as he adjusted that cravat like a hangman's noose.

He led me into a long stark room and bid me sit down right beside him. Then he shifted his papers, studied his notes, dipped his quill in the ink well and without even looking up, said, "So tell me Mr. Stewart, did you know you needed to check in with the American Embassy when you first came to Russia?"

"Well, no sir," I told him quite truthfully. "Nobody told me to do so, and how the hell would I know to do that!"

"No need to get defensive, Mr. Stewart." said the man with the black cravat, as he jotted down "hostile attitude" on his little piece of paper.

"Well, while you're busy writing down: hostile attitude, how about you call me colonel!" I told him quite tersely.

"Sorry, Colonel Stewart, but the fact remains, you should have checked in with the Embassy when you first came to Russia. Do you have anyone who can vouch for your whereabouts over the last two years?"

"Well, let's see, I've been with the next tsar of Russia nearly the whole damn time, and if you don't trust him, why don't you just wire my old friend Cassius Clay back in Kentucky? He'll vouch for my character."

"Friends in high places indeed, Colonel Stewart," the man said like he wasn't impressed, "but let me explain, this is a fact finding mission…"

"And you are?" I interjected. Doc had taught me to stand up straight, look a man in the eye, and shake his hand real firmly when you first met, but this man hadn't even bothered to tell me his name. Maybe it was the horse clothes I was wearing, or me cleaning the bottom of my boots on his chair, but the whole thing smelled like horse shit to me!

"I'm the Legation Secretary of the United States Consulate, Mr. Eugene Schuyler," the man said like I should be impressed. "What I need from you, Colonel Stewart, are the answers to some rather delicate questions."

"Go ahead ask away," I said with nothing to hide.

"Did your friend Modest Mussorgsky ever receive payment for services rendered to a Miss Fanny Lear?" He asked with his pen at the ready.

"Which services are you talking about? I know for a fact the sex was gratuitous!" I barked right back.

He put down that pen and whispered like the walls had ears, which they probably did since we were in a Russian Police Station. "Colonel Stewart, we are both men of the world, are we not? Mr. Mussorgsky told me he spent several months playing the piano for Miss Fanny," the diplomat said sternly. "Is that true, sir?"

"Well, that wasn't all Modest Mussorgsky was doing up there for Miss Fanny Lear!" I said, trying hard to get the Dutchman to smile.

"To the best of your knowledge was he ever paid for his services? Please, speak to the question!" he cross-examined like the lawyer he was.

"No sir, not one kopek!" I answered. "He got a roof over his head, maybe a meal or two, and all the good loving Miss Fanny Lear could bring to the table, or the top of the piano, or up on the window sill, but not one red cent did Modest ever get for any services rendered," l lied damn persuasively!

"How do you know that? The lady claims she paid him fifteen hundred rubles a month, and she wants the money back before she'll leave Russia quietly."

I started laughing like a hyena, for number one, Miss Fanny Lear was no lady that I knew of! And number two, it sounded like she was running a scam on the Russians, and had the US Diplomatic Service doing her paperwork!

"So again, sir, how do you know Modest Mussorgsky never received remuneration from Miss Fanny Lear?"

"Well, that one is easy, councilor," I said. "I was footing his bills."

"And why would you do that?" he asked like he never had a friend in need.

"Because that's what friends do for friends where I come from, Mr. Schuyler. Now, if you don't mind this meeting is over!"

We lay low in the barns after that for Miss Fanny had blackened the name of America for all of us. Her lover, the Tsarevich's own first cousin, had stolen diamonds right out of his mother's favorite icon,[154] and he was banished. Poor Modest was considered a persona non grata for his participation in the affair, and all he'd done was play the piano, while I was on thin ice for having introduced the Tsarevich to such an evil woman.

But Sergeant Yakovich and I were a happy pair in the Royal stables. Give us a good horse and a field to gallop in, and we were as happy as clams! The Naslednik's first born son, Nicholas, would come down to the stables and play with us "characters" as he called us. He was a bright little blue-eyed boy so slender and kind, and we taught him and his little brother how to ride like Cheyenne braves. Soon enough, his scrawny tutor, Pobedonostsev would arrive and ruin our fun.

"Sergeant Yakovich!" he'd squeak in that high raspy voice, "Nicholas Alexandrovich is to return to the Anichkov Palace at once!"

Little Nicholas would ask him why he couldn't stay and learn to be a great horseman like Redbeard the Magnificent and his friend, Sergeant Yakovich, and his gaunt faced tutor would look at me through those wire rim glasses like he wanted to murder me. Pobedonostsev considered me a heathen for my Episcopalian ways, and he hated foreigners as well, so he never would talk to me.

Then one day, my Boss and Count General Shuvalov when that scrawny tutor cut in. "All of Russia is calling the young lady the Odalisque, Count General Shuvalov. Do you think she has bewitched the Emperor?"

"I wouldn't go as far as to call her Baba Yaga,"[155] Uncle Peter answered, "but she does have some pretty skinny legs and can eat like a horse."

When the Emperor caught wind of the story, Uncle Peter was called in to His Majesty's study and left without his Secret Police job. Oh, he was too powerful to be exiled to Siberia, but the Tsar sent him packing under the guise of making him Ambassador to England.

Nadia and I saw him off and before the great man's ship set sail he took me aside and said, "First off, don't even try to ask for Nadia's hand in marriage, or I'll have you murdered in your sleep! Do you hear me?"

"That's not what I wanted to talk to you about, Count General," I lied. "I wanted to tell you it was Pobedonostsev who ratted on you."

"He did what?" said His Lordship who wasn't use to my American slang.

"He told the Emperor what you said about Princess Ekaterina's legs."

"Oh, I know how Pobedonostsev works, my little friend," the Count General said as he leaned over the ship rail and frowned down into the steel gray waters. "Divide and conquer, that's his game. You just try to keep your head on your shoulders. And don't you touch a hair on my niece's head, or I swear it won't be the Holy See[156] that kills you."

Nadia and I walked down the quay as his ship steamed away, and she looked into my eyes and asked with great excitement, "Did you talk to Uncle Peter about our marriage, Augustus?"

And what was I to say to the woman I loved? "He said to ask him again in a years' time," I lied.

That evening we headed out to the Gypsy Camp on Vasilyevsky Island where we ate dinner under the stars at a place called The Samarkand. We were surrounded by birch trees with strings of hanging lanterns, gypsy dancers, and violins taking us to a higher place, as we drank peach vodka and laughed like the lovers we wished we were. Uncle Peter's ship hadn't reached the western tip of Kotlin Island[157] before we were making love under the stars, for the summer of '74 was a season of love!

Chapter Fourteen

The Mukden Rifles

My trusty sergeant and I would have trained horses for the rest of our lives, but once more the wolf was at our door. In 1876 a wave of freedom swept through the Balkans, and the Sultan of Turkey sent Ahmet Aga and five thousand Bashi-Bazouk cavalrymen up into Bulgaria to teach his Christian subjects a lesson.[158] They burned down the schools with the children in them, and lay siege to the last haven the citizens had in a stone church in the little town of Batak. All of Europe knew of their dastardly deeds, and even the British Prime Minister, Gladstone, said, "Let the Turks now carry away their abuses in the only possible manner, namely by carrying off themselves."

But no one had the nerve to take on the Turks!

No one but the Russian people—that is, for these Orthodox Christians were their Slavic brothers! All of Russia (except for the Emperor) was chomping at the bit to go down into the Balkans and drive the Musulman back into the desert where they belonged. The Tsar, however, wasn't so sure he could afford a war with the Turks. But the Sultan was preparing to fight for every inch of Europe he could conquer. My friend Mike Kelley worked for the Winchester Repeating Arms Company and they sold the Turks over fifty thousand Winchester Rifles and two hundred thousand American made Martini-Henrys that year. In a cyphered telegraph message, Mike offered to sell the Russians the same guns at a twenty percent discount. But the Emperor said he couldn't afford such a weapon—not even at that price. And this, while Grand Duke Vladimir was building a huge palace, and his wife was buying a tiara worth fifty thousand rubles![159]

That was the straw that broke the camel's back as far as the Naslednik was concerned. Alexander II could sit up there in his Winter Palace and roger his 2nd wife before God until he was blue in the face, but someone had to go down there and save their Christian brothers! The Anichkov Palace became a place where plans for war could be openly discussed, and one of our first visitors was my old friend, General Gurko.

"Colonel Stewart!" he cried with a big grin on his fur lined face as he gave me the customary kisses and hugs the Russians all loved. "Thrown any Guard officers into Lake Dolgoye lately?" But what he and the Tsarevich were really up to was no laughing matter, for they wanted to form a Flying Column to go down and fight the Bashi-Bazouks.[160]

I was wearing my colonel's uniform instead of my old horse clothes as ordered—a naked chest where medals hung on the other two men, but we all had those shiny pogoni on our shoulders as the sun streamed in through the library windows. There was a big map of the Balkans lying on the table, and I got the distinct impression they had already put a few pins in it.

"How many men do you think it would take to ride down into the Balkans and scare the bejesus out of the Bashi-Bazouks?" the Tsarevich asked my little Polish friend with a mischievous grin.

"A hundred tops!" he said with his thick black beard waving.

Here was a short little bow-legged cavalryman that hardly came up to the Tsarevich's shoulders, talking of invading the lands of the Sultan, and according to him, a hundred men should do the trick! I was thinking by the way they looked at me, that this baby had my name on it, so I warned them that I was no military genius.

"We know dat," General Gurko said with a chuckle, "but what matters is you're lucky!"[161] And the Tsarevich nodded his head and smiled.

Then I asked the two great military minds, "How can we move into Ottoman territory without a declaration of war?"

"Don't worry my little red-headed friend," the Tsarevich answered. "By the time you've punished the Bashi-Bazouks and gathered the intelligence we need for our upcoming invasion, war will be declared."

"But how can a Flying Column cross the Danube River when the Turks watch every crossing?" I asked as I pointed at their map and wondered what they were smoking?

"Dat's de beauty of dis plan!" bellowed General Gurko. "We can cross anywhere we like, for we cross in de dead of winter!"

I swallowed hard and thought back to Fredericksburg with the snow covered bodies on a windswept hill, and the goosebumps spread all over me, though it was a warm day in June. No, there were a hundred good reasons not to fight a winter campaign, but they wouldn't listen.

"The Danube is near a mile wide, Sire!" I slightly exaggerated to try and get my point across. "And taking horses up into those snow covered mountains, why, you might as well shoot half of them now, and save yourself the trouble of shooting them later."

"You see what I mean?" General Gurko said as he slapped me across the back. "Dis boy has a great understanding of life in de field. Take all de mules and horses you want, Colonel Stewart!"

No matter what I said, they wouldn't be swayed! Colonel Augustus Stewart of His Majesty's Infantry was their man, and I thought to myself, oh, hell no! I wasn't taking a Flying Column through Turkish territory in the dead of winter as a damn infantryman—no way!

"You want me to sign off on this crazy plan, Sire," I exclaimed with the only bargaining chip I held, "then you best make me a cavalryman!"

"I told you the boy has brass balls!" cried the Tsarevich. "A colonel of Cavalry you are Augustus Augustovich—from this day forward! Now gentlemen, let's get on with our plans."

We spent the rest of the afternoon going over all the main points, and if I hadn't of been an old sergeant major, I'd have been lost in the details. "First things first, Sire!" I told His Majesty with all due respect. "I need to give my Sergeant Yakovich a transfer to the cavalry too, and while we're at it, could we make him an officer?"

The Tsarevich looked at me like he was gonna take my big brass balls and tie them in a tight little knot and pitch them into somebody's soup, though he did agree to make Yakoff a sergeant of cavalry. General Gurko just stood back and watched us haggle.

"We'll get you some staff officers and you can set up your Headquarters down at Gatchina where word of the expedition can't get out," His Highness said like they'd already decided just about everything.

387

"You go order all de horses, and mules, and supplies you need, Colonel Stewart." my little friend told me. "And tomorrow you can start picking out de best men for de job."

"One more thing, Sire," I said as I almost got excited. "May I wire up a telegraph line to one of those towers down at Gatchina so we can talk with St. Petersburg on a regular basis?"

"See, de boy has brains," cried the walrus to the ogre, as they smiled like a couple of underemployed undertakers.

But I really didn't have any brains at all agreeing to take a Flying Column across a frozen river in the heart of the Ottoman Empire, in the midst of winter. That was like playing Russian roulette, for if the Danube was a windswept sheet of ice when we crossed, we could lose two thirds of the Flying Column just in the crossing. And if our supplies were on the mounts that went down, how could we survive out there in the cold? And as I walked out of the Anichkov Palace that day, I realized there was one more person I needed to tell about this cockamamie plan, and she would probably kill me before the Turks ever got a chance!

Once a week, my lover and I would meet at the Nevsky Hotel. We'd have dinner, chat, kiss and hug, and talk about running off and living as husband and wife. But now I had to break the news to Nadia that I was about to go into harm's way.

"You're doing what?" she said with her face turning red and her emerald green eyes flashing fire!

"I'm going on a little scout for the Tsarevich, is all. It won't be dangerous!" I lied as I gazed at her beauty and wondered why she'd chosen me above all others?

As a Lady in Waiting to the Tsar's mistress, her Dance Card was always full, and I knew several Guards officers who would have liked to have married her, had she not kept them at arms' length. Then I remembered what she said out there on the snow covered trail to Tsarskoe Selo as the stars came down and swallowed us. "Lovers, who enter the Vertigo together, will be lovers through all of time!"

"Why you?" she said with tears in her eyes. "This isn't your fight!"

"Ah, but it is, my love," I told her. "When I was a boy back in Baltimore and slavery ruled my world, I was an abolitionist before I even knew what the word meant, for every man, woman, and child on this earth deserves a chance at their freedom. Those bloody Musulman are murdering innocent people whose only crime is wanting to be free, and somebody has to go down there and help them!"

She thought a minute and then she smiled and said, "If I could come along with you, Augustus Augustovich, I would. You go down there and I will wait for you, forever, if I have to!"

We said our farewells that night and in the morning I was Gatchina bound with my new cavalry Sergeant Yakovich, twenty handpicked men, and a mile and a half of telegraph wire. Oh, I told the bosses that there was no need to rush a thing like this, since all the supplies were up in St. Petersburg, but they swore all I had to do was telegraph them, and whatever we needed would be down on the very next train.

The first thing they sent me were boxes and boxes of those Baranov rifles with rounds that wouldn't fire and actions that jammed, and then they sent a hundred horses that the French wouldn't have eaten even if they were starving. Next they sent me a hundred men gathered up from the dregs of all the regiments in St. Petersburg. We'd strung the wire from the stone tower to the Admiralty Gate and then out to the railroad station and started training operators to send and receive in cyphered code. Up at General Gurko's Headquarters, his handpicked men were using an old Civil War cypher I'd given them to decode our messages, but they were having trouble breaking the code on the word "shit" I was using to describe those rifles. It seemed the Russians had the word covered seven or eight ways—none of which they figured I was applying to the Baranovs (though I'm sure all seven would have worked just fine). So I had to take the train up to the capital to clarify my complaints.

General Gurko kept me waiting in the anteroom to his office for about a half hour—not the best of signs, but the General was a very busy man. He had stacks of papers as high as me on his desk, and his staff was running about like chickens with their heads cut off.

"General Gurko," I said with my hat in hand. "If you and the Tsarevich want me dead, why don't you just shoot me?"

"What do you mean, Colonel Stewart?" he said as he twisted at his side whiskers like he really didn't have time for my bullshit, which was a whole nother word entirely.

"Well, so far, sir I haven't received a single thing I can use for our winter campaign," I said trying to sound like a friendly comrade—not a pain in his ass, which I was. "We have a saying in America, sir, shit in—shit out, and if you want me to ride down there in the middle of winter and give you good intelligence for next spring's campaign, then I need good men, good mounts, and good weapons, sir!"

"And what would you suggest, Colonel Stewart?" he said with a little sharpness to his voice.

"Once we get these cypherers trained on the telegraph, General Gurko, why don't we take this show on the road, say down to Kiev? We can buy our horses ten times cheaper down there, and hand-pick our men from the veterans of Tashkent. Armed with signed orders from you and the Tsarevich, nobody will tell us no, while here in the shadow of the Tsar the red tape is so thick we'll never put a Flying Column together before spring."

"Spring," he yelled! "We go dis winter!"

"And Kiev is eight hundred miles closer to our objective, sir." I answered. "So we can push on for Bucharest that much faster."

"Someone has been looking at de map!" he said with his blue eyes twinkling. "Let me show you dis, colonel." And he swept his pile of papers away to show me a huge map of Bulgaria. "We want to cross here at a place called Ruse," he said as he pointed her out. "And move south through here," which was a line like the crow flies to Constantinople, or Istanbul, as the Turks called it.

"You scout south beyond de Shipka Pass dis winter and head back for Ruse by May and we will join you dere on de banks of de Danube for one hell of a fight come spring! So you study dis area real goot, Colonel Stewart, and I'll sign orders to train your men anywhere you like!"

Lord how I loved my little Polish general, he was a fighting man's friend! We returned the crappy rifles, men, and horses, so they weren't charged to our Flying Column, then we wired the Military Governor down in Kiev with orders to find us ten big strong Orlov horses, and two hundred of the biggest mules they could find, plus feed for the men and livestock—all signed for by my two powerful friends.

Before we left Gatchina Palace, I climbed those steep stone steps to my Clock Tower cell one more time to put my little yellow Jesus back on his table. I tried to avoid the accusing eyes of Dead Tsar Paul, and to my smiling little friend I said, "I'm sorry, dear Lord, for any inconvenience I've caused you, but you're back home now and thanks for your help!" I didn't want the theft of a religious icon hanging over my head when we fought a Holy War against the Turks.

Mike Kelley came through with a contact in Odessa who could reroute the Sultan's weapons, and it sounded like a plan to me. So before we set out, I wired my old Kentucky friend and told him to set up the meet. We collected a hundred thousand rubles including a hundred twenty-five ruble gold pieces struck in honor of Grand Duke Vladimir's thirtieth birthday—all stacked away nice and neat in two big wooden crates that Sergeant Yakovich guarded like a hawk.

"This is my mother, the Empress of Russia's contribution to your Flying Column, Augustus Augustovich. Spend it wisely!" said the Naslednik as he saw us off in the late summer of '76. "It's twice as much as we gave Miss Fanny Lear to leave Russia!"

"And I didn't have to screw anybody to get it, Sire!" I said, forgetting that the big man didn't like vile humor, even if I was going off to war.

Save for missing Nadia, I was glad to see St. Petersburg pass to our rear. The place was a den of inequity, a sea of insanity, and a haven for bureaucrats with their plots and counter plots. We were off for Kiev, the mother of Slavic cities with plans to head straight down to Odessa once the weapons arrived. So with twenty mostly empty box cars on a Royal Romanoff train, we set off to start the Russo-Turkish War!

It was some four hundred miles to Moscow where we rested for two days. St. Petersburg might have been the capital of Russia for some, but

Moscow was the heart and soul of the great nation! Seeing the size of the Kremlin, the gold topped church steeples, and the giant cannons that protected her walls, I knew Moscow ruled the roost.[162] Then we were off for another five hundred mile journey through the breadbasket of the Empire, miles and miles of wheat fields and big work horses, with serfs working the fields like the slaves of the Deep South.

Once our train came into Kiev, we headed to a siding just east of the cemetery to set up camp. General Gurko had said to check in with the Military Governor as soon as we arrived. "Prince Dondukov-Korsakov is a fine man, he will see dat you are made ready for a winter campaign, Colonel Stewart," were his exact words.

So I brought out my brand new cavalry uniform and mounted Boris, as Sergeant Yakovich mounted Little Suli the Second. We were off to find my music Professor's long lost cousin, Prince Alexander Mikhailovich Dondukov-Korsakov. Lost for a while in that huge Ukrainian city, we got to see the Golden Gates of Kiev where the Mongols had fed fat their war horses. Finally, we met up with some well-mounted Circassians who directed us to the Governor's Palace, and there we waited for over an hour in a hall as grand as any in the city of Piter.

When the Korsakov prince finally entered the room, I saw the family resemblance immediately. He had that high forehead and deep thinking eyes of my trombone professor, but Prince Dondukov-Korsakov was an older man, and his thick gray beard had gone to seed and was flourishing in two great blooms beneath his noble chin. But just like Nikolai, he had a sharp nose that seemed to sniff things out.

"Nice uniform, Colonel Stewart," he said in his deep bass voice. "But it looks like it's new to me. Have you been in the cavalry long?"

"I've been a cavalryman since the age of fifteen, Your Majesty," I said with my eyes lowered. "But only as of late was I transferred back, Sire."

I had that sire thing down to a science. Some of the Royals were to be addressed as His Highness and some as His Majesty, while some didn't rate either title. But I could sire till I was blue in the face.

"And who is this great giant behind you?" Prince Korsakov asked. "Why, he looks as tall as the next Tsar of Russia."

"Actually, sire," I mumbled—tripping over my words, "Sergeant Yakovich is half a hand taller than the Tsarevich."

"Huge by anybody's reckoning," says the Prince with those bushy side whiskers bristling. "Has your colonel always been able to stretch the facts, Sergeant Yakovich?"

"Yes, Sire, indeed he has," Yakoff answered with great conviction. "A small Amerikanskiy with big brass balls, our Naslednik says of him, Sire." Yakoff liked that word sire too.

Prince Korsakov burst into laughter. "I like you boys, so I will help you get your Flying Column started, but crossing the Danube in the dead of winter, that's absolutely crazy! You'll need mules not horses to move through the Balkans, you didn't know that, did you, Colonel Stewart?"

I shook my head, no, but hell yes I did. A mule was stronger and would last longer on a trek like that, but we were definitely taking along eleven big horses. Boris was chomping at the bit to go down in the Balkans, and I couldn't disappoint my four-legged friend.

"Are you a Christian, Colonel Stewart?" the haughty prince asked, and I shook my head yes. "Good because you will need the Lord's blessings to survive out there in the snow! Have you heard of a Krivitza?"

I hadn't, but he happily told us a Krivitza was what the Bulgarians called a winter hurricane that swept down through the Balkan Mountains gaining strength as it came. "The winds will blow so hard they can pick up a fully loaded mule and carry him away, and as the snow piles higher and tries to suffocate you, it will snow some more!" he warned with that puffy gray beard blowing like a blizzard.

I was glad I hadn't stayed in St. Petersburg to train, for the Prince seemed to know the lay of the land, but being the Military Governor of Kiev must not have been much of a job. His Majesty showed up in our camp one morning with a tent the size of Barnum & Bailey's and took over. His organizational skills were way better than mine were, as he made every decision from the size of the mules (he liked the medium ones), to the class we chose our soldiers from.

393

In Russia they had two classes of people—the dirty poor and the filthy rich, but way down in the Ukraine, they had a third class—the middle class—shop keepers, teachers, and rich Yiddish folks. Prince Korsakov figured they made far superior soldiers. I wanted war veterans who had fought the tribes out in Turkestan, men who knew how to fight from a horse, but the Military Governor of Kiev wanted high thinkers and good Christian men, who could go down and save their Slavic brothers. Day by day he got on my nerves.

We'd moved our camp two miles west of the cemetery, with nice neat rows of white canvas tents and the Prince held court there like the King of Siam, as he saw to every detail. But when he said, "I don't see why you need to go all the way down to Odessa for your weapons, Colonel Stewart, when we have crates and crates of these marvelous Baranov rifles right here," I decided to mutiny!

I sent General Gurko an emergency message (in cypher of course) saying my plans were being hijacked by a well-known prince and could I please push on for Odessa? One hour later from near a thousand miles away, we got his answer: "Push on for Odessa at once, Augustus Augustovich, and God speed to you and your men."

He even telegraphed the Prince with a covering message that said I was to take whatever supplies, men, and stock we had gathered, and thanks for his help. So with two hundred slightly smaller than I would have liked mules, their harnesses and feed, ten big Orlovs (and Boris), plus the forty trainees including twenty bourgeoisie shoemakers, shop owners, and teachers the Prince had drafted, we were off for Odessa. We took tents, dried food, hospital supplies, and even one hundred and fifty Baranov rifles and a hundred thousand rounds, for the Prince wouldn't take no for an answer. And there in the Pearl of the Black Sea we picked out our final fifty men from the dregs of a military jailhouse.[163]

These boys were all experienced warriors—they could shoot; they could ride, and they knew how to fight, so near half our company was ready for action, and hopefully they could help train the rest of our men by winter. Mostly I used the brigands, as I called my fifty jailbirds for the weapons recovery team. Why gun smugglers like to meet in a church is beyond me, but just like that bandit, Cipriano Ferrandini, these gun smugglers planned to do their deals in a church. We were to meet them at the eight o'clock Mass at St. Nikolaus Cathedral[164] in downtown Odessa—only a few blocks from the central police station.

I was "to come alone and bring the money with me," but a Baltimore Stable Rat knows better than that! My men were stationed all around the huge stone church. One of our draftee school teachers even posed as a priest with a big Russian .44 under his Bible, and when I entered the cathedral, I lit a candle so they could get a good look at me.

Up comes a little African boy who says in the King's English as spoken in Savannah, Georgia, "Come follow me, sir!" which I did very cautiously.

We walked several blocks east towards the harbor through the nice part of town with the seagulls singing and ship's rigging clanging, then crossed the railroad tracks where we came to a tall stone wall with a sign pointing to the south harbor that said Quarantaine Hafen. Out in the harbor the boats were bobbing up and down and nobody seemed to be in a hurry to quarantine anything. Down a narrow path we went with old crippled Arabs staring up at my Grapeshot pistol as they held their hands out and begged. Then into a dilapidated warehouse we went, and as my eyes adjusted to the lack of light, a voice rang out in Russian with a deep Alabama drawl, "Did you bring your money along, Amerikanskiy?"

"Maybe in Tuscaloosa they teach you to pay up front, Johnny Reb, but where I come from we like to see the goods before we pay for them," I told him as I prepared to draw.

His confederates put their hands on their weapons. There were three of them, maybe a fourth one behind me, but the one-eyed Rebel (he had a patch over his right eye) just laughed and told his men to stand down.

"You mean you can hear my accent through all that gibberish? Mike Kelley told me you was a pisser, but I thought you'd be bigger than that," he said sounding a bit let down.

"Well, I ain't done growing yet," I said in a surly way, being surprised to see a Southern boy so far from his home. I moved my hand slowly away from my LeMat and said, "Tell me Johnny Reb, how did you wind up down here in Odessa?"

"The same way you got here, Billy Yank. Wherever the wind blows us," he said in a jolly mood, and we shook hands like long lost brothers.

"Enough of the niceties," came a voice from behind us. He had a strong Turkish accent with a high pitched squeak.

I turned to see a dark little Turk sitting in the corner sneering up at me. He had a long pencil thin mustache that stuck straight out like the quills of a porcupine, dark black hair—plastered to his head, and a tiny little black goatee. Dressed in loose fitting Arab garb with one of those red Turkish beanies on his head, he was all business.

"Mister Kelley said you would like to buy some weapons. How will you be paying for them?" he asked.

"With golden coins of the Russian realm," I told him. "But you'll not get one red kopek until I see the goods!"

"Gold coins," he said all excited like, for gold was worth ten times what paper money was this close to a theater of war. And with the Turks and the Russians gathering for battle, the Black Sea was definitely hot.

The Turk babbled something in his native tongue and six shirtless Africans came out of the darkness with boxes of rifles they carried like coffins—two men to a crate. They set them down in front of me and the Turk signaled to the one-eyed Rebel to unscrew the tops. Burned into the wood on the top of each box was: Winchester Repeating Arms Company New Haven, Connecticut, and out came a fifteen shot Model 1873 carbine that hadn't seen the light of day since it left the factory. There were twenty to the crate and those sweating Africans kept hauling them out until there was a total of five crates sitting there looking dangerous. The Turk signaled to his lifters to bring out a box of the .44-40 Winchester rounds that the rifle fired—a big square wooden case that held a gross of fifty round boxes, which must have weighed a ton, for the Africans were sweating bullets as they dragged them out.

The one-eyed Rebel unscrewed the top of the crate and the Turk popped out a long bullet with twice the kick of my Yellowboy. "I can let you have a hundred Winchesters with a thousand rounds a piece for ten thousand rubles in Russian gold," said the dark-eyed Turk.

The one in my hand cocked as smooth as silk, but ten thousand rubles in gold was like a hundred thousand in paper money, and the Turk knew it. He'd stolen them right off the Istanbul docks; Property of the Sultan of Turkey was stamped in Arabic on the rear receiver of each and every one of them.

"I'll give you eight thousand rubles in gold for the lot!" I said like the horse trader Doc had taught me to be.

He snapped back, "nine and a half," without even thinking, so I figured I was on the right path. "Nine and a quarter," I countered, and he countered back with a drive to ten.

"I tell you what," I said in a Christian mood, "I'll give you that ten thousand rubles, if you give me another thousand rounds per weapon?"

"Allah be praised!" He blurted out in surprise. "Are you going to war or having target practice?"

"A little of both," I answered and we both started laughing.

"Ten thousand rubles for a hundred Winchesters and one-hundred and fifty thousand rounds, that's my best offer," he goes like he was enjoying my company.

"Fine," I said, "Ten thousand rubles it is."

Then he popped back in with, "but I might have to make another trip to Istanbul to fill the full order."

"Well, whatever you can steal from the Sultan of Turkey is just fine by me, but its cash on the barrel head, is that agreed?"

He spit on his hand and we shook on it, then we moved on to the Colt revolvers that came out in short little wooden crates stamped Colt Manufacturing Company Hartford, Connecticut. Beautiful little six shot single action rear loading .45 caliber revolvers they called the New Strap pistol. That pistol was so powerful that they had to reinforce it with a top strap made of forged iron.[165]

"You even get a screwdriver with everyone of them," says my swarthy little friend who kind of grew on you as he picked your pocket.

"How much for a hundred of those pistols and say a thousand rounds per weapon," I asked, figuring you buy in volume, and the Turk would give you a break.

"You really are a bad shot if you need a thousand rounds for a pistol like that," he said as the wheels in his head started spinning. "But first let me show you this .45 caliber bullet," he begged like please let me give you my sales pitch. "It's a 1.29 inch killer," he bragged.

He was right, that bullet from my LeMat was but a pug nosed cur compared to that Colt .45 round he passed me. It was incased in cooper with a big conical slug that looked like it could bring down an elephant.

"I know what you're thinking," said the Turk as he smiled a toothless grin and took his little red fez off out of respect for the weapon. "This thing could knock down a camel, right?" which was close enough for me to want to pay him whatever he asked.

Then, like I wasn't drooling all over myself, he whipped out his little five inch model and blasted away at a rat in the corner. "Thirty grains of powder is all this thing needs to do that kind of work." He bragged, and he'd split that rat in half! "Look at this walnut grip! Smell it, son! It's the smell of fine American craftsmanship, is it not?"

Hell, yes it was, and I needed about a hundred and fifty of them—some in that sweet little five inch model he whacked the rat with, and most in the seven and a half inch version for riding up there on the men's hips. And didn't I need two hundred thousand rounds of that lovely long .45 caliber slug, for who knew how long the war with the Turks would last?

"I'll give you ten thousand rubles in gold for two hundred thousand rounds and one hundred and fifty Colt .45s," I barked.

"I only have a hundred Colts," he said sadly, so we bought a few dozen Remington shotguns just to round things out.

"What else do you have to sell me?" I asked on a roll, and he had the Africans go in the back and bring out a crate of .50 caliber Sharps— another fine Connecticut manufacturer.

Oh, my heart was thumping then, for I'd seen the Union cavalry use their Sharp's carbines on that first day at Gettysburg! But these Sharps were the .50 caliber Buffalo Model 1874, a real sniper's rifle! "We'll take twenty of them and twenty thousand rounds," I said, violating Doc's rule not to buy when you were excited.

"We've only got ten Sharps to sell you," says the Turk like he was gonna stick it to me, "and maybe five thousand rounds, but look at the size of this bullet!" Why, that .50 caliber round was as long as my finger and fatter than my thumb—I had to buy all he had!

"Ten Sharps with five thousand rounds will run you ten thousand rubles in gold," he said as he turned away so I couldn't see his face.

Out there where the two great religions of the World were coming together in a very violent way, it didn't matter if my gold was worth ten times what paper money was. What mattered was who had the best weapons that could shoot the farthest, and the straightest, and deliver up the most rounds—that was a simple fact of war.

"Sold!" I said before I even remembered the rifles we had to trade. "Have you got anything else you want to trade for a hundred and fifty Baranov rifles and a hundred thousand rounds of ammunition?"

"I could give you three dozen sticks of Dynamite," the Turk said.

Dynamite was dangerous stuff—I'd seen the Prussians blow up a French bridge with the stuff. But at least it went off when you needed it to, so we made the trade.

"Bring your wagons around tomorrow morning and we'll swap, but don't forget your money! No gold, no weapons!" He warned.

"We'll pick up and deliver tonight," I told him just to shake things up. And we'll be loading it all on our pack mules' backs."

"You'd trust a crate of Dynamite to a pack mule's back?" asked the Turk like he didn't trust the long-eared critters to do a thing.

Chester had taught me that a mule was the steadiest creature on God's green earth. He said that the mule's fetlocks (that bump down near his hoof) were what they called "night eyes" and they could see in the dark and on uneven ground with them. Doc said that wasn't anatomically correct, but I always believed my old free African friend. As long as we loaded the dynamite last and kept the Powder Mules in the back of the pack, what could possibly go wrong?

We picked up our trade goods and headed back out of town for the Romanoff plantation that the Empress had loaned us. The moujiks grew apples and cherries on Her Majesty's estate and had miles and miles of grain fields with a railroad siding where we parked our train. For the better part of the summer and into the fall, we built up our supplies and trained hard. We'd move the mule trains twenty miles a day, never coming to the end of the Romanoff estate. There were hundreds of serfs out there slaving away, and when we stopped they would ask us if we had any darning or other chores, for they always needed money to pay the Soul Tax the Tsar-Liberator had levied when he set them free. My men bought the Emperor's Cherry Brandy by the gallon before it was sent north to the markets; and we were living in the lap of luxury.

The mules and the horses were eating several fresh apples and pears a day as fall came on. They were growing out their winter coats as we came up with just the right blend of corn, grain, molasses, and dried sliced apples and cherries. By studying their excrement we could judge how the feed held up and were fine tuning them for the winter campaign, for we heard the Turks had swept the Balkans clean of forage.

My boys were beginning to pull as one and we could load and unload the stock from the royal train faster than Barnum & Bailey could unload their circus. Half the Flying Column could advance in good order whilst the other half laid down a withering fire, and we could ride our mules twelve hours a day without a single complaint from man or beast. But in the Balkan Mountains where we were heading, we'd be facing Old Man Winter for the very first time, and the Musulman had turned the countryside into a wasteland, so we had to carry everything we needed with us. Our school teacher draftees figured that to get us down to Bulgaria and back to the Danube with what we had in supplies, we'd probably starve somewhere around the 1st of April, and General Gurko wouldn't be down to rendezvous until May, so we needed a better plan, if we were to survive.

"What you need is twenty wide wooden sledges pulled by troikas of three mules each," Sergeant Yakovich told me.

400

"No," I barked. "We're going American all the way! We'll take two teams of two mules each for four mules per sledge."

So after the apples and cherries were all picked off the Empress's plantation, we put Her Royal Majesty's serfs to work building twenty strong wooden sleighs lined with fatwood (the better to burn in our winter campfires when they were emptied) while we rounded up more mules. The Ukraine was under Martial law (with the Russians being the marshal), so when the Cossacks helped us find our mules, it felt like Sherman's raid to the sea. The largest mules seemed to be owned by the richest folks and we just confiscated them in the name of the Tsar. We found some sand hills to train in near Odessa—hauling our mule sledges as if we were in snow up and down those long dunes as the mules grew stronger.

Our sharpshooters consisted of ten hand-picked men on the Buffalo rifles and they were all crack shots. They were mounted for fast scouting on our big Orlov horses, the mules being too small to carry the three giant Mongolians in the sharpshooter squad. The Sharps could hold a mountain ridge from a half mile, so we had a little friendly competition to decide who made the Sniper Team. Anyone who wanted to win a twenty-five ruble gold piece with gun-shy Vladimir aboard was welcome to try. Our best shot turned out to be a big Mongolian named Altan, which meant Red Dawn in his native tongue, and he loved me like I was his father. He was damn near seven foot tall, a big burly man who made the Sharps look small.[166] Altan could split melons wide open from three quarters of a mile out.

Naming the Flying Column in his honor was the least I could do since he'd come the farthest to fight for the Tsar. We were the Mukden Rifles, a name that reminded me of home, since Chester liked to hunt rabbits up around Monkton Mills back in Maryland. With Yakoff and Altan at my side, not a single trooper ever tried to kill me, which meant my leadership skills were growing by leaps and bounds. Oh, they were an ill disciplined lot, and as I limped by them on the firing line in my fine green officer's uniform with my pogoni shining, someone would inevitably mutter, "Want to take a shot there gimpy?" Although my reputation for being a crack shot was well-known, I kept them guessing on my current status. But my men liked me, and I liked my men, and the Orlovs and the mules—why they loved us all!

A mule is more like a dog than a horse. He'll lie down beside you while you sleep under the stars, or let you stand in his lee in heavy weather. So, with good comrades like that, autumn passed quickly as we grew into a tight knit band of brothers.

And then a decree came down directly from the Emperor that took the wind right out of us! "All Russian soldiers going down into the Balkans are to destroy their uniforms and resign from the Tsar's Army, effective immediately! All Russian insignias right down to the belt buckle, must be destroyed before moving south into Turkish territory. You will then proceed as volunteers with no support from the Russian government."

There was no mention of back pay (which we were all owed), no mention of money for new clothes—just leave your uniforms in Odessa, boys, and have a nice day! Alexander II was so frightened of the Sultan that we had to disguise ourselves to go down and save our Slavic brothers.

I sent my shopkeepers and my school teachers back to Odessa to buy all the winter clothes they could find. We had boots for the men in every size, thick warm coats of fur, and big fur hats, double layered pants, mittens, gloves, tons of long underwear, sun goggles, and hundreds of pairs of thick wool socks, all dragged through the muddy streets of Odessa in a cold November rain on our long wooden sledges. On the next dry day the clothes and accoutrements were laid out in a nice long line, and the Mukden Rifles gathered round me and the beer keg I was on as I hollered, "Men can I have your attention?"

Discipline was not my forte, and like a horse that learns your weaknesses faster than he learns your strengths, my brigands just kept on jabbering.

Then Yakoff bellowed, "Mukden Rifles, attention!" And his bellow was bigger than mine was, while Altan stood behind me with his arms crossed, just about head to head. These lads had just barely tolerated me when I was in uniform, and now we were all going to be volunteers with not a shoulder board in sight.

"Men," I yelled—up there on my bully pulpit. "The Tsar has said we must resign from the Russian Army if we want to go down and save our Christian brothers! Anyone who can't abide by that can ride for Odessa and be reassigned, but anyone who wants to go down and fight the bloody Bashi-Bazouks at my side can come and join me right here and right now. For too long they've been killing defenseless women and children, so let's go down there and kick some Bashi-Bazouk asses!"

Just like the Pulaskis before them, these brigands began to cheer Old Redbeard their Yankee commander, which gave me hope. Only problem was, not one of them started stripping!

These boys didn't know any other way of life (save for the draftees), and no matter how wayward they were, the Army had always taken care of them. I'd have had no men left if I'd kept on talking, so out of desperation, I started tearing off my uniform—first a pogoni at a time and throwing them into the fire. Piece by piece I stripped down until I was standing there in nothing but a sheepish grin and a pair of long underwear. The lads could see by my missing toes, that big scar over my eye, and that gash across my cheek that I was an old war horse, but I wasn't what you'd call the perfect picture of an officer.

The men seemed embarrassed for their scrawny little commander standing there in his long johns, but I roared, "Come on men—into the fire with anything Russian. True to the faith with saber in hand we will free our Christian brothers!"

And off came the men's uniforms—what parts they wore, for out there on the outskirts of the Empire we weren't all that particular. Off came the kepis and the tunics and the stiff Army boots, and the coats. All that would burn went into the fire, as we drank brown bread beer and cherry vodka and sang like a band of naked gypsies!

"Big men to the left—take your long underwear, socks, and new boots," shouted my shopkeepers to the dancing brigands as the balalaikas played and I wailed away on my trusty Hohner. "Mediums to the center—keep the line moving men; we have plenty of clothes to go round!"

I helped myself to the Smalls in the bins to the right and dressed like any other moujik—save for my lucky Garibaldi shirt which would remain with me through the entire campaign. And in the morning when we did the final count, not one of my Mukden Rifles had quit! Oh, I'd opened a big can of worms by not explaining what a Volunteer Corps meant, but two of my corporals wanted to explain it to me the very next morning.

You see the Mukden Rifles were a mix of Circassian Muslims, Mongolian giants, Poles, Belarusians, Ukrainians, and a few Russians all blended together by our love for a good fight, a draft notice, and or a paycheck (at one time or the other). But these two Russian corporals that waylaid me on the way to my first coffee of the day wanted to turn the Flying Column into a proving ground for their Bolshevik ways. One was a big bastard with an ugly twisted up smile and the other was his evil twin, for I swear I couldn't tell them apart. They caught me hung over and wondering where my pogoni had gone to.

"Good morning, Amerikanskiy. You're just in time for the elections," they slithered.

Well, the last time I checked I still paid the bills and when it came to fighting, I'd be the brains of the outfit—not these two overfed, and did I mention useless corporals. But they were blocking my way to that first coffee of the day and the first one said, "Since we're all volunteers now, shouldn't we be voting for what the Flying Column wants to do today?"

"That's right, Augustus Augustovich." says the other one blowing his bad breath in my face. "In America you vote for everything, don't you? Well, today we'll vote for an Executive Committee, then vote for what we want to do with the rest of our day," he yells to the men at their breakfast as they cheered right back.

So I'm contemplating how to disarm this bomb before it goes off in my face. Who knew what those corporals would do at the helm of my Flying Column? But they were circling me like crows before battle, so it was time to show them a fine American trait, which was to strike first and ask questions later!

I had a .45 caliber Colt revolver on my left hip all ready for that quick cross draw Mike Kelley had taught me so well, and up under my right armpit was another one of those chunky little five inch models in a shoulder holster. I stood up from my mush to seek out a match for my smoke, fumbled around a bit as I prepared to strike, and then realized if I pulled in that tent full of soldiers there'd be a shit storm for sure, and wouldn't that shit storm have my name all over it!

So I yelled, "I nominate Sergeant Yakoff Yakovich, Altan the Mongolian, and yours truly for the Executive Committee, all in favor say aye!" And we won by a landslide.

From then on we voted for everything! We voted for what we ate for breakfast, for whether we took a hard days' ride or a soft one. We even voted for if we wanted to skip voting for a day and pretend we were all back in the military. The other two members of the Executive Committee—the two evil corporals, even brought up a vote on whether I should be referred to as Augustus Augustovich or Redbeard the Young American (which they felt would show my lack of experience better). And after much debate, the nickname Redbeard had to go by the wayside—it was Augustus or Amerikanskiy from that day forward.

We trained on into the snows of December and saw that it wouldn't be easy to campaign in winter, but still the men stayed on as we counted the days 'til we were off. Our private train was all loaded and ready to roll. The sledges were tucked away in the boxcars where we could haul them out quickly, and we trained and we waited, and we wrote to our families as the clock ticked away.

Then one day I got a very disturbing letter from Nadia up in the Babylon of the Snows. A letter that almost made me quit the military and head north to murder the Emperor! It wasn't enough that the great Tsar-Liberator was banging his 2nd wife before God just a floor above his poor 1st wife (our Empress and benefactress), but now he was taking to exposing his bingerlini[167] to Nadia and her Freilini friends!

"What should I do, Augustus?" my emerald-eyed Snow Maiden wrote. "After all he is the Batiushka-Tsar," which meant Little Father, and all the more reason he should keep his bingerlini to himself!

"Why don't we buy a townhouse up on the English Quay and you can quit your Freilini job, and we'll start a family when I get home," I wrote. But what I really wanted to do, was hop on a fast train for Piter and clean the old man's clock! Maybe if he had a real job like the rest of us, he'd be too tired to let his bingerlini do his thinking!

405

But like a good soldier, I bucked up and Christmas came and New Year's went, as we continued our training. On February the 15th there came a cyphered message from General Gurko saying, "Mukden Rifles move out! Good luck and God speed!"

We were to head to Bucharest by rail, only Bucharest was full of Turks and lay some seventy-five miles north of our planned crossing. Why risk capture before we even got to Bulgaria, when we could skip a three day march with one small change in plans? If we took the rail line south out of Slobozia, we could bypass the Rumanian capital, but was that a decision we best leave to the brass back in St. Petersburg? Some on the Executive Committee thought so, but I sure as hell didn't! We were out there to make our own decisions, play it by ear was the name of the game, and Headquarters was a world away.

"What will we do with the Romanoff train when we get to our river crossing?" Yakoff asked before we brought up my plan to the Executive Committee.

"Well, I suppose we'll turn the train over to the Rumanians, they'll be fighting the Turks soon enough," I said, since I'd signed for the train.

My fur lined rifle scabbards were all the rage that Christmas, I had one made for each man. Fur lined inside and out to keep your weapon warm and dry, they were cushioned so when they slapped the horse or mule's side it was a gentle slap. And consequently, the vote went in my favor—we'd leave the train with the Rumanians.

When we reached our destination—perfectly timed in the dead of night, we unloaded the sledges and hitched the teams in maybe a foot of snow, as I prayed to Sweet Jesus that my secret weapon would work! The Danube was windswept and clear—just as I feared, and I couldn't stand the cry of a steed wounded in battle, nor one who had slipped on the ice, so I brought along ten extra sledges—all filled to the brim with a nice gritty ash from last fall's campfires. Good cherry and apple wood charcoals that would grind into the ice and form a safe walkway for the mules and horses to cross. We laid down a four foot wide strip and slowly crossed the moonlit river on a shimmering surface so slick it looked like a mirror with stars shining up from the cold depths of the deep blue Danube, as two moons lit our way south. And as I looked at the Rumanian shore in the bright moonlight, I distinctly heard the locomotive steaming for the little town of Zimnicea.

Then came one of my Powder Mule Monkeys galloping wildly down to the river bank yelling, "Run for your lives! She's going to blow!" Like he'd just mined the Tsarevich's train, which he had!

And if he spooked our long-eared friends out there on the ice, the whole herd would stampede, so, I signaled Altan to take him out. Down he went with his mule sliding to a stop sitting upright on his hind quarters at the edge of the ice wondering where his rider had gone to.

Even though the Executive Committee had voted three to two to save the Tsarevich's train, the two Red corporals had decided to play a trick on their old ex-colonel. The ground rocked and a great plume of smoke and flames rose in the air from where once there had been a Romanoff train. But the strange thing was, the light of that burning locomotive gave my men something to laugh about as we crossed into enemy territory! Still, the first thing I did when we reached the southern shore was arrest our two corporals, for democracy had no place in a Flying Column.

Slowly we brought the sledges through the deep snow as we headed for the mountains hovering on the horizon like a great gray cloud. The going was rough, but the muleskinners talked to their teams and when they were out of steam we'd stop and let them breathe, while we walked to get the blood flowing in our legs again. We pushed on through the moonlit night 'til at the seventeen mile marker; the map said we'd reached the town of Alexandrovo, only Alexandrovo wasn't there, for she'd been burned to the ground by the bloody Bashi-Bazouks.[168]

That silent moon lit night seemed to carry the voices of a thousand souls as we came to a place by the side of the road where crows were picking at a mound of what we figured was old cast off gourds. The mules and horses were hobbled close to the fires as our cooks made the first warm meal of the day over a roaring fatwood fire. As we ate, down rolled a head with a half a face missing, for it was a pile of human skulls that the Turks had stacked. And as we stared into man's inhumanity to man, there came a huge shooting star hissing across the heavens.

The religious amongst us said the Lord was guiding us into Tsargrad, the Russian name for the city of Constantinople, which the Turks had taken in 1453 and renamed Istanbul. It was time for the Christians to take her back again, and even the Circassians amongst us agreed.

The mules started getting restless as we prepared to break camp the next day. They began to bray and tried to break free. Within seconds a pack of ravenous dogs came charging in. There were thirty or forty—all howling like hungry wolves as they came on with murder in their eyes. And these weren't dogs that were afraid of man; these were dogs that had tasted him! They'd been feeding on human remains for several months and we fought hard to survive!

From then on, we put up a watch tower with a big wooden sledge buried upright in the snow—a torch burning on top with a watchman armed with a rifle and three shotguns. Two more men kept the torches burning, and that was the only way we kept the dogs out of camp.

The second evening we came into a burned out village called Whitechurch where there were three starving beggars standing by a gallows in the deep snow with a couple of frozen mummies swinging in the wind. They were staring up at their friends like they wished they could bury them, but the Sultan had ordered them to hang forever! We took them down real gently and their friend's snuck them off to some caves nearby.[169] The Turks had gone on a killing spree in Whitechurch and there were piles and piles of bones stacked ten feet high. And the call of the crows that circled us madly weren't the calls of birds that were afraid of man, they were the calls of crows that had tasted him. That endless Caw…Caw…Caw was worse than Poe's ravens!

Each of us soldiers led a second fully loaded mule with the supplies we'd need to survive should anything happen to our sledges. Every rider's duty was to keep his two mules well stocked and ready to break free at a seconds' notice. Oh, we'd protect our sledges to the last man if we could, for they meant we could have pancakes for breakfast, and hot coffee, and a bonfire at night. The longer we kept our fatwood sledges, the happier we'd be, but on the third evening out the sky turned dark and ominous, and the winds began to howl. It was a darkness I'd never seen before— like Death was coming for us all as it roared down out of the mountains, the snow and sleet flying sideways. We crossed a small bridge and headed south for the next town on the map, which was Veliko Tarnovo as we prayed for shelter.

Down that twisted trail we went with the snows blowing so hard I thought it would cast us off into the abyss. There was a rocky ravine and a river moving fast down there, and one slip in that blinding snow would have meant instant death! We traveled maybe five miles in ten hours and the storm grew stronger and screamed like a banshee. A Krivitza was blowing in at ninety miles an hour and the temperature dropped to twenty below. And there on the edge of a precipice we couldn't see over, we found shelter in an old abandoned church. It was the stony remnants of the church of the Patron Saint of winter, St Demetrius himself. All that was left of the place was a little wooden chapel and a few stone walls.

"We'll give you a shot from the Sharps, if we find a better place," I cried to the coldest ones who needed a fire the most.

"Somebody needs to scout ahead!" I yelled and half the party moved on with their colonel.

But the mules up in that graveyard smelled fresh buried humans and took it upon themselves to press on for parts unknown. We were coming down a steep mountain trail where you could hardly see your nose in the blinding snow when a mule would sashay by as sure-footed as a Jack rabbit on the Fourth of July. So we followed the mules down that damn near cliff, and those night eyes that Chester had told me about, must have been good in a blizzard as well, for there before us at the base of that rocky cliff was a red roofed mirage which offered us shelter.

Church grounds seemed like a good place to sit out a Krivitza—at least that was what the mules had figured, for they stopped at the gate and wouldn't go any further! It was nice and roomy inside and I wanted to say a little prayer to Sweet Jesus for getting us out of the storm, only there wasn't an altar, or seats, which seemed strange to me. We signaled the men above to come on carefully and brought the loaded sledges in and lined our supplies in well-protected nooks. Then we laid the empty sledges lengthwise at the outer arches to make a corral for the stock to bed down as the storm roared. We found wood and built fires to ward off the cold, and by holding on to ropes hooked to the ground by spikes the men got water from a nearby stream. Twice we had to go out and shovel the roof so it wouldn't collapse, and the winds stayed hard and blew havoc for days.

On day four of that powerful Krivitza the winds backed off and a couple of old Muslim ladies in their long black burkas came in screaming like banshees and almost caused a stampede. "Get out! Get out!" the old women shouted, and that was the first we knew that mules weren't allowed in a Muslim Mosque![170]

But what those old women saw next drove them into paroxysms of weeping and wailing, for our mules had the whole outside perimeter of the building as a nice cozy pen, and each of them was working on their own little private pile of mule manure. And apparently mule manure in a Muslim Mosque was frowned upon even more than Christians were!

We had to gather them up (the women of course—the mules were there first) and we tied them to a post just inside the front door with a blanket and a bowl full of mush. They had orders to stay silent or suffer the consequences, for we had a sinking feeling that we'd camped right amongst the Ottoman Turks!

Once the winds subsided, we could see that we'd parked right up under a great stone fortress, so close they could piss on us! The high stone walls of what they called the Tsarevets stared down as the snow kept coming. We were ready to let bygones be bygones and hold our fire until we all dug out, but they raised their mortars high in the air and brought rounds down all around us. And who was desecrating their Holy ground then?

But Sweet Jesus had thought of everything for us, for we were parked so close to those big stone walls (five hundred feet as the crow flies), that they couldn't hit us. There in that sanctuary our mules had found in the height of that blizzard, the two Muslim ladies and some Circassians were praying to Allah, as our Mongolian friends prayed to their little fat Buddha, while a pack of Russian Orthodox prayed with their icons in hand, and a parcel of heathens found God for the very first time, for there were no atheists in that non-denominational Church of the Forty Martyrs!

410

But if the Turks kept lobbing those mortar rounds down, someone was bound to get hurt, so we decided to go out and stop them. Altan and his snipers shimmied through the snow cracking away with their Buffalo Rifles and many a Turk went down. That didn't stop their mortar men though, and the shells were going over our heads and bouncing off the Yantra River—bursting great holes in the ice. The bang of the cannons echoed off the rocky bowl we were in and damn near deafened us, but on the tenth day when we could finally move out, our Powder Mule Monkeys blew the stone bridge to their fortress, and we headed south for the Shipka Pass with our ears ringing.

We took to using a block and tackle (like old Henry Knox and his Ticonderoga cannons), bringing the mules and horses along one at a time. We'd take one mountain peak and set up our gear at the top to haul everyone up the north face, and then switch it over to lower the sledges back down to the south—always the south, the warm south of Istanbul where we were all headed. We were lucky to make four miles a day in that fashion, and there on the last rise on the nineteenth day of our journey we saw maybe eight or ten men riding along laughing like lunatics near a mile to the south. Their high pitched giggles and big giant heads seemed to say they were the world famous Bashi-Bazouks, but we'd never seen a Bashi-Bazouks before, though who else would be out there riding about in the snows of March with a head the size of a full grown pumpkin?

"Can you bring down that front runner from here, Altan?" I asked my Mongolian friend, and with a blast of his Buffalo Rifle, down went the lead Bashi-Bazouk[171] as the rest spread out and ran like the wind. And with another crack of the Sharps down went a second Bashi-Bazouk with a high pitched shriek. Altan brought another round into the chamber and sighted in slowly as he sat his huge Orlov like a Manchurian warlord, and down went number three—all in a matter of minutes. When we rode up to their scrawny little bodies lying there in the snow with their short little pants hiked up to their boney little knees, we were amazed at the hat racks they wore. Some said Bashi-Bazouk meant bad head, well I know for a fact they had really bad hats—all covered in the things that they'd stolen from their Christian prey. We hunted the rest of those mad hatters down to pay them back for all the women and children (and barefoot

411

priests[172]) they'd murdered and we took twelve of them like rabbits that first day out.

After that we did our best to trap a bevy of Bashi-Bazouks every day, tricking them into chasing us into tight little canyons where we'd pop out and give them a good thrashing. One thing the Bashi-Bazouk loved was the promise of loot, so we only had to let them see our fatwood sledges to get them to attack. Using that Turkey Shoot technique, we'd take the last ones out first, as we decimated them like buffalo on the Western plains. Every day we came across Bashi-Bazouks in their brazen glory— riding at us like Cheyenne braves. Down the mountains they came chasing us as spring came on.

We bumped into an Ottoman outfit bigger than we were north of Stara Zagora and good old American fire power won the day. If they charged (which was rare), we used the Colts and the Remingtons at close range, while the Winchesters and Sharps emptied their saddles from farther out. We had a running battle for two days through the melting snows—losing ten men and fifteen mules as the melt turned everything into what Napoleon called the Fifth Element, which was mud.

It was really starting to feel like spring as we came across more and more Ottoman Turks, but we no longer had our sledges with us and we could move on a mere goat path, which mostly the Shipka Pass was. Down to under eighty men with one mule each, fifteen sticks of Dynamite, a captured Gatling gun—that liked to jam worse than the Baranov rifles, we raided a Turkish supply train and got fresh feed and ammunition as we moved south like Sherman's Bummers. And when we finally stopped in Stara Zagora, Stara Zagora wasn't there either, for the Turks had burned her to the ground and killed every last man, woman, and child!

So with the Sultan's Army now hot on our heels, we reentered the Shipka and headed north to make the rendezvous at Ruse. But there was no Russian Army at Ruse when we got there. His Horniness had not yet declared war on the Turks! We could stand there between the two great religions of the world as they prepared to collide, or we could get the hell out of their way—and toot sweet about it!

So we smuggled ourselves over to the Rumanian shore on the Nikopol ferry, swiped a German locomotive and headed for Calarasi, then on to Chisinau for a well needed rest. There was no use wiring General Gurko of our whereabouts for he had enough on his plate, so we rested and waited in peaceful Moldova as the days ticked away. I wired the Empress with our list of accomplishments and told her we were standing down until the Russian Army crossed the Danube to join in the fight, and she wired another twenty-five thousand rubles by way of expenses. Lord how we loved our Empress Maria Alexandrovna!

Odessa was but a hundred miles off, and with our own private train (though all the controls were in Turkish), we could cruise down and resupply at any time. But the best part of our plan was we were so far out of the loop, that the loop had no idea where we were! And if they can't find you, they can't get you killed, which was our motto and our mantra as we rested up. We were laying low—drinking whiskey out of bottles, nursing our wounds, and ready to rendezvous with General Gurko whenever he saw fit to come down and join us.

It was June before the Russian Army finally crossed the Danube River into Bulgaria, and they only let our little Polish friend bring ten thousand men for the drive to Istanbul, not the hundred thousand they'd promised him. We bumped into General Gurko (a little man on a big white horse) on a steep hillside near Plevna as the sun was just going down.

"Colonel Stewart," he barked like I was an Aide de Camp, "Where have you been, I've been missing you, boy!"

General Gurko always blossomed in the field—for one thing sitting up there on his big white Orlov, he was a true cavalrymen's cavalryman. You could see the light come up in his eyes when the Turkish cannons started to thunder! We were to be his eyes and ears out ahead of the advance as we headed south to kick the Sultan out of Europe. Up in the high mountains of the Shipka Pass the main Turkish lines dug in deep and we hit them from both sides via the goat trails we'd scouted. But once we got south of the Pass with summer in full bloom, the Ottoman Turks took to the offensive. We had lancers, and vedettes shooting at us daily, as the main Russian Army got stuck up north of the pass at a place called Plevna. Uncle Niki was in charge up there and he was dragging his feet, so we turned around and headed back north to help him. We took the Pass, they took the Pass, the Shipka went back and forth, and we were down to forty Mukden Rifles on thirty-five mules by the time the next winter arrived. And then our luck simply ran out!

We were up on a high bluff—maybe fifteen of us left when I was hit in the right shoulder with a .44 caliber round, which we figured, came from one of the Sultan's Winchesters. It knocked me off Boris and at first I thought I'd bought the farm, but when I saw there wasn't much blood to it, and it went in and out without breaking a bone, I knew I'd dodged the Grim Reaper once more! We were being overrun by thousands of Turks with their little red fezzes—giving as good as we got, when Altan went down right there beside me with a bullet to his head. And as the Turks closed in, Yakoff ran to my side and picked me up and threw me across Boris's back as the last of my Mukden Rifles went down all around us.

We rode back to General Gurko's Headquarters a few miles north and gave our report. "Can you hang on till you get to the hospital at Plevna, Colonel Stewart?" my little general asked.

"I can, and I will, sir," I told him. "But can I ride to Alexander Alexandrovich's side, instead?" And he nodded his head.

I'd survived my double lung shot wound because I didn't go to the hospital, and I saw no reason to go then. What I needed was a good clean place to stay out of the cold, so we headed for the Tsarevich like a wounded sparrow in high winds. Uncle Niki didn't want his nephew showing any military prowess, so he had the Naslednik guarding the left flank of the Russian Army three miles south of Plevna. We found him there—irate at some nonsensical order his uncle had sent, and for the first time, I saw him in a full brown beard.

"Augustus Augustovich, how have you been, my friend?" he said as he first laid eyes on me. Then he saw my arm was in a bad way and helped me down off Boris. He wasn't the same man he used to be, he was sleepless and baggy-eyed, and war-worn, like all of us.

"My mother keeps me advised of the Mukden Rifles marvelous feats," said the Naslednik with a smile as he poured me a cup of hot tea.

414

His hut was perched precariously above a rocky culvert and though he didn't have room in his lodge for Yakoff and me, His Highness said we could spend the winter under his shack. His doctor said I'd die of double pneumonia sleeping under that ramshackle affair, so the Tsarevich gave me a spot on the floor beside his cot by a roaring fire. Yakoff got a nice straw filled hole under the shanty with two colonels and a major like a team of sled dogs, but me, I got the place of honor between His Majesty's bed and a warm fire.

"You just lay there and rest till you're ready to stand," the next Tsar of Russia told me gently, and I knew I couldn't be in better hands.

Save for one night when the fever hit! My night visitor and I were up in the Clock Tower at Gatchina busy building a barricade to keep Princess Matilde (the pig faced Queen of Hearts) and the Knights of the Golden Circle away as they heaved flaming torches up into our love nest. I heard the Tsarevich slapping me awake in a whole nother world than the one I was dreaming in, and I knew I was trapped in a dream that could get me killed, should I call out my lover's name once more! But the woman beside me seemed so warm and inviting, I just couldn't quit, even though I knew if I called out her name and His Highness heard me in the world he was busy trying to wake me up in, I'd surely be murdered!

After that, I took to sleeping during the day while the Tsarevich was out inspecting his lines and staying up nights to read as he slept. He had miles and miles of trenches to inspect and Yakoff went with him like a loyal retriever. One cold day in December the Tsarevich came home with tears in his eyes and said he'd just carried his cousin's body in from the works where he'd taken a round in the head. The Naslednik had tried to get his brother Vlad to go out there to recover the body of Sergei Maximillianovich, but the Grand Duke had balked at the job. Yakoff had gone along in his stead without even being asked and the Tsarevich couldn't understand his brother's cowardice.

But there was something evil about Vlad, and we all knew it! He looked at me and hissed like a house cat when he saw I'd returned. "Are you still keeping that bed wetting Amerikanskaya at your side, my brother?" went the Grand Duke like I was a deaf man.

415

Grand Duke Vladimir bragged that he was the best candidate to rule Russia if and when his father ever died, and from a security standpoint, he was first on my list to crush if that day ever came. I loaded my Colts and walked around camp telling the Blue Cossacks to keep their eyes peeled for any plot he might try. He'd be just the kind of conniving coward to take out his father and his older brother, and then return to the Land of the Firebird as the next emperor of Russia!

The war with the Turks had been a colossal mistake with our dead piled high before the trenches of Plevna. Uncle Niki refused to press on for Istanbul until Plevna fell, and made attack after attack and butchered his men. And when Plevna finally fell and it was time to head south to push the Sultan out of Europe, the Russians held back.

The Emperor left the front for St. Petersburg on a fast train—no doubt missing the good loving his 2nd wife before God was giving him, while Uncle Niki wouldn't even let the Tsarevich go home for Christmas leave! There we sat in the slosh and the snow as the war wound down all around us—me on the floor of a beat up shack beside a nice roaring fire with the Naslednik in his bed—lost in dreams of his family.

Somedays as my wounds healed slowly, we'd walk the mud covered hills and gaze at the Turkish lines. I wished we had a sniper or two who could hit a target as well as my Mukden Rifles. But they were all gone, for I'd gotten the poor boys killed.

"What do you want to do when you get back home, Augustus?" the Tsarevich asked me one night as he scratched at his beard.

"Oh, I want to marry Nadia Shuvalova and retire to a little horse farm up in Finland and spend my days in peace and quiet raising horses and little baby Stewarts, if it suits Your Highness!" were my words of hope.

He just smiled off into the night watching the fire flicker and mumbled, "Peace on Earth, Good will towards men!" like he was talking to his wife and children a thousand miles away.

Chapter Fifteen

Slipping Into Darkness

"Colonel Stewart," His Majesty said to me one dark and windy night as I lay there on that hard wooden floor while the fire spit sparks in my face. "My wife and I weren't very close when we first met you, you know?" And that was way too much information for me!

"But as you prattled on in that wonderful Parisian, Minnie's spirits began to soar and she loved me more and more. She became a lioness in our bed, Augustus, a real lioness, I swear it!" He whispered and I tried to put that thought behind me too!

But this conversation had to end somewhere far from either of our carnal thoughts of Maria Feodorovna, for I couldn't afford to have another noisy nights' dreams! So, I said by way of distracting His Highness, "You know Sire; I once was a well-respected spy."

"What do you mean a spy?" he asked. His bed creaked as the big man rolled over to take a good look at me.

"Well, I was a spy for the Prussians in France till the Froggies took it upon themselves to start a war with my masters. Mostly I just reported on the latest French weapons, but from time to time I even sketched out a fort or two. But don't worry, Sire," I said as he fell silent above me. "I haven't been a spy in many a year, and never once did I spy on Mother Russia!" We both let out a little sigh for we were becoming fast friends.

We spent the rest of that winter traveling the trench lines with Turkish snipers and artillery trying to kill us. The poor Naslednik didn't even have a chance to buy his wife and children Christmas presents that year, but once the Treaty of San Stefano was signed, Uncle Niki finally let us go home! We went first by horse through Bulgaria, and then by Royal train at top speed for Moscow, and once we hit the city of St. Petersburg, the Tsarevich sped off for the Anichkov Palace like lightning on the wire, while Yakoff and I headed to the Winter Palace at near the speed of light!

417

Nadia stayed in her Uncle Peter's suite there on the third floor of the great palace that looked like a big gaudy wedding cake with blue green icing and pure white trim. Uncle Peter's suite was filled with tall Greek columns, sparkling marble floors, shimmering gas lamps, crystal chandeliers, and mirrors hanging everywhere. There stood Nadia at her apartment door—her emerald green eyes flashing I love you as I swept her off her feet. She was more petite than I remembered—possibly a bit shyer, but she let go of me and caught on to Yakoff's neck with a swirling hug and a kiss that somehow seemed better than mine was.

"You've brought him back home to me, Yakoff Yakovich. Thank you, my friend!" Nadia cried as she kissed his cheek over and over. "And without a scratch?" her eyes searching Yakoff's for confirmation.

"Oh, I may have gotten myself a little shoulder wound, my darling. But it's healed now," I told her as I raised it up over my head and smiled.

She took me in her arms and said with very sexy intent, "Well, we'll see about that shoulder wound, now won't we, Augustus Augustovich!"

"Oh, no we won't," I said like I wasn't an oversexed tramp anymore. "I won't besmirch our love with gratuitous sex—at least not till we're married!"

In my lengthy convalescence down in Bulgaria, I'd read this book that the Tsarevich had lent me called Lysistrata, where these Greek ladies were so tired of seeing their men go off to war that they withheld their love making until peace was declared. I figured if it worked for a bunch of Greek ladies,[173] it just might work for me, so I told her, "You'll never see this body again, Nadia Shuvalova—not unless you marry me!" And down on one knee I went.

"I'll be your wife tomorrow, Augustus Augustovich," she answered like she'd rehearsed it too. And we were a couple of cuddling fools the rest of the day and on into the evening!

The next morning, Nadia awoke to write her Uncle Peter a nice long letter. She told him she'd been in love with me from the first time we met, and after five long years of waiting, she could wait no longer. So with much gratitude for all he'd done to raise her, and understanding that he would probably disown her for marrying outside The Church, would he please just promise to never disown her love? That was all she asked. We bought a townhouse up on the English Quay with a lovely view of the Neva River and just two weeks later we married in the Anglican Church of Jesus Christ,[174] with Yakoff Yakovich as my best man, and Modest Mussorgsky as my Second. Nikolai Rimsky-Korsakov and his beautiful wife, Nadezhda (Nadia's Maid of Honor) attended as well, as did Alexander Borodin and his wife Ekaterina, while the Tsarevich and Maria Feodorovna came late for the cake. We sang and we danced till dawn. It was a wedding soiree to remember!

Then off for the cold North we went by Snow Train, for Nadia had a little surprise waiting there for me. About a quarter of the way up the western coast of Finland (some 400 miles from St. Petersburg as the crow flies), there sits the little seaport village of Vaasa. And there on a lovely little horse farm all covered in snow were the Gelderland stallion, his mare, and their foal—all tucked away in nice clean stalls.

"I wanted to surprise you, my love!" Nadia said as my heart melted at the sight of those dapple grays, especially the lanky little colt as he nuzzled his mother. I looked at that big-boned baby standing in his stall and almost wept. Why, if Doc and Chester could have been there to see him, they'd have cried too!

"We can take them back to the city of Piter when we go," Nadia said sadly like she wished we would never leave Finland. "But this farm and all the horses on it belong to you, Augustus. They are a wedding gift in memory of my dear Mother, who would have loved you like a son."

Nadia had never brought up her mother before. Oh, I knew her Uncle Peter had raised her, but we'd never talked about her mom. The Russian rich (Maria Feodorovna excluded) didn't participate much in the day to day raising of their children—that was a job for the servants. But my bride's mother had been right there by Nadia's side until the day she died, and a five year old girl knows her mother well, so saying she would have loved me like a son was really something!

419

We only had a few days before Nadia had to get back to the Tsar's 2nd wife before God, so our honeymoon consisted of setting the staff straight on how the farm should run. Lars, the big Swedish farm manager seemed totally incapable of understanding a single word (no matter what language we said it in), and finally we fired him and made the next Finn in line learn the job, which he did well for many years.

We'd be leaving the dapple grays behind in the peace and quiet of Vaasa, and we wanted them cared for well. It was still the dead of winter with drifts higher than a house and cold winds whipping down from Murmansk, so when we weren't out talking with the farm hands about the horses, we were holed up in our little twenty room cottage making love and trying to catch up on lost time.

"I wish I didn't have to go back to work so soon," Nadia said to me softly on the last night of our honeymoon. We were on our bed—naked as jay birds as she fed me sweets, and she whispered, "But Princess Dolgorukaya has been very unstable as of late."

"What do you mean unstable?" I asked. "Is she touched in the head?"

"Well, she's not sane," said Nadia like she knew her well. "But if I had a lover that went at me day and night like the Emperor does, I swear I'd cut his little bingerlini off!"

"He's not waving his little batiushka-tsar at you anymore, is he, my darling?" I asked with fingers crossed.

"No," Nadia said with a look of surprise. "He's after several of the other Freilini, but not me, Augustus. The Emperor would never risk a duel with Redbeard the Magnificent!"

And we celebrated right on through dinner and into the next morning!

But the day of reckoning finally came, and Nadia returned to her work, while I went back to the Anichkov Palace to see what was left of my old job. Maria Feodorovna was the matron of the Russian Red Cross, and all the wounded from the war with the Turks still needed lots of help, which cost lots of money. So she just up and sold the Naslednik's race horses to help pay for the good work she was doing. That's how we wound up with the Gelderland stallion and his brood, and there was not one race horse left in the Anichkov Stables. So I could either bring it up with His Majesty and he would have a baby with my name on it, and possibly demand my dapple grays back, or I could march right into his library with an entirely different plan—something that would razzle and dazzle the big giant, and require me to travel to Finland on a regular basis!

"St. Petersburg is far more dangerous than it ever was, Sire. Wouldn't you agree?" I asked His Lordship as he slowly looked up from his book.

He was wearing his size fourteen bedroom slippers and his peasant clothes looked like he'd slept in them, but he was a happy soul. At peace with the world and happy to be home!

"What are you up to this time, Augustus Augustovich?" he said with a look of kindness on that big bearded face, for we were old war buddies.

"Well, Sire," I answered with a small bow and my eyes hanging low, "Can I speak frankly, Your Highness?"

"Of course you can!" he said. "You can say anything you like. I am your trusted friend, Augustus Augustovich, and don't you ever forget it!"

"When Yakoff and I were down in Kiev training the Empress's Own Mukden Rifles, we came across two of those Bolshevik bastards that might have been members of the People's Will. Quite frankly, Sire, Kiev was rife with the Narodnaya Volya!" I gave that sad fact a little time to sink in, and then sprang my plan on him. "Russia is slipping into darkness, Your Highness, so why don't you let me bring back the Mukden Rifles? We can hunt the Reds like they're hunting your family. We'll set up camp in St. Petersburg, Moscow, Kiev, and Odessa, for we need to know who they are and what they plan, if we are to catch them."

And if our prey went north to Finland and dug in amongst the citizens there, we might have to add another country to the list. I'd tell Nadia she was needed for a baby making session, and she'd beg off her Freilini job and meet me at the Vaasa train station with a kiss, and a hug, and a roll in the hay—at least that was my daydream which was progressing quite nicely 'til the Tsarevich burst back in.

"And it won't cost me one red kopek, Colonel Stewart?"

"Well, not much, Sire," I answered after a pause and a hard swallow. "I'll trade your surplus rifles from the war with the Turks for operating expenses as I gather information all across your great nation."

Which took me right back to thoughts of Finland, though I squashed them and waited for the Naslednik to bite. Unlike the lies that were spread by the Reds, Alexander Alexandrovich was a pretty fast thinker.

"So, what will we need to get this operation started?" His Majesty asked.

I wanted to start negotiations by saying we needed a special kind of a train, but how do you bring up your need for a train when you lost the last one with such a big bang? So I asked him for fifty-thousand rubles to get us back on our feet with a brand new crew of maybe fifty or sixty. Some cypherers and telegraph specialists, some warriors, some spies, plus a hundred thousand Baranov rifles—delivered to an Odessa address with a million rounds of ammunition, no questions asked!

"And last but not least, Your Majesty, we need a special train with a battery room and a telegraph system aboard." I threw in at the last moment.

There was silence as he stared at me hard, and then finally the big man spoke. "I know what your men did to my last train, Augustus! They didn't have your blessings, did they?"

"No, Sire, they certainly did not," I said in my own defense. "And every last one of those boys (including the one Altan shot off his mule) is dead now, Sire. So, can't we let bygones be bygones? I'm here to talk about the People's Will and their plans to destroy the Romanoffs!"

And he bit on it, though he had one last question before he did. "First, tell me why I haven't seen you in uniform since your shoulder wound, Colonel Stewart?"

"You see, Sire," I told him all sad and truthful. "Your father ordered us to resign from the Russian Army before we went down into the Balkans. So technically, I've been a civilian (save for my honorary commission as a Red Cossack lieutenant, which they'd given me for being a good friend and a bad shot), for nearly two years now."

"Nonsense!" roared the Tsarevich in his angry bear voice. "You're a colonel of cavalry with back pay due you from the day you were forced out of the service! You were under my command, Colonel Stewart, and if the Emperor wanted you to resign your commission, he should have checked with me first!"[175]

And it was not just any cavalry regiment I was to be reentered in either, the Tsarevich was so mad with his father that he made me a colonel in the Preobrajenski Guard, and dared anyone (especially the Emperor) to disagree with him! Life was to be sweet again, for I could finally go to the Balls and dance with Nadia, and wouldn't old Redbeard look absolutely magnificent in his red and green Preobrajenski uniform! But there was one fly in that ointment, for in the new job I was proposing, I needed to be stealthy and out of uniform at all times.

"What if I work under cover till we clear Russia of the People's Will, Sire?" I asked with my eyes lowered like Mr. Salomon had taught me.

And that's how Yakoff and I gave up a position in the sports and entertainment branch of the Romanoff household, and became a couple of well-paid spies!

"First, you will come and talk with my mother about her beloved Mukden Rifles," the Tsarevich said with a broad beaming grin, for he loved his mother like he loved no other, and she loved Her Mukden Rifles. "She speaks often of the exploits of you and your men."

"And I speak highly of your mother, our Empress, Maria Alexandrovna, Your Majesty!" I answered respectfully for she was kind and wise.

She had looked after our Flying Column from the time we were formed, and now slowly dying in the same palace where her husband rogered his young lover, the old woman had little to live for. We met in her library, over stocked with gaudy furniture in the fine Romanoff fashion—the Tsarevich, the Empress, and I. It was a gray and rainy day and the poor lady was having trouble breathing as she sat their looking frail in a long black dress. She breathed faster and faster—frightened that the next breath would be her last. I suggested they quick run and get her a paper sack, which I then had her breathe into real slowly, and didn't she regain her composure.

"You Americans think of everything," she said like I was some kind of a wizard. "Who taught you that trick, Colonel Stewart?"

"It was my Fourth Grade school teacher, Mrs. Johnston, Your Majesty," I told the Empress as her color came back. "When we were kids back in Baltimore, someone would always work themselves into a tizzy and my teacher would dump out somebody else's lunch and make the heavy breather breathe real slow and deep in and out of that paper sack. It worked every time, Your Highness," and I bowed low to the sickly Tsarina and prayed that Sweet Jesus would come down and ease her pain!

We just sat there staring out the window—not knowing what else to say as she coughed and hacked her life away. Then, when the coughing stopped, she talked with her son and they smiled at each other. There were parts of their lives neither one of them could talk about, so they talked about the Naslednik's children, especially little Georgie, who was everyone's favorite around the palace. I just sat there with my head bowed low as the two of them talked, and when it came time to leave, she handed her son a check for fifty thousand rubles and clasped my hand in thanks.

"You keep our Emperor safe, Colonel Stewart, and I will pray for you like I pray for the Tsar!" she said and I backed out bowing low and with a high respect for her strength, her fortitude, and her unfailing love for her unfaithful husband.

Telling Nadia I'd be off for another special assignment was getting easier now that we were married. My lathery horse, my weapons of war, and my big mean friends didn't seem to bother her, for she knew I was the Tsarevich's right hand man, and we had a whole Empire to look after.

"You go with God," she whispered as she kissed me good bye.

There had been no Victory Parade after the war with the Turks. Austria and Britain had stepped in to rewrite the peace treaty we'd made. They even demanded a piece of the pie though they hadn't lost a single man. So without firing a shot, Austria-Hungary got Bosnia and Herzegovina (which later gave them the First World War), while England got the island of Cyprus, and the Sultan of Turkey got to keep Istanbul. And as for Russia, well, Russia just got the shaft! Two hundred thousand dead and wounded had paid dearly to push the Ottoman Empire out of Europe, and all for naught. Our leaders had let us down![176]

Pobedonostsev said things were going to hell in a handbasket because the people of Russia had lost their fear of the Tsar, but what the people had lost was their respect for their leaders! And into that void stepped The People's Will promising to bring Russia back to her former glory again. One of their members even shot the mayor of St. Petersburg, was captured, tried, and got away Scott free. Then the head of the Secret Police was murdered in broad daylight right there on the streets of St. Petersburg, while the Emperor was attacked near the Summer Gardens by a maniac with a pistol who chased him around a tree firing five shots as His Majesty weaved and went serpentine. And once more a member of the Narodnaya Volya got to meet Frolov, the red-shirted hangman, while the inteligencia took the terrorist's side.[177]

Down in Kiev, the terrorist meetings were so packed with the Bolsheviks that we recognized one of the plain clothes policemen who watched them plot. He would go through all kinds of disguises to trick the Reds and still somehow something would always give him away to us. For one thing, he had the biggest blackest beard on the whole planet. I mean this thing was pitch black and as thick as a brick! And no matter how he wore his wild curly hair or what kind of hat he had on that big lion's head—we could always pick him out of the crowd. Major Sudeiken was his name and he was as cruel a Secret Policeman as ever there was, though some said he could be quite charming.

425

Students from the University of Kiev, who met with him regularly, said he was a friend of the people, and the People's Will weren't real friendly with any policemen that I knew! So we set up a group of ten men and a telegraph system in Kiev to watch over him as we moved on down to Odessa. We dropped ten men off to spy in Odessa, traded some rifles to cover expenses, and then dropped ten more men off in Moscow on the way back home. And when we hit the Babylon of the Snows, we had eyes and ears on the ground for over twelve hundred miles. We could send or receive an updated report on our terrorist friends at near the speed of light, and the Tsarevich was impressed. That's when I convinced His Majesty that we best cover Finland!

"Those Finns are a finicky bunch, Sire," I told him—in all truthfulness having never met a Finn I didn't like—save for Vlad's big bully sleigh driver. "It might take me half the summer and well into the fall to infiltrate their ranks, Your Majesty, but I'll go up there and personally see that it's done."

After all, the Tsarevich needed some kind of a hobby to keep him out of trouble—look what idleness did to his father! Now that all the Naslednik's race horses were gone, we had to keep him busy someway, so helping me spy on the Bolsheviks sounded like a plan to me.

"You go up there to Finland, Augustus Augustovich," His Highness decreed. "And I'll keep track of St. Petersburg, Moscow, Kiev, and Odessa for you."

So Nadia packed her bags and we progressed on our private train to Vaasa with twenty brand new members of the Mukden Rifles horse racing team, which was a subsidiary of the Mukden Rifles Security detail. We had grooms, stable boys, trainers, and a few old warriors who were there to protect Sunset Hills, as we called our new home, for you could see the sun going down over the Gulf of Bothnia from our porch.

I didn't feel guilty at all! Spy work was a lot like muskrat trapping—you laid down your traps and waited for your prey to step in. So while we waited for the terrorists to show their faces in Finland, I began schooling the horses with Yakoff's help.

426

My old friend Boris stood there all concerned that the new recruits weren't up to his high horse standards, but the Gelderlands were coming along fine. The long-legged colt was learning to run at his God given pace of the gallop with those silvery spots dancing in the midnight sun.

Nadia and I took long walks in the pine forest and smelled the wild roses as we talked of having babies—or at least trying. That sweet summer of promise with the warm breezes blowing in off the Gulf and a bright blue sky overhead was the most wondrous summer in my life! We never wanted to leave the horse farm again, and as our love grew deeper and stronger, we even made plans to escape the Romanoffs. But by the end of that summer we'd found exactly one Marxist in all of Finland, and he was a pacifist Marxist with anarchist tendencies, so we weren't too worried about him.

We wired the Tsarevich: "Finland is clear of terrorists for the time being, Your Highness, but we'd like to leave a team up in Vaasa just in case."

The Naslednik tapped back that he had intelligence that the People's Will were making bombs and training five man teams just like Dostoyevsky described it in his book Crime & Punishment. And since most of the action was down in Odessa, we headed there at top speed, using two engines to haul our train. Our old friend, the Turk, reported that someone had bought a crate full of the Sultan's dynamite, but so far he'd drawn a blank on who they were or what they planned.

"Give me more money to cover expenses, and I will find your terrorists for you," he wired, but we needed boots on the ground!

The Marseilles of Russia they called Odessa, for her cries of freedom could be heard all across the Ukraine. So when we intercepted a coded message that said the People's Will were planning on blowing up the Tsar's train when he returned home from the Crimea, we dropped everything and searched for more clues!

The Tsar had taken his 2nd Wife before God (and all her Ladies in Waiting—including my Nadia) down to Livadiya for a summer by the sea. Traffic on the wire showed the People's Will were planning something big for His Majesty's return, and since we now knew they'd bought enough dynamite to sink the island of Cyprus (hopefully with the British aboard), they had a pretty good chance of annihilating the Emperor, and everybody else on the Royal train.

We telegraphed Livadiya at once with a message that said: "Do not send the Romanoff train back to Russia, there's danger on the tracks ahead!" But in typical Tsar-Liberator fashion, the Emperor ignored us and set off!

Only Providence saved them that day, for the terrorists figured the Emperor would be on the second train (as he usually was) and His Majesty had mounted the first one. I felt we had failed him since the bomb went off and destroyed the train he should have been on, but the Tsarevich said my warnings had probably caused the Tsar to lose his patience and set out on the first train he came across. Alexander II couldn't take directions!

"I want that Perovskaya bitch caught," said the Tsarevich when we returned to St. Petersburg.

Sophia Perovskaya was a young noble woman who had joined the Peoples' Will and was said to have signaled the bomber when the Tsar's train was blown up outside Moscow. Her pegging the exact car His Majesty should have been on troubled the Tsarevich immensely. The girl was a pouty little blond haired noblewoman in her twenties with hair brushed back across a long wide forehead, and the deep dark eyes of a cold-hearted killer. The police had stopped a woman of that description after the bombing, but she had been released—some say by that black bearded Secret Policeman we'd seen down in Kiev.

We were interrogating a captured terrorist in the Peter & Paul Fortress about her whereabouts, and he just laughed and said, "You will never catch our Lady of Death, Amerikanskiy! And why do you care?"

He was right too, I really didn't care if the Tsar lived or died anymore! But as long as Nadia traveled with His Majesty's entourage, and I'd promised the Empress I'd protect her husband, it was a personal matter.

Then up came a prison guard who said, "By order of Major Sudeikin, no one is allowed to speak with his prisoners—now be off with you!"

How did a junior officer from way down in Kiev suddenly command the forces of the Peter & Paul Fortress? It seemed very strange, so we started tailing him, and although his costumes were many and various—one being an Old Believer still dressed as in the days of Peter the Great with a thick wool coat down to his ankles, soft black boots, and a tall fur cap, Sudeikin still sported that thick as a brick beard, so he was easy to spot. We tracked him down to an elegant apartment at a busy corner on the Nevsky Prospect where we found a mother lode of sin, degradation, and quite possibly treason!

His apartment was over a little haberdashery at a Y in the street with steep stairs climbing up to the third floor where we saw him meet with little Nicholas's bug-eyed tutor, Pobedonostsev. In his late fifties, skinny and haggard with a pair of huge brass rimmed spectacles that magnified his evil stare, that scrawny old man was the most hateful person in Russia! He stayed maybe a half hour and left with a sick twisted grin, but we knew not why he was grinning?

We needed to get closer if we wanted to find out more, so we rented the adjoining apartment up towards the busy Nevsky. It had little odd shaped triangular rooms, and we snuck into Sudeikin's place one night when he was away and ran a little ear trumpet through a hole in the wall behind a painting of a moujik bringing his cows in from a storm.

The next visitor to Sudeikin's den of inequity was the gun-shy Grand Duke Vladimir. Taller and fatter than his older brother, the Grand Duke was in full military regalia as he slowly climbed the creaking stairs. Vlad usually looked down his nose at everyone, but on this occasion he was sucking up to Sudeiken something fierce.

"The Holy Brotherhood will give you all the support you need, Major Sudeiken," said the Grand Duke. "You want someone to disappear on you? We'll disappear them. You need money for a secret operation; you need only ask us. The Holy Brotherhood is here to help you!"

The Holy Brotherhood was kind of like the Knights of the Golden Circle back in Baltimore. Rich folks, stuck in their ways, and they weren't afraid to commit treason to have their views forced on the rest of us sane people! And now they were offering Sudeikin all the help he needed, but for what? That was the question!

The next visitor to Sudeikin's little third floor House of Intrigue was the Tsarevich's friend Nikolai Baranov—of the Baranov rifle family, and a young lady of maybe fifteen (and I'm being generous). And then the whole thing began to snow ball before our very eyes, for we'd made a little hole to see by, and there in full color was that big headed secret policeman and Grand Duke Vladimir's wife, the Grand Duchess Maria Pavlovna going at it like a couple of teenagers! They went at it that way three or four times a week, and when they got finished, they'd talk about how they were going to bring the Vladimirovichi, which was Vlad's branch of the Romanoff family, into the foreground of Russian politics.

"We need to stop the Emperor from ruining Russia," she huffed and she puffed as she struggled to get her bustier back on.

Pobedonostsev was right, we were all going to hell in a handbasket, but when that bespectacled old Holy man showed up disguised as a Yiddish salesman in a long black suit complete with a pair of faux louse ladders, I knew he'd been spending way too much time with Sudeiken! In came a homely young thing—probably half his age, with mousey blond hair and pretty blue eyes that popped out of a head that was way too small for the rest of her body. They chatted tenderly for maybe fifteen minutes and then they were off.

Next customer in to Sudeikin's House of Love was Grand Duke Vladimir's wife, Maria Pavlovna, only this time she brought along a brand new paramour. The two of them were in there hooting and howling for over an hour when Yakoff told me the man was the Tsarevich's new best friend and Deputy of Secret Police, General Peter Cherevin. There he was astride the Grand Duke's wife, and this seemed very strange, since the Naslednik hated his sister-in-law, and trusted his new best friend with all his best kept secrets. If the Tsarevich ever heard that his new buddy was making the double-backed beast with his brother's wife, he'd have cut off more than the man's pogoni!

You might think I was exaggerating when I said sex crazed St. Petersburg was what was bringing us down, but I swear there was something in the water! Pobedonostsev and that homely young lady with the pretty blue eyes and the tiny little head showed up next on the docket. First, they talked and then that scrawny old zealot ripped the poor girl's clothes right off her body and they went at it like a couple of rabbits! The Mukden Rifles took bets on the fastest sex they'd ever seen, and that was kind of strange too, since His Holiness was known for his famous quote, "In Russia all things must be done without hurry."[178]

The haberdashery down below must have thought they were having an earthquake, and not one that lasted real long either, for the Ober-Procurator was what you'd call a sprinter! Then it was Sudeikin and Maria Pavlovna's turn to go back in the saddle and of all the après sex conversations in that House of Sin, theirs' were the strangest. They lit cigarettes to recover from all that hard work, and first she complained that the Tsar was cutting her family's funds in half,[179] and then she went on to say, "Once we rid Russia of all her rotten apples, we will rise again to the heights of our greatness!"

It sent chills down my spine to hear her speak that way, especially after we saw her meet with an old friend of mine from my days in France. I had a Prussian handler who came down with my pay and new assignments from time to time. He'd signal me all quiet like at some lonely little tavern and we'd meet out in an alleyway where no one could listen. And there he was chatting with Maria Pavlovna in the remnants of the Tauride Palace while Nadia and I searched for a place to picnic.

But I couldn't just run and tell the Tsarevich that Vlad's wife liked to have sex with multiple partners—one being his new best friend and the other being the Secret Policeman who may have let Sophia Perovskaya go free. And oh yes, Your Majesty, your sister-in-law just might be meeting with a German agent. No sir, I had to get more proof than that before I could go up against a Grand Duchess!

431

But just as we honed in on all the comings and goings at Sudeikin's House of Love, a new job came along—one that seemed far more important!

"Augustus, I want you and your men to go down to Cannes with Count General Adlerberg (the Tsar's right hand man) to bring my mother back home to Russia," went the Tsarevich like he was unhappy with the plan, but what could he do? The Empress had gone down to a spa on the French Riviera for the winter, but now her husband—having heard she was dying, wanted her back home toot sweet.

We didn't talk with the Emperor's man on the way down for he was far above conversing with a foreign mercenary like me. And when we arrived at that fairytale spa with its warm green grass and bright blue waters—palm trees swaying in a fragrant breeze, I didn't want to go home either!

"You go in there, Colonel Stewart and tell the Empress she needs to pack her things and come home at once, by order of the Tsar!" was exactly how Count General Adlerberg ordered me to do it.

He was a tall princely man in a full dress uniform of dark Russian green with a sky blue sash across his proud chest and huge golden epaulettes flowing down his upright shoulders. His pure white hair was cropped short on that regal head, while his fuzzy little side whiskers met in the middle with two inches of bare chin sticking out. And that naked chin was quivering when he realized I wasn't there to do his bidding, I was there to look after our Empress!

Dressed as a Kievan trader in a long elk skin kaftan with two Colt .45s and a Winchester Rifle at my side, big loose fitting black peasant pants, and the high cavalry boots of a brigand, I probably looked more like an Indian scout than a Russian colonel. I put my weapons down quietly and knocked on the poor woman's door. Her aging Freilini let me into a darkened room that smelled slightly of stale urine, and there she was—a very sick lady in a small black dress with a brave smile on her proud face as she bid me hello. I kissed her hand in the fine French fashion and Her Highness almost blushed.

"Your Majesty we are here to escort you back to Russia by order of..." I started to say, but she interrupted me.

"I don't want to go back to Russia in the depths of winter, Colonel Stewart," she whispered in what was left of a very weak voice. "You won't make me go, will you?"

"Of course not, Your Majesty, but your husband misses you terribly."

"If he misses me so much, why is he not here to take me home himself?" she sighed, for she knew what was going on up in Babylon.

She was right too! It was warm and sunny down on the French Riviera and the healing waters of the spa were helping her gain back her strength—she thought. And if we were indeed the Empress's Own Mukden Rifles, then her words were our command. If she said we were to escort that huffy Count General back to his train and send him packing, well that would be an order I'd love to carry out!

"Has she agreed to come back with us, colonel?" asked the Count General with a glare when I came out of her sick room.

"Not yet, Sire!" I said with a look of disgust.

He had no respect for our Empress.[180] "You get back in there and don't you come out again until she agrees to leave, or I swear I'll have my Cossacks come pick her up and carry her out!" he snapped.

"She's asleep right now, Count General!" I said sharply.

He tried to pull rank on me and talked of my loyalty to the Emperor being in question. "Have you ever heard of Frolov, the red-shirted hangman? You get right back in there and get her packing, or I swear I'll have you strung up and hung for your surly ways, Colonel Stewart!"

"I serve the Tsarevich," I explained as calmly as a Scotsman can to an big bully like him. "His Highness has sent me here to make sure our Empress is brought home in the comfort and dignity she deserves. So you keep this rude behavior up, sir, and you just might be the one swinging from Frolov's rope!"

433

The big man didn't like what he heard from me, but what could he do? As long as the Empress had a breath left in her, no one would treat her poorly while Sergeant Yakovich and I breathed!

"Your Majesty," I said gently to her the next morning when she finally awoke. "Your son has sent me here to bring you home to Russia. He misses you terribly!" I said with tears in my eyes, and she gave in.

We sent the Royal Romanoff train ahead with the Count General aboard, hoping the Narodnaya Volya would blow him to hell, while Yakoff carried our sick little Empress to our first class car on the Moscow Express. We headed back to the Land of Snow leaving the palm trees and green grass of the Riviera behind us, and every step of the way she got colder and colder!

The Naslednik was waiting at the St. Petersburg Train Station, and back to the Winter Palace we flew with so many furs piled high upon her that some said it looked like an open grave. The palace fires were brought up to a high burn to keep our Empress warm, and as she looked out the icy windows to the frozen whiteness beyond, she sighed, like that would be the last sight she ever saw! And then she thanked us for bringing her home.

Yakoff and I left her room with tears in our eyes.

"Did the Empress tolerate her travels well, Augustus Augustovich?" Nadia asked me when I got home.

"Not really; it's a tad cold up here compared to the French Riviera, and she shivered the whole way home."

We were standing in our bedroom looking out at the frozen Neva with the winter sun poking through the thick gray clouds, and I said, "Someday I'll take you down to Port du Cros and introduce you to summer in winter and my second love, Signora Fungini. It's a special place full of special people—a land of warmth and sun, and the poor Empress begged me not to bring her back to this frozen place." I'd have said more, but Nadia would have given me a lecture on decorum unbecoming an officer of the Guard.

434

"We have some more sad news to discuss, Augustus," Nadia said with her eyes cast down. "Modest Mussorgsky has taken ill. He's in the Imperial Military Hospital asking for you."

So off we flew before we even had a chance to make love—that's how much we loved the Maestro! He was the salt of the Earth, the child we never had, the troubled soul who we all knew would never see fifty, and yet, in the light of his bright green eyes—even when they were blood shot and swollen, Modest Mussorgsky had the joie de vivre of a platoon full of Preobrajenski Guardsmen!

There he was standing in the corner of a long open ward in a tattered hospital gown as he hummed his latest tune to a couple of old soldiers. I bade him quite loudly that there was a damsel on deck and Modest and the rest of the old veterans ran to their beds and grabbed their thin sheets. They wrapped them around them like Romans at the coliseum.

"My friends," I bellowed. "I am Colonel Stewart of the Preobrajenski Guards," and they all laughed. "Fine, I'm Redbeard the Magnificent, anybody heard of him?" A few shouted and cheered hurrah, and a few just sneered at the brash little foreigner who dared to stand beside Modest Mussorgsky like his equal.

Yakoff and his corporal carried stacks of new warm blankets for the old veterans' beds, and thick wool socks for their feet, and chunks of nice Swiss chocolate, and fresh fruit just up from Cannes. "Gather round me men and take a blanket, and a pair of socks, and some fruit, and some chocolate, care of my beautiful wife, Nadia Shuvalova Stewart," I roared.

Nadia took a bow and beamed at the soldiers. "Thank you so much for your service to Mother Russia," she told each and every one as she handed out their presents with a big warm smile. Her new friends were wrapped in their togas and smiling away as they exchanged the customary kisses and hugs with my emerald-eyed Snow Maiden.

Modest walked over to the west window and signaled me over. "Look down there in that shack on the hospital grounds, can you see it?"

435

Nadia was busy kissing and hugging the old soldiers, so I humored him. When his old friends had called him a coward for not rejoining the Regiment for the war with the Turks, Modest had begun to drink more heavily. And now he drank on his good days, and he drank on his bad, so what he told me appeared to be the rantings of a drunken man.

"That's where the Secret Police do their torturing, Augustus." he said as he pointed to a little building not more than a hundred feet off.

There was an iron gate to the north up on Botkinskaya Street and Modest said he'd seen, "people coming in there sitting up on a sleigh with a Secret Police escort, then the night would be full of screams, and come morning they'd be taking the twisted bodies away on a sledge."

What could I say to a tale like that? I knew that the Third Section tortured their prisoners, but there wasn't a thing I could do.

"Let's get back to Nadia now, Modest. The soldiers are swamping her. Go tell her how you were kidnapped by Miss Fanny Lear or something from happier times," I said to him proudly, for we both knew he was a consummate wastrel and took pride in his work.

That evening as we got ready for bed, Nadia said she wanted to buy Modest a new bathrobe, for he would catch pneumonia wrapped in just a hospital gown and a thin little sheet. "One that's warm and fits him well, after all he is The Maestro," she said proudly, for we all loved him like a brother!

"And it must be in the green and red colors of his beloved Preobrajenski Guard, if you please, my dear," I pitched right in.

We fell asleep dreaming of the horse farm in Finland and then the devils came! There was that scrawny school master, Pobedonostsev having sex with the Bonaparte Princess under a swaying palm tree down in Port du Cros, while the Secret Police tortured Signora Fungini and her family to find out where I was hiding, which was under a bright red rowboat with the two Sulis gurgling away like a Maryland brook. The Secret Police started to chase us out onto the deep blue waters of the Mediterranean, and we rowed our little fishing boat for all we were worth. Then it suddenly became an Excalibur train doing damn near sixty miles an hour through a sea of deep snow heading straight for the city of Piter as Yakoff yelled, "She's going to blow, Augustus! Jump or die!"

I awoke in a pool of sweat and swore not to eat any more chocolate before bed, but what that dream was trying to tell me, was Russia was going off the rails—though you didn't need to eat chocolate to see that. And when the Empress's brother, Prince Alexander of Hesse, came to visit his dying sister in the middle of a February snow storm, the Empress sent us out to keep him safe, while the Tsar sent his two sons, and a squadron of Convoy Cossacks dressed in their long red cherkeskas.

The snow was deep and the train was late, but when Prince Alexander finally arrived near 6:00 PM in a roaring blizzard, we escorted him back to the Winter Palace—blinded by the blowing snow. The Royals dismounted and went into the Winter Palace, as Yakoff and I went back to the stables to cool the horses down, when suddenly a huge explosion rocked the ground we were standing on! There was smoke and fire coming from the Winter Palace—smoke and fire, and the smell of gas! I ran to the Palace's private quarters and started searching for Nadia. The old Empress was still fast asleep in her bed—all alone and quiet, while the Tsar was going about with a lantern calling for his 2nd wife before God like a lost soul in Hell. He never even asked how the Empress was!

The Tsar's mistress had been complaining for several months that she smelled the makings of a bomb in the bowels of the Winter Palace, and even though the Secret Police had a terrorist map with a big X in the exact spot where the bomb blew up, they somehow couldn't find it. Three hundred pounds of nitroglycerin had gutted the Yellow Dining Room and we were hours in there digging out the survivors and the dead. As I heard the screams of the poor wounded soldiers, it brought back memories of Baltimore and the B&O horses. Homo homini lupus, we were a race of murderers from one end of the globe to the next!

Twelve guards were killed that night and sixty were wounded.[181] Their funerals were almost too much to bear with the orphans and widows standing beside the coffins crying as they were buried in a snowy field. But the people of Piter didn't seem to care anymore! They were in love with the People's Will. That's when I mentioned to the Naslednik that the policeman with the thick as a brick beard had quite possibly set Sophia Perovskaya free. The Naslednik must have told his new best friend, General Cherevin, since he came at me with death in his eyes!

First thing he did was tell the Tsarevich that he knew for a fact that I was a German spy. "You bring me the spy master that manages that wild little Yankee," the Tsarevich told Cherevin, "and I'll have Frolov hang the two of them, but otherwise leave my good friend alone!"

So he turned his ire on Yakoff. We were just catching up on the ins and outs down at Sudeikin's House of Love one morning. Besides watching Pobedonostsev and his new girlfriend go at it like a couple of rabbits, the morning was quiet.

"Where's Yakoff?" I asked my Sergeant of the Guard.

"He didn't come in today, sir." He whispered as he peeked through the rabbit hole, which we'd named our little peep hole for the speed trials the Holy Procurator was running. But that was strange since Sergeant Yakovich had ridden to work with me! I'd come into our lair over the haberdashery to take my watch beside the hole in the wall, and Yakoff had ridden into the city to give Modest Mussorgsky his new bathrobe.

That was about 8:00 AM, so he should have been back, so I sent two men out to track him down, while I rode hard for the Imperial Hospital. And there was the Imp smiling away in Nadia's gift—a nice rich Preobrajenski green bathrobe with red facings and cuffs that made him look like a king, so I knew Yakoff had been there.

"How did Yakoff seem when he left here this morning, Modest? Was he nervous or depressed?" was my first question, for the war in the Balkans had been hard on us all.

"He was as jolly as ever when he left, Augustus, but I did see him talking to this strange looking character with a great big head and a big black beard. They went west down Botkinskaya Street."

That sounded like Sudeikin to me, but had he come at us head on because we were spotted at his House of Lust, or had his boss, General Cherevin, ordered him to pick up Yakoff? In Russia that double-headed eagle looked both ways at all times, so you never knew which face you'd see. But I put on a silent face that day, for someone was definitely hunting us!

Our contacts in the Secret Police were able to track Sergeant Yakovich to the Peter and Paul Fortress where he was being held on the orders of General Cherevin. And the worst news of all was Yakoff was to be a victim of the infamous Katorga![182]

I wired our spy stations for all the help they could send us and we stocked our private train for a rescue mission—took on extra coal, food, water, and ammunition. We were going to steal Yakoff back from the Secret Police or I wasn't the Tsarevich's wild and crazy American!

But first I spoke with Alexander Alexandrovich about how much Yakoff meant to him. How he'd taught Little Nikolaus and Georgie to ride their ponies like Cheyenne braves, and had carried the Naslednik's poor sick mother to the train in Cannes. Why, the loyal sergeant had even helped bring in the Tsarevich's dead cousin from the trenches in Bulgaria, and I added that into my story.

Oh, I brought tears to His Majesty's eyes, but he said no way would he interfere with official Secret Police business. "Yakoff was arrested because he lied about his religion when he entered the Army," went the Tsarevich with total certainty. "He's a half Pole—half Russian Jew, and the man had the audacity to play with my children!"

Yakoff had told the Naslednik all that at the time of my duel, and His Majesty was fine with it then. This was not the man who chatted with Yakoff and me over a bowl of borscht; this was a bigoted monolith that Pobedonostsev and his general friend were molding into their own private little puppet!

General Cherevin—in his wisdom, had decided it was the Jews that were responsible for all the ills in Russia, and that slippery Pobedonostsev was helping him sell it! I couldn't just sneak Yakoff off the plantation on the back of my horse like I had Little Henry, so my plan was to follow his prison train at a comfortable distance until we hit a place where we could (hopefully by stealth) steal him back again. And if stealth didn't work, we'd ram the prison train and board her with weapons drawn, for Yakoff Yakovich was the heart and soul of my Mukden Rifles! But that would have meant a life on the run, and what would become of Nadia, and Boris, and poor Little Suli the Second, and the dapple gray Gelderlands, and my beautiful horse farm up in Finland? The more you had, the less likely you were to stick your neck out! No, we had to follow Yakoff to wherever they took him and set up an alternate plan; after all, I was a married man with hopes of having a baby!

Then the sad news came that the Empress Maria Alexandrovna had passed away in her sleep. Her body was cold when they found her and what perturbed the Tsarevich the most was his father had left her all alone to go down to Tsarskoe Selo with his mistress! At Her Majesty's funeral, the winds blew so hard from the north that you could hardly take a step forward on the Troitskiy Bridge. And as the procession crossed the Neva to bury her, the sky was black and the rain poured down, and a great shaft of lightning struck in the middle of the road right there before the Emperor.

It was as if the Lord didn't want any part of the man, nor did the Tsarevich, nor me, nor Russia! The Naslednik wept for weeks on end and when the forty days of mourning was over and word leaked out that the Tsar had gone and officially married his concubine (a year was the customary waiting period), I saw murder in the Tsarevich's eyes!

"Can the Succession be changed if that whore is crowned Empress?" gun-shy Vladimir asked his older brother, as we waited for the Naslednik to haul himself aboard his big horse I called the Brahma Bull.[183]

There was silence, and heaving, and huffing, and puffing, then finally His Lordship sat up straight in the saddle like he was riding a cow and said, "Hell, yes he can change the Succession, you fool! Didn't Peter the Great do the same thing to his first family?"

That was the closest I ever heard Alexander Alexandrovich talk of high treason, but Vlad's wife, the Grand Duchess Maria Pavlovna definitely went farther than that every time she and General Cherevin met. They had become frequent members of Sudeikin's House of Sin, for who could resist such a glamourous man with his short-cropped hair and his thick caterpillar mustache? Not the Grand Duchess, and even while she was in the throngs of their lovemaking, she'd bark out orders!

"You need to make sure the Narodnaya Volya don't fail this time, do you hear me, General? Oh my God! Oh my God! Faster, faster!" she went like the two-faced harlot she was!

I asked myself many a time, should I tell the Tsarevich of this unholy union? But we'd heard nothing else to implicate the two of them—other than what I heard from the horse's mouth. And since the horse outranked me, I was dead in the water until I could prove her guilt. One wrong word and I'd be on the next train to Siberia with my ankles and wrists chained like poor Yakoff!

Then one day in late June our plans took a turn for the worse when we had a near collision of lovers that almost sent us all down the rabbit hole. We were up in our little corner apartment listening in, while the preacher's girlfriend took on a brand new lover, Nikolai Baranov, who'd moved up the age brackets to pretty near the legal age. He wasn't a sprinter like Pobedonostsev was, and the young lady was finally showing some signs of life. Their bed creaked loudly like a ship in heavy seas, but the next noise we heard was the squeaking of the stairs as His Holiness the Ober-Procurator ascended his own personal staircase to Heaven. Creak creak—went that bed, and squeak squeak went the stairs, and the two sounds were coming closer and closer together!

Luckily, Nikolai Baranov was a speedy character in his own right, for he heard His Holiness approaching and flew through an open window to a narrow ledge over the Nevsky as carriages and horses flew by. But there was the rub, for on his way out the window he'd slammed into our pastoral painting of the farmer bringing in his cows and exposed our little hole in the wall to Sudeikin's society of sex-crazed sinners! We left in a hurry and soon after my favorite Secret Policeman moved out. But the

441

collapse of Sudeikin's House of Sin meant we had nothing more to go on regarding a Vladimirovichi plot.

Nadia said that the Emperor's new wife, the Most Serene Princess Yurievskaya (she'd gotten a new title to go along with her marriage) had received a letter warning her that Alexander II would die that Sunday, the first day of March. So on that last day of February, 1881, Nadia was needed at the Winter Palace. And to help speed that last day along, Pobedonostsev had convinced His Highness that he should follow his heart and give up the heavy guard. "We must not let the people of Russia smell fear on you, Sire!" said the Grand Inquisitor to the gullible Emperor, and His Majesty bought it.

Usually my six sense picked up on impending doom like a bird dog picks up on the scent of a quail, yet on that morning of the first day of March, I awoke refreshed having slept like a baby. Usually we slept in on a Sunday, but lying there in that lonely bed looking out at the blue sky over the frozen Neva, I decided to get dressed in the only military uniform I had left—my Convoy Cossack's long red cherkeska and shiny black boots to go eat lunch with my favorite horsemen. Once a month the Cossack Convoy gathered in comradery at their barracks for brunch, and I having made so many of them rich, was always welcomed.

The Red Cossack barracks were but two squares from the Winter Palace and in the great hall where we ate they had a huge ham and long trays of freshly cooked blinis, and sauces of preserved fruits like apricot, raspberry, and cherry with a huge vat of sour cream. They hadn't seen me in a couple of months, and what with my wild red hair poking every which way from my undercover job, my appearance wasn't exactly top shelf. But my bright red cherkeska was freshly pressed, my tall black boots were polished to a Cossack's content, my long curved sword held a diamond in the handle, my Colt revolver sat in its nice black leather holster at my left hip pointing backwards, and I had my trusty Winchester on a strap across my back. I might not have been the best looking Cossack lieutenant in the hall that day, but I was certainly the best armed!

On the walls of the great gathering place were all kinds of Musulman flags they'd captured in the war with the Turks. The balalaikas played as we chatted about the campaigns we'd fought, and the friends we'd lost. We ate a hearty lunch and drank beer and vodka, as we laughed about how wild we'd been in our youth, but what these men of the Steppes really wanted to talk about was how the Emperor had stood them down to take only six men out on the streets of Piter!

"That's suicide, Augustus Augustovich!" exclaimed a toothless Cossack as he quaffed his beer. "The Batiushka-Tsar needs at least a squadron of Cossacks to keep him safe in these troubled times. Why, the whole city knows the Narodnaya Volya are out hunting him!" He screamed as he slammed down his black bread beer, and wiped his long beard on the bright red tablecloth.

"Well, I could stay and gossip all day, but I have a friend in the hospital that needs to see me," I told them—thinking of Modest Mussorgsky who had gone off the wagon again and was back in the hospital.

In the usual Cossack fashion, they gave me some food for the old soldiers—four dozen blinis on a silver platter, complete with a cherry compote and sour cream, which I balanced precariously on Boris's back as we trotted off to see the Maestro.

When I arrived at the hospital, the patients were lying on their beds in boredom. "Modest, my friend, I have come with some blinis care of the Convoy Cossacks! Where can I set them down?" I asked as he stared at the ceiling like he was planning an escape.

"Put them down over there," he said pointing to a table.

"Come men, the sotnik has brought us some food from the Cossacks. Dig in before the blinis get colder," he told the soldiers like he was bored to death.

They lined up in that land of the white. The sheets were white, the walls were white, the bathrobes—all but the one the Imp wore, were white as well, and they began to divvy out the spoils with smiles on each and every face, save for Modest.

443

"Where's your lovely wife today, Augustus?" the Maestro asked. "I want to thank her for this lovely gift," and he clutched at his bathrobe like it was the best bathrobe he ever had.

"She had to spend the night at the Winter Palace with the Emperor's new wife," I said as the men pricked up their ears.

"How is Princess Yurievskaya doing now that she's the official wife of the Emperor?" asked the Imp like he really didn't care.

"She is certain her husband will die today," I told him in a whisper and the room fell silent as a graveyard.

Old soldiers are a superstitious lot, and when they heard the Emperor's new wife was in fear that our Batiushka-Tsar would die that day, they all started to mourn him like it had already happened. Whispers spread through the ward like wild fire as Modest called me over to the window.

"Come here Augustus, I want to show you something," he said with a stern voice. "You know that building over there that I told you about?" and he pointed off to where he said the Secret Police murdered their prisoners. "Well, this morning a sleigh came in with a man and a woman prisoner aboard, and the man with that huge head and the big black beard was at the reins."

I was thinking maybe Modest was going through the DTs again, only his mind seemed clear. "Usually they bring their prisoners in sitting up and when they are done, they are stone cold dead. But this morning, the girl walked back out again! And I recognized her, Augustus," he whispered like the walls had ears. "It was Sophia Perovskaya, of that I am certain!"

"Sophia Perovskaya, are you sure?" I asked the Maestro.

"Well, she's brought me flowers back stage many a time in my life, and I've seen her face on the Wanted Posters. And there she was, right over there by that shaggy little pony hitched to the Secret Police sleigh."

The Tsarevich had told me that he and his wife planned to go skating at Tauride Lake. It was to be a romantic interlude that his brother Vlad had helped him plan, and although it sounded strange at the time, once I heard that Sophia Perovskaya was loose,[184] I knew something was rotten—and it wasn't in Denmark!

"Can you ride to the Preobrajenski Headquarters on Boris as fast as you can, Modest? Tell them they should ride for the Tsar down at the Fields of Mars—he's in grave danger!"

"And what will you do, Augustus Augustovich?" the Maestro asked like he figured I had a better job lined up for myself.

"I'll go steal that Secret Police sleigh," and I pointed to Sudeikin's little black horse and sleigh tied up by the torture chamber. "And I'll go and rescue the Tsarevich and Tsarevna at Tauride Lake!"

I figured Grand Duke Vladimir was about to take his father and brother out of the line of succession all in one fell swoop. The Vladimirovichi would finally rule Russia in the style they were accustomed to, and they'd blame the whole thing on the People's Will!

"Why do you always get the exciting jobs?" the Imp inquired as he dragged his feet. "Let me steal that sleigh and ride off to rescue Sasha and Minnie? After all, I am a Preobrajenski Guardsman just as you and the Tsarevich are, Augustus!"

How could I say no to the man who was so busy cinching up his bathrobe round his ample middle and preparing for the ride of his life? So off he ran in just a pair of long underwear, his hospital gown, a pair of warm wool socks, thick black felt boots, and nothing more—save for that green and red bathrobe he was so very proud of. I ran out and mounted Boris like the red-coated Cossack I was, kicked him in the side and headed for the Neva crossing. My job was to warn the Emperor!

The Tsar usually went first to the Guards review on the Field of Mars via his armored carriage, but it was after 2:00 PM and he was gone. So I galloped off for the Mikhailovsky Palace with Boris huffing like a freight train, but the guards said he'd headed west for the Catherine's Quay on his way home to the Winter Palace. So north up the Quay we thundered only to hear an explosion that rattled the windows and shook my teeth!

445

A cloud of thick black smoke rose in the air and I figured that was the end of the Tsar—only to see him standing there beside his damaged carriage as we skidded to a halt. A small boy was dying in the snow as the Emperor questioned a man lying by the side of the road.

"Get back in your carriage at once, Your Majesty!" I bellowed. After all it was bullet proof and still up on all four.

But the Emperor wouldn't listen to a lowly sotnik like me, and out of the crowd stepped another bomber who threw his explosives right at the Emperor's feet. The world went dark and when I woke up again, my left eye was on fire and I was lying in the snow with the ringing of a thousand church bells. Just to my left wreathing his life away was my old friend Boris, and there to my right was Alexander II, his one leg hanging on by a thread—his greatcoat blown completely off his body!

We loaded him up on the Police Chief's sleigh and prepared to make our escape. They piled the wounded on a second sledge and we were off for the Winter Palace as I watched the lights go out of Boris's eyes. We bounced along behind the dying Emperor with his blood dripping in the snow, and slid to a halt right there in front of the private entrance. But we couldn't get the Tsar through the Saltykov Doors, so we ripped them off their hinges and carried him up the red carpeted stairs on a blanket and got him into his study.

"Lay him down on his camp bed!" the major domo bellowed, as they pulled an iron cot out from behind a tall curtain.

We stood there behind the Tsar as he breathed his last breaths. In came a mess of doctors tut tutting that he should have been taken to the Military Hospital—not brought to the Winter Palace where he would surely die. Princess Yurievskaya came running in dressed in her nightgown and tried to mount the Emperor in a hysterical fit of undying love!

"Can't you stop the bleeding," she sobbed, which lit a fire under the doctors as they tried a tourniquet and brought in Oxygen. I remember the sky was turning red outside, as red as the blood from the Emperor on the

446

snow, when in came the Tsarevich and Maria Feodorovna still in their ice skating outfits.[185] The Imp had completed his mission!

Within an hour the Emperor was gone and they moved his body into an alcove with the Tsarevich holding his hand. Then came the cries of that black bearded Secret Policeman as he stuck his big head through the Tsar's study door and hollered, "Let me in you fools, I must talk to that Cossack lieutenant over there about the whereabouts of one Modest Mussorgsky!"

"Silence, can't you see our Emperor has just passed away," the next empress of Russia barked with fire in her eyes. "Guards cast him out of the palace at once!" She roared like a lioness.

"Go get Nadia Shuvalova and tell her to dress warmly for a night ride into Finland, and prepare the Royal sleigh for a long winters' journey," she bellowed to her Guardsmen. Then she said softly to me, "My God, Augustus there's a coat button where your eye should be!"

She went white as a ghost and hung on to me tightly until Nadia came and rescued us. "Can you drive a sleigh, Nadia?" she asked my emerald-eyed Snow Maiden with a look of fear on her face.

"I can, Your Majesty," Nadia told her.

"Take them to Finland at once and kill anyone who tries to stop you!" our Empress roared to her Cossack captain.

An eerie silence hung in the air as we thundered north in the last light of a blood red sunset. Grand Duke Vladimir's men had sealed the Viborg Gate, but our captain had them opened on Maria Feodorovna's orders!

We rode north through the night as the stars came down and surrounded us in their sparkling glory. And just as Miss Harriet had prophesized to a little boy in a May snow storm some twenty years before, one woman who loved me had set me free and the other was driving me off to freedom!

The End

447

Glossary

Amerikanskiy…..Russian for American

Badmash…..Persian term for an evil hooligan

Banya…..A Russian sauna

Banza.....The real name for a banjo

Basin…..The Baltimore harbor was called the Basin back in the 1860s

Batiushka-Tsar…..Little Father, the people's name for the Tsar

Bingerle…..Tsar Alexander II's favorite code word

Cherkeska…..A long tunic with crisscrossed pockets for bullets sewn on the chest that was worn by the Cossacks

Cocotte…..Prostitute, whore, tart, harlot, bawd, strumpet, trollop, working girl, courtesan, lady of pleasure, lady of the evening, hooker, street walker, etc.

Der Hintern…..German for buttocks

Digitus Impudicus…..Better known as The Finger or The Bird, an ancient term of disrespect dating back to the Romans

Freilini…..A Russian Royal Lady in Waiting

Full as a tick…..Civil War slang for stone drunk

Hauptfeldwebel…..German for Sergeant Major

Hetman…..A Cossack military commander

Hock…..A horse's back knee joint

Izvozchiki…..A Russian coachman, wildly dressed, and highly independent

Joie de vivre…..Joy for Life

Katorga…..A Russian system of forced labor that predates the Gulag

Krivitza…..A winter hurricane that sweeps down out of the Balkan Mountains

Losing my religion…..A southern expression for losing one's temper

Maior…..Russian for the rank of Major

Moujik…..Russian word for peasant

Musulman…..another term for a Muslim

Nancy…..Civil War slang for a homosexual

Narodnaya Volya…..a Russian terrorist organization translated as the People's Will

Naslednik…..The heir apparent to the Russian throne

Odalisque…..An Ottoman concubine

Palkovnik…..A Russian Colonel

Picklehaub…..A spiked Prussian military helmet

Pogoni…..Russian term for the shoulder boards an officer wears

Reitknecht…..German for groom

Rio…..Civil War slang for coffee

Rogered…..To have sexual intercourse

Secesh…..Short for secessionist

Sotnik…..A Cossack lieutenant

Toot Sweet.....A bastardization of tout de suite meaning quickly

Uhlan.....European term for a lancer

Weed…..Civil War term for a cigarette

Endnotes

[1] The Russians called such a star filled night the Vertigo of the North, and if you ever lie on a hillside and stare up into the heavens you can see the infinite nature of time and space, as you fly through the Universe at near 70,000 mph.

[2] In the troubled times of Colonel Stewart's youth, hatred and avarice abounded in both lands, and the Tsar-Liberator and the Great Emancipator were both murdered by their own people.

[3] Synesthesia is a neurological condition that allows for sensations to intertwine, for instance Nikolai Rimsky-Korsakov was said to be able to see visual images of the sounds he heard in his music.

[4] A double lung shot wound wasn't considered survivable by Civil War standards, as noted by Shelby Foote in his wonderful First Volume of The Civil War Narrative, where Major Roberdeau Wheat suffered the same wound and told his physician, "I don't feel like dying" and he didn't either.

[5] The building that housed the Maryland Line Confederate Soldiers Home in Pikesville, Maryland has served many purposes, from a Federal Arsenal back in 1818, to a State Police Barracks more recently.

[6] Just before the Stock Market crash that began the Great Depression, Herbert Hoover prophesized, "We in America today are nearer to the final triumph over poverty than ever before," which was followed by ten hard years of poverty.

[7] H. L. Menken was the real Sage of Baltimore, and he could have helped Augustus with his rant about Prohibition in Chapter Two with his quote, "Puritanism: The haunting fear that someone, somewhere, may be happy."

[8] Whether this was the actual photograph, I cannot say, but the old soldier in the left foreground (page 140) of Richard Cox's excellent book, Civil War Maryland is most certainly throwing someone the finger.

[9] While the Rebels called the bloodiest day in Civil War history, Sharpsburg, the Yankees called it Antietam.

[10] The Scopes Monkey trial made national news in 1925 when the state of Tennessee charged a substitute teacher, Mr. John Thomas Scopes with a violation of the Butler Act, which decreed that it was illegal to teach evolution in a state funded school. Three-time presidential candidate William Jennings Bryan prosecuted the man and won the case, with Mr. Scopes found guilty and fined for his audacity.

[11] William Surrey Hart was a cowboy star from the silent screen who tried to bring a sense of realism to the Hollywood scene, much to his downfall with the movie industry.

[12] Colonel Stewart is referring to the 2nd American Revolution as the southerners so patriotically called the Civil War, and Bolshevik revolutions in Finland and Russia.

[13] On page 41 of Festus Summer's fine book, The Baltimore and Ohio In the Civil War the author discusses the Luggage War the railroads were in.

[14] Fifty years later, another "incorrigible" boy grew up in this same rough neighborhood down by the Camden railyards in Baltimore, see: http://xroads.virginia.edu/~ug02/yeung/baberuth/born.html.

[15] Read what Frederick Douglas had to say about being a slave in a northern state, and see if they got any better treatment than the slaves down south @ http://www.historyplace.com/speeches/douglass.htm.

[16] Bluestone was copper sulphate crystals and it was considered bad form to recharge the crowfoot jars this way, though I'm sure it was done.

[17] This sounds like a lightning protector on the lines of one David Brooks invented using an iron water pipe wrapped in paper and then wound round with telegraph wires to ward off stray electricity.

[18] See: http://www.businessinsider.com/massive-1859-solar-storm-telegraph-scientists-2016-9 for more on the solar storm of Sept. 1, 1859. If such a solar storm hit today in the Age of Information our electrical systems would be fried.

[19] A chicken coop jump is a pyramid like affair made of wood, high enough and wide enough to keep a docile horse or a self-respecting cow inside the confines of a designated field, while still allowing a horse at the run to jump it.

[20] In an excellent case study of slavery titled Ridgely Compound of Hampton by Dr. David Taft Terry, the author mentions as many as twelve slaves trying to escape from that iron forge in a single year, so it must have been bad. See: http://slavery.msa.maryland.gov/html/casestudies/fifrh.html.

[21] Augustus wasn't the only one to think he'd seen ghosts at the Hampton House, for the strange goings on at the Ridgely mansion check out the following: https://www.youtube.com/watch?v=k2vIi3OOVIQ.

[22] If Captain Ridgely was referring to his 1st Lieutenant John Merryman, this would seem rather disingenuous, since after the bridges were burned around Baltimore, Captain Ridgley was to wave off his responsibilities by saying, "I think it not unlikely, the first suggestion of the burning of the bridges, emanated upon the occasion I have alluded to, by John Merryman."

[23] Later Mayor Brown was to find himself in trouble for ordering the bridges burned around Baltimore and he took the same tack—claiming they were out of his jurisdiction, though the Governor denied having given the order.

[24] Add veteran of the Mexican War and you have a description of Fort McHenry's black-bearded commander. For more information on the man who saved the Baltimore star fort, see http://www.nycivilwar.us/robinson.html.

[25] Coming to America after their failed attempt to change Europe's monarchist ways, the German "Forty-eighters" were staunch Republicans.

[26] Barnum's Hotel was a fine Baltimore establishment at the corner of Fayette and Calvert Streets that all the best people in town frequented. Down in the basement Captain Ferrandini plied his two trades of hair dressing and passing out diatribes against President Lincoln, not necessarily in that order.

[27] The 1859 McClellan saddle was a well-designed, light weight, rawhide covered affair that was said to be easier on both the horse and the rider, though the Prussians suggested McClellan might have lifted the design from them.

[28] What the boys thought was a cavern, was actually the Ice House. See: https://janeaustensworld.wordpress.com/2012/11/25/the-19th-c-ice-house-at-hampton-mansion/ and see why they could enjoy ice cream on the 4th of July!

[29] This is the actual French for the toot sweet Colonel Stewart loves to use, and it means right away.

[30] The Captain's wife was his first cousin, some six years his senior, proud Ridgely born from the next plantation over, and blessed with the same strong Ridgely jaw.

[31] I can find nothing to substantiate this plan, but when Confederate General Isaac Trimble took over the Maryland Militia on the day of the Baltimore riots, he renamed it the Volunteer Un-uniformed Corps, so Colonel Stewart could have been on to something! See page 57 of Maryland in the Civil War, A House Divided by Cotton & Hayward for further information.

[32] The gentlemen's rules for dueling, or Code Duello could be called into play for just such a challenge, and social rank had little to do with accepting. For details, see: http://www.pbs.org/wgbh/amex/duel/sfeature/rulesofdueling.html.

[33] Little Henry's escape is confirmed in Dr. Teary's wonderful article @ http://slavery.msa.maryland.gov/html/casestudies/fifrh.html, and it's true that the Afro-Americans on the streets of Baltimore made the best conductors for the Underground Railroad.

[34] South Carolina's palmetto flag displays a white crescent and palm tree on a dark blue background and was one of the first battle flags used by the Rebels in the Second Battle of Baltimore.

[35] Some may disagree sharply with Colonel Stewart calling Mayor Brown's book, Baltimore and the Nineteenth of April, 1861 a work of fiction, though the mayor's facts do seem a bit skewed.

[36] The Knights of the Golden Circle, or KGC, planned to take over all of the U.S. slave states, Mexico, and the Caribbean to form a brand new slave nation with Cuba as the capital—not the most patriotic of plans.

[37] Actually Captain Ferrandini was a Corsican like another half-crazed megalomaniac, Napoleon Bonaparte, my apologies to Italy for any confusion.

[38] Cipriano Ferrandini had gone to Mexico as a captain in the Knights of the Golden Circle in an attempt to conquer Mexico for their brand new nation, see: http://knightsofthegoldencircle.net/Introduction.html for details.

[39] Many rich Marylanders were involved in this un-American organization, including Mr. Winans' son, and Jerome Napoleon Patterson Bonaparte. For details see: https://msa.maryland.gov/msa/educ/exhibits/hicks/html/case5.html.

[40] If you doubt Colonel Stewart regarding the huge size of the Steam Gun see John W. Lamb's wonderful book, A Strange Engine of War .

[41] The Richmond Daily Dispatch (April 24, 1861) reported that two spies had been captured with the Steam Gun at St. Timothy's School, so these were indeed the Federal agents.

[42] See: https://www.youtube.com/watch?v=YKhLgPyymfU for a test firing of the Winans Steam Machine Gun on Mythbusters. This thing was wicked!

[43] In fairness to Captain George H. Steuart, who went on to make Brigadier General in the Confederate Army, I can find no proof that he committed treason or even frequented Houses of Ill Repute, though he did resign his Federal commission on the date in question.

[44] Ordinarily the passengers detrained at the outer train stations and came across Baltimore's inner harbor via the horse drawn trams of the City Passenger Rail Way Company—their stables located at Light & Wells Street.

[45] Whether these coins were left over from the KGCs' bribe, I cannot say, but the Knights of the Golden Circle definitely had a war chest in Baltimore. See: http://www.legendsofamerica.com/trs-kgctreasure.html for more information.

[46] Mayor Brown was to say that he was called away by the Governor at that very moment, but the Governor had troubles of his own; for Washington had just wired him that they knew there was treachery afoot.

[47] Colonel Stewart is referring to Nicholas Biddle, a 65-year old Afro-American Pennsylvania volunteer who was brutally beaten by the mob. See: http://www.phmc.state.pa.us/portal/communities/pa-heritage/nick-biddle-forgotten-hero-civil-war.html for details of this dastardly attack.

[48] Shortly thereafter, Major Pemberton resigned his Federal commission and joined the Rebels. But unlike Captain Steaurt with that extra e in his name, there was no subterfuge to it.

[49] The State's Rights Convention held on the evening of April 18th, 1861 may be a major smoking gun as to whether the next day's riots were premeditated as Colonel Stewart says they were, or spontaneous as Mayor Brown claimed in his book Baltimore and the 19th of April. Read their resolutions in Mayor Brown's book and see what you think.

[50] For illustrations of the Baltimore breweries (including Pabst, Miller, Muth, Hoffman, Bauernschmidt, and Brehm) with their lovely beer gardens shown on the side of the map, see: https://www.loc.gov/resource/g3844b.pm002540/.

[51] Marshal Kane's knowledge of the troop train coming in at this hour, which he notes in his own writings (see The War of the Rebellion Volume 1, page 629), is another big hole in the politico's story that they weren't advised by B&O management in time to protect the troops on the East End.

[52] This was the smelliest jailhouse in Baltimore, see: Our Police by de Francais Folsum (page 304) for the sordid details of this terrible place.

[53] The clearest evidence of a conspiracy to commit treason is noted by the telegrams Marshal Kane and the Rebel leaders were sending even prior to the riots. See Maryland Reports Volume 25 for a reference to their premeditated plan to obstruct Federal troops by acts of violence.

[54] Historians argue about the size of the mob, but this article: http://baltimorecitypolicehistory.com/index.php/our-police/riots-1861.html puts the numbers at ten thousand, and some sources raise it to twenty thousand.

[55] Major Watson and the tenth rail car to cross with Company K onboard were attacked and derailed three times as they headed west for the Camden Street Station. They were fired on, pounded with stones, and finally answered with volley fire at both Charles and Howard Streets some two blocks away from where the Mayor and the Marshal said they heard nothing.

[56]Corporal Sumner Henry Needham was the first soldier struck down in the Civil War, though he lived a week more without regaining consciousness.

[57] Lieutenant Lynde of the Stoneham Light Infantry captured the Rebel flag and was thus the first Union soldier to capture such a prize of war. See: http://www.stonehamhistory.webs.com/BaltimoreRiot/BaltimoreRiot1.htm.

[58] Seventeen year old Private Luther Ladd was said to have died in this fashion with his last words being, "All hail to the Stars and Stripes," according to John Wesley Hanson's Historical Sketch of the Sixth Massachusetts Volunteers.

[59] The first Confederate to die in the Civil War, died right there on the streets of Baltimore. See: http://www.hmdb.org/marker.asp?marker=71978 for further information on this South Carolinian artilleryman.

[60] On page 48 of Hanson's Historical Sketch of the Sixth Massachusetts Volunteers, an eyewitness said, "the brutes who killed him crushed him with clubs and rocks, so that almost all trace of humanity was beaten out of him."

[61] I found mention of Marshal Kane's Rebel bodyguard on page 167 of Frank Tower's great book, The Urban South and the Coming of the Civil War.

[62] With the legal definition of treason being, "The betrayal of one's own country by waging war against it or by consciously or purposely acting to aid its enemies." I would have to agree with Colonel Stewart.

[63] These horses were actually the first casualties of the day from Major Watson's rail car—possibly the booms young Stewart heard as he sat at the East End with his friends waiting to be towed to the Camden Street Station.

[64] 1st Sergeant John E. Ames was struck in the head by a paving stone and was so severely wounded that he was left behind in Baltimore. He was later returned to Massachusetts, but died of his wounds the following year.

[65] See: http://civilwarhome.com/jones.html and note that four men of the 6th Massachusetts died of their wounds, thirty-six were hospitalized, and one hundred and thirty were listed as missing. Plus a thousand Pennsylvania Volunteers that ran for their lives.

[66] The Rebels claimed a civilian standing in his doorway was shot without provocation, but the battle still raged when he caught the round, and if you stand close to the fire you're bound to get burned.

[67] In the Historical Sketch of the 6th by John Wesley Hanson (page 41), Captain Follansbee stated that, "Quite a number of horses were killed."

[68] Captain John H Dyke was saved by a Baltimore tobacconist named Dorsey who pulled him out of the fight at Howard Street with a gunshot wound to the thigh and hid him from the Secesh for over a week. See: Historical Sketch of the Sixth Massachusetts Volunteers (page 30), for details.

[69] In fact, word traveled so fast that the lawyer in question's friend down in the Deep South penned a poem after his friend's supposed death called Maryland My Maryland, before he learned that he had survived.

[70] It was reported in civilwarhome.com/marylandcmh2.htm that the lawyer in question, Frank Ward "was shot through both thighs," which would suggest Colonel Stewart's hypothesis just might be right.

[71] Google: civilwaref.blogspot.com/2013/10/cassius-marcellus-clay-born-october-19.html for full details of this true American hero and Son of the South who was dead set against slavery well before the Civil War ever broke out.

[72] Though Mayor Brown defends this man in his well-known book Baltimore and the 19th of April, 1861 (page 50), His Honor clearly states that the barrister "seized a flag of one of the companies and nearly tore it from the staff." Words that seem quite out of character for a supposedly Unionist mayor.

[73] On page fifty-one of Mayor Brown's book (noted above), he wrote twenty-seven years after the fact, His Honor finally got around to disavowing the fact.

[74] When the Secesh called for a vote to cast Baltimore with the Confederacy in 1861, they were surprised to see the majority were against them, see: http://www.nytimes.com/1862/04/20/news/a-year-s-changes-in-baltimore.html.

[75] The Dark and Bloody Dueling Grounds" of Bladensburg, Maryland were where Washingtonians settled their disagreements according to the Code Duello. Google: townofbladensburg.com/cms/dueling-grounds for more details.

[76] This aberration of the moon on Sunday April 21, 1861, was also noted in Richard Wheeler's wonderful book A Rising Thunder (p. 140) where it was reported by a band of New Yorkers coming up the Chesapeake Bay.

[77] Senator Henry Wilson was a well know Radical Republican from Massachusetts who wanted Emancipation to come as fast as possible, and he hounded Mr. Lincoln so much that the President was known to hide from him.

[78] Major Watson of the Fighting 6th said close to the very same thing—possibly even stronger when he spoke to President Lincoln with the Baltimore Mayor present right after the riots. See: History and Complete Roster of the Massachusetts's Regiments, Minute Men of '61 by George Nason, page 405.

[79] Cassius Clay had been appointed Ambassador to the Romanoff Court where he got along so famously with the Tsar that it kept France and England from supporting the Confederacy more vigorously. For more information, see: http://civilwaref.blogspot.com/2013/10/cassius-marcellus-clay-born-october-19.html.

[80] On page 68 of H. Edward Richardson's excellent book, Cassius Marcellus Clay Firebrand of Freedom he discusses Clay's rescue in this fashion by a man named Wash from Lawrenceburg, Kentucky.

[81] www.historicmapworks.com/Atlas/US/7166/Baltimore+and+Anne+Arundel+County+1878/ shows such a location in an old Annapolis map, but if this was where the boys took a bathroom break, I fear they were using it for the wrong purpose!

[82] When Harriet Tubman was a young girl, she was struck in the head by a piece of iron that left a permanent dent and a propensity for falling asleep mid-sentence. It also turned on her circuits for premonitions, as noted in Anne Schraff's wonderful book, The Life of Harriet Tubman.

[83] This appears to be right along the Gunpowder Falls near the boys' island in the stream between the little towns of Corbett and Glencoe, for details see: www.mdhs.org/findingaid/gorsuch-mitchell-papers-1698-1921-ms-2733.

[84] Annapolis actually had such an unusual snow storm on the date in question, for details see: https://sites.google.com/site/holdingfortmchenry1861/.

[85] This sounded unbelievable, but it is indeed true, and by my calculation that's over one million dollars in today's money.

[86] According to the Richmond Daily Dispatch of April 24th 1861, the B&O horses were taken by the Maryland Militia and the Baltimore City Police Department to be used for burning the rail bridges and policing the city.

[87] The Daily Exchange, a Baltimore newspaper of April 22, 1861 lists several dozen ships in port from the Deep South.

[88] General Butler had the very same theory when the Rebels demanded that he return their runaway slaves, saying since they had seceded they had no rights in our Nation, and thus their property was now his contraband. For details see the amazing Butler's Book by General Benjamin Franklin Butler.

[89] When Harper's Ferry was attacked by the Virginia Rebels just before the Pratt Street riot, they shipped their spoils of war to Baltimore to help with the upcoming fight for the largest city south of the Mason-Dixon.

[90] I can find no documentation of this plan for the Eastern Shore of Maryland to become a Rebel state, though shipments of stolen weapons were most definitely being sent to Snow Hill. See: https://ehistory.osu.edu/books/official-records/114/0571.

[91] Perhaps these were the same weapons General Butler found in Marshal Kane's possession when he took Baltimore back from the Rebels. See: https://baltimorecitypolicehistory.com/index.php/insight/george-proctor-kane-marshal.html.

[92] General Winfield Scott had planned for twelve thousand men to attack Baltimore from four directions to return the Monumental City to the Union, but on the wings of that storm—without one soldier dying from either side, Baltimore was freed from the Rebel horde.

[93] The Rothschild banking empire used the telegraph to keep track of the financial markets in Europe as far back as 1845.

[94] Whether the ship in question was the Monticello, I cannot say, but Richard Cox's delightful book, Civil War Maryland (page 60) tells of just such a loss.

[95] The Green Ferry is a reference to the mind expanding effects of absinthe which some have described as hallucinatory!

[96] The Second French Empire under Napoleon Bonaparte the Third (1852 to 1871) was a time when the French resurgence was strong in Europe and Nice was a very fashionable place to be seen.

[97] The victorious Union Army held a Grand Review on May 23 and 24, 1865 in Washington, D.C. with a hundred and forty-five thousand troops marching down Pennsylvania Avenue. See www.civilwarhome.com/grandreview.html.

[98] A photo of the 3rd Indiana Cavalry mostly dressed in civilian clothes can be found @: http://www.civilwarphotos.net/files/group_photos.htm Group Photo # 390.

[99] A well-known leader of the Knights of the Golden Circle, Jerome Napoleon Patterson Bonaparte was the first born son of Napoleon's youngest brother, and by all accounts he bore an uncanny resemblance to his half-sister, Mathilde.

[100] If you believe Colonel Stewart was being unfair to the Bonaparte Princess and her lecherous house guests, Google: The Princess Mathilde Bonaparte by Sergeant Philip Walsingham and see what an Englishman says on the subject.

[101] Though Psilocybe semilanceata (Liberty Caps) are definitely found in Europe, I can find no mention of them growing in the south of France. See: www.mushroomjohn.org/psilocybesemilanceata2.htm.

[102] Whether these were the same three German girls noted on page 80 of John Priest's excellent book, Before Antietam the Battle for South Mountain, I cannot say, but they were definitely made of the same metal.

[103] Though I could find mention of Man Killer in David Homer Bates' superb book, Lincoln in the Telegraph Office, there was no mention of the colonel.

[104] The Austrians called their hauptfeldwebel der Speer, which meant the spear—like the tip of the attacking weapon.

[105] Junkers were rich south Prussian families that supplied their country with the smartest/toughest warriors in all of Germany. With sword cuts across their faces from dueling with their Junker friends, they were the proud leaders of the Prussian Army.

[106] General Longstreet had no faith in Lee's plan for a frontal attack on the third day of Gettysburg and hoped to convince Lee to go around the Union flank. See http://scienceviews.com/parks/longstreet.html.

[107] Actually, these two linden trees shown in a photograph on page 339 of Quintin Barry's wonderful Road to Koniggratz were huge.

[108] Three times the Austrians were ordered to retreat from the Swiepwald and three times the officers on the ground begged Headquarters to let them stay! But finally—even though they were winning the fight for the high ground, they were ordered back to the east of the two giant linden trees, one of the great military mistakes of history.

[109] He also became the Kaiser of Germany; though Frederick William III reigned for just 99 days. See www.reformation.org/kaiser-frederick3.html for details.

[110] Actually, on page 305 of Quintin Barry's marvelous book, The Road to Koniggratz, it says that the two messengers survived, though they never made it to the walled city, nor did the telegraph message ever get through.

[111] To see how the Prussian mouse crushed the Austrian eagle, check out: https://battlefieldanomalies.com/the-battle-of-koniggratz-2/.

[112] In fairness to the Russians, I can find no reference to everyday Polish being outlawed in Poland, though it was outlawed in Polish schools, offices, and official paperwork. For further details see: Archives of Belarus History of the 1863-1864 Uprising @: http://archives.gov.by/eng/index.php?id=434588.

[113] http://bowieknifefightsfighters.blogspot.com/2011/03/cassius-marcellus-clay-kentucky.html provides more information on Clay's Bowie knife prowess.

[114] Forty years later the Russians were still sending out unciphered messages, which led to a debacle at the Battle of Tannenberg. If you doubt the Colonel, see: www.firstworldwar.com/battles/tannenberg.htm.

[115] Whether Tsar Alexander II supplied the gold for the church steeples from the sale of Alaska, I cannot say, but he did have two wives at the very same time in the very same palace, which shows you what a brave man he was!

[116] See this site for details of the graves of all the Romanoff rulers from Peter the Great on: http://www.saint-petersburg.com/cemeteries/tombs-of-the-peter-and-paul-fortress/.

[117] Frolov the Hangman was a well-known executioner who preferred to work drunk and in the fine Russian fashion you would be slowly dragged up off the ground with no need for a long uncomfortable drop from the gallows. See Bruce Lincoln's Sunlight at Midnight, page 182 for more details on him.

[118] Like America, Russia expanded into territories controlled by local tribes throughout the 1870's. See: www.scaruffi.com/politics/russian.html & www.russojapanesewar.com/clark18.html for further details.

[119] Peter the Great trained his troops by fighting war games right under his older sister's nose until she found out the hard way that his little "Toy Army" had teeth!

[120] Russia fought a series of wars with the Circassians and Caucasians known as the Caucasian Wars—mostly in Georgia, Azerbaijan, and Armenia. See: http://www.cutandparry.com/Caucasian.html for more details.

[121] Colonel Stewart refers frequently to his old nemesis Colonel Edward F. Jones whose rail car was drawn through Baltimore so fast that he didn't have time to order his men off it. See: www.civilwarhome.com/jones.html.

[122] Google: On the investigation of the possible remains of Field Marshal Iosif Gurko @ hrcak.srce.hr/file/94016 for details on the General's Belarus/Polish heritage and his rather diminutive size.

[123] This 1868 battle at the Arikaree Fork of the Republican River in Colorado is well documented and Major Sandy Forsyth was indeed a brave man.

[124] Seeing the elephant refers to having been under fire. See: http://wesclark.com/jw/elephant.html.

[125] Catherine the Great was the wife of Tsar Peter III, and when their marriage went south, she and her lover helped the Tsar move on to a higher place, and thus the strongest ruler in Russia since Peter the Great was a Prussian woman. See: http://www.biography.com/people/catherine-ii-9241622#synopsis.

[126] See www.polishamericancenter.org/Pulaski.htm for information on this fine Polish hero who came to America to fight for our freedom and paid "with the last full measure of devotion," as Mr. Lincoln describes dying for one's country.

[127] Captain Ridgely was indeed in Europe at the time that Colonel Stewart refers to and he remained there until his unfortunate death. For coverage of his ghostly return to Hampton House in a most Captain Ridgely fashion see: www.hauntedhouses.com/states/md/hampton_house.htm.

[128] On page 58 of Liliane and Fred Funcken's Arms & Uniforms the First World War Part 1 it discusses a Romanoff Grand Duke who was gun-shy, though whether this was a family trait I cannot say.

[129] According to Margarita Nelipa's wonderful book, Alexander III: His Life and Reign (page 154), the Tsarevich felt the same way about the Baranov rifles.

[130] The Siberian city of Omsk was founded in 1716 as a Fortress to take Russian exiles in as they came to Siberia.

[131] For a clear idea of the lay of the land around Gatchina Palace see this amazing site @: http://gatchinapalace.ru/en/gatchina/.

[132] Alexander Alexandrovich Romanoff really did have a private band, though I can find no mention of an American trombonist.

[133] The Grand Duchess resided in the actual palace that Tsar Paul was murdered in, though no one bothered to tell Colonel Stewart this fact.

[134] As noted previously, Professor Rimsky-Korsakov was what was called a synesthete, and you only need listen to his Flight of the Bumblebee to see how the notes he heard turned into a picture.

[135] This sounds very much like an early rendition of Rimsky-Korsakov's lovely Scheherazade though he didn't complete the piece till 1888.

[136] In Robert K. Massie's excellent book, Nicholas and Alexandra (page 13), he tells of how poor little Nicholas Alexandrovich (the Tsarevich's first born son) once was so hungry that he ate his Baptismal cross with a piece of the original cross inside.

[137] Though Harriet Tubman didn't get much respect in America, she was well-known in Europe after the Civil War and even received gifts such as a shawl from Queen Victoria, https://nmaahc.si.edu/object/nmaahc_2009.50.39.

[138] Several times, Colonel Stewart refers to Balaam and his ass—an Old Testament tale of an angel, a man, and a little talking donkey.

[139] On page 286 of Margarita Nelipa's Alexander III His Life and Reign, she expounds on the Tsarevna's dislike of Prince Mesherskii.

[140] Johns Hopkins alumnus Henry Gantt devised the term man-hour for the amount of work a man could do in an hour—not including any need for rest, food, or those pesky little trips to the bathroom, though Colonel Stewart may have invented the man-minute.

[141] For many years Modest Mussorgsky labored at his famous opera Boris Godunov, which I believe is the opera Colonel Stewart is referring to. See: http://www.favorite-classical-composers.com/modest-mussorgsky.html.

[142] Fanny Lear was a wild American who slept her way across Europe collecting Grand Dukes and Princes like some would collect butterflies from Borneo.

[143] Cesar Cui, Alexander Borodin, Mily Balakirev, Modest Mussorgsky, and Nikolay Rimsky-Korsakov were a band of composers striving to bring their own Russian touch to classical music. Also known as the Mighty Little Heap, or The Five, they brought a new light to music all across the globe!

[144] Since the times of Peter the Great, the Heir Apparent to the Romanoff throne was always the first colonel of the Preobrajenski Regiment.

[145] If you think a torn epaulette wasn't such a serious thing, check page 89 of Vladimir Littauer's autobiography, Russian Hussar A Story of the Imperial Cavalry 1911—1920 and see what a Russian officer thought on the subject.

[146] Actually, Princess Dolgorukova wasn't a concubine, for in the words of her lover, Emperor Alexander II, she was, "His wife before God" though his first wife was still very much alive.

[147] Tsar Paul had planned to be buried at Gatchina and had built a crypt there for just such a purpose, but his family chose the pomp and circumstance of a St. Petersburg funeral to show off his "peaceful death" to the doubting crowd.

[148] In Virginia Dentry's wonderful book, Family Genealogy of Edward T. Dentry, Jr. & Virginia (Bortner) Dentry the author notes that Captain John Stewart was a famous Baltimore duelist (page 52).

[149] The Russian saying is actually, "For a mad dog, seven versts is not a long detour." See: http://masterrussian.com/proverbs/russian_proverbs.htm.

[150] A horse can run between twenty-five and thirty miles an hour at the gallop, see www.youtube.com/watch?v=45hdjzNgLfc for a bird's eye view.

[151] This would appear to be the site of the little pedestrian bridge called the Bank Bridge with its four golden griffins.

[152] According to Coryne Hall in her delightful book, Little Mother of Russia (p. 59), the Persian Shah sat in the Royal theater box with his arms around the bare shoulders of the two Danish sisters feeding them sweets, as the Tsarevich looked on with displeasure.

[153] This sounded like an exaggeration to me, but this article found at: https://www.telegraph.co.uk/news/worldnews/europe/russia/1330890/3000-letters-that-spell-out-a-Tsars-love.html substantiates the Emperor's prolific correspondences.

[154] The diamonds were taken from the Vladimirskaya Mother of God icon—see page 306 of Margarita Nelipa's excellent work Alexander III His Life and Reign to see why Fanny Lear's lover was considered dead to his Romanoff family.

[155] See: http://www.oldrussia.net/baba.html and note that Baba Yaga is a Russian witch of folklore fame who is known for her scrawny legs and healthy appetite.

[156] Pobedonostsev's position with the Russian Orthodox Church and his propensity for stirring up trouble gave him the nickname of "The Holy See."

[157] By the map that's about twenty nautical miles, though to the couples' credit, ships traveled slowly in the great Age of Steam.

[158] To read more on the Sultan's response to his Christian subjects, see: http://www.thebohemianblog.com/dark-tourism-in-bulgaria-the-massacre-at-batak .

[159] The Romanoff gems Vlad's new bride bought were definitely fit for a queen or two; see http://weldons.ie/the-vladimir-tiara/ for the details.

[160] To see just what kind of warriors the Sultan of Turkey unleashed on the Balkans, go to: http://thelastdiadoch.tumblr.com/post/125264820395/ottoman-military-bashi-bazouk-infamous .

[161] Napoleon's famous quote was, "I would rather have a general who was lucky than one who was good." And General Gurko felt the very same way.

[162] See this 1908 moving picture of the city of Moscow and judge for yourself, https://www.youtube.com/watch?v=EPgbIK002us!

[163] As a Physical Therapist in the U.S. Navy I had the pleasure to treat an old Marine who was selected for a mission in the Pacific back in WW2 the very same way by none other than Chesty Puller.

[164] Torn down with great difficulty by Stalin's henchmen in 1936, Saint Nikolaus Cathedral was rebuilt when the Communists were kicked out of Odessa.

[165] I found this marvelous explanation of a top strap Colt .45 revolver @: http://dailycaller.com/2015/04/24/the-45-colt-history-and-surprising-facts-about-this-iconic-cartridge/.

[166] See Henning Haslund's excellent book, Men and Gods In Mongolia if you doubt Colonel Stewart regarding the size of his giant Mongolian.

[167] Actually Alexander II referred to his little friend as "mon bingerle" not his bingerlini as Colonel Stewart has so erroneously stated! For confirmation see Simon Sebag Montefiore's marvelous work, The Romanovs 1613 to 1918 (page 417) and see what a busy man the Emperor was.

[168] If you think Colonel Stewart was being too harsh on the Sultan's troops check out The Daily News of August 22, 1876 by J.A. MacGahan http://www.attackingthedevil.co.uk/related/macgahan.php.

[169] Take a closer look at this beautiful countryside where these fine people risked their lives to honor their dead @: www.travelsewhere.net/bacho-kiro/.

[170] Actually for the first five hundred years of the sanctuary's existence it had been a Christian church before the Muslims drove the Christians out. See: http://www.velikoturnovo.info/en/museums/sv-40-machenitsi-43/ for a wonderful article on this multi-denominational Church of the Forty Martyrs.

[171] If anyone doubts a shot like that could be made with a .50 caliber Sharps, read up on the Battle of Adobe Walls and see how Billy Dixon laid them down @ htpps://truewestmagazine.com/the-shoots-far-gun/.

[172] See https://www.revolvy.com/page/Bacho-Kiro and note the barefoot priest, who was captured by the Turks and hung for his faith.

[173] Luckily, the two lovers were in Europe at the time, for Lysistrata was banned in the land of the free and the home of the brave from 1873 thru 1930. For details see page 47 of the great magazine, History Revealed—Issue 38.

[174] Although closed by the Communists when they came to power, this Protestant church was home to many a good Anglican in the city of Piter.

[175] This was almost the same complaint that got A.P. Hill in trouble with Stonewall Jackson—nearly missing the Battle of Antietam.

[176] The head Russian minister at the Peace Talks was so senile that he presented his least acceptable terms first, and all the gains of the Treaty of San Stefano were lost in a heartbeat.

[177] On page 21 of <u>The Degaev Affair</u> by Richard Pipes, the author notes that Dostoevsky swore he would never report a terrorist even if he knew who they were, and he lived right next to a nest of them.

[178] To see more wonderful quotes from the great man, including the importance of child labor, see: www.cyberussr.com/rus/pobedonostsev.html.

[179] In a belt tightening measure after the war with the Turks, Alexander II cut the stipend each Grand Duke and Duchess got, one Grand Duke even riding about Piter in a donkey cart to show his adherence to the Tsar's program. But the Vladimirovichi had very expensive tastes and would not have been pleased.

[180] Empress Marie said it best when she said, "They'd treat a sick housemaid better." See page 436 of Montefiore's <u>The Romanovs</u> for confirmation.

[181] Had the snow storm not delayed the arrival of the Empress's brother, the Romanoffs would have been at the Dining Room table as the bomb went off.

[182] With chains on your ankles and wrists, kartoga meant you were sent into exile in Siberia for a life of hard labor with no chance of escape.

[183] To see the huge size of the Tsarevich's horse, go to: http://www.saint-petersburg.com/monuments/alexander-3rd/.

[184] The Illustrated London News (Volume 78) noted that Sophia Perovskaya escaped the Secret Police that morning just as Colonel Stewart said.

[185] This scene has been described in many ways, though on page 16 of Robert Massie's wonderful book, <u>Nicholas & Alexandra</u>, he mentions the ice skates Maria Feodorovna carried as she came in to the Emperor's study.

Made in the USA
Lexington, KY
02 December 2019